BROKEN BIRDS

A Novel
By
Peter Molnar

Listen to your sergeant!

listen to yourself.

BROKEN BIRDS

A Novel
By
Peter Molnar

ISBN: ISNB-13: 978-1-945263-14-9

For distribution, please visit
www.stitchedsmilepublications.com
or email
distribution@stitchedsmilepublications.com

FOREWORD

One of the greatest honors and distinctions a mentor can have is seeing a person's work come to fruition. Such is the case with Peter Molnar and this book, *Broken Birds*.

I began with Peter a few years back when I was a mentor for the Horror Writers Association. We'd come together by chance because I wasn't exactly assigned him. They asked if someone had the time to take on the project, and I jumped the gun.

Peter's imagination is unique. If I gave five people the same exercise, his would always go in a direction I wasn't expecting. Beneath it all, he's a good person. He's humble, soft-spoken, and his passion for writing shines through his hard work and dedication. I never had a complaint while working with Peter.

With all that said, it was I who asked Peter to submit this story to Stitched Smile Publications. I enjoyed the story and his writing style so much; I couldn't pass up the opportunity to follow through from "cradle to the grave."

Broken Birds is gritty and its characters are so well developed, you would swear you knew them from somewhere in real life. This is how real his story is to him, but to his credit, it is also how real his talent is.

When you're done reading *Broken Birds*, keep an eye on Mr. Molnar. He may hide in the dark shadows for now, but his anonymity won't last too long.

Lisa Vasquez

CEO of Stitched Smile Publications, Author, Writing Mentor

For my girls, Dana and Ani

PART ONE

No Benediction

"Life's
but a walking shadow, a poor player
That struts and frets his hour upon the stage
And then is heard no more: it is a tale
Told by an idiot, full of sound and fury,
Signifying nothing."

–Macbeth,
William Shakespeare

1. SHOW US WHAT YOU'VE GOT

Anyone who did not want to see Father Bingham grovel on his hands and knees was discouraged from coming. "You'll only get in the way," Bill Fielding said to the small cluster of locals in attendance at the Comstock Firehall, home of Ladder Nine. "It would be better if you stayed behind and watched your *Law and Order* reruns on TBS."

Fielding was Comstock's fire chief. He recently started teaching Sunday School over at St. Alphonsus. This made Father Bingham his boss, and that used to be all right with Fielding. "We're going there to frighten him right down to the marrow. Whatever it takes."

Everyone who attended the meeting was in. There were no *voices of reason*, although a few of the folks in attendance wished secretly somebody (anybody) had spoken up. They knew in their heart of hearts *frightening* the father was a slippery slope, especially when it came to a group of angry parents whose rage had swelled beyond reason.

"The plan is this," Fielding said, his hands spread out before him like he was delivering a sermon of his own. "I have it on good faith a number of the other priests at the rectory are away on a retreat up in Bethlehem. Bingham was told to stay behind by his superiors, in light of the … *allegations* leveled against him. He'll be there along with Monsignor Bigalow, and we know he's been sick and bedridden for the last couple weeks. Dan Bradley and I will ring the rectory doorbell and when Bingham answers, we're going to grab him. From there, we'll haul him over to the church and move everything inside."

One of them raised their hand, one of the mothers. She wore a rosary wound around her wrist and its little plastic black crucifix dripped down her arm. "Does it have to be tonight? Couldn't we wait on a ruling—"

11

Dan Bradley, a husky older man who worked as a volunteer fireman and ran a plumbing business in town, cut her off. "Word is they're looking to relocate Bingham as early as tomorrow morning. They're going to shuffle the deck, like they've done for decades. Instead of taking out the Joker's Wild card, they're just going to move him around. It's now or never, Melanie. Now or never."

Father Bingham had done them all wrong. Not one of the families in the man's congregation had gone unscathed by the lecherous, depraved actions he had visited upon twenty of their children. His light, lingering touches and tight, squinty blue "altar boy forever" eyes. It tore many of them clean through the fabric of their being to know they had all brought their sins to him and asked him for forgiveness, this man of the cloth who would later in the evening not only beg for *their* forgiveness but for his own miserable, stinking life. They would not relent. Ask any of the parents in attendance at that secret town meeting and they all would have professed themselves to be God-fearing Catholics of the old caliber.

"When we're done with him, folks; he'll never even look at another child without getting sick. Trauma can turn anyone around, as long as it's damaging enough to take root in his mind and heart." He paused, his lips a bloodless pair of lines. "And ... if it becomes obvious Father Bingham is invulnerable to such trauma, Dan and I will ... we will disappear him. The less you know about it, the better. For your own protection. Dan and I have already hashed it out. No one will be able to trace it back to any one of you," he concluded.

They looked at one another, buzzing here and there.

This lasted only a moment before silence returned. They turned their full attention back to Fielding, some of them switching their gazes between him and Bradley, who stood a few paces left of the speaker with his thick, hairy arms folded across his barrel chest.

"Any questions?" Fielding asked.

There were none.

"Last chance to head home."

Nobody moved.

Ask any one of them and they would have told you, even God would have wanted it to happen the way it did. The New Testament is interwoven with numerous instances where Christ invites the little children near to him. He wished to guard them from the fearful prospectors in their midst.

Fielding closed the meeting by leading the group in both the Lord's Prayer and the Glory Be, all holding hands and some even swaying in place. Then, he raised his eyes, "Show what you've brought with you. Hold them up!

12

Show your neighbors what you've brought to avenge our children, people!"

A soft murmur hatched in the center of them, then built to something louder and more sinister. Mr. Burton held up a carving knife, Mrs. Burton a garden trowel. Andrea Townsend, a small single mother who'd only moved to Comstock six months before to avoid an abusive husband across the continent, touted a large tire iron in the air. Mr. and Mrs. Kretzky brandished twin spears that had been hockey sticks two day ago until they were dismantled and sharpened to a spearpoint. Peter Hilton and his common-law wife, Sabrina Hadley, held up a ball pein hammer and a claw hammer, respectively. Bill Fielding nodded solemnly, tallying what he saw in his head: three fondue forks, two meat cleavers, one baseball bat, one nail gun, and surprisingly, the most popular item of all, gardening shears.

Trauma. Nothing more.

"Let's go," Fielding told them.

Bradley moved up alongside Fielding as the group filed out of the hall. The two men briefly exchanged words, then separated.

It was 9:30 at night.

2. WILL

Will Bentley didn't believe in writer's block. He'd read enough on the subject to assure himself it didn't exist, and if it did, it ought to be called by another name entirely—*pussying-out!* This was not the sort of coarse language he'd favor among his literary friends, of course. It ran the closest parallel to his actual way of speaking, but what could he do? After all, Will had awoken one day to find he suddenly had an image to protect. It hadn't always been like this for him. No, it wasn't until after that goddamn Pulitzer Prize nomination for *I Can Hear the Shiite Weeping* things started to get a little weird and exceedingly surreal for him.

Then, didn't he end up winning the Pulitzer after all?

Sonofabitch!

That pretty much summed it up.

Still, there were some things that stayed the same for Will, both before and after his overnight success. The Brother P-Touch typewriter sitting on the desk before him, for one. He relished how it hummed like a living thing. Will liked how it purred against his fingertips during moments of pause. He also insisted on remaining a social being, despite the loneliness borne of the writing act itself. The solitary aspect of the process had nearly sunk his aspirations before he edited down the first draft of his prize-winning novel. He liked people. He especially liked women, although he couldn't help hurting them time and time again. An old flame had actually sent him black roses one Valentine's Day after a messy breakup. He'd never fancied himself a *real* writer because he never thought he'd be able to cozy up to his own words, a purring, albeit mechanical typewriter, and a glass of scotch, with any consistent success. In the end, he came to embrace all three. The scotch during his darker, more private trials of the soul.

Will did not want to upgrade to some fancy PC or Mac. He'd thought about investing in a laptop so he could actually take his writing to another place, where he could actually be around other human beings.

I do not have writer's block. There is no such thing.

He glanced at the clock on the wall in the den. 9:25p.m. He didn't always write in the evening, but the "qwerty" called to him, and he answered. More and more frequently, the call to write beckoned him in the evening. The "qwerty call" was hard to ignore, like a lover showing one lovely breast to him in the lowlight and asking him to come on and do something to her. Sitting there in front of his P-touch, it was like that lover had covered back up under her nightie the moment he committed to taking her.

Will shoved back from his writing desk, stood up, and glanced around the shadowy confines of his writing room. He kept it dimly lit at night, a psychological thing he swore influenced his writing in a positive way.

It was time for a walk.

"Albie? Hey, girl!"

The door to the writing room wasn't shut for a reason. Will kept it open a crack. He heard the dog find its feet, and the twelve-year-old German Shepherd burst into the room. Albie stood to Will's thigh. She'd been waiting to hear her name and once she did, she burst into the room with her tail swishing, and heavy, rhythmical panting.

The other thing Albie liked to do was dance. Will took her front paws in his hands, and she raised the front half of her body. "All right now, remember I lead! I *lead!*"

Albie was powerfully built. She swiveled the upper portion of her body to the right, trying to work her master into some sort of spin. After a few revolutions, he slowed her to a stop and lowered her back onto all fours again. Will hugged the dog around the neck.

"Time for a walk. I have to get a thousand words tonight, or I won't be able to sleep. You know what that means. We gotta walk!"

14

Albie barked loudly. She backed off from Will and tried to snag her own tail in her mouth.

"What do you think? St. Alphonsus's per usual?"

The dog barked affirmation.

"I'll even let you run around in the field behind the rectory tonight, all right?"

Another bark followed up by a slow, soft murmur. That meant *Yes, please.*

That's when Will Bentley heard the voice in his head he hadn't heard in the two years since he'd begun taking his antidepressant tablets daily.

Sergeant Karns.

Them fields get mighty dark this time of night, soldier. You're gonna want to pack a lunch!

"Lunch, huh?"

Albie cocked her big head sideways, befuddled. Will strode out of the room without another word. Albie trailed behind him, her collar rattling around her neck like a ring of keys. He motioned for the dog to come to him when he paused at the bottom of the stairwell and snatched the leash off the banister. He attached the leash snap to the animal's collar, tugged to make sure it was connected, and led Albie over to the coat closet in the foyer. He swung the white closet doors open, and parted the hanging puff of jackets and coats.

Will opened the compartment in the wall at the back of the coat closet and felt around.

Pack a lunch.

He eased the small, black metal case out of the compartment and slipped out of the closet. Will took a knee with the case to punch the combination into its digital readout.

"The fields *do* get dark around this time. But I wasn't expecting to hear from you, Sarge. This ... this is a surprise."

The top of the case yawned open to reveal a well-oiled Beretta nestled amidst a black foam manifold.

Albie backed away when Will drew it out into his hands. First thing, he checked the safety was on. It was.

"Don't be afraid, girl. Just want to be careful some places we walk around. You never know, believe me."

3. BECAUSE YOUR SERGEANT SAYS

By the time Will and Albie hit the road, the clock struck 9:30 p.m. Albie heaved against her leash, pulling full speed ahead. Will was out for more of a slow meander. A quick walk would not help him unclog his mind like a dawdling stroll would. But the dog's will won out. When it came time to round the corner onto Heatherton Road, a dark and silent byway that intersected with Calendar Road where he lived in one of the three farmhouses, Will submitted to the dog's persistence and lifted his legs into a light and steady jog.

"All right, girl," he said to the dog. "For a little ways, anyway."

Albie grumbled and slanted off to the side, nosing her way onto the frozen grass.

Up ahead, the pointed white spire of St. Ephrem rose like a glowing clavicle above a roadside row of tall arborvitae. Every time he came upon the backlit spire of the church against an ink-blotted sky, he found himself wondering if the thing ought to have a blinking red air-traffic light attached to its point to ward off passing single-engine planes, or something to that effect.

Albie bustled along, dipping her muzzle down to the ground here and there, before moving on. Will's walk turned to something resembling a stagger. He was coming to *it*. The ever elusive *it* he'd gone on a walk to try and snag in the snare of his mind. A way out of his writing rut.

The white church spire swelled in size overhead as they walked along Heatherton, and he wrestled with the finer points of the book in his head.

Okay, so if Kent decides to have the bone fragments surgically removed from his bicep, he's going to feel this tremendous guilt because he's worried he'll start to forget about Sergeant Biltmore. After all, the fragments came from Biltmore when the rebel blew him up with a MiG-29. Kent was right next to him and received the spray of the bone ... okay ... but ... what is Kent going to do to preserve his buddy's memory if he has the fragments tweezed out of his skin? It's gotta read well on the page—

"What? What the hell is it, girl?"

Albie strained against her leash and started barking, her long snout whipping about.

Lost my thought ... ah, hell!

St. Alphonsus Catholic Church stood fifty feet from the road. The roof of the building was slate-grey shingles that converged around the base

16

of the spire. The brickwork used to be red but had faded to coral pink as the years passed since its construction in 1968. A two-story parochial school was attached to the church's foyer, and fifty-some classroom windows stared darkly downward at Will and Albie like many opal eyes. The grounds were peaceful, boasting the occasional gust of breeze that tickled the bushes lining the walkway and flanking the sculpture of St. Alphonsus himself, theologian and miracle worker.

When the sound of shouting and cursing carried itself to where they stood, Will chalked it up to a trick of the breeze whistling around the eaves of the old house of worship. Nothing more.

Albie's growl turned maniacal and spiraled upward into a desperate shriek.

He let out the leash a bit more, allowing the dog to lead him. The incomprehensible shouting became intermingled chants and taunts that sent a cold finger up the buttons of his spine.

"That's what you hear, girl?"

It was the voices of men and women, frenzied and ravenous. There was mention of the Devil and how they were sending "him" back. *Him?* Will doubted his own sense of hearing when one of them, a voice he thought he recognized but couldn't name, screamed "Gut 'im! Gut 'im! Gut 'im!" Then, the rest of the voices swelled with cheering, affirming their shared conviction.

Albie pulled Will across the driveway and closer to the building. The revelry softened some. Then, a horrible wail fanned upward and outward into the air.

"Jesus!"

The hasp connecting the leash to the collar around Albie's muscular neck snapped. Before Will knew what was happening, Albie cut around the corner of the school building and disappeared. Will chased after her, the gravelly voice of Sergeant Karns bubbling up in his ears like boiling blood.

Time to mow the lawn! Mow them all the fuck down, soldier!

4. A QUESTION OF BONE FRAGMENTS

Mow them down! Then we'll head back home, and I'll help you write your way out of yet another goddamn corner, soldier!

Will worked himself into an all-out sprint. The backside of his dog slid around the corner of the building, and he felt a rising stiffness in his knees. He ran through the pain. By the time he rounded the corner and reached the back of the school wing, Will heard his heart hammering in his head.

He slowed for a moment. The blacktop spread out all around him like an abyss. Pale, ghostly lines of parking markers divided the asphalt. He noticed he was standing at the foul line of the basketball half-court where recess was held, the yellow lines of the key glowing like spirits funneling out of the earth.

"Alberta! Dammit!"

The rear of the Church was a mere twenty paces away. A cement stairwell led up to the side door just off the altar. The door was propped open a foot in width. Will watched Alberta charge up the steps and grease her long, lithe body through the narrow opening.

"Albie!"

Get after her, soldier! Man's best friend!

The chaos of cackling women and frothing, growling men met Will's ears as he took up his sprint towards the side door. It was coming from inside St. Alphonsus. For some odd reason, it made him think of what a Greek orgy must've sounded like. Boundless. Depraved. Will saw someone run by within as he launched himself up the cement steps towards the door. A blur.

Will pounded up the stairs, forsaking the railing on either side altogether.

He wrenched the hydraulic door open and breached the interior.

The left side of his face tingled like its pores were screaming in unison, something Will thought he would've become used to by now.

No.

What he saw made Will Bentley slide his right hand inside the inseam of his jacket, finding the firearm holstered under his armpit.

5. SOMETHING ABOUT A SAMARITAN...

Will froze just inside the door, barely able to produce a sound other than something comparable to a phonograph needle scratching out of the groove. The Church was dark, aside from a lone beam of light shining down upon a hanging marble sculpture of Jesus on the cross, mounted above the altar. They were swarming around something at the base of the altar like bees around a honeycomb. Five of them, perhaps? They scattered like vultures rising off a lump of carrion on the side of a busy highway. They all wore ski masks. They disappeared before his eyes, swallowed by the deeper pockets of shadow so quickly Will could have imagined them. He heard weeping, a trickling as if from a slow-flowing brook. A handful of others (as far as Will could tell) lingered in the low light, moving *towards* him, rather than having fled from his judgment.

A male voice, fatigued and disenchanted, addressed him from a place that sounded both near and far all at once.

"Come get your dog, Bentley," the man said. "Then get out of here. She got away from me. From *all of us.*"

The voice belonged to Bill Fielding, Comstock Fire Marshall. He moved into the soft circle cast by the spotlight above his head. He kept his ski mask lowered, despite his unmistakable Southie Boston accent. A Louisville Slugger dangled from Fielding's right hand. The top half of the bat glistening a dark color, as if it had been dipped in paint.

"She came at me," Fielding said, "so I had to sedate her. Get her and go." He pointed the business end of his bat towards the left side of the church, drawing Will's eyes towards a crumpled heap on the ground in front of the first right pew.

Albie?

"Is that my dog, Bill?"

"We were going to scare him. Nothing like this."

"What'd you do, Bill?" Will inched closer, raising his Glock out before him.

Then he caught a glimpse of what the masked strangers had been crowded around; what they had fled from like the possessed suddenly awoken from the Devil's work.

"Is that ... Father Bingham?"

"He wouldn't admit it," Fielding said. "Just wouldn't ... *admit* what he did. Then, one of us ... we cut him. Real quick on the arm. Just to scare him. But ... he wouldn't ... admit what he did." Then, it was as if Fielding was suddenly roused from a waking nightmare. "I said *get out, Bentley! Get your fucking dog out of here!"*

Will's tongue tasted like wax paper, and it clung to the roof of his mouth. He switched his eyes between Fielding and the Father. The slightly rotund Father lay sprawled on his back against two risers leading onto the altar. He was shivering, his hands sliding over one another as he looked to be miming the act of washing them. His black coat had been peeled off. His black shirt ripped open to reveal a white tank top that gleamed red down

19

his belly, like he had carelessly spilled a full glass of wine down his front. Puncture wounds, varying in size, leered up at Will from the priest's chest and stomach like tiny smiles oozing blood.

"What the hell have you done?"

"Now *Will*—"

"We're not gonna tell you again, man!" Another man had come up behind Will. He spun around, training the Glock on the speaker. "Get! Out!"

This new stranger was flanked by a pair of masked individuals. One of them was a woman, judging by the slight projection of breasts beneath her black sweater. Then, her pert mouth turned to a black, raging O. "He doesn't have any children! He needs to go!"

"*Get outta here!*" Another one of them said from further down the aisle; another woman.

Behind him, Fielding sounded suddenly closer to Will, nearly on his back. "This is your last warning, or you're in this, too, Bentley!"

His left cheek lit up with a current of impossible electrical shocks. *Soldier, back up and squeeze them all into your sights as best you can! Don't turn your back on any of them!* Will pulled back, doing just that.

That's when two things seemed to happen at once.

Will saw the lump that was Albie rising behind Fielding, precariously finding her front paws then the back ones.

Father Bingham's low whisper became a muttering from his place on the risers. "*... and I detest all my sins because of Your just punishments, but most of all because they offend You, My God, who is*—"

Fielding exploded to Will's left. "Oh, you're praying? *You're praying?*"

Alberta strode towards them, the shadows peeling back off her brindle fur as she closed the short distance on wavering legs.

"*... I firmly resolve with the help of Your grace, to sin no more*—"

Will alternated his aim between Fielding and the others, who were closing in like a ravenous coven in black ski wear. "Now just *stay back!* Everybody just take a breath!"

Fielding lunged at Father Bingham, baseball bat raised above his head. "You're the devil, Bingham!"

The dog, Albie, moaned low in her throat. Then, a series of crazed barks and yelps burst out of her as she surged towards Fielding.

"Get off me, you *bitch!*"

Fielding spun around and swung the bat at Albie's head.

Will fired on him, his aim true and his thoughts clouded with the murk of confoundedness. Then the rest of them were upon him, and he knew nothing more for a long time after.

6. FALLUJAH/ LIVING IN YOUR BRAIN

Excerpt taken from *I Can Hear the Shiite Weeping*, by William R. Bentley, 2008,

Pgs.27-35:

Many of the men in I Marine Expeditionary Force (MEF) were overly confident about our chances when the attack orders came down and we were instructed to take Fallujah, coming from the north and unzippering the entire insurgent stronghold. Shaking them out of their hideaways like moths inside your favorite dress clothes. Major Natonski pressed on us, while we were to maintain confidence and hold faithfully to the crushing resolve of the United States Marine Corps, to go in there with too much bravado could compromise our chances of pulling off the mission. One of the guys in our unit made the mistake of calling Major Natonski a pussy under his breath after one of our briefings.

I fattened his lip for him. Another soldier cuffed him in the nuts, and that was the last insubordinate talk we heard from that guy, name of Silinsky, until he stepped on a landmine and his blown-up bits painted the side of a nearby shack. I remember thinking how somebody ought to stop at that shack after we take Fallujah and scrape off whatever remains they can from the side of the little shit building. Bury it. Bury something so his mother would have something to prove her son had once lived and died.

We went in 5,000 strong, Third and Fifth Marines, with our clean-up crew in tow, Seventh Cavalry. We swept down through the northern corridor and attacked the western quadrant with a ferociousness I had not seen as of yet during that tour. We were joined by the Regimental Combat Team Seven and the Army's Second Battalion. They went for the eastern portion and gutted that section of the city, efficiently and mercilessly. Iraqi troops joined our ranks, but we were sullen and cool towards them. After all, they'd lost the city we were now reclaiming for them. Zarqawi and his rebels had goosed them in the worst way, humiliated them; marginalized this new breed of Iraqi troops. If they couldn't hold their own, how could we ever hope to wave goodbye to them at any point in time?

We corked Fallujah from the inside, and we went to work smoking the rebels out of their holes. A few days before, this city had been 300,000 strong. Then, we warned the good eggs to clear out of Dodge before we went in to clean house for them. I heard Sergeant Karns mention something about 90 percent of the civilians having picked up and left at a moment's notice. They were scared, and they were obedient. They were holding out hope we'd win them back their lives.

I'm not kidding when I tell you these poor folks cut out of there with little-to-no regard for what they might be leaving behind. I wanted to believe this was because they all had such trust we'd make it possible to return to their homes like they'd never left. But, the more I think about it, the more I come to understand it was naked fear that drove them out without packing.

We were taking fire from every crack and crevice the ragged buildings around us could offer. We were treading light and pushing forward, holding to our formation until it was no longer efficient, nor smart, for any of us to do so. We fanned out, some to the left, some right. We started getting lucky and spotting them before they spotted us. By the time they could lay their crosshairs on our heads, we were cutting them in half with heavy, condensed firing. The sand was kicking up. When that shit coats the back of your throat, you learn how to swallow less than ever before.

Some of the locals who'd opted to stay behind, but held no ties to the insurgents, came pouring out of doors and scaling out of windows once they saw our earth tones tramping down the paths. We shuffled them to the back of our ranks and into numbers where no one bad could get at them. Then we rolled onto the highway, taking back the main train station in the city. Essentially, we would unclog the vein of troublemakers so Fallujah could fill with the lifeblood of Baghdad once again. Because of the stronghold the insurgents had constructed within Fallujah, the city had been forced to sit and putrefy and fester with little-to-no hope of becoming enriched from its neighboring city.

For the next couple of days, we went from house to house, clearing the rebels out. They fought back like children in the schoolyard who don't know what to do when they're being slammed hard and resort to slapping. They tried to slap us around with explosive devices and random booby-traps. We lost most of our men because of this primitive piecemeal bullshit tit-for-tat, but we also rattled them out of their tunnels and mosques. Their niches. We would bury our dead afterward. That is what made us men with a mission. They would probably leave their brethren behind after it was all said and done. This is what made them cowards and opponents unworthy of a victory.

Much of the terrain of Fallujah Province is flat, and it's relatively easy to gaze unobstructed down the street so long as there are no zigzags. The smoke of the mortars and the bombs blitzed the terrain, and we clawed our way through like we were pulling back a heavy gauze curtain that kept presenting itself before us. Some of our guys started seeing things that weren't there. Little shifts and swirls and disturbances in the smoke they automatically assumed to be an insurgent breaking cover to run at us with one of their fucking C-4 specials wrapped around them. I couldn't blame them, couldn't fault a one of them. Because by November 13, I found I was shooting at phantoms in the smoke too.

All I did was look for the earth tones in the shifting smoke clouds and if they never presented themselves, I shot. I was scared. I started seeing my mother's face everywhere I looked, and she was crying, waving me in towards her like she had a secret to tell me. Maybe Mom showed up and kept showing herself so I'd stop shooting at everything. I was lucky, although stupid and undeserving of such luck. I didn't hit any of my comrades. I could've killed one of my brothers with friendly fire.

Like there weren't enough motherfuckers hiding in windows and behind iron-grate doors waiting to do that for us?

It wasn't until I heard a dog barking on the second floor of a building we were filing past that I snapped out of this little daytrip. The place was split-level, about four-stories tall. There were balconies pushing themselves out over our heads and they made me think *hotel*. *Hotel?* Who the hell would want to bunk up here? Not now! Not ever, I remember thinking. Then, I heard what I took to be that same dog whimpering.

Then, it was whining.

Then, crying.

Then, something small, soft, and wet hit me hard across the side of my helmet. It splattered down in front of me, stopping me. I bent down to see what some shithead had thrown at me (morbidly surprised it had not exploded on contact) and forgot where I was or what I was doing for longer than thirty seconds since I'd shipped off to Iraq. Someone had thrown a newborn pup at me. It hadn't even opened its eyes yet, and it was dead at my feet. I suddenly understood why the dog up on the second floor of that Hilton from Hell on my left was shrieking the way it was.

When another pup carcass was hurled down to the street, it hit a soldier a few paces back, and he let off a slew of curses.

The dog had stopped screaming shortly after, and I thought the worst had happened. Until, this beautiful brown and black German Shepherd came barreling out of one of the openings on the side of Highway 10. It located one of the dead pups that had been thrown at us while we passed by. It bent to lick and kiss and nudge its baby. And the only reason I didn't cry was because the sand in my eyes had stopped up my eyelids and fucked with my sebaceous glands …

7. STELLA POST/ KARL TARLICK

On November 11, Stella Post spent much of the early morning sipping her cup of pumpkin flavored coffee and peeking out the kitchen window. *It might not even start. You hardly ever drive it.* But it would, and she knew it.

Yesterday, the sun had hurt her eyes and burned the back of her neck and hands in the short time she was out running a small but agonizing list of errands in preparation for this day. Stella was fair-skinned and freckled all over, but that wasn't why the sun had been her bane of existence the day before, and for so many days prior to that. It was not only a warming orb but a watchful one as well. It had no business marking and tracking her every move once she stepped out under its keening glaze. Then again, neither did the neighbors. The checkout boy at Shoprite. The hair salon lady who'd cut her hair the other day and tried, to no avail, to coax casual conversation out of her. The mechanic at Z Boys Service Station who'd changed the oil on her Taurus while she waited in the cramped reception area, covertly munching her nails down to the quick.

Either I do it all once, adding to a list over the course of days and weeks, or nothing gets done. Not ever.

That was not an option. There were plans in place. Plans she had procured with a man.

A man behind thick plate glass, through a phone connection strung between the barrier once a week for the last three years. It was the only *errand* Stella ever felt comfortable leaving the house to complete. In fact, her world had come to revolve more and more around this visit; this other man.

Once Stella had convinced herself she would have no problems with her transportation, she took up a vigil at her kitchen table, waiting with her hands curled around her Tracfone. A "burner" phone because her husband, Jack, insisted she have a phone with minimum capabilities and requiring the purchase of monthly minutes. Jack leased an iPhone 8, most likely due for an upgrade, while his wife subsisted on a flimsy flip-phone drug dealers used once and then tossed. He had only deactivated her phone once, after an especially harrowing argument. Stella made sure never to drive him to it again. Sitting there, her thoughts suddenly turned to the possibility Jack had found out about this other man, and the phone in her hands was deactivated again. *No, he wouldn't! We haven't fought for a while! At least, nothing worse than most days.*

Her palms wet, Stella sucked wind as she flipped open her phone and punched in the number for her house's landline. She hit the call button and waited with the earpiece crammed into her ear.

The phone on the wall nearby hung there, silent and despondent.

No-no-no—he wouldn't—not now! Not now! He—

Brrrrrrrrrrrrrrrriiiiinnnnngggggg!

Stella slapped her cell shut, ending the call and cutting off the wall-mounted phone's abrasive ringtone.

"Thank God," she said, squeezing her cell in her hands. Her chest unclenched. She remembered to breathe again. "So stupid. Why *would* he? No reason. Calm. Down."

She had been waiting for this day to come for ten years.

The cell phone vibrated in her hand. She looked at the number on the screen.

It read: *215-639-9082.*

She felt her pulse quicken, twitches at her wrists. She pressed the talk button.

"Hello?"

A man, his voice hoarse from cigarettes, answered her. "You picked up on the first ring. You desperate little whore, you!"

"Shut up, Karl. Or I'll let you stew over there in that phone booth a little while longer."

"Septa bus just dropped me off. I can see the halfway home bout' a half block down the road. You know the way here?"

"I did a couple dry runs to and from." *It was hard. I hate driving. But, yes, I did it. And it hurt. I mean, physically hurt my head.* "How much time do we have before the halfway house starts to *miss* you?"

Silence.

"Karl?"

"How come you been away from me so long? I don't think you been by for a month."

"The usual. It's been worse than usual."

She heard him sigh on the other end. "It's funny."

"What's funny?"

"Oh, I'll tell you what's funny soon as you swing on over here."

"You always did love keeping me in suspense. You shit!" Stella laughed, and was pleased to realize she was free of self-consciousness. Whenever she laughed, even so much as chuckled, in front of Jack, Stella always ended up feeling a gnawing embarrassment. It wasn't merely because Jack loved making fun of her laugh, but because he usually followed it up with a cutting insult that burned her to ash. "I'm on my way. Be there in a half hour."

"Well, you know that only leaves time for a suck-off in the woods. Any longer, they're gonna start beating the bushes."

"I know," Stella said. "I'll run some red lights."

"No you won't," Karl said. "You don't have it in you."

He's right. I don't.

"Stella?"

"Mm?"

"Love you."

"I love *you*, Karl," she told him. "I really do. Half hour. Maybe less."

Severed connection.

Karl Tarlick stood off the curb when Stella's car pulled onto the side of the road, his ratty yellow-brown suitcase beside him. He was Stella's height and equally slight in build, with small black eyes that stared out of a long, pale face. His oddly plump lips clashed with the other pinched features of his visage. The last time she'd visited him at Berrysburg Prison, he'd been sporting something of a five o'clock shadow, and now he wore a thick, black beard that grew in patches up the sides of his sunken cheekbones. His eternally-tousled black, curly hair hung down to just above his shoulders and managed to stand up in ringlets on the crown of his head.

The thing of it was, Karl Tarlick bore more than just a close resemblance to Cat Stevens. They could've been taken for twin brothers set up side-by-side.

Karl's nickname in high school?

Moonshadow. One of Stevens' many hits.

No, he looked the same as the day they passed down judgment on him in that cold Doylestown courtroom ten years before. He'd been a boy then. Only sixteen.

Moonshadow.

Stella could remember how, after he was arrested for the crimes that would land him in Berrysburg, Karl Tarlick's nickname had taken on more of a horrid double-edged meaning among the other students in their high school.

He rushed to Stella after she shut her car door and scooped her up in his arms like some gent in an antebellum romance novel.

"Damn, woman, you cold?" Karl set her down. His eyes were searching.

Stella was shivering inside her winter layers. "I'm fine."

26

"All right then," Karl said. "The woods are waiting, my lady."

She couldn't shake the feeling. It only intensified as she followed him into the forest.

8. MOONSHADOW

The unsettling feeling held while they tramped deeper into the forest. Stella started to consider her own death and how it would be handled. Would she be missed? How would she be remembered by those who'd known her? What music would they pipe into the viewing room the night before they lowered her into the ground for all time.

Stella always knew her secret relationship with Karl Tarlick would end in her death.

At his hands.

And that was okay with Stella. She had made her peace with God and her own mortality some time ago. Sometimes she wondered if she had somehow unknowingly shed the survival instinct some time ago. She felt its loss but did not mourn it. She couldn't channel what was such a base, primal urge. Self-preservation. A long-battered woman, beaten by words, Stella had come to prefer death to the living hell Jack Post put her through on a daily basis. If she were going to pop the escape hatch out of her miserable life, why not climb out with the likes of the lethal, poisonous Karl Tarlick.

After all, she loved him. But she loved how he would ultimately free her when the time came.

Karl bumped into her, pinched her thigh. "Right here."

He stopped, almost knee-deep in leaves and brambles. He unbuttoned his ragged army jacket, unzipped his brown corduroys, shoving them down a pair of chalk-white, hairless legs, and lowered a pair of dark boxers to the knobs of his knees. His long, thick cock slanted off to the left. Stella could hear the Delaware River some twenty paces to her left. Could hear the ice ticking, splitting.

His smile had vanished. He looked deep in thought.

"Come kiss it hello."

Breathlessly, Stella nodded her head and slunk to the ground before him. She suspected she would be called to honor many strange requests from Karl Tarlick from then on. Stella knew better than anyone Karl was not *cured*, in any sense of the word.

His cock shuddered and spasmed, and shot its gunk to the back of her throat.

Stella swallowed Karl's seed and gazed up into his squinty, black eyes. She said the first thing that came to mind.

"I'm sorry about your sister."

Later, Stella would wonder aloud what made her say such a thing at such a strange time. Blaze Tarlick had been Karl's younger sister. When Karl's crimes were unearthed, young Blaze was vilified at the high school where she'd begun as a freshman. As if low girl on the totem pole of the high-school food chain wasn't enough to contend with, Blaze had been forced to roam the halls amidst the jibes, sneers, and frequent pummeling at the hands of her peers. Many of them had been touched directly by Karl's terrible deeds. They showed her no mercy. The young girl's final chapter involved a self-made suicide snuff film that enjoyed a record-breaking, albeit brief, cult status on YouDeath before getting demoted to the Dark Web domain.

Karl yanked his cords up and buckled them. He gazed off in the direction of the frozen river. "Me too."

Then, without another word, he offered her his hand. She took it, and he hauled her to her feet. Together they filed out of the trees, and Karl walked to her car.

Stella came up behind him as he hauled his suitcase out of the back-seat. He slammed the door hard.

They stood there looking at one another for a second. Then, she leaned in and threw her arms around him.

Don't you say it ... don't say—

"I love you."

Karl nodded and grunted his agreement.

They separated.

He sniffed at the air. "Jack still mistreating you?"

Now it was time for Stella's normally green eyes to blacken. She looked away from him, jaw set and stiff with anger. She wanted to tell him, but something made her hesitate. Later, Stella would come to realize it was her fear and trepidation of setting this whole thing in motion. She knew once she answered him in the affirmative, she would not be able to call back this dog. She would not be able to hold him back on his leash, as it was made of tenuous fiber that would split with relative ease. As of now, she'd managed to hold the stick between this dog's teeth to keep from getting bit.

Stella felt her mouth run dry.

"Yes. Nothing's changed."

Karl nodded, glanced down the road towards the halfway house.

"You ever hear of *Santeria*?"

She shook her head.

He shrugged and started walking away.

"Do they have a phone there?" Stella called after him.

"Two tin cans and a string," he answered, turning and walking backwards for a bit.

"Fun-*ny!*"

"Yeah, there's a phone there. Monitored calls."

"Well, then," Stella said, winking at him. "Maybe I'll take you to get a phone like I have. Pay-As-You-Go."

"Why? You don't want them to hear some of the things you got to say to me?"

"Do you?"

"Fuck 'im," Karl said and spun on his heel to walk the rest of the way.

9. THE LONG HARD ROAD OUT OF HELL

One month after the events of St. Alphonsus Church, Will Bentley was only certain of two things in his life.

He would not move out of Comstock, no matter how much his girl-friend and his agent begged him to reconsider.

He would never fire nor handle another firearm for the rest of his life. The mere thought of it called immediately to mind how Bill Fielding's head had exploded like a ball full of bloody insulation when Will had cut him down, stopping him from battering Father Bingham with an already bloody, well-used baseball bat.

He couldn't worry over whether his agent, Claire Monasta of The McNair Literary Agency, would ultimately decide to pull away from him and his added baggage. Maybe start dropping his name to other agents in her circle perhaps better suited to deal with someone as stubborn and decidedly reckless as Will Bentley. Will thought he knew better than to imagine Claire leaving him before he'd been completely wrung out of literary liquid gold, but stranger things have happened.

Much stranger things. Will was certain the events that had taken place in the church would have resulted in charges against him. After all, he had shot three of the eight people there that night besides Bill Fielding. The others nearly fell on him with their weapons, an odd assortment as he would later discover, and he had been forced to defend himself against their onslaught. But the people who died left behind children. Husbands. Wives. Extended families. It was determined in a short time Will had acted in self-defense, as well as in defense of Father Bingham, who died at the scene as well from an assortment of bludgeonings.

Will's girlfriend, Mina, and his agent both wanted him to guard against something like *that* ever happening again. Hell, the world almost lost the next Tim O'Brien, for Christ's sake! Isn't that what *Time* and *Publisher's Weekly* had touted him as after the release of his prize-winning war memoir? His agent wanted him in Manhattan, having said something about Will "swimming with his own species for a little while." Mina wanted him over in New Hope, to warm up the empty side of her four-poster bed.

The night of the incident. That was the last time he sat down to write and could do it without his fingers cramping up and his mind blaring with a headache the likes of which he thought only cerebral hemorrhage victims could describe. Each time, he ended up slinking away from his writing desk, his Brother P-touch staring vacuously at him with its blank, bent white sheet of paper run into it.

Twice, Will was moved to tears in the weighted silence of his den.

He wasn't short on ideas. They just had a funny way of eluding him when it came time to sit down and type them up.

What do you have to say about that ... huh, Sergeant Karns? And don't hand me the same old shit you've been shoving my way for the last four weeks! I did not let you die, and I sure as shit didn't let Father Bingham die, either! By the time I got there with Albie, the damage was beyond repair.

Karns was obviously practicing the "nothing nice to say then say nothing at all" approach to things. Will searched for and grasped at words on a daily basis, and his Sergeant's input was few and far between. When Sergeant Karns did voice his opinion, and Will's left cheek stung with that same, familiar grid of electric shocks, it was only to berate him. To humble him. It had never been this between the two of them.

"C'mon, Karns ... you ... *flaky shit—*"

"Who you talking to, babe?"

He hadn't even noticed her filling the doorway to his den. Mina Cohen was beautiful and worthy of the interruption.

"No one, Meen," he said, craning around to her in his seat at the desk.

"Hungry?" She slipped inside and set a bowl of her homemade matzoh-ball soup down beside his elbow on the desk blotter.

His favorite dish of hers. "You better believe it."

"Any luck?"

"No," he said, gathering up the bowl and ladling some soup into his mouth. "But I still have—" he checked the Fossil watch strapped to his wrist,"—six hours before Dr. Phil."

"Oh really, smartass?" Mina said. "What's he got on his docket today?"

"You're going to love it, Meen. Convicts and the women who love them!"

Mina rolled her eyes. "I'll pass today."

"Suit yourself."

"Maybe you should think of passing on it yourself. Especially if you don't have anything down before then."

"Yeah, well, I told you just like I told Princess Claire at the agency … I've got an unfinished novel that gets finished before I'll even consider giving you guys what *you* want."

Mina's eyes widened, suddenly sensitive. "Hey mister, I'm not the one pushing for *that* book. I only said it could be therapeutic for you to get it all out."

Will slurped some soup, gazed at her across the lip of his bowl. "Too late. It's a part of me. There's no getting rid of it."

"See, I don't understand, Will. It's going to sound really silly and juvenile of me to say this in light of what's happened, but … well, you know how much I love *CSI* and *Law & Order.*"

"Their best writing's long behind them, I think."

"I don't know how true that is, but on those shows, whenever an officer shoots a suspect … whenever they're forced to discharge their weapon at another human being ... they're required to undergo a psych evaluation afterwards before they can return to work at full capacity so—"

"Honey," Will said, handing the now empty bowl back up to her, "I'll be fine. That's not how I deal with things like life and death."

"How would you know what you *need* until you sit down with someone, Will? Maybe they can help you back into a comfortable place where you could write again like you used to."

"I hate to come at you with an obvious rebuttal, but I'm a veteran, Meen. I had already taken plenty of lives before I walked into that Church looking for Albie."

"It doesn't mean you weren't affected by what happened that night."

"Of course, and I'd be stupid to even try and sell you such a line of bullshit."

Mina glared down at his upturned face. He relished the way her

31

green eyes flared when she tried to be stern with him. Ultimately, they would round out into big loving emeralds that made him feel like the luckiest man this side of Guantanamo. Her smile was infectious. When it broke her lips, he was powerless to hold onto his own frown.

"Can I ask you something?" Mina asked, brushing a thick loop of black hair out of her eyes and behind her ear.

"Always."

"You said you were done with guns after St. Alphonsus. Are you going to sell your collection?"

"I ... don't know," he told her. "But, if you and Claire really want me to get back to my *writing*, the two of you better start lumping your prayers together and making it a part of your daily routines, because if Albie doesn't come out of her coma, I think I'll be done writing for good. I don't need a change of scenery. I don't need Manhattan."

"I know."

"I just want her to wake up."

Mina reached out and laid a cool hand across his lowbrow.

"I've got to get back, honeybear," she said, smiling limply. Mina was the owner and proprietor of Marley's Bookstore on New Hope's bustling, prosperous Main Street. The cramped and drafty store was one of the staple stops for tourists by the dozens daily, yearlong, and second only to The Witch's Brew Shop for New Age. "We're having Scott Feldman in store for that live reading. Would you believe he actually called over a list of prerequisites to prepare for his arrival."

Will laughed. "Who the hell does Scott Feldman think he is?"

"Right now, he's got a pretty firm hold on the Number One spot on the New York Times bestseller list."

"You're kidding! Still?"

"Mm-hmm," droned Mina, rolling her eyes. "And to be perfectly honest with you, I've read *Sheep In Traffic,* and it smacks of Tom Wolfe before he started wearing his obnoxious white suit and still gave a damn about what he wrote about."

"Ouch."

"Big time!"

"I'd hate to overhear what you say about my book when I'm not around!"

"Oh, Mr. Bentley, you're one of the last great American truth tellers. I'll always bow at your altar, lover."

"Even if I never publish again?"

"Sure," Mina said, walking out. "But you and I both know you're a writer and sooner or later that itch will get scratched."

"Sounds more like a disease than anything else," Will said.

"Poe called the compulsion of the writer to write *the midnight disease.*" She beamed with gloating, bent to kiss his lips.

"Show off!" he called after her as Mina called her goodbye and hurried out.

Will gazed out the window above his writing desk. The sky was a luxuriant blue shot with purple veins that lifted up from behind the treetops of the small forest visible from his spot on the bed. Lately, he could slip into stubborn loneliness at the drop of a hat. Whenever Mina left him for the day, or he lay in bed panting after stirring violently from a vivid nightmare, Will found himself consumed by a stifling melancholy. It made him think of how lonely death must be for the one doing the dying. The one buried alone up on a hill with only a grave blanket to keep the dirt piled into their grave symbolically warm. He couldn't help but to entertain this dark string of thoughts. He hadn't thought so chronically about his own mortality since he'd done his last tour, and that was near seven years ago.

What was it?

Karns.

"At least help me get a sentence, for Christ's sakes!"

Nothing.

Will touched his hand to the left side of his face, where a small collection of what felt like acne pockmarks speckled the flesh. He felt the familiar tingle there. It felt like an awakening, the pores crying out with joy after having been unclogged. But Will knew better. He did not just feel the small craters in his face, but also the smaller, barely detectable bumps embedded there and boasting a subtle sharpness. The medics over in Iraq told him they'd gotten all of the bone fragments out of his face.

It simply wasn't true. They were still there and had been since the day they were blown into his flesh and lodged there for all time.

He could feel them.

They tingled.

"Just one goddamn word? Karns?" He traced his index finger across the rough skin patch, just below his sunken cheekbones.

You want a fuckin' word, soldier?

The entire left side of Will's face felt like it had caught fire. He cried out.

How about this one? You ought to know all about it!

Sloth!

10. JACK POST AT HOME

Jack Post hated being at home. The road spoiled him, and after only an hour of being back at the homestead with Stella he turned downright mean. After his third or fourth glass of Jack Daniels, Jack slipped religiously further into a part of his psyche that, once engaged, would not easily relinquish its power over him.

He became a sadist.

That night, it took hold of him little by little, a slow drip of adrenaline into his every muscle fiber. Jack took his place at the kitchen table, frowning down at the empty plate before him where a place was set and a sparkling glass of iced tea shimmered by his left hand. The house smelled of casserole and a mingling of spiced meats. His mouth had been watering for the last twenty minutes. His stomach was roiling. He hadn't eaten since lunch with the star quarterback of Ocean City High School and his parents, and even then he'd done more talking then eating. Ballantine University wanted Carnel Jenkins on their playing roster next year, and Jack was the college's go-to recruiter to seal the deal. He was close.

And now I'm home, and I'm starving!

Across the kitchen, Stella stooped and wrenched open the over door. A hot blast of heat fanned across the room, irritating Jack's skin and reddening the flesh. Stella reached into the oven with two oven-mitted hands, the heat lashing her face. She straightened up holding a steaming casserole dish before her and kicked the oven door shut with the heel of her sneaker.

Stella's movements were oiled and graceful. She usually moved about the kitchen in a series of rigid ticks around him. That night, Jack felt he could actually *hear* something different in her step, a certain specific excitability in her blurts here and there as she shoveled a big dollop of corned-beef hash onto his plate and then her own. She had even prattled on about how she found the recipe in one of those Rachael Rachael homemaker magazines Jack saw in line at the Shop Rite supermarket. Something told him he wasn't remembering Rachael's name correctly, and it only aggravated him all the more as he decided he would blame this on wifey as well. She must have said the name wrong to him, and he'd gotten stuck remembering it wrong now.

What did he care where the recipe came from? It was like wondering over which chicken laid the eggs that made his breakfast omelette that morning at the Best Western early bird buffet. The only thing that matters is the product, not its maker. Not the dreamer but the dream. Once Jack had dreams. He'd wanted to be a pinch hitter for the Phillies. Then, his father had beat his dream right out of his bones, quite literally, by breaking both his wrists during an especially violent beating in his teenage years. Now, Jack could hardly hold a baseball, let along sink it over home plate without suffering excruciating pain for days after.

"Great to be home, Stella," he said, voice too rich and singsong to possibly ring genuine. "Really, you run a helluva tight ship, my girl. Dinner fifteen minutes later than you said it was going to be. Your man at the dinner table, wondering if he'll ever have a meal when he expects to have it before he has to ship out again. Room service gets the food to your room when they say they're going to have it up to you. It's still hot, too."

"Isn't that their job?" Stella chirped, shutting the oven door. She smiled winsomely and set the casserole dish down on a wooden pallet in the center of the circular drop-leaf table.

"What'd you say?" he blurted. Jack followed her to her seat with his searching brown eyes. He snatched up his fork and plunged it down into his plateful of food. "Just what in the hell do you mean by that?"

The healthy-looking rosiness in Stella's cheeks faded to a cheese-cloth white, but a thin, bloodless smile held to her lips as she lowered herself down into her chair.

"Nothing else to say?"

She didn't say anything, only tucked her long red hair back behind her ears.

"Are you taking your meds again?" Jack pressed. "I swore I flushed all of them."

"I'm not taking anything," she said. "I don't have anything."

Jack was a statue in Perry Ellis. He licked his lips, applying a new sheen to them. His eyes never left her. "I hope you're telling me the truth. You gave me your word you wouldn't try to refill your Klonopin or the Prozac. They're designed to keep you sick so you'll get dependent on them. They keep you running on their wheel for the rest of your life like a dumb hamster."

"I know."

"Do you?"

"Yes," she said, in a small voice.

"It's like I told you," Jack said, finally turning his attention to his food, "all you need is love to cure depression. John and Paul were on to something."

Stella shrugged, digging her fork into her dinner and bringing it to her lips. She blew on it. Blew on it some more. Could not break the cycle of blowing on her food that should have led to eating it, and never quite made it to that point. She would not place it in her mouth until he stopped staring at her like he was, fork and spoon now standing up in his fat fingers.

Of course, Jack knew this game. He'd invented it. A mindfuck.

He licked his full lips. "What are you? Stuck in neutral?"

That's what he called it when he'd scared Stella so completely she took to repeating her motions over and over again, her brain and its impulses suddenly locked into a mode of personal protection above all other things. Stuck in neutral. *No sudden movements.* Jack loved her like this and wondered if one day he'd have her so frightened and wrung through with anxiety she'd be afraid to draw her next breath. Asphyxiate.

Getting *stuck in neutral* was borne of a particular time at dinner when Jack had been really ragging on her, digging in and cutting her with outlandish accusations and verbal assaults which were baseless as they were cruel. Stella, in a rare moment, had found herself strong enough to ignore him and to continue eating as if he were not foaming at the mouth across the table from her. Blowing on her food *and then* eating it. Repeat. All the while, Jack had kept at her, his voice climbing in decibel the longer she ignored him and blew on her food and swallowed it down. Morsel after morsel. Finally, Jack had lost it. He lunged across the table and curled his right hand around the bar of her larynx. A good hunk of the pot roast Stella had just spooned into her mouth became wedged in her throat. A smile had burst across Jack's handsome, chiseled jawline as his wife's eyes grew wide and terrified. She must have changed three different shades of purple before Jack decided to let go of her throat and perform the Heimlich.

Stella blew on her forkful of food a final time and then set it back down on the edge of her plate. Jack laughed at her, satisfied he'd gotten her *stuck in neutral* yet again. The nights he was home and off the road. It was ritualistic at that point.

Shaking his head, Jack dug into his food and started eating like he hadn't seen food in a month.

Stella stared down at her plate of food, now gone cold, and decided she would not eat.

Jack thought she was starting to look a little *depleted.*

After some time, Jack threw down his fork and wiped his mouth with his napkin. He flung that down too and it yawned open, showing the brown stain he had made there with his dirty lips. "I've got my appointment with Doctor Robard tomorrow at three, you know?"

"Okay," she said.

"Just *okay?*"

36

"I've been praying ever since you told me about it."

"I don't remember asking you to say a prayer for me," he said, shoving back from the table and rubbing the back of his neck. "You light a candle for me, too?" A dark laugh rolled out of him like the low rumbling of a chainsaw getting some gas.

Stella kept silent, hands folded in her lap as she stared dolefully down at her cold dinner dish.

Jack's laughter wound down to a growl. "I tell you Doc Robard called me in for a follow-up visit because he's concerned about my blood-work results and the only thing you can think to do to help me is to pray to the Man in the Sky?"

"You make it sound like I'm—like I'm some kind of primitive idiot. He's your Lord and Savior too! You don't believe He wants to help you?"

"Babe, you'd have to be some kind of primitive idiot to sit there and try to sell me on a God who saw the need to *turn* my blood irregular in the first place. So he can what? Show me some sleight of hand to remind me he's The Man? I'm unimpressed."

"That's fine," Stella added. "It's probably nothing. You shouldn't worry."

"You remember what your God let happen to one of His guys a little while ago?"

"I don't want to talk about it," Stella said, her cheeks reddening.

"My buddy, Ed Frankel? He works for Comstock EMT. One of the first on the scene out at the church."

"Jack!"

"He said poor old Father Bingham was pretty much a knife sponge when he got there—"

"PLEASE, JACK—"

"—and all on God's watch. Your Man in the Sky!"

Stella frowned down at her food as the image of Father Charles Bingham swirled around her head. Stella's years in Catholic school had trained her into trusting men of the cloth, even the women in their habits who wore simple wedding rings and when asked about them responded, "I am married to God." Stella used to wonder what such a wedding would look like, uniting a Supreme Being and an often homely looking woman ranging in age from early twenties to eighty. She imagined a chapel formed by fat cumulus clouds and bells ringing incessantly from every corner of the sky. She imagined a much older Man taking a nun's hand, sliding the ring down her finger and then flying in circles above her to demonstrate some superhero quality Stella could not help but to attribute to her God. Her God did not wear a mask or a cape, but she firmly held to the belief He was the only one who could help the helpless and have it mean something.

She had faith God would someday deliver Jack from her.

The thought of it frightened her as much as it made her swoon inside.

She did love Jack and still believed the man who had once wooed her, played Harry Connick Jr. standards on their upright piano after dinner when they were first married, still resided somewhere within handsome man seated across the table from her, with his hands steepled contemplatively over a half-empty plate. Back then, he would play and sing for her. He would play for hours, long after his wrists started to sing from the injury his father had given him that ended his prospects of playing professional baseball. Back then, Jack only told her after he had thoroughly melted her heart with his crooning and near flawless playing that his wrists hurt terribly, and he should put some ice on them. Back then, she would have tended to him and never let him get as far as the freezer. Because she had wanted to. For the man he had been and could be again.

Always eyeballing her like he longed to detect some hint of fight in her. Something to challenge him when he craved it like a hungry leopard.

Of course, such a look sometimes meant something else entirely. It meant he wanted something else. She could deal with the *something else.* Husbands and wives are supposed to long for the *something else.*

I'd rather that than have him go on and on about my shitty cooking.

Jack stood up suddenly, but his hand did not go to his fly as she anticipated.

"Man, I almost forgot! Mother-*fuck!*"

"What's the matter?"

"Ah, I have to get over to the hotel in Jersey where I was staying. I left my wallet in the room. They're holding it for me, and the lady who knows about it is leaving by nine. I'm going to be sitting in traffic unless I leave now and catch her. *Fuck!*"

"All right, it's going to be okay," she stammered. "Just ... go!"

"I'm going. You just ... I don't know ... put a finger in the page and hold the place or something." He hurried out of the kitchen with nary a glance back down at his wife.

Put a finger in and hold the page?

11. MINDMELD

Stella cleared the table of the plates, utensils, and the casserole in a fog. She dumped them in the sink. Jack's thunderous footsteps sounded overhead. Their bedroom was right above the kitchen. She knew he had other women. She also knew he had come home with his wallet and the story was a fabrication, one of his less effortful tales. When she had greeted him at the door earlier that day, after having not seen him for two days while he was away in Trenton, Stella had not just felt the press of his wallet into her breast as she hugged him, she had also seen it poking its little leather corner up out of his jacket pocket. Yet, even that was not what perplexed her. It would be the fact for the last month he had not touched her in a sexual way. Jack had always kept her well-sexed until recently, their sessions often rough and drawn out, but she had been on the same page as him. His meanness was not only welcome but expected during their coupling.

It was always better than nothing, which was what it had become.

Stella listened to the pounding of Jack's Timberlands along the ceiling and, satisfied he would not be down for a few more minutes, she hurried to the dining room. She located her handbag lying limp beside the leg of the dining room table and stooped to fish her cell phone out from amongst the stray tampons, gum wrappers, and her jangling keys.

She rushed back into the kitchen clutching her cell. The heavy footfalls continued above, and Stella quickly dialed the halfway house number Karl had given her earlier that day. Once Jack's footsteps died out, she would most likely have to hang up on Karl, but she knew he would understand. Hoped he would, at least.

A shrill male voice filled her ear after three rings. He sounded like a sniveling, birdlike man, and Stella couldn't wait until he quit with his little bit of awkward small talk to tell her Karl was *right there*.

Then Karl's eternally saccharine drawl drew the downturned corners of her mouth upward into what felt like a wholly involuntary smile. "What's the good word?"

The floodgates opened and Stella started babbling uncontrollably. She knew any minute Jack would come charging down the stairs, and she would have to go. "I'll tell you what's doing. Jack is a lying pile of scum, and he's on his way out right now to *fuck* another faceless woman while I soak the dishes and figure out how I'm going to scratch this sexual itch he just left me with. I think I'm going to *do* something to him, and it's just going to happen, and I won't even know it's done until I've got blood up my arms.

I don't sleep anymore, Karl. I lie in bed, and I wonder how long it would take him to wake up if I put a pillow over his face. Pinch his nostrils closed and clamp a hand over his mouth. I think about spraying his food with Lysol. I think about biting off his candy cane dick every time it's in my mouth. But then I realize I'll end up in the same place you just got out of. They won't have any sympathy for a battered woman. They never do on the shows I watch. But TV's bullshit, too!"

"Stell—"

"This is a *fucking* man's world, Karl! Count yourself lucky you were born with the right parts, because otherwise you'd be me in one way or another. I envy you. I am *green* with it! Because I *know* you would know exactly what to do with a man like Jack!"

"Stella? I had a feeling something was wrong. A buzzing in my skull."

"What are you talking about?"

"I'm talking about the fact you and me got some kind of a *mindmeld* going. We can feel each other's pain the moment the other one's feeling it. Like twins. You ever hear of it? That's us. We got a mindmeld."

"Are you listening to me, Karl?"

A little chuckle on the other end. "Follow him. That's what you do."

"Really?" she sighed, her chest tightening like a snare drum. She felt herself sinking. "You know that's easier said than done. Why would you suggest something you know I can't do? Anything else?"

She nearly missed the absence of Jack's footfalls overhead.

Silence.

Then there was the heavy stomping as Jack came crashing down the stairs like a wild herd of buffalo. "Stella?" he called from the other side of the first floor. Karl hissed in her ear, a serpent uncoiling. "Follow the bastard. Drive through the fear. You're afraid to leave the house, but you're looking for some truth about that prick husband of yours. You'll never get it unless you step-*drive* outside this comfort zone of yours. Just do it, Stell. Punch through the walls and just walk out. Do it!"

"I-I will."

"*Stella!*" Jack boomed.

Stella rang off.

12. THE CALL

Will Bentley turned the snow globe over and over in his hands and tried not to think about the fact in two hours he had only managed to lay down a few sentences that didn't embarrass him. The snow globe showed the Golden Gate Bridge against a bright blue sky, and a caption ran underneath it: *Winter's Greetings from San Francisco ... Not!* When he turned it upside down, snow fell in a heavy, swirling mist, and played around the bridge's red cables and supports like fairy dust. His agent had sent it to him while she was attending a meeting with a reclusive horror writer from Sacramento. "Yes, even *more* reclusive than you, my dear Mr. Bentley!" she had joked. The globe usually made him smile, but not that night. He felt untethered. Free-floating. The reason for this was too ghastly to admit, and so he did not give voice to it. He would most certainly not write about it, although he had recently started keeping a journal.

During his final tour in Iraq, Will decided he would never tell anyone about Sergeant Karns's voice in his head. He would never commit it to anything which could later be discovered upon the event of his death. No one would remember his body of work like they would remember the fact Will Bentley's muse consisted of a rough-hewn voice in his head, borne of the microscopic bone fragments embedded deep within the flesh of his right cheek. Poe never escaped the slander of his sworn enemy, Rufus Griswold, and his name was still synonymous with "opium addict" and "madman" when, in reality, these titles were nothing more than baseless allegations forged by a jealous literary colleague. *What would the world make of you, Karns?*

Nothing. Still, nothing of note from his *muse.*

The problem was Sergeant Karns, real or imagined, was a damn dependable internal editor for Will. Hell, the pushy, abrasive bastard had practically co-written his Pulitzer Prize winner with him. Sergeant's name was listed among the twenty other people included in the book's Acknowledgements section, and that was as far as Will was willing to go in terms of publicly tipping his hat to the man. No more.

Next step would be an extended stay at Friend's Mental Hospital. No thank you!

He set the snow globe back down on his writing desk beside a green-shaded poker lamp. He ran a hand along the underside of his strong jaw, relishing the prickle of a week's growth sprouting there. Then, Will leaned towards his Brother P-Touch and read the sentences he could live with again:

41

He doesn't walk with a cane anymore. It leans against the night-stand next to his bed, as if secretly rooting against his recovery so he might hobble beside it once more. He itches to pick up his guns again and to fire them now that he can walk, but just handling his Glock for a moment the other day reminded him of the church spire rising like a great, prehistoric bone into the black night sky, and of the screams of the "night parishioners" hidden within and hiding their devil's business.

He had let his imagination take him wherever it wished, and it took him right back to the very place and time he'd pushed so hard against writing about.

"Shit," Will said, pushing himself back from his writing desk. "Now, who's the reclusive horror writer? For God sakes, this is a damned *shivery* tale. No one's looking for a fucking *shivery* tale from Will Bentley." He shook his head. Critics be damned, he had to *purge.*

The funny thing was, Will's agent thought his next book was going to be about Albie, documenting the relationship between he and the German Shepherd that was forged while deep within the heart of a battle zone. She had even suggested a name for Will's as-yet untitled (and unwritten) memoir *Wardog.*

If Sergeant Karns were not *on mute* when she had suggested such a title, Will was pretty sure the dead man would have strung together a new and terrible string of profanities the likes of which would have made George Carlin blush.

Wardog ... Christ ...

He could not ignore the fact he was being tugged in the opposite direction creatively. Something inside Will begged to write about the night at the church.

The cell phone beside his word processor buzzed to life, skittering along the lip of the cherry writing desk. Will snatched it up and pressed the green Call-Connect button.

"Hello?"

"Mr. Bentley, it's Doctor Lanza."

Doctor Lanza was the veterinarian personally overseeing Albie's care at the clinic, where the dog was presently in a coma. Albie had been in a coma since one of the parishioners at the church hit her in the side of the head with his Louisville Slugger, the same one used to break Father Bingham's arms and legs.

Will's heartbeat leapt into his head as he suddenly lurched forward in his chair. "Is everything all right?"

Doctor Lanza sounded breathless, like she had literally sprinted a

42

mile to make it to a phone. "Your girl's awake, Mr. Bentley. She just opened her eyes and she is responsive. Can you come?

"Will?" Mina stood in the doorway to the bedroom, wiping her hands on a dishtowel. Deep lines had sprung across her brow. "What is it?"

"Oh, thank you God! Absolutely! We can come! We're on our way!"

He rang off and came out of his chair. He crossed the room and swept Mina up into his arms. Her moccasins left the ground.

"Alberta's back."

"I'll get our coats," Mina said.

13. TROLLING

Jack Post spotted her walking hurriedly alongside the shuttered shops of Tighe Street and started hunting for a spot he could slip into along the curb. There were no meters in this section of West Philadelphia, and he was thankful as he had nothing to feed them. Holding her within his periphery, he gunned the engine of his Prius and lurched forward until he was well ahead of her by a half-block. Then, as if providence were suddenly opening itself to his will, an open spot out in front of a corner bar called Curran's revealed i self to him. He eased his Prius into it and checked the rearview for the woman. At first, Jack feared he lost track of her. It wouldn't have shocked him. *These working girls are surprisingly elusive when they want to be. When they want you to see them, you can't miss them. They're trolling you before you even realize it.*

Then, she reappeared like an apparition, emerging from the slippery shadow as a streetlight broke across the top of her black roots and bled blonde down to her chin in unkempt tresses.

This one was fragile. He knew it. His sixth sense told him so.

She was in some kind hurry; fleeing something or someone?

Her bare legs bowed slightly with every wobbly step atop a pair of red stiletto heels. They were thick, tree-stump legs that widened all the way up into a tight, leather mini skirt which cinched her waist severely. Jack liked them nubile, but the meat on this one did not turn his stomach. More flesh to leave his handprints on. To knead. To pinch until she squealed like a sow. Her chest heaved beneath a leopard-print coat, and Jack recognized a Blondie t-shirt peeking out from underneath the no-doubt second-hand garment. The size of her breasts remained a mystery beneath the layering of clothing, but he enjoyed surprises. He liked them big, smothery and motherly. *Yes, motherly. There's no shame in tracing it all back to Momma, now is there? I think everyone can trace back everything that ever went wrong for them to their mother, and I am no exception.*

He killed the engine and climbed out of the driver's side just as she clicked past his car, the spikes of her heels stabbing the cracked pavement. Jack skirted the front of his car, pocketing his keys and buttoning his black peacoat.

"Hey, girl, where's the fire?" He hurried his step when it was evident she had either not heard him or chosen to tune him out. "I was driving past. You caught my eye. Looked like you could maybe use a drink."

She quickened her steps and widened her stride. Her head down-turned, she spoke without looking at him. "Leave me the *fuck* alone, Uptown. I'm off-duty."

"Good, because it's not what I'm after. You looked upset, and I thought there's a bar right here. Maybe you'd want to duck inside and talk about it?" Jack kept pace with her, even as she rounded the corner out front of Curran's Bar. The clink of swill-filled glasses and a Tom Petty song he barely recognized spilled out onto the street. He grabbed gracelessly for her coat sleeve and came away empty-handed. "Hold up a second. I know you don't know me from Adam, but could you take a breath? I mean you no harm. Seriously. I'm a good listener if you've got the time."

"Not unless you look like Channing Tatum and fuck like a beat cop," she muttered. "Now, I told you *fuck off*! I'm retired!"

"Mmm, you're not *listening to me*. I'm not after that. So you're retiring from what it is you've been doing?"

"I shit you not, Uptown! As of right now—"

Jack Post's hand shot out. "Will you wait up?"

This time he had her by the bicep. He dug his fingers into the fake fur, rooted, and found the lip separating muscle from bone of the bare arm underneath.

She shrieked, her left leg buckling and nearly spilling her over into him.

"Sorry to be like this, but you'll thank me for it later. You look like you could use a friend—"

"Hey! *Hey, motherfucker!*"

Before Jack knew what was happening, strong hands turned him around, and the center of his face exploded into white lightning. Blood ran thick and gloopy down the back of his throat. His hands flew to his nose. Warm and sticky, it fanned out from between his fingers, and he could not swallow as it coated his larynx like a syrup. The world swam in and out of focus. He blinked feverishly and then something ridged and rigid walloped him across the crown of his skull. Jack felt his legs turn to rubber bands. They gave way, but the cement did not rise up to meet him.

Instead, hands seized him by his shoulders and bore him upward.

The bulging, bloodshot eyes of a stranger rushed towards him. The chrome-dome of a bullish, bumpy, and bald head lowered, and those devilish eyes disappeared as his captor rammed his shorn skull up into Jack's dipping chin.

"Now! Motherfucker, what *now? Now I kill your ass—*"

"Walton! I told you *I QUIT!*" The girl's protests swirled all about. Then she burst out laughing.

She's laughing because I'm—

Jack vomited all over his captor's hands and down the front of his pea coat.

The girl's laughter pierced the night, louder now, and high-pitched as a haggling bird.

"Augh, what the fuck!" Chrome-Dome's hold on Jack lessened, and he shoved him backward, retching now himself as the stench hit his nostrils. "You serious with *this shit?*"

This guy's a PCP freak! The strength. The temper. He's going to kill me, and it'll feel like batting a fly because he's got no idea what he's into right now. Gotta think-gotta think-gotta—

His mouth now thick and gelatinous with the mixture of vomit and blood, Jack raised his chin like a recalcitrant child and hocked a fat, purple wad right at Chrome-Dome's wildly blinking eyes.

Chrome-Dome screamed. His hands came away from Jack and flew to his eyes. He dug the flats of his palms into them, gouging. "*I'll-I'll kill you, mother—*"

Jack kicked him square in the crotch, folding Chrome-Dome over neatly as a card table. Then, leaning over him, Jack shook his face down at him, sending all of the blood and bile and throw-up onto the back of Chrome-Dome's bumpy, bare skull. "Good luck with the HIV! I'm *crawling with it!*"

"Naaaaahhhhhhh! Cocksucker! *"*

Chrome-Dome groped madly for his legs, but Jack feinted right and sprinted off, rounding the corner of Curran's Bar and nearly turning an ankle in his Timberlands. The woman's laughter had turned to shrieking, and it made Jack's heart leap with joy despite the flaring pain radiating outward from his broken nose. He heard the shuffling of feet and the confused

45

mingling of people's voices as they spilled out of the bar. By then, Jack was not running, but walking as briskly as the prostitute had been when he had first encountered her. No use in drawing attention when the Prius was right there waiting for him. He fumbled his keys out and in moments was gunning the engine and heaving the hatchback out of its spot. The undercarriage of the car jolted beneath him as he pushed the gas and drove the needle up to 60. As the signs for the I-95 North on-ramp flickered in the glare of his head-lamps, a wild and unchained peal of laughter ripped out of him. He aimed the nose of his Prius onto the ramp and then sailed along the highway, weaving around the spotty traffic like a Nascar driver. He flipped on the radio, turned to the Classic Rock station, and then sang along at the top of his lungs to the closing chorus of Alice In Chain's "Would?"

He felt so damned good, crumpled face be-damned. *I feel like a hot coffee before I hit the ER. Christ, I really don't feel a thing. It's adrenaline for you! It's a shame I couldn't help the girl. I really wanted to.* Jack dug his hand down into his pea coat pocket, seeking his wallet. He would hit the drive-thru and thumb out a couple bills to have at the ready before they could ask any questions about his red-coated face.

No wallet.

Not in the other pocket. None of his pockets. Not in the console. Nowhere.

Jack Post stopped laughing and started to worry.

14. ON THE ROAD

The fact Saint Pio's Veterinary and Rehab Center was a little over fifty miles away never bothered Will until the night when he wanted nothing more than to get there. Alberta would be scared. She would be looking for him, seeking his face among those leaning over her as the world swam back into focus after a month of darkness. Jack could not help but think about the sorts of things Alberta may have had running through her mind as she lay prone and lifeless for all those weeks. He could only pray her memory didn't transport her back to those terror-filled years as a pup in Fallujah. *Don't let her remember what they did to her litter! Please, God, spare her that much!* The worst part about it was, there was so much about Alberta's life he didn't know and never would. Those things would remain forever locked away in her sub-conscious. A part of him was thankful the German Shepherd could not talk, could not tell him where she's been and what her life was like before Will and his platoon freed the city where she had been barely subsisting.

Why are you doing this to yourself, Will? She's back for God's sakes!

Mina touched Will's shoulder from the passenger's seat. "Where'd you go?"

It was a question his girlfriend had to ask him a couple times a day, but she never complained about it. She knew a writer's mind was prone to just standing up and walking out and stalking off without warning and that was its way. His way. *How could it not bother her? Shit, it would irritate the shit out of me if I knew someone was almost always half-listening to me!*

"I'm thinking about stuff I should just leave alone ... again."

"Like what kind of stuff?"

Will shook his head, wishing they were at least halfway there. "Why don't we have some music—"

"No, Will. Talk to me. What's going on?"

He could feel her wide, emerald-green eyes on him and felt their warmth. She would bring it up and out of him one way or another, and this was her gift; it was why he loved her.

"I'm just doing it again. I just get my thoughts stuck on one thing, and it's the one thing I ought to stay away from. But I keep going back to it and back to it like something buried in the sand that turns out to be a landmine. I don't want it to blow."

"Then, take a few steps back and let the desert winds clear away the sand until you can see what it is. Oh my God, now you've got me extending metaphors right along with you."

"Want to see how far we can stretch this metaphor before it snaps?"

"Don't change the subject, babe," she said, solemnly. "Tell me."

Will hesitated, itching to switch on the radio. But he knew what she was doing, and it was exactly what he needed. The book was supposed to be about Alberta, even though it was turning out to have little to do with her directly. This was not Sergeant Karns nudging him into the right direction. This was Mina. *I still think she ought to try her hand at writing. I think it's in her blood. I also think she'd bleed all over the page like a stuck vein, and it would be genius. Every word.*

"All right, Meen," he said. "But just grab my phone from the center console and record me. I might ramble, but there may be something I can use after a couple minutes of talking."

Mina grabbed Will's phone, swiped to the Recorder App, and set it rolling. She set it back down in the center console and settled back into the plush upholstery of the passenger seat, listening.

Will Bentley started to talk:

"So I was just thinking about whether or not a dog dreams when they're in a coma. I hope Alberta's mind was empty. I know there are a lot of snakes just waiting to bite her in the dark every time she shuts her eyes. I've actually seen it. Sergeant Jackson had a warm spot for the dogs roaming the desert where we were stationed, and he personally saw to it many of them were taken in by the Nowzad Organization. Nowzad is the first veterinary hospital ever established in Afghanistan, and they oversee the care and eventual adoption of all the 'lost dogs.' I owe the good people there a profound debt of gratitude. Those people are absolute *guardians of goodness.*" Will paused.

"When I got Albie home, she wouldn't sleep in the bed with me. She scoped out the coldest, most distant spot on the floor of the bedroom she could find. It saddened me because I knew she was so used to shivering and straining against an uncomfortable cement floor, that to even think about the luxury of lying on a mattress shocked the hell out of her. She probably didn't think she deserved such comfort, if that makes sense. The first week, I must have woken up to her frantic, frightened yelps and cries at least five-six times a night. I remember thinking back then what horrible things she must have been remembering in her dreams. And I couldn't do a damned thing for her except hold her in the dark and smooth down her fur. To tell her she was finally safe. Finally safe. It took her a long time to believe. A very long time. But I'll do it again. Mina and I—we'll do it again for her. As many times as it takes. She will have a quality of life. She will know love. Again."

Will motioned for Mina to stop the Recorder. Then, he groped for her hand in the shallow darkness of the truck cab and drove on, silently.

15. SOME KIND OF SUPERMAN

It is a wife's instinct to protect their husband in the event of an attack, no matter what kind of man (or monster) they have been. Some would say it is nearly as powerful an instinct as that of a mother to protect their child from danger or to snatch them free from the jaws of harm. Stella Post felt this. It lit up her arms, legs, and brain with bolts of electricity calling her to climb out of her Taurus; to run to his rescue. He would be killed right before her eyes. The bald man in the track suit was going to murder him right there a half-block away from the bright, strobing shamrock sign hanging over Curran's

Pub. She felt for the door handle and cranked it open.

Then, she stopped mid-motion and eased the door shut once more. She settled uneasily back into the driver's seat, and watched from across the street as her husband, Jack Post, shuddered in the bald man's grasp and then let loose with a spray of green vomit.

"Oh my God," breathed Stella, her chest tightening. "He's going to kill you for that. Oh *God.*"

Something else happened entirely.

She watched him suddenly lunge forward as the bald man dropped his hands and swung his upper body away from Jack. A broad, sweeping smile spread across his reddened lips and he spat a mouthful of what could have only been vomit and blood into the man's eyes. He shouted something at him, his smile bursting into rows of shark teeth glistening crimson in the moonlight. Jack straightened up like a man reborn, sculpted anew into a more resilient flesh and bone impervious to harm. Stella thought of what a superhero, your everyday run-of-the-mill *superhuman*, might look like right then. Triumphant. Resistant. Gloating.

Stella realized what it was that had kept her inside her car, away from the fray. She had been hoping for his murder. His death. A poetic end to a life of lies and bullying and abuse. She had been praying, the words hatching from deep within the dark pit of her being, he would get what he had been giving to her for so long and it would end him.

But he looked like someone who had only just begun.

This was a birth.

She didn't see him break into his sprint back towards the bar and around the corner to his waiting Prius. Stella turned the key and gunned the engine, propelling herself out of the parking spot with the lights off. She forgot to turn them on, and it wasn't until someone flashed her on the way home Stella remembered to flick their switch. Otherwise, she would have driven all the way home in an invisible killing machine.

16. IN THE DEPTHS

Stella waited until she got home to call Karl Tarlick, mostly because she could not hold her hands steady enough to hold the phone to her ear and drive. Once inside the kitchen, she stood in the dark and frantically dialed him on the landline, haphazardly dumping her handbag onto the tiles.

It spit out her cellphone and tampons, and a box of Altoids exploded curiously strong white mints across the floor. She clutched the handset with both hands, the plastic shell clicking in her white-knuckled grip. Absently, she wondered where Betsy, her overweight black and white cat, had been hiding all day. She hadn't seen it since the night before, and it hadn't shown up for its meal in the morning like normal. Typically, the fat cat carried on outside the bedroom door in the morning until Stella rose and filled her bowl to overflowing. Stella was about to call to Betsy when the line connected, and Karl's voice filled the earpiece.

"Karl? It's Stella. I followed the sonofabitch. And he's still alive. He's *still* alive even after all the evil he's done! How? Will you tell me—"

"Whoa—h-hold the phone there, Stell," Karl said. "Who said anything about the guy kicking the bucket? Were you expecting as much?"

"Well—no. No-not at first," she babbled, unable to pull back. "I expected to find him with another woman, or meeting up with someone. But not a streetwalker, for God's sake! He's been fucking whores all this time and for who knows how long!"

"They're all whores if they're lying down with a married man. Let's not split hairs, now."

"No, Karl. I'm talking a *bonafide* prostitute! I watched him proposition her, and when she wasn't going for it he grabbed her arm, and I don't know what he would have done if this—this guy—I guess he was her pimp or maybe some kind of drugged-out Samaritan—if he didn't show up—well, who the hell knows! I know what Jack's capable of. I've been on the receiving end of his bullshit for so long I think I know what he'll do next before he does it. He's been sticking his thing in diseased whores for however long and bringing it back home into our bed." Her voice had climbed to something of a frenzied shrill. "I don't think I'll ever be able to sleep in that bed again. Every time I pull the covers back, I'll see snakes and rats and things that bite and carry sickness, and then I'll wake up with welts and boils, and then *I will slit his throat in his sleep!* I swear to God I will!"

"He ever been tested?"

"Not that I know of," Stella said, winding down somewhat. Her breaths were still coming hard and fast, and she thought she might start to hyperventilate. "There—there was something abnormal about his blood work he mentioned. The doctor's checking it out. But I know it'll be nothing. The bastard can't die. He's got nine fucking lives. You tell me how the worst people seem to hang on forever, and the good ones die too soon? Tell me!"

"You talk about the guy like he's some kind of Superman. He isn't no 'Man of Steel.' I tell you, I sock him a good one in the back of his head it *will* leave a dent." Karl chuckled, a dry and brittle sound like pennies rattling around in a tin can. "We all went to the same high school, Stell, and I had some run-ins with Jackie-boy here and there before I had to leave. There was this one time in the Boy's Room. I don't think he knows to this day who done it, but I remember one day I went in there to take a piss, and I heard someone in one of the stalls. Grunting and huffing. Clearly jacking off. I mean, you could hear the slick slide of his hand up and down his rod, really going for it. He didn't much care *who* come in. He knew someone was in there with him, but it didn't slow him down one bit. So I snuck over to the door of his stall, and I kicked it in. It knocked him down, and I saw it was him because his head slid out from underneath. He didn't get a look at me though, cuz' I banged out of there faster than you could say *little pecker.*"

Stella, Karl, and Jack were classmates at Helms High School. Jack was a year older than the other two, his graduate year '09 to their '10. Karl would go on to embody one of the most infamous students ever produced by Helms. The things he had done.

What Jack hadn't the faintest idea about was Stella had any connection whatsoever to Karl, then or now. As far as Jack knew, Stella had not been asked to her Senior Prom, and she had stayed home and watched a "Friends" marathon with her mother instead. This was what Stella told Jack. Stella and Jack had not met until he was a sophomore at Penn State, and Stella met him at a fraternity party her gay friend Taylor convinced her to attend. As for the Senior Prom, Stella Post (formerly Stella *Warren*) had not only been asked but had attended and lost her virginity to none other than Karl Tarlick.

Then, Karl was gone, locked away a week after her deflowering. He had been gentle. Accommodating. Patient. He had been with five girls before her, many of them no older than thirteen. It didn't phase Stella as it should have. Little of what she had come to learn about Karl disturbed her, and she supposed a part of it related to the fact he had been *her first. You never forget your first. And you always forgive them whatever it is they have done wrong ...*

For Stella, she chose not to forget. Couldn't now if she tried, although for the first time she was put off by his casual treatment of her during what was clearly a terribly low point in her life. This was not how she had expected him to speak to her when she told him what she had just witnessed.

Not at all.

"I'm sorry, Karl, but *what the hell* does your story have to do with anything? All it shows is Jack's probably a nymphomaniac or something, and he started at a young age. Is this supposed to make me feel better?"

51

"I don't know," Karl said. "I guess I was hoping it would prove to you just how vulnerable Handsome Jack is. You're the one making him out to be some kind of superhero."

"Karl," Stella said, her voice suddenly measured and restrained. "Do you remember our conversation from earlier today?"

"After you sucked me off in the woods?"

"Don't be crude."

"Sorry. You were asking if I remember? I don't know. I said a lot of things. If I remember correctly, I never shut the hell up. Floodgates just opened up or something."

"You mentioned something in passing about Santeria. You asked me if I've ever heard of it."

"Yeah—'course," he said, dreamily. "You said no."

"What is it? A religion?"

"It is. From the bush. Africa. Then they brought it over, and it took root down south. It's alive and well and still steers the hearts and minds of many a Creole. New Orleans. You ever been?"

"No," Stella said. "Why did you ask me about Santeria?"

"Just curiosity, I guess. Although, it's looking like it could turn into a little more than that. I gotta do some more reading on it. I'm not so much interested in the accepted Santeria. A guy on the inside taught me all about one of the break-off disciplines. A practice called *Palo mayombe*—"

"I remember you got this, I don't know, thousand-yard-stare in your eyes when you asked me about it. What were you thinking about?"

"Stella—"

"Because you asked me right after I told you Jack was still abusing me. Is there some kind of connection?"

"What do you mean by *thousand-yard-stare?*"

"I—"

"Nah, what did you mean by it exactly, Stell?"

"Karl, what's wrong?"

"Oh, I think it's plenty wrong you'd used that turn-of-phrase to describe me. You know who looks around with a *thousand-yard-stare?* Fucking schizos and Vietnam vets still hung up on the Charlies. You think I'm like them? You think I'm fucking some kind of whacko? Speak now or forever hold your peace, cuz' I—"

"Karl, I would never say that."

"I got no time for a *dumb cunt like you* if that's the case—"

Stella slammed the phone down so hard into its cradle, the force of it ripped the whole thing out of the wall.

She screamed from the balls of her feet and let it tear out of her until every fiber of her flesh was raw and irritated. It broke in her throat, a sorry snapping off.

Stella slid down the wall until her ass struck the tiles, and her tailbone rang out in exquisite pain that rifled up the column of her spine. Her vision ran into watercolor softness as tears flooded and dribbled down her cheeks, carrying the thin layering of her eyeliner along with it in black runnels. She drew her knees up into her stomach and rocked herself back and forth. When Betsy the cat suddenly slipped into the kitchen and immediately set about rubbing herself along her ankles, Stella did not startle at the fat feline's touch. She moved into the animal, then reached out and scooped the bowling ball covered in fur into her lap, dropping her legs back down and burrowing her nose into the slightly matted fur of the animal's arching back.

The tile floor started to vibrate beside her. She turned to find her cell phone skittering around like a living thing. The face was lit up, framing it in white. After some deliberation, Stella grabbed up the cell phone and stared into the screen:

JACK CALLING

It would be Jack calling from either an Emergency Room or on the side of the road. He hated hospitals, and it was quite possible he'd skip medical attention and simply pull over to tend to himself. *No, he's at the hospital—definitely the hospital—and he wants you to come right away! You better answer it! Answer it ... answer it ... don't you—*

Stella cooed down at Betsy and sent the call to voicemail. She wondered why she felt so much more comfortable in the dark. Her mother and father were both drunks and they weren't secretive about it. All their friends who ever came over to the house (couples or not) were alcoholics themselves. No judgment to be had. Her parents had a strange thing they did where they would wake up together in the middle of the night for a drink. The first time little Stella had come down to pour a drink of milk for herself she found them sitting there at the kitchen table in the dark, passing a bottle of Jack Daniels back and forth. It scared the hell out of her at first and she cried out, but her father told her to pour her milk and sit down beside him and from then on, this had become one of many bizarre practices she came to consider normal. Things done in the dark were considered normal and oftentimes necessary in the Warren household where she grew up. What was decidedly abnormal was when Mr. and Mrs. Warren died within three days of one another when Stella was twenty-two. Twin cirrhosis of the liver.

Yet, Jack Post lives on and thrives. Reveling in disease and debauchery. *Oh shut up—you know you'd be lost without him.*

53

"This is the problem, isn't it, Betsy?" she asked the cat, who offered a low *murr* in response. "I have always known I would die by a man's hand. I just never could be sure which one. Karl or Jack. I was able to keep going because a secret part of me, something Jack could never get at—never knew even existed—could not be compromised. A happiness I watered and seeded in private and it grew and grew each time I went and visited Karl." Stella scratched that special spot behind Betsy's ear. "Oh, Bets, Karl's not a bad man. His mouth just gets ahead of his brain sometimes. So do his hands, and they have done terrible things, but for the same reason. His hands move quicker than his mind, his conscience. No one knows him like *I* know him. I know, what a cliché, huh?" Her hand stopped cold. She felt the cat tense. "You want to know what he did?"

Hackles rose up along the ridge of the cat's spine.

"No, I didn't think so," Stella said. "And I'm not ready to tell. It would make it all too real for me. But ... there was something different about him tonight. I had to hang up on him. He's never talked to me like that before. I mean, he has his days where he's like a zombie. He sometimes has weeks where he doesn't want to see anyone. He turned me away at the prison a couple of times. But I know it's during those periods he's remembering his sister. He loved Blaise so much. She killed herself, you know. He blames himself. But it wasn't his fault. Her classmates broke her spirit. *Those* bastards broke her, and they may as well have slit her wrists for her in that bathtub." Stella paused, listening to the house click and settle around her. "Tonight, for the first time ... he frightened me. Karl ... *frightened me.* With h-his hair trigger temper. I could hear the-the hate in his voice. It was like someone jumping out at me from a blind alley and just clubbing me over the head without warning.

"There was no ... warning. I'm ... I'm scared of Karl right now. What if—"

Stella cut herself off, dipping her nose once more into the cat's fur. Her thoughts were awash in visions of blood and coffins and open graves, and her limp body dangling from a tree that looked strikingly familiar to the one which stood in her backyard. A "climbing" tree that had come with the Colonial house. She had to finish her thought, give voice to it. It demanded to be set free of her lips. "What if Karl will be the one to ... to kill me? Not Jack."

You're so certain you'll die young? So certain?

"I am."

Then you are truly alone, and you know wha—

"—you have to do." Stella completed the thought aloud and knew

54

it amounted to nothing more than a fancifully dark daydream or a musing here and there.

This was a decision. Plain and simple.

Stella groped blindly for the cell phone on the floor and swiped the **VOICEMAIL** onto the screen. She pressed the Playback button and listened:

"Stella? It's your husband? Where the hell are you? What are you doing not answering your phone when you've been told time and time again you answer every call from me. *Every mother-fucking one!* I'm in the ER. I slipped on the curb outside the Marriott. Broke my nose on the goddamned concrete—dammit—you know I hate talking to voicemail—just get your ass down here, will you? All I do for you, and this is how you repay me? *Voicemail?* Hurry up and—"

"Go fuck yourself, Handsome Jack."

She sent the cell phone skating across the kitchen tiles. It struck the floor paneling and made a sound like a hockey puck dinging off the corner a goal post.

"Betsy? How's about we have a bath, huh?"

Stella rose with the bulk of her fat cat in her arms, its lower half hanging down the front of her like a white knapsack.

Beside her, the dangling wall phone started to ring.

She wrenched it violently out of the unseated cradle and put it to her ear.

"Stell? Just what the fuck was that all about? *I was just rubbing your tits a little, babe!* Playing a joke! C'mon, you know I'd never disrespect you for serious—"

"I'm glad to hear you say you're sorry, but it's just not enough for me right now. I think we need a break from one another. This is just all too much." Stella surprised herself by how measured she sounded in her own head and then realized this was part of a larger process she had just entered into.

A disconnection from any and all things.

"Seriously?" asked Karl, primly.

"Seriously."

All at once, Karl stuttered and stammered, a series of false starts before he found his words. "*It's all too much?* Isn't that the point? I mean, c'mon, you're just mad, and I said I was sorry. It was all just a rub, babe. You gotta believe me. And—"

"It doesn't matter."

"—and you asked what I was talking about. What Santeria's got to do with Jack. Well, let me finish my thought. I'll give you a sneak peek o' what I been looking into for you. Looking into *for you*, Stell. Cuz' I can't stand your fucker husband, don't see what he has, and one day he's going to just steal you away from the world."

Him or you. Him or you. She almost said it out loud.

Karl kept on. "I just mighta' found a way to humble the sonofabitch. You said so yourself, he's been a cheater all this time, but none of them women were innocent. You gotta know that, too! You lump them all in together, Jack *and* his bitches, and you dump them all into a pot of boiling water and that's really solving the problem. Hurting them all. Everyone involved. But in a way you can't never guess until I tell you. They won't see it coming. And you'll see once and for all Big Jack ain't no *superhero*. You're going to see once and for all if you set it up just right, he'll be the *anti-hero*. Then, after we're done with him, and he's had more than enough—we kill him."

"No, we won't, Karl. Now, I meant what I said. We need a break. I'll call you—"

"Don't you want to know? *Goddammit, don't you want to know?*"

"No."

Once Stella locked Betsy inside the bathroom with her, it was like the animal knew. The few times Stella had to give the cat a bath, it had proven traumatic for the animal, and Betsy exhibited an aversion to the bathroom from then on. The cat was no doubt spooked by the warm bath water Stella was running into the tub. Steamy tendrils lifted all around the two of them as the bathroom turned thick with damp. The cat crowded herself up against the door, mewling softly up at Stella while she undressed and stood in front of the full-length mirror attached to the back of the door. Stella *shushed* the cat, told Betsy she loved her so much, and then proceeded to examine herself.

The ruin her body had become without her fully realizing.

Her breasts, a full C-cup, did not disappoint her, and they never did. Stella considered them her best physical attribute. They stood at attention, the nipples high up on the swell of flesh. Dime-sized and a darker pink. She scooped them up into her hands and let them drop. They did not fall far. This was a wonderful thing. Then, her eyes settled on the slats of her ribcage that pressed prominently upward against the starved flesh of her midsection like twin xylophones on either side of her sunken belly. Her hip- bones jutted out on either side like the sticks of a kite. Malnourishment. Had she really been eating so little?

She had been paying little mind to her daily caloric intake, a neglect that often manifests in those who have come to concern themselves almost exclusively with mental survival. Every day above-ground a good day, she supposed. No longer good enough. Stella would not wait out the inevitable ending. She would take charge of the *when* and the *how*. All there is to it.

Betsy rose to full height and dug her nails into the white wood of the bathroom door. She screeched, a sound Stella had never heard from her before. It sounded remarkably like a child's cry, an infant's desperate coo.

The cat glanced woefully up at Stella and they locked eyes.

"What? Is your life really so great, Bets? *Really*? Christ, you haven't been outside the house since the day I brought you home from the pet store. You'd have a heart attack if I let you out the front door. The world is nothing but claws and teeth. Too wild for you, and too damned cruel for me. Trust me, dear, you won't be missing a thing."

The animal dropped its doleful gaze to the tile floor.

Stella flinched away from the mirror when her eyes found her face. Pockets of discolored gray flesh bunched upward into her hazel eyes, nearly closing them. Her full lips were thin, bloodless lines. The corners, down-turned. She rarely looked at herself naked in the mirror, but there was no avoiding her face on a daily basis, if for no other reason than to apply spare makeup or to wash up in the morning. No need to have another look. Soon, she'd look about as hot as a corpse could manage so what does it matter?

She stepped over Betsy and crossed the bathroom to where a radio was perched on the window sill. She picked it up and walked over to the corner of the bathtub, setting it down precariously on the edge. Stella sat down on the edge of the tub and skimmed her hand across the surface of the warm water. It was high enough to submerge herself to her shoulders. Good enough. Stella turned the water off and rose. She tweaked her nipples, softened by the humid air of the cramped bathroom, and they hardened to attention.

"Ready, Betsy?"

Betsy offered Stella one last pitiful *meow*. The cat crowded her body up against the door. Stella moved towards Betsy and scooped her up into her arms.

As soon as Stella turned to walk towards the tub, Betsy turned to a tangle of scrambling paws, extended claws, and snapping jaws. She swiped at Stella's face with one paw and dug the left front claws into the tender flesh of her bare bicep. Stella screamed. The animal screeched like an alley cat in a fight over dumpster scraps, the lower half of its fat, furry body a pendulum of rapid, frenzied motion. Stella, teeth bared herself, wrenched the animal away from her. Betsy took a sliver of flesh with her, carving a slice out of

Stella's upper arm. Stella bit her lower lip, tasting blood there instantly as she held the animal out to arm's length.

"STOP IT, YOU LITTLE BITCH! STOP IT! THEY'RE GOING TO KILL ME AND THERE WON'T BE ANYONE TO TAKE CARE OF YOU! DON'T YOU UNDERSTAND? DAMN YOU!"

Make the little bitch understand.

Karl's voice bloomed, opening like a lotus flower, inside her mind. It scared the hell out of her at first, and then she remembered what he had called this connection between them. *A mindmeld.* It was a real thing, and somehow he had inserted himself into her conscience, skewing her morality. Karl's voice cleared out quickly as it had come, the seed buried over within her consciousness. She held the cat firmly as she stepped into the tub. The water was wonderful around her legs. The cat continued to struggle, but now Stella felt as she had felt earlier when she had decided to stay in the car while Jack took his beating across the street. Someone else's hands had pulled the door to her car closed. Now, someone else's hands grasped the animal around her sizeable middle.

Stella dipped down into the calm, cooling waters of the warm bath.

Betsy screamed. This time, the animal sounded more infant than animal. It was unmistakable and anyone walking by the Post house just then would have paused at such a sound, fearing a child was being murdered inside.

Stella *shushed* the cat as she had before.

The animal moaned low in her throat. Her body stiffened, straight as an arrow. Stella felt the animal's entire body harden to a slippery stone. Goosebumps spread across her arms as she submerged the cat's lower paws. The cat renewed her fight at once.

She shoved the animal down under.

Water rose and splashed up and out of the tub, spilling across the tiles. Stella struggled with the animal.

Then, as she poked one foot up out of the water to nudge the radio off the ledge, Stella Post thought a second time. *This is more than a mindmeld, do you understand? You are killing your cat. Karl did the very same thing to other people's cats and dogs and rabbits, and he says he had good reason, but we both know he was sick and he was using heroin pretty regularly. Do you understand? You need to understand, and you need to remember who Karl Tarlick is. He fancied himself an artist, but his art teacher at Helms High School put it to him plainly; he* had no aptitude or eye *for it, and he never would. Karl worshipped Dali and Mapplethorpe and Van Gogh. When he brought in his portfolio to show to that smug art teacher, trying to con-*

vince her he was worth her time, she told him he was not Honors Art stock, but keep working at it, Karl! *Do you understand, or shall we go deeper down into the dirt and follow the hole further into the ground? Okay—your hand is still pushing your cat's head down under the water so here we go—do you remember the "exhibit" Karl put together in the woods behind his house? Is this enough, or do you need more? Stop-stop-STOP-STOP.*

Stella kicked the radio off the ledge, onto the tiles as her hand came up off the top of Betsy's head. The cat launched herself at the lip of the tub, scrambled stupidly with slick, sloppy paws at the side until it managed to anchor herself up and over. Out of the water. It bolted to the door, saturated to half her size.

"Betsy, I'm so sorry!" She scrambled out of the tub, bringing a wet wave of water up and out of the tub as she stumbled over the side and sloshed across the tiles to the animal. Betsy moaned low in her throat, bent her head low, and raised her eyes up to meet Stella's. There was no love there. There was a naked fear. The cat trembled from head to tail. "I'm ... so ... so ..."

It was no use, of course.

Stella opened the door. Betsy crammed her way through the opening and disappeared, wet paws slapping feverishly at the hardwood floor of the bedroom beyond.

No use.

"Okay," she said to herself. "I've stopped. All right? It's stopped."

She toweled herself off and placed the radio back on top of the bathroom window sill. She strode back into the bedroom, not even bothering to look for the likes of the cat she had just tried to drown. It was quite possible Betsy would never come out again, not even for food.

Moving around the bedroom with the mindless agility of an apparition, Stella shrugged herself into a warm sweater, jeans, and then hurried downstairs to pull on her winter coat. She returned to the kitchen and turned on the lights. The dark did not lend her any comfort as it had before, so there was no need for it. All things illuminated. Ugliness and all. She located her cell phone, dumped it into her handbag, scooped her keys out and made for the door.

I'm coming, hubby. You sonofabitch.

17. PERFECT WORLD

Saint Pio's Animal Rehab was a deceptively small-looking building of brick and mortar that, once inside, proved to spread out across two acres like a winding snake of hallways, with various wings and waiting areas. The night staff was scaled back by the time Will and Mina rushed through the front doors. The seating area stood vacant, and the reception desk was barren of receptionists. Will hammered his palm down on a small bell that would have looked more at home at the reception desk of a Best Western. A pretty, young black woman promptly appeared with a tired smile on her face and warm eyes. She led them through two doors which gave way to the Intensive Care ward of the center. Then as quickly as she had appeared, Camille (as her name tag read) vanished, and Doctor Lanza accepted the handoff.

Doctor Lanza was a short, athletic blonde, with a curt way of speaking that had taken Will and Mina some getting used to at first. She had been working beside another male doctor, taller and more fleshed-out. They both wore blue doctor's coats, and the man was leaning towards something on a gurney before him. Will and Mina barely heard Doctor Lanza's words of greeting, and it wasn't until the little blonde threw her arms around Mina and hugged her tight, they actually realized there would be a great deal to discuss with this woman. She had taken a special interest in Alberta and could be credited with saving the dog's life. Will looked through her when he realized what the gurney supported.

Alberta lay across the gurney, her long, brown body stretched out among a pink frilly blanket. The other doctor administered oxygen, gently pressing the mask over the dog's snout and rubbing her belly with disarming affection. The room was sterile white, and instruments reflected silver from seemingly every corner and coordinate. It smelled of wet fur within. Will stood there, half-hearing Doctor Lanza as she prattled on to Mina, and he found he couldn't tear his eyes away from Alberta until he actually saw the dog's open eyes.

Tears pricked at him. He turned blindly towards Doctor Lanza, and now it was his turn to sweep her up into a bear hug that lifted her nearly out of her white Reeboks. "Thank you, Patty! Thank you so much! This is *all you*! I know it! I knew you would never give up on her."

Mina was crying too. "And you never let us give up either."

"Time and grace, guys," Lanza said. "That's all it takes is time and grace. You remember I drilled it into your heads. Of course, our girl is going to have a long road ahead of her. I know you're both ready, and she's one hell of a fighter this one. How about you come and say good evening to your girl."

"Yeah?" asked Will, swabbing at his eyes.

Mina hurried along, slipping in beside Alberta. She leaned down and nuzzled her nose into Alberta's belly. "Hi, baby girl. So happy to see you. Hi, Albie."

Lanza touched Will's arm. He hadn't moved. He could only look on from where he was, like some outside observer peering in.

"Will?" Lanza said. "You okay?"

"Yeah, of course."

"This is real, Will. I promise. She's going to be okay."

Going to be okay. "Her brain function."

"Will—"

"She lost some of her—"

"Come on, Will. Let's go say hello. We'll talk later about all of this. Right now, this is the time for celebration."

Brain function, Doctor. The only reason I ask is because of what I saw when I followed her into the church. She was the first one in, braver than me even then. Always braver and showing it once again right here and now. I followed her inside. Some of them stood in a cluster around what I would later discover to be Father Bingham. Poking and stabbing and cutting and opening him up with their fucking little household weapons. Albie was nowhere in sight. Then I heard a series of growls, guttural and animal. My girl fighting with someone or threatening them with her teeth. I ran towards the sound of her and found her trying to wrestle a baseball bat away from Bill Fielding. A guy who volunteered as Comstock's lead firemen before deciding to help his friends and neighbors take a priest apart bit-by-bit on the altar of St. Alphonsus. I yelled to Albie, told her give it! Just give it, girl! *I had already sighted down on Bill and once she let him have his bat I was going to call her over and hold him off by making sure he saw he was in my crosshairs. And Albie did give it. Once her jaws loosened off the wood of the bat handle, Fielding moved faster than I had seen some of my fellow Marines maneuver out in the field of engagement. He choked up on the bat and swung it at the side of Albie's head. It connected right under her right ear. She did not collapse. She didn't even buckle. I had meant to fire at Fielding's knees, to fold him over. But I changed my aim and shot him in the heart. He collapsed. That fucker buckled. Albie started running around in circles. I moved towards her. She started scraping the right side of her massive head along the carpet of the church's center aisle. "Girl? It's okay! It's going to be all right!" She wouldn't stop—couldn't stop doing it. Moving in tight circles and burrowing her head into the ground. "Girl?" Then she straightened up, bolt-upright, and I saw something tumble out of her ear. Wet and gelatinous. "Girl?"*

"It's your girl. Come on." Doctor Lanza led Will over to the gurney. The other doctor hung the oxygen mask on a nearby pole and slipped away, offering Will a nod of encouragement. Behind Will, Lanza spoke up in a genteel voice. "We'll give you some time, and then I'll rejoin you both and we'll talk."

"Thank you, Doctor," Mina said, lifting her head for a moment and then leaning in towards Albie with a bright smile and glistening eyes.

"Hey, baby," Will said. He smoothed his hand along the starved, bony belly of his dog and took a knee next to the gurney. "It's Dad."

Alberta's tail lifted off the gurney, wagged to and fro slowly, and dropped.

"That's right, honey. I'm here. Mom and Dad are both here, and we're never leaving you again." His breath came in ragged, choking gasps as he bent in and slung his arms overtop of the dog spread out prone before him. "Almost lost you. Almost."

A rumbling within Will's brain gave way to the sudden, quick raggedy voice of Sergeant Karns in his prefrontal cortex:

There's a storm on the horizon, soldier. You'll be suiting up soon ...

Part Two

Palo Mayombe

"Whether the dogs have been used in specialized
operations or as traditional guard dogs,
they have been subjected to the same traumatic
events as any soldier and bear the emotional scars
upon returning home from their mission. Unlike
humans, they can't speak to what they have
witnessed, and so must be treated with special
care and intuition to what they have been through."

"Veteran dogs suffering from PTSD"
Joe Wilkes

18. GLYNNA / DOG WITH A BONE

(*One Month Later*)

Detective Glynna Rivells woke to the heavy-handed knock on the door to her apartment around two in the afternoon.

It was a great misfortune.

She had been dreaming of her mother, Louise Rivells, whom she lost to stomach cancer only five months before. Rivells had heard from close friends and family her mother would be around to say her *official* goodbye not long after her death. Mother had taken her time, as it was. Some of Rivells's relatives (Uncle Owen, Cousin Karyn) even claimed Louise had already visited them in that rare, magical REM realm behind the eyelids. Rivells couldn't help but be angry about this, whether it was true or not. She had read a smattering of articles about the phenomenon of loved ones appearing in their loved one's dreams, often much younger. Rivells wondered if she would have trouble recognizing her young mother when her time came to say goodbye in a dream. Louise Rivells had appeared to her only daughter as a thirty-something woman standing by the sun-brightened window of Rivells's childhood bedroom. Mother was drawing back the curtains, spilling more and more of the warming glow of day into the room. Mother was singing the day into being. She always had a beautiful voice, the kind of mournful and bluesy lilt that had sung Rivells to sleep after a hard day at school, post-breakup, or when she still lay in her crib. *Let the sun shine—baby—let the sun shine—because the world is just fine for you and I—gonna let it shine on in and say good mornin'!* The light was decidedly unkind as Rivells figured it. The light poured in, and it spilled across the upper half of her younger mother's body, face, and shoulders, erasing them from view. "Stop singing momma! You're singing yourself away! Please, just stay! Don't go! It's too soon, Momma ..." Rivells's voice was water-logged in the dream. Indecipherable. Still she begged. Still Louise spread the curtains wider and wider, and sang herself right out of sight.

The banging on the apartment door turned violent.

Rivells shot upright amidst her tangle of blanket and sheet, her mind still consumed by the dream.

It took her a moment to reunite her body with her mind, and once they came together, she was out of bed like a shot. Rivells had fallen asleep in her clothes. The night before had ended for her when the sun came up, and she finished typing up her report on a case she had finally closed after months of canvassing and frustration. Quite by accident she and her partner, a Latino with a calm demeanor to compliment her headstrong approach, identified "The Streaker." They were walking along Twelfth and Arch after Indian food at Aaliyan's when they found him standing in a phone booth struggling to button his pants up. He had just done his thing down in the subway, then rushed up the stairs and ducked into the nearby booth to fix his pants when Rivells spotted him from the corner of her eye and matched his face to the police sketch they had been working off for weeks. He didn't deny it, had insisted he was only channeling his long lost relative Adam. *Yeah, Adam as in the guy from the creation story who ate from the tree of knowledge and never wore clothes.*

"I'm coming!" she called, shuffling along the hardwood floor in her athletic socks. "Give me a minute!"

They kept hammering away as if they meant to bring it down.

"You wanna leave it on its hinges? Hold on!"

Rivells threw back the dead bolt but left the chain attached. She cracked the door and peeked out. "Yes?"

A short, elderly woman dressed in a long black raincoat stood next to a young and pretty twentysomething blonde girl in a brown tank top and pajama bottoms, whom Rivells vaguely recognized. It was a faint trace of recall, slippery as deja vu. The older woman had her arms slung across the girl's bowed bare shoulders and looked to be comforting her. The girl's eyes were traced in thin eyeliner that had smeared around cavernous sockets, puffy with red from what could have only been a previous weeping. She kept her head down, gaze settled absently on the auburn rug of the common hallway. The older woman's eyes flitted towards the crack, her eyes wanting and chin upturned like a recalcitrant child.

"Detective Rivells?"

"Yes?"

"Detective, my name is Gloria Dare," the older woman stated. "This

66

is my daughter Jodi. I need to speak with you. There's been a crime. Some-thing was done to my daughter. Can we come in?"

"The precinct—"

"I would rather she spoke with you first if you would be willing. We need your help and Jodi has said you seem like a nice person."

If anything, I have only ever passed your daughter in the halls. She must live in the building.

"Have you called the police yet?"

"No, can we please come in and speak with you. I don't want the other neighbors hearing any more of this than they have already."

Rivells nodded and undid the chain. She peeled back the door and ushered them inside. The older woman filed over to the loveseat in the living room. The daughter followed close behind her, precariously lowering herself down next to her mother and casting her eyes about the apartment before dropping her gaze once more and crowding in closer to her caretaker.

Rivells raked her black hair down into something presentable along the sides of her head. "Can I offer you something to drink? Some coffee? Soda?"

Gloria offered a winsome smile and asked for coffee. Jodi begged off from anything other than a glass of water. Rivells made quick work of preparing the Krispy Kreme coffee, light and sweet as requested, and then poured a glass full of spring water and brought the drinks to the mother and daughter. She perched on the edge of her LaZBoy with a mug of black cof-fee. There was a warmth in her gaze as she waited patiently for the two of them to settle in. She had conducted so many interviews with suspects and victims, but never in the living room of her home. It felt a little too close for comfort, but the girl looked ragged and ripped apart by whatever it was that happened to her. Rivells's thoughts turned to her mother for the quickest of moments, and she smiled inside at the already rapidly fading memory of her from the dream. Then, she began, slow and easy.

"What happened? Just take your time, and we'll get through this."

Gloria blew on her coffee, sipping cautiously at the mug's rim. "Jodi was attacked on her way home from work—"

"Mom!"

"What? That's what happened, isn't it?"

"Oh my God …" Jodi clapped a hand to her forehead, shaking her head and sobbing. "You don't just *come out* with it like that. It's still raw. I'm raw from it, and if—if I'm going to tell it then *I have to tell it in my own way.*"

"All right, okay." Gloria blew another plume of steam off her coffee.

"Your mother says you were attacked?" Rivells asked, gently inserting the prompt into the exchange. It was all about the timing and the tone of interviews that made them a success or an abject, crumbling failure. "Why don't you start at the beginning."

Jodi nodded morosely. For the first time, she met Rivells's brown eyes. "I work as a barista at the Starbucks on Germantown Avenue. I'm paying my way through college at Penn. I have a partial scholarship there. Studying Special Education."

"Teachers are the rarest of blessings, sweetie," offered Rivells. *Mother was a teacher. First graders. The only black woman on the faculty, and everyone there called her* Momma *just like me because she just had this thing about her that made you want to ask her for a cup of hot cocoa and a shoulder to cry on.* "My mother always said so, not just because she loved what she did for a living. It helps to love what you do every day for a paycheck."

Jodi cracked something that passed for a smile, and when Rivells saw those glacial-blue eyes, upturned and gleaming with something of pride, she knew she had calmed her enough to speak clearly and run it all the way through to the end.

"I was the last one out the night it happened. I locked up and by the time I left, the streets were pretty much empty. There weren't even really any tourists or college kids, like most nights. Mom and Dad make me carry pepper spray in my purse because they always say *you never know.* And you really *don't.* But, I mean, it's Society Hill! The richest section in all of Philadelphia!" Jodi paused, bit her lip, and went on. "I never really liked taking the bus. Not because I'm a snob or anything. I have a beater car, and I love it, and it still runs great so ... anyway, it was parked a little ways down from the store because I had a hard time finding a spot that night. Usually, there's a spot for me right there by the door. Pretty amazing how that happened, actually. I had my car keys out before I even started walking but I remember ... something hit me across the back of my head, and I lost my footing. I stumbled, and I thought I sprained my ankle. Thought I walked into a crack in the sidewalk. Then, there was a hand over my mouth and another around my stomach, and I was being dragged into the alley that runs between Starbucks and Beckel's Florists. I was—I was *right there.* But everyone else was gone for the night." Jodi stopped. She crossed her arms over her belly, as if trying to hug herself. She started to rock, ever so slightly. "He must have known I was there by myself because he pulled me all the way behind the store and dumped me down onto the disgusting blacktop behind the store dumpster. You can't see anything behind that thing. A couple of the guys I work with stand behind it when they're on their break and want to get high. Perfect hiding spot, I guess. He ... he ..."

Rivells didn't press her. She let the silence take up space and expand until the young girl crowded into her mother and clutched the older woman's arm. Gloria whispered something into Jodi's ear which made the girl nod and straighten somewhat. Jodi's mother smoothed down her bare, goose-bumpy arms while the girl gathered herself and continued.

"My head was throbbing, and my vision was going in and out of focus. I felt his hands around my throat, not squeezing. They were only hold-ing me there. He moved me over onto my stomach and then he sat on top of my back, pinning me. 'Scream and I'll cut your throat,' he told me. 'It's that simple.' I knew no one would hear me anyway. There is a row of three-story homes that overlook the rear of the store, but I never see any lights on in the windows when I take the trash out. It could be nobody lives there. I don't know. There's an antique store on the other side of the coffee shop, but it's only ever open three days a week. Real exclusive. I was all alone. I didn't scream, but I guess he wanted to be sure because before I knew it he fished something out of his jacket and crammed it into my mouth. It was a fuck-ing—*sorry*—it was a dirty sock. I tried to spit it out, but it was stuck in the back of my throat, and he took a roll of duct tape out of his jacket. He wound it around my head, over my mouth, and I couldn't spit it out."

"Jodi? You said you were on your stomach. Did you get a look at his face before he moved you into that position? Any defining characteristics? What kind of jacket was he wearing?"

The fog of recognition deepened the creases in her young brow. "No, it all happened too fast. Then he was fumbling around inside his jacket while he was sitting on me. It was a big bomber jacket I think ... and he ..." Jodi snuck a nervous glance at her mother.

Gloria patted her daughter's hand, "He—he took her driver's license and ... what else, Jodi?"

"He took my phone and got my phone number out of it."

Rivells leaned forward, barely sitting on the cushions. "He actually *stole* your license?"

Jodi nodded, primly. "He knows where I live," she groaned. "I can't afford to move, and he said when he was finished he would—he would be *seeing me*. It means he's not done with me—"

"Oh, sweetheart," Gloria said, "you'll come and live at home until the man is caught. Wouldn't you say this is the best thing to do right now, Detective?"

"Of course," Rivells said. "But I have to ask ... when did this hap-pen? It sounds to me like you waited because you were afraid if you talked to an officer or a detective he would come back."

Jodi turned her eyes to the rug, defeated. "A little over a month ago."

Rivells didn't say anything. She was not about to discourage a victim who had come as far as this, to tell her story. There were ways around this sort of delay, but a rape kit was key to securing a conviction once the suspect was nabbed and identified. Without the kit, she could already hear District Attorney Dagwood, already a pompous and entitled prick with ties to the mayor's bloodline, and the lecture he would lay on her like a wet, cold blanket. Still, Rivells had worked with far less, and her track record of decorations and arrest-to-convictions would not suffer under these circumstance either.

Like Mother Louise says, *Time to shine!*

"It's going to be all right," she told Jodi and her mother. "I'm not about to lecture you about how important it is to report a sexual assault because this guy clearly put you on the defensive from the get-go. We'll get the guy regardless of his weak, short-sighted tactics."

"And you'll live with us until then, Jodi—"

"Mom!"

Rivells inserted herself into the exchange to keep Jodi on target. "Can you remember anything else about him that could help in catching him? Any skin disorder? Fat face? Thin face? Anything?"

Gloria balanced her coffee mug on the edge of her wide kneecap. "I'm sure Jodi would be willing to sit for a sketch artist if she does remember anything. Isn't that right, honey?" She tried to continue on about something, but then it was the mother's turn to break, and she did. Her eyes suddenly overflowed and her mouth quivered as the weight of what they were actually discussing struck her across the mind. It was true, her demeanor up until that moment had been rather reserved for someone who has just discovered their daughter was sexually assaulted, but Gloria Dare's emotional mind caught up with the rational side and ultimately won out. "Go on ... I'm-s-s-sorry ..."

Jodi looked at Rivells, but there was a strange wariness in her eyes. "He pulled something out of his coat. It crinkled like plastic. I remember the crinkling sound, then a harsher sound. Rubber grinding against rubber, I think. Then he turned me over onto my back, and I could see him. He had a mask on. It was ... it was a fucking ... *a German shepherd mask*. Like one you could buy at a Halloween store. Through the mask I heard him say, 'Okay, before I do the doggie on you, you gotta *be the doggie too!*'"

"A dog mask," repeated Rivells. Suddenly it dawned on her she ought to be writing this down. She snatched up a blank yellow tablet of paper off the nearby coffee table and started scribbling furiously until she had near half the page filled. "Sorry, I wasn't thinking. Let me just get this down. I know shorthand for the job so ... only one more minute ..."

Jodi and Grace looked on expectantly until Rivells lifted her gaze from the page and asked Jodi to please go on.

"He said that, and then he ... the sick bastard made me wear a dog mask."

"Same type of dog mask? German shepherd?"

Jodi opened her mouth to answer and then clapped it shut. A mist blew across her eyes. "I dunno," she admitted, her voice squeaking a little. "I only know ... he pulled it down over my head."

Then Grace and Jodi were in each other's arms, rocking slowly and sobbing against one another.

"All right," Rivells sighed, letting them have as much time as they would need. "You did good, Jodi. You're brave, and you're strong. We're going to catch this freak. But, if you would be willing to come down to the station with me, I would like to get all of this on record. All of this—" *disease, sickness, depravity?* "—detail."

Rivells set down her notepad and pen. She stood up, and soon the mother and daughter joined her. Rivells took the girl by her bowed, bare shoulders and hugged her tight. "You came to the right place. The right person. I don't quit until I've got them. Like a dog with a bone. You understand? A dog with a bone."

19. ENGAGEMENT, MORE THAN ONE KIND

If Doctor Lanza had it her way, Alberta would have remained at St. Pio's Veterinary and Rehab Center for a month of observation following her awakening. Once Will explained to her he had brought a work crew in to completely renovate the garage, transforming it into another wing that housed a wave pool for Albie's daily exercise regimen, the good doctor was somewhat convinced of an earlier release after two weeks. Mina explained they had also hired a rehab nurse, a highly-recommended and profoundly dedicated middle-aged fireplug named Kathryn Danforth, to work with Albie in Will's home. Alberta returned home thirteen days after her revival from a month-long coma.

Lanza, of course, would have been remiss in her duties if she did not outline how the transition should unfold for Alberta. "For the first week, she will need to remain on an intravenous diet or the shock to her system will set her recovery back. She will also need a quiet, isolated area in your home where she can rest. I would set this area up well away from entryways or foot traffic. Have her feeding dishes right beside her when she does switch back to regular food." Then, there was the matter of the nasal implant she would have to wear twenty-four hours a day. The funny thing about it was it seemed to bother and annoy Will far more than Alberta, who was tasked with actually having to wear the uncomfortable looking device.

"It looks like a damned plastic twist tie for a trash bag," bemoaned Will to Nurse Danforth one morning over cups of black Columbian brew. "It just seems so damned medieval." Blowing the steam off the rim of his coffee mug, Will stared out the kitchen archway towards Alberta, where she lay prone on an oversized brown pillow bed, her large snout stretched out and over the side as she sighed and slept.

Danforth, ever the devil's advocate, sipped cautiously at the steaming brew in her hands as the two leaned on the kitchen divider in their casual meeting-of-the-minds. "Mr. Bentley, I'd say the more sadistic option would be to let your dog asphyxiate. Don't you think?" She footnoted this with the gurgling giggle of hers which had become something of a trademark. Danforth often laughed at her own jokes, even the corny ones.

"Touché, Danforth," Will said. "Touché, I say." Still in his bathrobe and slippers, Will shambled off towards his study. It was nine a.m., and the wheels of creativity had already started to grind. He would have to catch up to their motion and fall in line. They were well-oiled and trained to kick into gear at this time of day, whether he was ready and willing to meet the muse on the blank page wound down into his Brother P-Touch or not.

"Happy writing, Hemingway!" Danforth called after him.

"Yeah, yeah …"

You got yourself a foil in that woman, soldier. She won't let you get away with any of your bullshit!

Something else had changed in the last month. Sergeant Karns, scarcely heard since the ambush at the church, seemed to be making up for lost time. He never shut up, as it turned out. But the writing had never been better, and there was no use in denying this fact. Will was up to a staggering hot-and-sweaty five-thousand words a day quota. He knew he was back the first day a week and a half ago when, after a two-hour stint, Will looked up from the "hole in the page" and found the upper part of his body was slick with perspiration while the lower half of him remained cold to the touch.

After an hour-and-a-half, Will's body sang like a tuning fork as the voice of Sergeant Karns guided his writing. The sheaf of pages at his elbow slowly rose, as he experienced the hot and cold of the word flow. He had once described it to Mina as being second-best to a mind-blowing orgasm, and she had not taken offense at the comparison, surprisingly. In fact, Mina had gone so far as to say her "second-best-to-an-orgasm" was reaching the especially delicious reveal of a good novel. "A good book makes me wet, but that's only ever happened twice in my life ... really felt it down there." Of course, Will's next question was obvious to predict, and she had told him one of the books in question was indeed "one of your books, Mr. Bentley."

Will decided it was time to break. He looked out the picture window above his writing desk. Danforth and Alberta were in the front yard, a twenty-five by twenty-five expanse, enclosed by a quaint arrangement of cattle fences. Alberta lay in a pile of leaves and Danforth was bent over her, engaging her in some one-on-one fashion. It warmed Will's heart, the Norman Rockwell cliché of it all.

Mina was at her bookstore, teaching a new hire how to inventory. Will didn't expect her for a good two hours from then, which would afford him just enough time to hit his word quota and maybe, in fact, surpass it. He stood up, wrung his bones out with a good long stretch, and walked over to the door to his study. He shut it, soundlessly. His writing room boasted a surrounding bookshelf inlay and the spines of nearly two thousand books, all manner of fiction and genre and nonfiction and memoir, stared out at him from the cherry shelves. Will had not read everything on the shelves, but only Mina knew this. Three-quarters of it, which was not too shabby.

Will had just turned thirty-five. The way he saw it, there was time.

He had let Mina have at the organization of the books on the shelves and the result was a convenient, logical arrangement consisting of fiction and nonfiction, genre, and finally alphabetical order. Of course, Will's book was prominently displayed among the other dusty volumes, and backlit with a special spotlight hidden by a wooden fold overlap.

Jesus, the hubris!

Will approached the backlit first edition copy of his book, *I Can Hear the Shiite Weeping*. He took it down and tucked it under his arm. He retrieved a small black box from behind the stand displaying the book. Then, he replaced the book and returned to his writing desk. He didn't sit down. Will stood there; just holding the small box in his hands sped up his heart. He slipped the top off the decorative box and plucked out the gray jewelry container inside. He flipped it open.

When you gonna pop the question, anyhow? Sergeant Karns sounded more impatient than amused at Will's sluggishness. *Time's ticking. Always slipping away, soldier. Tonight, why don't you make it official?*

He held it closer to the natural light filtering through the nearby picture window. The stone seemed to come to life, every cut and angle of the stone inset jumping and dancing and leaping with reflection and refraction. Karns was right of course.

"Hold up," Will told himself. "Let's not put the cart before the ponies. Tomorrow night." He smiled, relishing the warmth of such a decision."Will that satisfy you, Sarge?"

His left cheek tingled, as it always did whenever Sergeant Karns spoke up from within. *Deeply and thoroughly, soldier. You bet.*

Will snuck another glance out the window at Danforth and Alberta. Danforth was still engaged in some sort of one-on-one interaction. Will wondered often if she spoke canine and kept such an ability secret.

His cell phone started buzzing beside the typewriter. It was set on vibrate, or *walk across the desk* as Will called it.

Will closed up the box. He snatched up the phone, the screen display read CLAIRE MONASTA. *The agent checking up on the writing, not the writer—hahahaha.*

"Hey, I already gave at the office, so—"

"Yes, but it turns out, Will, there's no such thing as 'The Human Fund,' so we're going to need another Pulitzer winner instead. We'll settle for a Man-Booker Prize this time around, of course."

"Love the 'Seinfeld' reference, dearie," Will said. "If not for those, I'd probably have to jump ship from McNair and McNair for Ellerby Literary."

"Bite your wicked tongue, Bentley!"

"Bitten, ma'am."

"How are you feeling, Will? And how's our Albie?"

Will burst into his month in review spiel, if for no other reason than he was shying away from the inevitable question of word count. Not that it was a poor number. Will just didn't feel like poring over statistics just yet.

"And the book, Will? How are we looking on deadline?"

Will raked his dark hair away from his forehead, driving it into black spikes. "Going swimmingly," he said. "I'm halfway in and digging out the other side. It's practically writing itself. I should have a draft for you by the middle of next month."

"Then you're right on target," Claire said. "I'll let the brass know." Will heard her stifle a violent, hacking cough and then sigh into the phone. "Sorry about that. A little under the weather."

"Tis' the season, huh."

"You betcha," she said. "So the real reason for my call is I have actually been getting inundated with calls for you to come and speak."

"Really? Shouldn't we wait until the next book has a street date?"

"Oh, you'll be running the circuit for it soon enough," Claire said. "These are university gigs. You'd be speaking to a room full of creative writing majors. NYU was the first to call, and then they just started pouring in. The latest call came in from Boston College."

Will set down the box and lowered himself into his chair. He gave it a whirl, spinning himself halfway around and then braking with his bare heel. "So ... how many dates are we talking?"

"Five in the next week. Spread out over the northeastern region. Nothing further west than Pitt."

"Pitt, too?"

"You know how these things unfold by now. One call turns into a slew of them. The power of synchronicity. You're still very much a hot commodity. The word is all of these schools are teaching your *Shiite Weeping* in at least one of their Lit or American History courses. By the time your next book comes out, every academic institution will be tripping over themselves to get you booked on their campus. And don't worry! Tell Mina I'll have you home by Christmas."

"You'd have to have me home by Chanukah for Mina to care as much," Will said. "She's Jewish. It's kind of her thing, you know?" He chuckled. Mina celebrated both holidays, her mother and father Catholic and Jewish respectively. "These are paying gigs, of course?"

"You'll be well compensated, to say the least. UMass mentioned six figures for an hour. That float your boat?"

Silence. Will opened his mouth to speak, to confirm. Something held him back.

"Ah, Will," Claire said. "Your silence is deafening. I understand what's holding you back."

"Do you?"

"I do, Will. You want to be there for Alberta. You're afraid she'll take some turn for the worse, and you'll be holed up in a Marriott in New England somewhere. Then you'll curse me seven ways to Sunday for sending you on this little tour. But I want you to run it all back. Everything you just told me about how well she's doing? How she's in such good hands with the live-in vet you have looking after her. There's Mina, of course. It's not like you'd be dumping her off at a kennel. That's a damned impressive support system you've got lined up for her."

"Claire, I hear you. Believe me, I do. But Albie just opened her eyes a little under a month ago." He looked out the window once more, surprised to find the yard, his view of it at anyway, vacated of both Alberta and

75

Danforth. "I'd feel like a supreme shit if I left now."

"Just give me five days. Rake in the money and inspire some wanna-be Faulkners. I'm giving you a guarantee you'll be home no later than the 12th of December. I will keep in regular contact with both Mina and Danforth. We'll both keep on top of the situation together. I promise if anything happens I'll get you off the hook for whatever gigs are left." Claire paused for a moment. Will heard something like faint whistling through the phone line. "So are you in?"

Will held off another moment, spun himself in the chair until he made two full revolutions. "I can't argue with that. All right, book it."

"Terrific! I'll call you later today with the logistics and pay grade. I'll have specific figures for you then."

"That'll be fine," Will said and rang off.

He picked up the box with the ring in it and thumbed it open once more. He must have sat there for ten minutes staring not at the stone but into it. It was hypnotic beyond measure. He didn't need Sergeant Karns to spell it out for him. *I have to wait until Christmas. I can't ask her to marry me and then hop in my car and hit a tour. No ... it will have to wait. I think she would want it that way, too.*

Will walked over to the backlit hardback copy of his book and hid the box behind it once more.

"MR. BENTLEY! COME QUICK! YOU'VE GOT TO SEE THIS!" Danforth.

Will ran in the direction of the vet's voice, traversing hallways and bounding out into the yard without a coat on. The sharp, whipping wind slipped its hands underneath the flannel and t-shirt he was wearing. Danforth was standing alongside the driveway. Alberta lay on her back, rolling slowly and stodgily around in a drift of leaves Will had been meaning to rake for the last month.

"She's rolling!" he cried, astonished.

Danforth walked over to Alberta and rubbed her long, brown belly. She glanced back at Will, "Oh, that's not all. Not nearly all." Then, she turned back to Alberta and gently eased her back onto her belly. "Call her, Will."

"Are you sure?"

"Just do it. Trust me."

Will stiffly lowered himself down into a crouch. He held out a hand to beckon and called to Alberta.

The dog took a moment to respond. Her tail lazed along the dead leaves, kicking them up ever so slightly. Then she heard her name on the third call. Her whole body twitched and this worried Will at first. Alberta tensed and rolled onto her right side. She tried to bark, but it seemed to catch in her throat. Alberta tumbled onto her belly and precariously drew herself first up onto her front legs. Her back legs followed suit, buckling like the limbs of a newborn fawn.

"Is this ... has she done this before?" asked Will.

Danforth shook her head, standing aside and watching with her hands on her generous hips. "Never. She's been trying, but nothing like this."

Alberta held back a moment, but she met Will's expectant eyes. The spark in the animal's gaze was unmistakable. There was a deep longing in Alberta's eyes, appearing nearly as eager as when she used to circle him in the kitchen every morning while he spooned out Alpo into her bowl. It was a primal desire. She took one shallow step towards Will, her stare never once wavering from her master's. Her tail was a furious fuzzy whip that swiped at the biting breeze and then she was coming along, the other paw slipping alongside the other.

Danforth moved down low and spotted Alberta along her left side in case she were to collapse. The animal was clearly favoring that side. "Slow and easy, baby. Slow and easy ..."

"You're doing great, girl," Will said, now beckoning Alberta with both hands. "Just a little further. You can do it. I know you can do it."

Alberta, snout open and snapping absently at the breeze, peddled along little by little. Back paw lining up with the other, followed by front left and right. Never faster than that, but this was more than enough. She was close enough to Will for both of them to join hand and paw, but Danforth waved Will to remain in place. She told him to let Alberta come all the way.

When she did, Will lunged at her and slung his arms lovingly around the dog's neck.

The big German Shepherd collapsed in his arms, her back legs folding under her flank. Will held her top half in his arms and tears were pricking at his eyes.

"Don't break her!" she cried. "We just put her back together again, Will!"

"Danforth!"

"Slow and easy!"

Alberta lapped at Will's black stubble, wriggling in his arms. When she barked up at him, the sound of it was crisp and true.

"My God, Danforth! After only a few weeks!"

"I know—I know—just take it easy—"

"Danforth?"

"Will?"

He looked up at her, his eyes bright and smiling. "Will you marry me?"

20. ROCKING CHAIR

Stella Post spent the next four weeks in the rocking chair her grandmother had passed down to her as a housewarming gift when the Posts moved into their split-level home on Calendar Road. According to Stella's grandmother, gone two years now, she had rocked Stella's own mother in the chair during an especially nerve-racking spot of colic.

She sat to the left of the back bay window, which looked out onto a meager, slightly sloped rear yard. It was twenty percent gray grass and the rest bald, brown dirt. She studied the pickets of the white fence enclosing the backyard and wondered how it would be if she were to drive one of those pickets deep into her husband's side. She whiled away each day in that chair, enjoying her meals and tea. She read her James Patterson novels.

It was the itch. The terrible, radiating itch she could not scratch as it lurked well beneath the cast of her broken right arm. This had been Jack's answer to her ignoring his phone calls that night a month ago. This was her torture, the special sort which threatened to drive her mad for the length of time she had to wear the concrete shell. Then, the doctor had sawed it off and it had been like a spell was broken. The spell that had held her, bound her to that chair staring dazedly out the window as she slowly and stiffly rocked to and fro. Even Jack didn't bother her much during those four weeks, surprisingly leaving her to her daily quiet, near-catatonic contemplation.

It's not to say Jack didn't mock her complacency. "You sit there day after day like you were the one with their nose smashed in. Look at this piece of cauliflower on my face! It'll never look right again." With a wink, he added, "I'll never be beautiful again." Stella knew better. Jack would never be short on vanity, although his nose did bend slightly to the right. She never said anything out loud about it, relishing her deep, hidden pleasure in the fact it looked like a piece of deformed vegetable. She would never tell him what she had seen that night in the city.

She *would* do something about it later.

The cast removed, Stella moved the rocking chair back to a far corner of the bedroom and set about planning how she would take him down.

There was no chance of strong-arming him in any way. He was just too powerful, no matter how much she wished she could clobber him and bust his nose, flattening it out and mashing across his cheeks like Play-Doh. When he walked into a room, his presence alone and the threat of caustic insults still unnerved her to such a degree, she needed time to shake her anxiety once he had gone out again.

So she did her *work* while he was gone.

Stella had never before dared to delve into any of Jack's belongings. It just wasn't *done*. But after what she had seen and all the time she had spent thinking and retracing the path of their lives together while sitting and rocking all those weeks, Stella had come to more than a few conclusions. The first was there was a certain freedom in knowing no matter what she did, she was at peace with the notion of dying young. Nothing to lose. *Why not muddy his good name and sabotage him somehow before I go?* Once she had managed to marginalize the threat of death in her mind, the rest was easy. He was involved with prostitutes, a crime in and of itself. If he had seen that line and crossed it so effortlessly, battling with whores and their pimps, then what's to say he hadn't taken things further and broken another law or two?

Jack worked as a talent scout for Ballantine University's athletics department. She possessed a limited knowledge of what Jack's job entailed, little beyond the extensive travelling all over the country and expensive dinners with prospective players and their families. Stella knew enough to suspect such a job could, and probably did, involve *payola* here and there, to give a player the nudge they needed to sign on the dotted line. Really, what sort of trouble could Jack get himself into with such a position? Perhaps a casual question here and there about his work would shed more light on his duties and activities? Unless, of course, Jack resented the fact she was asking about his *business* in the first place. That could get her other arm broken, could it not? It would depend on his mood. She dug out the back of his closet and after the revolting find of a dead mouse wedged behind a pair of forgotten Sebago slip-ons, Stella located the safe. It was built into a small compartment in the back wall. She knew he kept one because he hadn't kept this bit of information from her. He kept her social security card inside, as well as her birth certificate. He had demanded both documents from her early on in their marriage and she had relented, thinking nothing of it because they were husband and wife.

There had existed a vague notion the safe was located where it was because she had caught him on more than one occasion on his hands and knees, halfway inside the closet. Fumbling with something beyond the field of vision. He had scowled at her and slammed something closed deep within the closet, before storming out of the room, barking, "Jesus Christ, you don't *walk*, woman. You *creep!* All the time!"

Her success in having located the small safe ended when she tried to open its door and found it locked up tight. Jack hadn't left it on the last combination number. In high school she always left her locker's lock on the last number for convenience. Jack had no doubt spun the dial a few times.

She would come back to it. Stella left the safe alone for a few days.

She decided to pore through whatever papers she could locate with a greater ease. Jack's study was locked, but Stella breached the simple mechanism with a swipe of her supermarket card between jamb and door. From there, Stella emptied all of his desk drawers and spread each and every paper, loose as well as bound, along the hardwood floor. Bank statements. No significant spike in any of the account balances to hint at embezzlement. Credit card statements. Low balances. *The cheap prick!* Jack did not let her keep a credit card. Nothing she could use. She painstakingly reassembled each bound sheaf of paperwork, having kept them in order as she pored through them. She replaced all paperwork back inside his desk exactly how she found them, Stella wiped away any and all traces of her fingerprints with a hand towel. She rubbed out her knee prints in the rug, as well.

Stella crept off to bed and burrowed under the blankets until an hour before dinner, which she dutifully prepared for Jack's arrival home.

That night she dreamt of endless figures. Bafflingly long numbers stretching on and on into infinity, where typical human understanding breaks down.

21. A PILE OF GRAY

The Sergeant hissed in Will's ear. Usually, he was all bark.

It could not have been worse timing, this being the first night of his speaking tour.

Will stood just outside the auditorium doors of the Ballantine University Liberal Arts Building. His agent was busy fetching a bottled water for him while a pretty creative writing professor was in the process of introducing him to a capacity crowd of *young scribblers*. That's when Sergeant Karns blew a string of words and sighs across Will's brainpan.

Karns was damned certain he knew what Will was going to do before Will had even decided.

You tell those little fuckweeds about me and how I'm in your head, and I can promise you your little tour will be over before it starts! They will not *understand. Those coozes don't know nothing about what a* real muse *is. They write like they're constipated, forcing it out until they pop a couple blood vessels. None of them know how to coax the muse out. This generation doesn't wait for anything, and they'll never have to.* We can't trust them. Don't ... tell ... them!

Will's agent, Claire, pressed an opened bottle of Aquafina water into his right hand and slapped him on the back like she was sitting next to him on a barstool somewhere. "She finally wrapping it up?" she whispered. "Man, talk about a *superfan*, Will. She sounds positively weepy."

Claire cracked the door to the auditorium open wider. The department chair was winding up her introduction, and did indeed sound like a woman wrung out. "... and so we at Ballantine University are proud to present an evening with Will Bentley! Please give him a warm welcome! Come on out, Mr. Bentley!"

Dressed in a tweed jacket and black shirt opened at the throat, with baggy jeans and low-top black Doc Martens, Will walked up onto the low stage. He accepted an exuberant hug from the little blonde with the sodden brown bedroom eyes, before stepping to the podium which bore the Ballantine crest across its face. The department chair clapped herself down off the stage to join Claire. The entire audience was on its feet for the better part of a minute before Will waved them down with his big hands and proceeded to wrestle with the microphone holder. It hung low around his throat, and he tried to raise it to his mouth. A few chuckles filtered out of the crowd, and he couldn't help but laugh with them. It kept dropping down to where it was, and he had no choice but to shrug and begin, grasping the podium on both sides and bearing down on it without realizing.

"So, what I want to start out by saying is I always wanted to write. My father, an English teacher all his life, used to keep this electric typewriter on his side desk. It was blue. We called it 'Big Blue' as a matter of fact. Boy, I'll tell you, when you turned the sucker on, it hummed like a 65' Thunderbird under your fingers. I wrote a lot of things on 'Big Blue' but never anything I would dare have shown to anyone. Especially not my father, Mr. Ph.D who worshipped at the altar of Faulkner. I never could make sense of Faulkner, something else I kept from my Pop. I grew up teaching myself to write. I was too damned bashful and unsure of myself about showing my work to anyone else, but I worried a lot I might just be learning to write *the wrong way*. I knew I needed a mentor, but my insecurity kept me away from approaching anyone who might just help me to aim myself towards the light

81

of the sun like a tree in need of harnessing, pulled towards the warmth and the nutrients. I still think I write *the wrong way*, but I guess now it could also be called *style*.

"What I want to say to all of you is there is no *right way* to do it. Sure, there's mechanics. There's nuts and bolts bullshit. There's even craft, but most important is voice. Style. These are things which cannot be taught, because they're perfectly intertwined with your souls. Just try teaching your souls how to be, well, *soulful*. See what happens!"

Applause. A pause.

"In 2002, I enlisted in the Marines—"

"Hoo-aaah!" someone called from the back of the auditorium.

Will pointed towards the source of the sound. "That's right!" he said, smiling and swelling with pride. "You know it, my friend! Thank you! Anyway, I enlisted, and I did three tours over in the desert. A great deal of my time was spent in Fallujah, and I was there for both the first and the second battles which took place on its stage. I was over there for five years total. I remember the night before I left for basic training. I packed a journal my father bought for me at a local bookstore. It was a beautiful little bound book. Moleskine. He also fastened a fountain pen to it, and he inscribed it, which was his way. He wrote, *This is the journal of Private William Bentley—the pages are blank for want of the written deeds of a noteworthy life!"*

The next pause was entirely unplanned for. Will bit his lower lip, gripped the sides of the podium, and tried to hold back the tears pricking at the corners of his eyes. "My father passed one month after I shipped out for Iraq. I missed his funeral. But ... you know ... I'll tell ya, I never missed a day writing in the journal he gave me. And, it turned out to be a good thing, because from those journals I was later able to extract what would be the contents of *I Can Hear the Shiite Weeping*."

Applause.

Will sniffed and drew his reading glasses out of his breast pocket. He put them on and pawed the copy of *Shiite* on the podium open to the sticky-note where he meant to read from. "Chapter Ten, In Karns We Trusted"

"Sergeant Karns never used to talk about his brother Grant, even though they worked in close coalition with one another. We all knew he had a brother, and his name was indeed Grant, but that was the long and the short of it. Karns did say once, Grant was 'always smarter' than he was and the work Grant Karns did for the government was more interesting and meaningful than what our sergeant did. Grant Karns worked for Blackwater USA.

"Now, Blackwater USA was a private military contract organization. In July 2004, Blackwater was hired by the U.S. State Department under the

Bureau of Diplomatic Security's Worldwide Personal Protective Services, WPPS, umbrella contract, to provide protective services in Iraq, Afghanistan, Bosnia, and Israel for servicemen. They were the ones who kept the 'rain off our heads', as our sergeant put it. What he really meant was they were the ones who provided an added layer of security for all of us while we toiled to stay alive in the face of a hidden enemy. 'Much more interesting than leading a bunch of boys into harm's way and pulling off the impossible, don't you think?' our sergeant used to say. Very tongue and cheek was our sergeant, and it was what masked a secret pain. An insecurity in what his life's purpose happened to be.

"The 82nd Airborne Division handed control of Fallujah to our First Marine Division in February, and we were busier than ever before, fighting to hold the ground and the status quo. There was no time to talk about family or insecurity or sibling rivalry. Sergeant Karns was most happy when he was yelling at us and least happy when the focus was on himself and what secret shame he harbored. Strategy and maneuvering dominated our conversation, marginalizing our human sides for the better part of a month. We weren't men, individualized or special.

"We were a leviathan.

"In March, four American private military contractors from Blackwater USA were ambushed and killed in Fallujah. Images of their mutilated bodies were broadcast around the world. Grant Karns was among the four. When the sergeant viewed the footage, as much as his superiors had tried to block his access to it, his face turned the color of alabaster. Somehow, his shoulders lost their T-shape and sagged. He looked to have aged twenty years, and he was not a young man as it was. Then, he asked for a brief leave from a supporting officer and wandered off into the desert. He walked as far as he could before encountering our gated barricade. To breach the gate meant not only a court-martial, but certain death. The wolves were outside the gate. They would have gnashed the bones of a sergeant, greedy as you please. So our sergeant walked the entire three-mile perimeter of the barricade alone, and in the dark the searchlights could not reach. I have no idea when he came back, because I was catching winks in the buSenkhouse.

"The next morning, Karns caught me while I was readying the pack for Ammo, the dog we had liberated from a stronghold a few months back and who we had decided to keep with our infantry division as a sort of mascot. I was packing her snacks and also prepping my gear when the sergeant strode up alongside me. I expected his hoots and hollers to break across my back like a strong wave, but instead, he patted me on the shoulder and took a seat. He clasped his hands in front of him, cleared his throat, and started to talk about what kind of man Grant Karns was.

"'Better man than me, especially in death, soldier. What a fool I've been for so long. And I'll tell you something, I got this strange feeling. Just a strange predilection. I feel like Grant's calling me. Calling me out. To avenge him. I dreamed about him last night, and his face was all red, and he was stomping his feet and gnashing his teeth. Pounding one fist into his palm. He was demanding blood and retribution. Even ... shit, even my own blood if that's what it took to make it so.'

"I said, 'Don't worry about it, Sarge. We'll take care of it for you.'

" 'No,' he said, 'you won't. Never leave it to someone else. It's like letting another man plow your wife.' Then he stalked off, rubbing at his hands like he always did."

There were a few small snickers from the audience, instantly squashed by louder *shushes*. Will did not crack a smile, his face tight.

"Operation Vigilant Resolve, the first battle of Fallujah, may as well have been named by our sergeant. Vigilant. Resolve. Karns was hoping for a resolution, a resolve, but he didn't get it, not to his satisfaction. It took three weeks for our infantry to drive the insurgents out of the Fallujah province, and then the first conflict was done. We handed off the responsibility of keeping the rabble-rousers out of the city to the population, and along with Blackwater USA, provided for the safe instatement of a new local leader in the territory. There was talk our sergeant had actually somehow gotten so close to his kills he knifed them, savaged, and butchered them in the midst of battle. The insanity of the conflict masked these encounters, but not entirely. Our sergeant's behavior only added to what was becoming his growing myth.

"Our sergeant refused to wash off the blood he had gotten on him in battle. In between encounters, we couldn't wait to get the shit off our faces and off our gear, if possible. Karns wore·the blood of his kills for days. He told me it was his 'warpaint'. I knew it was his reminder of what he had set out to do. In the end, the first battle of Fallujah did not feed his bloodlust as he hoped.

"Word was also coming down he might be relieved of his duty or demoted in some fashion once the smoke cleared. His erratic behavior was not lost on his superiors, and he made no effort to hide any of it either. He started spending more and more time with Ammo the dog. Ammo was most partial to me, and I would eventually adopt and rename her Alberta after my grandmother. But Karns used to lead Ammo away from me with a handful of meat scraps, and I watched them walk along as if in deep conversation. Ammo kept stride with Karns, and I remember thinking he was probably telling Ammo the things he just couldn't confide in any human being at the risk of sounding weak.

"To this day, I wish my dog could talk. I would have liked to know what our sergeant's final days were like and what his state of mind was.

"The coalition forces had to sew up the all highways and entryways into and out of Fallujah. The insurgent forces were swelling in number by the day to five hundred "hardcore" and two thousand plus "part-time" enemies, and by November the numbers were doubled. Think of Fallujah as a pipe which carries clean water, and we had to keep the dirty water from pouring in. It was all about 'fresh water,' Sergeant Karns used to say. We knew there would be another battle, and somehow every damned one of us was certain it would end many of us. We all did our part to patrol the highways and entryways, and they were clogged pretty regularly with Iraqis who wanted in, either to find refuge or their loved ones. We had to search every car, taxi, bus, whatever damned thing ran on four wheels. Of course, we even searched the ones on bicycles. It was piecemeal, but it was necessary. Sergeant Karns was with us during one of our highway patrols.

"It was October tenth. We were patrolling a four-lane highway. Two lanes going north and two lanes going south with a median in the middle. We were Bravo Team. We had a bus northbound and there were about twenty-five Iraqis on board. We had to search everyone as well as the bus itself, inside and out. We made them all line up along the median and wait in a line. It took hours, because we had found a suspicious-looking device clamped around the back shocks. No one was coming or going until we could ascertain just what in the hell it was. Two hours in, this teenage girl started crying very loudly. She was holding her stomach and before we knew it, she was vomiting, and when we moved her away from where she was standing, we saw a pool of blood she had left there. Her robe was saturated. It was obvious this girl had no idea she was having her first period. We were a bunch of men, paranoid, on-guard, and none of us had a daughter old enough to have gone through this yet.

"Sergeant Karns, as it turned out, had a son in the military and a daughter who lived to be twenty when leukemia took her. I didn't know anything about them then. His widow would later tell me about Sasha, the daughter they lost. Karns stepped up to the girl. He asked her where her mother was, her father. In her language and in ours. She didn't understand a word of either one. The other people who had been standing around her gave her something of a wide berth, and our sergeant stepped into it and slung his arms around her. He whispered into her ear, but none of us heard what he said—"

85

Then Sergeant Karns was in Will's ear, his tone seething. *What is the point of reading* this *part to a bunch of snot-nosed kids, soldier? What do you think you're teaching them with this?*

Will paused, wet his lips and continued. His delivery slowed to a near-crawl. "The girl was getting more and more amped up. I moved to step up and lend a hand when I was lifted up and off my feet. I was driven back and down into the tarmac as if by the hands of God. My face was on fire, and the left side felt like it was quite literally rolling down off my skull. Then there was an electric current there, lighting me up. I was knocked out for a few seconds and when I came to, the first thing I saw made me wish I had never opened my eyes again. Our sergeant lay on his side a few feet away from me. Half his body was ash, and the other half was exploded into a mess of twisted bone and charred flesh. The girl was in pieces scattered all around the highway. One of the Iraqis had been sitting on the median, waiting to board the bus again when the young girl blew herself and our sergeant up. He was just close enough to the impact to have been quite literally transformed into a sculpture of ash that depicted him leaning down to tie his tennis shoe. Frozen in the moment. His shape held for a moment before a soldier stomped through it, and the ash collapsed into a pile of gray.

"I felt for my face, expecting the worst. I thought most of it, if not half of it, would be blown away. Precariously, I felt my forehead, the ridge of my nose, and my lips. It was all there. I reached for my cheeks. The right cheek was tender and gouged open. My finger recoiled from it, and they crept to the left side, just along the cheekbone.

"There was a hardness there. A rigid line of bumps. It felt like pebbles embedded in my cheek, and they screamed at the touch. I screamed. Then there were hands on me, and I waved them off halfheartedly, demanding they see to our sergeant.

"I fought them and fought them until the strength went out of me, and I blacked out."

Will paused and closed the book, which gave way to thunderous applause and the crowd to its feet. He felt small, and their applause only managed to box him in even further until he could barely stand there another second. *I am a little man standing on a stage, and they are clapping for me because I am alive. Doesn't make sense, and it never will.*

"Please ... stop ..." he muttered, his lips grazing the microphone. He sounded like a modest, polite man, but his words were those of a pleading, drowning veteran. "Please..."

Will sucked wind and wet his dry lips. He waved them all back down into their seats. This was not the first time he had done a live reading.

This was, however, the first time he had come this close to outing Sergeant Karns to a room full of people. Sergeant Karns was surprisingly silent right then, when Will expected Karns to be railing against him. *So close ... too close ...*

"Can I take some of your questions now?"

The hands shot up like white weeds in hyper-motion. Standard protocol at these events required for the speaker to only answer fifteen to twenty questions, no more and no less. There were a sea of hands, and Will had never grown used to the enthusiasm of the readers and writers at these events. He simply did not believe he was special enough for any of this. He decided to use the age-old boy-girl-boy-girl alternating method of calling on people. He started with a tall, young brunette in a dark pantsuit third row back. She did not stand up, the Apple laptop in her lap acting like some sort of seatbelt for her.

"Mr. Bentley, I was wondering if you would comment on the current trend in Washington and Hollywood, even on a lot of 'Mainstreets'," (complete with 'air quotes') "which maintain the Iraq war was a mistake, and we had no business being over there?"

Will saw his agent raise her hand in protest from the side of the stage. He waved her back and bore down on the podium a little further. "Well, Miss—"

The young woman's blue eyes flashed up at Will behind her Coach-style glasses. "I found it curious you went out of your way to *not* voice any sort of opinion on whether or not you felt you should've been over there in the first place, so—

"Me? Personally?"

"Well, you know—"

"I was one of thousands of brave men and women who answered the call. Have you ever been moved to do something you didn't quite understand completely inside and out, but you believed in enough to lay down your life for it? That's passion. That's allegiance. Love of country. If you're asking whether or not I sat down and read everything I could over a series of weeks about the millennium-old conflict in the Middle East before making something of an *informed* or *justified* decision, I'll tell you I didn't. I didn't join the Marines so they would pay for college. I wasn't looking to *get something out of it*, unless you count the sense of pride in being a part of something noble and bigger than myself."

She didn't hear a word of what you just said, soldier. She was already reloading while you were firing, waiting for her next chance to speak.

Pantsuit raised one dainty finger in the air, calling for a follow-up,

87

but Will was already capping the exchange with his final word. "Don't write to be the smartest person in the room. This is not the role of the writer. I hate to break it to you, but the role of the writer is to fade into the background of real life and then to report on it in a fair and accurate manner. We observe and report. Then, we smear the lines just enough to form fiction apart from nonfiction. You want to inject your own opinions or make your *point*, don't do it at the cost of your own soul. Asked and answered. Who's next?"

There's always one, isn't there, soldier? Always one in the bunch ...

22. AND SO IT GOES

The next day, Stella vowed she would fight her anxiety harder than the day before. There would be no *off to bed* at late afternoon, wracked with the certain fatigue anxiety breeds over a short time. There was something to learn, stones to turn over and daytime was precious. She wondered how deep Jack's rabbit hole extended? She imagined breaking into his briefcase and finding nothing inside but a banana and the bagged ham and cheese sandwich she made for him. They would not have been able to hold onto their house or stock the fridge or make car payments if not for Jack's income. Stella had not worked since before she got married, when she temped doing title work at a car dealership during her late teens.

No, the bastard works! Whether or not he actually travels as often as he claims, I would have no idea. Unless ... unless ... another tail on the way to the airport? *Maybe?*

Ultimately, Stella exhausted herself once more after poring over her husband's papers with closer attention and rifling through every one of his clothing drawers. She came away with nothing for the second day in a row. If there was something she missed, it was something she simply would never find.

That night, over ziti and vodka sauce, Jack announced he would be going away on the coming Saturday through to the following Tuesday. "Flint, Michigan," he said. "A senator's son who might sign on with me. When I get back, I'm going to put my piano on the market. Get it tuned. Polished. Make a nice chunk." The piano Stella had been waiting for him to touch, to caress, to play Harry Connick, Jr. on for her, like years before.

A message? "Ok, if that's what you want," she said. *You'll sell the piano, and I will suffer for days after. But then, I'll plan for your suffering ...*

Stella felt all the more desperate after he told her of the pending piano sale to find some damning evidence she might make use of. It would be something which would tear her down in its implications, but she expected it. What other sort of proof was there, if not something which would crush her? Of course, after she recovered from whatever proof of a double-handed dealing she unearthed, Stella trusted it would be covered over, buried by malice. Mercilessness.

Stella trusted her previously broken heart would solidify, shrink and blacken like bad fruit.

It would harden. Mummify. Petrify.

Sell the piano. Go ahead. You're coming to an end, and you don't even know it.

23. "YOU'RE GONNA DIE ... BIG TIME!"

It wasn't Will's idea to bring along his Glock .9mm on the speaking tour. Sergeant Karns had been the one to more or less guilt him into packing his gun along with the change of clothes and the toiletries. Now, sitting at the small circular table in his hotel room at the Boston Radisson, his laptop open and glowing before him, the fact he had brought it along bothered him.

You won't ever really be able to call yourself healed until you can hold a gun in your hands again, let alone fire one.

This was also what had Will starting off with a glass of Kentucky Bourbon at the hotel bar and then moving his solo party upstairs with a six pack of Corona. He called Mina, but it didn't help his mood when he sensed the preoccupation in her tone. Granted, he had gotten her at the store because her phone at home rang and rang. *Could be she's in the middle of doing inventory or haggling with a customer?* He thought either could be possible, but her tone nagged at him. *But it's not her, it's me.*

He turned his attention to writing around eight at night; an episode of *True Detective* muted on the tv.

His relationship with Sergeant Karns was as frustrating for him now as it was in the trenches of warfare. If anything, Karns became more cumbersome to carry around in his head. It was why Will had come so damned close to *outing* Karns right there in front of a college crowd two days ago. It would have been like releasing a pressure valve. His mind was compromised, and he knew it. It was a pipe leaking steam and fit to burst. But Karns was the one who had gotten him writing again. Not just *writing*, but laying words down he could actually be proud of.

"You sure you're not maybe giving *him* too much credit?" he asked himself, sitting there and casting his alcohol-slowed eyes about the room. They caught on the goateed Matthew McConaughey on the tv screen, lingered absently, and returned to his beer. He took another slug. "I'm not so sure. If you're my muse, Karns, then I'm starting to think I'm fucked. Really fucked." He took another swig of his beer. "May be time for an exorcist. Why'd you talk me into bringing a fucking gun on a *book tour?*"

Hold it right there, soldier! I belong to you. I suggest. But you? You're the one who executes!

"I'm sitting in my hotel room ... and I'm talking to my imaginary friend. There's something wrong here, and I've been denying it out of fear." He tipped his beer before him, as if tapping it against the bottle of an invisible drinking partner across the table from him. "It's good of you to finally admit *you* belong to *me*. That can only mean my writing ability does too. You're the equivalent of a writer's block placebo. A salve that's ninety-nine point nine percent water. Tell me I'm wrong—no, *wait*—I know I'm right so don't bother. You're in my head. And I think I'm going to have to deal with this when I get back home."

You think so, soldier? All right, I'm gonna go off the grid for the night then. Let's see you write a goddamn sentence that doesn't make both of us want to puke, eh?

The left side of Will's face, the profile speckled with scars and miniscule bone fragments, jolted with pain. It was quick and alarming, like an old aunt pinching your cheek over-affectionately.

He decided he couldn't sit there and stare at the screen any longer, not without some junk food to dip into while he typed. The beer was a heavy, acidic puddle sloshing around in his stomach and not getting along well with the bourbon from before. He had seen a 7-Eleven not two blocks from his hotel during his drive into town.

The real "Cheers" bar was five blocks north of the college where he had spoken earlier. Boston University. The audience was the most attentive he had encountered in the four engagements he'd done so far. Mostly young women, pens poised at the ready, or parked behind an ear as they listened to him with rapt attention. It had been nice. Thinking back on it, Will felt his body warm. It wasn't the alcohol. Success is comfort, and he would not let it be the alcohol for the rest of the evening. Time to buy up some food to sop up the suds. He needed a clear mind.

Because Karns was not going to be right come morning.

He would write, and it would not *suck*.

Hurriedly, Will bundled himself into a pea coat and ski cap and hit the cold streets. A cutting wind felt its way beneath his coat and t-shirt, goosing his bare flesh and calling goosebumps across the muscles. He stuffed his hands deep into his coat pockets, turned up his collar, and stalked along with a strange sense of insecurity crawling in his gut. He couldn't help replaying the brief and cursory conversation he had with Mina earlier. Things like this rarely bothered him, and he was acutely tuned in to shifts in tone. She had not been thrilled when he told her about the speaking tour, as short as it would prove to be when all was said and done. He shook his head, trying to shake the preoccupation, and dodged a pair of giggling college girls as they nearly walked into him, their heads bent to the glowing screens of their cell phones. Then, his thoughts turned to the deafening silence of Sergeant Karns.

Stop thinking of him as if he lives and walks! He's in you!

"Yeah, well, this is a neuroses I have to deal with," he muttered to himself.

A car sighed by him and eased into a spot close by. It backfired and nearly sent him clear out of his skin. He sidestepped, finding himself hanging inside a dark and vacant entryway to a shuttered storefront. Before he knew what he was doing, his hand was inside his coat, feeling for the holster that was not there. The gun he left up in his room.

Something's happening. Something is happening to me. Why now? Can't be now?

Will knew what a panic attack was. He'd never had one and pitied those who suffered them. He had friends he served with who were plagued so profoundly by anxiety they lived locked-away lives, their hearts fluttering at the sound of something as commonplace as a ringing telephone. But this was not his condition. Couldn't be. Still, he lingered in the darkened doorway until his breathing returned to a normal rhythm. He smoothed down his coat, ran a coarse palm along his jawline, and squared his shoulders as he rejoined the walkway.

The street was otherwise silent, as if the backfiring car had banished everything and everyone within a one-mile radius. The neon-sign of a Japanese restaurant across the way seemed to burn itself into the side of his face as he hurried past. *Or is it burning Karns having a bit of a tantrum?*

"Fuck, fuck, fuck …"

Will Bentley was never so happy to see the green and red sign of the 7-Eleven as it slipped into view above his head. He laughed to himself, a small sound of stones stirring at the bottom of a mason jar, and entered the convenience store.

The fluorescent lights made it feel at first as if he were walking into the center of the sun. He turned around in a semicircle, gathering a lay of the land and where everything was stocked. A short, elderly woman in a long ratty coat that whispered against her flip-flop clad feet, stood before a red rack overflowing with throw-away romance novels. She began slowly turning it, drawing an annoying squeal from its hinges as it spun before her. She glanced half-heartedly over at Will, who smiled thinly at her before surging into the second aisle on the left. He grabbed a bag of sour cream potato chips, turned it in his hands, then frowned at the calorie count. Yes, these things still mattered to him, no matter how much he wanted to be bad and eat crap! He begrudgingly stuffed it back on the shelf and turned to where the baked Wheat Thins boxes were stacked. Flavorless wafers that tasted about as good as Communion at church, minus the spiritual influx. He took a box in his hands and knew where he was headed next.

Beer. More calories. God knows. Still, maybe there's actually something to this drinking and writing thing all the greats used to put into practice. So long as I realize when I'm a few days out from putting two barrels of a shotgun in my mouth, I should be okay. Dark humor. Dark mood. Fuck, fuck, fuck—

"You think you're big time?"

Will had just opened the door to one of the coolers, reaching for a six-pack of Heineken when he heard it. The cold blow out of the cooler slid up his sleeve and brought color into his ruddy cheeks. Yet, when he tried to retrieve his hand bearing the six-pack, it remained where it was. He thought of it, concentrated on it until his focus became a virtual laser beam, but he could not bring it back out again. Behind him, a young male voice, touched with Spanish inflection, exploded down the aisle from him.

"YOU GONNA DIE *BIG TIME!*"

Familiar. I've heard this before. Don't know where ...

It wouldn't have mattered anyhow if he could remember. He heard the swift clicking of flip-flops against the tile floor of the 7-Eleven. The woman who had been looking at the pathetic paperback rack was hurrying about. Why? *Because something is happening. You felt it in your stomach before you even got here. Something bad. Here it is. Here ... it ... is.* He slowly drew his hand out of the cooler. He gently allowed the rubber to meet rubber, sealing the door again. He quickly turned and dove for cover behind the right row, the one nearest him. He ducked down onto his haunches, his heart between his teeth and beating savagely. He angled his head around, just enough to gain some vantage point for what was happening at the register.

92

A tall man with a short black crew cut whose upper body bulged out like an inflatable person in a billowing, grey ski jacket leaned half in and out of what was a plexi-glass enclosed booth. Will could not see the cashier. He imagined them behind the register, the thief pressing the nose of a gun into their temple as they tried to open the drawer with palsied hands.

"You're not moving fast enough, cocksucker! Stop shaking! Keep your *motherfucking self* straight and open it up—"

"Trying—I'm trying—"

Will could hear the cashier crying. A young-sounding male. Early twenties. Maybe even a student paying part of his tuition.

"TRY HARDER! GET TO THE SHIT 'FORE I BLOW YOUR MOTHERFUCKING HIGH-AND-TIGHT OFF YOUR HEAD!"

The flip-flop's slapped the floor all the way to the door.

Wait—he let the old woman leave during a robbery—she must have seen his face.

Will's chest felt like someone had strapped him into a straightjacket. He felt his legs going numb. He soundlessly slid one of the Heineken bottles out of the package, turned it upside down in his hand, and skirted around alongside the candy rack out of view of the cashier station. His knees and ankles clicked like a typewriter, and he could only hope the Top 40 radio station piping out of the ceiling speakers would drown out.

The cashier cried out in pain. He was crying so loud now, it almost sounded like something else entirely—

"Now—pussy—NOW PUSSY."

Christ, I'm pumping blood right now! Spots. Spots? What is happening to me—what is this?

Will angled himself around the front of the aisle. Big Ski Jacket was three feet from him now. He was off his feet, looked to be trying to climb his way inside the narrow opening into the enclosed cashier station.

He straightened up some, coming up directly behind the robber.

He raised the bottle over his head, his arms jumping with adrenaline.

Then he saw it. The cashier's head rose up above the straining body of the robber as he tried to climb into the booth.

The cashier, a young man with a blow-dried drift of blonde hair, was not only smiling—

But laughing. Belly-laughing, his pale face red with the strain of it.

Will felt his mind shudder under the strain of resetting itself, given the new information. The vital details.

He saw the robber's hand, fingers splayed in the shape of a gun as he waved it all about.

Will couldn't lower the bottle. It held there. Then, his fingers loosened just enough for the bottle to slide out of his grasp. It smashed to the floor, sticky beer exploding outward and upward.

Friends? A ... joke? I almost—I—almost—
(had a heart-attack?)
(clubbed a wise-ass over the head?)
(and if you had a gun?)

The robber wheeled around on Will, still frozen with his arm up like a wax sculpture. He smirked at Will.

The cashier looked on, blinking vapidly. "Hey ... man?"

Will never heard the *man* part of the question. He pushed out of the double doors of the store.

The cold slapped him hard across the face. It was then he remembered where he had heard those words from the "robber."

Fucking Scarface. Al Pacino. They were playing fucking Scarface.

Will had to stop after a couple steps to duck into the same storefront he had only five minutes before. He had to do it, because the nausea wrung out his stomach all at once and he vomited on his knees, in the dark of the storefront, not caring who saw him.

No one did.

24. THE REAL AUDIENCE

As far as Will was concerned, his *real audience* were the veterans who came to his readings and pressed his flesh afterward at the meet-and-greet. He especially enjoyed speaking with the veterans who brought their "rescue dogs" with them, as it reminded Will of back home, Albie and Mina (hell, even Danforth). It was a bittersweet feeling, though.

The engagement at Wilhelm University in Massachusetts the next evening brought a smaller crowd than the other two. The committee in charge of advertising the event on campus dropped the ball in terms of getting the word out. At least, that was how it was explained to Will by the English chair, a small, dark-haired woman with pinched eyes named Yancy Gradel. Will's agent confirmed this, though through a terse expression which seemed to say to him *never again at Wilhelm, not even if they paid triple!* It was all right with Will. The smaller draw did not bother him nearly as much as they both thought it did. He was tense, but not for the reason they assumed.

94

Will couldn't shake the 7-Eleven incident back in Boston. He wasn't completely committed to the reading at Wilhelm, much of his delivery dull and flat. It was good the turnout was so meager. Perhaps Will would be able to maintain his reputation for being an engaging and passionate speaker among publishing and academia circles. This wouldn't hurt him. What gouged at him was the fact he had not recognized the quote from *Scarface* the kid in the convenience store had used while hamming up his robber routine. *I must have watched that movie a hundred times. I know the dialogue backwards and front. But it's like the bottom of my recall just dropped out, leaving me with nothing.*

Not to mention, Sergeant Karns hadn't breathed a word since that night. Will had told him in so many words to *fuck off.* He hadn't really expected the headstrong sergeant to do as he was told. It was never Karns' style, certainly not in life. He didn't heed advice; he rammed it down your throat, and you asked for another bit of it or you got the hell out of his desert sand. But no one ever hated him for it. They never begrudged him his hardness, for it was a contagious condition and one which every good soldier adopted and grew into like a suit of added armor when the bullets dropped like bludgeoning rain. In death, the sergeant was fickle. *This is why I can't really call him my muse. He's so damned cagey.* Will imagined Karns hunkered down in a darkened corner of his unconscious, arms folded over his barrel chest and head down, chin burrowed into his red, round throat. Sulking.

Will stood by his decision to have Karns removed from his cheek. It could mean a psychic break in the bond between himself and the sergeant, but it was a chance he would have to take. The thing of it was, for all of the confidence and word-weaving Karns afforded him, Will was not certain the sergeant in his ears was also the gasoline shower on the little flame of anger and unresolved rage which had only recently shoved its way fully to the forefront of his brain like a dodgy theater line cutter. Will was suddenly certain of the recipe he required to heal himself, and perhaps Karns understood what it would mean. Hence, the silence from within.

Therapy.

Surgery.

The long-overdue burial of a man blown to bits by a dirty bomb nearly a decade ago. The remains Will had been carrying around embedded within his fleshy cheek he would bury and pray over and then walk away, wiping his hands on the seat of his pants.

The auditorium had been hot. Crossing through into the receiving hall was a pleasurable thing as its great, refreshing breath of cool air blew across his brow. He followed along behind his agent and the English chair.

The two of them were haggling over something he could distantly grasp, the matter of pay scale. He tagged along, feeling very much the obedient talent. He had shaken hands, signed roughly ten or twelve trade paperback copies of his book, and even received a wet kiss from a pretty blonde coed who then saluted him with a sharp slash of the hand to her brow. "Your book saved my father's life," she told him. "He felt like a monster for so many years. The things he had to do in Vietnam. Your book released him from his guilt. Taught him his guilt was what made him human. He's doing well, and you gave him back to my mother and I." Will thought of these words as he slipped between the two squabbling women before him.

"Mr. Bentley?" A gruff, Southern male voice sounded behind him.

Yancy, the English department chairperson, angled herself around Will to address the owner of the Southern-drawl. She sneered at the man, greatly appalled. "You can't have your dog in here! I'm sorry, but you'll have to take him outside!"

Will turned to find the target of the woman's ire and felt his cheeks sting at once with anger. The man in the wheelchair switched his gaze away from the woman, Yancy, over to Will. He tugged at the leash of a rather old, somewhat weathered brown Labrador who had no doubt been grace in motion years before. Now, it knew only the pull upon its leash and allegiance to the man in the wheelchair who tugged the animal gently enough to draw him near so he could scratch affectionately at the standing scruff of its head. The man looked to be a full ten to fifteen years older than Will, but the black baseball cap with yellow lettering across it sitting on his head revealed his age and service all at once: OPERATION DESERT STORM VETERAN.

The dog nuzzled down low along the man's pant leg, drawing Will's eyes down to where the glint of steel and black molded plastic comprised the man's prosthetic foot. He wore a battered green army jacket with his name stenciled across the breast pocket: LINTELL. He was a big man, even seated, and appeared constrained by the tightness of his clothing. Will surmised the man had probably not worn his army jacket in many years and had squeezed himself into it for the occasion.

The man held Will's gaze, speaking out of the right side of his mouth at the woman who had come up alongside him with hands on hips. "Sorry. I-I didn't know. We were just leaving. He's my—"

"Therapy dog," Will said, reaching down to shake the man's hand. "I've got myself a war dog at home. She offers me therapy as well." The man shook with Will, a strong and sturdy double-pump that marginalized the daunting presence of the wheelchair altogether. Will turned towards the woman, feeling the eyes of his agent boring a hole into the side of his head and praying for his cool resolve to override the temper flaring in his eyes and face. "I know you and Claire have been going back and forth over what my speaking rate ought to be, even though a contract was signed."

Yancy blushed, clasping her hands together in a way which was more admonishing than gracious. "No-no-no, there's no confusion. You're locked in for the rate we agreed upon. We're so honored to have you here. I was only trying to appeal to your and your agent's sense of fairness, as we were expecting a much larger turnout for your reading and lecture than this. The admission fees were meant to cover the majority of what we had agreed to pay you. Our projections were off significantly. I merely proposed to your agent, if it wouldn't be too much trouble, you wouldn't mind coming back when your next book is released and, perhaps, speaking for free so we could break even."

"It might not be for another year or so," Will said.

"Oh, no doubt it will be worth waiting for. I hope this minor disagreement, this *misunderstanding* hasn't offended you in any way. We are so happy to have been able to host you."

"How about this, Yancy," Will said, feeling for the old dog's head by his thigh and rubbing it. "You not only let my friend, Mr *Lintell* is it?"

The man brightened, sitting up straighter in his seat. "Well, Lieutenant—"

"You got it! You not only let *the lieutenant* remain indoors with his dog so I can have a conversation with him, but you make a point of advertising on and off campus—and I mean wherever you can pin a poster or paper a billboard in town—the price of admission to my next reading and lecture will be free for *any and all veterans.*"

Claire tugged at Will's dark sweater elbow. Through gritted teeth she said, "Will?"

But Will kept on. "And their therapy dogs. War dogs. Even their lap dogs, if they so please."

Yancy stiffened, cords jumping out across her narrow throat. "I-I would have to check the health codes—"

"Please don't bother, ma'am," Will said. "Otherwise my offer to waive my speaking fee for this evening and for the next one on down the line will become null and void as neat as you please."

"Mr. Bentley, I—"

"Please, Yancy?" Will was one of those men who knows they are handsome and shrinks away from the notion like it were the most offensive of things. Women often complimented his long, dark eyelashes, envious of their curl at the ends. A natural perfection. His strong, low, and dark hairline.

The way his cowlicks lifted around the crown of his head like a child's does. It made women want to mother him, before they fucked him, at least. In that moment, Will counted on his *alleged* good looks to see him through to a successful bargain. He even clenched his teeth behind his sealed lips, thereby accentuating the deep grooves of his high cheekbones.

Yancy glanced around as if fearful someone would hear her strike a deal she had no authority to make, and then extended her hand to shake with Will. He took it in pure Victorian-gentleman fashion. "Agreed. Of course, that would be fine."

"Wonderful," Will said.

"Uh, Will?" Claire bristled beside him. "Remember me?"

Yancy smiled, eyes squinted shut and lips bloodless. "It's been a pleasure. Would you mind signing my copy of *Shiite Weeping,* and perhaps signing a new contract to include your next reading?"

But Will had already taken a knee in front of the old dog, his hands smoothing down the animal's bumpy back. He spoke towards the dog, but his words were for Yancy. "I'll come find you after I'm done. Where is there a nice quiet place Lieutenant Lintell and I can have a word?"

"Well," Yancy said, her sneer returning only not as boldly put forth, "by the concessions. There are tables and chairs set up. I would just have to ask you keep the animal away from the food stands."

"You were bitten by a dog before, weren't you?" Lieutenant Lintell suddenly spoke up.

Will nearly laughed out loud, but bit it back. *I was thinking the same thing.*

Yancy blanched towards the man in the wheelchair. "Excuse me?"

"Nothing to be ashamed of. I can sort of tell these things. You can tell who the *dog people* are, and who hate dogs on sight. You're not a big fan. It's all right. But what I'll say is I never met *anyone* in all my life hates a dog unless something happened with a mean one before scarred them in some way."

"I can assure you, I don't have a problem with dogs, sir."

"*Lieutenant—*"

"Lieutenant," Yancy said, seething. "I'm more of a cat person."

"Cat person?" Lieutenant Lintell laughed. "It's like letting a bum live in your house. For free!"

A red flush crept up and out from under Yancy's navy blue turtleneck as she turned completely away from Lintell, towards Will and Claire. "Why don't I fax over the paperwork when we get closer to the date of your next speaking engagement? How does that sound?"

"Much preferred," Claire said icily. "Oh, *Will?*"

Will stood and took Claire's hand. He gazed openly into her eyes, batted his long eyelashes, then cracked up laughing. It was too much to hold in any longer. "I know. I'm in trouble."

"You betcha', asshole," Claire said through a tight smile. "You shut me out like that again, and I promise you I will personally deliver your next manuscript to Harvey Michael, Michael, and Davies Inc."

"Not Harvey Michael," Will said, grinning. "The guy who turned down *The Godfather* and nearly jumped out his eighteenth-story window the day the movie came out?"

"The one and only. Don't force my hand, Will." Claire's grin turned sexy and lascivious. "I don't want to get into a habit of waiving fees. I still need to hatch out a living for myself, you know. You waived *my* fee just now. Not only yours."

"No, I didn't. I'll pay you for your trouble."

"We'll discuss it later," Claire said, buttoning up her long black overcoat and knotting a red splash of scarf at her throat. "Meet you back at the hotel?"

"Yes, you will."

"I need a drink, you shit!" she said, and sailed off through the double doors and out into the college quad.

When Yancy and Claire were gone, Will moved behind the wheel-chair and started to roll Lintell towards the neon lights around the corner where a Nathan's hot dog stand was set up, as well as a Stewart's Root Beer station. Will asked Lintell if he was up to a float and a dog. Lintell was enthusiastically game. Even his dog, who smelled the meat of a hot dog more acutely than the men, seemed to lather into something of excitement. Will ordered two dogs, both with mustard and ketchup, and two root beer floats. He rolled Lintell over to a nearby table and took a seat across from him. The dog took his cue to drop down beside the right wheel of his master's chair.

"Thanks, my friend," Lintell said. He bit into his hot dog, chewed thoughtfully. Smiled. "Hope you didn't make trouble for yourself on my account. A man's gotta eat. Gotta pay the bills. I know this is your livelihood."

"Don't even trouble yourself about it, Lieutenant. I won't be back here when the next book comes out. It was already a foregone conclusion before the little altercation. I have no interest in speaking any place whose people would treat a veteran that way. The only difference between you and I is I wrote a book a couple years ago. We're the same man. Hell, I almost threw the final draft of *Shiite Weeping* into a trunk, locked it, and stored it away. It was a memoir. A way to make sense of what I had seen and felt. It

99

was never meant to see the light of day. It's the God's honest truth."

"You don't gotta convince me, Mr. Bentley."

"Well, I feel like I do. I especially have to convince those who served of that fact. A lot of authors who achieve fame beyond anything they expected start to feel a sense they should back away from success. Distance themselves. Even go so far as to say they never wanted it. I don't know why they do it. But I'm telling you, I never wanted this."

"Well, you got it ... for better or worse, Mr.—"

"Call me Will. Come on, Lieutenant. We're sharing a hot dog dinner. This automatically moves us into the realm of the first-name basis."

"All right," Lintell said, slipping the last nub of his hot dog under the table. The dog lifted its upper half and snapped its jowls towards the hunk of meat and bread. Then, it was gone. "Then no more of this *lieutenant*. I only ever remind people I was a *lieutenant* when it seems they need reminding. You, on the other hand, don't. So call me Edgar"

"Why is that?"

"You never forget. About yourself, or about any of us."

"I just hope I've given proper voice to all of the fallen and the survivors. There's been so much written on the subject of war, and so damned little on its aftereffects. People only seem to want to read about the conflict and the artillery and the strategy and the casualties. The sexy stuff, right? But what about when we all come home. Nothing sexy about it."

"Oh, I don't know. I think I'm looking drop-dead-gorgeous with these wheels."

They both laughed, drawing it out as long as they could until it wound down to nothing more than an awkward rumbling from their depths.

Thankfully, it was Lintell who burst the bubble of silence and dragged the real reason for this impromptu dinner out into the light. "You look like a man who's been chewing on something for some time. Can't swallow it because you don't know what it is."

"You'd be right there."

"Here's what I can tell you," Lintell said. "When you sit in a wheelchair and move around the world in it, you got no choice but to slow down and pay closer attention to things. You gotta negotiate the world more carefully than most, and it not only makes you more attentive, but a better listener."

"You married?" Will asked, then wished he could run in the opposite direction of the question.

"Divorced," Lintell answered. "Twice. Seeing somebody now."

"I'm going to be popping the question pretty soon."

Lintell's face lit up. He slapped the table, joyously. "Terrific. My advice to you would be only do it once. Stick with it. Unless your beloved comes at you with a knife one day, or you wake up in the middle of the night to find her hovering over your head with a pillow, she's a good one."

"Should I ask?"

"Better not," Lintell said, shrugging his wide shoulders. "That's not what you been chewing on, though. Why you're hanging back to talk to me in particular. Oh, I'm not complaining. You're my favorite author, and one of my favorite human beings. There aren't many around who could understand. Especially not *on-campus* eh?"

"Ok ... well ... I am ... full of dread. Wrung dry from it."

From there, Will went into all of it. He hashed out a good bit of the experiences he had in Iraq, and these bled into the subsequent bouts of depression he dealt with. He didn't take much pride in the fact he was functioning pretty well despite the blues he experienced pretty regularly. Lintell was quick to remind him he was indeed *more than functioning and dealing* from an outsider's point of view. Will accepted this, but didn't really believe it. He nearly outed Sergeant Karns, but something inside of him, a well-hewn aversion to speaking about the "voice in his head" and its connection to the rough patch of skin running up the side of his left cheek, kept him from doing so. He spoke of the events at the church. The shootings and the priest sacrifice. Albie's injuries and coma. He mentioned his fear of using a firearm borne of the church's nightmarish events. This led him rather seamlessly into his account of what happened at the Boston 7-Eleven a few nights before.

Lintell's bushy grey eyebrows seemed to dip further down from the moment Will spoke of his fear of guns until they practically erased his small green eyes. By the time Will finished speaking, he himself was drawing shallow breaths and recovering from the sudden realization he had been talking for twenty-minutes straight.

Lintell laced his hands together on the lip of the table, considered them with pursed lips and contemplating eyes. The dog by his wheelchair sighed, lifted his maw and then dropped it like it weighed too much to hold up. Then, the older veteran looked across the table at Will, who was busy raking his fingers through the black tuft of thick hair atop his head.

"Son? You don't think those two young kids at the convenience store are a little bit to blame for your reaction?"

Will shook his head. "They were just acting like stupid college kids."

"Now, you tell me, Will. If it were anyone else and they realized maybe *too late* these boys were kidding around and socked one of 'em over the head with a beer bottle, they'd be carrying around as much guilt as you are now when you didn't even get to the point of *socking 'em!*"

"That's the problem," Will said. "It was like a switch thrown inside my head. I turned into the creeping, stealthy guy I was when I was snaking my way through sand on my belly, trying to keep my AK out of sight of the enemy. I slipped into that mode just as easily as I did when I stormed the church."

"They had your dog, sir. I would have done the same damn thing, even in this chair. I would have done something. I carry a concealed weapon. Bet you can't even see it."

"I can't."

"I never unbuttoned my jacket. If I had, you woulda' known. I just don't feel the need to advertise. No one will expect anything of me if shit hits the fan. They also won't think of me as some *gun nut*, on the other hand, either. They'll just see me. Like you did."

Lintell smoothed his hand down across the stitching of his name, accentuating the bulge of a gun beneath. Then he held up his hands, plaintively. "You even said you got three shots off in the church, and it was to put down the people who were trying to hurt you. Then, you stopped shooting."

"Sure," Will said. "Three was bad enough."

"You, my friend, exercised restraint. Just like at the 7-Eleven. So what is it you're worried about?"

"It came over me too easily, I guess. It was too, instinctual."

"What? Survival?"

Will knew he had him there. The ghost of a smile flitted across his lips. "Sure."

"What came over you is as old as the hills, my friend," Lintell said, folding his arms across a barrel chest. "You stopped shooting as soon as you were fairly certain *you* and *yours* were safe. This is what you should be concerning yourself with, not saving the rest of the world or the people who need saving. If you just so happen to help some people out of a jam they can't get themselves out of, it's all well and good. But don't go looking to save people because what you need to understand is you are *off the clock* for saving people who *aren't you and yours.* You understand? You fought for everyone's freedom and their way of life and you done it just as fervently and passionately as the rest of us. But an old, retired warrior knows when it's time to retire and to guard his homestead above all else. That's your job now, and there ain't nothing wrong with guarding the homestead—" he quickly unbuttoned his army jacket, yanked it upward and away from his right rib cage where a Magnum glinted in its holster—" through the use of a firearm. This world is cruel. Getting more so every day. But it ain't people overseas we should be most afraid of. I'm telling you, it's your neighbor. Guard yourself against your neighbor. You learned the hard way when you went into the church. I know I'm preaching to the choir, but still I hope I'm resonating."

"Anything like this ever happen to you?" Will asked. "Any anxiety or depression?"

"I hide it well," Lintell said. "My Lexapro and my Xanax help me out. Otherwise, my hands shake, and my eyes feel like their leaking every other minute. Sometimes, it hurts so bad, I feel like I may as well be crying blood. You should look into talking to someone about what it is you're feeling. But, it don't make you any less the warrior. You understand? So long as you understand a warrior never gives up his spear. Neither should you. Guard your homestead, and you will feel fulfilled. You will be a happy man. You said you're fixing to get married soon? It'll be one more thing worth guarding with your life ... against the rest of the world as things crop up."

"The dog helps?"

"Yessir, indeed he does," Lintell said, then his eyes fell to the dog, and there was sobriety in them. "But I'll be losing him soon too. Cancer. Rheumatism. Bad eyes. Blind in one. He's not much longer so we're going to enjoy each other until the sky opens up and claims him."

"Oh no," Will said, turning his attention to the dog, who must have sensed this, as he suddenly strained to stand back up. It took some time for the animal to turn himself around so he could arrange his head beneath Will's waiting hand. Will plied at the dry fur around the dog's crown. "Oh no, this is a strong fella right here. I don't see anything putting him down anytime soon. Isn't that right, there, good boy?"

The dog moved into Will's fingers, pushing up against them. Then, he jabbed his sagging maw upward and his eyes, lined in strands of red and yellow, locked eyes with Will directly.

They were not looking as much as they were all at once *showing* Will.

Will Bentley suddenly felt himself being drawn somewhat forcefully into the black pupil of the animal's eye, deeper and deeper until he was no longer inside himself.

He had slipped seamlessly behind the eyes and into the mind of another being altogether. By *being*, Will could ascertain immediately he was not inside the mind's eye of a human. His vision had turned a swirling and dizzying array of grey and whites and subtle nuances of each, with no hint of color to behold. *Color blind?* He drew in short, shallow breaths and heard himself panting. He felt as if he were crawling on hands and knees, his belly low to the floor as he moved along. His motion was slow and stalking and calculated. Every muscle jumped and jerked with adrenaline and an incredible tightness made him feel as if his entire body were tuned tight as an overwound guitar string.

He was stalking. No doubt. He heard himself growl low in his throat. He could not speak, only a guttural drone, and then he saw the dark shape on the floor before him. It was moving. A long and slender shape on the ground and the closer he crept towards it, the more agitated the shape became. It slithered backward. Then the shape grew a face, and he recognized the nakedness of the woman right before she screamed out loud, a weakened and pathetic sound. The reality of her bared breasts and womanhood were concealed by a slick layering that slathered the woman's entire body like a shiny second skin. Another hiss from her as she slipped and slid around in her own gore, struggling to get away from him. He willed himself to stop, to take stock of what he was seeing. To make some sense of it. But something, a dark and heated instinct, overrode this. He kept coming for her. He drew close enough to see her stomach was opened up in a jagged wound spilling out loops of intestine. Stop! Stop! I need to stop! I *have to stop* myself! *The woman was crying, foaming, and slobbering at the mouth. She tried half-heartedly to sweep some of her innards back up into her stomach. All the while, and much to his building horror, (Will) kept coming—*

"Mr. Bentley? *Will!*"

Will found himself down on his knees, his hand still moving in the air now where the dog's head had been moments before. He blinked and blinked, and the world swam back into focus. Lintell had Will by the shoulders, the lieutenant's deep-etched and tanned face right there before him. Eyes wide with alarm. The dog had slipped back behind Lintell's wheelchair. The animal peeked out from behind, badly spooked.

"Will, you need me to call someone? You with me?"

Will's eyes roamed aimlessly before they found and locked with Lintell's. He nodded, stiffly, and eased himself back into his chair. "No-no ... what the hell just happened?"

Lintell studied Will curiously. It turned into wariness. "Some kind of blackout. I don't rightly know. You ever blackout before?"

"No," Will sighed, his mouth dry and tongue sticking to the roof. "Never."

"Well, after this especially, I really hope you will take my advice and visit a doctor. For mind *and* for body. Just to be sure."

Will could only nod. He was tongue-tied. He glanced around. *Sure hope there wasn't an audience for whatever just happened.*

"No one's the wiser, Will," Lintell said, as if reading his concern.

"It was subtle enough I was the only one who saw. Well, myself and Brewster. You two have some kind of psychic something happen between you just now? He was letting you pet him one minute, and then I saw his whole body stiffen like he was afraid of you. Before I knew it, he was moaning and groaning behind my wheelchair, and you dropped down flat. Couple of seconds. I thought you were stroking out or something."

"Call it lack of sleep," Will said. "Lack of productive sleep. It's a part of what I've been telling you."

"Yeah," Lintell said, suspicion in his tone. "Yeah, I guess you might have left that part out." He felt around inside his army jacket and produced a small notepad and pen from what must have been his inside shirt breast pocket. He slapped it down on the table, flipped past a page Will could see bore the items which would comprise a minimal market shopping list, and scribbled on the next clean page. Then, Lintell tore it out and handed it over to Will, who took it absently. "This is my cell and my home. You made a friend today, and I think I did too. Something we both can benefit from, if I could be so bold. I want you to call me in a couple of days to let me know you made it to *two doctors*. Not one. *Two*. You don't have to tell me how it went, just *you went*. Fair enough?"

It was. Will reached to shake with Lintell and stuffed the paper down into his pants pocket.

After some silence, which was not uncomfortable and entirely necessary, Will offered to wheel Lintell out to his car. The lieutenant accepted and guided Will out to the general parking, between the swirling gusts of winter winds that had kicked up between then and now. Will rolled him alongside a white Cavalier, helped him into the driver's seat, and the two men promised to talk in a few days. Will would not have had it any other way. He stood there long after he shook hands with the lieutenant, tapped the top of the car roof, and gathered his thoughts into something bearable. He did feel a strange lightness of being. It came from having divulged the things he had to a new friend. He felt purged of the heavy burden of unresolved issues, and his stomach was unknotted. He felt a warm center of light within and could only attribute it to having made what he now knew was a meaningful connection. The only thing he regretted was not having told it all, even about Sergeant Karns in his head.

I've got his number. We'll be talking. And once I talk to a professional about Karns, I'll feel a lot better about sharing with anyone else.

Will stuffed his hands into his pockets and trudged back towards the college quad. He would sleep well that night. He would shower and he would write and he would deal with Karns, should the old grizzled sergeant return out of the darkness. He would also do something else. Will would take the gun out of his suitcase. He would handle it. He would hold it in his hands for as long as he felt comfortable. He would hold the faces of Mina and Albie and Danforth in his mind while he held the gun in his hands, then he would put it away. He would do this once a day, until the shakes subsided.

Of course, just as Will crossed back into the auditorium, the exchange of cold with heat blowing the skin of his face back delightfully, Sergeant Karns suddenly bloomed in his left ear like a snatch of music. A grinding, ear-whig waltz.

There's an enemy coming, soldier. A new *enemy. Coming round the bend ...*

25. YELLOW LEGAL

Jack sailed off to work an hour after the first snow of the season, Stella found what she was looking for.

Sort of.

It was a breadcrumb, if anything. The beginning of a path to be navigated.

It had happened quite by accident. Stella decided to take another look at the items in the top drawer of his desk. When she rolled it open, the whole thing came off the track, and she barely rescued it from spilling out all over the floor. Then, she would have no idea where things belonged in terms of organization, and would be forced to stow them back inside the drawer recklessly. She would be caught, and she would be dealt with. Stella slid her hands deftly underneath the drawer, stabilizing it so she could lower it onto the rug.

She felt something, a piece of paper taped to the bottom of the drawer. Her fingers grazed it. She might have missed it if not for a significant piece of the tape having unraveled. It came off in her hands. Then a corner of the paper dropped down.

With an even greater care than usual, Stella slid the drawer off its hinges and out of the desk altogether, and laid it down on the floor. She would have to empty out the items, to arrange them on the floor next to the drawer the exact way she had found them *inside* the drawer. A perfect reflection. She knew the drill by now.

Two minutes later, she had all the items beside the emptied drawer and arranged as they had been inside. Stella took a deep breath, and flipped the drawer over.

Taped to the bottom was a single piece of yellow Legal Pad paper, the writing facing away from her. She set to work with her neglected finger-nails, bringing up the bordering of scotch tape until the paper came away in her hands.

Stella bit her lower lip and turned the page over.

In a tight, bookkeeping script was written a series of what looked like initials and coinciding ten-digit numbers. The first such listing appeared in this way:

T. S.

2675762928

Her heart was a panicked bird behind her breast bone and her mind went to work. Why hide it in this way? Why write these up instead of typing them into his cell phone or work iPad? Stella had no idea, but she let her imagination wander for good measure. *Let's see ... prospective client's initials ... yeah ... this could be a client list, could it not? Then it would most certainly have a better home in his computer files, would it not?*

Only one way to find out. Call one of them.

"And say what, exactly?" she asked herself. "Hello, has a representative from Ballantine Athletics been by to wine and dine you lately? Really? What's his name?" Exactly.

"It's ... it's ... okay, so what if it *is* a cell number. The *two-six-seven* is a dead giveaway. Some of the area codes are different, though. Three-oh-two? Four-One-Oh?" Stella bit her lower lip, ruminating. "I'm not going to call. At least ... not right away." She rushed out of the study and returned with a piece of notebook paper she had torn out of the pad beside the bedroom landline phone. Quickly, Stella scribbled down all twelve of the listings. Then, she made short work of replacing the papers under the drawer, applying the same border of tape (with some new strips to hold it in place). She restocked the drawer precisely as it had been and closed it. Then, she wiped down the drawer's handle with her blouse sleeve and exited the study, mindful to lock the door on the inside before easing it into place with a delicate click.

25. THE DEATH OF TWO VETERANS AND A SHINING STAR

Will's hotel room phone started ringing at 8 am. Will turned over, his mind tight and clouded, and wound himself into a cocoon of heavy hotel quilts. He grappled blindly along the bedside table for the phone. He nearly toppled the lamp before laying hands on the phone and snatching up the headset.

Will dragged the phone under the covers with him, pulling the hem of them up and over his head.

" 'lo?"

"Baby?" Mina said, chipper as ever at such an hour. "Oh my God, you sound like an animated corpse!"

Up with the birds, this one!

Will drew the covers back. Stretching and yawning, he made sure it filtered right into the mouthpiece. Loud and obnoxious. "Why, hello, I love you. What's your name?"

"My name is *lonely girl*. Thanks to you."

"I know. Right there with you. I miss you too."

"How goes it, darling? You giving those college kids one or two things to grow on?"

"To be honest with you, the college kids are a bit standoffish with me. They want to know if I ever killed any civilians by accident. A lot of them seem like they're there to play *gotcha* with me, and when I try to appeal to their sense of reason, they end the exchange. They always preface these types of questions by saying 'Well, I want you to know right off the bat I support the military, but ...' The older people? Veterans. Academics. People off the street. They're the ones who came to listen and maybe learn something. I don't know."

"Oh, I'm sorry," Mina said. "You know, the topic of war. It's a lightning rod in and of itself."

"I know it," sighed Will, drumming his knuckles along the headboard. Soft, ethereal light had just begun to filter through the sheers across the room. It only reached halfway across the queen-size bed. "Makes me wish I wrote children's books. No one ever gave Shel Silverstein this kind of shit. Hell, Dr. Seuss wasn't even a real doctor, and no one ever called him out on it."

"I don't know. Maybe choose a selection from your book that'll make them laugh. Something lighter."

"Like what?"

"Oh, I know. What about the part where the one private, the one with the rosacea—"

"Carter Bagwell."

"Yeah, him. The time he dropped his little hand mirror and it broke while he was getting ready for lights out, and the whole platoon heard about it and thought they were going to have seven years bad luck."

"Yeah," Will said, smiling. "And Carter was so gung-ho about winning over there he thought we'd be out in a month, and the bad luck would stick to the enemy when we left. There's a thought."

"Although," Mina said, "maybe you want to measure it out with the grit in there. Don't sugarcoat it for them. That's not what I'm saying."

"Oh, no, I know. But it *is* a good idea. Let me see what I can do. So, how you doing, sweetheart?"

"I'm ... I ... have something I wanted to run by you."

"Sounds serious. What's the matter?" He felt his body stiffen. He pulled himself up into a sitting position.

"Well, I don't want to upset you. It's why I'm asking you first. I need your opinion and your blessing, babe."

"Okay," Will said, his cheeks burning.

"Everything's fine. It's just ... a reporter from the *Philadelphia Inquirer* called the house looking for you. They're looking to do a story about you and Albie."

"The *Inquirer*, eh? They want an interview? What about?" *I already spoke with all of the newspapers, digital and print, in the whole tri-state area after the Church Incident. I told them everything, more than I ever thought I could even remember. More than I wanted to remember.* He clenched his right hand into a fist. "It's only been a little over two months. Back for more?"

"Well, something prompted the reporter to revisit the ... the incident at the church. The reporter who called said something happened she thinks will revive public interest in your and Albie's story. She's the same one who interviewed you before. Nancy Springer. She wants to do a follow-up, 'Where Are They Now' type of story."

"Hmm ... it's very *Oprah*, don't you think?" Will tried to keep the seething sound out of his voice, but it was inescapable. He stifled a yawn and swung his legs off the bed. He stood and spread the sheers of his room opened wide. The downtown Baltimore street was surprisingly stripped bare of all but the most forlorn-looking pedestrians toting tote bags and cups of Starbucks. "When?"

"Well, this is the thing," Mina said. "She wants to make the Saturday Edition and it's Friday. She was looking to interview today and get it into print for the weekend."

"That's going to be impossible. I've got two more lectures. University of Maryland tonight, then Villanova tomorrow night. I'll be home Saturday night. Late."

"Then why don't you let me interview on your behalf."

"You'd *want* to do that?"

"I already proposed this option to her because I knew you wouldn't be back. This Springer lady, she seems nice enough. I don't think she did a bad job with the first story. She was very fair. You came out like the hero everyone knew you were, babe. I don't know. And you know I'd tell it like it is, without making you uncomfortable in any way. If there's anything you would want me to treat as out of bounds, just tell me. If you're comfortable with the idea."

"Of course," Will said, now fully awake and firing on all cylinders. "No, it sounds like a great idea. Do the interview."

"Okay, good. I promise you'll be pleased. I'll make sure to throw in a few stories here and there about our six-hour tantric sex sessions."

"I'm sure this Springer lady wouldn't mind that at all. Whatever will help her move some papers, right?"

"You know it."

God, I miss you terribly. My body aches. If you were here, right in front of me ... I don't know if I'd be able to hold myself back ... miss you ...

"Just steer her away from any talk involving my next book."

"Oh, don't worry," Mina said. "I know you want to keep the two things separate."

"I mean, if it should come up."

"It will. You know it will."

"Christ."

"Don't worry. As long as you're sure."

"Yeah, go for it," Will said. "You know what happened. You're Albie's mom."

"I am, aren't I."

"Oh, Mina, I almost forgot. You said something happened? Something sparked interest in the story."

Silence. "Will, it's just so ... it's creepy."

"Tell me."

Then, he heard the sound of fingernails clacking computer keys. "Why don't I read the article to you. I have it up. Nancy Springer wrote this one also. It's dated a little over a month ago. Are you sure?"

"Why wouldn't I be?" Will let his eyes tumble downward to the street once more. This time, nausea answered him, knotting up his stomach like he was standing out on the ledge rather than separated from a long fall by a thick pane of glass. "What the hell happened?"

"The headline reads: **"COMSTOCK KILLERS" DISTUR-BANCE AT BERRYSBURG PRISON BARELY CONTAINED, 3 PRISON GUARDS DEAD'."**

Will forgot to breathe. He felt his head swell to popping like a balloon, and it wasn't until he exhaled that his thoughts swam back into focus. "They're still calling them the 'Comstock Killers', huh?"

A pause, then Mina began to read:

"Three prison guards are dead after an evening of bizarre behavior in Berrysburg Prison's General Population wing, which culminated in a small uprising among certain inmates. At approximately 9:15 pm on November 22nd, five inmates began exhibiting manic, hyper behavior in their cells. Three of them, Peter Hilton, 25, Raymond Burton, 39, and Thomas Kretzky, 42, started throwing themselves against their cell bars, one of them bashing his own head against the wall until he had given himself a serious concussion. Two women, Betsy Burton, 39, and Sabrina Hadley, 25, both painted the walls of their cells with their own menstrual blood. The women both smeared unrecognizable symbols on the walls, which have, as of yet, not been deciphered as anything more than nonsensical writings. Three guards on duty responded to the disturbances in the cells and a struggle ensued between the five inmates and the officers. The three officers were overpowered by the inmates. Two were stripped of their firearms and one officer, Don Tully of Bristol Township, was fired upon and died from the blast. Another officer, Bruce Reed of Yardley Township, was pistol-whipped with his own firearm until other officers were able to aid and assist. The third officer, Dan Stahl, a rookie officer, was bitten by one of the female inmates along his carotid artery and bled to death before paramedics could arrive. According to inmates on the scene, the four inmates were "howling like wild animals" throughout the siege. When additional guards reached the site of ambush, they were able to contain the prisoners and all four are now in solitary confinement. Warden Adrian Miller gave a statement later that evening, stating, 'All security measures will be re-evaluated, augmented, and adjusted as necessary to make certain something like this never happens again. We lost two veteran officers tonight, and a new shining star. We mourn them all as fallen brothers. All five inmates comprise the now infamous quartet of convicted murderers known as the 'Comstock Killers', themselves the surviving members of an assault which resulted in the ritualistic murder of a Catholic priest in Bucks County this past October. Funerals for—"

"Stop there," Will said, flatly. "That'll do it."

Mina's voice cut off. "Are you all right?"

Will pulled the sheers back together, closing out the sunlight. He turned away from the window and began to pace. He couldn't remember having seen any of the four people, the inmates, the night inside the church. He remembered the maniacal barking of Albie, followed by a dull thud as a baseball bat connected with the side of her skull. When he shot the ringleader, the one who'd struck Albie, the shadows grew arms, legs, faces, and torsos surging towards him. Their hands bore sharp objects, aimed at his heart. His head. Aimed at him, seeking to rip him away from the very life that moved him to squeeze the trigger over and over, blasting at the shadows come to terrible motion—

"Will?"

"Yeah," he said, breathless. "Yeah, I'm here."

"You don't sound good. I shouldn't have read it to you."

"No-no, it's all right. I'm all right."

"What are you thinking? Talk to me."

"What am I thinking?"

"Yes, baby."

Sergeant Karns's voice crackled to life, like a dead ham radio finding its frequency once more. Will twitched at the sound of him between his ears, sounding somehow stronger after his respite of silence.

You're thinking if only you'd shot those five motherfuckers and done away with all of them right there the night at the church, three men would still be alive tonight, soldier. And you know what? You'd be right!

"Oh, what the hell," sighed Will, squeezing the bridge of his nose. He shut his eyes.

"What? Will?"

"Hey, Mina, someone's knocking at the door. Can I call you back?"

"Um ... sure."

"Right back. Stay by the phone."

"O-kay."

"Love you," Will said, and punched the disconnect button.

You ready to start showing me the respect I deserve, soldier?

Will could only laugh, a raucous noise anyone would have mistaken as a sign of insanity.

I'll take that as a yes. Now, it's time I reminded you of your oath. You remember the oath you made, the promise you made to your weapon during Basics? Let me hear it. And don't you forsake your weapon again. You're going to need it. And this time around, you're going to take em' all out. No

112

prisoners. No survivors. C'mon ... this is my rifle ... there is only one like it ... I love my rifle, and my rifle loves me.

Will said his oath, the oath of a Marine for life. Then, he took a long hot shower and emerged from a steamy bathroom with Karns gone from his head altogether. It was no surprise. The bastard had certainly said his peace, made his point. Will called Mina in his towel, feeling oddly invigorated himself. Whole again.

"Two more appearances," he said, listening to the phone ring on the other end of the line. "Then, I'll be home in your loving arms, Mina. Just two more."

26. WORKING-CLASS ANTI-HERO

Stella had known before she scribbled down the listings the previous day she would call *him*. She hated herself for seeing the need to wait a day until she could muster up the nerve to actually do it. *Am I doing the right thing? Should I leave it lie?* There was a very good chance he would refuse to speak to her. She had tossed him aside like a stranger and they hadn't spoken in four weeks. What frustrated her the most, perhaps, was how easily *he* had, in turn, given up on *her*. He never called. Not once. Karl Tarlick was proud.

He's a man, isn't he?

Stella stood by the phone hanging on the wall in the kitchen, taking stock of where she and Karl had come from, and where they would be going should she call him right then and there. She hadn't fucked him yet. She thought of what it would be like, the violence of it, barely held at bay. Lingering behind his eyes.

Her nude body spread out before him would act as the equivalent of a hooked and hanging slab of raw meat before a starved animal's drippy jowls. She would feed him and he would be hers, because there was a *mind-meld*. He had been right. The way it sounded when he described it before, Stella had felt like she was somehow ensnared by him. Powerless to it. It frightened her; he was so certain he was living rent-free in her head, and she was helpless to this. But Stella understood now she wielded a power over *him* twice as unyielding and merciless as his influence over her. She had never seen it in this way before, the angle. Her angle. She decided to engage it, to call it out before she dared dial the phone. With one hand, she clutched the headset as it hung in its cradle on the wall. With her other hand, she

113

unbuttoned her pants and slid her hand down inside her already moistened panties. *Make sure it comes across when you have him on the line. Make sure he can hear it in your voice, and it's true.*

She dialed with one thumb, and pleasured herself with the other.

It rang three times before an abrupt, no-nonsense Southern voice trampled over her. "Yeah, who is it now?"

"Can I speak with Karl?"

"Augh, he ain't here right at *this* moment. This is Bluto. This *Stella?*"

Her hand froze down below. *How does he know my name? Karl talks to them about me? Bluto?* "Not there? Where is he?"

"You know, we don't have many lady friends call in. Whaddya' need from him?"

"Do you know where he is?"

"Working. I think so. Yeah. Henry? Creepy Karl workin'?" A faint response. "Yeah, I was right."

Karl? Working? Of course. It was part of his release agreement. He had mentioned it to her, how much he loathed the idea of busting his hump for minimum wage, as well as having to disclose his past to a stranger. Stella tried to imagine what line of work would have the likes of Karl and couldn't. In that moment, she could only envision Karl at the prison, leaning in towards the glass divider with that sideways smile of his, or cracking his knuckles with a sudden, lavish movement while he held the phone to his ear to talk to her on the other side of the partition. She could see him (although she would rather not) standing in the forest behind his house, amidst the dead animals he had arranged into elaborate poses through the use of tent poles and sticks.

Bagging groceries? Stocking shelves?

Not him.

She pulled her hand out of her pants and wiped it off on her thigh. "Do you know where?"

"Christ, ma'am," drawled Bluto. "We're trying to watch the Pac-quiao fight on DVR right now. You oughta know where he's working at—"

"Please ... his mother died. I'm his sister."

A cold shiver whittled its way up her spine. This had to be bad karma for her. *Playing Karl's dead sister?* This *could get him plenty mad if he was to find out his* dead sister *called for him! Now, I have to find him, and I have to explain ... IDIOT!*

"Well, shit ... uhm, why didn't you say so? I'm really sorry, ma'am. I didn't mean nothing by any of this. Creepy—I mean *Karl*—is working over at Mac's Car Wash. Just started yesterday I think."

"Where is that?"

"Oh, well, I think it's at the intersection of Russell and Vine. Bensalem. You know it?"

"I know it," she muttered, anxious to cut the line. "Thank you."

"Again, I'm mighty sorry—"

Stella hung up the phone hard.

I gotta go there. I gotta talk to him. Now I don't have a choice. Gotta explain. I just came out with it—I don't know—STUPID—STUPID—STUPID!

Mac's Car Wash was a small, whitewashed brick building with a teller barricaded behind thick, bulletproof glass and two gas pumps that looked like they hadn't been used since the Nixon administration. Clearly, the business' money maker was its surprisingly elaborate and busy car wash operation, which seemed to vomit an endless stream of clean, gleaming vehicles every two minutes. Stella parked across the street in a pharmacy parking lot. She had on the twenty-four hour Christmas music station and drawing some small comfort from Bing Crosby and David Bowie's unlikely but moving rendition of "Little Drummer Boy." Her tired grey eyes roved over the cluster of men hovering just outside the car wash exit. As each vehicle rolled out of the car wash exit, wet and slightly spotty, the four or five men fell upon it with their blue towels like some violent obsession drove them rather than minimum wage and tips.

Karl Tarlick was not among the towel men. They were mostly twentysomething men, with a rough-looking sixty-something thrown into the mix and barking at those around him like some kind of alpha dog.

She sat there, warm inside her Taurus. She sipped at a Dunkin' Donuts cocoa and waited, and it was hard to deny she somehow sensed him nearby. But the waiting is the hardest part, like Tom Petty says.

Then, Karl Tarlick, wrapped in a secondhand ski jacket and a mesh baseball cap with the Flyer's logo on it, emerged from behind the building. His long, dark curly hair ballooned out the back of his hat. He was rubbing his bare hands together, trying to bring warmth to the palms. His personal blue mopping towel hung out of his jeans pocket and he snatched it out with obvious irritation. He fell in among them as if he had been there the whole time, swatting at wet windshields and digging the towel into the ornate crevices of hubcaps.

He's probably just coming off of break. Well, he'll have to have another quick one with me ...

Stella killed the engine and emerged from her car. She crossed the street with care, clutching her hot cocoa to her chest. He didn't have the time to look up. She clacked up the driveway towards him on low black heels, which drew the attention of two of the other moppers. They seemed to like what they saw. Perhaps five years ago, she would have blushed at their prolonged, lustful glances. Love is a funny thing, though. It gives one the strangest tunnel vision.

Is that what this is?

Karl didn't notice her until she was practically upon him. He snapped his towel off the back bumper of the white Chevy Caprice and spun around to find her standing there, one hand holding her cocoa and the other thrust deep down into the pocket of her khaki winter coat.

His mouth dropped open, not out of shock or surprise, but because that is what it usually did a couple seconds before he was ready to speak. He didn't say anything right away, his hands absently feeling their way through the coarsening fabric of the towel in his hands. He cast a quick, squinty look up at the slate-gray sky, pregnant with either rain or sleet. The snow of the earlier morning had tapered off an hour ago.

Stella was about to break the uncomfortable silence when Karl cut in. "Guess our *break's over?*"

At first, Stella was confused by his words then she remembered she had wanted a break. "Yes, if you're game, it is."

Karl measured her with his small, black eyes. His hand was still and dead inside the towel. "Mm ... break's over, because *you say so?* That how it is with us?"

"No ... no ... I was wrong to treat you like that," Stella said. "I—"

Karl seized her by the arm and led her away from the other men and the next car as it rolled under their snapping, blotting towels. He walked her, somewhat forcefully, over to the side of the enclosed cashier booth. Stella could both see and feel the eyes inside the booth as they burned into the two of them. *It's gotta be the boss inside there. I don't want to get him fired his first week.*

Then, the speaker right behind where Karl was standing bloomed to static life with a burly man's angry voice.

"You! Tarlick! You just took a damned break!"

Stella pawed at Karl's ski jacket sleeve. "I don't want to get you in trouble!"

Karl waved her off, turning slightly toward the booth. "Nah, I'm getting right back, sir. *Right back!* This woman wants to know if you're hiring for part-time work in there."

116

The voice cleared his throat. "Well, she can talk to me, and I'll send her out an application. Always looking for a helping hand. *You* get back to it."

Karl nodded, and leaned into Stella. His hot breath stimulated her as her own probing finger had done a short while ago in her kitchen. "Next time you want to take a break, you break it clean. I know I'm alone in this world, but I'd rather keep it that way than to have someone pulling me in and out like a goddamn rubber band."

The static voice erupted behind them. "*Karl! KARL!*"

He went on. Stella felt his hand stiffen around her wrist. "You want my help with your sonofabitch' husband, or is he a turned-over leaf now?"

Stella nodded, quick and clipped motions.

"KARL! YOU GOT FIVE SECONDS!"

"Stell, you wait for me. Give me a minute."

"KARL!"

Stella turned to him. His cheeks were pulled back, tight as white sheets. "He sounds like he wants you back at work—"

Karl wheeled on the cashier booth and launched himself at the bulletproof glass. He pressed his face up against its filthy surface, laughing wildly. "I quit! I quit! And this lady wouldn't work at this shit-trap if she only had two pennies to rub together! *Fuck ... you!*"

"YOU ROTTEN LITTLE CREEP! NO TAX CREDIT IS WORTH THIS SHIT! WAIT RIGHT THERE SO I CAN KICK YOUR ASS DOWN THE ROAD FOR YOU!"

Karl grabbed Stella, and then they were running. They booked it across the blacktop, all towel boys' eyes on them as they fled to Stella's car.

Beside her, Karl was bursting with laughter. "Well, Stell. They're gonna come for me now. I broke the deal with them I had to hold a job, and look what I did. They're gonna boot me out of the halfway house, and they're gonna put me back inside."

"No. No, go back and apologize—"

"Nope, nope! I'm your responsibility now. Not going back. Now let's get to work. Let's get it going and then follow it where it leads us."

27. THE VISITOR

As soon as Stella and Karl entered the Post home, Stella started tallying in her mind all the ways she would have to cover their tracks for when Jack came home. Karl's every footfall on the living room carpet amounted to a thorough vacuuming to erase the imprints of his boots. He might have tracked something in and she regretted not having him remove his boots beforehand. She sniffed at the air as he strode casually over to where the cat, Betsy, lay across the center cushion of the sofa. *With his long hair, will Karl shed on the sofa? A strand? That would be all it took!* Jack was finely attuned to any changes in his homestead. He could walk into a room and instantly call into question any number of subtle changes to the environment.

This was his environment. His *castle.*

"All right, I guess this makes us friends again," he chortled, lowering himself down onto the sofa. Stella flinched as his narrow backside crushed the left cushion. When he turned and scooped Betsy up into his arms, she nearly cried out. Betsy was skittish as it was, a different animal altogether since the night of the bathtub. This stranger's hands on her could transform her into a seizuring mess of white fur and flailing claws. She hurried over to the sofa, almost striking her knee along the lip of the coffee table.

"Wait! She's a little—"

Betsy's tail curled at the end as she allowed Karl to maneuver her onto her back, into his arms. He held her like a newborn. The big white cat glanced up at him with eyes of kindness, not hatred.

"What?" Karl said, playing kissy with the animal in his arms.

"I-I was going to say she's been a little ... she hasn't been herself."

"Mm, if this ain't kitty—like then I don't know what is, Stell," Karl said. "Despite popular opinion, animals *love* me. Don't you now, you big ball of marshmallow?" He nudged the top of the cat's head with the ball of his nose.

She stood there, hovering and rubbing her hands together.

"Why don't you come sit down?" Karl said. His eyes crept over to the front door. "What? You expecting him home now? It's the middle of the day. Jack working banker hours nowadays?"

"No. But he's been known to pop in unexpectedly here and there. I don't know."

"How often?"

Stella shrugged. "Not very often. I guess."

Karl smiled wryly. He scratched behind his right ear and cast a glance around. "Well, I got my protection right here. This cat loves me. She'll do anything for me, won't you? I bet she'll come to your defense if big bad Jack comes walking in the front door, all bothered about something."

"I don't think you're right."

"Come sit down and stop looking so scared."

Stella nodded stiffly, then walked back over to the front door. She attached the chain, threw the deadbolt, and thumbed the doorknob lock into place.

"Still scared?" teased Karl.

"No," she said, turning around slowly and walking towards the sofa where she gently lowered herself down onto the edge of the cushion. "No, that was to slow him down. Just a little bit."

"Good," Karl said. "You should always lock your doors. Even in the middle of the day, sorry to say." He dumped the cat onto the cushion beside him and moved closer to Stella. "The cat ain't the one who's skittish, either. You afraid of me?"

Stella looked at him. "No ... no, of course not!"

"You think I did a dumb thing today?"

She opened her mouth to answer, knowing what she thought but also what she couldn't say without it sounding clip and judgmental. She shook her head. "I think ... I made a mistake coming to your work."

"Why's that?" asked Karl, propping up his head along the top of the sofa.

"You just started a new job. I showed up unannounced, and I spooked you."

"Spooked me?"

"Well, I think I might have thrown you off to the point you did something you should have thought about first. You know, the repercussions of doing something like quitting your job when it's tied to the conditions of—"

"—my release. Oh yeah, *my release*."

"You said they're going to throw you out. You won't be able to stay at the group home unless you have a full-time job."

"That *is* in the handbook. It was explained in just that way before I left the prison. You are correct."

"Where will you go now?" Her whole body stiffened, fearing his response.

Karl frowned, looking very much like a stumped first grader. His dark curls dropped into his eyes like big sausages. Then he lifted his chin, and the hair dumped away from his face. His eyes were squinted.

"You mean we can't do what we said we were going to do when we were high-tailing it away from the car wash? I can't stay?"

Stella studied his eyes, searching desperately for some tell which would reveal the joke of his words. She could find nothing of the sort and felt her chest tighten. She positioned herself on the edge of the cushion, her ass cheeks barely holding on. "Oh, Karl, it was exciting. Don't get me wrong. It was a lot of fun pretending for a minute there we could just run away, and no one would miss us. No one would come after us. Sure, it would take them some time to realize I'm gone, but you?"

"Four thirty. Two hours away according to the clock on the wall. I get off work then. So ... you give them a half hour for me to get home by Septa bus. Not even counting traffic. You take on another fifteen minutes for good measure. Then, I report back in. Sign the book and check in with my sponsor on the telephone. Really, they'd come to miss my ass by 5:30, no later."

"All right," Stella breathed. "Then there's time to go back to the house and explain what happened."

"Too late."

"Why?"

"You don't think that douchebag at the car wash dialed my house manager before we even made it off the lot?"

"You think he did?" Stella's eyebrows arched downward.

"Course," Karl said. "And it's safe to say he probably told them I left with an *accomplice*."

It took a moment for it to sink in, but when it did Stella was off the couch with a start. "Then, I have to take you back. Come on, we have to leave right now before things get any worse." She stooped, grasping for his hand. He dodged it, playfully. "What are you doing? You want to get me in trouble?"

"Is that what you think?" Karl asked.

"I *think* we should *go!*"

"In a minute," Karl said. "Aren't you going to offer me a drink after a hard day's work?"

Stella felt her cheeks burning hot. The same familiar anger she had felt for him a month ago returned, bright and blazing, and she wondered what in the hell she could have been thinking. Did she really need him there to check the phone numbers she had procured in Jack's office?

Karl stood up. "You don't want me to go. I know exactly where ... you want me." His voice adapted to a slow burn. He stepped up to her and slipped his arms around her waist. He must have felt the stiffness of her body, for he set her with a curious stare, one eyebrow cocked and that crooked smile of his slanting his full, feminine lips. "What's the matter? Huh? I thought you liked me again. Feels like I got my arms around an elm tree. What are we gonna do about this? How do we reconcile properly?"

Stella turned her face aside.

Karl smirked. "Why am I here? You wanna let me in on that at least?"

You want to talk about accomplices? What if Jack has done something illegal? He's a man who will somehow find a way to grab onto your leg on his way down into the swamp and you know it. Both of these men, the men you have chosen to surround yourself with, will bring you down and here you are making certain of it one way or the other. You need to return him to where you got him from, and then you need to end this because he has nothing to offer you except codependency. All the things that ran through your mind while you sat in your rocker and studied the picket fence like a math problem, and here you are ready to see it all undone. Tell him about those numbers, and he will see to it you call them. Then, somehow he will grab onto your foot or Jack will. They're both just strong enough to drag you into the muck and feed you to the alligators. Don't tell him—

"I-I was going to leave Jack," she blurted out. "I was coming by to say ..."

Karl waited. "To say what?"

Nothing.

"To give me the big fucking kiss off too?" Now it was Karl's arms that stiffened around Stella's body. "Is that it?"

"No, I ... I—"

Don't lie.

"I was going to pick you up, and we were going to just ... leave." She looked at him, straight on. "Together."

Karl stared back, uncertainly. Stella hated the look of it, of him, and she knew of only one way to break the spell of what they were talking about. She moved into him, pressing her full breasts into his narrow chest. She loved how her flesh gave way against him, somehow crushed, and then she had her mouth on his, and he shoved his tongue past her lips. He took the hem of her sweater and worked it up past her ribcage. He flipped the cups of her bra upward and suckled her, biting her. Above his head, Stella swooned, her words unexpected even to herself.

"We ... oh God ... we need to call some ... phone numbers ..."

Karl was far too swept up in what he was doing to answer or to acknowledge he had heard. They dropped where they stood, naked in moments, and then a swarm of arms and legs and mouths and wetness, then softness and a light doze.

At around three in the afternoon, the doorbell started ringing like a demon had taken possession of its mechanisms. There were fists hammering at the door. Then, there were hands wrestling with the screen door handle, trying to rip it out of its frame. From their place on the floor of the living room, Karl and Stella thought at first there were easily two or three men grappling to get inside. Men, or animals.

Karl shot up onto his knees, steadying himself along the coffee table by his bare thigh. Stella rolled around onto her stomach, wrapped in their clothing. She stared across the rug at the front door. It was rattling around. A large head and squared shoulders pressed in against the screen, pushing it back against the glass of the storm door. The shape of a large man.

They exchanged fevered glances, suddenly aware of their nakedness.

"We know it's not Jack," Karl whispered. "He's got a key."

"Oh, Karl—"

"Ssssh, hold on," he hissed at her, his eyes dark and wild. He climbed to his feet, naked and practically hairless, save for a diamond patch of black tufted hair spread across his breastbone. In the midst of their lovemaking, Stella had barely noticed his hairless privates, only he was smooth and slippery down there while she moved over him. "I'll get out of sight," he said. "But I'm going to need some company. Don't know how long I'll be in the shadows for, and I'm not one for loneliness."

Karl moved to where Betsy lay, her spot on the center cushion of the sofa. The spurious and sudden nature of his motion as he moved towards her and scooped her up against his naked chest alarmed the animal. Her tail turned to a black bushy stick and her eyes flashed up at him. Karl hugged her against him, and slipped past Stella as she rose and quickly hurried to dress herself.

Karl and Betsy the cat had indeed made themselves scarce. She felt badly frightened, having no idea who was knocking so angrily at her door. He had left her there to deal with whoever it was.

"Karl?" she called in a low hiss. "Hey?"

Nothing. *Where had he gone? God, I can't even peek out at them through the curtains to see who it is. They'll be looking right back at me.*

Stella gathered up Karl's clothes and stuffed them back behind the sofa. She kicked his shoes back behind there as well. She was ready. Stella smoothed down her sweater and jeans, held her breath, and opened the storm door.

The visitor had backed up some from the screen door.

When Stella laid eyes on him, her memory blanked. He stood there for a moment, as if allowing her the time to remember him.

Then, she knew who he was. The enlarged, bulbous and previously-shaved head that now sprouted a few patchy gray hairs along his crown. He looked different. He had a neck now, clearly the result of skipped meals. Starvation? His eyes were rimmed in red and lined in circles, his lips colorless. His black tracksuit hung on him like clothes on a clothesline snapping in the breeze. When she had seen him before, his body mass and muscles filled out the slippery fabric almost to tearing. This was an emaciated, somehow shrunken version of the man she had seen.

The one who had beaten her husband on that Philadelphia side street a month before.

Sickly, although his eyes revealed little deficiency in the rage he had displayed so effortlessly that night.

Now, he would show it to her firsthand.

"I'm looking for the man of fuckin' the house," the visitor said, stepping up to the screen door once more. "He here?"

Stella froze. "No ... he-he's at work."

"Where's he work?"

"I-I—"

"You gonna try to tell me you don't know?"

"No ... I ... he's away on business."

"Bullshit."

"What? No-no bullshit—"

"I'm calling bullshit," the visitor insisted. Then his hand curled into the screen door's handle, and he started rattling it around. "Let me in. Unlock this shit. This flimsy-ass shit, or I'll rip it out!"

"What do you want?"

He pressed his wide forehead up against the screen like a bull lining up his charge. "Open the *motherfucking* door, twat!" He pushed his head up against the screen, stretching it inward. The mesh distorted his features, carving lines into his forehead and driving his thick, dark eyebrows dramatically downward. The screen gave easily. "I'm calling bullshit on you, and now I see I gotta get it outta you some other way. You're making me do this," he pulled back and then snapped forward again, driving his head through the screen, tearing it away, "you're making me do this," he felt along inside the door frame and unlocked the door hasp—"YOU'RE MAKING ME DO THIS!"

Stella dipped down and bit the man's hand, sinking her incisors into the hard ridge of his knuckles. He gasped, but didn't cry out. Then he swatted his hand aside and with it, Stella as well. She felt the side of her face smack the doorjamb and then he peeled back the screen door and shoved her aside, moving into the house. Stella screamed and screamed, launching her meager weight at him and looping her arms around his throat to try and pull him down to the ground. He was an immovable boulder standing there in her foyer, and he shrugged her off, accenting her trip back down to the rug with a backhanded slap across the jaw that rattled her from head to toe like a human tuning fork. She landed on her right hip hard and rolled over onto her side.

Above her, the visitor slammed the storm door shut. Bolted it.

From the floor, Stella cried out. "What do you *want?*"

"You know something? I'm not even fuckin' surprised you got no idea where your man is. If you only knew. *If you only knew.* He left his wallet, the dumb fuck. I tracked him here. I waited ... but motherfuck—I couldn't wait any longer." The visitor threw Jack's battered brown leather wallet down at Stella on the floor.

Moaning, Stella rolled over onto her back, gasping for air and sucking it down in quick, short slurps. "I ... know ... who ... *he is*—"

"Do ya?" She suddenly felt the visitor's hands seize her by the arms, bearing her back up onto rubbery legs before he pinned her hard against the wall. He cross-barred his meaty right forearm along her windpipe. "Do you fuckin' really? You know he bangs prostitutes? You know he likes to manhandle them? That's what he woulda' done to one o' mine, and I think he woulda' killed her and dumped her right there in the gutter if I weren't trailing her cuz' she just tried to pink slip herself! You don't know shit! Your man's got two faces. Two *fucking* brains! Dark and fuckin' *reaallly* fuckin' dark! I can't eat! I-I-I can't sleep! I tried to jump off a bridge two nights ago because I can't stand the fuckin' crazy thoughts I got in my head. You wanna know why?"

"Gggaaaaaahhhh—"

"YOU WANNA KNOW WHY?"

The spots danced before Stella's eyes, waltzing and spiraling and multicolored. Black closed in from all sides of her vision, advancing rapidly. Closing out the world.

"Cuz' I don't know if I'm dying or not!"

Black shutting out the whole shitty world and Stella was willing to go along with it. She would let go.

"You gotta tell me cuz' I gotta know! Does your man have AIDS? *You gotta tell me right now so's I know!* I got no health insurance. Can't see a doctor, but I'll raise some kind of money if you'll just fuckin' tell me if he's got it! He spit on me! You hear me? *Spit on me* and then he said he had AIDS. Shit got in my eyes, and I couldn't blink it out! I flushed my eyes all

124

night long, but I could still feel something there! Something I couldn't get at! Something that already got me! *You gotta tell me! TELL ME!*"

I always knew it would be a man—just never knew for sure—which.

Then, Stella heard the high, piercing screech of a cat and Betsy appeared on the visitor's shoulder. The visitor's arms flew to the animal, and then Karl Tarlick, naked and still holding the cat from behind, came around and smacked the visitor in the side of the head with a rolling pin.

The visitor went down.

Stella slid down the wall, slowly remembering how to breathe again.

Then, there was no time.

Everything happened so fast.

28. A VERY DIFFERENT KIND OF WATER-BOARDING

The earthy swirl of shadings comprising the color-scheme of Stella's living room swam back into focus. The edges of things sharpened. She remained in a crumpled heap against the wall beside the television console, her throat throbbing. The sounds nearby were terrifying. They only intensified the longer she hunkered there. A cacophony of feline screeching and mewling intermingled with the far more wrenching sound of a man shrieking and begging for *it* to *stop*. She rolled her head along the wall, the flurry of motion and the struggle between Karl, the visitor, and (Betsy?) on the ground beside her calling the hairs on the back of her neck and arms to attention.

What she saw made no sense at all. A vision so surreal as to be mistaken for hallucination.

The visitor was on his back. Karl grasped the cat by its scruff, which had turned the cat into a tight wedge of fur in midair. He had his legs on top of the visitor's arms, pinning them to the rug. Karl sat across the man's chest, and the visitor could not seem to free himself from this strong-arming arrangement. Karl had always seemed to Stella to possess the same sort of surprising strength most small, sinewy men harbor, and then let loose at the right and proper time. This was that moment. Karl was silent as could be.

Cold silent as he held the cat in the air above the visitor's face.

Betsy shrieked and wailed, her body was a white and fuzzy bullet frozen in mid-air. She was staring with a terrible pinpointed focus down at the visitor, and the visitor was straining to break his gaze away from the cat's. The visitor was screaming, whipping his head around. Left to right.

Left to right.

The cat mewed and shrieked.

Then, suddenly the visitor was mewing and shrieking. He ceased trying to avoid the cat's eyes, and his head went still on the rug.

The cat and the visitor were quite literally staring into one another.

Betsy spoke.

Stella came to then, her spine stiffening and eyes widening. She looked over at the cat and watched it speak in what was not quite a human voice, but just clearly enunciated enough to be mistaken for something damned close.

Betsy said, "Drowning."

Stella felt sick to her stomach. "Oh my God—"

"Sssh!" Karl said, driving the cat's face down further into the visitor's, closing out any and all of his remaining peripheral vision. Karl leaned into the cat's ear, uttered something and then drew back.

"*Drow*-ning ..." Betsy said, in a high whine that now sounded more like an infant's tone than an animal.

The visitor mewed low in his throat, shrieked once more. Meowed.

Then he was a frenzy of bucking and struggling, the slippery fabric of his black jogging suit wisping along Karl's naked legs. The visitor broke the cat's line of vision, the damage done. The transference complete. The visitor screamed, and it was thoroughly feline. Nothing human of its tone remained. He was gasping, spitting, trying to draw a breath. He spit up. His broad but sunken chest started hitching and spasming, so much so the motion threw Karl clear and he landed on his side. The cat, Betsy, lay down beside Karl, catatonic. Karl pet the animal, but Betsy did not move.

The visitor, no longer pinned, didn't make any motion to stand or to break for the front door behind him. He couldn't. He raised his arms up over his chest and looked like Betsy sometimes does when she is sleeping and dreaming about running (or trying to break free from having her head held underwater).

He can't breathe. He's suffocating. Drowning.

Karl climbed back on top of the visitor. He slapped the visitor's hands aside as they pawed at the air. He leaned in. Spoke into the visitor's left ear, something Stella couldn't hear even if she wanted to.

Then, Karl turned to Stella. "Hit him with the roller! It's right by you on the floor there."

"Karl, I—"

The visitor moaned. A human moan, produced by human vocal cords.

What produced the cat sounds he had been making seconds before?
Karl stood up and stepped away from the visitor.

The visitor rolled slowly, stiffly onto his side. He came to face Stella. She recognized a small light of knowing blooming in his eyes. Then, she saw the malice and fear hit her heart like a jackhammer.

"Stell, hit him now!"

She grabbed for the rolling pin.

The visitor moved to raise his hands in a pitiful warding off gesture. "Naaaah—"

Stella hit him across his forearms, collapsing them. Then, she clubbed him in the side of the head with the rolling pin, and he rolled over onto his back, unconscious.

She shut her eyes, prayed when she opened them she would not see anything other than the ceiling of her bedroom and hear the sound of Jack snoring beside her. The windows darkened by night. The emergence from a dream state.

But Stella was used to living without refuge. This would prove no different.

Instead, she heard the slow build of Karl Tarlick's giggling, from a small chuckle to an all-out riotous roar of amusement. One would have thought George Carlin was holding court there in the Post living room.

This was real. Dear God-dear God!

Karl leaned against the wall opposite her, naked and unashamed. He held Betsy in his arms again. The cat was prone, unmoving.

Dead? Oh dear God is she—

"Dead? Is she dead? What did you *do,* Karl?"

Karl's laughter wound down. He smiled broadly. There was the fire of a new knowledge burning behind his small black eyes. "It worked. It actually fucking worked. That was some dry run, Stell! He came just at the right time. Served just the right purpose for our needs."

"Wha-what needs are you talking about? What the hell happened, Karl?"

"Shhh—you'll wake Sleeping Beauty, and believe it, he needs his rest after that."

"What did you do to him?"

Karl beset Stella with a squinty stare, smiling his sideways smile. "Babe, I should be asking you the same question?"

"What are you talking about?"

"What the hell happened to this cat? Did Jack try to hurt it?"

Stella fell silent. She knew.

"Did you?" pressed Karl. "Try to ... I don't know ... drown it or something?"

Stella flinched at his words, her eyelids twitching. She rubbed viciously at the bridge of her nose, trying to clear the remaining haze from her vision. The living room stunk of sweat and another far more acrid, stinging stench Stella hadn't smelled in her home since they first brought Betsy home as a kitten, and she had her accidents here and there before learning how to locate her litter box in the laundry room. Stella moved away from the wall, crawling on her hands and knees. Her nose stung as the scent intensified, and it became clear the visitor had soiled himself with urine, as well. She looked at the crotch of his pants and saw the dark stain spreading there as it saturated the black fabric of his jogging pants.

Crawling along, careful to skirt the comatose visitor with piss down his leg, Stella suddenly bristled at what Karl had said. "Of course I didn't do anything to my cat. What the hell are you talking about? She's my cat. You—"

Do not complete that thought, Stella! Don't fucking do it!

She was within a hair's breadth of calling Karl out for his past transgressions against his former neighbor's pets when the wind went out of her, and she clapped her mouth shut. She could only hope he hadn't caught on to what she meant to say. She had only given him one word. *You!* He was the one who insisted they shared in something called a *mindmeld*. She hoped it had broken down, temporarily at least.

When she slid up alongside Karl, the sudden sound of weeping, like small stones inside a small glass, drew both their attentions towards the visitor. Quite a paradox to hear. The man had been intimidating, heartless. Capable of murder. Reduced to this lump of incontinent, weeping sludge.

Karl offered her the cat in his arms. The moment he lifted it to give to her, Betsy sprang to life as if someone had goosed her with a cattle prod. She shot past Stella, disappearing into the kitchen area beyond. Karl shrugged, trying not to eyeball Stella beside him. "Guess you guys are on the rocks these days."

"What ... what happened here, Karl?"

Karl raked the black curls of his hair away from his low forehead, smirking with a raw sense of pride. "What the hell did you expect me to do?" he asked. "The guy woulda' killed you."

"No. No-I don't think he would have. He was here for Jack."

"You ever seen him before?"

"Why would you ask me that? You think I associate with guys like him?"

"Guys like what? What is he?"

128

"He's ... he's a *pimp*."

"How do you know?" Karl asked. Curiosity burned in his eyes. "See, I knew it. I knew you seen him before."

"How did you know? What? Is this more of your *mindmeld* shit?"

"No," Karl said. "I'm just attuned to how people talk to strangers instead of how they talk to people they know. People they seen before. I was listening to you from the kitchen and you? You sounded shocked to see him, but it faded away and something else took its place. You knew what he was, and you knew what kind of threat he was bringing. It was all there. In your words. In your voice. So I—you know—I talked it over with your kitty cat, and we came to an understanding something needed to be done. She was game. At least, I think she was. She done a great job. Gold star for following directions."

Stella chewed her tongue. "So you ... you somehow sicced my cat on this guy?"

"Come on now! Don't be silly! You can't *sic a cat* on nobody. That's a dog's territory." Karl turned toward Stella, reached for her hands, and tickled the palms with his fingertips. "But, you *can* chase any animal's essence right the fuck out of their body with just the right words. Leaves a void. An empty vessel that begs to be filled. And it'll latch onto whoever the fuck is there in the general vicinity. The essence leaves through the eyes. It also enters that way. Enters the vessel. Fills it."

The whole thing sounded ridiculous, and Stella felt herself stiffen as Karl went on. If he were joking with her, she vowed she would turn him out right then without so much as a backward glance. The thing of it was, Karl spoke of these things in a respectful, deeply humble manner. He might as well have been talking about some spiritual revelation or impossible encounter with God. He did not so much tell Stella about what he had done as he recited the words. They poured forth like a prayer he had spoken time and time again on his knees, pious and still aside from the soft and supple movement of his lips.

Still, Stella had no idea what else to do. She couldn't help but laugh.

Karl suddenly smiled his sideways grin. He appeared bashful suddenly. Self-conscious, even. "All right," he said. "Have it your way. I'm probably not explaining it right. To be honest, to even try and explain it is like trying to tell a blind man what the color red is. I don't think I'm going to try. The guy who showed me, didn't *tell me* either. He gave me his book. He gave me a warning about it. Told me not to be *fucking stupid* about it. Then he walked back into his cell at the prison, and I never saw him again. I think he mighta' shipped out right before I did. Strange thing of it is, he never came back to get his book from me. I know he didn't forget. Couldn't have. It's a fucking beautiful leatherbound piece. I know I'd never forget to get something like this back if I handed it out on loan." Karl rubbed the sharp, angular line of his narrow jaw, thinking. "No, I'm guessing he wanted me to have it. And ... well, he could very easily have found me at the halfway house if he got half a mind to. He never came."

"Is this ... what you were talking about?"

"What? When?"

"Santeria? Is that what this is?"

"Oh no," Karl said. "No, Santeria gets a bad rap. It gets lumped in with splinter sects that take its messages and practices steps further beyond what was ever fucking intended by the original practitioners. Nah, this is *palo mayombe*. This ... this is for the black hearts." He looked at Stella, a small sadness standing in his dark eyes. "You a black heart?"

"I-I don't understand."

"Yeah you do," Karl said. "If you're not already there, your heart's real close to turning black as ink. Maybe Jack beats you *one* more time, and you'll be there. Black as *bad fruit*. Then you'll understand, and we can get started. And you ... you want laugh at any of this like you just done? You'll starve for it."

They sat there looking at one another for much longer was comfortable with Stella. Then there was only the sound of the visitor as he started to weep again, only this time it was a snot-clogged sound. His body shuddered from head to toe, a long rippling wave coursed through him like an electric shock.

This snapped Karl to, his attention turning to the visitor with full attention. "When's Big Jack get home? You can *actually* tell *me*."

Stella glanced towards the door. The sheers in the storm door were no longer lit with sunlight. They had gone grey with what was a sudden cloudiness. "Another two hours, I think." She looked over at the quaint cuckoo clock hanging on the wall at the foot of the stairwell clear on the other side of the room. "Looks like its quarter to four?"

"All right," Karl said and stood up. He crept towards the couch and his clothes, with his flaccid penis dangling hypnotically between his legs. He felt around behind the couch, locating his underpants and jeans first. "We gotta dump this idiot somewhere. In his car. He's got a beater Chevy parked out in your driveway. I'll drive him in it and you follow me in your car. We'll leave him at the airport parking lot. Not Philadelphia International. You gotta pay."

"Northeast Airport."

"Agreed," Karl said, fishing around behind the sofa for his shirt. "That's good. And on the way home, you can tell me why you tried to drown your cat. Lay down on the couch for Dr. Tarlick, and just *let yourself go.*"

29. KEEN EYE FOR DETAIL

Rivells slipped out of the interrogation room, a cramped eight-by-eight space with walls of exposed brick painted a gunship grey, and nearly walked headlong into her captain. Captain Manfred Toulon was one of those police administrators who looked very much the part of his title. He stood six feet two and filled out every inch of his pressed white shirt and charcoal slacks. The clothes he wore looked as if they were asphyxiating against his firm and swollen upper body. He was also one of those rare administrative breeds who reddened in the face when heaped with praise of any kind and preferred to hand off said praise to his detectives like it was a hot potato. He was standing before the one-way glass that looked into the interrogation room. This would have been expected had Rivells not been told earlier the captain's wife had taken a turn for the worse with her *condition* and no one would see him until around midnight.

It was barely five in the evening.

"Oh, Jesus," Rivells blurted, dodging him at the last minute. "Sorry, Cap. I didn't see you there."

Captain Toulon laid his palm against the one-way glass and smiled thinly. "Then I guess we don't have to replace this just yet. I don't know the budget would cover it anyhow." He paused, crossing his barrel arms over his chest, the sleeves rolled clear beyond the elbows, and glanced back at the twentysomething girl slouched in the iron chair and table in the room. "She looks tired as hell. How long you been working her?"

"Believe it or not, a half hour. She's wearing three inches of eyeliner around her eyes. That's part of it. Plus, I just found out she hasn't slept in almost a week, and once I found that out I decided to halt the interview for the time being. Wouldn't want her lawyers to say her senses or her judgment were impaired when she confessed. I'm thinking we let her catch some winks in the bunk, manacled of course. By that time, her lawyer should be here."

"She invoked?"

"Nope," Rivells said. "But her mother, a bleary-eyed mess herself,

131

said she'd be making the call while we were taking her out of the house."

"Where's your partner now? I heard something about bad Indian food at lunch? "

"You heard right," Rivells said. "He didn't have me for his lunch date this afternoon. I would have steered him away from Arahad's if I were there."

"I'm sure you were catching some well-deserved winks, Rivells."

"A couple hours. Double cappuccino. Repeat. Here I am."

Captain Toulon tried to conceal a yawn by rubbing at the bottom half of his face. Salt and pepper stubble covered his maw. He never let it go that long, his face usually shiny from a daily shave and layering of Aqua Velva at all his morning briefings. Rivells was worried. Toulon had been the one to personally pluck her from the obscurity of the beat-cop rank and file after an especially impressive collar a few years back involving a series of subway abductions. From then on, Toulon assumed something of a mentor and fatherly role for her, without allowing for the indulgence to cloud his sense of command. Rivells never knew her real father. She knew he had another family down in Atlanta and she left him to it, harboring no ill will. He left her in the cradle. Toulon, a bulging German-Frenchman, was the *wrong* color but of the *right* heart. That was how Rivells saw it.

This was why she could get away with touching his shoulder and looking at him in the darkened room with something of sympathy without Toulon flinching away and reminding her of her place. It was why she could dare ask him how Rebecca was doing.

Poor, wasting Rebecca.

"She's back in the hospital," Toulon said, expelling the words as if they had been choking him for hours.

"Oh, I'm so sorry."

Another yawn, rubbing at his mouth. "I don't understand it. Everything we try carries these horrid side effects that outweigh the benefits. She's been on everything, and I do mean *everything*. The fatigue. The night sweats. Brain fog. I mean, Christ, this is a woman who used to teach AP Calculus. Now, she reaches for words like she's just learning the language." His eyes twinkled in the darkness. Wetness. Rivells squeezed his shoulder. "She took my car keys last night and ... well, and she didn't want me to drive to work today. She thinks the neighbors cut my brake line. When I found the keys, she snatched them out of my hands and almost ... she tried to hurt herself with them."

"Captain—"

"A Three-Oh-Two order this time," Toulon admitted. "I have been trying to avoid three-oh-twoing her. I can't commit my wife. I didn't want it to go on her record so she would be able to teach again when this ... this *shitstorm* passes us by. But ..."

"You'll be able to get it expunged."

"Right," Toulon said, turning away to peer blindly into the interrogation room. "Right-right." His voice quavered. "So, have an officer escort the girl into the bunk room." Then, his voice was even-tempered. It was impressive. "If they don't cuff her in there, I will have their ass. Make sure you tell them, whoever does it."

"I can do it."

"Not at the moment, Rivells," Toulon said. "You've got a visitor waiting for you. Detective Jones from Special Victims?"

Now it was Rivell's turn to say it. "Oh, right-right-right—"

"The rape vic from your building?"

Rivells nodded. "I won't be long," she said. "I hope you don't mind. I handed it off, and I asked he keep me in the loop if they had any new info to share."

"Just don't step on any toes over there," Toulon said. "They can be very territorial."

"Wouldn't think of it, Cap. If you could have seen this girl and her mother. I just want to know they're doing everything they can to catch this sick bastard."

"No reason for them not to, Rivells," Toulon said. "When you finish up with him, we'll talk about this young lady and roll over what she's given us so far. If anything."

"It's spare so far, but there are some things."

Rivells strode out into the hustle of the station house proper, nodding and smiling in the direction of the four or five colleagues who hollered their congratulations at her. Riviera wanted to fuck her, and had wanted to ever since he divorced his wife (perhaps, Rivells had been the reason for the split) a few months back, and so his hooting and hollering rang out the loudest, and perhaps the most hollow. The upstairs floor, a small landing where old files and frustrated detectives lingered with their sour station brews, bustled with activity. She saw Nolan's blonde, frizzy bun above the stacks, followed by Primm's dyed jet-black pompadour as they scoured the files as a tag team. The water cooler in the far corner burbled loudly as Thompson, the oldest and oddly least-decorated detective, filled his cup. Then, she saw her partner, Jim Tyler, shamble out of the men's locker room looking like he'd just been through a war in the trenches. He didn't walk so much as he slid along. *That will teach you to pick a lunch place without me, pardner!* He glanced over at her, his face white and eyes hollowed. He must have lost more than a couple of meals to the porcelain God just now. She nodded at him and raised a finger to let him know she'd rejoin him shortly. He nodded back, wandering off.

The noise of the station floor sometimes worked like a corkscrew in her ears. It annoyed as often as it comforted. Right then, Rivells wanted to hear good news from her visitor. She skirted the rows of desks and found Detective Jones standing at her desk like he was afraid to sit down in the chair alongside it. Jones was an athletic-looking, solidly-constructed African-American with green eyes Rivells immediately found herself staring into in spite of herself. *Falling into is more like it!* She had only talked to him on the phone and seeing him, shaking his hand and standing close enough to admire the perfect white of his dental work, was an altogether different and decidedly dizzying experience.

Is it so wrong to be looking forward to keeping in contact with this one?

Her mother would have said, "Hell, naw, darlin'."

Rivells agreed. Momma was never wrong.

"Detective Jones," she greeted him warmly.

"Darnell, please."

"That's fine," Rivells said, waving him over to her side of the desk. "Detective Glynna Rivells." No need to have him sit down. She was curious of the cologne she could smell faintly wafting off him. He came around, unzipping his black tote bag and producing a brown folder from within. He laid it down on her desk and flipped it open.

Polo. It's Polo. Not my favorite, but good enough. Okay, back to it.

She looked down at the opened dossier and found she was staring down at a police sketch. *Holy shit! HOLY SHIT!* "Is this what I think it is?"

"Your German Shepherd Perp Pig," Jones said, stabbing a finger down at the page. "The Gods are smiling on this case. No doubt about it. They want this prick found and stopped as badly as we do. No to mention, this comes with a story you may find interesting."

"Tell me," Rivells said. She waved him down into the seat beside her desk and lowered herself down into hers.

Detective Jones sat down, leaning in. "We cased the neighborhood surrounding the Starbucks where the victim works. She reported having been dragged behind the coffee shop, and she was assaulted there behind the dumpster where her coworkers smoke during their break. There's a single light on a green wood post that stands directly overtop the trash bin. It has a spray radius of only about two to three feet in diameter, but that was just enough, as it turns out. The perp didn't pull his mask on until after he had his vic pinned. The seconds leading up to when he pulled her along the concrete, his face was in plain view. The light wouldn't have caught it for very long but it was just long enough someone got a look at him."

"Thank God," Glynna sighed, settling back in her seat. "Tell me more."

"There's a row of townhouses just beyond the chain link fence that separates the rear of the store from the back porches. The thing about these particular townhouses is, the second and third floors both have balconies off the upstairs bedrooms. These elevated porches present an unobstructed view of the entire rear area of the Starbucks shop. I stepped out onto the porch while we were conducting our interviews, and it's a clear shot across the blacktop leading right up to the back door of the shop. The thing of it is, the people who live in these townhouses rarely ever go out onto the third-floor balcony. They shut the blinds at night. There's no light up there once they close their blinds or pull the shades. People are only ever up there sleeping, for the most part. Not so much as a sliver of light to give our perp any pause before committing the assault there. He thought he was alone to do what he wanted. But it just so happens someone *was* out on her balcony the night our vic was assaulted."

"Reliable witness? Wouldn't they have to've been sitting out there in the dark? How could they see anything clear enough?"

"Our witness is about as reliable as they come," Jones said, almost gloating over their good luck. "She's a painter. An artist. You know where I'm going with this? Someone who possesses something of a keen eye for detail. More so than most eyewitnesses. Now, hold onto your hat, Detective. She was working on a piece out on her balcony when our perp appeared with the vic. She showed me her sketchpad. She was working out a rough scaled outline of the rooftops. She said it was a *blood* moon that night, and she felt compelled to capture it sitting all fat and red overtop of the skyline. Thing of it is, she preferred to work *in the dark* so the artificial light of her balcony wouldn't interfere with her sensitivity to texture and shadow. Our perp never even knew she was sitting out there, let alone drawing."

"What did she do when she realized what was happening down behind the store?"

"Nothing."

"Nothing? Why the hell wouldn't she call the police? Afraid to let it interfere with her art? Christ—"

"Hold off on that, Rivells," Jones said. "Her name's Rosario Diaz. She lives there with her son and his family. Moved in with him when her husband died. She's a native of Juarez, Mexico. Born and raised there. Her son was born there, but he's a naturalized citizen. An investment banker with Morgan Stanley. She's undocumented. You get the picture?"

"I'm afraid I do. How long did it take for you to get the information out of her?"

"I asked the same question you just asked me. I put it to her son and to her through him, since he translated for her. Their silence was telling, to say the least. I knew right then and there what I was dealing with. I promised them we weren't there to bust her. We don't owe ICE a phone call, and they wouldn't be getting any tip from us. As far as we were concerned, Ms. Diaz's name would be kept out of the papers, and we would conceal her identity if and when she met with a sketch artist. At first, they thought I was blowing serious fucking smoke. It took a while to get her to commit to and describe our perp for the artist and even then, I had to consent to have the artist come to her. She wasn't about to come down to the precinct. It would have been like walking into a lion's den for her. She's a smart woman. Pretty damned talented, judging by her work. While we waited on our artist to show up there, she showed me her artist nook and took great pride in sharing her work with me. She sculpts and sketches. Natural talent. God-given, I'd say."

Rivells rubbed at her temple, already sensing the migraine coming on. They were something she had come to live with begrudgingly in the last few months. Her doctor said she needed glasses. She thought she needed a stiff shot of bourbon. It usually worked, off-hours of course. "You know it will have to come out if and when this goes to trial. Defense will demand to know the identity of the eyewitness. Our wizard behind the curtain. What then?"

"It will never come up," Jones said. He raised an eyebrow, leaned in towards her. "At least, it doesn't have to if you're game."

Rivells's nostrils tingled against Jones's cologne. "Meaning ... what?"

"Here's how it went," Jones said. "I orchestrated the whole damned thing. Before the sketch artist got there, I had the mother sketch out a rough drawing of what she remembered about the perp's facial features. She put it all together pretty quickly. Her hand was a lightning stroke across the page. Really a wonder to behold, Detective. Then, I had the son study the drawing the mother had sketched out while we were waiting for our guy to come and render his own sketch. Her son sat there with his mother's drawing for almost a half hour before the doorbell rang. Then, we hid the sketch his mother made, and I had *her son* sit with the sketch artist and describe our perp, drawing from his memory of what his mother's drawing depicted. *If and when* the time did come for the eyewitness to be outed, we could claim it was the son sitting out there who saw the whole thing go down behind the

136

coffee shop. Not the mother. The legal citizen. No harm. No foul—"

"You would have done better not to share this with me, Detective."

Jones shrugged. He didn't say anything, instead sliding the newly minted police sketch closer to her side of the desk as some form of reprieve. "I got a vibe from you."

"What sort of vibe? Should I be insulted?"

"A *truth-seeker* vibe."

"At any cost?"

"Does it bother you, Rivells?" He squared his shoulders, and before she knew what he was doing, he had slapped the dossier closed before her and scooped it back up into his hands. "I could lose the sketch. It would hurt, but it won't hurt me. It'll set me back. Piss me off. How would you sleep knowing we had this key piece of the puzzle, and we suppressed it for the sake of ... what would you call it? Transparency?"

"The words *cutting corners* come to mind," she said, her eyes flashing. "But ... fuck ..."

"You kiss your mother with that mouth?"

"My mother's dead, God rest her," Rivells said drily. "I wish she wasn't. More than ever before. Then she wouldn't see me right now. She wouldn't hear me when I say the latter part of this conversation never took place. Now, play nice and let me have a look at the ... the *son's sketch.* Jones set the dossier back down before her, flipped it open, and settled into his seat while Rivells pulled it closer.

Her first thought—*Good looking guy.* It killed her to think this, but her mind went right to it. Defaulted. She wondered why a guy with looks like these, a certain ad-exec quality with hair long enough to fall into his face, felt he needed to steal sex from women. To violate them, when, in fact, most women would be willing to lay down for a face like his? It didn't add up. His wide, almond-shaped eyes. Proletarian nose that looked sharp enough to slice olives. A sculpted v-shaped chin, sunken cheeks, and plucked eyebrows. Ears that lay flat against the sides of his skull. Dark hair, swept and sprayed up into a neat swirl then lightly brushed to the left. Shaved, clipped sides. A *high-and-tight?* Rivells thought it was the style. He looked somewhat like a movie star, or his *doppelganger. Can't decide which movie star, but the name's right on the tip of my tongue.*

"I know," Jones said. "I know. Handsome *fuck.* But it means he'll stick out. This city's got a pretty dense population of *ugly* dudes walking around. It will be real easy for someone to spot this pretty boy *asshole* in a crowd. We'll get him."

"Every newscast in the tri-state area?"

"I was waiting on your go-ahead."

"You didn't have to wait on me. This is your case. You're showing me courtesy by even being here."

"You've got a direct line into this whole thing," Jones said. "I say we pool our resources, and see this one through together. Your Captain's game if you are."

"What do you mean *my Captain's—*"

"Turns out my captain and yours are blood related. Third cousins or something. A weird French-German conglomeration, the two of them. Mine called yours, and it's already a foregone conclusion. So I'm hoping to hear a *yes*, Detective Rivells."

"I'm wrapping up a case right now. Letting the perp sleep. Been something of an insomniac, but once she's gotten some winks and she's lucid ... maybe by tomorrow morning ... I should be able to take her statement, type it up, and send it off to the DA for processing. Then, I'll jump on full-time."

Detective Jones stood up, his smile blinding ivory. He had appeared perfect to her only moments before, but right then Rivells's eye went right to the one slightly turned canine nestled within his top row of teeth. *Not handsome anymore. Ruggedly handsome now.* This was just fine with Rivells. Perfection is a lie hiding a crucial truth.

"Full-time," Jones said. "I'll wait to hear from you tomorrow." He reclaimed the police sketch, zipped it back up inside his leather bag, and shook firmly with Rivells, who rose to put her own muscle into her pump.

It wasn't until two minutes after she watched him weave his way around desks and water coolers, out the door of the precinct Rivells remembered she had something to share with him. Something she ought to have handed over to him, as Jones was still for all intents and purposes the lead investigator of the case. Rivells rolled open the top side drawer of her desk, took the item in question out, and laid it on her desk blotter. Rivells had asked for it from the rape victim, Jodi Dare, and the young girl had handed it over like the tainted little block of technology it had become for her.

Jodi Dare's old cell phone. A silver iPhone with a pink, hardshell casing.

30. LIVING IN YOUR LETTERS

When Karl climbed into Stella's passenger seat and they were rolling through the exit of the Northeast Airport Parking Lot, she felt she could breathe again without it hurting. She had to hand it to him, Karl had seen to everything. He had even been the one to come up with this little cover plan of theirs. It excited her how mentally well equipped he was to deal with such surprises, as well as how to resolve them. It also made her nervous how calculating he seemed to be. All these things she had felt while they drove to the airport, her following Karl, who drove the visitor in his own car.

With the intruder dumped inside his car in Spot E3, Karl rejoined Stella. She found she could shove the other feelings of dread aside, leaving room only for her relief in being back in Karl's company.

On the way back to Comstock, Karl sat cross-legged in the passenger seat. He reminded her of how swamis were portrayed in films and paintings, exuding a zen-like confidence. His voice was airy when he spoke. "He won't remember anything about what happened today. He won't remember how to get to your house, and we got Jack's wallet back. The door's closed."

"How can you be sure?"

"It's simple," Karl said, suddenly lunging forward and flipping down the glovebox. He searched inside, and his hand came away with a small pouch of chewing gum. He thumbed one out and popped it in his mouth, chewing contentedly. "He's still a cat. And Betsy is somehow trying to figure out just what in the hell she is. Her brain is half the size of his, and most likely she isn't capable of thinking of herself as a man who wears stupid looking tracksuits and pimps out women."

"I ... I don't understand what you're saying." Her hands clutched the wheel, knuckles bone-white. "What are you *saying*?"

"For now, I'll just keep it simple. The guy we just dropped off will be himself again in a couple of days. Betsy, a little longer. Again, because she's got a smaller brain. It'll need more time to rebound. Right now, I'll bet she's probably hidden away somewhere in your house. She's probably doing what animals do out of instinct when they sense they're about to die. It feels like that for Betsy, I'll bet. But I think she'll be surprised when it doesn't happen."

"This is that *palo* ... I don't remember what you called it—"

"*Palo mayombe*, Stell."

"Right ... right."

"Now," Karl said. "We both saw what happened to the guy when I did the switch."

"The switch?"

"First, I want you to tell me what you did to Betsy."

Stella glanced at him fretful and checked the rearview absently. "Nothing."

"Stella, I'm not going to pass judgment on you. Christ knows, if there's anyone in this car who ought to have judgment passed on them, it's me and you never done it. Never once. Maybe in your heart, once or twice, but I don't fault you for it if it's even true." He paused, wet his lips, and blew a bubble with his gum that popped back against his lips before it could really get going. "It's more about trying to understand what exactly the switch *does*. Call it research. I want to know all there is to know about what the switch *does*. Don't want nothing to go wrong. I want to have complete control over the whole thing. Don't want no surprises. So ... tell me what happened."

Her next thought surprised her so much she inadvertently applied the brake out of instinct. Her foot tapped it before she knew what she was doing, and the car shuddered a bit before she returned her sneaker to the gas and kept them rocking down I-95 North. *Telling him what you did to Betsy won't make you* anything *like him. The things he did to those pets, they're horrible things. What you did was terrible, but you stopped yourself. He never would have stopped if he wasn't caught.* You *are not* like him! *(you sure?).*

Stella started, her words gradually building a steady momentum. She began with the tail of Jack into Philadelphia. She explained what she saw in the city. The trip home, the bathtub, the second-guessing. She hesitated often. The tears sprang to her eyes almost immediately, and she felt Karl's hand on her arm. She drew small strength from his touch. When she finished, Stella expected Karl to dive right into the silence, but he held his tongue for a while, and they remained this way for perhaps two miles. Then, he blew another bubble, popped it back, and sucked wind.

"Do I gotta worry about you?" he asked.

She didn't say anything. She shook her head, like a cold chill had just taken her. "No. No."

"Yes," he said. "I do. I've been. Worrying about you. Even when we weren't talking. The way I feel for you, Stella? It don't just shut off like a night light. You can't just power it down, and it goes away."

"It'll be okay," Stella said, sniffing. "One way or another, I have to hold onto that thought."

"What if Jack's got AIDS, Stell. It'll be all right then, too?"

"He doesn't have—he doesn't."

"If he does, you know he got it from one of these skanks. These fucking tricks of his. You told me before he's been cheating since the marriage started four years ago. Makes me wonder why he even decided to marry when he had no intention of keeping it in his pants. I don't know. Maybe he just wanted someone to warm his bed for him when he gets home from doing what he does. He's got you doing the same job as an electric blanket. You been a comfort to him. Now you tell me? What's he ever been to you 'cept a serial abuser and a captor. *Your* captor."

"I could leave."

"You could? Why haven't you then?"

"It takes planning," she said. "Money for a lawyer. Money he has all tied up in *his* investments and a bank account I'm only allowed to touch with his permission." She shook her head, her cheeks reddening. "I went out to buy a new blouse one day a few years ago, before the fears took hold of me. I wanted to work, to at least *try* to get out of the house. I know shorthand. I know Office Suite. I picked it up as a title clerk. Let's just say I knew enough to fake it until I made it, you know? Whatever new updates or software came out since then, I figured I could just teach myself along the way. I got an interview at a doctor's office. I needed new clothes. I only spent thirty dollars on the blouse at Macy's. But he found out, and he removed my name from the joint access account. It's been in his name ever since, and he runs me an allowance. It covers groceries. Gas. Just enough money to cover those things, and little else. Then, he convinced me to toss my meds. He told me they were making me want to do *too much too fast*. He told me I'd overdo it and have a heart attack. He told me I should be homebound until I got these crazy ideas out of my system. I obeyed. I learned how to fear the outside world. So, how do you ask your husband for the money to pay a lawyer so you can sue him for a divorce?" She laughed at herself, and then a fresh bout of tears overtook her, and she wept over the steering wheel. "Jesus Christ—I—*am*—stuck!"

"The hell you are," Karl said, angling his body now to look fully on her. "You're out now, and you're driving around. Not hiding inside the house, twitching behind a curtain, sneaking a peek out the window at the big bad world on the other side of the glass. Without me, it'd be a different story. I know. I'm happy to heal you just by being around. But I also still believe in taking up for women, even the ones I'm not in love with. Well, love and *lust*. Ain't such a bad thing. I *do* believe you got yourself a deviant on your hands. I don't know yet about calling him a predator, but there's definitely some kind of sex addiction working here with Jack."

"So, so what?" Stella said, fire in her eyes. Just enough to burn away her tears. "So I should pity him because he's got an addiction? He can't fucking *help himself?*"

"The opposite, Stell. I would think of it more as an alternative to therapy. A new treatment, but one I am damn certain will snap him out of this addiction forever."

"Why are you being so damned cagey about this *palo*—"

"*Mayombe*—"

"MAYOMBE—WHATEVER THE HELL!" Stella reined her temper back, panting slightly. "What you did back at the house with Betsy and the—the pimp? Is this the therapy you're talking about? Because I think it's safe to say Betsy's been through enough of my shit. Now today's shit? I don't want to involve her anymore in this, whatever it is. And that's only if I agree to any of it."

"Oh, Stella, a cat just isn't gonna cut it for our means. No, ma'am. Not at all. You don't have to worry."

"FUCK, KARL—"

"'I remember how the forest was wet with rain, and my butt got all sticky. I remember when I stood up when we finished, I had leaves stuck to my cheeks, but it was erotic. It turned me on, not just because we had just been each other's firsts. The leaves tickled my ass. I hope you're not laughing out loud at me right now while you read this. Then again, how would I know? Laugh away, asshole! I'll keep writing to you, and when you finally are allowed visitors (finally?) I will tell you things in person because sometimes my words don't really come across the way I want them to when I write them down. Like for instance, you wrote to me you can't understand why a beautiful suburban goddess like me would want to drop down into the mud by writing to someone like you. Well, because you held me, and you were sweet to me my first time, and I remember how you said you wished our first time could have been in a grand hotel. You were bagging groceries at the Q-Mart so you couldn't spring for it at the time. I don't care now, and I didn't care then. But I will say the way you treated me our first time, and the times after before you were taken away, I have never forgotten it. Sure, Jack is my husband, but a change has come over him. He's turned mean, like a dog hit with a stick too many times and just suddenly bares its teeth. I never hit him. I do know his family background is well-hidden and always has been since we met in high school. I don't know where the evil comes from. Yes, it is evil. And I do believe you are basically decent and good and what you did was the result of a lapse in judgment. I believe I married the real "monster," and my prince is the one locked away. And how ironic? I have only ever been with two men, you and Jack, in my life. Therefore, my limited

142

experience only allows me to go by what the two of you have shown me. One has shown his fists, the other his love. So I hope this is why I decided to seek you out. Until we can see each other for the first time in years. I guess until we come to that time, I will just have to live in your letters. Love and affection, Stell xoxo.'"

Stella looked out onto the highway, not really seeing it. It had taken her a little bit of time to realize it when Karl began, but as he got rolling and Stella started to recognize turns of phrase she used regularly in her letters to him, she suddenly understood what he was doing. What he was quite literally reciting for her, word for word, like she had to do in sixth grade with Lincoln's "Emancipation Proclamation."

"God," she sighed. "Karl, I—am I really so ... *sappy?*"

"Yep!" Karl cackled, playfully nudging her shoulder. "You betcha!"

"Icky sweet! Yuck!"

"Oh come on! Give yourself a break. Your letters kept me putt-puttin' while I was away. The letters from my mother turned to a trickle of every couple of months when I first went in. And then my sister died ... they stopped altogether. You were the only one ever wrote me. I think I would have tied myself off somehow, turned myself into a hanging sack of meat, if I didn't have your letters. Then your face. Then your—" he suddenly fidgeted towards her, driving his hand down into her lap, "hoo-ahh."

The car swerved into the left lane. The sign for their exit rose into view, and Stella nearly missed the off-ramp altogether. She wrenched his hand away, laughing with utter abandon. "You kook! Let me drive!"

"Sure thing, ma'am! I mean no harm." Karl settled back into the seat, arms folded and satisfied. "Quiz me."

"Quiz you *what?*"

"You want to know the date of the letter?"

"What? You want to show off, now?"

"Of course. Ask me."

"All right," Stella agreed. "Month, date, *and year.*"

"November. Thirteenth. 2013."

Stella giggled. "Seriously?"

"Sure thing it is. You just turned twenty-one a week before. Married to Jack for six months."

"Twenty-five years old now. The two of us. We're quite a fucking pair, huh? The mess we made of our lives."

"Maybe so," Karl said. "But we got our youth. So we run the reset button. Don't you agree, Stell?"

"Sure," Stella said wryly, making a wide hand-over-hand turn which

143

took them off the highway and into downtown Comstock with its dizzying array of roadside store signs. "But all it does is put me back to my original question, which is how do I surgically separate myself from my husband? I'm broke. No money of my own. Ever since the thing in Philadelphia happened, he's kind of backed off from me. You'd think he'd batter me twice as hard, but he's given me this wide berth. Like I'm tainted or something. Either that, or he's done with putting his hands on me."

"The second you really believe this, he'll kill you for sure."

"Why do you say that?"

"Well, tell me you honestly believe his tiger'll change his stripes, and you can just let me out on the side of the road right now. I'll walk to Denny's down the road and make my way back to the halfway house."

"Karl, why would you say that?" She groped for his coat sleeve, and he pulled away.

"If you're telling me right now you plan on being a professional fuckin' victim for the rest of your life, I don't want no part of it. Or you."

"KARL—"

"I won't stand over your grave a year from now, wondering what I coulda' done different. I won't do it, Stell!"

"What'd I say? Jesus, Karl!"

"He ain't never going to change, you hear me? He's just—I don't know!"

Stella looked at him, fear in her eyes. "Just *what*?"

"He's dormant! Like a volcano! But it don't mean his erupting days are over!"

"Please stop yelling."

All at once, Karl's voice dropped in register and volume. The cords standing up along his throat unclenched, dropping down below the level of the taut flesh. He rubbed his jawline. "You tell it to them. Their bodies of ash. You want my help or not, Stella? There isn't no other reason you reached out to me all those years ago than to know, even in the back of your mind, I was the only one could help you do what *needs* to be done to Jack. No one else would have the stomach for what I'll do. With you. To give it all back to him, what he's been putting on you all these years."

"I started writing to you in the hospital because you were my first love. There—there was never anything else I had in mind. You were my first—and my *best love*. You make me out to be so cold and calculated, and I'm not. *I am not!*"

"Then why else would you tell me about him in your letters, knowing where I was. Locked up. No real power to help you or protect you. You knew you were just throwing food for thought into my cage, and when I did get out I'd make up for all this bullshit he put you through these past years. I didn't know if I was ever getting out of there. Still don't know what possessed them."

"All right," she relented, nodding. "Okay."

From there, Stella explained the list of numbers she found taped under the drawer of Jack's study desk. She spoke of the snooping with a glint of pride in the work and persistence she had put into it, like a child seeking validity from her father. She talked of the time she spent in the rocking chair in her bedroom, staring out across the sprawling backyard of the Post home and the sharp, menacing look of the picket fence spikes bordering the property. She even divulged her deepest, darkest reveries whereby she fantasized impaling Jack on a couple of those very pickets, the fence shooting up through his chest like a big white incisor. Karl held his silence. He was the best listener, to the point his attentiveness made the listener nervous. Then the stretched-out silence, which always seemed to follow one of Stella's long narratives. He did not disappoint, sitting there in the passenger seat until he noticed Stella was coming up on the driveway of his halfway house.

Karl straightened in the passenger seat, pulling himself up like someone hiking up his puppet strings. He stared at her, unblinking. "I almost forgot this is where I asked you to take me. I blanked out for a second."

"Did you hear everything I said?"

"You know what those numbers are, Stella," he said. "You don't need me to tell you what you already know." Karl reached behind his seat, locating the small belt bag he wore everywhere. It contained his identification, as far as Stella could predict. He whipped it around and secured it around his waist, taking a deep breath. "Man, what was I thinking having you drop me back here? There's no way to patch things up. I fucked up so many things in one afternoon."

"We could just keep going," Stella offered in a small voice. There was no commitment to her tone. It was brittle, flimsy.

"No, no we can't. Not yet, at least."

"When will you tell me about *palo mayombe*. When will you explain everything?" Stella shifted into park after easing down into the slab of gravel serving as the halfway house's driveway.

"Sooner than you think, Stell," Karl said. He cranked the passenger door open and climbed out. Then he bent to look in on her. His eyes were stern and serious as they regarded her. His lips were pulled back into thin white slivers. "Call one of the numbers. Dial one of them up. I'd say the last one on the list. Start there. The most recent. My guess would be you've got the master list of phone numbers for all the skeevy cunts he's been sticking. I'd also wager one of them on the list gave him his AIDS. Worst part is if he's got it and he knew about it, he could have been infecting all the other people he's fucked since. He's a loaded gun, Stell. And if I never hear from you again after this, I'll understand. Either way, get yourself checked. For you."

"I will call you later," Stella said, kissing her hand and holding it out to him.

"No promises."

"I promise."

"Don't."

"You'll see."

"Yeah, guess we both will."

Karl slammed the door shut and stalked up the slope of front yard leading up to the screen door of the house. It banged open and shouting erupted from within as he stepped inside. By that time, Stella was pulling away and trying like hell to remember when the last time was she had her blood drawn.

31. THE NUMBERS

Stella made sure to start the chicken stirfry on the stove before she did anything else. It was coming on 5:30 in the evening, and Jack would be home in a half hour. He would be hungry, aligning his *starvation* with those who can only dream of bread and water in some third-world country. The smell of chicken and sesame oil permeated every room of the downstairs when Stella decided she would make the call. Karl had advised her to dial the last one, as it would prove to be the most recent of contacts. He failed to tell her what she should say if or when someone answered on the other end. *I could stay silent. It'll creep them out, and rightly so. They oughtta be. It would plant a small seed of dread in their head, someone calling them up and then breathing. Just ... breathing. Nothing else.*

Stella crept up the stairs and into the bedroom. She threw open her closet doors and stepped onto the low stool arranged on the floor before her hanging clothing. She craned on her tiptoes and brought down the circular white hat box stowed way up on the shelf, close to the ceiling. Then, she stepped back out into the bedroom with the box, laid it down on the bed, and popped the top off. The smoothed, unfolded yellow legal paper bearing the twelve numbers (Karl was *certain* they were phone numbers) lay atop a purple felt cloche hat she wore once to one of Jack's business dinners. She remembered feeling very much the Zelda Fitzgerald to his F. Scott and just as anxious among his friends and coworkers as Zelda must have felt in the grips of her very famous psychoses. *I'll never wear this ugly thing again. Should throw it away.* Instead, Stella kept on task.

She took out the yellow paper and strode over to his side of the bed where the telephone rested on a nightstand. She pulled the cord out all the way and walked it around to her side of the bed where she took a seat on the edge of the mattress.

Stella swallowed some air and took her time breathing out. She shut her eyes, sniffed the air, and blew it out fleetingly like cigar smoke. Her heart dropped back down into her chest. Her hands stopped shaking. She found she could smooth the paper down before her on the nightstand. She picked up the headset of the portable phone, traced one finger down to the last number entry, and dialed: 215-874-2002.

"Silent," she told herself, clutching the headset with both hands now until her knuckles felt cold. "I'll stay silent. And ... I'll see."

The bedroom was chilly. She drew one hand away from the headset and wound it round herself, trying to contain her body heat. To keep it from somehow leaking out. The phone rang. Rang.

Rang. She let it ring for so long it started to sound more like a bee buzzing dangerously close to her ear than anything else. Still, she held fast to it while she hugged herself. Waited. Stella started to rock absently to and fro on the edge of the bed. Still, she waited.

She couldn't be sure, but Stella suspected she finally hung up the phone around the thirtieth ring.

No, just not good enough. Not at all!

Stella checked the clock on the bedside table. Quarter of six. Fifteen minutes left before Jack came home.

Fifteen.

Stella did not lunge for the phone again right away. She whiled away the next three minutes, paralyzed. Stuck somewhere between action and a building nausea chewing at her stomach.

Then, she snagged the headset in her hands and dialed the number with stiff fingers. She listened, vowing this time not to hang up until 6pm struck. Under no circumstances. She would be a nuisance to the owner of the phone. She would disrupt them, and she would not be ignored because it was only fair and just, was it not? This whore on the other end of the line?

147

They would know and they would understand without Stella having to say a word. It would wash over them like a scalding shower, they are known. Found out. Marked.

The forty-second ring broke halfway through.

She nearly said "Hello," and bit back the word at the last second. *Silence. You let them say something. And even then ... even then, you say nothing.*

The person on the other end held their silence, also.

Well, now just what the hell is this? Why aren't they saying any-thing? They have no idea who I am? They might not recognize this number, but you still say something, don't you? You ask what this is about? Who are you? Something—

"Who's calling?" the woman on the other end said, a firmness in her voice which disarmed Stella for a moment. She nearly answered, something about the woman's assertiveness demanding a response.

Say nothing, don't breathe.

"Is it you?" the woman asked. "Is it? Mr. German Shepherd?"

What? Mr. what—

"All right. If you're feeling shy then just make sure you listen to what I'm about to tell you, Dog-Boy! We have an active trace on this call, and we know where you are. We will come, and we *will* put a leash on you. I'm sure you'd like that, so I'll make sure your leash is a little too tight for you to draw breath. You understand what I'm saying to you? You sat back, and you held your silence, and while this is your right you still managed to lead us right to your dumbass. So, sit tight. Don't go anywhere. There's no way out of this. We'll be *right there—*"

Stella hung up the phone, now not just hearing her heart in her ears, but tasting its bitterness between her teeth.

Downstairs, the front door banged closed, announcing Jack's arrival.

32. THE RINGING DRAWER

The gods were clearly smiling down on Detective Rivells when she stepped out of the interview room at 5:40 p.m. The female insomniac perp had awo-ken in her cell after only an hour, but it had been enough rest and, surpris-ingly, enough time for the girl to weigh out her options and opt to confess her crimes to the detective in full. This freed up Rivells's evening, the earlier part of it anyhow, as it landed her back at her desk where she would be typing up her report of the interview and the finer details surrounding it.

She hated this part of the job, the narrative portion. She always hated English class and felt like a student wandering in an academic fog, until her senior year when she was finally able to take a college credit course in Forensics. It was not until then Rivells felt connected to the material put before her. She was a fast typer (60 words per minute), but her internal editor often slowed her pace when she drafted reports. She labored over almost every word, like an insecure, unseasoned novelist. *These are hard facts. No grey areas. No fucking similes or extended metaphors or any bullshit. Cold. Hard. Facts. Boiled down. Nothing else.*

"This isn't *Huck Finn*, Glynn," she told herself, hunched over the typewriter at her desk. It buzzed like a living thing beneath her fingers. Her precinct had not yet caught up with the twenty-first century, and all reports were still drafted on an electric typewriter. She had already typed a good portion of her report down on paper. But now, Rivells was cognitively blocked.

"Coffee," she decided, and shoved back from the typewriter. She switched it off, comforted by the snatches of conversation spiraling around her as other detectives and beat cops circled the floor, weaving and bumping into one another verbally with bits and pieces of casual conversation. Rivells smiled at those in her path, exchanged cordial retorts, and retreated into the break room where a near-empty pot of coffee waited for her. She dumped two packets of Splenda into a Styrofoam cup, smothered it in non-dairy creamer, and dumped the swill of the bottom brew overtop. The smell of it turned her stomach, so powerfully bitter and pungent.

The taste was not much better, a tar coating her tongue and the roof of her mouth, *Oh the rush when it hits your brain stem!* A coolness she felt to the very ends of her fingertips.

She leaned against the nearby countertop, tilted her head back, and shut her eyes.

No sooner did her thoughts slide away into a sweet temporary blankness, Taggart, another detective who had been there longer than the precinct's captain, ducked his salt-and-pepper crew cut head inside the break alcove.

"Rivells!" he said, a smile playing about his non-existent lips. "Your cell's ringing."

Rivells sighed, dropping her head back down. Her chin dipped downward into the supple pocket of her smooth throat. She returned a half-hearted grin. "Let it ring. I'm not expecting any calls—"

"No, Glynn, the *other* cell phone. With the cutesy pink shell. I know

149

what your cell looks like. Silver shell with the Batman logo on it?"

Rivells's eyes brightened, and she dumped the remaining coffee into the trash can. "Holy shit! Thank you, thank you, *thank you Tagg*!"

She hurried back to her desk only to cast a doleful glance down at the pink shelled iPhone lying faceup and now silent on her desk.

"Fuck!" she cried. Then, she snatched up the phone, and engaged the screen to light it up. "What about a number?

Missed Calls. *Restricted Number.*

"FUCK!"

"They'll call back," Taggart said, tagging her on the shoulder. "Whoever they are."

"That's just it, Tagg," Rivells groaned. "It's key I not only answer the phone but run a trace. There's only one person who'd be calling this number, and they're a person of interest in a rape case I'm working."

"How do you know it'll be the perp and no one else?"

"This is the victim's cell phone. She gave it to me and told me she updated her new cell number with everyone in her phone list so they wouldn't call this one. She's on the *Do Not Call* list for telemarketers, so it wouldn't be one of them either. That leaves our perp, who took her cell and retrieved the number after he assaulted her. This will be him. A direct line to the sonofabitch. But he's gotta call back. Has to!"

"Sweeney's here," Taggart said. "In his office. I'll go give him a head's up to ready his equipment to run a trace on the caller's number. They'll call back."

"I think they will," Rivells said, staring blankly down at the phone in her hands, willing it to ring. "They didn't leave a message. I think they wanted to. They'll call back."

"Damn right. I'll go alert Sweeney. Maybe we'll get lucky, and it'll be a landline."

"In this day and age," Rivells said. "Better chance at seeing God."

"You never know, kid," Taggart said, hurrying towards Sweeney's darkly-lit nook in the corner of the precinct floor. "Maybe have your sunglasses ready just in case!"

In what seemed like seconds, Taggart and Sweeney were both leaning out of Sweeney's office, waving Rivells over with the cell phone. Rivells hurried inside the somewhat cramped room, its walls piled high with dormant iPads and lifeless aged-out printers and desktops. Sweeney was a tall, gangly man who wore Buddy Holly glasses and completed the look with a blonde ducktail. He took the phone from her, removed the back casing shell and proceeded to transcribe some numbers from inside the phone into a few fields on his computer screen. Then, he laid the cell phone down at his elbow, busied himself with some other equipment Rivells had little knowledge of.

The three of them, crowded inside the tech's office, exchanged expectant glances seeming to convey the same intention: *Now, we wait for the call back. We pray for the landline, because then we won't need as much time for the trace. It will be near- instantaneous.*

When the cell phone started to buzz and inch towards the edge of Sweeney's desk, Rivells almost didn't believe it. It somehow seemed too easy to her. There might have been a bit more agonizing over whether it would ring again.

Sweeney handed Rivells the phone, made a motion to *roll with it*, and she did just that, answering the call.

Someone silent on the other end. Soft, shallow breathing.

Don't say anything right away. Try to get them to say something first.

Nothing. Seconds ticked by. *I don't want to lose them, or bore them. Guess it's gonna have to be me first—*

"Who is this?" Rivells asked.

33. SET IN MOTION

Stella eased the door to the bedroom shut and slipped down the hallway on the balls of her bare feet when Jack called out to her a second time.

"Stella!" he called. "I—"

He broke off abruptly, the next sound the ever-familiar clump of his briefcase as he set it down on the floor beside him. It sounded to Stella like the body of a small child slumping over, dead. The sudden silence was unsettling for Stella, and she froze at the top of the stairwell. *Please, say something. What's wrong? God, help me, what is wrong now—*

"I'll be right there!" she called to him, slowly descending the stairwell. Her ankles buckled and bent as she went.

"Uhm ... no ... I'll come to you," Jack said, his voice clouded and murky with preoccupation. "Stay where you are."

"I made your favorite," she said, moving downward to the lower riser. It creaked beneath her meager weight. "You smell it?"

"What did I *just say*? Stay. Where. You. Are."

"What's wrong with you?"

Jack appeared at the bottom of the stairwell. He gazed up the incline at her, half of him blacked out by the absence of light along the stairwell's bottom landing. They stood staring at one another, a band of light from the bathroom window behind her illuminating the top of Stella's face, digging her sunken eyes out of their crevices to reveal the real fear seated within them. Just outside the window nearest where Jack stood, a strangling sound of two wrangling cats fighting to the death filtered through the pane and poured through the hunter green curtains, muted but nevertheless horrid in noise. Stella had not seen Betsy since the altercation earlier in the afternoon, and her thoughts touched briefly on the animal's whereabouts. *I hope she's all right—*

"I'm coming *to you*," Jack said, and switched on the stairwell light. "I want to show you something." His pale blue shirt was still tucked neatly into his charcoal, pleated trousers. A canary yellow tie was yanked downward away from his throat, and it hung askew to the left, like a loosened noose. His black loafers, the shine off them, clomped up the steps one by one, making a leaden sound Stella felt in every bump of her spine. "Something on the floor—you left." He did not sound menacing. He sounded consumed by his own thoughts, barely stringing words together. Stella heard it in his voice.

My God, it's fear. Fucking fear!

Before Stella knew it, she was saying it. "You sound scared, Jack? You scared?"

The subtle fog in Jack's eyes cleared. He saw her again, crystal clear above him. "What the fuck did you just say?" His free hand, the one not slipping up the banister, came away from his side.

Stella saw the leather wallet he held up to show to her.

The wallet the intruder had come and thrown at her once inside the house.

Jack's wallet.

It did not stop her from repeating herself. "You scared, you cocksucker?"

"You're going down for good tonight, you defective cunt," he seethed. Four risers below her now. "This is a long time coming—"

"So's this!"

Stella ripped her sneaker off her left foot. As Jack lunged upward towards her, she smacked him in the face with its rubber sole. It made a flat, dull sound against the side of his head. He swatted at her blurred hand a second after her shoe had already knocked him off balance. Then, the hand on the banister slipped away and his other hand raked the stairwell wall as he struggled for a purchase which was not there. It dawned on her Jack was perhaps eight risers up the stairwell and about to go ass-over-end back down them.

The fear in his eyes swelled them to twice their size as they swung away from Stella and outward, his attention flying wide as he tumbled.

It happened without Stella realizing it. The startled look in her eyes right after she smacked him, followed by the ever-widening smile which burst across her face and squinted her eyes as the crown of his head glanced off the banister. She heard the *crack* of polished mahogany splintering and splitting as his full weight thrust itself upon it. He let out a weakened moan as his body crumpled. Then, his spine struck the stairs as he turned over and over. Spine then head. Spine and head. Over and over.

By the time he lay sprawled at the bottom of the stairwell, along the cool wooden square of the small landing, Jack Post lay prone and silent.

Stella stood, frozen with anticipation. She waited him out a minute, and when he showed no sign of coming to, she slipped down the stairwell the rest of the way. She angled over him, mindful to keep her legs clear of Jack by a foot or so. She had seen enough of *those* types of movies to know he could very easily snap from his brief unconscious state to grapple her ankles with superhuman strength.

Karl's voice bloomed in her head, opening like a lotus flower. *He's no superhero. He can be killed. He can be made vulnerable. You just can't picture it. But you will. Oh, you will.*

Why don't I just kill him right now? Claim self-defense?

"Because my bruises have been healed for almost a month," she told herself. "He hasn't laid a hand on me for that long."

Do it to yourself? Have Karl catch a Septa bu,s and have him come over and punch you around some? He may not want to do it at first, but you could always goad him into it and then apologize later.

The landline phone in the kitchen, designated as her *phone of choice* for communicating with Karl, started ringing. Stella jumped at its sound. She turned to check Jack on the floor, terrified the bell had awoken him. *He's not sleeping, you idiot! He's unconscious! You can't just rouse him with an alarm clock, for God's sake!* The reason the bells sounded much louder right then was the cordless phone, the one she never used, was also ringing. A few steps away, on the sofa side table beside the coral lamp. She had to make it stop. Now!

Stella seized the cordless phone and hit the Answer button.

"Yes?"

"Hey there, Stell," Karl said on the other end, through a connection which sounded more tinny than usual. "Small problem."

153

"You're fucking telling me," she hissed into the phone, working her way into tight circles as she walked blindly about the room. She cupped the receiver. "I hit Jack. He fell all the way down the stairs. He's knocked out right now. Right near me."

"Ho-leee *shit!*"

"Yeah, holy of fucking *holies*—what if he wakes up?"

"You pin im'."

"How?"

The connection crackled, like kindling snapping in a fireplace. Stella's heart stopped, fearing she lost him. Then, Karl piped up again, halfway through having said something. " ... a chair and you line it up overtop of him—"

"*I don't understand what you're saying—*"

"You take one of your sturdy kitchen chairs, and you set it down overtop of him. You line up his throat under one rail and his arms under the left and right rails. Then, you sit on top of it."

"I don't know if I can hold him down."

"Well, you try it, and you see. Go on—set the phone down. If he isn't on his back, you kinda' nudge him a little until he falls flat. Then, you arrange the chair over his throat and his biceps. Go on. I'll wait."

"I don't *know*—"

"He wakes up, and he *will* gut you, kid. What don't you know?"

Jesus Christ!

"Okayokayokay!"

Stella set the phone down on the coffee table and rushed into the dining room. She yanked one of the dining chairs away from the table, eyeballed the wooden slats along the bottom of the legs and finding them suitable, hauled it over to Jack. She lifted the chair and hesitated. She couldn't move. The slats looked low enough to the floor when she laid one across his throat, it could choke him. Wake him. *Would it be the worst thing? Yes, it would because then the self-defense motive goes all swirly! Test it—test it! And if he moves, you jam the fucker down and you pin him.*

It shocked her still for a minute more, the way that last thought of random consciousness struck her as sounding so much like Karl's it could have sprung from his prefrontal lobe and jumped right into hers.

Mindmeld.

Thankfully, Jack was already on his back. She nudged his arms, holding her breath until it looked like they were splayed in just the right way. He looked like a crucifixion nailed to a cross on the ground. Then, baring her teeth, Stella lowered the chair legs down overtop of her husband's still and silent body. Her lips were dry, her teeth sticky as she lowered the chair legs, pinning his left and right biceps. There was still his throat. She feared the slat would be too low and it would—

Easy—

Stella eased the slat down lower and lower—

EASY!

The chair legs touched down on the rug.

The wooden slat crossed over his throat, a quarter of a centimeter above his prominent Adam's apple.

The air rushed out of her in a quick hot burst. She grabbed the cordless off the coffee table and put it to her ear again.

"Ok, I did it."

"Are you sitting in the chair?"

"What?"

"*Are you sitting in the chair?*

"I-I—"

Behind her, Jack groaned low in his throat. Unintelligible words dribbled out of him.

"*I hear him, Stella! Grab the poker from the fireplace and take a seat! DO IT NOW!*"

The fireplace ledge was a couple feet away. The poker and leather blower were assembled on a gold stand. Pinning the cordless to her ear with the point of her shoulder, she grabbed for the poker. The stand and blower toppled over in a great clamor as both rang out against the granite of the hearth ledge.

Jack's eyes were fluttering wildly. He had already curled his hand around the slats.

The chair was rising.

Stella launched herself at the chair, landing painfully on the knobs of her knees. The chair slammed back down. Jack gurgled, his hands falling away from the slats. She swung the black, blunt business end of the poker around. She aimed it at the supple curvature of her husband's throat. She touched it to the taut skin. Somehow, she had managed to hold the cordless in place at her ear. Karl's voice exploded in her right ear, reminding her he was still with her.

"Got 'im?" he cried.

"I got you, you *fuck!*" she screamed.

Jack's eyes goggled up at her. He opened his mouth to say something and produced barely a gasp. She had somehow damaged his windpipe when she had come down on the chair, driving the slat into his neck.

Karl cackled into the phone, a dry sound not unlike the bad connection of the phone line itself. "All right. I'll be right there. I'm down the street in a phone booth. The halfway house won't have me, and I got away before they could remand me back to prison. I saw his car and held back. But looks like you got things well under control. So, I'll be there directly. It's time."

"Time for what?" Stella said breathlessly. The poker edge had pierced Jack's throat. A red bead developed at the point of contact.

"Time for Superman to die."

34. GONE, BUT NOT FORGOTTEN

Rivells knew better than to expect anyone to be at home when she reached the Post residence. Right after Rivells hung up on the woman on the other end of the cell phone, she called over to Jones and told him what happened. She thought he would have been more upset she had held the cell phone back from him, but Rivells already had her story in place. She simply explained the witness was just located it that morning, and it started ringing on Rivells's desk in the afternoon, but she had *absolutely* planned on driving it over to Detective Jones later. So Detective Jones could not possibly be angry, only mildly peeved.

What slowed them down was not the quick and frantic assembly of a team to bring with them to the Post house. They were always ready at a moment's notice to perform searches and seizures, as necessary. The warrant was the sticking point. The DA had a profoundly difficult time securing it from her judge downtown, as he was *off the grid* while attending a couple's therapy session with his wife. Finally, DA Osborne tracked down the judge on his cell shortly after his session wrapped and secured the warrant, quite literally, in the parking lot of the judge's therapist. From there, she met up with Detectives Jones and Rivells who then assembled their team and headed over to the Post residence in a town called Comstock, twenty miles north of Central Philadelphia.

Detective Jones scoffed at Rivells's disappointment in finding an empty house. "What are you down about? They're not here, so they won't get in our way. I much prefer when they're not hanging about, lecturing about how fragile this sculpture is or how much those sofa cushions are. We can tear the place apart more thoroughly, and without interruption. Shame on them for flying the coop. Boys and girls! Turn everything upside-down!

156

Inside-out! And I'm talking every shirt sleeve and pant leg to boot! Go-go-GO!"

The house was modestly sized, a standard Colonial in a development that mingled A-frames with this model as liberally as most suburban neighborhoods. A white picket-fence, the sight of it causing Rivells's inside to tingle at its clichéd irony, enclosed the front and back yards of the house. A climbing tree mushroomed twenty-feet high out of the rain-softened ground of the rear yard. The interior of the home was dustless and nurtured by what Rivells called overly-attentive "housewife hands." Every window treatment was thick and drawn across, leaving each room dark and deep. The wooden floor was covered over with oriental throw rugs large enough to accentuate an entire wing. The kitchen was the most spotless of all the rooms, and it was where Rivells gravitated towards for a reason she could not identify at first. Call it intuition. The woman of the house had "housewife hands," and Rivells took that one step further, fleshing out the woman's character with guesswork and experience, along with time-tested profiling. She named the woman Housewife in her head so as to have something concrete to refer to while she spoke out loud. Detective Jones climbed to the second floor, along with three other officers. She stood there alone in the kitchen, speaking low and wispy to herself.

"Housewife keeps all of the rooms in the house spotless," she said. "Of course, there is a certain pride and compulsion which goes along with this type of household cleanliness. I can't help but to think there is also intimidation from the male of the house that drives the Housewife to keep things so neat and orderly ... to a fault." Rivells stepped to the kitchen sink. She traced a finger along the bottom of the basin, near to the drain. When Rivells examined her fingertip, it was clean. No gunk. No residue. Nothing. "And Housewife is not someone who will order out every night and place the cardboard carton before her husband when he sits down to dinner. No, this woman cooks for her man every night, or there's hell to pay. Then, she scrubs the hell out of the kitchen sink. Comet and a bristly brush. Maybe a Brillo pad. But she has to make sure the stainless steel basin is so clean and shined to such a high polish at all times her reflection is *always* visible in the surface. Otherwise, Big Daddy is going to beat her. And if Big Daddy is who we think *he* is, those beatings are as sadistic as they are frequent. The guy is no doubt, a *Mindfucker.*"

Detective Jones was at her elbow just as she stepped away from the basin. She turned and nearly walked into him.

His face appeared mildly amused. "Call in SWAT," he said, rubbing his goateed chin. "We found two dead cats in the back yard. Within a foot of each other. Clawed all to shit, one more than the other. There was a definite victor. Big white cat. Looks domesticated. Healthy. Could have been their family pet. Ugly, ugly scene out there."

"Lovely," Rivells sighed. She waved her hand all about the kitchen. "It's clean and bright as a sterile zone in here. You could eat off the drain if you wanted to. Shit you not! Compulsive. I'm gonna say *sick*."

"Just because you maybe don't pick up after yourself doesn't mean—"

"I'm calling BS, Jones. I'm right about this. Explore it."

"Yes, ma'am," Jones said. "I will, just as soon as I verify with the DA the family safe upstairs is included on the warrant. If so, we're going to need a locksmith to come in." He slipped his phone out of his khaki trouser pocket and swiped it on. He addressed her from the corner of his eye, lingering nearby. "You fairly certain we won't have them wandering in while we're in mid-search?"

"Oh no," Rivells said. "I gave the caller a head's up we traced her call. It was the landline. Took less than a minute. I made it clear to her we were on our way."

"Sure, an hour later."

"This place would have been emptied out if we came from down the lane, Jones. Their silence on the other end of the line was panic. If they had said anything at all in response, I would have given it more of a fifty-fifty shot they thought they were either above the law or so guiltless they'd welcome a police visit. The silence translates into the person on the other end of the line going back into their head and trying to figure out what their next move is going to be. And *fast*!"

Jones turned his whole body away from her, then stalked into the adjacent dining room where he exchanged a few hushed words with the DA on the line, and then quickly rang off. He stepped back into the room, his eyes dancing with elation. "The safe's fair game. And our DA will have a locksmith en route in ten. You gonna hang around?"

"Wouldn't miss the big reveal. You kidding?"

"Dinner after we wrap up here?"

Rivells kneaded the ridge of her nose and sighed. "Sure."

"All right, then. Ho Wah's Chinese. You been?"

"Have not."

"Mm, you haven't lived."

"I'll bet," she said, then added, "So we've got two dead cats. One domestic, one wild. Anything else upstairs?"

"Let's see," Jones said, and posed the question to one of his investigators upstairs by way of a burping CB.

The CB belched the response of the investigator back at them. "We got some signs of a hurried exit. They're subtle, but they're there."

"Do tell, officer," Jones said.

Burp. "I'm in the upstairs study, and it looks like someone was rifling through the desk. Maybe looking for something or hiding something. The drawer that runs across your lap is off its track on the right-hand side. It's hanging askew, and if someone left it this way, they were definitely disrupted while they were looking inside."

"What's in there?"

Burp. "Papers. Ledgers, looks like. This guy was crunching some numbers. We'd have to go over these with a closer forensic eye. Nothing damning at first glance."

"But signs of a quick getaway."

Burp. "Roger."

From the living room, two rooms away, a male investigator shouted. "We've got blood! Throw rug under the coffee table!"

Jones and Rivells looked at each other with something of mingled dread and excitement, the latter winning out and moving their feet into twin sprints towards the living room. *Foul play! The beginning of a journey. Here we go. I've seen it start this way time and time again. I only hope it ends better than most of the others.*

They found an investigator hunkered down beside the edge of the oriental rug closest to the stairwell. Another older and more grizzled looking investigator with a face worn from skepticism and regret in equal fashion hovered above him. Jones went to them, and the investigator closer to the ground (and the stain) started framing the small section of rug in question with his plastic-gloved fingers.

"It's barely there, but you can see it if you're looking for a break in the pattern. A disruption. The red threading most prominent around the rug border is practically non-existent in this area right here. You can see the white and blue and aqua and even orange looming here, but *that* red right there? Blood. Not spatter. A pooling."

Rivells bent over for a closer look. "Like someone might have been laying there?"

The investigator looked up at her, a twinkle in his eye. "It's from a head wound. I'm almost certain."

Jones crowded in now. Rivells moved aside, giving him enough room to have a good, hard look. "How can you tell?"

"Because the blood is deep-set into the fabric. It ran out into the rug

159

quick and thick. Characteristic of a scalp wound. They bleed endlessly."

"Well, then that would fit, wouldn't it?" the older investigator said, bushy salt and pepper eyebrows rising and falling as he stepped away and slipped halfway up the stairwell. He splayed his arms wide as if trying to embrace the white wall before him, and spoke over his shoulder. "Come have a look at this. I thought it might have been an imperfection in the paint job or simple flaking off over time. But when you look at these marks and consider them along with the blood on the floor down there, a timeline starts to develop. We got a story here, folks."

"How so, Willy?" Jones joined the investigator, Willy, sidling up next to him on the stairs. He craned in, his eyes following Willy's fingers as they traced something in the wall before them.

"You see these? Deep-cut into the drywall."

"Scratches," Jones breathed, sneaking a glance over the railing at Rivells, whose eyes were widening by the moment. "That's what they are. Someone trying to steady themselves along the wall, but their nails cut into it and then slip away. And then they …" Jones stopped talking and turned around to face the wooden railing running up the stairwell. He curled his hands around it and started moving it. The rail moved generously in his hands, groaning back and forth like a loose tooth ready to pop out of a gum. Then, everyone nearby heard the snap of wood, a dry and brittle noise not unlike a bone breaking under skin. "… then they grab for the railing, and they loosen it so it's barely stabilized. Moves like this. Then down they go."

Rivells clasped her hands before her belly, a thing she did when the wheels were really turning and grinding against one another. "He hit his head on the hardwood at the bottom of the stairwell. Maybe against the closet at the foot of the landing. The doorknob. Something."

Jones charged back downstairs and stopped at the foot of the stairwell. "You smell that? Jesus, you *smell that?*"

The investigator on the ground stood up, although it made little difference for his height. The man was barely five-feet tall. "Bleach. I thought I smelled it over here. Floor cleaner. Most likely bleach."

"*Fuck-in'* bleach, people!" Jones cried and dropped down onto his hands and knees. He lowered himself even further until his nose grazed the wooden floorboards. He sniffed enthusiastically at the floor, and his movements as he inspected the boards soon resembled that of a dog caught by a scent. He turned round and round on his knees, and it wasn't until Jones nearly had everyone laughing at him and he himself worked into a corner did the detective stop cold, his nose crushed against the hardwood floor. He popped his head up, stabbed one finger down at the spot he just sniffed.

160

"This area right here's been treated. Cleaned. This whole spot right here. Recently. Maybe less than an hour."

"So we literally just missed them," Rivells said.

Jones nodded. "This is proof of foul play. It's time to dig further down, see how deep this rabbit hole goes. I believe we are only just peering down into the ground at the moment. We need to call in more detectives and have them canvas the neighborhood. Ask around about these people. This kind of knock-down drag-out fighting cannot possibly have escaped the notice of the neighbors on either side. This was a noisy dust-up, and some-one may have ended up dead at the end of it. I want to know what people heard, even if it's nothing more than a mouse fart in their pantry. Anything and everything! Willy, call in to the field house and get four more suits out here." Then he turned to Rivells and winked at her. "Let's have a look down basement while we're waiting on the locksmith. I've got a feeling that safe is going to yield up more than we could ever have asked for."

Rivells nodded. *The Post House. Who are they? Or I guess I should be thinking of them in the past tense now they're on the run. Who were they?*

35. IN THE WHEAT AND THE WEEDS

Who am I now?

The question plagued Stella incessantly as she rested her head in Karl Tarlick's lap, and watched night darken out the car windows and sweep the field where they had parked her gold Taurus. Earlier, Karl had needed to drive when it became evident Stella's hands were shaking so badly they kept slipping away from the wheel. They pulled into a Texaco as far from the pumps and teller window as possible, and switched seats. Stella sat with her legs pulled up into her chest.

It was as obvious as it was vital they leave Comstock. Karl doubted at first Stella had actually gotten a police officer, let alone a detective, on the phone when she had called that number off of Jack's list.

"Whoever it was that answered your call was bluffing you so you wouldn't call again," he had told her. "Question is, why would she not want you to call her again? What's she got to hide?"

Stella had insisted it sounded like a legitimate intercept of the phone call by the authorities. It wasn't until Karl said what he said that Stella started to shake to the point she quite literally had to sit on her hands

161

to make them still.

Karl had said, "I'll tell you what the bitch on the other end of the line had to hide, Stell. Sorry to break it to you, but she don't want her boyfriend's wife to be calling her on the phone. Boyfriend, or *fuck-buddy*. I'd be willing to bet you all them numbers belong to the women he's been screwing on the side. I think you knew that too. Didn't need me to spell it out for you."

Who am I now?

They had hit the road with no particular destination in mind. It was a dangerous and reckless way to set out. Stella knew this, but she couldn't think straight, and she had left a lot of the thinking and decision making to Karl. She had been more than happy, and relieved, to relinquish any and all control to him. But he could only think to hold his foot on the gas, to get them onto the interstate as quickly as possible, and to disappear into the steady flow of traffic for as long as it took them to think things through. Comstock gave onto Bensalem. Bensalem gave onto Richboro. Richboro softened into more of a sweeping landscape of open fields and waving trees, tilting and nodding in the breeze like sleepy old men. As houses turned all the more rare on either side of the road, then downright endangered in favor of rolling hills and untouched greenery, and deep stands of trees in abundance, it was Stella who recognized the sun was going down and New Hope was close. New Hope could offer them any number of places to park their car in the total dark of a wheatfield, unnoticed and anonymous. The sleepy, artsy little town was known internationally for its haunted atmosphere, borne of having endured both the Revolutionary War and the Civil War, and its dead, in equal bloody measure.

So it was Karl who simply chose to angle the Taurus onto the side of the road at a spot clear of any houses for at least two miles in either direction. Then, with Stella's approval, he rolled the car off the road altogether, and they were dipping down a steep grassy slope which nearly tipped them head over end before smoothing out. Karl got a lay of the land and when he was confident enough there were no trees in their direct path, he shut off the headlights, shut off the engine, and kicked the car into neutral. The Taurus rolled, smooth and easy, offering a slight jolt to Stella and Karl here and there. They shook it off.

In the moment, Stella had forgotten their circumstances and slipped into the excitement of the unknown; rolling along in a dark car, in the ink black of a winter's evening.

The feeling might have held, if not for the scream from the trunk that ripped through the car, muted but nevertheless terrifying. Stella cried out. Her hands flew to her ears. "Oh God, make *him* stop! *Please!*"

162

Karl squawked, annoyed. "I can't rightly do that and steer the car away from the trees. Don't worry, he'll shut up in a minute. If he don't I'll give him good reason to."

He quickly switched on the headlights and then doused them when they were coming up on a deep stand of elms and yews. He pumped the brake gingerly so as not to spin the wheels or dig them down into divots they wouldn't be able to drive out of come morning. Then, he angled the car alongside the perimeter of forest, and the Taurus stopped. The flurried screams of bats spun out around them as the feral creatures dipped and rose among the treetops, an ebb and flow of diseased creatures. There was sound. There was no sight. Stella stared unblinking out the side window, cherishing the silence of the trunk. She knew it was temporary.

Unless he's dead back there, and it was his death cry we just heard.

The thought of it knotted her innards, massaged them uncomfortably. She hated this response. She hated Jack, but her physiological response betrayed this. Betrayed her. She wanted the heady feeling of elation Jack's death ought to inspire within her. Instead, she mourned him, and loathed herself for it.

Jack screamed, and it unfolded and unraveled seemingly without end until Karl and Stella heard it die in the man's throat. It shook the inside of the Taurus and stung their eardrums. It was not the trebly shrill of a helpless human. No, this was the battle cry of a warrior who is not about to go down without a final confrontation. This was Jack and she had always known it. He was not someone to lay down and die. He was ruthless and everlasting. A *(superhero?)* super-fiend.

Karl shot her a dark glance. His eyes looked like two pieces of coal jammed into the sockets. "I am gonna mount his fuckin' head on our hood right now! Fuck the plans! He's gonna get us caught carrying on like—"

"No!" Stella cried, trying to stay his arm. "Just put him out. Don't kill him. He's dangerous. We need to restrain him. Put him out so we can tie his hands and legs. The rug's not holding him. I can hear him moving around."

But Karl was already cranking the driver's side door open and climbing out in a flurry of motion. "Fucking jock *asshole!* Can't abide you! Can't no more—"

"Karl!"

He slammed the driver's side door, cleaving off her protest.

Stop this! Stop this now before it gets completely away from you! You can still *stop this!*

Stella cranked her door open and scrambled out into the darkness, just as Karl raised the trunk open and surged down into the opening, hissing unintelligible words as his upper body descended.

From there, things happened very fast.

She came around to the rear of the Taurus just as Karl was ending his struggle with what looked at first like a man-sized centipede he had wrestled out of the car's trunk. He squawked as it dropped down on top of him. Then it unfurled and a man emerged from the rolled-up rug like a chrysalis from a cocoon. Jack was wobbly on his feet as he stood there, freed from the restraints of the rug. He looked like he might topple of his own accord and Stella held back, crouched down beside the bumper. She was waiting him out, as well as waiting for Karl to regain his feet and put Jack down once more. Karl was still. Stella feared he had struck his head on a rock submerged in the ground. Jack slowly turned around in place. A sliver of moonlight slashed across his face, digging out one of his eyes. It was caked in blood, black in the moonlight, and she remembered how Karl had struck him repeatedly in the face while Stella sat on the chair in the living room. Karl hit him and hit him until Jack's smile and dry, brittle cackling stopped cold. Then they had rolled him up in the oriental rug from underneath the dining room table.

There was no way he could see her there, hidden alongside the rear of the car. Yet his muddled gaze seemed to settle upon her like she was in plain view on a sunny day. Jack was tall, but right then he looked larger than life. Rising as high as the elms in their midst, her mouth pulled apart in a silent scream as he smiled, a cold and stiff lifting of the corners of his mouth.

"Augh," he moaned, swabbing the corner of his mouth. "*Auggghhh! Always knew—I* always *knew you would snap—*"

Stella shot up, as if spring-loaded. "You brought disease into our bed, you filthy fucking pig!"

"You ... you *wanted* him? You can *die* with him." Jack started shambling towards her. Stella took a blind step backward and stumbled over a tree root sticking out of the mud. "I'm going to leave your bodies out here to rot and then, I'm going to walk *all the way home*. Wait an hour and call you in as missing. They'll do their *work*, and I'll grieve like a widower when they finally find you two. *I'm always going to be smarter than you, stupid-Stella!* What my mother used to call you when you weren't around. *Stupid-Stella!* If she could see your dumb ass now—I'll always be one step ahead of you."

Behind him, Stella saw Karl rising up onto his feet. She nearly reacted to this, called out to him. Some elation in her face nearly shined through for Jack to read, but at the last second she held it all back and showed her fear to her husband. She worked up some tears, a quiver in her bottom lip.

164

All the while, Karl was searching for something inside the trunk. Silently. *Maybe Karl hurt his ears or ruptured an eardrum when he was beating Jack earlier. How can he not hear anything behind him? Even I can hear it!*

"Why did you marry me?" Stella begged, straining to measure her every step backward. "You're nothing but a sadistic bastard, Jack! That's what your *mother* used to call you when *you* weren't around. She told me *all about you!*"

"Lying *bitch!*" He made a wide grab for her and hooked his bare foot under the protruding root Stella had nearly fallen over seconds before. He went down, shock gathering in his eyes before he struck the ground face-first with a dull thud.

Karl was standing right behind him. He stood there like a ballplayer at bat, a tire-iron from the trunk in his hands rather than a Louisville Slugger. They locked eyes for a moment and in that moment, Stella understood there was indeed an unmistakable unspoken unit between them. There was a secret, organic language in how they looked at one another, and she had no idea such communication was forming and hatching over time. This was the mindmeld he was referring to. She had only ever thought it was the occasional flare-up of Karl's voice and prompting in her head at times of uncertainty, but it was much more than that. This was some sort of psychic bond, and there would be no escaping it. Did she want to? There could come a time, but she had re-established the connection when she had gone and stolen him away from his job at the car wash. She craved the mindmeld. *Without it, I spent a whole month near-catatonic in my rocking chair, staring out the window at the grey, dead yard and the white teeth of the picket fence. Without it, I was a zombie.* She was alive now. In the car, she had her second-thoughts. She had her conscience, and it screamed at her to stop it before there was no return from this.

That was then.

Stella nodded at Karl.

Karl's dark curls lifted off his head as he smashed the tire iron down into Jack's legs. The pale steel of the iron glinted in the moonlight until blood muted its shine. Jack no longer cried out like the warrior he had been, rolled in a rug and stuffed into the back of a sedan, still with the use of his legs and his brute strength. He whimpered and whined like a child for the nipple. It wasn't long before Karl straightened back up after what seemed the ceaseless rise and fall of his upper body as he struck downward at the man on the ground. By that time, Jack's legs were shattered and twisted and bent inside the blood-soaked fabric of his Brooks Brothers slacks. Then, all was silent and still.

Even the bats in attendance seemed frozen in the moment, nesting in the upper treetops with baited breath.

Jack's cries turned to watery gurgles low in his throat as he clawed at the grass, tearing out great tufts as he struggled to pull himself along in a futile attempt to escape Karl. Karl and Stella watched him wiggle along, trailing his dead legs along behind him. Stella was paralyzed, and it wasn't until Jack swiped one hand towards her ankles and nearly seized her leg, she snapped to and dodged backward.

"I thought," Stella said in a small voice," I thought—we were going to—*tie* his legs."

"Yeah," Karl said, winded. He spun the tire iron in his hands. "And his wrists. This is better, don't you think? He can't run now. Can't even stand. All he can do is, well, all you can do now, Jackie is *weep-weep* like a little bitch, right?"

Jack drew his face up out of the dirt, craned his neck to the left. "You ... y-y-you better *kill me*—"

"Can't do that, my man," Karl said matter-of-factly. "We need your brain. We need you to be able to experience pain. We need to keep your pain receptors firing at peak performance, so—*sorry*—no easy way out for you. We'll decide when you can die."

Jack Post dropped his head. A small trickle of what could have easily been weeping or laughing drifted upward from his prone form. He raised one feeble fist up and smashed it down into the tall grass. It made no sound.

"Here," Karl said, holding out the tire iron to Stella. "Get his arms."

Stella looked down at the tool, silent and still. "But I–I—"

"C'mon, show some commitment to the cause, will you?"

"But I don't see why we can't just *tie* his hands—"

"Because we got no twine. Forgot to stop at Home Depot, so we gotta improvise. No big deal."

No big deal—no big deal—no big deal—who am I—

Stella shook her head, but her hands reached out and grasped the handle of the tire iron. She was still shaking her head as the tears skated down her cheeks. She was shaking her head, although not as vehemently as she had at first, when she stepped on Jack's right wrist, pinning it to the ground.

Jack raised his head, somehow managing to twist his face upward to look towards her. He could not meet eyes with her, and it might have made all the difference.

"No-no-Stell—what are you doing? Stell–Stell–*Stell—you don't*

166

have to do this–I'll cooperate–I'll be—"

She let out a whooping war cry as she smashed the butt of the tire iron down onto his bicep. The snap of bone brought vomit into her mouth, but she swallowed it down and screamed and screamed as she destroyed Jack's right arm. She felt the blood speckle her face once the tire iron tore through his once pressed-white button-down shirt, revealing the gleam of bone and torn flesh. Then, Karl stepped behind her and seized her by the arms. She kept battering downward, like a piston gone awry, and it wasn't until she heard Karl's voice in her ear and Jack's cries and intermittent sobbing, she slowed and stopped in mid-motion like a car out of fuel. Karl guided her away from Jack's right arm. "Step away and then ... then do the same to his left arm."

Jack lay with his face turned aside on the ground. His mouth was pinched into a rictus grin. His eyes squinched shut. "Pleeeaaaassssseeee ... augh ... auugggghhhhh ... you better KILL ME!"

Something about Stella's downward thrust was far more vicious than with the first arm. She didn't hold back, and in a matter of a minute, she had ruined Jack's left arm, and far worse than its twin. She had nearly separated the bicep from the forearm at the elbow before Karl flung his arms around her middle and yanked her backward, whispering unintelligible words in her ear she could barely hear. The drumbeat in her ears of a profoundly raised heart rate shut out all sound, and she couldn't even hear herself sobbing in Karl's arms as he drew her down to the ground. She felt the tire iron, slippery and lubricated with blood, drop from her grasp with a thud. She felt her body collapse against Karl as they both dropped, hers pulsating with intermingled grief and terror. Karl smoothed her hair away from her forehead, but she was not there.

Stella Post was reciting her vows on the altar, holding hands with Jack before a small gathering of loved ones inside Grace Catholic Church. It had only been four short years since they professed their eternal love (*in sickness and in health—good and bad*). Father Strahling had wrapped his big, liver-spotted hands around theirs, sealing the bond with the blessings of God. He had also cemented the fate of two early twentysomething people sick and tired of hearing how the divorce rate tipped the scale of fifty percent "so what's the point, really?" Jack and Stella had shrugged this off. Jack had shut one of his uncles down, telling them "Let us be one of the lucky few couples to tip the scales the other way." She had believed him.

Now, Jack's beaten and battered body sprawled out before her, and she wondered how it was he could have sounded so sure. And yet, so deceitful.

Slowly, Stella felt herself slip back inside her own flesh and blood.

167

She returned to the moment, and it was gruesome.

Karl whispered in her ear, his words gaining volume once more. "Gonna put the tire iron back in the trunk. I'll stow it away under the spare tire. You lay here. And if he tries anything—don't think he can—but if he *tries* anything, you call me."

"H-he won't do anything. You g-go get rid of this."

"We will" Karl said, taking the tire iron and stalking towards the back of the car. "On the road tomorrow we'll dump it. And we gotta button our lips for the rest of the night. We done enough screaming. This area looks secluded enough, but, you know."

Stella lay in the damp grass, staring up at the black sky. A flock of bats suddenly screeched, bursting from the trees in a mad dash and flurry of wings. She watched them bump into one another as they shuddered and shifted across the dark canopy above, and her eyes grew heavy. She heard the sound of Jack's sobbing at her feet, no longer begging for anything. No mercy. They were past that. She heard the sound of metal scraping and clanging against metal as Karl rummaged in the trunk, pulling up the false floor to get at the compartment where the donut tire sat pinned in place.

Sleep eroded her feverish thoughts, silencing them little by little—

"Uh, Stell!" Karl cried, from the rear of the Taurus. "You gotta come see this!"

Stella's eyes flashed open. She gouged them with the balls of her fists, digging sleep out, and slowly rose to her feet. She made her way over to the Taurus, careful to skirt Jack and allowing a wide berth around him. He made no motion to grab at her. If it wasn't for the broken sobs coming from him, Stella could have very easily thought him dead. She circled to the back of the Taurus just as Karl came up from the trunk. He was holding something in his hands, a plastic oven bag it looked like. The outside of it was mottled in grease.

"This was stuffed down underneath the jack and the spare tire, bunched up. I almost missed it but my hand grazed it while I was feeling around inside there."

"What's inside?" Stella was shivering now. She hugged herself, trying to contain some shred of warmth beneath her thin coat and sweater.

"Trying ... to ... see." Karl felt around the edges of the bag. His fingers found the Ziploc edge, and he tore this end open. "Here we go." He dug around inside, drawing the items out. He motioned for Stella to shut the trunk, and she slammed it closed. Karl laid each item down on the trunk surface.

To Stella, the things looked like baseball cards at first. They were in a small stack and Karl fanned them so they could be seen for what they actually were.

She leaned in, still hugging herself. "Driver's licenses? Is that what they …" Her voice trailed off. Her hands flew from her sides, and she scooped them up.

"What the … fuck?" Karl exclaimed beside her. He laid another item on the trunk. "That's it. Shit, that's enough, I'd say!"

Stella thumbed through the identification cards in her hands, barely bothering to look up at the last item on the trunk. "Who are these women? They're—young. Madison Winslow … she's from Hartford? What … I don't …"

"IDs?" Karl asked, leaning in. "Can't see. You got your cell phone? The light from it."

Stella absently dug her cell phone out and handed it to Karl. He fiddled with it and soon the phone's flashlight spilled bright, white light across her hands and what they were thumbing through. "Six altogether. Three–three girls from Philadelphia. Dana Malone. Uhm, Maureen Smith. Jodi Dare? Then you have … Connecticut … New Jersey … fucking *Maine?* Who the fuck are these people? Why are they in *my car?* Why do I have these?"

"It's pretty obvious hubby hid them in *your* car for a reason. But, Stell–*Stell?* You gotta look at the thing on the trunk. Here, hand me those IDs. Have a look at this fucking thing here!"

Stella handed the IDs to Karl and reached for the thing on the trunk. She took it in her hands, a rubbery and sticky texture. It reminded her of what those cheap Disney Princess Halloween masks felt like and how uncomfortable they had been when you wore them for a few hours and breathed into them until they were sticky on the inside and out. She had worn her share as a child, trick or treating as Belle or Cinderella or The Little Mermaid. It was all stuck together. She unfolded it and then splayed it out flat on the trunk.

A German Shepherd mask. A fucking Halloween mask. And driver's licenses. Hidden in my *trunk.*

She could have killed Jack right then and never thought twice.

Not once.

36. AND NOW THIS ... FROM A VAPING TEEN

The locksmith team of Touring and Son arrived at the Post residence a little before 7:45 p.m. The elder locksmith was a starved looking, middle-aged man with greasy, thin white hair he repeatedly smoothed back along his scalp as he worked, and the younger Sonny Touring hovered in the background like a fern while his father worked. At a little before 8 p.m., Old Man Touring cracked the small fireproof safe in the closet of Jack Post's study.

Twenty-five miles away, Jack was having his arms and legs crushed and destroyed at the hands of his wife and her lover.

If Rivells knew what was happening to Jack Post right then, she might have secretly applauded the torture inflicted upon the man of the house. But she had no idea and only had eyes for what the safe contained. She asked Jones if he wouldn't mind allowing her to do the honors. He was fine with it, not the standard greedy detective who savored and protected his collar and all evidence gathered therein for their sake of their own glory at the close of the case. So the moment Old Man Touring gathered up his tools and backed away from the now yawning safe, Rivells swooped down on her hands and knees. She started digging inside the safe, the giddiness of discovery fluttering like butterflies in the pit of her stomach.

She laid item after item on the rug beside her, bearing each with plastic gloves. Detective Jones crouched beside her, inspecting each of the contents as quickly as she removed them and handed them to him. She removed a small banded sheaf of papers and once Jones opened them, he announced they were stock and bond certificates. She removed a manila envelope, labeled with a meticulous-looking handwriting, which seemed alien to any man she had ever met, with the words: BIRTH, MARRIAGE CERT./ STELLA GAY AND JACK POST. Rivells felt dirty handling them, even if they were contained inside an envelope and she was wearing gloves. Like she needed to wash her hand tout de suite. Beside her, Jones sounded a similar reaction.

"Ah, these. Damned shame they ever met each other."

Rivells shook her head, reaching deeper into the gaping black mouth of the safe. The smell of fabric softener and moth balls swam up her nose and her eyes watered slightly. She grasped a smaller envelope, letter size, and removed it. The outside was marked JACK ALLEN POST-LAST WILL AND TESTAMENT. Her intuitive mind immediately seized upon the obvious and she turned to Jones.

"See what she might gain from his early demise?" It sounded cliché in her ears once she said it, but often enough people tend to prove just how accurate clichés turn out to be. Rivells reached in, groaning a bit as her bad knee from an old high school softball injury sent shimmering waves of pain up her inner thighs.

All she felt was the cold steel bottom of the safe's interior. "Seriously?"

"That it?" Jones asked.

Rivells slid her hand around, then along the sides and the top. The tip of her index grazed something there. She grasped it, a small book of some kind, and drew it into the light of the bedroom. It was stowed atop a small shelf inside the safe, and they would have had to haul the whole damned thing out into the open to see it otherwise. She stared down at it. A small photo album, no larger than 5x7. Black exterior lined in felt. Jones held out his hand.

"Curiouser and curiouser," she said, handing it to the lead detective with a forced grin.

Jones thumbed it open. A sense of knowing crept into them and he rubbed the sharp underside of his jaw with the large in-seam of his palm. "Glynn, come have a look at this."

Rivells stood, dusted her dark slacks off at the knees, and crowded in beside Jones. He smelled of Christian Dior cologne. She knew her men's colognes, having spent the better part of her late teens and early twenties working a perfume counter at Macy's before entering the police academy. When she saw what the photo album contained, her awareness of his scent fell away like two sides of a curtain.

"Bigamist?" Jones asked.

The first insert of photographs inside pictured Jack Post in a slate-grey suit. He was holding the hand of a pretty blonde woman, considerably shorter than him, but busty and voluptuous nevertheless. She was not exactly wearing a wedding gown, more of an ensemble for a bride who has just tied the knot at City Hall. A pale blue dress. She didn't hold a bouquet in her other hand and it dangled at her side, holding fast instead to a simple white accent purse. They stood before a small archway of flowers that would have looked most at home at a Senior Prom.

"No," Rivells said. "They're at some sort of event. Maybe business. I saw one of his business cards on the refrigerator. He's a sports talent scout over at Ballantine University. A gala, maybe. An *away* gala? We've got a Don Juan here, who dabbles in sexual assault on the side. Oh, and let us not forget the fact he's somehow managed to hold a marriage together the entire time."

171

"Their marriage was held together by safety pins at best," Jones said. "It looks like the spurned wife finally put her foot down tonight. Could be she's been stepping out on him, too."

"Tit for tat. Or they've come to some kind of understanding."

"Something *I'll* never understand."

"More people than you'd think have come to just this type of *understanding*. Sex is cheap. Love costs more."

Jones sighed. "Couldn't be his sister?"

"Not unless he dabbles in incest along with everything else on his resume. If it was his sister, it'd be displayed on the wall or a shelf. It wouldn't be locked away in a safe like some dirty secret."

"Handsome guy. Gotta say. Doesn't make sense he would feel the need to force himself on women when it's quite possible he could have charmed them right into bed."

"Jones, you're thinking like a man."

"I know, just talking out loud. I know sexual assault has nothing to do with sex and everything to do with power. Still, I've never been able to wrap my head around it."

Then, maybe you ought to go back to being a beat cop, sweet Jones! Think on it a little while. Rivells did not work in sex crimes, yet it never ceased to amaze her how easily a man's mind strained to reconcile itself to a rape charge when it involved a handsome man or a stunning woman as the perpetrator. Too often men cannot seem to remember rape does not know attractiveness, it only knows force of will and soft targets. "What's on the next insert?"

Jones flipped to the next page. "The same woman. Looks like they're standing outside in line for some event."

"A slate building, looks like. New York street."

"Right," Jones said. "Souvenir shop across the way. 'I Love NY Keepsakes, Inc.'"

Jones jabbed a thumb down at the photograph. "See the sign above their heads."

"I see a part of it. Looks like the rest of it is blacked out."

"Not at all," Jones said. "That's the *whole* sign."

"What ... looks like ... cat's eyes?"

"Think NY. Think Broadway—"

"*Cats!* Shit, never been. Never seen. Don't like musicals."

"I ... love them," stammered Jones, looking sideways at her. "So, I guess I should return our tickets?"

Is he serious? She glanced at his profile as he turned the page. There was no way of reading him. "Either way," she said, sneaking another glance at him and then reining in her focus once and for all. "We see he had a woman on the side. This has been established. We need more. This makes him look like nothing more than a guy who's unhappy in his marriage." She motioned for him to flip the page.

The next insert showed something far less intimate than the previous two, but the same woman remained the focal point of the two 3x5 photographs wedged into place, and pinned beneath the clear sheet. The two photographs showed the woman obviously unaware of her photographer. She appeared candid, crossing a busy urban street and clutching her bag, while she adjusted a pair of Hollywood-starlet sunglasses over her eyes with her other hand.

"Far removed, huh?" Rivells said. "If this is in any kind of consecutive order, it would appear our Don Juan went from cozy with the woman to someone who can't get near her. Why?"

Jones had already thumbed to the next page, where more photographs stared up at him with a beckoning sheen. A different woman, photographed from a distance, ordering a coffee in a local shop. The picture was snapped through a storefront window, its photographer further removed. This woman was a tall redhead, her porcelain skin glowing, even behind the plate glass. Rouge looked roughly gouged into the deep divots of her high cheekbones. Drawing attention to the unmistakable heaviness of a frown weighing down her mouth. Another photograph on the same page showed another woman sitting on a park bench with a brown paper bag in her lap and a far off look in her downward stare. The small photo album was filled from cover to cover with candid, far-removed snapshots of women, unaware of the photographer. Getting into their car; walking out of a grocery store with two yellow plastic bags weighing their arms down; even a streetwalker in the mix, huddled in a record shop doorway that looked like a South Street location in Philly, where fringe music stores and headshops reigned supreme.

"These women ..." Jones said glumly, "they ..."

"If you suggest it's their *time of the month*, our chances of having dinner together just evaporated."

"Of course I wasn't going to say *that*, but—"

"They all look ... lost."

"Like their best friend just died. Or their puppy, for God's sake."

This was how I must have looked to my friends and coworkers for the better part of two months after Mama died. If I hadn't taken the advice of one of those friends and met with a therapist, a great lady I still meet with from time to time, I think I would have slipped into an inescapable malaise.

173

A deep well without a ladder and water up to your neck ...

Jones thumbed back to the beginning of the small photo album, to the petite blonde clutching Jack's tanned, oversized hand. "Take a look at this one. Take a look at her smile. Tell me it doesn't look like he's got his hand up the back of her dress and he's working her strings."

Rivells stared down at the 5x7 and was surprised to not have recognized it before. "It looks pasted on. Forced. They all look miserable. But this one, it looks like she was the most intent on trying to hide it."

"Because our photographer didn't catch her in a candid moment, like with the other women."

"How many more photographs are in there?"

Jones thumbed to the back of the book, ticking off each number with a shallow nod of the head. "Twelve. Twelve women in all, and—"

"Jodi Dare? Did you see her in there?"

"Right, right." Jones flipped back a couple glossy pages, stopped on one of them. Then, he shook his head, held the book out to Rivells. "It could be her, but I can't be sure. What do you think?"

She lifted the page closer to her eyes, blinked a few times, and was suddenly certain. "That's her. Different hair color. She's a brunette in these pictures. Hair a little longer. To her shoulders. And she's got a little bit more meat on her. She must have dyed blonde since. Stopped eating. It fits, her altering her appearance and starving herself. It fits a rape vic's response to the attack. Depression and an inherent need to disguise themselves any way they can. But that's our Jodi."

Jodi Dare was behind the counter of what was clearly a Starbucks, mopping her hands with a white dish rag, and talking to another young girl with black hair in pigtails and a silver drink mixer canister in her hands. Jodi's eyes were glistening. She had been crying or recently stopped. "He would have been able to snap these pics unnoticed with his cell phone. Right from the serving counter if he wanted."

Rivells smoothed her palm against the back inside panel of the book, searching for anything else peculiar, as if it were not a strange item in and of itself. She felt it there, just beneath the felt inlay. *There's scratches or cuts underneath it.* She inspected the edge of the felt with her fingers. After some prodding, the felt peeled back as if it were barely held in place. Beneath it, the words were etched into the plastic covering, hidden. They looked to have been carved there with a paring knife, or some other crude blade:

WHO WILL UNBREAK THE BIRDS, IF NOT ME?

Jones was staring down at the album.

"Unbreak ... the birds? *Unbreak?*"

"Detective?"

Rivells turned to the two uniformed officers as they filed inside the master bedroom. Two young men with olive and rosacea faces respectively. Sturdy, lean builds alluding to the possibility they worked out together and even spotted each other during reps. They approached them with their eyes and attention set squarely on Detective Jones, as if Rivells weren't even there. *I get it. I'm not even supposed to be here. Nevertheless, dicks, I remain!*

"What'd you find?" Rivells asked, snapping the book closed and handing it to a forensics woman nearby who disappeared with it.

Olive-skin spoke first. "We spoke with five different couples on the block. Ages ranging from late thirties to early seventies. Guess which age bracket was the most talkative and knew the most?"

"The golden oldies?"

"And his wife. She broke out the biscotti for us and everything. According to the elder couple, the husband, Jack, 'respects his elders.' The old lady's words. Jack helped her husband repair his workbench in the garage one summer when it collapsed while Jack was outside mowing his lawn. Jack ran right over, helped the old man rescue his tools, and then he hung around until near midnight reinforcing it for the guy with new studs. The other neighbors pretty much confirm the fact Mr. and Mrs. Post are, for the most part, private people. Jack was more inclined to come out of *his* shell every once in a while. He attended a few of the block parties and even met with a couple of the other young guys at Bailey's Tavern in town for March Madness couple years in a row. But other than that, it was common knowledge he was, and I quote, 'tending to a sick wife.' People seem to think without that responsibility he would have been more sociable. Most of the people on the street claim they knew *of* his wife, but rarely, if ever, actually saw her. She had a car, but they hardly ever saw her drive by. It just sat, for the most part. One of the young ladies said this house actually spooks her, and she crosses the street now when she walks her dog."

"Spooks her?" Rivells asked.

Olive-skin flinched in her direction, and went on. "She says one too many times she walked past this house, and she saw Mrs. Post peeking out at her from behind the curtains. Just staring. The girl felt sorry for her at first, but when it kept happening, she started to get a bad feeling. And I quote, 'I always knew something was happening in that house.'"

Jones glanced around him, his lips bloodless for an instant. "Were you able to find out anything more, like maybe what kind of illness our Jack was *tending* to so faithfully?"

Rosacea-Face adopted a constipated expression as he bristled beside

175

Olive-skin. "What was the word one of them used?"

"Agoraphobic," Olive-skin said. "One of the neighbors is going for her Masters in Psych. Made a point of telling us so we wouldn't dismiss her outright. But it sounds like it could fit."

"So ... a fear of the outside world," Jones sighed.

"Well, when you're married to a control freak like Jack Post, the poor woman was terrified of what the rest of the world was like, if her own husband treated her like dogmeat. I'd even go so far as to theorize he conditioned her to never want to leave the house unless he needed her to. It's another form of control. This guy was her captor, not her husband."

"Yeah," Jones said, "and we've got ourselves an uprising and a jail-break. We'll hold off for now on a psych profile. We should be focusing all our efforts on getting this guy into custody, alive, if that's even an option at this point. His wife could have killed him by now."

Olive-skin piped up. "Yeah, well, she wasn't alone. She had another fella with her earlier."

"What?"

"We got an eyewitness next door we think you'll want to interview more in-depth. She's waiting on you. We came to get you, Detective."

"Lead the way," Jones said. "Rivells, you coming?"

Rivells snapped to. "Yes, of course."

A young looking female uni (uniformed officer) headed them off at the entrance to the bedroom. The uni held what looked like a slim, glossy book against her chest like she meant to guard it against any and all harm. *She looks like I did the first time I unearthed what I hoped to be case breaking evidence by accident! Ah, the memories!*

"Officer?" Jones prompted.

The newbie handed the glossy book over. "I found this when we were tossing the bookshelf downstairs in the living room. I like birds. I have to say, it's the only reason I even paged through it in the first place. My father and I used to bird-watch when I was a kid—"

"What about the book, officer?" Jones scanned her name plate. "Officer Dugan?"

"Anyone just leafing through it would have missed it at first, the way the writing is inscribed onto the pages in sections of the bird photograph where it would blend into the background color. I caught it when I stopped on the raven photograph, a quarter of the way in. I saw it. Calligraphy writing. They took some time writing it. But I found an inscription on twelve pages of this book."

"*An Enthusiast's Aviary Handbook,*" Rivells read the cover, which featured a breathtaking zoom shot of a whippoorwill in mid-chirp or song. "Broken birds." The last part she whispered than saying outright.

Jones was already shuffling through the book. At page twelve, he bit his lower lip. "I don't see anything–"

"Right there! See it?" Rivells poked the opened page with an index finger. "Can't see what it says though, but it's there."

The newbie made a half-hearted grab for the book. "You have to hold it up close to …"

Jones did. His eyes widened. "Hot damn," he breathed. He passed it over to Rivells. "Officer Dugan, this is going in your jacket. Congratulations."

The newbie had been right. Whoever inscribed the inside of the book had done it in spots on the bird photographs which would easily camouflage the writing. They had even gone so far as to use the same color ink as the color they were writing on. The photo depicted an American Goldfinch, a bird whose bright yellow plumage drew the eye with little effort. The inscription was literally carved into the yellow, with yellow ink. Rivells thought she knew just the style of pen the writer would have used, because her mother carried around the same kind. It had eight different colors of ink in one, and all you had to do was to depress the specific color's button and *voila!* Yellow becomes brown becomes blue becomes red becomes orange becomes purple. So on and so on.

The yellow ink blended so perfectly, Rivells had to shift the book around in her grasp until it caught a certain play of light in the bedroom. Then, the inscription looked to lift itself up off the page:

T.S.

5619082121

B 021517 U 032817

"Officer Dugan? You said you found twelve etchings just like this one?" Jones asked.

"Yes, sir," Officer Dugan replied. "Initials. And a phone number. Cells, most likely. Don't know what the third line means."

"Good work, officer," Rivells said. She leafed deeper into the lightweight book and discovered four more, all of which were easily undetectable if you weren't looking for them. "Twelve's our magic number here, looks like. Twelve entries. Twelve photographs of twelve women."

Jones crowded into Rivells, trying to gain a better look at the page she was opened to. "The third line? Any idea?" He studied the etching in the book. "Looks like military times? But ... the B and the U?"

"Let me think on this," Rivells said. "I'll get this."

Her mind seized upon the words etched into the back of the photo album. Two words, more than the rest: *Unbreak ...* and *... bird. Unbroken bird.*

"Glynn?"

"Yeah?" she answered, her fingers clutching the book edges so hard they had begun to curl under.

"Hand it off to evidence so we can go interview our witness."

Do I have to?

Before they were properly introduced to the teenage girl eyewitness, Rivells and Jones knew her as "The Vaping Teen." They met her on the screened-in back porch of the next-door neighbor's house. Night was dark and thick around them, and The Vaping Teen seemed creeped out by the ink-black darkness of the evening, more so than nearly every teenager Rivells or Jones had ever met. She stood on the porch hugging herself, and when she saw the two detectives and two officers coming around to the back yard, she joined them. She was a tall, waifish girl with straggly, dirty-blonde hair and long, stilt like legs that barely filled out her black yoga pants. A gray, baggy Ballantine University sweatshirt billowed around her upper body, yet she shivered like she was naked.

Olive-skin shook the girl's hand, pumping it twice. "These are Detective Jones and–uh–"

"Rivells," Rivells snapped, meeting the girls pinched blue eyes with her own disarming warmth. "What's your name, honey?"

"Greta," the girl said. "Simms."

Jones shook with her, then Rivells. "Good to meet you, Greta. Can you tell us what you saw?"

"Sure," Greta said. She slipped one hand into the front pouch of her sweatshirt, brought out what at first looked like a black finger in the moonlight. "You mind if I, you know ..."

"Smoke?" Olive-skin grunted.

"No, vape. I quit a month back when my mom caught me with some friends at the mall. She bought this for me to help me stop. I guess it's working."

"Vape to your heart's content, Greta," Rivells said.

Greta smiled. "I'll just show you." She clicked the vape's engage button. The contraption hissed in her hands, and she sucked a mouthful of whatever it had to offer down into her lungs. Then, she turned her head away from them and blew out what was a smoke billow the size of a cumulus cloud. Another smile when she turned back to them. "I don't vape right out here. I walk down along the hedge side of the back yard there. Then, I cut in. I can see right into *their* backyard. All the way up to their back porch. Straight shot. They must have never seen me doing it there, or they would have chased me away. It's probably their property. Their backyard is hidden on both sides by the hedge. Guess they like their privacy."

Jones dismissed the two officers, who held off a moment before trudging back across the lawn to the Post house. Jones and Rivells fell in line behind Greta. She led them along the tall hedge, easily eight feet tall and still hardy with lush green leaves that held on even through the harshest winter.

The backyard of the house where Greta did her babysitting opened into a vacant stretch of dirt patches and tall grass. She led Rivells and Jones to the left, coming along behind the back perimeter of the Post backyard. Their feet squished along in the soft, sodden earth. The remains of a white picket fence that had once closed off the rear of the Post yard lay crushed and driven down into the mud. The pickets were broken and splintered in some spots. At the foot of them, two deep grooves were cut into the swampy ground leading to the battered fence.

Greta looked at Jones, expecting him to meet her eyes. Instead, he stepped over the remains of the fence and into the Post backyard.

Greta held back, blowing big, fluffy smoke rings into the cold night air. "They drove a car back here. They didn't bother to take apart the fence or anything. Just ran it over and then backed the car up to the back porch."

"And big, tall hedges on either side," Rivells said, coming up behind Jones as he crossed the yard and made towards the soft, ethereal glow of the Post rear porch. He had his head pitched downward while he walked, and Rivells recognized he was looking at the tire marks running all the way up to the house. "They backed up the car because they didn't want anyone to see them hauling a body out and stuffing it into the trunk. Lucky you sneak your smokes back here, young lady. Otherwise, no one would have seen a damned thing."

Greta held up her vape, beaming with a simple pride. "Least I can do."

"Come on," Rivells said, waving Greta along to follow them.

The girl nodded and went along.

"So," Jones called back to the young girl, "they backed the car to the back porch. You saw them do it, and you hung back to see what they were going to do next?"

"They moved pretty fast," Greta said. "Backed up the car and then they were really hustling. I wasn't done vaping so I hung out, to finish what I was doing and ..."

"–and to see," Jones said. "It's all right. I would have done the same thing. What did you see?"

179

"They left the car running and went back inside. They must've had the ... the body already wrapped up and waiting at the back door because they went in, and then they came right back out."

"Now, you said *wrapped up*," Rivells asked, now officially annoyed by the squelching of her sneakers in the mud of the yard. "Could you see what the ... thing or person they were carrying was wrapped in?"

Greta nodded. "Looked like a rug. One of those fancy ones with the really detailed stitching?"

"An oriental rug," Rivells said. *They had oriental rugs laid all over the first floor. Jack Post must have had a hard-on for them. But I didn't notice any areas where it looked like a rug was pulled up.*

"Pretty sure," Greta agreed.

"You get a good look at them?" Jones asked, stopping at the base of the cement steps leading up to the small back porch. "I know you were all the way back there, but ... any identifying features?"

"The woman has red hair. But I knew because I've seen her looking out her window most nights. She's really skinny. Pale. Irish-looking. And ... sad. Just looked sad as shit." Greta paused, as if she had depressed herself somehow. Then, she went on. "The guy was kinda small. Skinny. Wearing a lamb's wool jacket. I got one just like it. Long, curly, dark hair. Dark eyes."

"Dark ... like brown or black eyes?"

"Probably black," Greta said. "They popped in the dark. Even in the dark. Black eyes. Yeah."

The three of them stood there for a beat before Jones extended his hand once more to the girl. They shook, Greta with her free hand.

Jones smiled. "This will help. Thanks for your time. I guess your ride home is coming soon? And the people you babysit for. They expected home soon?"

Greta shrugged. "Dunno. Running late I guess."

Rivells shook with the girl next. She held the girl's hand a bit longer than Jones. "Greta, just one more thing. It's okay if you couldn't see, but was the rug *moving*? Like the person was ... *moving around inside.*"

The girl thought about it, clicked off her Vape, and shoved it back inside the front pouch of her ballooning sweatshirt. Then, she brightened some. "They were kind of struggling with it. You know, getting it down the steps. And ... I think I saw the rug jerk. Not like if one of them was losing their grip. No ... it *jerked* hard!"

Still alive. The fucker is still alive!

After Rivells walked the girl through the side yard back to the neighbor's house, she came back and found Jones still standing where she had left

180

him. He started talking even before she crossed through the gate back into the Post's back yard. "So we got a rough description of the accomplice. Squirrelly little bastard from what the girl told us."

"There's desperation at play here," Rivells said. "Why else would she go from the hottie hanging on the wall in the house to a *squirrely looking bastard,* as you put it? He's our man. I can feel it. But I know a feeling doesn't mean shit. We've got a rapist wrapped inside a kidnapping, with an ugly little bow. We track the kidnappers to the offender and it'll be like Christmas in ... well, it's that time anyhow so it'll be like Christmas in December."

"Works all around," Jones said. "We have Stella Post travelling with an accomplice, and what is most likely a groggy Jack Post locked in the trunk. Only thing left we need is the car. Make and model. There's gotta be some insurance paperwork in the car that's still sitting in their driveway. Maybe there's a breakdown on the policy in there also, and we won't have to dredge anything up inside. We can get the other insured car's info off it. Unless Jack Post is a real prick and decided not to insure his wife on account of she never leaves the house."

"No, she'll be on there. Her car." Rivells felt the knot in her stomach tighten, and it almost always told her the worst was yet to come. "She left the house tonight. Whoever this guy is. However much she hates her husband. It got Stella Post to actually *leave the house.*"

37. DARK REFUGE

At the hardware store, Stella fully experienced the threshold of her anxiety pressing her down into the ground with great, invisible hands. Her heart knocked against her ribs like it had suddenly turned to a maniacal bird in a too small cage. It was nearly 9:00 p.m., and the store would only be open for another half hour. The customers were few and far between, the employees even more scarce. A small cluster of workers were huddled around one of the cashier stations up front, four young men trying their best lines on a twentysomething, attractive Spanish woman who seemed to be reveling in the attention. The logical part of Stella knew they were no doubt still standing there flirting up front, but she felt an equal certainty they were actually peering out at her from each corner of every aisle she walked, Karl just a few steps before her. Karl knew what they needed, and he wanted to work quickly. Stella carried the little red basket in her hands and he tossed things in as he found them on the shelves.

"Karl?" she rasped, hurrying her step to catch up with him. "We have to get out of here. I think they know." She moved into him and tried to curl her arm into his, to link to him.

"*Who* knows? Nobody knows shit! Take your breaths. You're forgetting to breathe. You're too tense. You look guilty as hell."

"They know something is wrong. Don't you see them? They're following along behind us."

"No one's doing that, Stell." He angled closer to the left of Aisle Five and grabbed a five pack of plastic-wrapped fifty-pound capacity burlap sacks. He tossed them into Stella's basket, kept moving. He had already selected a big ball of twine, duct tape, and a pair of box cutters. "No one."

Oh, but they are! She glanced down at herself and was reminded once more of another reason *they* would be following *them*. Why *they* might think *something is off!* Stella's tight blue jeans were matted with mud from the knees down. Deep stains darkened her kneecaps where she had knelt to help push the car out of the mud in the New Hope field, where the two of them had broken Jack's bones and discovered the elements comprising his *other* life.

Karl's pants were far worse than Stella's. They had taken turns steering the car and giving it gas while the other pushed from behind. Jack whined and wept from the trunk where they had dumped his limp body, complete with spindly, dangling arms and legs. Karl had been the one behind the car pushing when the Taurus's engine growled and lurched forward out of the deep divots in the mud. Karl went facedown into the wet earth and grime coated the front of him, from the tips of his boots to his low hairline. He wiped down his face with a bunch of napkins in the glovebox, but they were dry and only smeared the mud around. Needless to say, Karl stalked the aisles of the hardware store with dirt streaked cheeks, mud caked shirt and slacks, and stained motorcycle boots.   *Another one! I see you, asshole!* The round face of a teenage boy with a brown buzzcut and acne scars on his cheeks stared out at her from between a line of paint cans. Karl took her hand, but she could sense his impatience with her. It flared off his skin like fever warmth. He smiled at her, dark, greasy ringlets hanging in his eyes.

"Just hang in there," he said to her, squeezing her hand. "Just need to find one more thing then we can head out. In the meantime, I been thinking we should maybe hide in plain sight, if you know what I mean."

"Plain sight?" He guided her around the bend into the next aisle to the left. "You mean, stay in Comstock?"

"They're after us. No question about it. Or ... they're after you. They might not even know about me, but the blood on the oriental rug we couldn't soak up? That raised their eyebrows, and you can bet on it. They're expecting us to run. Far away. So, of course we're gonna stick close until we know where we're going. If you can think of any spot around your way where we can hide out undisturbed, we can get down to making some serious plans. Taking steps. You know of any place?"

Stella knew very little about how the map of Comstock would have changed in the last couple of years. She could not be deemed a shut-in. She went out only when it was absolutely necessary. The procurement of food at the supermarket. Mini errands by which she was there and back within a half hour. Those types of runs she could manage. It was the prolonged exposure to the social elements that quickly sloughed away her skin and scraped at the bones underneath. No doubt Comstock had seen some of its stores shutter, its residential houses foreclosed upon and left vacant for lack of a timely buyer. But she and Karl lacked the luxury of time to hunt around Comstock for such places to hide.

Of course, she knew for certain of one location not only closed but condemned and slated for demolition within the month.

You're not actually going to suggest going there, are you?

"St. Alphonsus Church," she said.

Karl glanced at her and smirked. "A church?" He led her over to a nearby shelf and grabbed a coil of bendable copper wire. Into the basket with a metallic *thunk!* "You serious?"

"I know it's empty. It's supposed to be. There could be squatters there. Kids smoking pot. But ... the church is closed down. Boarded up. For two months. They're going to tear it down. I read it in the *Courier Times*." It was on the tip of her tongue, but she just couldn't bring herself to explain it. Then, Karl was standing there looking at her with expectant, black pinprick eyes. "Horrible things happened there. A priest. He was ... he was abusing some children in the parish. The parents found out about it. The whole thing was kept quiet and swept under the rug. The priest was going to be relocated to some church in Indiana. It's what they do, they shuffle the deck whenever one of their cards is bad. But ... the parents weren't having it. They went to the church the night before Father Bingham was set to be transferred and they ..."

"No ... *shit!*" Karl hissed, his eyebrows jumping like Groucho Marx. "They banded together and they–"

"Yes."

Karl crowded in towards her. "How many of em'?"

"I-I don't know," Stella stammered. Suddenly, it felt like there were bugs crawling all over her hands. She shuddered. *You brought your Xanax bottle. You only need a moment away from him to take one. Just hold on ... hold on.* "I don't remember. A-a famous writer who lives on the outskirts where the church stands was walking his dog on the church grounds when it happened. He tried to save the priest, but it just ... my God, it turned into a bloodbath. The papers carried the story for a week straight, like it was the worst thing in the world ever. The pictures. Oh God–you don't really want to *go there*, do you?"

"Gotta get somewhere. And fast."

You opened up this can of worms, Stella! Time to live with it now! Stella nodded her head stiffly. Behind her, she felt the cold and curious eyes of another teenage employee standing behind them–staring–giggling. She fought with everything she had to keep from wheeling around and cursing them.

Karl touched her neck, smoothed the prickly skin there. "Hey, it's gonna be all right. You don't look so hot."

"Yes ... yes ... I'm all right."

"Good. Good. Let's check out then, Stella-baby. Getting late and we gotta get to church."

The duct tape over Jack's mouth turned the man's whelps to muted moans. With the radio on and tuned to the classic rock station, they couldn't hear Jack at all above the raucous grind of "Them Bones" by Alice in Chains. They rolled into the driveway circling around to the parking lot of St. Alphonsus Church. The church was almost completely obscured by a tall and lush row of tall arborvitae forming a natural privacy wall. Karl switched off the lights, his eyes well-adjusted to the pitch night by then.

Still, he nearly missed them.

The driveway was blocked off by two cement pillars and a piling of dropped branches, for good measure. Karl hit the brakes and sat there in the dark with the same mystified expression that had come across his face when Stella had told him the story of the church and its dark recent history.

"Shit, it's like the place doesn't want us anywhere near it. Look at all that!" He drummed the sides of the wheel, clapped his hands together, then steered the car off the path towards the trees. The tires rumbled and skidded over the frozen grass as he steered the car around the concrete barriers and beyond, to where the top spire of the Church rose into the air, a dinosaur tooth stabbing upward at the chilled, stirring heavens. "Let's hope we don't get stuck in the mud this time around. I gotta leave with the car as soon as I

184

get you and Jack set up in the church."

"What?" Stella cried. "You're going to leave me here with *him?* Where are you going?"

"I gotta swap this car out for another one. I'm sure they're probably already looking for your Taurus, and it's *no bueno.* Actually, I gotta to make a couple snatches."

"I could come with you–"

"Someone's gotta babysit Jack," Karl said, palming the wheel as he wound the car around to the rear of St. Alphonsus. "You know that. Christ!" He sucked his tongue, casting a wide-sweeping glance out the driver's side window at the dark, hunkering monolith of a church standing forlorn and somehow ashamed of itself. "Man, look at this place. Black as a bunghole at midnight. I got a sense for these things, and there ain't no one in there waiting to surprise us."

"I told you there could be squatters inside. Teenagers. And, some talk of *ceremonies* there."

"Where would they have written about such seedy shit? The good-ie-goodie folks of Comstock wouldn't want to know anything about that stuff! It offends their delicate sensibilities, don't it?"

"Strange things," Stella said, staring warily at the church. "Bored teenagers with ouija boards. Alcohol. Orgies. Kids don't believe in God any-more. And something has to fill the void. They don't always turn to Buddha or the Dalai Lama. Sometimes, they turn away from the light."

"Holy shit, you telling me good ol' Comstock has itself a devil wor-shipper problem?"

Stella stirred uneasily in the bucket of the passenger seat. "I read an article or two online about it. It could be sensationalism to get some more clicks. Revive a dying local rag. I don't know." She angled her body towards him, her eyes ringed in deep ringlets of worry. "What I know is I don't want to be left here unless you've got something I can hold onto to protect myself. I don't know a tire iron is going to cut it against teenagers."

"We'll do a sweep of the place," Karl said. "Together. C'mon."

They crept alongside the cement base of the building and rounded the left corner. Stella guided Karl towards a stairwell leading down to the basement door. He would have missed it if she didn't point it out. Karl led the way down, Stella holding close to him. The basement door was sealed over with a piece of plywood nailed in place. Karl found it had some play in it. He curled his hands around the right side of it, where it had warped away from the jamb. His ring finger grazed a rusty nail and skittered away from it. He yanked backward, gritted his teeth, and planted his boots. He yanked and yanked. The wood groaned in his hands and ripped away. Karl went with it, almost spilling down to the dirty cement of the landing. He braced himself against the red brickface of the building, panting. He cast a sidelong glance at Stella and smiled to set her at ease. She stood there looking at him like he was going to savage her. To cut her down with words, with misplaced frustration. She couldn't help it.

The inside of the basement was a black, yawning mouth.

Something metallic crashed to the ground within. Stella's scream came out as a squeal.

Karl giggled like a schoolboy and nodded at her. "Flashlight?"

Stella nodded. She fished her cell out of her back jeans pocket. The screen lit up in her hands. Her battery power was rapidly draining away. It was at twenty percent. She had no idea how much power the flashlight feature would take out of it, but damned if she would follow him into the basement without some sense of what surrounded them. She switched the light on and handed it over.

Karl aimed the cell flashlight, throwing light into the opening, which washed over grimy pale tiles and a black mat, half curled up before the entrance. He licked his lips and stepped into the breach.

The light's throw was surprisingly wide. It did not merely light their way, but the periphery on either side. Stella grabbed for Karl's hand. She clutched it. He barely squeezed her hand back, guiding her along. He stepped over what sounded like broken glass. It crunched under his boots, and he led her around it. The floor was littered with lots of broken, shattered, and abused things. Things someone or a group of people had seen fit to hurl against the white pillars here and there. Against the wall. At one another, perhaps? Folding tables lay on their sides, turned around at odd angles in some nonsensical labyrinth leading to nowhere. A few of the tables stood upright; one had a filthy white sheet draped over it. Karl's light played over it and found a tabby cat perched there, squinting back at him. Its back was arched painfully upward, and it screamed at the two of them before darting out of view and upsetting unseen, breakable items in its blind path.

Karl mocked the animal with his own pitiful imitation of its noise and drew Stella further along. He kicked aside a small circle of different colored candles on the floor. They were arranged on top of a swatch of cardboard with a crude drawing sketched into it. It showed a man with his face wrapped in what looked like mummy bandages and wearing a plain dark suit. His arms were outstretched like someone offering *death's embrace*. Stella shuddered.

"Ho!" Karl cried, the light in his hands playing across a nearby pillar.

"Looks like you were right, Stella!"

"*Ssssshhhhh–*"

"Oh come on, there's no one here except for Mister Fucking Whiskers, and he just skipped out."

"What are you talking about?"

"The pillar?"

The words were spraypainted in big, capitalized lettering on the pillar: THIS WAY TO SATAN'S SIDESHOW! ⌧

"Where's it lead?" Karl splashed the light off to the right, following the arrow's direction. "You know?"

"Can we go? Someone's down here."

"No one's *down here*! Will you cut the shit? You know this place, right? I need you to keep me oriented. Now, we keep walking this way, what are we going to run into?"

Stella pictured the basement as it had been before the atrocity had taken place at the church. She had made it to a pair of bingo games, each time forced to leave early when the anxiety sank its claws in. She remembered the folding tables. There had been folding chairs to go with them, all in a row. They were nowhere to be seen. She remembered there was a small stage set into the rear wall of the basement. It was where the bingo moderator, usually a wrinkly old woman with a sparkling disposition, stood and rotated the steel cage containing the bingo balls. The church committee also held teen dances down in the basement and talent shows with spare, wanting acts on display.

No ... no-no-no! Satan's sideshow? I don't want to see the stage, Karl! You can't make me!

Karl swung the light to the right. It washed over the ratty beige curtains of the stage. The light banked across the stage and illuminated something in its center that stole Stella's breath.

"Holy *Jeezus!*" Karl gasped. "You weren't kidding, Stell!"

The fawn's empty, black eyes stared out over the mess that angry hands and bored boys and girls had made of the church basement. The same angry hands had stolen a couple wooden slats from a cattle fence and dragged it down into the basement. The baby deer was impaled through its narrow belly with one of the slats, and the way the fence pieces had been hammered back together, the animal was projected up into the air and over the lip of the stage like it were taking flight. Its hooves dangled five feet above the tile floor, broken and bent into odd angles. Stella could see in her mind Jack's arms and legs and the odd angles she and Karl had hammered them into out in the New Hope field. The choking acid of bile stung the back of her throat.

The worst part, at least from Stella's point of view, was the animal's entire head had been spraypainted the same red as the graffiti words on the pillar.

Satan's Bambi.

Stella swallowed her vomit. She did not want to be sick in front of Karl. She straightened, sucked wind. "Monstrous," she breathed. "Can we go upstairs? Please?"

Karl didn't move. He had turned to a statue, his eyes fastened to the gory arrangement up on the stage. The flying fawn.

"It's gotta be here," he said, his voice flat. "This ... this is the place."

"What are you talking about?" gasped Stella.

Karl broke away from her. To her horror, he approached the horrid display and stood directly beneath the hanging animal. He held his arms up to it like he meant to drag it down into some kind of embrace. He started laughing, and it built to such a height of treble Stella thought it might drive her mad. His arms outstretched, like a Beach Girl worshipping the sun as it turned her skin a golden bronze.

Then, Stella understood.

He would worship something like this, wouldn't he? How could you have forgotten about the things he did to land him in Berrysburg in the first place? The way he kidnapped neighborhood cats and dogs. Dragged them back into the Livengrin Woods. Cut them open and inserted copper wire into their legs so he could pose them for his– what did he call it? His Gallery! Yes, that's it! Now you remember who this man is. Somehow you made your-self forget because he was your first, and you've never loved like him since then. This–This right here is art to him!

She watched him turn around, grinning from ear to ear. He felt around his crotch and broke into a newer, somehow stranger laughter. "I'm fucking hard as a rock. Here, come feel this!"

Stella turned away. "I'm going to go wait out by the car. Inside the car. Could you check the church to make sure it's clear before you go."

"Something tells me there isn't much to see up in the church proper. Down here is where it all goes down. But I'll make sure. Why don't you go grab the bags in the car and bring em' down here. This is where we're gonna keep Jack when we're not using him."

When we're not using him?

Stella nodded complacently. She slipped back up the stairs, thankful for the cold nipping at her nose and the fresh air. The basement had smelled like a tomb, musty and rotten, like a fleet of rats died in the walls. She stood beside the car and stared out across the adjacent open field. The wheatgrass waved lazily at her in the winter breeze. Before self-consciousness could stop her, Stella waved back like they were old friends wishing her well. She laughed softly to herself, shoved one hand deep down into the pocket of her jeans, and strode to the back of the Taurus. Being out of the basement and back out in the open, Stella felt much lighter in mind and consciousness. *Dare I say, playful? I'm ... feeling playful?* She stepped to the trunk.

Knocked three times.

"Anybody in there? Knock, knock?"

Nothing.

He's playing possum. That's all!

"Fine! Don't say anything. But you know you've had this coming for some time, Jack. You *know* it." She slammed the flat of her palm against the trunk.

Still nothing. Not so much as a whimper or whine. *It would have scared the hell out of me if he did it to me!*

Stella felt worry flood her gut. She hated herself for this reaction. Why should she care either way if he died in there? Wouldn't it be a blessing in the grand scheme of things? Then Karl would be put off from whatever it was he had planned for Jack.

She hesitated and knocked three times on the trunk.

Then, three more times.

That's when Jack let loose with a scream sounding like it tore him in half from crown to heels. It held and held until Stella bolted away from the car, her fingers plugging up her ears. She tripped and barely braced herself from slamming her face into the ground. She went down and rolled over, scuttling backward on hands and feet like a crab. The Taurus was shaking, the whole frame. The scream held. And held.

I need a pill! I have to get to my pills before he comes out—

Karl planted his hands on her shoulders. She nearly rocketed clear of her body.

"Hey-hey-hey-HEY! What the hell's going on out here?"

"He won't stop screaming!"

"Well, what'd you do to him? He had electric tape over his mouth!"

"I didn't do anything!"

"Goddammit, Jackie! Shut up! Gimme the keys!"

Stella fished them out of her jeans and flung them at Karl. He charged over to the trunk, unlocked it, and yanked the hatch violently upward. "I told you to *shut the fuck up! Put the tape back on, asshole!* We're not ready for you yet!" He punched downward into the opening, five quick jabs that did not so much silence Jack's screams as they crammed them back down into his mouth. Jack made a series of slushy, guttural moans and fell to weeping.

Karl leaned in. Stella assumed he was reapplying the swatch of tape over Jack's mouth. Then Karl slammed the trunk shut again.

He dusted off his hands like a landscaper after planting mums in a front yard bed. He slowed, saw the stains on his palms. "Blood. Dammit. Got his blood all over my hands. Pussy." He strode over to Stella, wiping his hands on his muddy chinos. "You all right?"

Stella approached the Taurus, hand flattened across her forehead. "Yeah. I think I am."

"Good. The church is clear like I said. A big ass elm tree dropped right through the roof, but other than that the upstairs looks like a church hasn't seen some action in some time. Jesus is still hanging out over the altar. The pews are untouched. Saw a couple more red graffiti tags along the walls, between the carved wooden Stations of the Cross. Inviting visitors downstairs to *Satan's Sideshow*. We already been there. Done that. Good show!"

"Karl?"

"Yeah? What?"

"I wanna go with you."

"I was thinking about it, and I'm gonna let you come along. You'll drive after we swap cars. I'll make the snatches. You're gonna keep your foot on the gas and your head in the game because once I fill the burlap sacks, and I come running with em', you gotta be ready to go! No second thoughts! No walking around inside your remorseful little head. You promise me?"

"I promise," Stella said. "But ... what do you mean *snatches*?"

"It's gonna be trial and error at first. We're gonna need more than one puppy dog to work the ritual before it takes."

"Puppies?"

"Dogs, woman! Not *puppies*! Just casually talking. They have to be big dogs. Quick to anger. Even that doesn't matter so much. We'll turn em' if we have to. Every goddamn dog's got a wolf inside em' just waiting to be called out. We'll get it right. You? You just make sure you're the getaway girl, and we'll get it all right!"

Stella looked past Karl. She stared with hooded, tired eyes out into the field which had so softened her a short while before. The wheatgrass was still, their stalks straight, no longer offering her the warmth nor refuge of nature. They regarded her, an army of the cold and dead.

"No ... no, I'll stay here and get everything ready," she told him. "Tell me what preparations we'll need. I'll have everything in place. But you have to promise *to come back*."

"Fine," Karl resigned. "Now help me carry that big bulk of shit you call a husband down into the basement, and I'll fill you in."

38. NIGHT TERRORS

Alberta dreamt of the men with their faces covered. They were dreams without a bottom. Her fevered brain free-associated the memories of her time in Fallujah, stitching them together into a series of scenes from her life.

The life before she became a war dog.

When she was an eater of the dead.

It was not borne of anything evil contained within the animal. Alberta entered the world with all the normal capacity for canine kindness and loyalty. It was the rough hands and the harsh words and the beatings, and finally the murder of her puppy litter which completed the separation of the animal from her former, innate self. She saw the wariness and the question in her master's eyes. The kind man with the five-o'clock shadow and spiky black hair, who sometimes looked down at her, as if to ask, What are you capable of, really? *She could not tell him of course.*

The dreams came to her after so many years of peace and restful sleep, and a sense of safety and love and kisses and hugs from the man with the black spiky hair, and the girl he kissed a lot with the lighter hair and a white streak in the front. The night terrors revisited Alberta the first night Black Spike Man left, and they haunted her every night since. She hoped he would come walking back in the front door soon so he could frighten away these terrible nightmares. She suspected only he could do it. Only Black Spike Man had the power to free Alberta from the curse of memory.

She snapped awake around midnight, the nice lady with the gray, helmet-like hair lying in the big bed a few feet away. The woman farted in her sleep, and sometimes they were so loud as to rouse the dog from the nightmares. For this, Alberta was thankful. She could not seem to wake herself up, and while she tried to keep herself awake in her big pink dog bed in the corner of the big bedroom, the dog found sleep would not leave her be. It just kept submerging her, pushing and holding her head down under the water of REM rest. Then deeper. Drowning. Suffocating. Dreaming. Remembering.

She was running with a new pack. She was a few months pregnant by a wandering mongrel which had taken her by surprise amidst a trash heap beside a burning hovel. A violent, feverish rape complete with bites on Alberta's ear as the distressed animal filled her with its seed, and then bolted after a rabbit that caught the corner of his eye. Alberta needed to eat, and she took up with the new pack, trusting they would lead her to food. She knew she needed to feed the burden in her abdomen. It was crying out to her, this life inside her she did not ask for. Alberta wandered with this pack, even though she knew they were different. She longed for this sense of belonging. She hoped they would share whatever food they found and not shut her out. Alberta followed along, and at nightfall, the pack of ten dogs came upon the Crucified Man and Woman just inside the northern border of The Sunni Triangle.

The dogs did not wait. They did not signal to Alberta what they would do. They were different. This sense of the abnormal was not verified for Alberta until the first two dogs snapped into mad dashes towards the Crucified People. The first dog to reach them launched itself at The Man, jaw wide and teeth menacing. It snapped its jowls shut around The Man's side, clamping down into the starved brown flesh of him. The dog hung from The Man's flesh, chewing and chewing until it dropped with a hunk of bloody gore between its teeth. It hunkered down to work on this bit of human meat. The Man was dead. He didn't scream. He didn't resist. His essence had long since departed, and the shell remained as if to say to the pack Do what you will with my remains! Stay alive! I'm not here!

The second dog gained much more altitude and lifted itself so high it locked its jaws around the throat of the Crucified Woman, tearing away her larynx and bone and ligaments.

The Crucified Woman's mouth opened up into a soundless scream. She had been holding on. Somehow. Could not scream.

The second dog hunkered down beside the other, eliciting a growl from it before it got to work on its own bloody take.

From there, the rest of the dogs attacked the two Crucified People with abandon and frenzy. They flew at them, locked onto them, and tore them apart piece by bloody piece. The Crucified Woman fell away from her cross, dangling precariously until one of the dogs tore her arm clear of her hand. Then the Crucified Woman fell into the sand, and the dogs tore her to shreds.

Alberta felt the cries of her babies in her belly. They cried out for her to mix in. Mix into the lot of them. Mix in! Mix in, or we will all die!

The Crucified Man fell onto the sand next, kicking up a cloud around the scurrying and snapping pack of dogs. Alberta trotted uneasily to the group gathered around this dead human flesh. Instantly, saliva gathered at the corners of her mouth. It dripped to the sand, dimpling it. She felt her stomach heave. Scream. Her mouth was gummed up with saliva, and she moved in amongst the shifting shapes of writhing animals. Another dog knocked into her. She snapped her teeth at it, and before she knew what she was doing, Alberta was wresting a loop of intestine free of the Crucified Man's rapidly emptying stomach cavity. Then there was sustenance. She knew it was good ...

"–baby girl, you mussed yourself–*shhhh-shhhh*–it's all right. Come on, let's get up. I'll clean you, Albie." The Gray-Helmet-Haired Lady was out of bed and on her knees next to Alberta. The dog was shivering, despite the warm urine she had been lying in for the better part of twenty minutes, along with her feces. She had felt it happen, but the taste of the meat had been so strong on her tongue, between her teeth, Alberta could not wake herself up. She hadn't wanted to. Not just yet, truth be told. When she came to, she realized what she had done and whimpered. Alberta felt ashamed, even though White-Helmet-Lady spoke calmly to her and smoothed down the top of her head between her ears.

"It's all right. Just a bad dream, honey. It's all right. We'll get you all cleaned up, okay?"

Alberta felt she loved the White-Helmet-Haired woman almost as much as Black Spike Guy. *Almost.* She allowed the woman to draw her up onto all fours. The woman led Alberta into the bathroom adjoining the guest room. She drew a warm bath, brought forth an army of bubbles that floated above their heads and popped delightfully. Alberta climbed into the bath, docile and submissive. The woman washed her whole body with a big sponge, sloshing the warm, lovely water down over Alberta's brindle-furred back. *Yes, I do love you too. I do. I do. Thank you!* Alberta swooned and when it was all over, she nuzzled into the warmth of the towel the woman wrapped around her. The woman hugged Alberta around the neck, and spoke kindly.

I taste the blood and the flesh, and it is good. It's good ... blood and flesh ... the Man and the Woman in a T shape.

"ALBIE!" screamed the woman.

All of the dog's muscles clenched. She dropped her snout and tasted blood on her front teeth.

The nice woman's finger was bleeding. Alberta could smell the strong, acrid scent of the oozing and felt her eyes roll backward. The saliva pooled in her mouth. But she somehow remembered herself and drove her snout downward. Downward and away.

"Ow-*shit!* Ow-ow-ow ... ah ... it-it's all right, baby. It's ... it's okay. Just give me a minute to bandage myself, and then we'll go for a walk. All right ... just ... give me a minute." The woman rose and dug in the medicine cabinet until she found a fluffy roll of gauze and medical tape. She covered up the blood.

Alberta's muscles unclenched once the coppery scent evaporated into the air. She whimpered again. It was her way of saying *So sorry! I'm so sorry! So-so sorry.*

"Come on now, darlin'," the kind woman said, and led Alberta back out through the master bedroom and all the way into the breezeway where the dog's leash hung on a peg in the wall. The woman fastened the leash to Alberta's collar. Alberta felt her breathing call itself back into a calmer rhythm. She walked alongside the woman and whimpered, as if to say, *Thank you for forgiving me–I love you–I love you–I do!* The cold air was welcome and reviving.

Then, Alberta saw the white spire of the church rise up above the border of elm trees. It was not backlit as it had been that night. The night the bad man hurt her across her skull and drove her down with two strong hands into a long darkness. Alberta pulled away, yanking back on the leash. The woman laughed at first, regarding the dog with something of a doting parent. "Oh come on, what's got you, honey? What's the matter?"

Alberta could hear them. People at the church.

The hackles on the back of her neck rose to sharp, ridged prominence like a furry fin.

Their voices. The crying. The arguing. The laughing. Here to hurt me again.

Alberta started barking, her jaws snapping so violently her fangs rang against each other with a dull cracking sound. She barked until the woman gave in, showing the first faint signs of annoyance that evening, and led her back to the Bentley farmhouse. The dog did not stop barking until she laid back down in its pink bed, and even then she wet itself twice more before dawn.

39. THE TRIALS

Stella knew Karl had successfully swapped her Taurus out for another vehicle when she heard the sound of a gunning transmission endlessly clearing its throat as it approached. He pulled the car behind the church. She had done her best to prepare the altar of the church as Karl had instructed, and stood at the entrance to the church like a child waiting for a pat on the top of her head.

While Karl was gone, Jack's screams from the basement (the electrical tape wouldn't stick to his mouth any longer) carried up the stairs and echoed terrifyingly throughout the hollowed-out belly of the church. Stella resorted to turning on the Pandora radio app on her phone and tuning it to the classic rock station. She was never so happy to hear AC/DC's "Thunderstruck" and Nirvana's "Aneurysm" among others in her whole life.

Karl climbed out of the driver's side of what looked like a decent vehicle, aside from its snarling transmission. An older model beige Cutlass. The driver's side window was smashed in.

"Couldn't pick the door lock so I had to break the glass," Karl said. "It'll have to do." There was a clear edge to his voice. It was unfriendly and temperamental. Stella didn't like the sound of it. He hurried around to the trunk, jiggled something that had already been inserted in the lock. Paperclip, maybe? The trunk door rose. "These mongrels tore my arms up good. They put up one helluva of fight, both of them. But I bested both the bitches."

"Two females?"

Karl sighed, cursed under his breath. "Nah ... one of them's a boy but I don't got the patience to sort out their gender for you at the moment. Leave it be, will you? Not right now!"

"Sorry," Stella muttered. "Let me have a look at your arms. Maybe I can do something to bandage them."

"There's no time, and frankly I'm more annoyed by what I had to go through to get the fucking car than the fucking dogs. They were easy, aside from the nips and the claws. I don't give a fuck. Let em' fight. I bested em', like I said. No, I fucked up my arms breaking the glass in the car."

"Well, let me see!"

"Is everything ready? That's all I need to hear from you right now!"

"Don't talk to me that way, Karl," Stella said evenly. She kneaded the palms of her hands nervously. "I did everything you told me to, and it wasn't easy. You show me some respect, and I'll return it."

Karl snorted and slammed the trunk door shut.

"I didn't hear any barking," Stella said, scratching the back of her neck where a fly quickly lighted and flew off into the field. "Why are they so quiet?"

"Because I found your stash, and I made better use of it than you would have."

"My stash?" But she knew. Stella knew *damned* well. "You mean, you took my–"

"You taking those fucking pills again? Those brain-fuckers? Since when? I thought we were on the same page about what those things do! You made a promise to me! I don't take mine, and you don't take yours!"

"You had no right to go through my bag!"

"This is how we keep our *mindmeld* connected. You get back on your meds, and it'll compromise our little closed-circuit. You *really* want to

195

sacrifice what we have between us for a little false relief? If that's where you stand, I'm going to need to borrow your cell to make a call to some more reliable help! I know a couple guys I can depend on if I dangle the right size carrot in front of them, so—"

"YOU HAD *NO RIGHT!*"

"I don't want to talk about your rights, you hear me? I'm not interested. We're on the run now, babe! We got no rights until our business is done! We got no rights until Jack pays what he owes! Rights? Not the kind you're used to, so you tell me what you're going to do from here on out! *Are you on the med wagon again, or aren't you?*"

A loon hooted, and an owl answered deep within the woods north of the field. It was a spooky conversation ending with the squeaking squall of a cluster of bats as they burst out of one of the treetops.

Stella burrowed her right fist into her left hand until the small bones nestled beneath the webbed flesh flared with pain. She knew for certain none of the men she had ever known wanted Stella at her best. They much preferred the challenged, feeble and obliging *Stella* who lived according to the whims and wants of others. She suppressed her own comfort to bolster those of the men in her life.

"Did you use all the pills?" she muttered.

"Would it matter if I did?"

Stella thought about it. She felt the bottom of her stomach drop out like a trapdoor. *I am still deciding. I may kill you. You may kill me. But I am still deciding. Either way, it will be up to me.* She said, "No, I guess not."

Karl stepped up to her, separated her fidgeting hands from one another and squeezed them in his. She felt stickiness embedded there in the skin. He touched his forehead to hers, smiled widely. "Then, just know I put your Xanax to good use, and those dumb fucking dogs are dosed. But they won't be for much longer. Show me what you done inside, and then if it's up to speed we can get going."

She led him into the church and across the altar.

Karl had explained to her earlier the significance and function of the items involved in the *conjuring of the enfulmbe,* or "spirit," which would assist them in their efforts and complete the process. "It all starts with the *engange,* which is a pot you set up in the center of the altar." Stella had wrested one of the brass bowls out of its wall fixture just inside the church entrance. Parishioners would dip a finger into a bowl, usually filled with holy water, and they'd bless themselves on their way into and out of the church for Mass. Her stomach churned when it came away in her hands. *This is the Holy Spirit damning me.* The bowl was not very big, but it would serve. She set it up on the floor of the altar, directly under the hanging crucified Christ.

Stella bent down to more closely inspect her handiwork, the items she had arranged inside the *engange*, the pot. Her stomach lurched once more, somersaulting behind her ribcage. A series of spindly kindling overflowed out of the pot. The church smelled of earth. Stella had to walk among the elm trees bordering the front of church property and root on the ground for anything dropped from above. She had an armful of twigs and brambles in less than ten minutes.

It took her longer to gather the second required implement. Grave dirt. Behind the church, the remains of its founder Monseigneur Musial were interred in the ground. A simple stone marked the spot and was easy to miss if one weren't looking for it. Stella briefly belonged to the parish years ago. She was familiar with the gravesite, the only body buried on the premises, in accordance with the Monseigneur's wishes. The reason this took longer than the gathering of the tree branches had a great deal to do with the "Catholic guilt" that suddenly consumed her before she dug her hands into the dirt of the Monseigneur's grave. On her knees, she hesitated. A chill wind blew her ginger hair away from her brow and tickled her wide-open eyes. She wept, and her eyes were damp again. Her vision was warbly and warped, and this was better because she could not see what she was suddenly able to do. To dig her nails into the ground. To burrow deeper and deeper into the tough, frozen ground, casting tufts of grass behind her as she dug deeper and deeper until she had enough dirt to fill her hands cupped together. Then, feeling suddenly sick and cold, Stella slunk away from the grave and returned to the altar, where she spilled the grave dirt into the pot.

Of course, there's more, isn't there?

Two more items to gather.

There was. She decided to leave the worst for last, as far as she was concerned. Stella exited the church proper and crossed the front hall adjoining the church to the classroom wing for Grades One through Five. The hydraulic door wheezed open with barely a push, its mechanisms obviously disabled. The long hallway stretched out before her smelled of lingering incense mingled with a more overwhelming smell of musty neglect. *In only two months time? Crazy!* She quickly darted into the first classroom on her right, the door standing open and yawning into an abyss which, on closer inspection and a widening of her irises, revealed discarded items scattered across the tiles. A colorful banner curled up on the floor with only a portion of its message staring up at her … DREAM AND DISCOVER WHAT …

The sight of the crumpled banner hurt her heart. She hurried over to the chalkboard on the wall on the right side of the classroom. Blindly, she traced her fingers along the ledge where the teacher had once set down her chalk pieces. Stella walked the length of the ledge, her fingertips discovering nothing until she nearly reached the other end. Then, a nub of chalk touched her index finger and she snatched it up greedily. Thankful to exit the school wing and its heavy air tugging downward upon her shoulders.

Stella re-entered the Church. She went to the altar and set about inscribing the symbols on the outside of the pot, according to Karl's instructions. "You'll draw ohs and plus signs all over the outside of the *engange*. They represent the positive and negative … uhm, what was the word Shambe used? Yeah, polarity of existence. Our world and the spirit world. ohs and plus signs. Our world and the world of the *enfulmbre*. You get it?"

Karl's backward, lazy way of speaking sounded completely at odds with the language of *palo mayombe*, so much so that when he spoke its words, Stella felt amused and unsettled at the same time. *Karl, it's possible I understand this more than you do!*

There was something else–something else–I don't know I can—

"Oh, look at what you done," Karl said, hunkering down beside her, "you little devil-worshipper you!"

"Don't call me that," Stella said, rising up and turning away from him.

Karl laughed to himself, examining the pot and its contents. He moved the tree branches around, looking for something. Stella knew what it was because she knew what she had neglected to include in the pot. A part of her had been hoping he wouldn't notice.

"Oh, Stella? Where are the bones?"

She waited, considering what to say. "I couldn't do it. You said to cut the bones out of the deer downstairs but, I couldn't. I would have gotten sick everywhere. You want to smell puke for the rest of the night?"

Karl stood and turned to face her. "There's no time for this bullshit, and you know it! I asked you to get it done, you should have damned well done it!" His black eyes searched hers, boring into them like twin drills threatening to carve into her frontal lobe.

She met his stare and would not let herself look away, no matter how unnerving his glare. "Don't look at me like that! I'm not built for certain things!"

Karl whipped his denim jacket off and flung it on the ground. He wore a ratty black t-shirt underneath. It was a tour shirt for the band Danzig, complete with a smiling skull glowing across his chest. His arms were bloodied and torn up, just as he had described them. The dogs had put up quite a fight and gotten a few good gashes in on him. He shoved past her, and she watched him disappear. She stood by, her mind empty, and a small flicker of pride stirring within her having stuck up for herself. This was dashed to pieces when he reappeared in the church, the light of the blood moon filtering through the stained glass windows on either side and tattooing him with indecipherable shapes and images. It highlighted the gleam of wetness down the front of his shirt and across the underside of his hands. He was carrying what at first looked oddly enough like more sticks and branches.

Of course, not.

"Here they are," he stated, shoving past her. He placed the items inside the pot beside the branches. "Wasn't hard at all. I mean, you never went hunting with your daddy? Never? Shit, you're really not used to getting your hands dirty, are you? You sure you're up for this, babe?" He stood up, and Karl was very much the sight up close. He looked like he had just cut his way through a jungle of bodies with a machete and come out the other side.

"My father wouldn't have been able to handle a gun without blowing his face off. He was a drunk, remember? I told you."

Karl waved it off. "Neither here or there. What matters is we got what we need. Now, we drag Jack's sorry ass up here, and we carry in the dogs."

"Why *two* dogs?"

"Because this is trial and error, babe. We gotta make sure we got what we need for a second go if we fail the first time."

"What happens if we fail?"

"To us? Probably nothing. But … the dogs? Jack? Who the fuck knows, but I don't want to think about it. Let's accentuate the positive, huh?"

One of the dogs was awake, the other still groggy from the Xanax. Karl dragged them in one by one, the lively dog howling and growling and kicking at the confines of the burlap sack. He hauled the unconscious dog before him like an unwieldy sack of potatoes. He arranged both sacks o' dog on the left and right sides of the pot respectively. Jack barely fought when Karl and Stella dragged him up through the vestibule and bore him to the altar. They spilled him down before the pot of sacred items, all hanging dead arms and legs. He let out a *whoosh* sound, his lungs violently deflating.

Karl made to strike Jack, and the beaten man flinched pitifully. Karl laughed at him. "Now, I just got to bind the first doggie with some more twine. He's a big boy and a bit of a wild one. So, don't go running off anywhere, Jackie! Wait a second … where the hell you gonna go? With what legs? Your bones are nothing but chalk dust by now. Aren't they?"

"Karl—"

"Well, they are!" Karl kept on, playfully. He flew to the rustling burlap sack just as it turned over and spilled down off the top riser. He straddled the sack between his legs, blocking Stella's view of his struggle with animal.

The thing inside that sack looks a hell of a lot bigger than a big boy, *as Karl called it. It almost looks like he's got another human being knotted up inside.* Stella glanced down at Jack. She found Jack staring up at her. The look in his eyes hurt her heart, and she hated herself for it. Yet, there he lay, resembling an overgrown baby with blinkless eyes and simple, naked pleading in his eyes. They looked at one another. She could not tear her eyes away from him. She sensed this was the last time she would see this spark of life and personality in her husband's eyes ever again. From then on, as it had been explained to her by Karl, she would not see Jack as he was ever again after the ritual. The man's character, everything that made Jack who he was and shined through his big, brown irises, would be pressed back behind the eyeballs and another consciousness would fill his eyes and his stare. A terrible swap.

Stella almost apologized to him. She bit her tongue, holding it back. She sensed he was waiting for it. For her to intercede. She turned away from him, angling her body just enough to get her point across. *There's no stopping this.*

Karl's shoulders rose and fell, and he panted furiously. "Whoa, there doggie! *Whoa there!*" It sounded like he was trying to break a horse right there on the altar. He nearly toppled backward off his knees as he wrestled with the animal before him. The dogs front and back legs were tied together and jutted out on either side of Karl. She watched him nimbly wind another thick binding of the twine around the front and back limbs. Stella felt heartsick. The dog let out a quick series of angry barks in quick succession. Karl must have wound the duct tape around the animal's snout, for it wheezed and whimpered defeatedly then after. She heard Karl laugh, a mirthful belly-laugh she had only ever heard before from her father when he was deep in his cups and laughing at one of his own stupid jokes.

He is good at this. Manhandling an animal. Breaking its spirit. Muscling it. Someday, that dog will be me ...

He stood with the big dog in his arms. Karl was not a big man, more scrappy and tightly-wound. Coiled. He turned around with the beautiful brown Greyhound in his arms. The dog jostled and fought against him, wriggling its body about. The dog whined. "All right ... ah ... *shit!*" He looked at Stella, standing by with a washed-out look. "Stella, there's a pack of matches in my back pants pocket. Get it out and light the branches in the pot."

She snapped free of her rapidly descending thoughts. "Oh, right."

The dog stirred violently, forcing Karl to square his shoulders and plant his feet more solidly. Stella skirted the dog's taped muzzle and quickly

200

fished the book of matches out of Karl's chino's pocket. She hurried over to the pot, struck a match, stared at the flame as it winked at her, and touched it to a stem sprouting brittle leaves. The leaves caught instantly and flared with a fire which quickly began to eat through the contents of the pot.

Karl stepped up to the left side of the pot and set the dog down on the floor. It rustled about, its eyes rolling white. Black. White. It arched its back, and Karl placed his bootheel into the animal's back, steadying it.

"Stella, one more thing."

"What? What else?" *I want this over with or not at all!*

"You got a picture of this prick in your wallet?"

She had to think about it. "I … I think so." Stella took out her wallet and unsnapped its hasp. She thumbed through the plastic sleeves and found a miniature wedding picture of The Posts, only four years younger, yet two vastly different folks. She pulled it out of the sleeve and held it out to Karl for inspection.

"Nah, you gotta tear yourself out of the picture. It can only show him. Otherwise, something'll happen to you too!"

"What? Like *what*?"

"You wanna find out?"

"Well, all I know is you're giving me a lot of *I don't knows,* and it's starting to scare the hell out of me, Karl! Are you sure you know what you're doing? Because it's feeling more and more like we're playing with fire here!"

Karl looked at her, all humor having vanished from his features. "All right. Put it in the pot as-is, Stella. *Go right the fuck ahead!*"

"FINE!" she cried and without thinking anymore about it, Stella tore the bride away from the groom.

"Burn it."

She felt her breath hitch in her throat. She stepped forward, sighed, and pitched it into the flames. She could have sworn she heard Jack start to cry but when she looked at him, his eyes were dry and wide and staring, ready for death. Submissive.

Things happened very fast from then on. One minute Karl said it was time to begin, and the next he gathered the rustling, wriggling Greyhound back up into his arms. Stella's hand went to her quivering lips. Her eyes welled up as she looked on, her stomach sick and excited at the same time. Karl struggled with the animal in his arms but managed somehow to turn it around so it was facing downward. "Look! Dammit, Jack! Stella, hold him still! I dunno how the fuck he's even moving around with broken arms and legs! *Hold him still!*" Stella went to Jack. There was no mistaking his tears or blubbering for anything other than weeping now. She somehow managed to hunker down beside her husband and pin his shoulders against the floor of the altar.

"BITCH! YOU BITCH! YOU FUCKING BITCH! HOW COULD YOU? BIIITCH!"

To think I felt sorry for this bastard.

Stella dug her fingernails into the divots between Jack's chest and shoulders. He screamed.

Karl walked over Jack with the straining, whining Greyhound in his arms. Then, he squatted down. The Greyhound descended. Karl aligned the animal's body with Jack's upper body. The dog kicked its tied legs downward at Jack's abdomen and drove the wind out of him. Stella tried to turn away while bracing Jack in place. It didn't work. She had no choice but to look on, up close and intensely personal. Karl gripped the dog's muzzled snout and angled its face downward until Jack and the Greyhound were quite literally eye-to-eye. Jack turned his head away.

"Turn it back around, Stella! Hold his fucking face if you have to!"

She grabbed on to his ears and steered his head back around.

Karl leaned in and did just as he had with Betsy and the fat enforcer in a black jogging suit back at the house. He spoke soundlessly into the animal's ear. Stella was thankful to not have heard a syllable of it.

The Greyhound's long, lean body wrenched itself upward. The arch of its back disappeared into a perfect and painful line as the animal appeared to seize into this position. Karl spoke into the animal's left ear. Then, the right. He alternated in this way. Left. Right. The Greyhound looked like it was concentrating completely on Karl's words. Stella looked down at Jack. He had squeezed his eyes shut. A bloody line traced itself down the side of his face. He had bitten his tongue. When he opened his eyes, he looked up at Stella, yet somehow through her. He could not lock onto her. Jack gazed impossibly through her.

Jack barked up at her, his teeth snapping together with a crisp click like an icicle splintering against the sidewalk. It was by no means a poor imitation of a dog bark by a human.

It was thoroughly canine and utterly terrifying.

Stella heard a woman scream from what sounded to be a great distance. She only realized the scream was ripping upward and out of her throat when Karl himself let out a distressed squawk of sorts and fell back across Jack's dead legs. The Greyhound scrambled haphazardly about, trying fruitlessly to gain its feet which were bound in an inch of twine.

Until, they weren't.

The dog made a horrid sound like its heart was trying to rocket out of its chest. The twine around its back legs started to split, centimeter by precarious centimeter. It burst apart and the Greyhound kicked outward. It lifted its head, its gaze hooked jaggedly upon Stella. It studied her, black eyes crawling over her face, inch by inch, with a sense of horrid recognition before the dog produced a heart-ripping sound once more, and the tape around its snout split apart, still clinging to the small hairs of its snout.

"Oh Jesus! Oh God! Karl! KARL!"

"Stella, back away! Back. Away!" Karl crawled away like a lobster, retreating to the far left side of the altar where a statue of the Virgin Mary stared down in patient adoration.

Oh God please get me out of this, and I promise I will call this whole thing off!

Stella backed off in a lumbering crouch and hid herself behind the wooden front kneeler wall of the head pew. She hunkered there, shivering and trying to rein in her thoughts as they kept banging into one another. Her base, curious nature got the better of her, and she peered out from behind the kneeler wall.

She did not *want* to see. She *needed* to see, if for no other reason than to verify for herself the animal was not walking towards the front kneeler wall she hid behind.

It was not. The Greyhound had no regard or notion of Karl behind it or Stella hidden a few feet away.

The dog lay on its right side. Its whole body shuddered and spasmed as it worked its snout into its left flank. Tearing at itself, it would seem. The jerky motion of it reminded Stella of when Betsy had fleas one summer and could not keep from biting at her own fur for hours at a time, toiling in vain to free herself of the invisible biting bastards staked out beneath her luscious mat of white belly fur. Stella knew better, though. When she heard the same terrible tearing sound of something wet and slippery, she was painfully aware.

Brown Greyhound's snout flicked away from its side as if springloaded. A gaping, gleaming red maw of opened flesh winked at Stella. Then, a loop of intestine burst out of it and thumped on the floor of the altar. The dog clenched another half-foot of its own intestines between its bloodied teeth and with one snap of its head backward, it made its own gizzards disappear down its throat. Then, it hauled itself up onto its back legs while it worked on the twine around its front paws with its teeth. In no time, the animal freed itself.

It lingered there on the altar. It appeared deep in thought, sorting out the finer mysteries of existence when the animal's stomach dropped out of the opening it had torn away.

Stella screamed and screamed.

But it would not be over.

The dog turned towards the pew where Stella was hiding. She swiveled her head back around. This did not save her from hearing the padding of the animal's paws as they slogged along the rug. Closer and closer. She swore she could hear the animal's breath in her head, felt hot stink-breath of blood and gore break across the nap of her neck while she hid.

The dog stopped, its paws still and silent.

This moment held on like the last heartbreaking, tremulous note of a painful symphonic piece.

The dog cried out.

It did not bark. Its words were not well articulated, actually malformed in their delivery. But she understood them well enough, and a cold finger tapped its way up every bump of her spine.

Brown Greyhound shrieked, "Stellllllllaaaaaaaaaa ... you biiitch!" Then, it dropped where it was and bled out across the crusted altar rug.

Stella kept herself behind the safety of the wall. She couldn't bring herself to come out, to lay eyes on the aftermath of what the animal had done to itself. It had cursed her. In a human voice, albeit impeded. She had heard her husband bark as convincingly as any dog she had ever heard or come across. The dog had called her by name. *Cursed me!* She believed in the power of such a curse. This was an ungodly, unnatural act, and it would have consequences. The whole damned thing was already cursed, and those involved. She knew it.

"You all right?" Karl stood over her, his hand extended down to her. "I knew this would happen."

"You ... *knew?*" Stella gasped. "You knew *what?*"

"I ... well, I told you. That's why I grabbed two dogs. Trial and error, remember?" Karl spoke like a child trying to reason with his mother to avoid punishment. He must have realized how petulant he sounded because Karl shed the tone instantly, favoring his previous headstrong demeanor. "Take my hand, will ya'? We just gotta try again. Now we know what we can expect. It's a helluva lot different with a dog than with your kitty Betsy. Dogs got wolves in them. And the wolf jumps right into the driver's seat as soon as we give it room to. Now we know—"

"Fuck you, Karl!" Stella cried, pulling herself up by way of the low wooden wall before her. "This ends right now!"

"What?"

"I can't *believe* I ever took it this far with you! I need to have my damned head examined!"

"You already done that! And lot of good it done you! We are not *done!* What do you think this is? You're a wanted woman!"

"No more than you're a wanted man!" Stella said, pushing past him out of the pew. "You're out on parole, asshole! They want you back a hell of a lot more than they want me. I can claim self-defense with Jack, and they'll take pity on me." Stella stalked down the center aisle of the church, her shouts ringing off the wood and alabaster of the church sanctum.

"Self-*defense?* You shitting me? It's one thing to knock him down the stairs when he came after you, but it's another damned thing to break all the bones in his arms and legs! Some seriously fucked-up, Biblical shit there!"

Stella stopped but did not turn around. "You made me do it!"

"You were *dying to do it,* Stella! Don't you lie to yourself, but lie to me all you want! Just like you're *dying for* THIS!"

"Karl—"

"But don't you worry!" Karl said, his voice choked with saccharine. "I'll take care of the whole thing. You go hide yourself away from the cruelness of nature. Go sleep in the car for all I give a shit! Have a nice rest! I'll do the man's work, and you dream your pretty little dreams! I'll come get you when we're in business, Stell! Nighty-fucking-night!"

She stood, lingering like someone stranded on a strip of land separating two deep, dark crevasses dropping off into nothingness. The church was cold, but she felt her blouse sticking to her chest with a dampness that had also accumulated across her brow. She thought of running, or taking the car. She would need the keys, and there were no keys as the car had been hotwired and stolen in the dead of night. She was *wanted*, and there could be no explaining the cruel and calculated way Jack's body had been broken. She could take a step back towards Karl or closer to the vestibule of the church. Either way, Stella found she would take a fall. She could plummet and perhaps her body would strike bottom with a great splash and explosion. Or she could drop, on and on further into a despairing state which would not allow her the grace of death and unconsciousness and peace.

In the end, Stella strode towards the vestibule. Before she passed through the doors, Karl began to whistle just loudly enough to be heard.

He was whistling "Inna-Gadda-Da-Vida." A great shudder took hold of Stella and it did not let go of her until she had safely shut herself up inside the stolen car outside and zippered her coat up just below the supple curve of her throat.

Karl had left the two wires he touched together to hotwire the car poking out from underneath the wheel. It was easy enough for Stella to bind them together, and the car thrummed to life after a brief, wheezing instant by which she held her breath and prayed. There was a robotic quality to her prayerful intent, and she felt like she were praying to a God she had just struck across the face. She switched the heat to max and opened all the front vents wide. She cranked the driver's seat back and relished the hot wind breaking across the bridge of her nose while she shut her eyes. It wasn't long before she stopped shivering inside the layers of clothing. Then, she felt her mind unclenching and lightening so her previously feverish thoughts stretched out into more of an easy, free-association of lingering thoughts and words and feelings. Surprisingly, the horrors she had seen back at her house and inside the church receded further back into the corners of her mind. Sleep stole over her.

At one point she snapped to, her upper body lurching in a myoclonic jerking motion. The images of what had frightened her hung in her mind like a negative of a photograph, slowly fading away. Karl stalking her through the woods nearby, ducking behind trees and parting bushes to leer at her while she ran from him. His head gone, replaced by the head of the Greyhound, which had eaten itself to death. Greyhounds always struck her as an anomaly, with their decidedly human-looking head, skinny bodies, and sometimes human mannerisms. The particular breed spooked Stella, and she wondered as she passed back into sleep if she had ever confided this information to Karl and he had decided to use it against her by choosing a Greyhound.

Nope, Stella. You're conversations with him during the prison visits mostly consisted of double-entendres because the two of you were so desperate to fuck.

The second time she slipped into a deeper rest, her eyes flitted over the digital clock readout in the dash. It floated before her, disembodied in the darkness. 1:17 a.m. She fell asleep, dreaming of climbing trees as an eight-year-old tomboy, with skinned knees and no hint of the mental illness which would come to cripple her during her late teens. Such a carefree time. A bee flew down her throat one summer day while she was picking tomatoes with her grandmother in their garden. Her grandfather made her drink a glass of vinegar to try and drive it out. The bee stung her stomach before it must have succumbed to her stomach acid, a self-preserving physiological response. Oh the pain of that bee as it lanced her stomach lining.

"Epic fuck-ing fail."

"*Whuh?*" Stella mumbled, clawing her way up and out of the cob-

206

webbed tunnel of sleep. She turned towards the sound of his voice, her eyes unfocused. She saw the outline of him, the lean and tight frame.

Karl had his arms crossed over his chest, normally sunken but bulbous beneath his bulky denim jacket lined in sheep's fur.

"The second dog," he said. "Must've had a heart-attack. Dropped dead right afterward. Right there on the fuckin' altar."

"Oh," Stella said, wishing she were still asleep.

"Yeah," Karl said. "It was a smaller dog than the Greyhound. Female. English Setter, I think. Body prob'ly couldn't take it." He turned himself towards the window, away from Stella. "Fuck it. Tomorrow … maybe we think a second time about the whole thing."

"Yes?"

"Yeah," he grumbled, shrugging his shoulders. "But I'm killing Jack. I earned it. You can watch."

40. "WHERE ARE THEY NOW?"

Will's dreams were strange, and he awoke wound round and round in his bed sheets. The stiff, overstarched quilting lay in a pile on the floor next to the bed. He had woken up many times in the night to fool with the thermostat in the room because his body temperature seemed to fluctuate from cold to burning, seemingly in accordance with each new transition into another, more bizarre dream. They were not quite nightmares. These were dreams which bore a stitch of queerness just noticeable enough to be tugged on and pulled at, until the normalcy of the dream itself came unraveled. By morning, of course, it didn't matter he couldn't recall specific details of what he had dreamt about. Just snatches of things circling his mind as he lay there in the darkness of his hotel room. The heavy drapes were pulled, but the nightstand clock showed it to be well past nine in the morning.

I had a sex dream with Mina, Claire, and I. All scrabbling and grabbing arms and legs. I do remember Danforth was there, too. But she was more of a referee, calling out the word foul *every so often for whatever reason.*

Will lay there thinking about what else had been especially unsettling about the dream with the two main women in his life. What started out as a tangle of arms and legs eventually turned to disembodied limbs crawling and writhing overtop of one another while Will, Mina, and Claire stood

207

beside the bed watching with a detached curiosity. Detached limbs, greased and slithering like pale serpents whipped into frenzy.

Will unwound himself from the sheets and slipped off the king-size bed. He sensed stickiness around his groin, extending down his legs. His bottoms stuck to him and he was shocked to find his dream last night, the one he remembered more vividly than the others, had been *wet*. *Christ, I haven't had one of those since I was nineteen!*

"Well, I'm just going to have to rock Mina's world when I get back," he said, massaging his jawline. "Of course, there'll be reason to celebrate if she says *Yes!*" There was no reason for her not to, other than the fact he did not fuck her nearly as much as a woman like Mina deserved to be. Smart, sassy, sexy, and poised.

This was the last day of Will's speaking tour. Claire had managed to arrange it so his final engagement and signing would serve and feel like a homecoming of sorts. Villanova University. Will obtained his Bachelor's and MFA from the university and they were proud beyond measure to be able to lay claim to their native son the likes of Will Bentley. He loved the college, and it never ceased to love him back, so to speak.

He was not in Philadelphia yet and wouldn't be boarding the United Airlines flight until 1 p.m. He was awake in Baltimore. Will had his morning planned already. He'd shower, an activity especially dire due to the state of his pajama bottoms. Then, he'd probably check in with Mina to see how she was, how the doggie was convalescing.

After a continental breakfast, Will was going to the firing range. He had passed one on the way to the Marriott in town with Claire. His brain bookmarked the place in his mind. He had oiled his gun the night before and dry-fired it a couple times to get the feel back.

He was peeling himself out of his bottoms when the phone rang, one of those clanging noises he thought died with the rotary phone. Claire or Mina. Will felt the shame of his dream scratch at his conscience as he snatched up the headset and greeted the caller.

"Will?"

Mina.

"Darling! Sunshine! How ya' livin'?"

"Somebody's in a good mood! I'm good! How are you?"

"Good. I'm good. Last day, then I'm coming home to you."

"I *know*. It's going well?"

"Off to a rocky start, like I said at first. But, then I made a friend. Another vet. And he's got this really cool service dog reminded me of Albie. He gave me just the kind of perspective I needed."

"Mind if I ask what you were so confused about?"

"Little heavy for a first-thing-in-the-morning talk."

"I'm okay with it."

"All right," Will said, scratching at his black tufts of hair standing up around the crown of his head. He started to pace without realizing. "The best way I can sum it up would be to say, in no uncertain terms, I am finished with the guilt and the lingering feeling I still have to *save people* and *deliver people from the bad* because I'm a soldier for life. I'm not a *soldier for life*. I *was* a soldier. I'm a writer now. And among all my pursuits, I just want to be a good man."

"You're right," Mina said. "This is peace time. I'm glad you finally let yourself go about this. You lived it. Now it's your job to spread the word about the heroics you saw while you were over there. To shed light on the exploits of the good men and women who you were there with and didn't come back. You're telling their story. It's your job now to *report back*. Not to look for another fight locally or wherever you see the slightest injustice."

Mina always had this keen, enviable talent for augmenting what were Will's thoughts and turning them into something more profound. It was why he never *dared* send out his manuscript to his editor until she went over it with her red marker at least three times. *Never.*

"And I've decided the only people I care to protect or fight for is my family. You. Albie. Even Claire."

"That makes me so happy," she said, then paused. "So I did the interview yesterday afternoon with the *Inquirer*."

"And?"

"Amanda Somers was really nice. She knew which things to stay away from. She read me very well, and absolutely fell in love with Albie."

"That's great! When should I be looking for it?"

"It's online. Right now, if you want. I think you'll be happy with it."

"I have no doubt."

"They used the picture of Alberta and I on the sofa in the living room. I had a feeling Amanda had her heart set on the one I hated. I didn't protest. She was really a cool chick, so …"

"Babe?" He heard the sudden trepidation in her voice. It baffled and unnerved him all at once. "Everything okay? Everything *else?*"

"Oh … yeah, yes. Nothing to worry about."

"But?"

"Danforth told me there was an issue with Albie last night. I couldn't stay over last night because I got hung up with store inventory. Albie had an accident in her bed. A couple of them. She was doing the whining thing in

209

her sleep she did when you first brought her home. Sounded like crying. Just like you described it."

"Is she okay?" Will felt his intestines start to constrict.

"Yeah," Mina said. "Danforth said she cleaned her up and took her out. Albie wasn't having any middle-of-the-night stroll like she used to so they went back home. She barked up a storm. But Danforth said she would keep an especially close eye on our baby all day today. Apparently, when Danforth woke up, she found Albie lying on the cold hardwood floor next to her nice, warm doggie bed."

"Well, it's understandable if she just pooped and peed in it."

"No, Danforth swapped out her pink soiled bed for the other one. Just as comfortable. But I remember Albie also slept in the cold corner of your bedroom when you first brought her home. That's two reversions back to the way she was before."

Will harbored no illusion about the fact Albie would have these flashbacks every so often, and that was just the way it would be. What hurt was he was not the one to comfort her last night. Of course, he hadn't left her with a complete stranger. Danforth had become like one of the family. *Home by tonight, then I'm not leaving for a while!* "She's better today, though?"

"Yeah," Mina said. "Like nothing ever happened. She woke up with the sun and they had their time in the wave pool. Later, they'll have their walk and some more exercises in the garage."

"That's good. Nice to know our money is paying for what it should."

"Will, you cannot blame Danforth for what happened last night. Our Albie is working through some things and if you ask me, Danforth is the best thing to happen to our baby post-coma. I know you agree."

"I do."

"Good. Then I'll let you go. Call me at the store when you land in Philly. And remember I love you."

"Love you."

"Oh, and *please* tell Claire I love her too, and we will *all* get through this with her!"

"All right."

"Much love!"

Disconnect.

Will took a quick shower, spending most of it with the hard pressure jets hammering the back of his knotted neck. The water worked some of the kinks out and by the time he was dressed again, in a Villanova sweatshirt and blue Levis, Will felt like a much younger man. He switched on the flatscreen, tuned it to a twenty-four hour news station, muted it (which Mina

210

never understood but accepted as one of his quirks), and opened his laptop. He Googled his way to the *Philadelphia Inquirer* home page. The image of his lovely Mina stirred an equal measure of pride and horniness within him. Mina sat with her bare feet up on the comfy beige sofa as she nuzzled into Albie beside her, with her eyes dancing and mouth open in what was clearly a playful laugh. The cover photo was at the top of the page, its headline: **GETTING ON: ALBERTA THE "MIRACLE DOG"AT HOME WITH HER FAMILY!** Even Albie appeared to be smiling at the camera. Will was one of those people who believed dogs can smile, and this seemed to bolster his belief all the more. He touched the screen and smiled to himself. *How I love these two! One more day!*

He started to read. By the time he finished the interview, Will was wiping tears from his eyes and nodding to himself. Mina had done him proud and told their story as if she had been the one to charge into that church two months ago and discovered a virtual *mouth of Hell*. She was there for the aftermath, which was what the article seemed to concern itself with exclusively. The interview was about moving forward, upward and onward. It was good.

Sergeant Karns stirred within him and spoke up in a cool, groggy but nevertheless assured tone.

Fools smile more, and they die easy! Remember that! Wipe your eyes and let's get to the range!

41. THE RACK

Karl slept in fitful stops and starts, but he did not dream. He couldn't remember the last time he had. It was like the part of his brain that used to provide him with such nightly delusions and unconscious delicacies had broken or wound down like an old transmission. When he was a boy, he dreamt so vividly it was often hard to tell when they ended and his waking life began. In the two years leading up to his crimes, Karl could remember how this seamlessness became so complete for him, he started to actively work on carrying over the events from these dreams into his waking life. Most people would have called the dreams Karl had "nightmares," but not him. The visions of mutilated animals. The mock poses and the puppet shows starring countless dead dogs and cats animatedly acting out strange, detached stories and their legs working while the death stood in their eyes, milky and distant. Karl carried it all over from the dream realm into his waking life. *I did a pretty damned thorough job of it, if I should say so my damn self!*

He had tried to explain this to his lawyer. The court-appointed psychiatrist who had done a comprehensive markup of his mental state. He had even tried to explain it to the judge. His counsel had thought if he tried to explain the way he had come to killing and posing all of those neighborhood pets in the woods behind his home, there was no way he wouldn't escape prison in favor of a lifelong stay in a mental institution.

The thing of it was, the things he had done to his neighbor's "property," as their pets were deemed, constituted a felony in the state of Pennsylvania. Jail time was a sure thing in the end.

He hadn't slept longer than three hours for the last five years. Everything around him when he was awake had taken on a permanently soft, cottony effervescence along the edges. He spent every day in a waking fog which could not be remedied. He tried and tried to get used to this as well, but that morning it not only bothered him especially, it made it damned difficult to drive the fucking crappy Cutlass down the road, let alone into town.

He had done much better with the car last night. This morning, Karl felt like he could barely see a car length in front of him as he crawled down the mostly empty side streets leading into the next town over, some small village called Crestfall Township. Stella could only offer Karl a skeletal breakdown of what Crestfall was like. Sleepy or bustling? Early risers or midnight oil burners? In the end, Karl told her in as soft and solemn a voice as he could muster, she would have to get out of the Cutlass and sleep off the rest of the morning in the church.

"I gotta run into Crestfall and find a convenience store."

He also asked her for her cell phone.

"You need to call someone?" Stella had asked him, arming away a big yawn that contorted the bottom half of her face into something monstrous. "Who?"

"You got internet on it, right?" Karl asked, a hint of impatience having crept into his tone. "I need to check the local news. See if we made the paper. If our pictures or anything is on the wire, we'll have to leave sooner than later."

Stella hesitated, then her fatigue won out. "All right. You know how to access it?"

Dammit, I don't. "Show me."

"Hand me my purse on the seat."

He did, and Stella rummaged around until her fist hit the bottom and she snatched the iPhone out. She ran Karl through a quick and cursory tutorial of how to access Safari and then Yahoo, her search engine of preference. Karl smiled up at her winsomely, took the cell out of her hands, and cranked the Cutlass out of park.

"Give us a kiss, Stell." She leaned down and pecked his cheek, roughened by the coarse black hairs blooming there.

Karl had eased the Cutlass from behind the church, then brought it to a stop beside the cement pillars that had failed to block their entry into the driveway the night before. He nosed forward a bit, craned his neck to look right and left. The crossroad was empty. Saturday morning, he had expected more traffic than this.

Once the white clavicle spire of the abandoned church slid out of view in his rear mirror, Karl slowed his speed down from twenty-five to a fifteen-mile-per-hour crawl. Switching his attention between the road before him and the cell phone in his right hand, Karl thumbed open the Phone-Dial option. He punched in a number from memory, and when he was certain he could speed up again without feeling distracted Karl gave it some more gas, and the Cutlass lurched forward, devouring a good bit of road quickly.

The phone rang seven times before the roughhewn, hard-knuckled voice of the halfway house's coordinator came on, causing Karl to revert to what was his impression of a Boston Southie accent. "Yeah, Dean-o," Karl said. "George Sira-vo cah-lling for Henry Bahst-wick."

"I'll get 'im," Dean Dougherty said, in his usual disinterested way. *Dean-o sounds a bit preoccupied this morning. Might have something to do with the fact the shepherd seems to have misplaced one of his lambs.*

Henry came on, sounding as tired as Stella had moments before. "I didn't think I had to check in with you on Saturdays."

Karl smiled, continuing his vocal impersonation of Henry's parole officer, the nasally and rather nerdy George Siravo. "Ya' offend me in a dream, ya' bettah' wake ah-p and apah-logize, Bahst-wick. I call whenevah' it suits me!" Karl had only ever met Henry Bostwick's P.O. once when he stopped over to the house to meet with the ex-convict charge. Yet, the Southie accent seemed to have stuck in Karl's mind ever since, the New England inflection of it. Karl liked it. He practiced it, not knowing why until that moment on Stella's cell phone.

What's the shit called?

Sinner-nicity? I think.

"Uhm … sorry—"

"Asshole, it's *Karl!* Update on the buried treasure you, me, and Bluto talked about a while back. Turns out **X** still marks the spot, like I suspected.

213

Pretend you're talking to Beantown George and just listen. Everything's changed ..."

By the time he rolled the Cutlass carefully onto Maple Street, a long avenue just beyond the handsome wooden sign on the roadside announcing his arrival inside Crestfall Township (Population: 1,428-Businesses Welcome!), Karl had a migraine pulsing behind his right eye. A *concentration headache.* He rubbed at it, trying to ease the pain. This only exacerbated it. The light of a pale, late-Fall sunrise hurt his vision. He was so happy to find the Crestfall Convenience store sign when it slid into view, along the right side of what was a strip of shops. Most of them privately owned and operated. He pulled off, his hand over his right eye to shield it from the sun-glare slashing across the windshield. He eased into a spot and sat there for a minute or two, breathing shallowly and trying to call the pain in his head off. To slow it. To stop it by sheer will of the mind. *Ignore the nerve-endings. Just ... go away.*

Karl opened his door right into the passenger side of the silver Mini Wagon beside him. It clanged and glanced off the other car, eliciting something of a shout from Karl. He hadn't opened his door but an inch and *whammo!* Then, he realized he had pulled his Cutlass in way too close for comfort next to the Mini Wagon.

"Fuck a duck! *Fuck. A. Duck!*" He pulled back out of his spot and sidled back in, leaving a foot of clearance on his side. "Fuck!" he cried, staring out at the brown dimple his car door had carved into the Mini Wagon's silver passenger door.

Whatever you do, do not *give their car more than a casual glance if anything when you get out!* He knew the rules. The second time around, Karl eased his door open and stepped out into the sharp slice of a cold wind as it goosed him around the throat and slapped him across the face. He shivered in spite of himself and clawed at the sheepskin collar of his denim jacket, yanking it up to his chin. Karl's turkey neck became swallowed up in the plush of cottony softness.

Karl shoved into the store and towards the nearest aisle, its shelves choked with canned goods and packages of bottled spring water. He surged forward and skirted around the back corner into the next aisle.

He so happened to slip into the pharmaceutical aisle next. He grabbed two boxes of Benadryl tablets. Stella's Xanax stash was not gone as he had intimated to her, but it was low. Now he had no choice but to buy something over the counter causing marked drowsiness. Karl gathered gauze pads, a box of Band-Aids, antiseptic (all to treat the scratches up his arms from the dogs last night), and a twenty-pack of wire-hangers. On his way up to the register, he spotted a rack of ski caps, colorful and assorted. He quickly rummaged through them with one hand and located two caps which converted into masks. He grabbed a navy one and a beige one, unmindful of the colors.

He slunk out of Aisle Seven with his neck bent, his head down. Awkwardly hugging the assorted items against his narrow chest, he lunged towards the checkout to find he had two people in front of him. He saw the two customers in front of him had two to three items. This would go quickly and quietly.

One customer sailed out the door on a sea of *thank-you* and *come again* from the cashier before she turned her attention to the next customer, a quiet and conservative little man with a bad salt-and-pepper combover and swishy eyes.

In a matter of moments, the comb-over man hobbled away from the register with his items already bagged and dangling from his short, stubby right hand. Karl stepped up to the counter, a friendly enough grin on his face. He made sure not to let his smile dip down into a slant like it tended to do without his realizing.

"Hiya–"

He was just about to spill his items across the countertop separating him from the clerk when the newspaper rack snagged his attention and did not let go. The front page of the *Philadelphia Inquirer* Weekend Edition pictured a big, friendly-looking German Shepherd sitting oddly prim on a sofa next to a pretty, dark haired young woman with a blonde streak in her hair that framed her pale, heart-shaped face.

Karl's heart sped up when he read the headline - *Where Are They Now? Comstock's Four-Legged Hero Saved a Priest Six Months Ago and Nearly Gave Her Life for It-But Now She's Back and BETTER THAN EVER!*

He snagged the newspaper and riffled through it until he came to the first page of the *Where Are They Now?* article.

He barely heard the chorus of clearing throats behind him from the people in line.

"Un-be-*leev*able!" a woman whined.

Karl's eyes skipped and scanned the columns of words, stopping on such clipped phrases as "abused" and "rescue dog from Fallujah" and "War-Dog" and "coma" and, most importantly "rapidly on-the-mend." When Karl saw that last one, it felt like the tumblers in a lock falling into place. The door clicked open.

"SIR!"

Karl tore his eyes away from the print and lowered the paper to find the twenty-something cashier gazing at him expectantly. His other items were already rung and bagged. *Did this little drink of water just raise her voice to me? Hell, I ain't even mad. God bless her, and the devil keep her.* He swallowed a lump the size of a jawbreaker down and laid the newspaper down as well. He couldn't possibly yell when things had taken such a weird and wonderful turn for the better in an instant.

"This too. Didn't mean to gum up the works here." He fumbled cash out of Stella's purse and handed a twenty over. "You're really quick back there with the ringing and the … the bagging … all by yourself!"

"Have a nice day, sir." The cashier held the bags out to him, her other hand blooming with change in bills. Her smile circled around pleasantry, not quite finding it.

Karl nodded. He felt all eyes on him, even if the lot of them belonged to meandering and henpecking mothers and elderly, ornery folks from the unfortunately-named Crestfall. He slunk away from the counter, stuffing the change of bills down into his chino pockets.

The sun was high and bright, a floodlight he visored his eyes against as he shuffled back around the driver's side of the stolen Cutlass.

In his mind, he was Karl the Kreep again (that's how they had spelled his nickname on the bathroom stall walls and etched it into the windows of the first floor just outside the gym entrance). Karl the Kreep was not always The Kreep. Other kids at Wilson Junior High started calling him that after the one day in Biology Class when he, along with three other girls, worked on dissecting a cat. He had shied away from the knife, and after the other girls poked casual fun at him for it, the smallest and spunkiest girl cut right down the center of the fat tabby's stomach. The sound of the scalpel digging in had made a slight popping noise Karl thought only he had heard. Then, the intestines and other surrounding organs peeked out at him from the slitted eye of the incision, and Karl felt the strange, sudden stab and spasm around the base of his spinal column. The crotch of his pants was tented, and he hadn't even realized it. Then his crotch was sticky and wet, a dark stain spreading just below the zipper. He had tried to hold it in, but the moan could not be contained, and the girls heard it, and they saw his pants, and they screamed and fled to the other side of the lab where the teacher, Mrs. Apfelbaum, stood with an expression of sheer bafflement. Then, the whole class was looking his way, some of them laughing and others muted by their own disgust.

Friend, you are not supposed to be free. You know this! Go back and tell them they made a mistake and to throw away the key this time.

Karl stood next to the stolen car for much longer than expected.

When he snapped to again, he found himself staring through the front plate glass window of the convenience store. The people in line were staring back out at him. *Karl the Kreep, right? You know my name? Maybe I know some of your names too. Bitches! Clucking hens! Sooner or later, the farmer's gonna come for you an he's gonna cut off your beaks, and then you won't be looking at me no more. You'll be waiting for your severed head to hit the dirt. One by one.*

He climbed inside the car and slammed the door shut. He snuck one more sidelong glance at the people inside. He felt his sideways smile come across his lips, only this time he embraced it.

Karl was also just fine with reversing his car out of the spot at such a haphazard angle the left side of his car smashed into the passenger side door of the SUV. He kept reversing and his left fender scraped a straight, brown scar across the silver finish of the SUV. Once clear, Karl gunned it. From the corner of his eye, he saw one of the women in line now running out into the street behind him shouting at him. Her words muted. Mouth a black hole of anger and confusion.

He hit fifty-miles-an-hour and held the needle there all the way back to Comstock.

42. UNTIL IT ALL MELTS AWAY

Tewk's Sporting Goods and Firing Range was empty aside from its proprietor and his son when Will Bentley strode in at 10 a.m. and politely asked for a shooting booth in the back. Bob Tewk, a soft-spoken and slender black man with the kind of casual accent comparable to a Southern summer afternoon, grabbed a pair of eye guards and earplugs and led him into the back bowels of the store, where the bright light deadened into a dim, nightclub murk, and the walls were big bricks painted the cold color of slate. Tewk asked Will if he had his own weapon. Will did.

"Legal firearm?" Tewk asked. "Standard clips?" Will said it was. "You wanna try anything out in the store you give a holler, and I'll have my boy bring it into you directly."

Will nodded. He liked Tewk, the kind of guy anyone could take an immediate liking to. But he wanted nothing more in that moment than for Bob Tewk to leave him be.

Tewks put out his hand to shake. Will offered the old man a *fist bump* and smiled. Tewk laughed. "What do you call it? Seems like a teenage thing."

"I-I … damned if I know," Will said. "Spur of the moment."

"Well, I'll take it. Long as it don't mean *go fuck yourself* in some secret sign language." Tewk wandered out of the range.

Will stepped up into Booth Five in the dead center of the range. He laid down the small cloth satchel, unsnapped it, and rolled it open to reveal a greased and beckoning Glock. He slid the box of bullets out of their pocket divider and arranged them beside the gun. His breathing hitched in his chest. His hands slipped and jolted as he handled the weapon. He had to put it down again. Will braced himself on the shelf before him at waist level and lowered the upper half of his body down so he looked more like someone stretching or meditating before a 6K Marathon rather than man about to fire a gun.

You've got ghosts, soldier. No doubt about it. They're all gathering around you right now, and they're going to try and fuck with you and throw off your shooting eye because they want to be heard. But not for the reason you think. They're here to forgive *you, soldier. There will be ghosts at first. Just hear 'em out. It's all ghosts ever really want from the living anyhow, only we scare folks too easily, and we don't get the point until maybe the fourth or the fifth haunting. You're going to get the point right here and now, and they're going to leave you alone after this. As long as they're confident you get their point, they'll leave you be from here on out. Don't be afraid. The shaking in your hands is only them shaking your hand in* hello. *Now, load your weapon, soldier.*

Will traced the barrel slowly with his index fingertip. His hand shuddered, and his finger slipped down the side of the gun, stabbing down hard on the canvas wrapping beneath it. He was determined to do this, and without the guidance of a bunch of miniscule fucking shrapnel stuck deep down in the flesh of his left cheek. He bit his lip, grabbed up the gun, and hammered the clip into place with the flat of his palm. The calm and coolness of the motion reverberated through him like a note through a tuning fork.

From the entryway, Tewk called to him. "You all right in there? Need help?"

"Nope, I'm good! Thanks!"

"It's just I ain't heard no firing at all, and you been back there ten minutes. You meditating?"

"Don't know how," Will said. He couldn't help but smile.

"Some guys come in here, and they do this meditational thing before they get to firing. Like it's some kind of yoga studio. I dunno. Let me know if the button sticks when you wanna bring in the target."

Will said he would.

Well, you know the drill. Breathe in–squeeze the trigger slowly while breathing out.

"I know, you pushy fuck," Will muttered and lined up his sight with the head of the paper target twenty-fiver meters down the alley. "I know."

No, you don't, soldier ...

The paper target was not paper at all, but a woman backlit in red. The lighting behind it framed her black mass in red, and drew him out of his body and back to the night in the church. When the woman shouted at him, he knew her by the scratch of her voice. *"Don't shoot, Will!"* Lois Tillman. One of the parishioners there that night. Lois had brought garden shears with her, and Will had shot her through the left thigh moments before those sharpened steel blades would have scissored into the side of his head. Lois was a greeter at the Yancy Supermarket at the intersection of Third Avenue and Cleave's Mills Road. Lois was the only elderly person there. Her grandchild Larisa went to the Bible School there, and so Lois must have assumed she had been among Father Bingham's victims. Later it would be determined, Father Bingham only had eyes for boys, but Lois had no idea back then She only knew her Larisa had trusted the priest, like the rest of them. Confessed their sins. Taken the Eucharist from his dirty hands. Shared the wine chalice with him every Good Friday.

One Saturday afternoon, Lois had brought Larisa into work with her, and Will walked in to the supermarket for a dozen bananas. Lois had stopped him at the entrance and lifted up Larisa to plant a little kiss on Will's cheek.

"That's how you treat a veteran, honey. Thank them whenever you can, darling." A sweet moment, and one Will held onto with kind recognition until the night Lois Tillman rose up from the shadows of the church pews, aiming to cut his skull in half with a pair of gardening shears. Then, he had shot her crotch away.

The target shuddered, the old woman shaking and the red outline framing her meager form like some gamma ray. The rail above his head thrummed to life. The target moved towards him. He hadn't pressed the button. She swept towards him. Lois Tillman. He stood there, eyes transfixed upon the old woman as her features came into view. Her hands were empty. At her sides. No gardening shears to be seen. Closer and closer. Will held his ground, gun aimed. She moved to within an inch of the Glock's barrel and stopped cold. Lois Tillman reached for him with her bare, flabby arms sticking out of her runner's jacket. "I forgive you, Will Bentley. You hear me? Someone had to stop us. We couldn't hold ourselves back. We. All. Forgive. You."

What do you make of it, soldier? You believe her?

The gun shook in Will's hands. The worst thing about the whole damned thing of it was, if he and Mina had a child of theirs under the care of Father Bingham and then the truth about the man had come out, who was to say he could not have ended up among the other murderous congregants with the weapon of *his* choice. This was something Will wrestled with ever since it happened. He had journaled about it, then burned the pages in the backyard firepit when Mina wasn't around. He had written down a few sentences and then scribbled them out so damned hard with the blunt point of his charcoal pencil, it tore clean through the page and four underneath. So this was unexpected, but not entirely unbidden by his previous actions.

In a way, Will wanted this *confrontation* of sorts. He wanted to be forgiven.

It was why he raised his gun and nodded at Lois until she retreated back into the recesses of the range. Then, she turned back into the paper target she had been. This lasted only for a few seconds.

The target paper then transformed into what first looked like a small, stooped child wrapped from neck to toe in black scarves. They wore a white kerchief over their small, birdlike skull, and it was knotted at their throat. The track above Will's head churned to life once more, but the small, stooped figure did not come to him nearly as quick as Lois Tillman had. They *crept.* Hobbled, even. As the overhead spotlights dappled their face, Will saw the deep grooves etched into its leathery hanging flesh. The slitted, onyx eyes with their eternal squint against the harsh Iraq sunlight. He couldn't see her hands, and it was this aspect of the small, stooped Iraqi woman which jogged his memory completely. He couldn't see her hands *back then* either, when she had come out of one of the many doorways on either side of Will and his platoon. They were sweeping a street in one of the Fallujah provinces and this old woman had appeared, her hands hidden under her black, flowing garments. The platoon's designated interpreter commanded the old woman to show them her hands. She started shaking but kept coming, just as the paper target continued towards Will. The interpreter repeated his warning, but she kept coming with her hand stuffed inside of the layering of black scarves over her heart. The soldier a few men back from Will started to panic.

"Do we shoot? Call it! Make the order—" and before the man had finished his rant, the soldier to Will's immediate left fired on the old woman. Will's trigger finger twitched in response to the gunfire, but he swore to this day he held his fire. *Or did I? I feel like I might have blocked it out. Attributed it to the man next to me. O'Reilly. Later on it had come up, and neither of us could recall.* The bullets drove her backward, laying her out flat

220

on her back. Her arms were spread wide in the sand on either side. The right held a grenade inside of it. Someone had secured it to her palm with a heavy layering of duct tape and staples driven right into the flesh. *It was not her idea.* The man they later smoked out of the room she had come out of was the one who deserved the rain of bullets. He had gotten it. It most certainly rained for him, as well.

But her?

The paper target fluttered, but Will saw only the old woman's crinkly brown eyes as they peeked out at him from beneath the white kerchief. Her cheeks gleamed lines of tears. She had not wanted to kill *anyone*. She stood an inch away from the nub of the Glock's barrel. She nodded, said in worn, broken English, "Forgive ... to ... you." Will lowered his gun and bent his head, the tears coming hard and fast. Unexpectedly.

This time, the paper target did not roll backward on the tracks in the ceiling. It fluttered there before him, and he heard the sound of the paper flapping, but how the target appeared to him was not only different, but downright dizzying all at once. He lowered his Glock and braced himself with one hand along the shelf before him, feeling nausea tickle his insides with a simple, white feather. The face of the old woman, of the target, turned into Sergeant Karns.

The old comrade's crystalline blue eyes sized him up from within the deep, lined caverns of their sockets. His lips were snarled, not in an aggressive way but just in a way simply belonging to who he was. When his mouth transformed into something of a grin, teeth yellowed from the cigars he favored as often as downtime in the desert would allow, Will couldn't help but smile back through a shimmer of tears.

"You couldn't have known about the girl on the bus, soldier. You couldn'ta known. For Lord's sake, *forgive yourself.* You don't need it from me. Means nothing from me," Karns said

Will nodded, wiped his tears away and sniffed at the air, still ripe with yesterday's cordite.

Sergeant Karns's face and body faded away from the target, leaving the simple white, body paper shape with its standard black outline for two arms, head and torso. Will reached up and pressed the button, sending the fluttering target back to the rear of the firing range. It glowed there in the darker recesses of the alley.

"All right," Will breathed.

Now, you know the drill. Breathe in with the lungs ...

Will lined up his sights, aiming for the heart of the target.

... and out with the finger–slowly–slowly.

The end of Will's Glock burned brighter than a Roman candle as he cut up the paper target. He did it through another fresh curtain of tears. He blinked them out of his eyes and emptied his barrel.

Then, he reloaded.

The tears were gone, already dried on his cheeks.

But, he didn't smile. *You don't smile when you're firing a weapon. It's like laughing at a burial.*

43. PENNSYLVANIA BREADCRUMBS

Rivells found Jones bent over a Macbook with a side garnish of scattered papers at his elbow when she met him in the back booth of the Denny's Diner. He raised a small mug of coffee to his lips, and when she slipped into the booth beside him Rivells found, much to her chagrin, a mug was waiting at her place along with a menu. She wore deep pockets under her eyes to match Jones'. *To think all this started with a knock on the door a couple days ago from a neighbor in my building.*

She slunk into her seat, offering Jones a fleeting smile.

Muttering over the brim of his raised coffee mug, Jones recoiled from the beverage. "Mine's cold and dead. Don't thank me yet until you tasted yours. I made them wait before bringing yours, but they must've gotten antsy because they set it down at your place a few minutes after mine."

"Doesn't matter," she said, hoisting her mug and sipping. The diner smelled of grease fires past and present, along with the cheap, over-applied perfume of the wait staff. The coffee tasted burnt, but lukewarm. When she set it down again, Rivells noticed she had sipped a mere inch shy of an imprint of lipstick. "It's fuel. Nothing more."

"Order something," Jones said, meeting her eyes before dropping his gaze back down to the glowing screen before him.

"Grabbed a bagel and scarfed it down on the way over."

A short, squat waitress, bulging in all the wrong places of the suffocating folds of her yellow and brown uniform, appeared at Rivells' elbow. She reached across and snatched up the menu. "Just coffee then?" Without waiting for a reply, the waitress disappeared.

Rivells shrugged. "You start calling the numbers?"

It took Jones a while to answer. When he did, he lowered his laptop screen closed. "Yeah," he said, sounding more like someone admitting to having told a white lie. "I've been researching the providers for each number. Got up something of a workable list here, but I anticipate a lot of pushback when I start making calls to them, asking for their names. As it stands now, the numbers we found inside the Bird Book are either deactivated or still in use but assigned to another person altogether. There's no way of knowing if the people who *do* pick up the phone are the victims and they're too scared to admit its them. We have to get their names, and we've got to get their new numbers." He scratched the back of his head, blew out a breath. "We have to get around the privacy agreements these women signed when they first got their cell phones."

"We have to warn them," Rivells said, her stomach rumbled. "We can compel the carriers to divulge the identities of the cell phone number owners. We have to find all of them. The carriers wouldn't want to obstruct what could very well prove to be a serial rapist case."

"A warrant's not going to get them to talk to us. The federal courts hit walls of obstruction when they tried to compel Apple to unlock a customer's cell phone after he committed an act of terrorism."

"It'll be hard," Rivells said. "Not impossible. We squeeze them. I'll be damned if this is going to be the thing that stops us." She saw their waitress scuttle past out the corner of her eye and flagged her down. She pointed at her coffee mug and winked at the woman. The waitress nodded stiffly before hurrying past at twice the speed as before. "District Attorney is a hawk. She'll make some calls, say all the right things to all the right people, strong-arm all the holdouts, and we could have our warrant within a couple hours."

"We don't have a couple of hours."

"Then, we start with running the photographs from the photo album through the facial recognition database. See what matches, if anything. While we're waiting for the warrant and the carrier's cooperation, we'll touch base with those whose identities we are aware of. Send some uniforms over to their houses. Question them. If necessary, round them up and store them in a safehouse until we've nabbed Jack Post, and the other two people of interest."

"Our couple may have already killed and dumped Post somewhere."

"Then, we're down to tracking the two. The only difference would be we'd be hunting for two murder suspects, instead of two kidnappers and an alleged serial rapist. Honestly, would it be so bad if they killed Post? Save the taxpayers a chunk of change if there were no trial for the bastard. No chance of walking on these charges, either."

"You can't think like that," Jones said. "As tempting as it is."

"It's not a matter of temptation. It's street justice. It's … Wild West."

"I heard that about you."

"Heard what?" But she knew. Her reputation preceded her, and she damned well knew it. She was not the least bit ashamed. There was simply no need. Her brown eyes twinkled.

"You're a bit of a cowboy with your methods. Your execution."

"*And?*" Rivells smiled, the first glimmer of one she had used since this whole thing started.

"*And* ... you love Spaghetti Westerns. Vintage Clint Eastwood. Sergio Leone behind the camera. *Hang 'Em High. The Good, the Bad, and the Ugly.*"

"It was a simpler time. Less red tape. More black-and-white scenarios. Horse theft. I have no problem rooting for Jack Post's death. Preferably, his execution."

The waitress swung around to their booth and laid a carb-heavy plate of bacon, scrambled eggs, and hashbrowns in front of Jones, but he didn't dig in. He sat there, staring at Rivells with something of fascination, like she was something preserved behind glass. Then, hastily, he set about slopping his hash browns with a heavy layering of ketchup. Jones didn't lift his eyes. "This ... this *approach* you take to cases ... it ever bite you back?"

"Not yet," Rivells said. "But if something were to happen in the midst of apprehending an especially nasty *perp*, it'd be worth it." *Of course, Mama would be turning over in her grave if I got fired without pension or leave!*

"Yeah, well," Jones said, a forkful of hash brown poised before his mouth "I have to say after having gotten one of Post's victims on the phone last night and talking to them ... I'm rooting for a slow and painful demise of the sonofabitch." He paused, then added. "The fact is, I learned a good deal more about Post when I talked to this person on the phone. This is a guy who needs to be put out of his misery. He's mentally defective. I don't know there's a word for guys like him. Their motivation. But it's strange as it is twisted."

"Tell me."

Jones chewed and swallowed, thoughtfully. His features hardened. "The woman's name *was* Hannah Shearing. Yeah, I said *was.* I called the cell phone number, and her husband answered. Guy named Walter. He told me everything, but he prefaced his story by telling me flat out his wife took her own life a few months ago. She hung herself out in the shed behind their house. According to her husband, Hannah was a bipolar depressive. Their marriage was ... he called it *challenging*, but he kept saying he loved her and never would have given up on her no matter how difficult things became for them. Hannah became promiscuous in the last year of their marriage, and Walter had his suspicions early on she was cheating on him with another man. Lots of hang-ups on the house phone. He found her side of the bed empty in the middle of the night and her cell phone gone from the nightstand. He found her pacing out on the back porch in the middle of the night on her phone talking to someone, and when he questioned her she flew off the handle and melted down, and he had no choice but to let it go before the neighbors called the police."

"Then Walter said it was like his wife had some kind of *grand epiphany,* and the next thing he knew Hannah was meeting with her therapist again after six months of refusing to go back. She started taking her pills again, and Walter thought she was right with the world. He thought they would make it through. Then he said he came home from work one day and found her in bed at two in the afternoon. She refused to get out of bed. Her arms were bruised, but she would not tell him what happened. She said she did it to herself. Walter knew it was impossible for her to have done it. But Hannah wouldn't tell him anything. She wouldn't get out of bed. No more therapy. No more pills. She cut herself off from the things which gave her back her life. Walter took a leave of absence from work because he was afraid to leave her home alone. When that ran out, he started talking to her about maybe going into a mental care facility. 'Just to hit the reset button is all', he told her. She seemed like she would do it until Walter found her hanging in the shed one morning. She did it while he was asleep. Walter said he tried to stay awake. He was afraid to go to sleep. He didn't know what to do. He turned himself into an insomniac, but even insomniacs eventually fold under the pressure to sleep. He did. And Hannah Shearing killed herself during that time."

Rivells had no idea she was holding onto the table leg so hard until she let go of it, and her knuckles cracked sharply. Her eyes burned, and she sniffed at the air, concentrating on holding back the tears of anger threatening to breach the corners of her eyelids. She felt her face, hot and stinging. Her blood pressure was up. It had jumped while she was listening to Jones. She imagined this faceless woman named Hannah dangling from a noose, the family lawnmower and maybe even some pool floats on the floor of the shed at her dead feet. Quickly, she shoved the image aside and brought herself back.

"Son of a bitch. We have to get him. Yesterday. *Dammit!* It's a mind-fuck with this guy! He fucks them in the brain, breaks them, and then leaves them to wilt."

"You're more on-point than you think," Jones said, shoving his plate away half-eaten. He had killed his own appetite.

"What do you mean?"

"She had a note pinned to her nightgown. In her handwriting. Red marker."

"What did it say?"

"Not much," Jones said, meeting her eyes unblinking. "'I'm a broken bird. Forget me.'"

"A broken *bird*?" She sat there, tasting the words on her tongue and disliking their flavor. They tasted salty. They also sounded vaguely familiar to her. This pairing of the two words. They meant something. *I have heard that phrase before.*

He motioned for the waitress and pantomimed signing a check in the air. Then, he looked at her again. "I already have a call into our staff psychiatrist. I want to get a psychological profile worked up on Jack Post. And I think this piece of the puzzle … those words … they'll tell us a helluva lot more about Post when our shrink hears about them. It smacks of something of a mental health term. I'm waiting for her call back—"

Rivells watched Jones suddenly flinch, like some unseen hornet just stung his inner thigh. Then, he was fumbling in his pocket under the table. "This could be her now. Although, it'd be a new record for her." He brought his cell phone up to his ear. "Yeah?"

I know those words. I know those words.

"No *shit!*" Jones cried. The waitress appeared beside their table, and Jones quickly asked to borrow her pen. "Give it to me," he said into his phone. The waitress obliged, and he immediately set to scrawling something on the back of one of the papers scattered at his elbow. Rivells could see it looked something like a plate number. The unique combo of letters and then numbers. "All right, thanks, Johnny-boy! This pans out, I'll make sure this ends up as a star in your jacket." Jones rang off, then quickly fumbled out his credit card and handed it over to the surprisingly patient waitress.

"Johnny-boy? Guess it wasn't *her* then?"

"No," Jones said, his big brown eyes dancing in his skull. "Officer John Whitaker. Comstock Police. Said a stolen Cutlass just had a hit and run incident in the next town over. Some guy pulled out of a parking spot in front of a grocery and sideswiped the SUV next to him. The lady tried to flag him down, but he sped off. In the direction of Comstock again. Curly dark hair. Scrawny."

"Our guy?"

"Fuck yes, *our guy*. He's back in Comstock. In a hurry about something, apparently. Time to box him inside the town limits."

"Unless he drove on through Comstock and kept going," Rivells said, hating to play the devil's advocate. But it was necessary.

"No, my gut tells me no."

"Why's that?"

"Because Stella Post wasn't in the car waiting for him. No one in the passenger. He was heading back to her. And I got a feeling she's hiding in plain sight. I got a feeling, and I trust that shit. It's never failed me."

Rivells nodded. Jones had a way of selling her on things without any substance behind them. She found herself trusting his gut as much as he did, but caution still gnawed at her gut like baby teeth.

"So we split the difference then. We change the APB to track the new license plate on the vehicle. Thirty-mile radius? And we work with the Comstock police to pinpoint each and every abandoned building, lot, forest, and open field. Every mousehole they could possibly cram into within Comstock limits. Comstock isn't a terribly large town, so there probably aren't many places to hide. That would make our job easier."

"The thing about a small town is nothing stays hidden for long."

Jones flung a wad of bills down onto the table for a tip, stuffed his laptop back into its leather tote, and stood. "Let's go follow some Pennsylvania Breadcrumbs."

44. SLINGS AND ARROWS

Stella knew she was dreaming but it did not deter her from moving into it. She dreamt she was walking through a dense forest. The canopy of naked, interwoven branches blocked any feel of sunshine or fickle, filtered rays from dropping down across the crown of her ginger-haired skull. She raised her tired eyes upwards, and a single raindrop tapped her between the eyebrows. Then, another and another, until she felt the odd and unexpected sensation of her sanity fissuring, and she dropped her gaze to the earthen floor made lumpy with scattered underbrush and uneven dirt. The forest reeked of damp and decay. The bottom hem of her white nightgown was dappled with mud that splashed up. Her feet were bare and squished down into the disgusting squelch of earth. Stella nearly stepped on it and would have if it hadn't cried out in profound alarm.

"Stella! It's me!" Jack's head protruded from the ground like some strange, talking mushroom. She made a strange, birdlike sound in her throat

227

at the sight of this. His face was slathered in mud so thick, none of his olive skin shone in his cheeks or forehead. Only his wide, chestnut eyes served to identify him for who he was.

"What are you doing down there?" Stella asked him. She gathered up the bottom of her gown and took a knee in the slushy mud next to Jack's head. He couldn't turn his head to look up at her directly, but answered with a vehemence typical of Jack's impatient demeanor.

"Nevermind! Dig me out! Dig me out, and we can go back home! We'll go home and play house! I'll be the doting husband, and you can be the wife who flits behind the curtains all day, watching the world pass you by outside day in and day out! Isn't that what you want? Then dig me out!"

"I want to start taking my pills again. I want to go back to Church. I want to start back up with my therapist." Stella said. She turned her face to the canopy, and her staring eyes caught raindrops. She blinked them back, annoyed. "I'll reap you. But this is how it's going to be, Jack! We forgive each other for what's happened so far?"

Jack laughed weakly. "I'll try really, really hard not to cut your throat while you sleep."

She laughed. "Not if I cut yours first."

With that, she began carving out the mud and bramble from around his head. She drove her fingers down into the ground and cupped the sludge, bringing it out until Jack told her to stop. By then, she had freed him down to where his neck ended and his shoulders spread.

"Now, pull on my head," he told her. "It's all right. Just ... pick me! That's all you need to do."

"Pick you?"

"Yes."

Stella hesitated, shrugged, and placed her hands on the back slope of his skull and the jut of his chin. She pulled upward. He screamed, and she felt the breath of it, hot and sticky against her wrist. She continued to wrench his head upward. She gritted her teeth. The long unused muscles along her upper arm writhed and danced. Then, she was falling backward with Jack's head in her hands. There was no body attached to the head. Long, grey tendrils of squirming snakes writhed and slid overtop of each other, attached to the flesh and bone of the opened chute of Jack's throat. They dangled as one living, shining, and hissing mass which, once freed from inside the ground, now began to separate. Stella lay sprawled back in the mud, still holding Jack's head in her heads. With a detached fascination, she could only watch in horror as the hundreds of snakes, fat and thin, dainty and imposing, suddenly formed a coat of slithering and slimy tendrils around

228

her upper body and down past her hips. Jack's head was still in her hands. She turned it around to ask it why. His eyes were eaten through to holes, his nose a triangular indentation, and his mouth jittering with the garter snake moving behind his lips. It shot out all at once, and its fangs sank into Stella's bottom lip–

"Baby! Baby! Wake up! Look what I got! Come on, now!" Somebody was shaking her by the shoulders. Her eyes sprang open to find not a face above her, but the front of a slightly crumpled newspaper cover seeming to dance before her eyes. The smell of excrement and urine came to her slowly, but when her senses returned to full capacity, she felt the vomit rise up her throat.

Stella barely recognized her own voice. "What … what's that horrible smell?"

"Well, now that's our fault," Karl said, his hand retracting the newspaper. "Jack must have had a couple accidents down in the cellar. We probably should've slapped a diaper on him. Bought a pack of Depends or something. Wasn't really taking his comfort into consideration. Neither were you, to be fair."

Now the abandoned church smelled like the remnants of incense, wood polish, and human waste. She rose slowly off the hard, unforgiving floor of the church altar. She gouged her fists into her sleep-worn eyes and tossed a foggy gaze all about the dimness. Karl was on his haunches beside her. He thrust the newspaper back at her and waited for her to retrieve it.

"Please … please give me a minute to—"

"What? You're awake now. You gotta see this. It's the answer."

Stella pulled herself up into a crossed leg position. She spread the paper across her lap and tried to focus her eyes on the image and words blazing across the front page. They swam in and out as floaters flecked her field of vision. "We should clean him. The smell is horrible."

Karl laughed grimly. "Not my area, lady. A wife's duty. But you'll have to step to it because we got some plans to execute. We gotta strike while the iron's hot. The man will be back soon, otherwise he woulda' done the interview himself. It says so in there. He'll be back today or tomorrow. Writer was probably speculating. But we gotta move, because we don't want him in the equation. Motherfucking ex-Marine. We don't need that."

"Marine … what? What are you talking about?"

Karl pinched the edge of the newspaper in her lap and shook it playfully. "Read it!"

Her eyes were watering from the stench. She breathed through her mouth and read the interview. The photograph of the big, friendly German

Shepherd sitting on a couch next to a strikingly pretty woman who looked like an art curator, judging by her hair and style of dress. Stella hated her on sight. The posh surroundings of the woman and her dog in the photograph warmed her blood, then brought it to boil. This was a woman Stella once thought she could have been, in another lifetime. Maybe with different parents than the ones she had. Two drunks who passed their own daughter like ships in the night and during the day as well. Stella once imagined when she graduated from high school leaving her hometown and her alcoholic parents. She had even saved a considerable amount of money in a Sanka can under her bed she planned to use for the first year's tuition to Bucks Community College. Then the can had disappeared when she went to find it one afternoon. She knew what happened to it when she saw the bottles of new, top-shelf alcohol arranged in one corner of the kitchen countertop. Already half-emptied, the lot of them. Then Jack had come along, and he promised her he would find a way to *put her through some technical school once their finances leveled out.* Stella looked at the caption beneath the photograph and tasted the blood in her mouth as she bit her tongue.

Mina Cohen. Mina? Really? As in Dracula's girlfriend *from the novel? I bet the bitch never even read* Dracula! *Doesn't even know where her name comes from! Bet she's never read anything heavier than* Redbook! *Mina ... and ... oh ... Alberta? Alberta the dog who lives in a big, beautiful house in Comstock, and probably eats scraps of filet-mignon mixed into her Alpo!*

She blinked down at the page. Much of it she had already known. She knew of Will Bentley and the dog who had been knocked into a coma. Why should it matter now? *Why?*

Karl bristled beside her. "That's our dog, Stell."

"What?"

"We gotta get our hands on that dog and press her into service. Look at her background. Born in a warzone? Traumatized? Tough existence. Memories probably still rattling around in her head like a couple of diseased pennies? There's a killer inside that big dog just waiting to be called out. That dog is the one!"

Stella could only sit there, staring at him. Karl's eyes were black opals, glittering madly inside his long, slightly bearded skull. His scrawny body jittered with energy.

"What? You want to kidnap this dog?"

"Mm-hmm?"

"*This* one? It's been to hell and back?"

"Yeah, because the thing about going to hell and back? You bring a little of it home with you, and that's what we'll use!"

230

The horror show of last evening's events bled back into her brain, and she felt even more nauseous than she was. She flung her arms around herself, desperately willing this sick feeling to cease. "To hurt a defenseless animal. It's … it's even worse than hurting a human being. Don't you feel it? How does it not affect you? What we did last night was … it was revolting!"

Karl pushed out his right cheek with his tongue and nodded slowly. "Okay," he said. "I see. You want some answers from me. And I think it's perfectly fair. You wanna know why I was able to do what I done to those animals back in the day. Those *poor, de-fenseless* household pets—"

"Karl—"

"Shut up! I'll tell you because I can't stand watching you fish for the answers."

He turned his eyes aside, as if returning to the moment he meant to recall. "I went to Howard Elementary School over in Bensalem. You know it? Figured you would, but I don't remember seeing you there. We didn't meet until junior high. Maybe you were there but too young to catch my eye." Karl smiled thinly. "I was a horny grade schooler, and I had my share of girlfriends even that far back. I felt the *itch* as early as third grade, but the girls were slower to feel it for themselves, so there wasn't much I could do with any of them except play wall-ball, suicide, or sickball. Anyways, there was this big open field behind the school. Bordered by a forest which used to stretch for miles in every direction, until an industrial park sprouted up back there, and then a townhouse development."

He stalled somewhat. "The time I'm talking about, the forest was deep and dark, even on a sunny day. One day, me and a couple of friends, because back then *everybody* liked each other the same, we were throwing a football back and forth by the back treeline when we heard a dog barking. Real close by. Close enough I grabbed for my crotch on instinct, because it sounded mean. We dropped the football and crowded in to peer through the trees. A Doberman Pinscher was chained to a tree about ten feet in. We didn't think nothing of the fact it was just chained there with no one around. It made sense to our soft little brains. Nothing suspicious. *Maybe the owner tied him up so he could go off and take a leak.*

"So we stood there. We waited. Ten minutes of recess dripped by. No one come back. By that time, the dog had worked itself into quite a lather about us standing there just staring at him. He barked and these ropes of snot just kept flying off his face. We laughed at that. *Maybe he's got the rabies thing where the dog starts killing people for no reason. The owner might have tied it up so it wouldn't bite his face off.* I thought it was a good enough explanation. The one boy ran off to go get the football so we could

231

start playing again. I looked down and saw a pile of stones dumped into a stand of weeds just inside the perimeter. Some kind of dark, jagged-looking shale I think it was. I picked one up and started tossing it up and down. Thinking. Then, before I knew it, the third boy did like I done. Picked up a stone and started just tossing it up and down. We both stood there. The idea was malformed in our heads. It was growing, but it took some time to shape up and become something. A thought. An impulse we never even knew was there, waiting in the backs of our lizard brains to be called forward. I like to think of it as our caveman ancestors whispering to us; when things get quiet enough inside our minds we can hear the commands of our primal DNA. I don't remember who threw the rock first. But it all started happening faster than I thought it would. I heard laughing. Children's laughter. I saw the dog dancing and jerking against its chain, trying to avoid the stones we were throwing. I do know it was *my stone* drew the first blood. It bonked the old dog right next to its right eye. Couple inches it would have taken that eye. Red gleamed there, and I felt a hunger. Not talking vampire-like, the sight of blood. Just a hunger at the sight of it. I kept grabbing and throwing, aiming the best I could. And a funny thing happened, Stell. The boy standing beside me? I looked at him and saw five other boys and two girls were joining in the fun. Grabbing stones on down the line. Throwing. And the Doberman's back legs folded under him. He made a face like his body just betrayed him. Condemned him. I saw it jerk at its chain, teeth long and bared. A stone bent its front right leg, and it made a graceless header down into the dirt.

"By then, I could sorta' hear the adult voices screaming at us. Getting closer and closer. *Drop the stones! STOP! STOP! WHAT IS* WRONG *WITH YOU ALL?* Closer and closer. The dog was jittering in the dirt, but its movements? I don't know. They were … honest. True. No pretense. It was beautiful. I don't know. I don't know. The dance of the dying. I threw my last rock, and it smashed the top of the dog's skull. Killed it. The dance stopped. It stopped. Then, the dog started jerking around again on the ground. The dance wasn't over! I watched. Hell, I even clapped! The most beautiful dance I had ever seen! Then there were big hands on my shoulders, and I was being dragged away. But I was laughing. Crying, too! Something changed inside me. A switch turned. I was a lover of *beauty*. The dance. Stella, you never seen it, but when you do … you will laugh, and you will cry just like I did. All those animals I sculpted in the forest those years back? They all danced for me in their final moments. And the way I posed them in death, they were in dancer poses. A tribute to their honesty. Those final seconds of their lives when they were the most honest creatures walking the earth."

Stella blinked the tears out of her eyes. They spilled down the slope of her cheeks. She didn't say anything right away. She didn't look at Karl, preferring to study the hands she kneaded in her lap. What could she say, really? The silence was deafening, and she knew she should stamp it out. But the words, no matter what they were, would ring false and even sympathetic. She felt a small twinge of sympathy, but for the first time in Karl's company she felt something else. Fear. *I knew once I took up a pen pal relationship with him I was doing a dance with the devil and I would end up dead in the end, but ... I don't know that I want to die.* The realization shocked her. Then she remembered.

The anti-anxiety pills from home. Karl thought he had taken her whole stash away from her. Stella had anticipated such a power grab and stashed four pills in the pocket of her jeans. She had snuck one in the morning while he was away. She felt her mind opening up and strands of clarity worming their way in.

Clarity. Shame, also.

Fear.

All things she had been numb to for so long. Alien feelings.

"Stella?"

She returned to the moment and found Karl had moved in towards her. So close she could smell the morning rank of his unbrushed mouth.

"Mm?" she muttered, turning her eyes aside from him. She sniffed at the putrid air. Tears came hot and stinging, and she could not hold them back.

"Stop your crying! What? You feeling bad now?"

"I-I—"

"You shedding a tear for poor old Snoopy and Lassie from last night? That it?"

"K-Karl—"

"I should have known," he said, and slunk away from her. Then he wheeled around, and his screams blew her hair back. "WHY DID YOU COME TO THE CAR WASH THAT DAY? WHAT WERE YOU AFTER?"

Stella looked at him then, her cheeks fluttering and mouth barely working. "We're friends. We're ... we're *lovers*. And I was unkind to you. I took you for granted."

"Well what the fuck you think you're doing to me right now? And you're lying to yourself if you think you come back to me because we're *so much in fucking love*! Come the fuck on! I want you to say it! I want you to *say it*, because I ain't the only sicko here and the way you're looking at me right now I could put you through a wall and then drag you back out again. You wanted me off my chain! I'm useful to you! I want to hear you say it!"

233

"Say what—"

"I'm not going to feed you the words like a fucking ventriloquist."

"Karl—"

"You want your pills back? Then you say it!"

Stella's words hitched in her throat. *I do. I want them back. I want to get well. I want to walk away from this, and I can't without a level head. I do. I want—*

"You *do* want them back don't you? Unbelievable. You idiot!"

I do-I want-I do—

"I wanted you to make Jack suffer."

"That's not all, and you know it! You want them back?"

"I-I-I-I wanted you to kill him and take your time with it!" she cried out. Then, Stella dropped her voice to a conspiratorial whisper. "Now ... please ... I want my medicine."

Karl laughed, low and throaty. "Too bad for you. All gone. Last night."

Four left you don't know about!

"Don't say it, or you'll be sorry for a long, long time, Stella."

I don't have to say a thing; I know something you don't know!

Karl said, "We're both bad. We're both *really* bad people. Now we established that, you're going to listen and I'm going to talk." He stood up and stalked away from her, down the center aisle of the church.

Stella Post vomited down the steps leading up to the altar until it all turned to painful dry heaves. Before she joined him, Stella fished a Xanax pill out of the skintight front pocket of her jeans, dry swallowed it, and slunk down the aisle toward the vestibule.

45. THE CULMINATION

Mina Cohen loved owning her own business and being her own boss. The freedom it afforded her, as well as the wealth of having a successful venture, was something she found she might never get used to. She had been under some employer's thumb only five years before, working as a paralegal and dragging her MFA in English behind her like what had previously felt like useless luggage. Then she got her Bachelor's in Business online and decided to take the proverbial leap of faith by buying a struggling little bookstore on New Hope's Main Street, attracting national authors to include her rapidly burgeoning and newly-improved "Mina's Dusty Page Bookstore" on their tours, and through blessed word of mouth, watching as her store became for tourists a quintessential stop second in necessity only to the internationally famous "Ghost Tours."

When Danforth told her Albie had her "accidents" the night before, and had spent the night generally "spooked" according to the live-in vet nurse, Mina cursed her responsibilities as a successful business owner. Mina decided she could not and would not leave Danforth by herself to care for Albie that day. Mina handed over the reins to the sadly reluctant assistant manager at the bookstore, and did not hang up before giving her a sort of pep talk involving lots of "You got this" and "It's only a day … or two. Open to close. Inventory. You *got* this!" Any important calls from authors, agents, or publishing houses were to be forwarded to Mina's cell phone directly. The assistant manager, the epitome of a bookworm, named Naomi would have to step up.

Danforth urged Mina to go in to work, but soon understood Mina was about as stubborn and assertive as the old vet nurse herself. Two antelopes kerranging their horns together, making a spark.

"All right," Danforth relented. "I may as well run you through the ropes and the regimen from soup to nuts. What do you say?"

It became clear after the first hour Mina could have gone into work. Much of the regimen required only one person to supervise and assist Albie. This frustrated Mina at first, but after putzing around the house for a couple of hours, dusting and varnishing the wood surfaces and engaging in generally useless "time fillers," she adapted to a kind of inner peace. Danforth was best for this. There was no shortage of genuine love and affection for the dog on Danforth's part either. Mina was quite certain of that and grateful for it.

Of course, once Danforth knew she had passively proven her point to Mina, that two caretakers were a crowd, a certain resolve crept into the older woman's demeanor.

Mina prepared some tomato soup and grilled cheese for the two of them, but Danforth begged off at first, saying she'd have to eat it a little later after Albie's wave pool therapy. Mina ate alone and munched and sipped her lunch, preferring her soup in a mug rather than a bowl, and half-listened to an NPR show on her cell phone. Sitting there, chewing and swallowing slowly, Mina heard the drumming fingers of rain along the eaves and the kitchen windowsills. It built very quickly to a full-on assault of flattened palms slapping the stone sides of the house like a threatening siege.

She heard Albie bark from the garage, a muffled sound, as the dog walked through the little wave pool. Strengthening her limbs more and more as the days passed. What a miracle!

Mina crept into Will's writing room and scanned the rather extensive library on his wall-to-wall bookshelves for something to read while stretched out on the sofa. She decided upon Hosseini's *A Thousand Splendid Suns*, a book she'd read many times and now sought to have it lull her into a nap while the rain carried on outside. She settled in among the lushness of the sofa cushions, rested her head on a billowing throw pillow, and read the first chapter and a half before slipping into a shallow doze.

Albie's bark, then much closer, roused her. Danforth and Albie were standing over her, the dog's leash dripping out of Danforth's hand as she held it out to Mina.

"I was going to take Alberta for a walk now that the rain stopped," Danforth said. "Thought you might want to come along. Then I saw you sleeping and decided I'd let you go, but Little Miss German Shepherd here wasn't having it and barked you right out of your nap. So what do you say?"

Mina felt a tug of love and affection on her heart at the sight of the two of them. A feeling cherished for its rareness. She rose up, quickly rescuing the opened book lying across her chest, and stood up with a spring in her movements borne of a good doze.

"Absolutely."

The air still smelled of ripe rain, its cloying mist like another weighty layer draped across the women's backs over their winter coats. Not unpleasant, and actually relished by them as they started up their walk. Danforth had bundled herself up into a heavy wool coat, buttoned up to just below her wattle chin. Mina wore one of Will's navy blue Villanova University hoodies. They moved down the street in silence at first, the only sound that of Albie's steady paw falls as her black claws clicked along the blacktop of the street.

Danforth handed Mina the leash. "You know, I've worked for a lot of families. I can honestly say you and Mr. Bentley are among the most devoted dog owners I have ever met."

Mina didn't thank her right away. She nodded, chewed her bottom lip. "Will and I decided if and when we ever got married, there wouldn't be any children. We'll just have litter after litter and that will be fine. Albie is like our firstborn."

"Mm," Danforth said, smiling. "A pet out of wedlock. In this day and age."

Mina laughed with the older woman, enjoying the gentle tug of the leash in her hands as Albie inspected something lying close to a sewer grate. "It's not that I can't have children. We just don't know if we'll *ever* have the time to devote to children. It's a full-time job. As the cliché goes. Dogs … cats even? They learn fast how to take care of as much of their lives as they can."

"Cats more so. I honestly think cats believe themselves to be the dominant one in a human-feline relationship. They have it in their little ping-pong-ball-sized brains they're actually *taking care of you* Not vice-versa."

"Probably why I've never been a cat person."

"You like the idea of being needed … to a certain degree? That isn't so demanding?"

"Probably, yes," Mina admitted. "I guess children would require too *much* of mine and Will's time. Cats demand little to none. Dogs? Like Goldilocks says … dogs are *just right*. They ask for just the right amount of affection and attention Will and I can offer."

Danforth was silent. "You want to know what I see?" she asked.

"That I'm preoccupied?"

"I'd say Will not only wants to have children with you, but he also wishes Albie needed him a little bit more than she does. I think a part of him wishes the two of you didn't need me to have to come in and do what he believes, for himself at least, to be his job. Big, tough ex-Marine."

"Oh, they never stop being *Marines*. That's the blessing and the curse of it. They need to be *needed*. They need to save the day in some way. Not because they're looking for a *thank you*. It's almost like bootcamp adds another strand of DNA to what they're born with. The *kick-ass* gene. The *hero* gene. They have a very difficult time denying its impulses."

"You want a child too," Danforth said, sneaking it in.

"I want Will to seal the deal," Mina said, laughing. "No escape hatch anymore by keeping me attached to the *girlfriend* tag. Otherwise, it's putting the cart before the horse. And I *do* want a litter of pups." She paused, flushing, and feeling it. "I think about it sometimes, though. Little boys or girls mixed in with pups skipping along behind them. Weaving in between their wobbly little baby legs."

"Well, never close your mind to anything you're not one hundred percent certain you'll never want. That way, you won't have to feel awkward when you realize you've wanted it the whole time."

The young, petite ginger woman appeared seemingly out of nowhere.

"Can I pet your dog? She's a beauty!"

She couldn't have been more than twenty-two or so. A small hatching of lines had already formed in the corners of the woman's deep blue eyes. Her lips were thin and pale pink which stood in small contrast to her washed-out complexion. She appeared bird-like, with shoulders sunken beneath a sky-blue parka and white t-shirt underneath. Her hair was pinned back into a ponytail, with countless flyaways that twitched in the soft winter breeze. Mina recognized her as someone with a kind heart who had somehow found her way into a "bread line" after years of telling themselves "it'll turn out okay in the end … you'll see."

Danforth took a deep breath, a little behind Mina now. "I don't know that's a—"

"Of course, you can," Mina said. After all, the woman was already inching forward and crouching down before Albie. Her smile looked painted on. "What's his name?"

Mina smiled. "*Her*, actually. Her name is Alberta. We call her Albie for short."

The woman snorted laughter. She smoothed back the narrow tract of brindle fur between Albie's antenna ears. The dog moaned low in her throat, retracting some rather than moving into the touch. Danforth saw it. Mina did not. The older woman was more attuned to such things.

Danforth took a small step towards Albie and the stranger. "She needs to be fed. We should head back, Mina."

"I read the article about your little hero in the paper this morning. Hope you don't mind, I just wanted to meet her up close. I'd ask her for an autograph but … I'll settle for yours. After all, you were in the article too."

"That's right," Mina said. "Only I don't usually bring a pen or pencil along with me when we go out walking with Albie."

Albie ducked her head down and under, away from the touch of the stranger. The girl cast a look behind her right shoulder, quick enough to have been perceived as nothing more than a tic. Then, she edged in closer to Albie and started running her hand along the dog's back. The arch of the dog's back stood up, rigid as a tree branch.

Danforth moved in closer. "Mrs. Bentley, I think Albie's a little spooked. Could we—"

"Ma'am?" Mina said. "Do you have a pen and paper I can write on? You said you wanted an autograph?"

The girl turned her bright blue eyes up to Mina. "Oh yeah." She stood up, still a couple inches shorter than Mina, and just above eye-level with Danforth. She fished inside her parka pocket and brought out a small square of folded paper, along with a pencil. The end of it was a nub, barely usable.

Just then, Mina grabbed the stranger's arm and tugged her towards the curb, along with Albie. "Watch! We have a car trying to get past and here we are hogging the road."

238

The girl stood there like a sculpted thing, her eyes oriented to the right just as a tan Cutlass slid past. She did not blink, and it looked almost as if she was holding her breath until the car turned into a driveway a half-block down. Then, she held the pencil and paper out to Mina. "Can you make it out to Cara Mooney?"

"Sure, but could you … would you?" Mina motioned for the girl to turn around and stoop. "I need to lean on your back, or it's going to look like chicken scratch."

"Surely, surely." The girl positioned herself.

Behind them, Danforth spoke up. "Albie! Come!" She called to the animal stern as a drill sergeant. "Come here."

The stranger: "But I wanted to pet her some more—"

"*Albie!*" barked Danforth. "*Come!*"

Mina kept trying to make a mark with the nub of graphite at the end of the pencil. Her patience was wearing thin, but she would hide it. "Sorry. Hope I'm not digging into your back. It's just … this pencil is pretty dull."

The girl muttered something incomprehensible.

Mina leaned in towards her. "What'd you say, hon?"

"Behind you," the girl said.

Mina whirled around, her hand tightening on the leash instinctively. She turned just in time to find a man with long, curly black hair raising a tire iron over his head behind Danforth. The old vet turned just in time to raise her hands up in front of her face. The backs of her forearms bore the full brunt of the iron when the man brought it down in a severe arc. The sound was like tree branches splitting under the weight of a cumbersome animal. Danforth screamed.

"Danforth!" cried Mina. "Help! *Help!*"

The man shot a furtive glance at the girl now standing behind Mina. "Grab the bitch!"

Danforth gathered her broken arms into her heaving, considerable chest. She barely dodged the second blow aimed at her head. She ducked down and to the left. "Hold still!" the man said through gritted teeth, and swatted the tire iron downward and to the left as Danforth sank downward, her knees bending and shuddering beneath her. Mina could only stand there in horror and watch as the tire iron did not so much slap Katherine Danforth across the face, as it gouged into the side of her skull, catching up in bone and tearing back a flap of skin just above her right ear. The sound it made was nothing comparable to a breaking branch or a snap. This was the sound of murder.

A sound all its own.

Danforth's body shuddered in the grass, part gran mal seizure and death throes.

"GRAB THAT BITCH!" the man cried, standing above Danforth with the tire iron slung across his shoulder.

By the time Mina wheeled around on the strange girl with the fly-away red hair, she was suddenly caught in a bear hug of sorts. The woman had flung her arms around Mina, pinning her arms at her sides. Then the woman's hot, sour breath was in Mina's ear. "Don't shout and he won't hurt you—"

"Help!" Mina cried. She judged the woman's grip around her as just loose enough Mina could spin herself around, at least a halfway revolution. It was all Mina needed. She turned and jabbed her elbow into the woman's stomach, knocking the wind out of her, .and then drove the elbow upward into her breastbone. The woman's hands fell away. Mina pivoted into her. "*Help!*" Mina craned her head sideways to bring the man into her periphery before she did what came next.

The man, a *short shit* by Mina's standards, lunged towards her with his tire iron raised above his head. With a blinding motion she had only just learned in her judo class last Thursday, Mina Cohen drove the unforgiving flat of her palm up into the jutting cliff of the woman's chin. Mina heard teeth come crashing together, breaking or splitting. Mina duck-walked out of the way just as the man brought the now crimson-gleaming hooked end of the tire iron down on top of her skull. The man stopped mid-strike, only barely missing clubbing his partner in crime at the last minute.

Mina's feet criss-crossed with one another. She tripped herself up and toppled down onto her side. That's when she heard the wheezing, strangling gasps of her dog by her feet. She raised her head up just high enough to see.

The man had Alberta's leather leash wound around the dog's neck, asphyxiating it. Albie offered what little resistance she could with a shortage of breath. She kicked her back legs out at the man. She whipped her massive head all about, but the man for all his short stature looked to have a wicked strength in his hands and arms. It was unyielding.

Albie's big brown eyes bulged, White and red stitched the upper corners as she tried in vain to look up and back at its attacker.

Mina moved to grab at the man.

"I'll yank this so hard it'll pop your dog's head off!" the man told her. "You want me to do that? No?"

Mina shook her head. Her blood was pounding in her brain. The first new raindrops of another coming storm dappled her cheeks. "No! Please!

She's not well! Why are you doing this?"

"Don't worry. I'll bring her back. Just have some work I need her to do, and she's the only one for the job."

Just then, Mina noticed the strange girl was gone.

"Oh, you looking for my lady?" the man said, tightening the grip on the leash in his hands. Alberta squeaked out a small resistant sound. "She's just bringing the car around."

"Don't do this! She's weak! She just came out of a coma!"

"I read all about it. And I'll tell you something. The picture in there didn't do you no justice. You got an ass to inspire sodomy, baby! Just might take a bite out of it when I return your dog to you."

She screamed wildly in her mind. *THINK—THERE HAS TO BE SOMETHING YOU CAN DO TO HIM!*

"She's got a microchip in her neck, you bastard! You won't make it a mile before the police track her down, and then you're *fucked*!"

"Lady, come on now," twanged the short, curly-haired man, "we got the police running every which way a fucking dog isn't even gonna show up on their radar."

"The hell they won't! Everyone around here loves her, and I can guaran-fucking-tee you they'll be all over your ass the minute I put in a distress call."

"Then, do it," he said, his petulant smile vanishing. "Right now. Take out your cell. Make the call."

The sound of squealing, bald tires slashed through the quiet of the late, wet afternoon. She knew it was the woman with flyaway red hair. *The deceitful piece of shit! Probably a crack-whore!* It was time to play the bluff before the car pulled up alongside the two of them, and the man disappeared into it with her Albie. She fished into the gaping mouth front pouch of Will's sweatshirt. Brought out her cell and swiped it on with a palsied hand.

"Here," she said, eyes wild and flashing, "watch what I do!"

Mina dialed and showed the screen to the man.

"Nine-one-one, motherfucker! That means *right fucking now!*"

His eyes fixed on the screen, Mina launched herself at him. He made a surprised, squawking sound. Mina punched both fists into the sides of his head. Her knuckles split and the blood from his scalp mingled with the blood from her hands, but she kept going. He punched her in the side with his free hand. She gasped violently but didn't let up.

Then, Albie's teeth were mere inches from cutting into his neck.

The dog growled, a guttural tearing at the base of her throat.

The Cutlass's metal hatch-work grille and bumper struck Mina in the shoulder and right thigh, tossing her off the man. He was shoved aside also, halfway onto the curb. His left arm swung wide and clubbed Albie in the side of the head, just under her left ear. The man climbed on top of Mina and hammered down at her face, mashing her nose and fanning blood upward across her eyes and brow. She grabbed for her face.

She would regret it for the rest of her life. Grabbing for herself, her broken nose.

Albie slumped onto her side, seizing. The man had hit her right where the bat had struck her last October inside the church.

Mina grabbed for him. "No-*no-noooooo-help*—"

The man drove the tip of his motorcycle boot into her stomach, cutting off her wind and her cries. She folded over in the grass of a neighbor's front yard. Mina could not straighten up.

"Hey! What the hell is going on out here!?"

Fred Perkins. This was all playing out right at the edge of his sprawling front yard. Fred the retiree from Proctor and Gamble. Late sixties. Widow. Lots of grandchildren. And a pacemaker for Christmas last year, as Mina remembered it. He would die if he got into it with these people.

Yet, Mina could not hold back. She was desperate. "Fred! HELP! HELP!"

Fred high-stepped it stiffly across the expanse of yard. "What are you—goddammit—*where you taking Albie*?"

She cleared the blood from her eyes just in time to see the man cradling the shaking dog in his arms as he hustled up to the passenger side.

Mina pulled herself achingly off the ground just as the passenger door slammed shut. She lunged at the side of the car as it started to roll. She got hold of the handle and felt it slip out of her hands as the car picked up rapid speed. The handle was slick with rain.

Albie was seizing—ohdeargod-ohgod-no-no-no—

Fred reached her just as the car rounded the bend. Mina Cohen fell into his arms as he hunched down beside her. She couldn't draw a breath.

Not one.

PART THREE

Broken Birds

"What good is it, my brothers if a man has faith
but has no deeds? Can such faith save him? …
Faith by itself, if it is not accompanied by action,
is dead."

James 2:14-17

46. JACK POSTS FINAL EPIPHANY

Jack Post lay in the darkness of the church basement, a filthy sheet flung across his body and over his face. He listened to the pomp and circumstance of an angry thunderstorm on its approach and shook like a fretful leaf as it exploded seemingly right over his head. He lay in the filth of urine and shit, caked to his inner thigh like putrid mud. The exquisite pain of moving any of his limbs so much as a hairsbreadth engaged his sphincter even though there was nothing more to expel. The rumblings in his stomach were not the typical hunger pains one experiences shortly after missing an afternoon lunch. This was a coiling inward of his midsection, combined with the altogether stranger sound of his organs devouring one another. An incessant, tunneling sound like a wild, groveling animal tearing him up from the inside out. Death was feasting, and he knew it.

Here and there, he prayed for one thing in particular, however it came to pass. He prayed for the end. It was already there in the room with him, holding off for whatever terrible reason. He understood it would seize him like a pair of Centurion guards, and it would squeeze him until the life dribbled out of him like toothpaste out of a rolled tube. It knew more than Jack, and he hated Death for that reason, among other things. It drew him further and further towards the precipice separating the want of survival, and the body flying outward into the windless dark. *Death, you're a motherfucker!*

Jack heard only the skittering of rodents from all around.

As Death held him in suspense, Jack's emotions fluctuated out of sheer frustration and a great deal of time to think. His thoughts snapped like a pendulum between an over-the-top will to survive and put up a fight, and the sinking feeling of submission. *If I can somehow drag myself out—which*

245

is going to involve pain which could very well throw me into shock—I still have my voice, and I have a set of pipes all of Bucks County would be able to hear. Just ask Stella, huh? Every time she started in about wanting to resume her sessions with that quack therapist I shut her down with very little words and a whole lot of volume! My father was a screamer. Mom was a screamer and a bawler. Just thinking, his thoughts spiraling round and round, exhausted him, and he found he had to force his mind into some kind of silence or it would fracture. There is such a thing as burning out the motor of one's mind. He'd done it many times.

Jack's broken birds tried his patience even more than Stella. He let his wrathful voice rain down upon their quivering heads and for the same reasons; he had to deal with his wife in such a way. *They always want to fly away too soon! They want to leave the nourishment of safety, a refuge I provided for them. All of them. The thing about the women, just like broken birds, is they don't think about damaging their wings by spreading them too soon after having snapped the bones. They need to be told; they need to be convinced to embrace their fragile state. Live inside of it. Learn to love it, long enough at least for their bones to heal. By then, I'm ready to fly with them rather than watch helplessly as they crest the horizon, leaving me in their wake like something used up and discarded. I only wanted to bring them to heal! To convalesce, at my wise discretion.*

"That's what I do," he said to himself, muttering in the dark like a whimpering child trying to explain himself in the face of guilt, "I bring them all to heal. It's not my fault they flock to me. It's how it's been all my life. You going to tell me that's an accident? Every woman I've ever known, been friends with, married, become intimate with, came to me broken. Why? Because they know they'll become my *project*. I *need* projects. The problem is, and always has been, they all grow far too eager to fix themselves when they *know* I'm the only one who can repair them. They flap their wings … and I shout them back down into the nest." He paused, breathless. His broken arms and legs sang their dry, brittle chorus of lament, and he bit his tongue so hard wet copper spread across his lips. "Then it's only suitable I bring them back down to earth. Break them all over again, if need be. They come to me broken, like a sports player comes to a doctor with a broken leg or arm. The doctor has to *break it a little more to reset it*. Don't you fucking understand?" *They need to have their wings broken again, and reset, when they fly too soon and damage themselves all over again.*

Waxing poetic? Jack didn't think so. He never fancied himself as anything special, no more than a healer toots his or her own horn. He read his Chopra, even his Dr. Phil, and Jack tossed them aside after only a few pages.

246

I don't need to write a book to let anyone know how smart I am or valuable my advice is! They come to ME! ALWAYS COME TO ME!

If I'm talking to Death, consider this my trial and judgment, and I myself acting defense attorney on behalf of yours truly! Ha ha! That's the ticket! "I know what you're thinking, and let me just … just deal with the argument right here and now! A *pimp* breaks down his bitches and builds them back up in a busted-up, drugged-out, and sniveling shell with a gash who proves their worth. Me? I torch the phoenix. I tend their ashes. I wait and, in time, the great bird rises from her ashes, and she's got me to *thank*! Thank you, Jack! For sitting by and brooming the ashes back into a complete pile when the wind creeps in between the eaves and tries to scatter them. To divide my essence! Thank you, Jack, for bearing witness and never judging me. The depressive. The bipolar. The nympho. The molested. The battered. The abused. The simple. The anxious! The helpless! S'why I came to you, Jack! You're a magnet. The Statue of Liberty drew immigrants by the millions over the years. I'm your Statue of Rehabilitation, ladies, and you flocked to me. You *came* to me!"

Then, the tears full of rage, and growls and moans tapered off into *poor me* snivelling as he tumbled just far enough onto his back to not aggravate the pain in his limbs.

He thought of trying to ward off Treacherous Death with prayers. The Lord's Prayer and Hail Mary burst from his lips in breathless gasps, and then he remembered his Act of Contrition, the one his mother told him growing up placed him back within the realm of God's grace no matter his trespasses. "But … I'm not bad, Mama. Really, I'm not *so* bad." He spoke the Contrition anyhow, repeating it over and over until it lulled him into a restless, shallow doze. In this state, he envisioned long arms reaching out for him from the black. Alabaster colored hands opened outward to him. White, flowing cuffs dribbling down off the wrists. A swooning from unseen lips. Swelling into something resembling a welcoming, an invitation. *Death won't let me come to you. I want to go. But … I don't? I don't know. Why are you hiding from me?*

Mother was notorious for her *white lies*. She relied on them. She told him *they* were A-OK with God and what made Jack human. Animals don't know the need or the necessity to lie when it means to save another's feelings or misguided intentions.

"Am I misguided? If so, that would make me redeemable. My soul … redeemable." *Fuck off, Jack! You're going to make it! Why are you lying there like a sack of shit! They can fix your arms! They can fix your fucking legs, but you have to act now! ACT NOW! The Lord helps those who help themselves, so get crawling. The pain will make you stronger.*

His mind had compartmentalized the memories of when Stella and her man had broken his bones with the tire iron. It seemed like so long ago, in direct correlation with how quickly he had come to bear the excruciating pain of it. The details of the attack were shut away, but as he lay there he dared to coax some of them back into the forefront of his mind. In essence, he needed to figure out how thorough a job they had done smashing his bones.

"Mash em' into a powder!" the little man had urged Stella. As Jack remembered, it became apparent the little man saw the need to press her on because her strikes with the tire iron were weak and half-hearted. Stella had pulled her *punches* so to speak, like two brothers will do when a fistfight breaks out between them, but the bloodline they share holds them back from all out savagery against the other. *Okay, we can use that bit of knowledge, can't we?*

Stella did my arms, the bitch! work on with the tire iron? Gotta test out to see how bad the damage is. Something tells me her blows were soft, and there's still a good bit of usable bone left I can lean on. The pain won't be as bad.

This required him to delve even further into the black incident. He concentrated and after some time, snatches of the attack flashed before his eyes. He tasted the mud in his mouth from the valley floor. He heard his own girlish weeping and begging, detesting himself for allowing them to bring him to such a pathetic state of mind. No one had ever made Jack beg for *anything* before, not even so much as a bit of kink. His broken birds, his wife even, had never denied him even the most depraved sexual requests. *I was laying on my stomach. I tripped over a root sticking out of the ground, and that's when they had me, the motherfuckers! The little guy–and goddammit I know I know him from somewhere—went right to work beating me. H-h-he was standing right next to the car, and he worked on my legs. Stella did a piss-poor job on my arms. Especially my right one. My good arm! Goddammit, this isn't over! I knew it wasn't!*

This sorted out, Jack knew what came next. He ground his teeth together, holding fast to the momentum and the anger of what he had just determined. He held onto the hope and the audacity of revenge, a hot and thumping pulse in his veins.

Two things happened at once.

Jack Post tested his right arm, this time pressing the effort further than before. Pushed through the pain and the white lightning as it radiated up the side of his body, violently massaged his heart, and lit up an endless circuitry of anguish centers in his brain. He felt the grind of shattered bones as he drew his right arm off the cold cement. Drew it up. Extended it. The black crowded out his vision as he came close to passing out. Jack held his partially bent arm up in the air, a quivering and mangled appendage still obeying despite the trauma.

The other thing.

The door to the basement banged open, letting in a rectangle of hazy light. The little man and Stella were arguing. Jack dropped his arm with a grunt and managed to arrange it across his heaving chest. They were really having it out. Jack smiled a rictus grin. *I'm going to get the fuck out of here. I'm getting out of here. You won't know it until I'm gone. You'll still be fighting amongst yourselves like this. A regular Ozzie and fucking Harriet! You two ... you two deserve each other!*

Their motives and movements were as bizarre as they were random. Jack's mind had also compartmentalized the events which had transpired the night before on the altar of the church. He remembered a dog, snapping its jaws and terrible, elongated teeth mere inches from his face. The rest bled black in his recall. He was thankful for this. As for Plan B? *You're one helluva talker, Jack! It's how you coaxed and some would say even coerced forty high school football players away from their many other "suitors" in favor of playing for Ballantine! Some of those fuckers were downright standoffish at your meetings with them. But you almost always boarded your plane or hopped in your car with a signed contract stowed away in your briefcase! The broken birds? You used your words on them for their own good, and now it's time for you to serve yourself with that same gift for negotiation. Now, it counts more than ever. Talk-talk-talk-you fucker—like you've never talked before—hit them with webs of words—ensnare them in your expertise and confound them. After all, they're not exactly Monsieur and Madame Curie you're dealing with!*

Stella's foot grazed his left shin, and she shrieked. "Christ, there you are! I'm sorry!"

"What the hell you sorry for?" the little man asked. "The little prick's probably starved for some kind—any kind of human contact. Been down here all alone ... in the dark. And just think, Jackie, it's only been ... oh, a day and a half. Imagine we left you down here with your broken little brain for ... oh, a month? A *year*, even?"

Jack heard the tremor in his wife's voice. "We're not going to do that. Of course not." She was getting herself *stuck in neutral*, only this time without any help from him. Something else had gotten her gears all jammed up. It was time for Jack to take the wheel, free up her gears, and *talk her out of this shit.*

249

He swallowed hard, and started. "You wouldn't, Stella. Not to me. Not after all we've been through together."

The little man erupted. "Stella, why you letting down your side? We gotta carry her all the way! No time to waste so you can catch your breath! Pick it up! *Now!*"

Gotta carry her?

Jack gathered his thoughts. "Stell, what the hell has this little *weasel* gotten you into? You've got to stop this! Don't you see you're being led around by … by the … I don't know. Have you actually *slept* with this … *person?*"

"Oh, Jackie," the little man cackled, "if I didn't know better, I'd say you're trying to outfox the fox. That's what you think you're doing here, right now? You got less than a little wriggle room to spout off at the mouth with more of the same reverse-psycho bullshit! I'm here to safeguard Stella from your horseshit once and for all. Won't work. You got nothing to use here. Even less to say to make a difference at this point."

Jack paused, wet his lips. "Stella? Is this *guy* some kind of master hypnotist he'd convince you to—to trade *down* from your husband. That's what you're doing. There is nothing you and I can't … work on and work through … hell, if I'm willing to forgive you for all *this?* Then, we've really got something solid we can build on and—"

He expected the boot in the side as long as he dared *talk* and *talk* and *talk*, but he was not prepared for the sickening sound of something breaking at the impact. A rib? He could still draw a breath, so if it was a rib it hadn't punctured a lung. *Or did it? I can't breathe deeply … of shit-talk-talk-talk–to Stella–marginalize the "little man" by cutting him out of the conversation altogether—it'll enrage him, but it'll also show Stella he's vulnerable and his plans are not foolproof or Bible-talk-talk—*

"Stella, I want you to take your medicine."

The little man sniggered. "Oh, she's been taking her medicine behind *both* our backs, it would seem. Huh, Stella?"

Jack sighed. *Now what?* "That-that's *good*, Stell. I-I was wrong about all of it. The Xanax wouldn't help you? That it's a … a placebo. I was wrong. I've seen you on it. You were … lucid. You knew what you wanted."

One of them yanked the ratty sheet away from Jack's face, then Stella was nose-to-nose with him. "You were only satisfied when I was weak and disoriented. You were nothing but a vampire sucking the life out of me so you could thrive, you sonofabitch! Now *I* do what I want!"

"Pick up your end again before this dog gets free of her ties!" the little man said.

Jack heard a soft, canine whimper nearby and a rustling of something that sounded like burlap. *What the hell have they done now?*

Stella's breath was sour as it broke across the bridge of Jack's nose. "I'm taking my medicine. When this is all over, I'm going back to Doctor Howell, and I'm going to see her every week. And not you—not even you, *Karl*—is going to hold me back from my life! Not one second longer!"

The little man scoffed. "Yeah-yeah-yeah–whatever you want, Stell! Now pick up your *goddamn* end and leave this asshole until we're ready for him!"

Talk-talk-talk—surrender if you have to.

"I'll get out of your way, Stella. I promise. I-I'll go to couples therapy if you want. You're in charge. I swear to God you are!"

Ah, there it is! I can see it in her eyes! She's coming-to! The dawn is breaking behind those baby blues! Come on, honey! Just a little bit more! Jack looked into his wife's eyes. She snapped her head back, away from him. He grabbed for her with his right arm, the one he had just moments before managed to lift in the air without losing consciousness. The pain was immediate and blinding, but he somehow managed to curl his fingers around the cuff of her sweatshirt. "I had a lot of time to think about what I've done. All the manipulation? I've been so very fucking bad, but … I want to get to better. I want to *do* better by you. You're my wife!"

"Jack—"

"Why don't we cut right to it, then! You got AIDS, Jackie?" the little man asked.

Stella ripped her sweatshirt cuff out of Jack's hands, recoiling. Jack turned his head so his eyes could seek out the little man who had just lobbed an IED into what could have been a peaceful communion. The little man's hair hung in his pale, horse-face. Long, frizzy brown ringlets. A slight hunch in his stature, shaving away vital inches for a man so short. The little black eyes darting about like a tweaker. The full lips, at feminine odds with the dark, patchy beard framing them. *In high school, Steve Benson and I used to know a kid—real psycho, it turned out—with big girly lips. Steve called them DSLs. Dick-Sucking—*

Karl! Karl? Tarlick?

Fucking-*Karl! I know you! I fucking knew I knew you—I knew I knew you! Hair was shorter—at your chin—now its down your back, but it's you.*

Jack stared unblinking at the little man, no longer a stranger but a ghost from his past given flesh once more. "Karl … Tarlick. Holy shit! Of all the people … when did they let you out? Or, more importantly, *how the fuck did you get out?"*

"Turns out if you're a *really, really* good boy they favor that kind of shit! Out in eight years."

"Still a crazy fuck, only now multiply it a thousand times!"

"Yeah, you may be right," Karl said. "What does that say about you, Mr. HIV? The fact I could give your wife more attention and affection behind bars than you cared to give her when you were playing house? You gotta admit, I may have fallen off my rocker here and there, but I never ever failed at treating a woman kind."

"*Shut the fuck up!*"

"*You* shut the *fuck up,*" Karl said, sternly. "You know me now. You *remember* me now. But before this is all over, Jackie, you're not only going to remember someone else but you're going to pay for your trespasses against them. See, I got a name in my head. Sometime very soon, I'm going to whisper it in your ear, and you're going to remember what you did to them. Then, it'll all come clear to you. All this babbling you been doing, has been a complete waste of time. Even if Stella recovers something of a soft spot for you, I'll never let you live your life. You never had a chance. Being down here in the dark, maybe you got to thinking there were ways you could save yourself. There's no chance. And before I break your right arm for good … since you were good enough to show me you could still use it … I want you to tell your wife you have AIDS. It's really the least you can do, Jackie."

"I-never-I-*never*—"

"Did you bring HIV into our bed? Knowingly?" Stella demanded.

"Stella … I …"

"*Did you?*"

"I-I told you I-I was sick. The doctor saw something with my blood—"

"You knew! And you KILLED ME!"

"Stella, I swear I didn't touch you once I knew!"

"YOU KILLED ME, YOU BASTARD!" Stella was crying, screaming. Then, she was on him, throwing fists at his face. Landing some of them. One of them tagged Jack's nose, and the center of his face exploded.

Karl seized his right arm, drawing it out from under the sheet.

"Nononononononono-don't—"

Karl held firm to Jack's arm. "Hold still and take your beating! Her fists'll draw your attention away! You oughtta thank your wife!"

Jack feebly tried to turn his face away from his wife's raining fists, only to watch as Karl Tarlick lifted himself up a little bit and brought his hard, knobby knee down on his right arm.

The sound of something splitting, like kindling collapsing in a burning hearth.

Stella punched her husband on the side of the head, and he knew no more.

47. CUT SHORT

Will was a third question in to the Q and A following his reading from *Shiite* when the vibrating started against his upper right chest. It took him a moment to realize what it was and it put him off for a second. It was not long enough for anyone in the audience at the Villanova University speaking event to notice, merely a brief pause. Will tuned out the buzzing inside his black suit jacket. He wished he had left it in his winter coat, back in the meet-and-greet area.

The young female coed wearing librarian glasses and one of those colorfully knitted hats with the earflaps waited patiently for Will for finish his answer. Her question: "Do you believe part of the writer's craft is paying mind to not starting consecutive paragraphs with the same word, or even paragraphs on the same page?"

"Elaine, was it?"

"Yes," she said, beaming.

"Elaine, when you write your first draft you shouldn't be shackling your creative mind by forcing it to pay attention to things like, well, how do the words *look* on the page. The first draft is for story, story, story. Without the raw materials, you've got nothing to revise or to make pretty on the page. But, yeah, the craft of revision does involve to some extent making sure your words not only read well inside the heads of your readers, but they look pleasing to their eyes. I know it sounds strange, and I see some of you out there looking a bit baffled by Elaine's question, but here's what I can tell you. She's light years ahead of where I was when I wrote *Shiite* in asking such a question. You rock, Elaine!"

Brrrrrrrz ... brrrrrrrz ...

Elaine offered him a courteous bow and sat, her smile stretched from ear to ear. Will called on the next hand up, two rows back and to the left by a Fire Exit. An older gentleman with grizzly white sideburns reminiscent of Asimov stood with a slight grunt and smoothed down his brown corduroy suit jacket with something of a strange grin before asking his question.

Brrrrrrrrz ... brrrrrrrz ... brrrrrz

Will slipped his hand inside his coat and depressed the button on his cell, shutting off the vibration. "Yes, sir? Your name first and foremost?"

"I'm a professor here, Mr. Bentley. *The Bildungsroman Novel.*" He blinked up at Will through a pair of thick bifocals, as if waiting for some validation. Maybe a golf clap?

I have no idea what the hell a building-roman is, gotta be honest!

"Welcome, and you are?"

"Stanley Howard," he answered. "I was just wondering if there was a catharsis for you when you wrote *I Can Hear the Shiite Weeping*, sir? How did you suddenly decide you would write about perhaps the most painful moments in your life? Did you do it for yourself, as a kind of purging of the nightmares onto the page, or was there the motivation in your business mind the war novel is ... how would you say it? *Hot?* With the arrival of Tim O'Brien's *The Things They Carried* and its success. Was this book conceived from a business sense or simply to tell the true story of war's atrocities?"

"I'm not sure I understand the question?" *I really don't. But I can sense this guy is grandstanding and is probably showing off because he recognizes some of his students in the audience, and for once they're not at the mercy of his no doubt long-winded lectures!*

"Did you write this book because you thought you could sell it with little trouble because of the state of the publishing world and how they embrace the war novel? Did you write it for the money, Mr. Bentley?"

An audible gasp swept across the audience followed by a nervous titter towards the back. Then a few more hands went up, as if to diffuse the discomfort somehow. Will took his eyes away from the professor and he smiled an *aw-shucks* sort of smile. He rubbed his mouth with the underside of his hand, sniffed off-microphone. He snuck a glance over at Claire, his agent, standing just off the left side of the stage. Claire was on her cell phone. She was looking right into his eyes and when he nodded at her, she did not return it but rather turned away from him and plugged her other ear with a finger, just as the audience began to buzz with anticipation for the speaker's answer.

"No, it's a fair ... it's definitely a fair question. After I wrote the book, I seriously considered keeping it for myself. Treating it like a journal, not meant for public consumption. I felt like I was selling out my buddies who didn't make it back by writing about them without their permission. It almost became what Stephen King calls a *trunk book.* Something to be retired, maybe for a later time when it might be more appropriate. I didn't think I was the one to write about something like this, not because I had no credibility. I obviously do, and I've got the scars to prove it. But because I never fancied myself a *writer* who could actually pull it off—"

"Yes," the professor interrupted, "but ultimately you did decide to publish. What I'm asking is if you were thinking of the notoriety it could bring. The money. A contract."

"Mr. Howard, is it?"

"Yes—"

"Mr. Howard, I came to realize I had written a tribute. Unless you've been there in the trenches, you have no idea how many feats of heroism, big and small, take place and often go unnoticed. And the soldiers don't do these things because they hope a guy like me will give them credit later on after they're gone. They do it because they're inherently good men and women, and they not only know their job but also one of their tasks … perhaps the most important job of all … is to make it home to their families." Will took a breath, snuck another furtive glance over at his agent. Claire was just stuffing her phone back into her pocket book. She was looking at him again, only this time she did not turn away. No, Claire Monasta met and held his attention. They were wide, wet. Shocked.

Will gave her another nod, this time to confirm everything was okay when she returned it.

Claire did not nod, but rather glanced out across the audience. Then she came up onto the stage and stood beside him.

The professor was just about to launch into his next round of interrogation when Claire leaned into Will, whispered in his ear. Stanley Howard waited, holding onto his doozy of a question.

"Will, we'll have to cut this short."

"What happened?" Will placed his hand over the hot mic and leaned into her.

"Just apologize. Thank everyone for coming."

"Claire?"

"Just. Tell. Them. Please."

They took it better than he thought they would. After all, he had done the meet-and-greet before the Q and A. They were not entirely let down. He shook their hands in a fog, nodding and smiling as his guts churned.

He did not realize he left the stage and was standing before Claire in the empty auditorium until she spoke to him. "… you okay?"

"What happened?"

"She tried to call you while you were up there."

"Who?"

255

"Mina. Call her back."

"Christ, you're scaring me—"

"Call your girlfriend back," she told him, taking his hands in hers. "There's been an accident."

She stood by him, and he was thankful. Will reached into his suit jacket and took out his cell phone. The screen showed a *Missed Call* from a number he did not know.

"She's calling on a hospital phone. Call it back."

He looked at Claire, appraisingly, and hit the *Call Back* prompt. After three rings, a woman answered.

"Doylestown Hospital. How may I direct your call?"

"Uh, yes, my girlfriend is there, and she just called me. Could you connect me with Mina Cohen?"

"One moment, please."

Synthesizer music filled his ears for a few seconds, and four rings later, Mina's quavering voice answered.

"Mina?"

"Will, we were attacked," she sobbed.

"Attacked? Who the hell attacked you?"

"I don't know who they were."

"Tell me what happened. I'll be there. I'm an hour away. Are you all right? Is everyone all right?"

"It was a man and a woman. They looked young. Maybe, ah, mid-twenties. Danforth and I took Albie out for a walk together and they just-just—the woman said she wanted to pet the dog. She was … so strange. Skittish. Then, the guy … he came out of nowhere, and he had a tire iron … he … he killed Danforth."

"Wait a minute … hold it-hold it—Danforth's dead?"

"They just told me she died on the operating table. I tried *so hard* to fight them off. I almost … I think I could have if he didn't hit me—"

"I'm coming," Will said, his heart in his throat. "I'm coming. Right now."

"They took Alberta!"

"They *what*?"

"She's gone. Will, please! Danforth's daughter is on her way, and I can't do this alone. Please just get here!"

He was already out of the auditorium with Claire in his wake, calling out to him. Wanting to know what happened. His feet kept on like he had stepped onto a treadmill. They carried him out of the English Building and the cold wind lashed his cheeks as it whipped around the edges of the brick building.

Then he was running, running, running.

48. DARK SUCCESS

The dog fought harder than the man when Stella and Karl carried each of them into the church and arranged them on the altar.

Jack hung limply in their hands as they bore him to the place of his fate. He didn't spasm or wriggle while they carried him. He moaned and muttered against the duct tape over his mouth. If his eyes bulged any wider, Karl joked with Stella "those things would've ended up on my sleeve like a couple of squishy golf balls." When he heard Karl, Jack screamed his face redder than the blood trickling out of his shirt sleeves and pant cuffs. Stella thought her husband might stroke out.

The dog was another story. Alberta had come awake from her concussed sleep by the time Stella and Karl came for her. She was struggling to stand even though her paws were bound together with twine. They stood there for a couple seconds, watching her from afar as she nearly balanced herself before dropping back down onto her side. Karl laughed. Stella blinked back tears. The animal's struggling reminded her of her cat Betsy. Stella hadn't seen the cat since the day the fat pimp in the jogging suit showed up at her house. *How long ago was that? I've lost all sense of time.* Karl called her over, commanded her to take the dog by its back legs. She did this. The dog lifted its upper body in the twitch of an eye, and her jaws snapped like a bear trap, just shy of Karl's arms as he took hold of her front legs.

"Goddam! I like this bitch's fight! I told you she was the right one!"

It wasn't all. Not by a long shot. The dog frothed and barked and growled, snapping at Karl's arms again. "Ho-ho!" The dog must have called on every muscle of her body as it shifted and strained in the air. They carried the animal by her legs, suspending the dog like she was on a fire spit. Albie bore herself up, over and over. Karl had to stop a couple times, each time the dog's teeth bit at the air around his wrists. Once into the vestibule, the dog's whole body clenched from tail to skull, and she extended her neck, opened her jaws, and closed her teeth around Karl's left forearm.

"Mother-*fuck!*" cried Karl. "Set her down! *Fuck!*"

Stella set the flank of the animal down on the cold tiles of the sacristy. "Give me the twine!"

She had to think for a second, then remembered she had it last. She had stuffed it into the front pouch of her hoodie. She took it out, tossed it to Karl, then skirted the animal as it wriggled around furiously on the ground. The dog's mouth was a bear-trap, echoing all around as it slammed shut over and over again. Karl unwound twine as long as himself and bit it off with his teeth. He handed it to Stella.

"Once I get my hands around her snout, wind the twine around it until you run out. Then knot the fucker! You gotta move quick. I don't know how long I can hold her!"

"You're not going to be able to—"

"Fuck that!" Karl hovered just above the dog, arms outstretched and fingers opening and closing as he waited for his moment. A break in the animal's rhythm when she would attempt to catch her breath. She would need to breathe, to flood her muscles full of new oxygen or there would be no more fighting from her. He waited and the second the dog stalled in her movements, her tongue dropping out of the side of her mouth, he seized her around the snout.

"*NOW!*" cried Karl.

The dog's tongue disappeared back into its mouth right before Karl used his hands like a vise to hold her jaw shut. He knew dogs, especially this German Shepherd, possessed a jaw strength amounting to a couple hundred pounds of pressure, and while the exact number escaped him, the reality of the statistic presented itself as the animal tried to open its mouth to break his grip. Stella got the twine around the dog's snout and quickly wound it around eight times before knotting it off with trembling fingers.

This drove the dog's growl, a guttural and demonic groan and burr, back down into the animal's throat. It radiated further down into the animal's whole body. The animal pulsed with a humming malevolence which offered the unmistakable threat of any second breaking free.

Stella saw Karl's hand as he clutched it against his chest. His shirt glistened with blood from the deep puncture wounds, thick with gouts of red that stood in the bite marks along the inside of his forearm. The part of the arm rich with a blue webwork of veins. Stella knew if the animal had pierced one of them properly, Karl would bleed out as if he'd opened up his wrists in a bathtub. She knew this, but she didn't know how to feel about it.

She made a half-hearted attempt to help him.

"It's fine!" Karl growled. "This is nothing! Believe me!"

"You've got to clean it out!"

"You think we got time for that, much less running water in here anywhere? I'll tend to it when we're done. It'll clot by then."

"It's not going to clot!"

"Then I die, and you take the reins for the remainder! You wanted this just as much as I did and if it comes down to it, you better see it through!"

Stella looked at him as the reality of what he said sank in. *He dies and this is over! He really thinks he has that much of a hold on me he could command me beyond death? Who the hell knows what he read in that book he got from his guy in the prison. My God, what if he knows how to ... holy shit ... not a chance ... can't be ...*

The eaves of the vestibule settled around them, like an old man flexing his tired, arthritic limbs. The dog continued to conduct her dark, full-bodied tone like a giant tuning fork on the tiles between them. Karl licked his lips lasciviously as he gazed down at the animal. Then he took a knee and grabbed at one of the frayed bottoms of his chinos. He yanked at it until a thin swatch of it tore away. He pulled upward, extending its diameter some and when he was done, Karl had torn the material away to just below his right knee. A long, chewed cut of the fabric dangled from his hands. "Come here and do this."

She went to him, feeling the heightened thrum of her pulse in her wrist. Stella wrapped it around the wound and knotted it tight as the twine around the dog's snout, only for a different reason. This was a tourniquet. Karl cried out, and even this painful utterance turned quickly to a maniacal laugh as he drew his wounded arm away and inspected it. Satisfied, he stooped and lifted the dog once more by its front legs. She circled back around and followed suit with the back.

They hobbled with the twisting, writhing German Shepherd between them, crossing back into the church and hauling the animal down the center aisle to the altar. Jack Post lay partly on his side. He was sobbing into the mildewed red rug. The lectern near his head leaned precariously. Vandals had unseated it from its post and smashed clean through the wood with something for good measure. Maybe a sledge. The gold cross once inlaid into the front of the lectern lay on the floor. It was bent all out of shape.

"Lower her down," Karl said.

They lowered the dog down. She twitched and snorted. Karl stalked past Stella and kicked Jack in the gut, forcing him to roll over onto his back again. He stooped down beside Jack.

"I know what you're thinking. But it's going to work this time around. You've had a good amount of time to think. About the things you done. To your wife. To your ladies. Did you tell them you were catching? No, if I know you, none of them knew you were shooting flames out of that dick of yours. Right?"

Jack lay prone and silent, his eyes slitted and swollen from crying and cast upward to the woodwork of the high, vaulted ceiling above.

"*Right?*" Karl stood and kicked another boot into Jack's ribs. "What about what you done to me?" He turned to Stella. "Go ahead, tear the tape off his mouth. I want to hear him beg. I want to hear his last words. A man is entitled to his last words, no matter what kind of monster he's acted his whole life."

"He'll scream his head off," Stella argued. "What if someone hears?"

Karl shook his head at her and did it himself. He tore the duct tape away and it made a sound like Velcro coming apart.

Jack started in right away. "You? *You?* What the *fuck* did I ever do to you to deserve all this?"

Karl swept his long, curly hair back out of his face. He looked positively anorexic. His cheeks were gouged out beneath the dark tufts of patchy beard. His thin face looked downright oblong without its hairy dark frame around it. His plump lips were the only fleshy aspect of his visage. His eyes were squinty black pinpricks below a pair of thinned, almost feminine eyebrows.

"You know me, *motherfucker*," Karl said. "My hair wasn't near this long when you did, but you remember me. You all called me Moonshadow. You remember now? You were one of those rubberneckers who looked on while they carted me out of the school in handcuffs. You were afraid of me. When they walked me past you in that busy hallway, I saw the look in your eyes. And you dreaded me. You musta' known what they were taking me in for. The stories spread like wildfire. At least, this is what my mother told me … on one of her handful of visits. But really, weren't you afraid because you knew I knew what you done to my sister? And a *crazy* motherfucker like me wouldn't just forget, no matter how long he spent locked away?" Karl paused, nodding his head in quick jerky motions.

"Karl?" Stella called to him. "What are you talking about?"

"Oh … *Christ* …" Jack looked at Karl and seemed to see him for the first time. "Oh … Jesus … *Christ* … you're blaming me? For her?"

"Her name was *Blaise!*" Karl cried. "But you knew that. You knew her biblically. I know you raped her. Took her out into the soccer field behind Poquessing High on a rainy Saturday night. She told you she loved dancing in the rain. Blaise was … she heard her own drummer boy, and she obeyed him. So you … oh, Jack … *you* talked her into dancing in the dirt. You got her to trust you by playing her game. Falling in line with her drummer boy's beat. Then when she got too dirty from the mud, she asked you to take her home so she could change her clothes. You weren't having it. Your dick was

260

up. You knew she was … what's the *word* … a little touched? Blaise had her problems. And you? You were gonna have her, or you were going to add to those problems, weren't you?"

Jack's quavering voice rang out like a wounded animal choking on its own blood. "We dated. She probably didn't tell you because she knew you were the one who was fucking *touched! And* I tried to *help her!* She told me all about you and your mom and your dad! Fucking Manson had a more normal family"

Stella shrieked behind them. "Karl? Jack? What the hell is this?"

Karl stood up and stooped a little bit, like a court jester without his bells. He jerked a thumb down at Jack.

"See, now I knew he'd say that! *I knew he would!* Goddam, I'm a regular Dr. Phil McGraw! You know what Dr. Phil would say to you, Jack? You know how he'd psychoanalyze what you just said in defense of your raping a sixteen-year-old girl? He'd ask you if you said you were sorry to her after you done it? So I'm asking you, in pure Dr. Phil fashion, did you *apologize* after?"

"Rot in hell … if there's a god, you'll rot—"

"God ain't here no more, Jack," Karl said, standing with one hand on his hip like a pompous prince. "No, see God moved out after what happened here. He didn't want any part of this place after the dirty, devilish things that went down here. This ain't a church. It's an above ground cemetery." He paused, as if gathering his thoughts or lamenting the absence of God. "But it's been established, and there ain't arguing at this juncture. Don't even try it, or I will ram a spike through your fucking skull. Now you tell me? *Did you apologize afterward?*"

"She was off … the path … she needed guidance—"

"BECAUSE YOU'RE NOTHING BUT A FUCKING PIMP!" Karl screamed, and kicked his motorcycle boot into Jack's cock and balls. Jack reeled with a pain that cut off his wind so he could not scream. "Let me break it down for you … because I have given this a lot of thought, and I had nothing but time on the inside to read whatever I could get my hands on about this. You'd be surprised how many magazines have hit on this subject we got here."

Stella grabbed Karl's arm. "Karl, what are you doing?"

"Sit down … and listen."

"*Karl!*"

"I said sit the fuck down! This concerns you, too, Stella! You'll want to hear all I got to say before we do this thing."

Instead, Stella froze. Karl seized her by the shoulders and drove her downward until she had no choice but to bend at the knees and lower grace-lessly into a sitting position.

Karl walked with something of a swagger between the husband and wife on the floor of the altar. "Jack, you're a goddamn pimp, and Stella? Sorry to tell you this, darling, but you … and my sister Blaise, god rest her soul … and all these other ladies he's been with? You're all broken in one way or another. You needed someone to come along and talk you up, build you up … *then, break you down!* Then … build you up in an image he could be comfortable with and make use of. Like a pimp does to his … oh, I don't want to use this word but what else can I do … like a pimp builds his bitch-es."

"You …" Jack was laughing now, a hideous surprise for both Stella and Karl. "You … don't have a *fucking clue*. Not a hint!"

Stella swallowed the sizeable lump gathered in her throat. "I am *not* anyone's bitch," she stated, flatly.

"Oh no, honey," Karl said, bending down and squatting in front of Stella. "It's not your fault. It's Stockholm Syndrome. The Pimp Version. You had no idea what was happening. Someone like me needed to come along and bring it to your attention. It don't make you a bitch, or a bad person. But I'll tell you this, Stella! You don't punish this man for what he done to you and your gender … and to my dear, touched sister … and I will treat you like the victim you decided to make yourself into, and I will not only follow through with the plan, but I'll also put you out of your misery. I got a stacked deck so it won't mean a damned thing to me. You wanna know why?"

She bit her tongue, sucked the blood it brought forth.

Karl smiled. "Because I'll be damned if I'm going to sit back and watch you settle into your victimhood. You'd be better off dead."

Stella hugged herself and started to rock to and fro without realizing. "This is ludicrous. This poor dog."

"You're missing the point of this," Karl said.

"Then tell me, for God's sakes!"

"All right," Karl said, "let me tell you. You're gonna *love it*.

"When the transference happens, don't think Jack and the dog are just going to swap bodies. It wouldn't mean shit and wouldn't teach any kind of lesson. No, Jack's conscious mind is going to squeeze itself into the space inside the animal's conscious mind. Whatever part of the dog's con-sciousness is pushed out by this will just find a new home inside of Jack's hard-headed skull. The dog will still work on instinct, and it will still have a good bit of its memory in place to guide it and help it make decisions. But Jack is going to be in there somewhere, too. I'm thinking once we get

262

rolling with the plans, and we're deep in it, he'll be desperate to find some dark little corner of the dog's mind where he can cover his eyes instead of having to look out the animal's color-blind eyes one more second. Jack is going to be the dog's *passenger*, and like a *passenger* he will be powerless to do anything to stop what he's seeing. He can only watch … and if all goes well … in absolute fucking horror." Karl paused, leering over at Jack. "Now that … that'll teach a lesson. Then, Jack will have our permission to die. Not one minute before."

It was Jack who spoke next, a bit of the old bravado having somehow found its back into his voice. "You know something, Karl? You're still the same gullible, deluded shithead I remember from high school. Who told you this was even possible, this little psychology experiment of yours? This is why you brought me here? Are you serious? You are a *dumb fuck!* Why don't you quit while you're ahead, leave town, and let my wife drive me to the hospital so we can undo some of this?"

Stella braced herself for Karl's temper to once again show itself. She couldn't tell what unnerved her more, the fact he spoke next in a measured tone or he held back his anger so effectively.

"Have it your way, Jack. Believe what you want. Hell, if it means you're going to humor me and not put up a struggle then have at it. When it's done, I'll look for you in both bodies. I'll call for you and whichever body, man or beast, answers me then we'll know who knows shit and who doesn't! How about it?"

"You'll find me right here … in this body. When you do, you leave town and Stella drives me to the ER. My wife and I never hear from you again. You want to wager, let's fucking wager!"

"Good deal," Karl said, "I'd shake hands with you but I doubt you'll have any grip. So we'll just talk it into being." He turned to Stella. "Cut some more twine. Two lines. About five feet long each. Then, have them at the ready and come help me with the dog."

This might not work. It does sound completely ridiculous. And I came all this way … allowed myself to be led by this man, and all along he's had this in mind as the endgame? No wonder he was so stingy with the information. I think a part of him knew I could laugh at him for even suggesting something like this could work.

She did as Karl told her. She would not take Jack to the hospital, but she wouldn't leave town with Karl either. She would do just that. It could be fun, assuming another name and slipping into the sweet anonymity of a new, untarnished life. Suddenly, she felt herself rooting within for the whole damn thing to fail. For Jack to answer Karl in that sardonic voice of his, gloating over the failure. *I would probably have to kill Karl, but I think I have it in me now. No, I know I do ...*

It was surreal as it was strange, Jack laughing instead of freaking out as Karl and Stella walked the wriggling, writhing animal over to him. They kept the dog's front and back legs bound, her snout as well. Karl told Stella only the animal's eyes need remain free and accessible. "The whole thing will happen between the eyes."

So ... ridiculous, Stella thought. *Oh ... Karl ... come on—*

They set the dog down on top of Jack, lining up the dog's bound snout with Jack's chin. Karl held the animal in this position. "Eye-to eye," he muttered to himself, eye-balling how the man's and beast's gaze lined up. "Perfect." He snapped at Stella. "I want you to lift Jack's upper body just enough to get the twine around him."

"Why?"

"We're going to tie them together. Bind them."

Jack jerked as the dog suddenly lunged its snout down at his nose. "Jesus, you want to keep Lassie from biting my face off? You want to keep her *out of my face?*"

"You scared, Jack?" Karl said.

"Fuck you, hillbilly. Family of fucking hillbillies. The fucking Tar-licks. You remember, Stella?"

"Shut up, Jack," Stella said, coming up behind his head. "I'm going to lift you so work with me here."

"Oh, sure thing, wifey," Jack said, uneasily.

Stella slipped her hands under Jack's armpits, counted down from three, and drew him up with a grunt. The animal growled from the depths of its soul as Karl maneuvered her to coincide with the arrangement. He told Stella to run the twine around the dog and Jack. She walked it around and around the two of them, Jack laughing weakly and the dog moaning. She pulled the twine taut enough she could fit a finger under it, but no more. She knotted it at the supple downward slope of the animal's back where it gave upward to the rise of its brindle-furred neck. She held Jack's lower back down, the dog bound to him like some horrid missionary-style bestiality display.

Jack cried out this time, shedding some of his previous nerve. "Keep that fucking dog's teeth out of my *face!*"

Now, it was Karl's turn to laugh at him. "No can do, Jack." He turned to Stella. "Now, bind them around the neck. Loose enough they can still look into each other's eyes. Tight enough they can't turn their heads away. And they're going to try to do it once this gets underway."

Stella said to Jack, "Lift your head up."

"Keep the dog out of my face!"

"Don't be childish, Jack. Be a man." It felt so good when she said it, Stella felt a twitch between her thighs. "Lift."

Begrudgingly, Jack lifted and Stella slipped her hands behind his skull. She told Karl to hold the dog steady, and he did so. She wound the twine four times around the dog's and her husband's necks. Karl lined up the eyes of Jack and the dog and when he nodded at Stella, satisfied with what he saw, she tightened it just enough for Jack to curse her and for the animal to burrow its snout into the small of his throat. It nosed around, greedily and full of suppressed anger.

Jack was screaming now: *"Fucking dog is going to rip out my throat!"*

"Shut up! Be a man!"

Something happened on the altar.

It sounded like an assembly of invisible people in the pews, a congregation, inhaling all at once. Stella was so convinced of the unsettling sound's reality she gazed out across the tops of the pews. The unseen parishioners held their collective breaths, as if waiting for the impossible to be made possible. Thunder exploded above their heads, then a quick and blinding light pierced the stained glass windows lining the side walls and illuminating the abandoned, atrophying interior of the church. Karl told Stella to step back. She was quick to do so, retreating down a pair of steps to linger by the front right pew. The hairs on her arms and along the nape of her neck stood at attention as she cast another wide glance from one side of the church seating area to the other. Still searching for those who waited with baited breath for ...

What? For what?

Stella returned her attention to the altar while rain sounded like the drumming fingers of a giant thrummed along the church roof and the red brick. The windows. The doors. She felt a light spray of wetness fan across her face and wondered where it could be coming from, before realizing two of the windows to her left were gone, leaving only open and empty steel frames which let in the elements. She listened while the thunder clapped its hands over and over, as if some great god above approved of what was looking more and more like an abomination unfolding across a once blessed and sacred Catholic altar. Stella watched Karl bend and crane his neck around the side of the dog's head and whisper something into her ear. He spoke into the dog's ear for what seemed like a long time. As he spoke, the dog's body seemed almost to shed some of her rigidity. Her back sloped downward. She

265

ceased struggling against Karl. At the same time, Jack's screams clipped off jagged as the page of a book torn in half.

There was only the rain and the thunder for a moment. Nothing else. Stella felt as if she were watching a silent movie unfolding on the altar.

Jack howled. There was nothing of the *man* left in the sound. It had turned thoroughly canine and monstrous. His scream held for so long Stella nearly succumbed to instinct and gouged her fingers into her ears to puncture the drum within.

The dog's jaws snapped the outer layering of twine around its snout and the pieces burst apart as if spring-loaded. A man's voice, not quite Jack's as it was much lower in register and bore a speech effect not unlike a deaf person, poured out of the animal's snout.

"KILLME-KILLME-KILL-MEEEEEEE"

Oh no–dear–God-this isn't possible!

The unseen congregants in the pews exhaled as one, slow and deep. Jack and the dog slipped into silence. For a second, there was only the rain again before Jack resumed howling once more. Karl hovered over the two of them, man and animal. He stared down at them with the same look of awe in his eyes Stella imagined Edison must have shown when he first lit the light bulb.

He wasn't expecting it to work either. He doesn't know what to do next.

Karl stood there a moment longer. Then he did as he said he would. He hunkered down next to Jack, who had gone back over onto his side, now whimpering like a puppy underfoot and fighting for air. Karl lowered himself down onto his belly and spoke into Jack's ear. "You in there? Jackie? Tell me if you're in there. Go on. We got a wager on this."

Jack lunged up off the floor, his mouth opening and closing at frightfully menacing rate. Teeth gnashing against each other. His bite snapped shut a mere inch from Karl's throat before he recoiled, gathered his wits, and punched Jack in the side of the head with a sloppy hook. Jack swooned. He sank back down to the moldy red carpet of the altar and curled up into himself.

"Holy shit," Karl said, just catching his breath.

"Are you okay?" Stella asked, holding her position and safe distance.

"Let's see." Karl crept over to the dog, spoke into her ear. "Jackie? Jack? You in there? Here's your chance if you can make those doggy vocal cords say the words. Your chance to tell me to *go fuck myself!* I'm guessing you won't be able to make that happen. So … how about this? Tell me again what you want me to do for you. Hell, maybe in the end I'll grant your wish. Go on … say it again."

The dog lifted her head, moaned in a warbly and terrible baritone, *"Killme! Killme!"*

"Hot damn," Karl said. He glanced over at Stella. "Hot damn! It worked!"

Stella was speechless. She had soiled herself without realizing, a small puddle standing just beside her left Reebok sneaker.

49. RIVELLS MEET MINA

When Detectives Rivells and Jones reached Mina Cohen's ER examining room at Doylestown Hospital, they were met by Sergeant Coombs of the Comstock Police Department, and a twentysomething responding officer who seemed all too comfortable to fade into the background. The ER was hectic, and the two detectives had to skirt three gurneys on their winding way to meet the sergeant.

"This is the nearest hospital," Coombs said. "We got an Urgent Care in Comstock, but that's it." He shook hands with Rivells and Jones, and rubbed his pale, soft jawline. "Thanks for coming out so quickly. We don't see much of this kind of thing where we're from." He sounded to the detectives like someone describing life on another planet. Rivells and Jones understood. Comstock felt a lot like Mars in comparison to their street beat in Philadelphia's Society Hill section.

"You say she described her attackers, and that's why you called us in?" Rivells asked.

"We got an APB out on the two you're looking for. They haven't hit any of our ins or outs yet which tells me they're still in town. The balls on the two of them, hanging out here like they got nothing to fear."

"Comstock have a lot places to hole up? Abandoned houses? Underpasses? Just driving in, you can see there's a lot of woodland. It poses a challenge," Jones said.

"I got guys on my team can walk every inch of our forests with a blindfold on. If they're sitting around a campfire somewhere in Cantrell Forest or Tanner Woods, we could find them within the hour."

Rivells glanced inside the ER room, seeking a glimpse of the woman inside, lying across a blanketed gurney. The voices of two attendant physicians asking questions and explaining what they were doing to Mina Cohen filtered into the hallway through the small opening between the sliding glass door and its jamb. Their words were mildly obscured by the sounds of beeping machines and nurses shouting at one another as they crisscrossed the ER tiles on soft, silent soles, dipping into and out of other exam rooms.

"How is she?" Rivells asked, turning back to Sergeant Coombs.

Coombs rubbed his jaw again, an obvious tic. "Miss Cohen is beat up. She took it on the jaw and a couple kicks to her stomach. Fractured ribs. From what we gather, she put up a pretty good fight. Apparently, she's been taking judo classes. Never thought she'd ever have put them to use but thank Christ she had the know-how, or we'd be looking at another fatality."

"You got an ID on them?" Jones asked.

"Name's Katherine Danforth," Coombs replied. "The male perp hit her in the back of the head with a goddam tire iron according to Miss Cohen. They lost her twice in the ambulance, then they lost her for good after fifteen minutes in triage"

"Fuck," Rivells said, ignoring the shocked expression of the two Comstock locals. *What's the matter? You've never known the release of using that word? You haven't fucking lived!* "You said something about Miss Cohen's boyfriend? He's something of a celebrity around here?"

Coombs smiled thinly. "Not just around *these parts*. Will Bentley's a superstar in the literary world. He wrote *I Can Hear the Shiite Weeping*. I'm not much of a reader, but if you're from our town it's become something like required reading. Won a whole slew of awards. A Pulitzer. Heard it's like an actor winning a goddamn Golden Globe or something. Our victim, Miss Cohen? She's his girlfriend. As for the fatality, she was their live-in vet nurse. Been taking care of Mr. Bentley's dog, who this whole town loves just as much as our favorite author. Named Alberta. Beautiful German Shepherd."

Jones had his pocket memo pad out, his hand a blur across the small page as he penciled in the information in expert shorthand. "Interesting," he said cursorily. "I can understand the town loving its favorite son, but his dog? Any particular reason for the fondness to extend to his pet, too?"

There was clear hesitation on the sergeant's part. For the first time during the exchange, Coombs looked to the officer at his elbow for some kind of support or prompt. Where to begin, perhaps? Coombs lowered his voice and explained the events which took place six months prior at St. Alphonsus Church. He shared the details as if he were one of the townsfolk in attendance at the brutal torture and murder of the priest. When Sergeant Coombs wrapped up his story of the massacre, someone threw back the curtain of the exam room. Two nurses stepped into the hallway, one of them peeling off a pair of rubber gloves. Rivells and Jones produced their credentials, his hooked to his belt and hers hanging from a dog-chain around her neck on a lanyard. The nurses waved them inside with the casual warning both detectives had come to know by heart. "Just a few questions, because she needs her rest."

They were surprised to find Mina Cohen in there by herself, without the inimitable writer-boyfriend by her side and clutching her hand in his. A stab of resentment hit Rivells' gut at this. It made her want to hug the woman propped up on the gurney by a slew of pillows and wearing red and blue bruises along her jawline. Mina Cohen's Fifth Avenue beauty seemed to defy and downplay her injuries. Her bright green eyes refused to soften despite the attack she had suffered, but they watered over as soon as the detectives stepped inside the exam room. Her black hair was clipped to the bottom of her earlobes and a single white strand framed the left side of her face. Rivells thought *Art dealer? Artist? Writer in her own right? Something creative? Her boyfriend's a celebrated author and birds of a feather do flock together, so ...*

Jones handled the introductions. Mina armed her tears out of her eyes, nodded with a strained smile, then spread her shaking hands in her aproned lap. "Did you find our dog?"

"May I sit?" Rivells asked.

Mina waved her down onto the edge of the gurney. "Of course."

Rivells took Mina's hand in hers and squeezed. "Okay if we ask you some questions, Mina?"

Mina nodded.

The first question sought to corroborate what the sergeant had already conveyed to them. Mina's explanation went deeper, which was what they were really after. "The girl was a ginger. I'm going to say early twenties. There was something a little off about her. I don't know, she was ... a *tweaker*? Twitchy and over-excited. She explained she saw the interview I just did with *The Inquirer* in today's edition. It featured Albie, our dog, and I ... and we talked about how we were all doing in the wake of the St. Alphonsus attack. Will's on a speaking tour right now, so I agreed to handle it in his absence.

"She was acting like Albie and I were a couple of celebrities because our picture was in the paper. I let her pet our dog." Mina paused, her eyes growing distant before she returned to her train of thought. "Now I remember Katherine must have gotten a bad feeling about the encounter because she started trying to rush us back home. Saying Albie needed her bath. Something like that. I can't remember exactly, but she *sensed* something was wrong. I should have followed her lead. Why didn't I ...?"

"Take your time," Rivells said, giving Mina's hand another squeeze.

269

Mina nodded primly. "The guy came out of nowhere," she said. "Actually, no ... no I can't say that. He ... he drove by in a car. I remember now. He must have parked it down the way and, I don't know, backtracked to us? I was busy talking to the girl and trying to extricate us from the encounter. One minute Katherine was behind me insisting Albie needed to get home. Then she gasped, and I turned around just in time to find the man from the car hit her ... *oh God ... the sound it made.* I can't get it out of my head."

"That's all right," Jones said. "You're doing fine." His hand was paused overtop of the small memo pad in his hand, pencil laid across the small page. "Did you put up a fight?"

"I-I tried *so hard* and the girl ... I was able to get the better of her. But the man? He had a tire iron, and he got it against my throat. Pulled it back. I couldn't breathe. The girl ... I got her good. A couple hits at her face. She pulled herself together enough and got a hold of my dog. The guy must have made me black out for a minute there. The next thing I knew, the car was parked right there. The girl must have run and gotten it. Driven it back down the road while the man held onto my dog's leash. Katherine ... she must have been unconscious. They took my dog. Pulled away with her. And she ... that *bitch* ... do you know what she said to me before she got in the car and drove away?" Mina's lips became a thin, bloodless line. Her eyes glazed over with anger. "She said she was *sorry about all this. Sorry ... about all this.*"

"All right," Rivells said. "Well, that's a *good* thing, Mina. The woman showed remorse for what she and her man did. Her heart probably wasn't all the way in it. Maybe the man threatened her, and she had no choice. But I want you to see this as a very promising detail, because if this woman feels bad about what she did, then the chances she may come to protect your dog if it comes down to it are *very* good. You understand?"

"Oh please, Detective—"

"Rivells."

"Detective Rivells, you've got to bring our dog home safe. She's still not one hundred percent, and if they push her too hard she could break, and I would never forgive myself. She's had such a shitty life and why this had to happen, I just can't understand! Alberta really needs to come home to us. She's our child. Our damaged, fragile child!"

Jones closed his memo pad and parked his pencil behind his ear. "Miss Cohen, I've got two rescue dogs at home. Greyhounds. Arnold and Willis, after the two kids from *Diff'rent Strokes.* They were race dogs. Abused. The things their eyes must have seen. Their bodies must have had to stand up to. When they came to me, I could count every single one of their ribs. I know exactly what you mean when you say Alberta is your child.

Those two are probably the only two kids I'm ever going to have, and it's all right with me. I wouldn't have it any other way. So I want you to trust my word when I tell you Detective Rivells and I are going to do everything in our power to bring Alberta back home safe to you. All right?"

Careful, Jones. Watch your promises! Rivells was so confounded by Jones' well-meant but potentially harmful vow, when he nodded down at her satchel she had slung over her shoulder, Rivells had to think about what he meant by it. Then, she came back around.

Rivells unsnapped her bag and withdrew two glossy sheets from within. "I know your nurse is going to be chasing us out any second. Do you feel up to looking at some photographs? Maybe making a positive ID of the man and woman if you see them?"

"Yes, let's do it," Mina said, accepting the first glossy from Rivells. It showed six photographs, four of them female mugshots; one a photo of Rivells' niece, and one in the upper left corner of a ginger-haired girl Rivells had retrieved from a hanging portrait in the woman's house. Mina glared down at the six photograph squares and almost immediately stabbed her index finger down onto the half-smiling face of Stella Post. "That's the *crazy bitch!* Definitely!"

"You're sure?" Rivells pressed, following protocol.

"I'm positive."

"Good," Rivells said, retrieving the first glossy and handing Mina the second one. "Now, I want you to look at these six and tell me if you see the man who attacked you tonight."

Mina studied the six mugshots. Her cheeks reddened, and just as Rivells told her to "take her time," she gasped and pointed down at the mugshot in the second row, center. "Him. His hair's shorter in this picture, but those eyes? Oversized lips. Creepy-looking bastard!"

Two-for-two! Rivells' heart punched out at her chest with anticipation. *We got them, the two fuckwits!*

Sergeant Coombs poked his pink, round head inside the exam room. "Detectives? A moment?"

Rivells met Mina's eyes and patted the bed. "I don't want you to sit here making yourself crazy thinking about what you could have done differently to prevent any of this. Do you hear me? Your job is to get well and meet up with your man when he gets here. Our job is to make this right."

"Thank you, Detective."

Jones smiled warmly down at Mina and exited to the hallway where Sergeant Coombs and the silent officer stood. Coombs motioned to the officer. "Officer Carver just got a call on his radio about a stolen car in town."

Officer Carver accepted the lead-in. "Over on Butler Street. Retired Air Force sergeant by the name of Willis Grimby reported his Cutlass stolen just now. He's something of a homebody. Doesn't take the car out unless he needs something from the grocery store or a new carton of Pall Malls. Says he drove the car yesterday afternoon, so it could have been taken any time between then and now."

"All due respect, but I don't get the tie-in," Jones said.

The officer squared his shoulders. "The car thief dumped another car two blocks down from Mr. Grimby's house. Silver Taurus. Registered to Stella and Jack Post."

Sergeant Coombs swiped a palm across his bald, pink pate. "Grimby didn't hear a thing when his car was reversing out of his driveway? Was it parked on the street? I just can't imagine it would take this guy so long to miss his car."

"It's a setback," Jones said. "They could have blown right out of town without so much as a second glance from your men. Unless they're more brazen than we could possibly imagine and they're coming to and from Comstock without a care!"

"They're still here. I know it in my gut," Rivells said.

Sergeant Coombs scratched the webbing between the thumb and index of his right hand. "I've already got patrols out and about checking the forests. Any vacant locations. The parks. Playground at the middle school and senior high."

"Can you keep someone posted here until Miss Cohen's boyfriend shows?" Rivells asked.

"Positively, Detective," Sergeant Coombs replied, raising his three chins towards Officer Carver. "And I've already updated the APB with the stolen vehicle's information. You two look like you're itching to get away from here. Don't worry about offending us! Go do what you gotta do!"

50. DRY RUN

Stella stopped cold, pulling backward on Jack legs. "I don't understand why we have to dump him back down in the dark again! Can't we just ... I don't know." *I was going to say, leave him in the light.*

"What?" Karl asked, impatience flaring in his voice. They had gotten as far as the vestibule with Jack's body between them. "You think he's gonna have a problem with this? He's not *here* anymore!" Karl jiggled Jack under the arms where he had hold of him to accentuate the point. "This is nothing but a vacant address, and we just forcibly evicted him from it. How many more times I gotta remind you of that?"

She straightened up, and her lower back clenched into an unforgiving fist. If what Karl said was true, that must mean the ritual (whatever it was) could, in fact, be reversed. They could return Jack's consciousness to the gray folds of his brain once more, like returning a filched wallet to an oblivious woman's pocketbook. The proposition stood poised on the edge of her thin lips, and she nearly spoke the words. But Stella knew better.

Turning this over in her mind, the belief was solid. It was flaking away, shedding motes of dust like a human body little by little over a lifetime. This could not be denied. She thought back to all those sweet words Karl had shared with her during their prison visits, at first through a telephone separated by thick glass and then gradually face-to-face as he gained more privileges for good behavior. The dirty words, too. The filthy talk he whispered to her about how he would *fulfill* her and *fuck her blind*. Both sides of the coin excited her, always had. Better to have two sides of a coin than to come up with an empty change purse, which was what her marriage to this dead weight between she and Jack had been for the past four years.

Karl's voice cut through the brightness of her reverie, like a machete through hanging vines. "Pick up your end, and let's be done with this shit. I don't want to touch this motherfucker any longer than I have to. He's got AIDS blood, and I'm not exactly wearing latex gloves. Neither are you, now come on!"

AIDS blood.

It was like a palm-slap against a horse's backside. Stella stooped, ignored the fist squeezing her bottom vertebrae and then opening, as she gathered up Jack by the ankles and continued backing towards the door leading down the shallow stairwell into the pitch dark basement. Any concern for Jack's well-being fizzled at the reminder of his previously reckless, lethal behavior.

Death was living inside of her.

Stella freed a hand to turn the knob to the basement and throw open the door. Sour breath sighed out of the opening as they crossed the threshold.

"You know the saying?" Karl asked. "Goes something like *you'll never walk alone?*"

Stella walked a few paces inward and let Jack's legs slide down the front of her and come to rest on the tiles with a thud. "It's a song." *More like a hymn, but a song just the same. Something about God never leaving your*

273

side? I call bullshit!

"Yeah," Karl said, dumping Jack carelessly. Stella saw the flash of his white teeth in the dark as he relished the pitiful shriek from her husband when his head struck the ground. "Yeah, the song. *You'll never walk alone!* Well, if the song were about us, it would go like *You'll never die alone!* That's you and me."

"I don't want to talk about it," Stella said, blindly feeling her way past him and back towards the doors to the vestibule. "It may not be true. And even if it is, I'm not ready to *laugh* about it."

He was on her heels, perhaps itching to get back into the part of the church where at least a little light reached. *He'll never admit he's scared of a damned thing ever! Never show weakness, not to me!*

Two things happened at once as Karl was propping the door to the entrance hall open for Stella to cross through.

They had only just laid Jack down there in the basement when the ravenous, unhinged barking erupted just beyond the bottom of the stairwell. Stella thought a dog was trapped down there, and they had somehow missed it. The sounds of a dog in distress. Then it broke in Jack's throat, and he sounded once more like a man merely attempting to imitate a rabid canine.

"Shit!" Karl said, beside her.

Stella shut the door to the stairwell, all too willing to close off the sound. She turned to Karl, eyes wide and terrified when she saw what Karl was cursing.

A pair of light beams played about the interior of the entrance hall, crisscrossing one another as they penetrated the glass of the front doors and washed over the wooden arches leading into the school wing. They bled across the floor. Broke across the ceiling tiles. One of the beams nearly touched the front of Karl's left motorcycle boot, and he edged his way out of the line of sight, grabbing for Stella's hand. She gave it to him, drawing some small comfort from the grasp of his strong fingers.

"Follow along close to me," he whispered.

Stella nudged her way into him and kept contact with the side of him like they were Velcroed together. The light beams swelled as their bearers closed in on the front doors to St. Alphonsus. Karl slipped through the glass door leading back into the church, mindful to brace it as it slid closed behind Stella so it wouldn't clunk shut.

A flutter of wings beat madly up in the eaves above the altar. The late hour meant bats, and Stella's skin crawled at the thought of one of them swooping downward, dive bombing her and tangling tiny claws in her red hair. Snapping tiny fangs at the pale, exposed flesh of her cheeks, her throat.

274

She ducked instinctively as Karl led her up the two steps onto the altar.

Then his voice was in her ear, hot and flustered. "Go and duck down behind the lectern. Don't come out until it's all over. One way or another, it will be."

"We could go out the side door over there and get in the car," she whispered to him.

"We're not done here. And they're not gonna rush us. Go to the lectern."

They stared at one another, Karl's gaze unyielding and certain compared to Stella's disbelief and dread. Stella shook her head and cast her eyes to the floor. She crept over to hide behind the lectern. It was hanging over, unseated from its base by some vandals with bats. She dipped down until her head was below it and watched from the hiding place.

The sounds of two men rang out in the vestibule. Their flashlights skimmed the tops of the pews, darting about like untamed spirits.

Karl went to the dog. He bent low to the animal and whispered in its ear. Stella would have given anything to know what words he was uttering to the animal to somehow affect her brain, calling it into line and command. The dog whimpered. The next sound she made quickened Stella's pulse as before when she was certain the dog had spoken in a human tongue. It was a word, the thrust of the consonant and roll of the vowels but damned if she could make sense of what it was.

Jack speaking through the animal.

Pleading? Bastard!

Stella watched Karl clip the twine from around the dog's front and back legs. They sprang free. She fully expected the dog to kick and fight, to catch Karl with one of her long claws. Instead, the dog rose onto four legs, wobbly at first, until Karl steadied the animal where she stood. He took hold of the dog by her collar and led her back into the recesses of the altar, to the left of the sacristy which was now a gaping hole where once the host and wine were housed under lock and key.

The church doors wheezed open. The lights spun about. The chatter of the two interlopers bounced off the wide-open space. Cold sweat squirted across her brow. Her heart was a rhumba drum between her ears. They were police. Of course, the police. Who else? Wilding teenagers? Not tonight. She craned her head in the direction where Karl and the dog had hidden themselves away in a deep pocket of shadow.

So deep even she could not find them with her tired eyes.

The spray of moonlight filtering through the stained glass lining the walls on either side illuminated the men just enough to reveal their stature and the khaki color of their uniforms. Stella always thought cops in Comstock dressed like SS officers. One of them was a good foot taller than the other and lumbered like he was traversing the center aisle on stilts. The other was stocky, but his face fully materialized as they closed in upon the altar, and Stella could see the freckles, a heavy spray of them from cheek to cheek.

Both patrolman had their guns at the ready. They held them directly under their flashlights like city cops searching a drug den.

Stella held her breath. Waited.

It will all be over one way or another.

The panic attack came on fast. Stella felt her heart racing, her palms slick. It felt like a heart attack. Always like a cardiac arrest. She would die. She would. Oh yes, she would.

The tall cop stopped cold five feet shy of the first step up onto the altar. He hissed at his partner. Their twin beams converged upon the altar, trained on something up against the rear wall.

Tall Cop cried, "There in the back! Hands up! Do it now!"

Freckle Cop bolstered the command, his voice far more trebly. "Now! DO IT NOW!"

Stella saw Karl and the dog awash in the wide, twitching oval of the flashlight beam, like some bizarre vaudeville act awaiting their cue. Karl was hunkered down behind the dog, his arm slung around the dog's neck. Holding her back. The dog was calm. Obedient.

Tall Cop: "Is the animal on a leash?"

"Nah," Karl said. "Don't need a leash."

"HANDS UP NOW!" Freckle Cop was antsy, trigger happy it would seem.

Karl's hand slid up around the dog's muzzle.

"SIR, SHOW US YOUR HANDS OR WE WILL SHOOT YOU!" Tall Cop took one long, lumbering step forward.

Stella heard something snap and knew what it was right off.

The twine holding the dog's snout shut.

The sudden wet glint of fangs as the dog leapt.

Tall Cop never saw it coming until the dog's teeth were in his throat.

Karl fell upon the other cop and wrestled the gun out of his hands. The look of shock never left Freckle Cop's face.

He couldn't bring himself to fire on the animal.

Dog lover.

Stella knew it.

Her thoughts detached, she watched from another place and time. Far removed from what unfolded mere feet away from the tips of her dirty Reeboks.

So very fast.

51. TERROR

When the human mind needs to reconcile itself to a state of being it is unfamiliar with, it will try to fit that concept into a framework which will allow for it to render such a state into something recognizable and plausible. A safety valve for the mind. That is how Jack Post guarded against his consciousness from unraveling in the moment. But it's not to say he wasn't screaming the whole ride like a man with his hair on fire. The moment Jack had felt himself ripped clear of his body, like a driver snatched out of the driver's seat of a wrecked vehicle by the jaws of life, there had been an immediate sense of loss and regret the likes of which he had never known before. It felt like some small death, his essence slipping his body, only to burrow itself into the folds of the animal's brain before the dank-smelling air could tamp it out or weigh it down. There was also the sense of his having unseated and, in the plainest terms, displaced a portion of the animal's consciousness. Jack had no idea where it could have ended up, the entire process like the space a body takes up in a bathtub where too much water has been drawn. The water splashes up and dumps out over the side, drenching the bathroom tiles and the tub mat.

That shred of the animal's consciousness was the water on the tiles.

That is the thing about forcing an entirely alien state of being to adapt to some construct a human brain can come to understand. It is a bit like forcing a screw into a nail hole with a hammer. The wall could crack. The brain could shatter. Jack's essence hammered home, snugly. It was all he could do to summon a recognizable form of himself when it happened. The summoning was not perfect, of course. Imperfect, Jack would say. Rather than Jack using the dog's tongue to taste, or its impeccable sense of smell to sniff things out, Jack Post's consciousness sorted this new situation, his new abode inside a canine mind, by casting himself in the role of the prisoner locked inside the top of a prison tower. He came to inside the dog's mind, feeling like an imprisoned political prisoner from the Dark Ages stirring inside a cell with rats squirreling in and out of his legs as he leaned against damp, wet stonework. He was a captive inside the dog's skull, with only the animal's color blind eyes to act as windows into the world before her.

Jack had screamed for a seemingly endless period of time after his small death. He had hurled himself against the invisible confines of the black cell imprisoning him, and then an overwhelming urge and desire to lie down and sleep had taken over. The small death had exhausted him beyond measure, the fatigue pressing him down into the floor of his cell at an unprecedented rate. He had fallen away, entertaining simple pleas to whatever God could help him, that he be allowed to wake up in his bed when he opened his eyes again.

Please, dear God, put me back in my bed, or kill me in my sleep! Have mercy!

He could feel the dog panting, the shucking of its body as it strained to breathe through its nose only. For Jack, it felt like he was sitting inside a car with a dying transmission.

I'm a fucking prisoner! Captive audience!

What are they planning for this dog? For me?

Karl Tarlick appeared in the dog's immediate periphery, as if Jack's thoughts somehow summoned him. The filmy windows of the dog's eyes revealed Tarlick to him, looming large as a godhead in his own right. Jack sprang up off the floor of his cell, a great surge of anger lighting him up. He launched himself at the filmy windows, fist pumping in the air.

"If you can hear me, cocksucker, stop what you're doing and listen closely!" Tarlick did not stop what he was doing in the slightest. The dog looked down the side of its long, lean body, and Jack watched through the filmy windows as Karl cut the bindings around the animal's front and back legs.

"You can hear me! I *know* you can hear me! You think you can keep me in here like this? You fuck! I *will* find a way out of this. And when I do … I'm going to gut you! I'm going to rend your fucking flesh, and I'm going to eat your *goddamn* heart like a fucking warrior because you're weak and stupid, and *I'm the man*! I have always *been the man!* Look at me! LOOK AT ME, YOU PIGFUCK! YOU WERE A LOSER TEN YEARS AGO AND TIGERS DO NOT CHANGE THEIR SPOTS! LOSERS DON'T GET TO WIN! EVER!*"*

Jack's skull throbbed from the effort. *Speakpleasespeakjustspeak*

There could be no denying he heard it. The animal had formed a word, struggled to produce it despite the binding around her snout. He felt the animal pin its tongue to the roof of its mouth as it tried to enunciate.

Like a human being! I did that! I know I did! The dog tried to say

278

what I wanted it to say, one of my words at least! Loser! Hot damn, that lit-tle prick unties the dog's mouth, I'm going to have this mutt hurling insults and threats like a mafioso! It did not give Karl pause of any kind. He cut the dog's back legs loose and leaned in towards what could only be, in Jack's estimation, the animal's ear. *Sweet nothing, Tarlick? I've got some choice words for you, fucker!*

Karl's words made no sense whatsoever. There was no explanation. He was not speaking to the dog in another language. Jack was quite certain no language, no matter how primitive, could possibly exist within the slow, atonal sounds which filled the confines of his dark cell like a siege of terrible, soulless cacophony. Karl's message was lost in translation once it entered the dog's ear canal, sifted down into the dog's cerebral cortex, and from there proved itself utterly confounding in its meaning. It occurred to Jack, this is most likely how humans must sound to a dog when they are prattling on and on to the animal.

The dog raised itself into a standing position. Karl steadied the ani-mal when it wavered a little. The dog cast its gaze in the opposite direction, and Jack spied through the filmy windows the two dancing beams of what could only be flashlights. Black, white, and grey, but they were enough. All he needed. *The police are here!*

I have to get this dog to say something! They have to untie the dog's mouth! They have to do it right fucking now! Use those jaws, dog! Open your mouth! You know? MOUTH!

Jack stood in the middle of his cell like someone trying to wave to a 747 passing overhead at ten thousand feet. Arms wide and high. He screamed over and over the same word, like somehow through repetition the animal would come to understand its meaning. *You don't have a dog biscuit to work this angle anyway! You've got no reward or anything to tempt her with! Just angry words! Shouting! Don't shout at her or you may upset her.*

It was not the man crouching down behind her who tensed Albie's muscles fit to snap. He whispered into her right ear here and there, but the delivery of those words were soothing as they were indecipherable. Albie could make no meaning of what the man behind her kept trying to suggest, to deliver directly to her frontal lobe like an untarnished and universal command to hurt and harm. The man could have been saying anything, and Albie would have heeled. She had been tired, and the sound of the man's utterances did not work her up. She had only wanted to lie down, to splay herself across the mildewed red rug of the altar and snore for a spell.

Then of course the screaming started.

The voice she heard sounded directly between her ears, and she felt herself clench. Froth formed around her muzzled mouth. The man was reaching around her with some sort of lethal looking instrument. It looked sharp at one end, dull and grim in color. Albie rolled her eyes back from the instrument, away from its danger. She dug her nails into the rug, and her heart started to build into a gallop. The screaming voice in her head did not match the man's voice behind her. When the screaming from one man and the whispers of the other man collided, filling her brain and overloading it, Albie thought at first, the screaming man was perhaps hovering nearby. Another one to contend with. She whipped her head around from left to right. Skyward. No one lingering within her narrow periphery.

Albie's skull started to buzz as the screaming man's voice ricocheted around her brain and grinded into and aligned itself with the nerves. One more glance around. Then, the man snipped the thing wound around her muzzle holding it shut. She snapped at the air, her incisors clicking harshly together like the heel of a woman's shoe breaking against the sidewalk.

The man she was no doubt looking for, the one screaming at and menacing her, slipped into the lowlight of the wide, sweeping the room they were in. His mouth did not move, but the screaming did not cease. It hammered at the size of Albie's head like twin sledges taking turns left and right. Another one drifted into the light behind the first man. Then there were two. Could they both be yelling at her? A chorus of rage. A terrifying cacophony she suddenly understood as it summoned a former dread into her mind, crowding all other impulses out in favor of the instinctual need to survive …

… to protect her newborn pups.

The two men were always with the raised voices, never silent. They did not creep and made no effort to conceal their presence, for they seemed to fear nothing. Always with the yelling in another language, but the first she had ever heard or become accustomed to before the good man came and taught her a new series of words belonging to another place and time. The men first took her when she was wandering the mountain ranges along their perimeters. She could not make it up any further along the faces of the elevated terrain because her belly was more often empty than not, and the energy was rarely ever there. Even when she came across a dead human in her travels, the remains were picked clean by the vultures and her quicker peers. Albie had no qualms about eating human flesh if that's what it came down to. Another band of men had forced her to feed on dead human flesh and without her trying for it, the taste for salty human meat had become forever stamped upon her mind as one more possible food source.

When the two men seized and trapped her inside an oversized potato sack, Albie was pregnant. They wore the light-shaded clothing. Both men wore black belts which bulged at their sides with an item they would occasionally take out and brandish in Albie's face. The item was not sharp at its end, but had an opening that smelled like sulfur and oil. She knew those smells. They swirled about the cities of men like a death fragrance. Sulfur and oil. The two men did not let her sleep. They fed her slim pickings, usually dogmeat. Albie had no idea. She had a notion, but it was a weak one. They made her fight other dogs in the middle of an enclosed space. Other men circled around them, their fists in the air and papers bloomed out of them. The other men screamed and yelled like the ones who took her out of the mountains.

Men were always with the yelling. Albie came to believe men are never happy. They only know rage and how to apply it to those around them. Other men and animals. Albie had felt that first bite into her neck where it joined with her right front leg. A tear into her tendons. By the end of the first fight, the other dog who'd bitten her was a still, silent pile of darkened fur in the center of the enclosed space, and Albie was full up with the intestines of her opponent. She had not eaten so well in a long time. Albie's days turned to a gnawing series of hours by which she longed for the next fight so she could eat as well (or better) the next round.

The men beat her with straps, and they stuck the thing in her mouth that smelled of sulfur and oil, and Albie heard the sound of dry click right before they laughed and hid the smelly thing away again. This was the way of men. Even their laughter is angry and desperate. Albie adapted to it, and the fights multiplied.

Then the soft stirring in her belly became something more as time wore on. It turned to a rumbling, a rustling inside her gut she knew to be her little ones. They survived, somehow. Fed on the protein and the nutrition and the rich, oxidized blood of Albie's opponents. It was not long after Albie's condition became known to the two men who yelled. They took her and hid her away inside a dark room, not nearly as large or looming as the one she was standing in right now. The windows were covered over. They did not beat her once they knew of her condition.

What made perfect, maddening sense to Albie was she was not fighting anymore. This meant she was starving again. Dying, perhaps.

They came into the dark room, both of the men. One of them crossed in front of her as she lay on her side against the harsh wooden planks of the floor. He peeled something away from the wall and a column of bright and glorious light spilled across the ground and up the side of the far wall like the hand of God to intervene on her behalf. The pressure around her flank built at an alarming rate, from a small discomfort to a flaring, overwhelming sense of being torn apart. Alberta whimpered and strained, her eyes fixed to the light bursting through the black wall. Her back legs were sticky and wet. She sloshed around in the warm liquid pooling around her flank. The pressure reached its first critical mass, and she felt the first of her pups exit the breach to slip down onto the dirty mat she had been lying on for so many days. The first pup let out a supple cry. Albie gasped, as the next round of tearing and tension seized her by the belly and squeezed with its iron fist. The man by the door rushed over to Alberta, hollering more of the same flurried words. If relieving the pressure would come to mean a beating, Alberta knew she would have to abide. Submit.

There was no stopping the excruciating process. The man stood at her hindquarters, stooped, and scooped up something from the ground. He barked something at the other man who had let the sun shine in. The other crossed over to where his partner was, accepted what he was holding, and rushed over to the opening in the wall where the day burst through the endless night of the room.

Alberta watched through pained, tired eyes as the man brought the first pup up into the light and pitched it out through the opening. She squealed. Tried to angle her body impossibly towards the man. To stand. The man by the opening took the thing off his belt, the item smelling of sulfur and oil, and aimed it at Alberta's head. He yelled at her, his voice breaking in his throat from the sheer demand of the high octave. Her flank cramped up, and she felt herself expel another pup. This time, the man standing at her other end snatched the pup out of the air and tossed the whining newborn over to his partner. The partner threw the second pup away, his voice a gravelly drone now.

The other man, hand hitched into his thick, dark belt buckle, hunkered down. He stared intently into Albie's inner thighs. When the next pup came, he snagged it like a baseball catcher grabbing up a foul ball, hurling it to third base where his partner stood. The third pup did not even have time to protest before it was thrown out, given over to the light.

She found her voice and used it, barking and growling ferociously at the two of them. How could they do this? They must be stopped! Another pup was breaching and she could not—would not—let them kill what felt like her final birthing. The last pup broke through. Alberta gathered all her might, sucked wind, and launched herself at the man standing before her flank. Her incisors broke the flesh of the man's forearm. Hot blood coursed down her throat. The man screamed. Alberta disconnected from him and wheeled around to lunge towards the other one. He was fumbling with the thing fastened to his hip, and it appeared to be stuck. Alberta angled her head down and to the side. She sank her gored teeth into the man's ankle and tore away a thin flap of hairy skin and flesh.

They were both screaming now.

The universal language of pain and suffering.

The dog's eyes showed the officer's look of shock as he crumpled to the ground beneath it. Jack heard the gun in the officer's hand skip across the ground. It did not occur to him to cover his eyes or turn away until the dog growled low in its throat, and its teeth punctured the officer's throat. The officer's scream turned to a gurgle in an instant as blood fanned up the dog's snout and sprayed the windows of its eyes.

"No," Jack moaned, curling into a ball in the farthest corner he could find. "No! Stop ... please ... *stop.*" He heard the firecracker shot of what could only have been the other officer's firearm before Karl cried out, and the sounds of a struggle sounded in the background.

I can hear it. Oh God, I can hear *the blood flooding its mouth ... God!*

Jack tried to shut out the sound of the dog's throat as it hitched and swallowed flesh and gargled the officer's hot blood. It seemed to run ceaselessly, an endless flow like a river beneath the cell where Jack was imprisoned.

52. THE RETURN

"Mr. Bentley!"

Will had not stopped or slowed since he handed his agent her cell phone back at Villanova University. He could not have put the brakes on if he tried, not even at the sound of his name being called by a gruff sounding man whose footsteps suddenly squeaked behind him along the white, polished tiles of Doylestown Hospital's ER wing. The nurse at the desk had directed him to the fifth examining room on the right and damned if anyone was going to hold him back.

"Hold on a minute, Mr. Bentley," the man called. "Need to talk to you. Police business!"

The headache which had been nudging at his temples during his ride out of the city was a boulder inside his skull, crushing his brain flat as a pancake. He grabbed for the bridge of his nose, squeezed. It relieved the throbbing. *Police business. No shit, huh?* Begrudgingly, he made a slow turn towards the portly officer who had begun to follow him down the hallway once Will caught his eye by the nurse's station. He had been talking up a pretty orderly in the vicinity.

Will raised his hands as if to say *Okay, I'm stopped! Can you state your business?*

"Sergeant Coombs," the officer said, raising a hand to shake. "I was hoping to intercept you before you went in to see your girlfriend. You almost slipped me. *Almost!*"

"If it's all the same to you, I'd rather do this after I've seen her."

"Well, if it's a matter of her safety, I got an officer stationed right outside her room."

"Wait. Are you saying there's still a threat?"

"I'm not saying that at all. Just wanted to put your mind at ease. The people who did this are no doubt on the run. It's procedure to guard our victims until the threat is neutralized. We're working on it now. I got some units out there combing the town, and other precincts are using their manpower to scour around their stomping grounds also. Fifty mile radius of scope. The suspects are not going to get very far, especially since they exercised the ultimate dumb perp chutzpah by hiding in plain sight."

"Who are they?"

"We been working with the Special Victims Unit out of South Philadelphia. They were looking for a suspect to question him about a recent rape, and he hails from Comstock, as it turns out. From there, all our interests sorta' dovetailed once the suspect's wife and her male accomplice abducted him a little over twenty-four hours ago. The house where the woman and the rape suspect were living showed signs of definite foul play, but the more this plays out the more questions crop up. Faster than we can answer them. Like why they saw the need to abduct your dog and assault your girlfriend and your—"

"Her name was Katherine Danforth," Will said, somewhat surprised by the sudden sense of loyalty for the vet he had not known before this mess. "She was living in my house temporarily to oversee the rehabilitation of my dog. *Our dog.*" *Our dog. Christ, I'm losing time with Mina when we could be doing this briefing fucking afterward!*

Katherine would be alive right now if she wasn't working for me. Will knew the train of thought was illogical as it was destructive to his own mentality in the moment. Yet, the train kept on rolling, and he stood there with vacant eyes and an empty expression tugging on his cheeks and the corners of his mouth as he silently thought along these lines. *She was always just Danforth until right now. But Katherine Danforth would have been making plans to travel right around this time. Now that I know where her daughter and her family are coming from, I know she'd be laying down her money for a round-trip plane ticket to Steel Town, USA. Thanksgiving holding her grandson while she pushed around a plateful of food she knew was not good for her cholesterol levels. Lying down in a mountain of Christmas wrapping paper with that same grandson—*

"I can walk you to her room if you'd like to say your goodbyes," Coombs offered.

"I'll find my way there. I just want to see Mina first."

"Understood," Sergeant Coombs said. "Before I leave you to it, those Philly detectives asked me to show you a couple photographs of the people your girlfriend picked out as her attackers. I wanted to see if you recognized them. Would you mind taking a look?"

Let me see these motherfucks! "Sure," Will said.

Coombs gave Will the two glossies Mina looked at earlier. "The circled man and woman are the people Mina gave a positive ID for."

The first thing Will thought was they were no more than kids. The girl looked malnourished, maybe a meth head or a shut-in? The man looked like someone who would cause Will to inadvertently feel for the gun holstered under his suit-coat. Black, squinty eyes that looked a little cross, off-center. Full lips which would have looked much more at home on a woman than a man. Small, shriveled nose. Long rat's nest of brown hair. *I don't know either of them, but they're going to come to know me really well when all of this is said and done. I promise you!*

Will shook his head. "Never seen them before. They're from Comstock?"

"She is," Coombs said. "Stella Post. Husband's Jack Post. As for the young guy … we're piecing details together as we go."

"But this is a mug shot. He's done time?"

It was obvious Sergeant Coombs didn't want to be pressed in such a direction. "He did nine years in Berrysburg Prison. Just got out about a month ago."

Will felt the blood burn his cheeks, and his heartbeat accelerate. "Sonofabitch—"

"Now, I don't want you to let it worry you. We got the whole town sealed off tight as a drum. No way out, and like I said, if they do slip the breach they'll have to avoid the eyes of some forty officers in surrounding townships. I know you writers can't help it when ideas start cycling around

285

upstairs, but you gotta fight the impulse when it comes to this. Can you do that?"

Will smirked. "Know a lot of writers, do you?"

"The wife," Coombs said, smiling. "She fancies herself the next Barbara Kingsolver. You bunch are a special breed, I'll tell you that."

It was not a compliment and Will knew it, but the sergeant was trying to lighten the mood by any means necessary. "You have my cell?"

Sergeant Coombs nodded, tapped the small black tablet in his shirt pocket.

Will started to walk away when he turned on his heel and glowered at the sergeant with an odd expectancy in his eyes. "My dog?"

"Oh … yeah," Coombs said, casting his eyes downward like Alberta was already dead.

Will took a step towards the sergeant. "I need you to bring her back home to me. Unharmed." He paused, then added, "She's already seen hell. Lived in it for the earlier part of her life. I can't let her go through it again."

"I understand, Will."

"No," Will said, "this isn't a wish list I'm giving you. I'm saying I want you and your men to search for and rescue my dog—her name's Alberta—like she was a human being gone missing. She ought to be treated with the same sense of urgency and given the same sense of priority as if it were Mary down the lane. I want your word you will spare no expense or opportunity to save her." Another pause. *Yes, of course she is. It should be mentioned.* "Alberta's a veteran of a foreign war. That's a fact."

"I know," Coombs said. "I read your book. I admire your work very much."

"She's a hero. A war dog. War hero."

"I know her story."

Will raked his dark hair back off his brow. "I'm sorry. I'm just … I don't know. Just get these two and … *don't let them hurt my dog.*"

Coombs met Will's burning gaze with a calm, but noticeably fatigued and sagging stare. "I'll do my best," he said. "Now, go be with your girlfriend. We'll be in touch as soon as we know something."

There was nothing left to say or do, at least not in the moment. The sergeant had just placed a finite period at the end of their exchange, and there was nowhere left to go with the matter at hand. As much as Will Bentley wanted to believe the sergeant and to take him at his word, the gnawing in his gut would not let him. He smiled, all teeth, which is how he did it when he had already moved on to thinking about something else.

Will's mind skipped along to what he would do to ensure the safety of his missing dog. He could not just leave it to the Comstock Police Department. Aside from the murder at the church, his hometown police force had been more at home with writing out parking citations or moving violations to meet month-end quotas. There was no *drug scene* in Comstock, and a modest one at best in neighboring Russellville, which never seemed to find its way twenty miles east without fizzling out due to little-to-no demand. Comstockers didn't kill each other. The men did not beat their wives or smack their children in public. Any fights among neighbors were usually alcohol-induced and spilled out the front doors of the two bars in the town at such a late hour, none of the residents ever heard about it unless they were there to witness it.

He did mention something about Philly leading up the investigation. That's a good thing. I'll have to ask the name of the lead detective and reach out to them. I think they could offer me the peace of mind I'm looking for with this.

Sergeant Karns added to Will's train of thought. *The only peace of mind you're going to find is the one you make for yourself, soldier!*

"Christ," Will sighed. He knew it was only a matter of time before he heard from Sergeant Karns. Will's left cheek had been tingling up a storm the whole ride over to the hospital, so much so the skin went numb after twenty minutes. "Not now. Let me see my girlfriend. I only want to hear her voice now, not your two cents."

Fine—fine—but you just remember our agreement. The one we struck back at the firing range in Boston, soldier. In case it slipped your mind, I'll refresh you later on—but don't wait too long.

Will slipped into the exam room, and the arms of Mina. He did not let go of her until they had both stopped weeping into one another.

53. ALBERTA IN CHAINS

Framed by another set of circumstances, Alberta would be nodding off to the gentle massage of a moving vehicle as its undercarriage pulsated beneath her. She always enjoyed her rides in the truck with the man who had taken care of her before all of this. She liked riding in the woman's car even more because she drove a car where the front seats were opened up during the warmer months, and Alberta could sit bolt upright in the woman's passenger seat and relish the rush of wind across her jowls and the area on top of her head between her ears. Alberta loved the sun on her face and a scratch behind the ear or along her muzzle as the woman or the man drove.

The good man before. The good woman before.

Where the New Man and New Woman were keeping her, the sun could not reach Alberta. She had no idea if the sun was even out, or if the white fingernail moon hung in its place. Alberta could not lie flat where they had stowed her away. She was folded into a cramped, painful position. She could not lower her flank in any kind of relaxed arrangement. So there was no rest; she could not shut her eyes or close out the discomfort by transcending to a far more pleasing dream state.

If she could only sleep, Alberta could have achieved a temporary reprieve from the memories of the things she had done back at the church. Try to discard the strange, renewed hunger she felt for salty, sinewy human flesh. Her belly had stopped rumbling after she feasted, and she could not deny the satiated feeling for what it was. Satisfaction. Pleasure.

She had forgotten the taste of human flesh. Now, it was quite possible she would never forget her craving for it.

The craving was quiet for now, but she would be hungry again soon. The New Man and New Woman would have to see to the craving once it reared its head again. God help them if they fail to meet Alberta's needs in this respect.

The New Man had wound something around her muzzle. She couldn't even yawn if she wanted to. The New Man had whispered something in her ear and the words had an effect on her mind and body in equal measure. The words, although she had never heard them before, coaxed her flesh into a sudden *oozing* sensation. It was the best way Alberta could understand for herself the feeling the New Man's words elicited from her. A complete and total melting away of any and all anger and rage, as well as a stopping-up of the adrenaline ducts flooding the dog's limbs. The New Man's words were a lullaby for Alberta, and they sedated her to silence and submission.

Alberta whimpered, tried once more to lie flat and bumped her head against the obstruction beside her in the darkness of her confines.

She tried to rotate in place while still hunkering down. That's when something yanked at her throat and she heard the metallic rattling of a chain. Alberta lunged at the thing around her neck and thought to snap her jaws at it. She groaned. She whined. The thing around her neck was cold, unforgiving, and too tight all at the same time. She could draw breaths. This wasn't the problem. The thing around her neck carved into her matted flesh, digging divots into her neck in a circular pattern. The Man and Woman Before used to take Alberta out for walks and they would fasten something around her neck which was attached to a long line they held to tug at her or keep her close by. It was soft and there was enough room for Alberta to strain a little against it without cutting off her own air.

She raised her head too high and struck it against something hard and unyielding above her. Alberta saw spots in front of her eyes. She crumpled as far down as she could go. So cramped. No room.

The ground beneath her continued to rumble, jump bumps and changes in grade. It droned on.

Alberta wondered why The Man and Woman Before gave her to these new people. She had tried to be good. She worked so hard at doing what the older Other Woman told her to do. Alberta wanted to walk and run just as much as The Man and Woman Before had wanted it for her.

She whined loudly enough, her small space of her confines threw the sound back in her face.

Someone nearby, muffled but angry sounding, screamed, "Shut the fuck up, or I'm gonna drag you behind this fucking car by that chain around your neck!"

She couldn't stop. It was all she had, her own lamenting sounds.

Suddenly she heard the voice of a man, more near than far. So close, Alberta shook at the sound of it. Between her ears. Inside her head. She had heard this man's voice inside her mind back at the church, but back there it had been hard to tell for sure. She thought she had heard someone screaming inside her head, reverberating within her poor skull. There had been so much screaming, everywhere she had turned back at the church, Alberta could not possibly have known for sure where it was coming from.

This was the Inside Man. Inside her.

The Inside Man told her, "Stop crying. He's a fucking maniac. He *will* do what he said he's going to do. Listen to him. Or we're both dead."

Albie felt the scurrilous butterflies in her midsection flutter to life as the transport carrying her veered a razor-sharp left. She had heard the rubbery-smelling thing near her head shifting the entire ride; an inch here, an inch there. But it had seemed well seated and pinned in place.

Then it rammed into the side of her skull. Alberta knew no more for the better part of an hour.

The transport rode on.

289

54. SCANNERS

The only peace of mind you're going to find is the one you make for yourself, soldier!

Will would have argued the point with Karns if he didn't believe it himself. While a soldier respects chain-of-command, and Will most certainly did even when it came to law enforcement, he could not find any comfort in allowing for someone else to look for Alberta. To "keep him updated as things develop." Coombs had said something along those lines. Will knew he meant well in saying it. Coombs seemed like a good man, but a good man is not the same as a seasoned professional. Yes, there had been the St. Alphonsus nightmare, but the Feds had come in and assumed a leadership role right away once talk of investigating it as a "hate-crime" against Catholics developed.

For all intents and purposes, Coombs and his men were not prepared for a manhunt like this.

Will couldn't shake the feeling Sergeant Coombs was humoring him when he promised to return Alberta safely. The sergeant made the vow, but the old man's eyes said something else—*All due respect, Mr. Bentley, if it comes down to saving a person or your fucking dog, well, you know which way the wind is going to blow!*

While he was sitting with Mina in her exam room, he couldn't help but lose track of what she was saying because he was chewing on Coombs's words. Remembering the dismissive flash in the sergeant's gaze. Will had somehow managed to catch the gist of what Mina was saying so there was no embarrassing instance where she had to call him out for not listening to her. They wept together. They met with the attending nurse who briefed them on Mina's condition, which consisted of a mild concussion, and would include an overnight stay at Doylestown Hospital for observation. He had kissed her hand, kissed her lips, and said he'd be back soon.

Will had entered the hospital in a waking fog. He walked out with a spring-loaded step and an ever-sharpening focus as he decided what Coombs had promised about Alberta was not enough. He felt it in his bones, a terrible certainty.

Zipping his bomber jacket all the way, he made for his truck and got behind the wheel with his mind made up. First things first, he whipped out his cell phone and Googled the number for the Comstock Police Department. He got an officer on the first ring and introduced himself. Will asked to be patched through to Sergeant Coombs. The officer told him the sergeant was out in the field. Will asked for his cell phone. The officer balked, and Will understood the resistance. More protocol.

"Officer … I'm sorry, I didn't catch your name."

"Evans, sir."

"Officer Evans, I get it. Could you possibly give me the cell for the detective out of Philadelphia who's working the case? Sergeant Coombs mentioned they were working with someone from one of the North precincts. Some kind of connection to another case?"

"Mr. Bentley, I wouldn't have that information on hand."

"What about their name? Anything? I don't think I need to tell you I wouldn't be pressing this if it wasn't important."

Silence on the other end. Then, Officer Evans blew out a breath which turned to static in Will's ear. "Let me see what I can find out. Hold the line."

Will heard a soft tick sound that did not give way to any hold music. He was grateful. He plugged his key into the ignition and engaged the engine.

Coombs is out of his depth here, and we know it. But if I can talk to a detective, who deals with these types of crimes on a regular basis, it could turn out I won't need to inject myself into the investigation. If the detective gives me a good feeling about bringing Albie home, I'm not going to get in their way. Jumping into this half-cocked could also get Albie killed. Foiling what could turn out to be a calculated and systematic approach to ending this, well, would haunt me for the rest of my life. We don't run into the sands blinded by rage, or by fucking sand, right?

"Mr. Bentley, I was able to get a hold of Sergeant Coombs on his phone, and he gave me the go-ahead to put you in touch with the lead detective on the case."

"That's really great of you, Officer Evans."

"You ready?"

Will flipped down his glove box and pulled out a small ringed notepad. He kept one in his truck and in every room of his house in case an idea struck him in the midst of something else. A black pen was linked to the rings. "Go ahead."

"Lead detective's name is Darnell Jones." Officer Evans read off the number. "If you can't get him, the sergeant gave me the cell for his partner on the case. Woman named Glynna Rivells."

A minute later, Will punched in Detective Jones's cell and waited through five rings before a voice mail message came on. He thought of leaving a message, but ended the call before the sound of the tone to start recording. Who knows when Jones would be able to return the call, especially if he

291

was working a lead or (God-willing) slapping the cuffs on this Bonnie and Clyde pair of fuckwits. Will nodded to himself and punched in Detective Rivell's cell number.

Fourth ring. "Rivells."

"Yes, my name is Will Bentley. Sergeant Coombs gave me your contact information. I wanted to touch base with you about the attack on my family earlier this evening."

"Mr. Bentley, good to hear from you. Sorry we missed you at the hospital."

"I was wondering if there was anything more you could tell me about where you are with the people who did this?"

"Didn't the sergeant fill you in?"

"He did—he did—but I wanted to see if you were any closer to tracking them down. Our live-in vet passed away in the last hour. My girl-friend fears for her safety. She's scared they're going to come to the hospital and hurt her. I'm just looking to put her at ease with any new information."

"I'm sorry to hear about Mrs. Danforth. Truly sorry."

"She was a good lady. This is a nightmare for her family. For us, too. She was working for us, and I feel responsible."

"I understand. I do. We're following the leads we have at this junc-ture. The suspects are still at large at this hour. I can assure you we will keep you in the loop as events unfold. But I want you to give my best to your girl-friend and let her know she's safe. There should be an officer posted outside her room."

"Yes, there's an officer there. He looks barely old enough to shave." He knew what he had to do. He knew what he had to say, to convey in the strongest and affirmative terms possible without pushing any buttons. No doubt the investigators were taking this quite seriously, but he needed to hear from Detective Rivells she would work to insure Alberta's safety. *Come on, you're a writer! You're good on paper! Come through!*

"Alberta. She's our dog. They took her. She's fragile. She just came out of an extended coma, and I'm very worried about her safety. I know how I probably sound saying this, but she's a member of our family. An indis-pensable member. It's like they kidnapped my child, and I'm going out of my mind with worry—"

"Mr. Bentley—"

"Don't get me wrong. She's a fighter. She was a war dog over in Afghanistan. That's where she's from. I adopted her. She served her country. I can't stress that enough. She's brave as they come. She's tough as nails, but I don't know if she could stand up to any further abuse. She's lived a hard life."

"I hear what you're saying," Detective Rivells said, a hint of frustration having crept into her voice. "We're working towards the best possible outcome. This is a round-the-clock search and tracking investigation. We're working within Comstock's city limits right now, and we're turning over every stone. I promise we'll be in touch with you throughout the investigation." Will heard her cup the headset to talk to someone nearby. Then, she came back on the line with more of a hurried delivery. "Anyone you can think of who'd want to hurt you or your family, Mr. Bentley?"

"No one."

"Made any recent enemies?"

"None."

"Sergeant Coombs show you the photos of the suspects?"

"Yeah. I don't know either of them."

"All right, Mr. Bentley. Keep your cell handy. I've got your number stored in my phone now. I'll be in touch soon. I'm sure I'll have more questions for you."

"I will," Will said. "Please, Detective. Bring my girl home—"

"*What? Christ!*"

"Detective—"

"*Okay, I'm ringing off now—*"

"Detect—"

"Gotta go. We'll call you soon."

"I was just saying—"

Call ended.

Bring my girl home.

He sat there feeling the same sense of dissatisfaction and helplessness he had felt after his conversation with Sergeant Coombs. He sat there looking down at his cell phone screen, the *Call Ended* icon fading to black as it timed out. It didn't help the truck cab was now a hothouse from the high heat breathing out of the console. He switched it off and set the cell down on the passenger seat. An impulse came and went, that of getting out of the truck and smashing his iPhone against the blacktop of the hospital parking lot. He knew the sense of joy to watch the device splinter into hundreds of small parts and minute mechanisms would prove fleeting at best. Then, he would only be left standing there wondering what the hell he was thinking.

Not to mention, Sergeant Karns would have something to say about a stupid move like that. The Sarge would not mince words. Will could feel his presence lingering just inside his mind, like a stalker hovering just behind a corner's edge. The tingling in his cheeks felt like a soft ocean breeze

293

blowing across the taut, scarred flesh. This was The Sarge also, of course.

Detective Rivells had not come out and said she would do whatever she needed to do to return Alberta home safely to him. Will had heard her say something *along those lines*, but hadn't it also been delivered in an irritated tone? Alberta's life would no doubt be treated as secondary to preserving the lives of innocent bystanders and any captives the two nutcases might take along the way.

There is a big difference between understanding it and *accepting* it.

"So then let *them* protect the public," Will said to himself, staring out the windshield as a light silting of flurries touched his windshield and disappeared on contact. "I'll look out for my dog. Take the pressure off of them." It made such perfect sense to him, he wondered why it hadn't occurred to him when he had been talking to Sergeant Coombs. Then, he started to realize the implications and responsibilities which would come from this division of labor. It was overwhelming for a moment, the things he would have to do. To find ways around any roadblocks.

Will shut his eyes and focused. "I need to track the movements of the detectives and the officers in town. I need to know where they're going. What they're doing. I need to trail them, but not far behind. I need to be on their *heels*. Nipping at them if need be. And, at the same time, I need to stay out of sight.

"A police scanner," he said. "Dark clothing. All my guns."

Sergeant Karns bristled behind his forehead. *"Atta' boy, soldier!"*

"And if by some stretch I happen to put together some pieces of the puzzle the detectives couldn't … well, then I'll go ahead and share my findings with them. If it's a matter of saving lives or bringing this to an end sooner than later. I gotta promise myself I will do what's right if it comes down to it."

Wrong, soldier–

"It's not debatable, Sarge."

If it comes down to you and yours, you have a responsibility to protect it all! Alberta is your main priority, just like if it was Mina out there! You don't owe them any intel! Let them gather their own fucking intel! You protect the home team. This is your charge!

The thought of sacrificing someone's mother or father or child for the sake of protecting only Alberta made Will sick to his stomach. "I'll work to see *no one* is harmed. Protect who I can. Family and strangers."

He knew this would demand so much more from him, and he could come to have a good many balls in the air before long, but to traverse the situation any other way would haunt him for the rest of his life if anyone died because he had turned his back.

Don't fuck up, soldier!

"Sarge, I love you, but if you don't ease off I'm going to tweeze the rest of you out of my face, scarring be damned."

They were both laughing, on the inside and out, until it sounded like a strange, sickly stereophonic noise echoing around outside the hallway to a rubber room. Will peeled out of the parking lot. He turned up the classic rock station and kept it loud while he ran his errands. The DJ, a toneless robot voice who had replaced "Moonman" Jones a year back much to Will's dismay, turned out a block of Black Sabbath hits for Will's drive.

When he drove back to Doylestown Hospital with an overnight bag packed for Mina, the falling snow had thickened into something approaching a whiteout. While he was sitting on the edge of her bed, a startling thought took root in his brain—*There is the possibility I might never see her again.* He thought about the engagement ring he had been holding in his hands in the silence of his writing room only a few days before. How he had decided to wait because surely there would be more time and a better moment! *I should have brought the ring and done it right here! Bent the knee right next to her hospital bed!*

Mina grabbed his hand. They watched the windows for a few minutes in silence as snow gathered on the windowsill. "I love you to the moon and back, Mina," he told her. "I won't ever let anyone hurt you again. I promise."

She smiled at him, more like a patient parent than a lover.

"I promise," Will insisted, kissing the top of her hand. He laid her hand down beside her blanketed body and stood with a groan. "I have to go."

"No, stay."

"Visiting hours."

"That doesn't apply to family—"

"They told me you need your rest, Mina."

Mina nodded, stiffly. "All right," she said. "You'll be back tomorrow morning?"

"Yeah," he told her, and hated himself for the lie. In reality, the course he had charted for himself didn't allow for a return visit as early as the next morning. He had no idea where the chase would lead him, across how many states, or what sort of altercation awaited him. He only knew the ending, and it could only involve the survival of Alberta, even if it meant his end. The dog would have Mina. This realization startled him when it formed at the base of his brain, the peace he felt in having arrived at a decision between life and death. *I'm not going to add to her anxiety by telling her about my plans. It's better if when she sees me next I have Alberta, and our world isn't tilting so severely on its axis any longer.*

Will stood beside the bed and looked lovingly down on her. He grabbed her blanketed feet, offered them a doting squeeze. "I love you so much, Mina. Please don't ever forget that."

She was gazing up at him, smiling, when suddenly it went away. Her brow broke into a cluster of lines, and her eyes widened with alarm. "Are you going to be okay?"

It's written all over my face, isn't it? Will nodded. "It's all going to be okay."

They had been together for going on five years, and Will could confirm he had never shown Mina this side of himself. The only people who had seen this side of Will, a seething dread which flushed his face of color and pinched at the corners of his eyes, were the men and women he shared a foxhole with during his tours in Afghanistan. The blistering blasts of mortar exploding all around. Rockets, propelled by launchers, exploding bodies into sludge and ragged pieces of chewed flesh. The smell and threat of death. *I may have made my peace with sacrificing myself for Alberta, but I made peace over there before I entered the war zones. And I can tell you, making peace with death is not the same as throwing your arms wide open and trying to give it a big hug. The primal urge to run away is always there, just compressed into a gnawing rather than an overwhelming impulse.*

"Tomorrow," he told her. The list of things he had to attend to rose in the forefront of his mind, glowing yellow and red. Pressing him to get to it. *C'mon, soldier!*

"Tomorrow," she said.

At approximately 9:30 p.m., Will walked into "B. Whetstone's Electrical Boutique." Whetstone's survived despite the Targets and Walmarts and Best Buys springing up in all the adjoining townships like stubborn weeds hellbent on closing out the ripened proprietors in their midst. The electronics shop kept later hours, to further compete with the larger chain stores which never closed.

Will asked the attendant, who had been watching him from the corner of his eye while stocking shelves, if he could tell Will about their stock of police scanners. The attendant, a hipster millennial with tortoise-shell rim glasses and black spiked hair with the tips bleached out, explained the ins and outs of what each device had to offer. The upsell approach was obvious, but Will didn't fault him for it. In the end, Will settled on a powerful and *sporty* scanner, the Uniden Bearcat BC125AT Police Scanner. Will liked it was a handheld, wireless device with a docking station you could mount on your car console deck, in case he needed to carry it out beyond his car and into the field.

Ryan, the Bleach-tipped salesman, explained further, "It's got 500 channels to choose from, with full VHF and UHF signals. You can catch all Air and Military Channels if you want to know what they're up to. I don't know about you, but I'm always interested in what Big Brother is planning. What I like most about this rollout is the *Do-Not-Disturb* function. It shuts out the signals you don't want, cuts down on their interference, *and* it amplifies and clarifies the signals you *do* want. Then, the signals you want to store, you can. Name each one as you save them into your banks. Those are your presets."

Will shelled out the cash and walked out the door with a strong current running through his insole. He was building an edge on these motherfuckers, the kidnappers, piece by piece. After the electronics store, he stopped home and changed into a black hoodie, black Dickie slacks, and black combat boots laced all the way up. In the mirror, Will thought he looked too much the terrorist or guerrilla militant. The only thing missing was the lampblack on his face. In the end, he stuck to the outfit.

He filled a leather duffel bag with all of his guns, a fine load-out. He laid them across his bed, on top a couple of old towels. Five firearms in all. He favored the handheld weapons, and they comprised the majority of his stock. His Glock handgun, the gun he travelled with during his speaking tour, lay there beside his .357 Magnum, a Beretta SRX he hadn't fired since he purchased it three years ago, and the only long-range weapon he owned, a black Blaser Tactical 2.300 Win Mag Sniper Rifle. He disassembled the long weapon and fitted it back into its case. Then he tossed the case into the duffel. He took all his ammo along for the hunt, as well. In the event he would need to stage interference to disorient the perpetrators, Will gathered a few flash and smoke grenades. He bundled them into a brown Panera Bread paper bag and zipped it all up inside the duffel with the rest of the artillery.

The smell of the artillery flooded the bedroom, pungent oil and steel. The bag must have weighed a hundred pounds easy, when he carted it out to his truck and stowed it in the passenger footwell.

One more thing.

For when I get her back.

In case she's ... not Albie! Will hurried back inside and down into his three car-garage. He took the dog crate down off the wall beside his workbench. Folded up, it looked big as a shark cage. The crate was lightly used as Albie was a gentle soul. But Will could only guess what state of mind his poor dog would be in when he rescued her from her captors. She might require containment, and he wanted to be ready for anything. Will walked the cumbersome crate out to his truck, tossed it up into the cab, and secured it with a webbing of bungee ties.

He crowded into the cab of his truck once more and did not begrudge the voice in his head when it bloomed behind his forehead once more. The voice with the steadfast counsel and guidance. He had spent his share of hours upon days upon years wondering if the voice of Karns actually belonged to the long dead sergeant and truly resided in the microscopic skull fragments blasted deep into the flesh of his left cheek, or if he had developed some kind of alternate personality deep within his war ravaged mind and assigned the identity of the dead sergeant to this alien consciousness.

Fire up the scanner and let's see what's dancing on air out there, soldier!

Will unboxed the scanner and the dock station. The station had two adhesives on the bottom, and Will stuck it to the lip of the console jutting out over the two air vents. He ran the power cord from the dock station into a power source, in this case a cigarette lighter located in the center console between the driver and passenger seats. He seated the black and yellow scanner onto the charging adapter of the dock and thumbed it on. Then, with the instructions fanned open across the passenger seat, Will tuned the scanner, adjusted the volume to a suitable level, and in ten minutes, he had stored state, local, military, and air to presets. He also stored a free-floating search tuner to a preset. This one would steadily and rapidly seek out any random radio waves which could not be classified according to any of the other options. Will imagined the two Philly detectives would be conducting their conversations mostly through the use of their cell phones, and the scanner couldn't pick up cell calls. He would have to rely solely on the transmission of messages within the police switchboard exchanges.

The mission would require the ability to adapt to a changing situation or a change of locale. He would have to retune if it came to leaving the state or the township, and he would have to figure out a way to perform this change-up as quickly and efficiently as possible. The learning curve presented something of a challenge, but Will was up to it.

Will pressed the preset for state police first. He started to drive, angling his truck down the lane of farmhouse estates which comprised his small and rather exclusive development. The signal was a steady, throbbing burp at first. This gave way to a warbly exchange between two officers. Will listened to the conversation. It was curt, between a male and female officer. The female officer called in a "ten-twelve." Will pulled over and fumbled out his cell phone, kicking himself for having not thought of this before. He needed to translate Police Code in order to understand what they were saying over the scanner. He Googled a quick-start guide to Local Police Signals and Codes, located the "ten-twelve" and found it to mean a registration lookup request. Just as he translated that code, the male officer used another code, "ten-eleven" in response.

"'10-11' … it's … all right, it's *Repeat Transmission*."

Sure enough, the female officer repeated her request.

The male officer told her to proceed. The female officer must have been trailing a vehicle and encountering difficulty running their plate for any possible infractions or outstanding warrants. The female officer read out the tag number and got three *alphas* in before Will snapped to and selected the next preset, local police.

This preset was alive and kicking.

The voices on the wire, frenzied, and rushed.

Just listening to it brought Will back to the sounds of the transmissions sent and received in the midst of a firefight with the insurgents overseas. It sped up his heartbeat. He thumbed the volume knob all the way up, turned off the heat in the cab to silence the hiss of air passing through the vents, parked in a narrow breakdown lane, and killed the engine. This called for total concentration.

"… Ten-Twenty-four, what is your location?"

"Ten-eighty … Ten-eighty … officers down! I repeat—Ten-eighty, Ten-eighty, Ten-eighty—two officers down at St. Alphonsus Church—"

"—thirteen … requesting transport by ambulance … location St. Alphonsus Catholic Church—"

"—ah goddammit–GODDAMMIT—Ten-forty-five—" The last part of the call was too garbled for Will to understand.

"—Ten-eleven … repeat transmission   did not copy-repeat—"

"Ten-forty-five–Ten-forty-five–fuck me … request coroner … fuck ME!"

In what had seemed like an instant during which Will had tuned in, someone was presumed living and then presumed dead. It tugged at his heart, tried to unseat it from its place in his chest. He had heard the words *Officers Down*, plural as in more than one. Then, of course, Will heard the location as being St. Alphonsus Church. It chilled his blood.

"Holy shit, I'm a block away from this crime scene. And it sounds like all hell is breaking loose there." *Gotta get there! Gotta get there!*

Will turned on the engine and pulled a U-turn in the middle of the sleeping country backroad until the nose of his truck was once more facing northeast; towards his farmhouse, towards the church in question. A chill rattled his spine when he peered through the windshield and saw that tall, white church spire. The spire was no longer backlit. It pierced the night sky, but now it resembled more of a dead tooth, gray and blackening as its root died.

He drove the truck back down the road. All the while, the police scanner buzzed with back and forth exchanges between two frenzied parties. As his truck drew ever closer to the large copse of tall, leaning arborvitae concealing the church and the long winding driveway leading up to it, the signal strength of the police exchange crystallized until it sounded almost like both the calling officer and the switchboard operator were sitting in the truck's cab with him.

"… Ten-twenty–Officer Manto and I have sustained … ahh … numerous lacerations … bludgeonings … over."

"Ambulance Twenty-Five … Ten-twenty—officers bludgeoned with lacerations—"

"—we were mauled by a dog … most likely … rabid … proceed with extreme caution upon entry … ahhhh—for Chrissakes …"

Will's left cheek tingled. *I think you're only half-listening to what's being said over the scanner, soldier. Seems you missed a pretty important piece of intel, or you're just trying to ignore it.*

"Fuck off, Sarge," Will muttered.

Just then, he noticed to his right the feverish play of red, white, and blue lights as they danced around the grass of St. Alphonsus's long, rambling front yard. Police dome lights. There had to be at least five police vehicles throwing their lights at the surrounding elm trees, the bordering forest, and the arborvitae wall. The previously darkened and abandoned place of worship was now alive with luminescence and the flurry of men in Comstock standard beige police uniforms as they scuttled in and out of the Church. Will inched the nose of his truck to jut out just beyond the arborvitae wall and killed the headlights. This gave him enough of a view to what was happening on the grounds of the church.

It was mayhem. It doesn't matter where the police are from, a sleepy one-horse town or a major metropolitan area, when one of their own (or, in this case, two) are cut down in the line of duty, it is like kicking a hornet's nest. The stingers come out, and the bloodlust for revenge pulses in each and every one of the surviving officers' veins like shots of an overly potent, near life-threatening street drug.

Will leaned over and dug in his glove box. He pulled out a pair of handheld binoculars Mina had given him as a stocking stuffer two Christmases back. She had the beginning and end dates of his first tour in Afghan-

300

istan etched into the left side. When he held it up to his eyes, his fingers felt the fine etching, and he thought of Mina in her hospital room. How small she had looked underneath the layering of starched, blue blanketing, and the even more stiff sheets swaddling her beneath. *Whatever I do from now on, I do for you!* He slid down lower into his seat. He adjusted the focus of the glass lenses until the back fender of one of the cruisers came into full, clarified view.

Its driver stood beside the cruiser, his hand itching at the standard issue weapon holstered at his side as he looked on. Will followed this officer's sightline and found a cluster of three officers gathered just inside the glass doors of the church's vestibule entryway. The way their mouths moved in conversation, tight and rigid while their eyes flared with fire and rage, Will knew they were close to quite literally frothing at the mouth over the scene inside the abandoned and condemned church. The clutch of officers standing in the doorway parted neatly, two off to the right and one to the left. Sergeant Coombs emerged between them, as if the door had just given birth to him. He said something to one of the officers, a ginger with porcelain skin and a blush rising out of his collar, borne of either a reprimand from his boss or the rising tide of anger in what they were bearing witness too within. Sergeant Coombs stalked through the dizzying kaleidoscope of thrown dome lights. The reds and blues and whites swept across his face, digging out the deep circles around his eyes for just a moment before he ducked down into a nearby cruiser to talk to an officer inside.

Then, as if by magic, Coombs's gruff and jagged voice burst out of the police scanner.

"Update all APB units currently stationed-proceed with added vigilance … I repeat—Ten-nineteen … Proceed with caution when confronting the two suspects. Suspect One is male, long dark brown hair, curly, short stature, slight build … travelling with Suspect Two, who is female, reddish-blonde hair, straight and to shoulders, slight build. Suspects are roughly the same height, travelling in the same vehicle as previously specified. Both suspects wanted for a Twenty-Five Oh-One … attempted homicide of two police officers … repeat—suspects wanted for a Twenty-Five Oh-One, attempted murder of two police officers. Suspects also wanted for the kidnapping of female suspect's husband, who is most likely with them."

"All due respect, motherfucker, but what about the abduction of my dog?" Will hissed, blood boiling inside his cheeks. "You gonna mention that over the radio waves or doesn't it factor in?"

"—Suspects are most likely travelling with a large canine, proceed with caution when approaching the animal as well. Ten-Nineteen—proceed with caution when approaching the dog … answers to the name Albie or Alberta."

"Proceed with caution? What the fuck does that mean?"

There was no time to consider his own question or attempt to reason it out. Will looked out the windshield. There were no police car dome lights casting their spiral spray around the church grounds. *They're not here yet, but they will be any minute. Two of their own are down.* He had parked his truck at such an angle, the arborvitae concealed the red bulk of steel enough it would go unnoticed for when the authorities converged upon the scene. Will hoisted the black gym bag onto the passenger seat, unzipped it, and removed his Glock. He loaded it and checked the safety. Next, he unseated the wireless scanner device from the docking station and clipped it to his belt buckle. The back-and-forth static squawk erupted from his hip now.

Will exited the truck into the cold, wind-screaming evening, and stormed the church grounds in mid-crouch.

An electric shock rippled across Will's left cheek. *You know what it means, soldier. You just don't want to fit the pieces together … you're gonna have to right here and now before we move forward—*

"Alberta didn't kill those officers! She can barely run, let alone walk. Or attack!"

You know how unpredictable an animal can behave when they're feeling threatened or deprived of food! They find strength inside even they never knew was there before. It's a reservoir of adrenaline. Her vet at the clinic told you and Mina about it. Bursts of energy. You remember it?

"No, I don't believe it for a second."

Yeah well, soldier, the truth doesn't need to be believed. It's just the truth, no matter what—

The police scanner swelled at Will's hip with Sergeant Coombs's voice as he hurriedly crossed the sweeping front yard of the church. "—animal should be treated as dangerous … approach animal with caution … animal may be rabid—"

"Rabid?"

The work of an animal! Your animal! What the hell do you expect them to think or do when they're faced with this kind of evidence?

"They're going to shoot her and ask questions later!"

Will padded down the front walk leading up to the church doors. He grabbed for the door handle and eased the squeaky door outward. He slipped inside. The musty, neglected smell of the vestibule stung his nose in contrast to the crisp winter air he had just come in from. While he hadn't exactly expected the pregnant silence of a boarded-up church, in light of what he had heard across the police airwaves, the sounds of agony and suffering hit his ears like a terribly familiar cacophony. A disjointed jazz piece he had heard before and remembered for the way it had quickened his heart rate and frightened him. The hardened, grizzled sound of Old Man War filling a soldiers ears with the sounds of death, pending and evident, filled the emptiness of the church. Only, Will was not on a battlefield or fanning out across some sandy overseas province. He was tracking the sounds of human wails and cries and screams from the vestibule, where such horror sounds were mildly muted into the church proper where they rang off the marble and brass like the sounds of a platoon dying rather than one or two men.

"Who-who's there!?" a warbly, wet-sounding voice begged nearby. *One of the downed officers. Alive.*

"I'm coming, officer." Will rose up. He held the Glock out before him, sighting down all four corners of the church proper as best he could. *A lot of nooks and crannies. Lot of blind spots. They could still be here.* In the moment, Will wondered what would happen if he happened to cross paths with Alberta right then. *What would she do? Would she know me?*

Enough, soldier. Get to the wounded and see what you can do!

Will found one officer, a tall and starved-looking older man, whose body was half in the aisle, half concealed behind the wooden arch of a nearby pew. He realized more quickly than he would have preferred, the man was beyond saving. Will hunkered down beside the officer. "Where are you hurt?"

"Who's that?"

"Just save your energy, officer. I'm going to do what I can for you. Medics and support are already on their way—"

"Will Bentley?"

"Yeah, and you're Officer Joe Ferguson. I heard your call over the wire. How's Officer Manto? Where are you hurt?"

"Beans … and … and …"

"Franks," Will said, understanding all too well. "Clean off?"

"Afraid … to feel."

"Doesn't matter. They're going to put you back together again. Don't worry. Just lie still. Don't try to talk. Lie your head down. It's all right." Will cupped his hand under Officer Ferguson's head, lowered it down softly to the rug. Officer Ferguson let out a watery wheeze, sighed from the soles of his shoes. "There you go. What about your partner? Officer Manto?"

Officer Ferguson rolled his head from side to side along the carpet and sniffed forlornly. "The dog ripped his throat out—"

303

"Are the suspects gone? Did you see them leave?"

"I-I—"

"Are they still here?" Just the thought of it, the possibility caused Will to cast a wide, sweeping gaze around the darkened church. His finger itched at the nub of the Glock which would disengage the safety feature.

Officer Ferguson's hand clamped on Will's wrist. The old soldier nearly jumped out of his black flak jacket. The officer lifted his chin upward. A grin peeled his lips backs into fine, bloodless lines. "They left the dog ... downstairs."

"What? The dog is still here?"

"Down ... stairs. I been hearing it ... whimpering ... barking ... sounds strange—"

"Strange? Strange how?"

"Like ... like someone doing an imitation of a ..."

"I don't understand!"

Suddenly, Officer Ferguson gripped Will's arm with his hands, digging into the steel-plating of his flak jacket. The officer's eyes were wild, bloodshot even in the lowlight. "Imitation ... like ... ruff-ruff-ruffruffruffruff-ruff-ruff—"

Horrified, Will ripped his arm free of the officer's limp grasp. He recoiled, stood, and took a few steps clear of the officer.

His mind is gone, soldier. You've seen this before. The mind goes right before the soul departs—

"Ruff-ruff-ruff-like that! Ruffruffruffruff—"

"Help ... helps on the way," Will stammered, before turning and running out of the church.

The downstairs.

The basement.

Albie.

They'll be here any second.

55. JODI

Jodi Dare was still getting used to smoking, and they still made her cough viciously, but it hadn't stopped her from ultimately buying a pack of her own. One of her coworkers at Starbucks turned her on to the heady feeling of pulling toxic smoke down into your lungs during a five-minute break two weeks ago. Carlos knew Jodi was having a hard time, what with the shakes the patrons pretended not to notice or her coworkers had learned to tune out. He had invited her out back behind the dumpster for what was her first puff-puff. Jodi thought she was going to die the first time. Her cough was so ragged it bent her over for a good five minutes. But that was all it took. From then on she began what would become a deliciously dangerous dance with nicotine, bumming every day from Carlos until he casually suggested she maybe buy her own pack.

That's just what Jodi did. His brand became her brand.

Newports.

She was living at home with her parents at the time.

This was a temporary arrangement, something her parents insisted on after she was attacked, and it was revealed her attacker had kept Jodi's driver's license for what could be a follow-up visit. The Dares lived in a large Colonial in West Chester, five miles north of the college and just far enough away the drunken college kids did not bother them or their cul-de-sac neighbors with noise or debauchery. Jodi had grown up there, an only child whose parents doted upon her at every turn. There was a time she loved it there, being the center of her parent's universe and oftentimes their ultimate obsession.

It had pained her to leave when the time came, and she cried for days even though it had been her idea. Jodi was an aspiring artist and wanted to plant herself in the center of Philadelphia's Arts District for inspiration and exposure. Years later though, Jodi learned the age-old adage, "you can't go home again," to be as wise as it was timeless. Jodi felt like a fish-out-of-water while living there. The transition, albeit temporary, from the steady and forward-moving bustle of the city to a calm and sedated suburb made her want to break away early on. To return to her apartment, threats be damned. Her parents wouldn't hear of it. So she simply existed, texting with friends, instant-messaging on Facebook, and sneaking her cigarettes in the side yard or just inside the forest tree line bordering The Dare's backyard.

A week into her stay, Jodi discovered her mother snooping around her social media pages on her laptop. She had screamed so loud in the middle of the day at the woman who had given birth to her, the neighbors called the police, and a mortified Mrs. Dare sent them away with the promise it was only a small mother-daughter disagreement and had already been diffused. Of course, it would not be diffused until Mr. Dare got home around nine in the evening. He worked in Manhattan at a brokerage firm and took the train to and from, hour and a half up and back for the last thirty years. Jodi appealed to her father's softened nature, in comparison to Mrs. Dare's domineering approach, and within a half hour Jodi was promised a new car on lease to be paid for by her parents.

Mr. Dare thought this would keep his daughter safe if she insisted on returning to her apartment in the city. "No public transportation," he told her. "Not anymore. There's all kinds of lurkers down there you don't know about until they're already on you. Savages, all of them. They defecate where they eat. In public. No shame. They do everything in public. You'll drive yourself everywhere. Even if it's a block away."

Of course, Mr. Dare hadn't made it to six figures by being an idiot. He knew how to negotiate, and Jodi had to agree she would enroll at Moore College of Art & Design next semester.

"No matter what, I want to see your registration paperwork and your first roster as soon as you obtain them. You'll meet with an advisor this week, Jodi. Or no car."

By then the deal had been struck, and Mrs. Dare had wandered into the office at the tail end. While the arrangement enraged Mrs. Dare at first, she adapted, which was often the case when it came to her dealings with the two of them. But Mrs. Dare did insert a condition of her own.

"I want you to meet with a psychologist and a psychiatrist. I already know of an office located near Independence Mall where you could make appointments for both. I'll give you their names and numbers. You have to meet with them within the week and provide us with a receipt."

Jodi balked. It was like they didn't trust her. She had said so to her mother.

Her mother shook her head, "I don't doubt you'll enroll at school, but I also know you, and if I don't hold you accountable for making an appointment for your mental health, you'll simply put it off. This can't be put off." Then her mother looked her dead in the eye. "I mean, for Heaven's sakes, you're smoking now? It's just not you, Jodi. The incident and the pain you're feeling need to be addressed before you graduate to—"

"All right, dear," Mr. Dare cut her off before she embarrassed herself. *She was going to say heroin, she really was!*

Jodi usually thought about what happened back home when she stepped out onto the front steps of her apartment building for a smoke. She was thinking about it as night swept the sidewalks up and down her block with winds whistling in and out of alleyways, screaming along the sharp edges of the marble and granite edifices in every direction. Clutches of tourists, natives unafraid of traveling alone, and couples walking in comfortable silence traipsed back and forth in front of Jodi's steps. Her street was so overgrown with trees, the night seemed to reach her long after it had already darkened the sky.

But it was there now with her.

Darkness.

Just in time for the second shift at Starbucks. Her boss was working on getting her an earlier shift, but it would take time, according to him. In the interim, Jodi would have to bear it. If Carlos lived closer, she would have asked him to walk to and from work with her so she didn't have to take out the car *again*. But Carlos lived over in Fishtown, and it wouldn't work. If her parents knew she was still working second shift after she had told them it had been changed, they would have come up there, abducted her, and dragged her kicking and screaming right back to West Chester.

Nope, I will grin and bear it!

The nightmares. They were another story, though.

Once she started having them, Jodi found herself spending more and more time on the stoop of her apartment at all hours of the night. She had the first one her second night back in her apartment. The same night, on the stoop after it happened, Jodi upped her daily cigarette count in a matter of minutes, by chain-smoking five Parliaments before finding the nerve once more to go back inside and try to sleep. Before the nightmares, Jodi was a rather conservative smoker, taking in no more than two a day and spacing them out over time. She woke up from the dreams with her t-shirt and box-ers stuck to her body and the blankets wound around her like loops of ma-licious vines trying to trip her up. Waking up alone in an empty apartment, in the dark and terrified, was terrible, and some nights downright crippling for her. She woke from the dreams positioned in the exact same way every time, with her hands at her throat. Feeling around, inspecting absently, as the grogginess unspooled from her mind and the reality of her surroundings drew into focus.

Inspecting her throat with her hands. Feeling for wounds.

Bites.

Bites?

In the nightmare, an animal was attacking her, tearing at her throat. It was relentless.

Jodi's nightmares were short clips of violence. There was no build-up. No story, not even so much as the atypical "dream-story," where random events and people are somehow seamlessly blended into a disjointed, bizarre chain of puzzling events. It didn't matter. No amount of buildup could soft-en the impending animal attack which seemed to stretch on endlessly into minutes of extreme agony before she woke up. The other thing which was strange about these nightmares, as if their content wasn't enough, was she did not wake up before the worst of the attacks took place. Growing up, whenever she had dreams of impending traumatic death, say *falling from a great height* for instance, Jodi always woke up right before her body came crashing down to the ground. Her brain used to protect her from such traumatic events, to safeguard her from the sensations of death.

With these new nightmares, it was as if her brain was on vacation and had no interest in saving her from the terrible visions.

She lay in darkness in the dream, her hands and feet bound by some unseen restrictions. Then, the growling sounded at her feet. It swelled in volume as it approached her. Red eyes shined in the black, sidling up alongside her. The animal did not lunge at her immediately. No, it took its time, psyching her out, tenderizing her poor brain. Jodi struggled against her restraints. No room. Then, right when her brain would have normally stirred her awake, the creature's eyes came alongside Jodi's face. They looked into one another's gaze, and then Jodi broke away screaming. This was what always seemed to throw the creature into immediate, terrible motion. The eyes darted towards her, rolled back. The white teeth, elongated and dripping with saliva, lunging downward. The awful pricks of them as they pierced her throat. Hot stickiness dripped down the side of her neck, and she screamed until the second lunge of the creature. This took out Jodi's voice box, and her scream became a gurgle as her voice abandoned her in favor of a welling up of hot, coppery wetness in her mouth. Drowning in her own blood. Suffocating.

And then, only then, was Jodi allowed to wake up.

The damage done.

Then, the front steps of her apartment—her smokes, the shakes, the tears.

What is wrong with me?

She had kept her word. Jodi had gone and found herself a psychologist. She needed to hash these dreams out with a professional, and the sooner the better. The appointment was set for the following Tuesday afternoon at one. Jodi pulled long and deep on her cigarette, the night chilling her and goosing the knobs of her spine under her shirt. She dropped the cigarette, stamped it out with her foot, then picked it up. She walked down the steps and tossed the mangled butt into the trash can. Her car was parked on the next street, so she crossed the blacktop and made her way down the side street, trying to rein her thoughts in. They had become more difficult to control these last few days.

"Hey there, Jodi!" someone called to her.

I'm late. Can't stop right now.

308

Jodi turned to find her landlord striding towards her. If Tom Daniels didn't always wear a three-piece suit in any array of colors from charcoal to rich, hunter green, Jodi would have assumed he was running late as well. To the opera or the symphony at the Mann Center. He had the whitest teeth she ever saw this side of a periodontist office. They looked wide and lascivious as ever when he flashed that expensive smile of his, hand outstretched for a shake. Jodi found she couldn't tear her eyes away from his shark-teeth. Werewolf-teeth. *My nightmares. Here it is, walking right up to me to shake hands.*

Clutching her handbag across her shoulder, Jodi offered Tom Daniels a limp shake and realized she was not smiling back at him. "Sorry ... I'm running a little late for work."

"Still working the night shift, eh?"

"Oh, it's not forever," she said. "I have some other resumes out there. Once I move, I'll be closer to many of these other places. They tend to close their doors and offices up after dinner, so no more night excursions."

"I see," he said, nodding down at his shoes. "I heard what happened. To you."

Jodi flinched. Her eyes tightened inside their sockets. "Oh ..."

"I just wanted to say I'm sorry, and if there's anything I can do for you—"

"Oh ... I'm ... dealing with it. One day at a time." *Who would have told my landlord I was fucking attacked? The only person I spoke to about it was Detective Rivells, and I know she wouldn't go telling my story to our neighbors. I mean, she* can't, *right? There's a privilege there!*

"I wanted to make sure it's not why you're moving," Daniels said. "Because I can assure you whoever it was that attacked you, they could never get to you inside those doors. I made sure the security in your building is state-of-the-art years ago, once the murder rate in this city really started to spike."

"No-no-no, not at all. You've been a great landlord. The neighbors are wonderful. Quiet. Friendly. No-I'm just looking for a change of scenery. I want to be closer to Moore College, also. I'm enrolled there for the spring semester."

Daniels smiled again, uncinching the tightness that had crept into his lips as he made his promises to Jodi. "Ah, an artist! Oh yes, I remember. You told me when I first showed you the unit. It was years ago. But ..." pointing a playfully accusatory index finger at her, "I never forget what my tenants tell me."

Unless they need a late night maintenance call to get their central air fixed.

Jodi nodded, slow and easy.

Daniels fell silent. After a beat, he grasped her hand in his once more and leaned in closer than Jodi had ever let a man do in quite some time. "Good luck to you, then."

"Mr. Daniels?" she suddenly chimed. "Has anyone expressed an interest in my apartment? I'm looking to leave in the next few weeks. Maybe less. I know its contingent upon your finding someone to take the place since I'm *technically* leaving the lease two months early."

Daniels's eyes flashed. He ground his upper and lower rows of pearly white teeth (complete with four surprisingly pronounced fangs) together, a tic of his. Jodi could have sworn she could hear the sound of the teeth grinding together. It sounded to her like two coins scraping. *Oh Christ!*

"Ms. Dare, we're right on schedule. I have someone coming in tomorrow morning to my office to sign a lease for your unit. No worries. Good night."

Oh Christ ... God ...

Jodi burst into a run as soon as Daniels disappeared around the corner, and didn't stop until she was standing beside her new black Ford Explorer and fumbling to get her keys out of her bag. It was as curious to her as it was frightening, her heart pounding between her ears. *I don't know if I'm running away from the fucker who raped me or 'Cujo' in my dreams!*

It didn't matter either way. The terror was real, and transferrable.

56. STRANGE TRANSMISSIONS

Will pulled his cell phone out of his pant's pocket, engaged the flashlight feature, and tucked it down into the collar of his flak jacket so three-quarters of the illuminated screen shone considerable light around him. The basement's floor tiles were shattered in spots, grimy and discolored. A rat carcass, fat and greasy-furred, lay on its back beside a column. Its back and front claws stuck rigidly upward in the air. The beam showed him a number of sheets and drop cloths flung all about, like the basement had once doubled as an artist's studio, and they had recently flown the coop along with their works. The air inside the basement cafeteria was a damp, tangible presence, and Will did not so much walk through it as he waded within it. A scattering of what looked like cheap, decorative Halloween masks, the kind you hold up to your face by gripping a stick attached to it, lay here and there. One of them was partially burned away, its edges brown and charred. Will kept moving and stepped inside the remains of a small, makeshift campfire that had been crudely assembled with a pile of larger framing firewood and a layering of charred, wasted kindling. Bits of white and gray ash coated the kindling like dead skin.

His right foot snapped the pile of kindling as he stepped. It felt and sounded like he had stepped on a dead bird, the soles of his boots collapsing its bones. He flinched away from it. The beam of his cell phone light spun wide, whitewashing the floor and walls as he regained his footing.

Come on, Albie! Make some *noise! Let me know where you are!*

He nearly missed the flash of the word *BINGO* in faded red lettering as his light beam illuminated it for an instant. He caught it in his periphery and snapped his head back towards where he thought he saw it. The light beam followed his head movement.

"Holy shit."

The board lay on its side, but the words running across the top of what was the ever-familiar square of smaller squares with letter-number combinations in them stared back at him from the shadows.

BINGO PARTY BOARD!

They're coming, soldier! Do what you gotta do!

Will lifted the Bingo Board and laid it off to the side.

What he saw hidden beneath the board brought the hairs on the back of his neck to sharp attention.

Then, the thicker hairs along his arms followed suit.

He immediately thought of *The Shroud of Turin*. It was a stream-of-consciousness moment for him. The shroud believed to have been Christ's funeral sheet as he lay in his tomb, and somehow imprinted his bodily image onto its very cloth in a mystical miracle. An adult-sized fig-ure lay prone beneath a piling of the same sheets and plastic throw covers Will had tread through as he navigated the basement. It was a tall *someone*. Perhaps an inch or two taller than Will. He pressed in closer, his heart ham-mering between his ears and blood pumping behind his eyes, twitching the left one. He hunkered down beside the shrouded figure on the cement floor of the basement.

The area of the sheet covering their face billowed upward, ever so slightly.

Breathing. They're breathing.

Then, Will saw the sheet covering the chest billow so slightly, as to

311

be barely detected. The motion was stilted and rigid. Their breath was hitching. They were gasping.

They. Are. Coming. MOVE IT, SOLDIER!

Will drew back the sheet.

The man under the sheet shuddered as Will drew the linen away from his face. A surprisingly good-looking twentysomething man with thick, dark hair that looked like it had been pomaded into place, and time and torture had undone the coif, transforming into a gelatinous looking sea wave. His eyes were wide and wild, nostrils pulling tightly together, then flaring painfully apart as the young man strained to breathe effectively. His jawline was checkered with a raspberry and blueberry discoloration just below the ear, where someone must have struck him repeatedly with a closed fist. His lips were chapped, the skin split and scaled.

"Don't try to talk," Will said in a whisper. "Ssh." He lowered the sheet down just below the man's sternum.

The man turned his head aside. He let out a soft, lilted whimper. Will stopped dead. The sound of it, the lament of it, was more animal than human. Not just any animal.

Canine.

Like someone doing an imitation of a dog—ruffruffruff.

Dammit!

Will bent low and spoke into the young man's ear. "I'm guessing you can't walk. You would have walked—*run* right the hell out of here if you could. I'm going to carry you out. We have to move quick. Now, do you have any other injuries I should know about before I lift you. Broken bones? Cuts? Gashes?"

Right then, the man grunted and started to shake. "*N-n-not much time b-b-before she wakes up. Then–then-I won't be able to t-t-talk–only f-f-f-fucking bark!*"

57. THE SHALLOW DOZE

"*N-n-not much time b-b-before she wakes up-then-then-then-I won't be able to t-t-talk-only f-f-f-fucking bark!*"

The Inner One didn't rouse Alberta entirely from what was a blackout brought on by a tire iron to the side of her skull. Her mind still skimmed the outer recesses of unconsciousness. She had seen through the Inner One's eyes. She felt what he felt. Panicked as he panicked, in the form of one of her legs kicking out, like a dog will do when they dream of chasing a rabbit down a hole. The road beneath the moving vehicle she was locked inside had slowed. Alberta could feel it, just as she felt every damned bump and slight rise in the terrain as the car ran over it. If Alberta knew what shocks were, let alone cars or anything engineered or pioneered by human ingenuity, she would have blamed the weak-ass shocks of the Cutlass itself.

"N-n-n-n-n-no wait! I know—I know we have to get the hell out of here, but you got a cripple on your hands. I'm ... I'm a fucking cripple now!"

Alberta understood human emotions more than anything else about them. She understood sadness and how the sounds of someone sniffling and a quavering vocal change signaled inner turmoil. That was how the Inner One sounded right then. He was talking to someone else, but Alberta only heard him and his side of the exchange. She wondered who he could be talking to. She didn't like having the Inner One inside her head. When she had first heard him tell her not to whimper or make a noise, or the New Man and Woman would kill them both, she dug her ear downward, grinding it into the unforgiving texture. Then, she had done the same with her left ear. It was how she dealt with the occasional fly that buzzes into her ear, or even worse, the hornet or wasp. It happened a few times at The Man Before's house, during the warmer months when she was allowed to spend more time nosing and adventuring around the big backyard. But as much as she had tried to drive him out, the Inner One remained.

He was no house fly.

"All right, I-I'm ready. No, no need to count off. Just do it. Don't warn me. It won't make it any more bearable. Okay—okay—waitwaitwait. Count off—I want to count off after all. All right, down from three then you lift me." The Inner One was panting, his breaths labored. They flitted around in Alberta's head like a yellow jacket circling and bouncing off the bone of her skull. *"Okay ... one ... two ... ther-eeee ... aaaaahahaha, Jesus Christ! Jesus Christ-JesusChrist-Jesus ... aaaahhhh ... aaahh.."*

The sounds were nearly enough to drive Alberta completely out of her mind, unconscious or not. She saw red. She smelled the salty, pungent stench of torn flesh and saliva flooded her mouth and dripped down the back of her throat. Somewhere along the way in her life anger and hunger had fused themselves together within, and she could not extricate them from one another. She had not experienced this dual response to stimuli. Not for a very long time. The Man Before had been younger and looked younger.

The Inner One would not leave her alone.

The Inner One was talking to someone. Who?

Then, she heard it.

"Will ... thank you, Will ... thank you ... but ... why are you here? Why are you doing this for me?" the Inner One said.

Will.

Alberta knew that word, not so much it was a name. She did know it was used constantly in the presence of The Man Before, the nicer man. The Woman Before said *Will* a lot to The Man Before, and it always got his attention. Made him turn his head towards her. Smile. Not always, but most of the time. Smile.

The Man Before.

The Woman Before.

"Where we going, Will? I need a hospital, or you can give me what I really want, not what I need."

She heard the high-pitched scream and peal of sirens in the distance. The Inner One and The Man Before heard it a couple seconds after. The Man Before shouted something in a loud, angry voice.

Alberta whimpered, loud and with utter abandon. Her brain burrowed back down into the depths of her subconscious, scrambling to escape an unseen terror.

"You can kill me, Will. I see you got a gun. What's say you donate a bullet to my cause. Put one in my brain so this can be over?"

58. THE CONFESSION

Will knew he couldn't bring the broken man from St. Alphonsus to his house. Sheltering the stranger there would have tainted his home forever. The stranger and his terrible wounds bore the residual traces of the evil that had traumatized his family and stained his once peaceful life. It would have been like letting the man and woman who stole Alberta into his living room, having them for a cup of Earl Grey or coffee. The stranger was inextricably connected to them, victim or not. Will drove to the Mall Motel five miles north near the on-ramp to the PA Turnpike. He could only hope the major highway had not filled the motel rooms to capacity by the time he arrived with the stranger.

He drove with a heavy foot. He wanted the man out of his cab, out of his truck. There was something about him Will could not put his finger on. He said very little, aside from the steady and incessant query as to where Will was taking him. At one point, Will posed his own question to the stranger ("Does it matter? You're still alive!") and it seemed to shut him down for the remainder of the ride, aside from the screams of pain bursting from him every time the truck rattled over a bump or a pothole.

They rode in tenuous silence for the last five minutes of the drive.

I started out feeling sorry for the guy. Something happened between then and now. It's only a feeling, but I can't shake it. This guy's a ghoul. He's not blameless here.

He parked the truck across the small parking lot from the main office, pleased to find most of the spots were empty. The Vacancy sign was unlit, but Will was optimistic. He told the stranger to sit tight, and he'd be right out with the keys to a room. The stranger balked at this.

"I'm dying, man. Why aren't you taking me to a hospital?"

"Later," Will said. "I've got questions. And you've got the answers."

"My arms ... my legs ... I got bones sticking out everywhere, you selfish fuck!" The stranger tried to sit up, to raise himself off the seat using only the square of his shoulders. "Shit ... sorry ... I mean ... can we—can we look at them once we're in a room? If they're green. Infected. If they look bad. You've got to promise me you'll drive me to the hospital. I—"

"Not yet—"

"I-I-*I'll* tell you everything you want to know on the ride to the ER. I swear to Christ I will!"

Will slammed the door. He paid for the room in cash, secured the key, and trotted back to the truck. He made sure to ask the attendant in the office for the room directly in front of where his truck was parked. It was obscured just enough by a stand of bushes growing across the office's main windows. There was no clear view out, but Will would still have to work fast in transporting the broken man into the room. He couldn't be certain the attendant wouldn't poke his head out the office door to have a look at him and what he was up to. Motel attendants have nothing but time during the smaller, darker hours of the evening, and they most likely look for and welcome any kind of distraction.

Casting one last wary glance towards the main office, Will unlocked the door to the room and left the door standing ajar. He hurried to the passenger side of the truck, hauled open the door, and was immediately met with a flurry of profanities, which first set him back on his heels before he realized how time sensitive the task at hand was. Will slid him out of the cab, certain if the man were still able to use his hands and fists, they would have rained down on his head or battered his chest the whole time. The stranger cursed

315

him so exhaustively spittle formed in the corners of his mouth. Will set him with a look of pure contempt, black and impatient, that quieted the stranger as he dangled in Will's arms and was carried into the motel room.

Will dumped him down on top of the quilt. He locked his truck, went back inside, and slammed the door to the room. He slid the deadbolt, attached the chain, then slid the only seat in the room away from its little desk carrel in the corner of the room. Swinging it around so he could lean across the top of the backrest, Will did not waste any more time.

The stranger grimaced and blew out a belabored breath. "I could use a stack of pillows under my head. It'd be thoughtful, at *least*—"

"Something tells me you don't deserve any kind of added comfort."

The stranger laughed, a gurgle low in his chest. "The fuck does that mean? You don't know me."

"I'm about to know everything about you if you ever want to make it to the hospital before your crushed arms and legs send an embolism to your brain. Why don't we start with your name."

"Oh … sure … sure … I'm Jack, and you're Will. Nice to meet us, eh?"

"Jack?"

"Mmm?"

"How did you end up where I found you?"

"How? They fucking hobbled me, *Will*! Then they smashed my arms from hands to shoulders."

"Who?"

Jack groaned, straining to turn his head towards Will. "You swear you'll take me to the ER if I tell you everything?"

"Why wouldn't I?"

"Because … *because* some of the things I'm going to tell you may be misunderstood. You could decide I'm not worth saving after I lay it all out for you. But I'm saying right here and now … I *love* women. Love-love-*love* them. If I took certain measures with them, these were things I thought would strengthen them. I'm a firm believer when something is broken, you have to break them down to the sum of their parts and then build them back up stronger than they were before."

"You a psychologist?"

"No … no, this is *common sense*, Will! If only more people were open to this sort of thing. We'd have less depression and anxiety running roughshod through our population. You want me to break it down to statistics for you, my man?"

"How do you know the people who did this to you?"

"Well, *one of them* is my retard wife, who I did everything for even

316

though she was a useless piece of turd! And … her—I guess she's been fucking him—her boyfriend? Yeah, he's a retard, too. But he's worse than her, because he's a convincing retard. Some kind of sociopath, the way he got into her head and got to living there rent free for who knows how long. I know he's been in prison. He sacrificed a bunch of pets from his neighborhood when we were all in high school together. Kidnapped them. From what I heard, he posed them in the woods behind his house with a bunch of coat hangers and duct tape, so it all looked like some kind of weird-ass exhibit. The papers all said he fancied himself some kind of avant-garde artist who thinks he's way ahead of the curve and everybody thought his *artwork* was sick and savage. So … that's the guy who's been fucking my wife's mind and her body! Other than that, I'm living the life."

Will didn't catch it at first, the mannerism was slight. Then, Jack made a sound that was unmistakably animal. Canine? A whimper? A sort of quick and desperate gasp that lifted into a whine and cut off abruptly.

"You all right?"

Jack made the sound again, then he laughed at himself. "They … did something to me back at the Church. I don't know *how* they did it, but it worked."

"What are you talking about?"

"I couldn't talk for a while there after they did it to me. This—*fucking*—this kind of weird ritual. I don't have much of a memory of it. Just— just strains of what happened. All I know is I remember they held a dog overtop of me. They lined its head up with my face. It snapped its jaws at me. Only inches away. I could smell its breath. Then … *shit!*"

"Keep going," Will pressed, kicking the side of the bed.

This elicited another whimper, more prolonged than the others. Tears squeezed out from Jack's eyes. "I got ripped out of my head. Everything I am. My thoughts. My self-awareness. It all became clouded. The lines blurred. And I was inside this cramped, dark space. There were two windows. I thought they were windows until I got a mind to have a look out of them. I realized … I … *realized they belonged to someone else. Something else.*"

Will launched himself out of his chair, and his hands were at Jack's throat, encircling the taut flesh. "Are you fucking with me? You think this is a game we're playing here?"

"No-no-no*! This is the only way I can explain it!* It's not like it makes any sense but that's what happened. It's how I see it."

Will pulled his hands from Jack's throat and straightened. "See what, you pathetic shit?"

317

"What they did to me? They made this kind of swap, I guess you can say. Don't look at me like that! I'm trying to tell you! They sent my consciousness into that dog's mind, and I guess it squeezed a shred of the dog's consciousness out. It had nowhere else to go so it went back into me. My empty brain sopped it up. It's why I keep making these stupid-ass sounds. I can't help it! What do you want me to do, huh?"

I should kill him right now for wasting my time like this!

"You want proof?" Jack cried.

Will bristled. "How are you going to provide me with any proof? There is no proof for this fantasy you're blowing up my ass!"

Another whimper. "Okay ... *okay, all right* ... what's your interest in this? I-I bet I can give you *s-something*?"

Will swallowed the lump in his throat. His patience was paper thin, but he knew he had to play along for a little bit longer or this will have been time spent in costly vain. "Your wife and boyfriend ... they murdered a friend of mine. Attacked my fiancée ..." *it's just easier than saying 'my girlfriend,* "and they kidnapped my dog."

"All right. See, I can bet your dog is the one—"

Will balled his hands into fists. "Tread lightly—"

"No-*no!* I-I-I—"

"Don't say it!"

"But I saw things in your dog's head. Things only I could have seen! Maybe even things you didn't know were in there."

I know he's evil. I'll cup his nose and mouth, and it'll be over— gather my intel some other way—

Will leaned over Jack, murder in his eyes.

"SAND! A-A DESERT! THE DOG'S BEEN IN THE DESERT! COMES FROM THE DESERT, GODDAMMIT!" Jack screamed.

Can't be! No way!

But it was enough for Will to stop cold. "Tell me *exactly* what you saw."

Jack's mouth strained to work, but only a ghastly hiss fanned Will's face. Then, he found his voice.

He told Will about Albie's exploits in the desert and the crucified Middle Eastern Christians on the side of the beaten sand path. He described in a prickly voice how Albie had eaten the flesh of the crucified people. "She was sickened by the thought of it at first, but she hadn't eaten in days. She was ... ravenous. She fell on the dead bodies. Tore them off the T-shaped trees and ... well ..."

In a voice that sounded apart from him, issuing from across the room

318

or another dimension, Will pressed him further. "What else?"

"I-I felt your dog's hunger. It was insatiable. Unstoppable. No, nothing could have held her back from what she did as soon as her memories from the desert—the human flesh—they … they connected to what was happening right in front of her."

"What?"

Jack hesitated. "You have to promise."

"*What?*"

"*You* have to promise before I go on you'll take me to the ER. I don't even care if you dump me right outside. But you at least have to let them know I'm out there—"

"I promise. Now. Talk."

"Your dog … she killed the two cops upstairs. Mauled the shit out of them both."

Will felt the bottom drop out of his stomach.

Jack went on. "Tore them to pieces. And … I had to watch. Those windows I thought were windows. They're her eyes. *I had to watch.*"

Instinct nearly won out over reason for Will. He envisioned himself delivering two quick downward punches right into Jack's nose, sending a shard of bone and cartilage up into his brain. A death stroke. He stuffed it down just as the adrenaline squirted into his arms and sped up his heart rate. He focused on his lungs, filling and emptying, slowing them down, and bringing them to heel. The red he saw faded to a softer shade of greys and blues. Bearable colors. He stood up, cracked his neck and shoulders, then pulled the chair back over so he could straddle it again. It was time to gather the meat of the matter. *Where are they going? Does this guy even know?*

Will's cheek tingled.

Ask him what he did to the women he was talking about earlier! It's all connected, or I'll be damned!

"There's no time," Will muttered to himself.

"Huh?" Jack asked.

Do it, soldier! Ask him!

Will did so.

Jack looked up at him at first with wide, astonished eyes before moaning low in his throat, then turned his face away. "All my life, man. All. My. Life. They've been coming to me. I've always attracted them, no matter how hard I tried not to. They must sense something in me. Early on, they were able to sense I was the one who could … fix them. Repair them."

"You're not making any sense."

"I'm trying—"

319

"Start making sense, or I'm going to snap your neck—"

"YOU PROMISED!"

"START MAKING SENSE!"

"Ever since I was a teenager in high school, the damaged girls flocked to me. Some of them were actually hot. Others, just zombies in black clothing and layered sweaters. They sought me out. Talked to me. Took me into their confidence. Early on, and I'm talking freshman year, I already fucked two of them. They were always so eager for the dick. But … also, for *abuse*. It wasn't my idea. Not at first. But it wasn't long before I realized they all wanted a smack here. Hair pull there. Nasty words. Name calling. Dirty talk. So, I made the connection and started giving it to them before they even had to ask."

"Before *who* had to ask? All your little high school girlfriends?"

"They were all my *broken birds*," Jack said. "And all the women who came after them were my *broken birds*, too. They all came to me. I threw them a bone here and there, a compliment or a heartfelt kiss. Stroke their hair. Touch them with something like *love*. But I learned I had to mingle it with the violence and the abuse, or it just didn't help them. And this is what I want you to keep in mind, Will. No matter how this all sounds, I was trying to help them. All of them. They came to me, and I thought I owed it to them. They trusted me. And I'll tell you another fucking thing, Will! My wife's boyfriend is going to insist I *raped* his sister, but that wasn't how it happened! She was a hard case. I couldn't get through to her. She came from a nightmare of a family. Her brother was a psychopath-in-training. I tried everything that worked with the other *broken birds* at the school. She didn't respond to any of it in a productive manner.

"Karl Tarlick, that's his name, and his sister were both fucked up beyond repair. And his sister, Blaise was her name, she wanted me to rape her. She said she wanted it to hurt. She said she wanted it in every hole. For Christ's sakes, this was a junior in high school, and she wanted me to fuck her up the ass! She said it would *wake her up*. I did it. I'm not going to lie and say I didn't enjoy it. I think she did too. Then her brother's crimes were found out. She … fucking killed herself soon after.

"The *bird* … the one that *got away*. Flew away.

"After high school, I married a *broken bird*. My wife. I didn't want to, but she got pregnant, and I had to do the right thing. Wouldn't you know it … a week after we stood before the Justice of the Peace downtown, she miscarried. Fucking believe it? Missed it by a week. Of course, after that I couldn't bring myself to cut her loose. She was still *my responsibility*. One of my flock. I wasn't going to lose her like I lost Blaise. I kept her. Mixed the love in with the abuse until the two elements were virtually indistinguishable from one another. This approach always worked in the past with the other *birds*. I figured, why mess with a good thing. And I'll tell you another thing, in case you're wondering if I feel responsible for Blaise killing herself, I'll tell you right here and now she did it because she was shamed by all her classmates once her brother went away. It wasn't what I did to her that made her do what she did. It *wasn't* me.

"I started to realize I could pick out the *broken birds* before they even came up to me," Jack said, with an odd glimmer of pride in his tone. "I travelled a lot for my job. I'm a sports talent scout for Ballantine University. A lot of time spent at the hotel bar. Bar-hopping. Night clubs. I never felt contented just staying up in my hotel room. I'm a social animal, man. And you'd be surprised how many of my *little birds* I discovered swaying to trance music in a dimly lit club, or knocking back all the shots guys lined up on the bar for her. All walks of life. Strippers. Librarians. Prostitutes. Cashiers. Paralegals. Teachers. Moms. *Broken birds*. All of them. And I always found my way to them. Or they found me. We met up somewhere in the middle.

"A relationship would ensue. The codependency. The love. The hate. The hate-fucking! I was able to juggle them one at a time because I was on the road anyway, and my little broken girl at home didn't ask a whole lot of questions as a result. But these women, they *all* wanted the strange, dangerous fuck! You can imagine how a *hate-fuck* could be misinterpreted by a damaged mind as something like *rape*. It wasn't. I never raped any of them. But, I will admit … these were a different type of damaged woman from the high school girls I was accustomed to. They were more complicated. They were … resourceful. Worst of all, they used *me* up and threw *me away* once I outlived my usefulness. I was helping them to heal, my *birds*. It wasn't enough for them after a little while. They eventually sought out professional help. And that professional *help* … they recommended to *my birds* they cut *me* loose. They said *I* was *unhealthy* for *them*.

"*I* was *unhealthy* … for them.

"You can't imagine the fucking betrayal I felt. Yes, the anger. I admit it. The worst thing of it was, I *knew* … *I* fucking *knew* these quack shrink motherfucks were unhealthy for my *birds*. They were tricking them. Brainwashing them. And if I wanted to save them, I was going to have to undo any of the work these *quacks* had done to my *birds*. I had to break them down … allow for them to pick up the pieces on their own … and then come calling for me again. Then, and only then, could I really pick up where I left off with them. Then I could repair them. Continue the work."

Jack paused. A soft, brittle sound escaped his lips. His forehead gleamed with a glaze of sweat when he turned it towards Will. "They were … resistant … when I came back around … you know, to tear them down. I used the element of surprise because otherwise they'd *really* fight me. Fight the *process*. I knew the only way for them to take me seriously, and to force them back and clear of the cliff they were hovering over, I would have to … *threaten them*. Traumatize. Hit the healing reset button. Harm their lives. Their families. I took their state IDs. They never knew it was me. I wore a mask. Made them wear a mask. I said very little if anything to them during the … the *breaking down*. I disguised my voice. I left them afraid, but more importantly, *broken* again. See, Will, sometimes you have to *reset* a bone that healed all wrong. You gotta break it all over again and *realign* it."

Will felt the grime of the man's words rub into his skin, oily and slick. "You broke them down?" He sighed, paused. "You're a … I just rescued a serial rapist? I knew—goddammit I *knew* there was something fucked about you!"

In a flurry of motion, Will exploded out of his chair, sending it careening across the room and upsetting the coat rack in the corner. He strode slowly towards the door, raking his hands backward from hairline to crown through his black, greasy hair.

From the bed Jack started screaming, the shrieks interspersed with animalistic yelps and snappy barks. "You can't leave! Where do you think you're going?"

Then Will was suddenly pressing the barrel of a Glock into Jack's left eye. Really pressing the eyeball deeper and deeper into the socket.

Jack moaned from his toes.

It was entirely canine.

Will was a blur above the bed. "What does this have to do with my dog?"

"Everything! *Everything, man!* Ow-owwwwww—your dog's a loaded weapon now! And they have those IDs I stole from my birds! They—they're going to track them all down—a-and—aim your dog at them, and they're gonna pull the trigger just like they did with the cops at the church! I can't see—I CAN'T SEE-I!"

"And they're going to make you watch! Aren't they, you miserable shit? That's their revenge?"

"I CAN'T SEE!"

"You set this entire freakshow in motion!"

"Nonononono—"

Will jabbed downward with the barrel. An ocular muscle nearly snapped before springing back like a sponge. "Oh yes, this is all you."

Will's face tingled.

Don't you do it, soldier! Don't you become a stranger to yourself! There won't be any coming back from it if you do. Relax the steel.

Damn you, Sarge!

Relax. The. Steel.

Will whipped the Glock away from Jack's eye. He stood swaying for a moment as the reality of the situation set its claws into him. He blinked rapidly, swabbed at his eyes to clear his spotty vision. His gaze wandered, unmoored, around the room. He managed to close out the mournful cries of the man on the motel bed. Then, he gathered his focus enough to walk to the carrel in the corner of the motel room. He rifled through the drawers and found what he was looking for. A pad with the motel's logo running across the top in a blocky, unbecoming script, and a pen with the same blocky logo wound around the center of its cylinder. He uncapped the pen and turned back to the bed.

"Shut up," he commanded Jack through gritted teeth. "You're the last one who should be crying."

Jack sniffled to himself, his washed-out face turned to the ceiling, eyes glassy and wide.

"Now," Will said. "I want all their names. The women whose licenses they took from you. Fast as fucking lightning. And here is where you better *really* drag your memory. I want their addresses. And don't tell me you don't know them off the top of your head. I *know* you know all of them like the back of your hand. You're the type of guy who covers all his bases. You've got their names and locations stored up there in that big, sick brain of yours." Will tapped the barrel of his Glock against his temple and smiled darkly. "Time to do the right thing, and I hope to God you still remember what it is."

"H-h-hospital—"

"How about the morgue?" The Glock was suddenly digging into the side of Jack's head, Will a dark and looming shadow above once more.

"Come on, man!"

Will disengaged the safety.

The names and addresses burst from Jack's lips fluently and all at once. Will barely had time to lay down his gun and start writing.

By the time Jack begged off, claiming exhaustion and coughing a thick wad of bloody phlegm onto the side of his face, Will had the names and addresses of four women scrawled across the cramped memo pad.

The addresses were as close as North Philadelphia and as distant as

Maryland. *This piece of shit really did spread the love around. Quite a wing span!*

Will pocketed the pad and pen, holstered his gun inside his flak jacket, and stood by the bed long enough to terrorize Jack for a few minutes more.

"I should kill you, you know," Will admitted softly.

"Ah … fuck you," Jack said, rustling on the bed. "You were never going to keep your word. I should have known." He laughed, a weak and desperate cackle. "No point in going on anyways. Dead arms. Dead legs. And a death sentence to boot. There's a goddamn doomsday clock counting down inside. HIV. So, if you think you're punishing me by leaving me here, you should know I'm already dead. Fuck you! I hope they serve up your dog on a spit!"

Don't do it, soldier!

Will's face lit up like a live wire. He flinched and sucked wind.

Then, he silenced Jack with a punch thrown wide into the side of his skull.

He slipped out of the motel room.

59. QUICK AND YESTERDAY

The scene from St. Alphonsus was still bleeding across Rivells' brainpan when she and Detective Jones strode into the Philadelphia SVU field office for Captain Tonelli's briefing on the case.

The sight of the big captain instantly tore Rivells away from her waking nightmare. She welcomed the reprieve. The captain was square jawed and barrel chested, with a large shorn skull and olive skin, which did not hang over his face but rather clung to the bone, tight and sculpted. His green eyes lit his face like emeralds catching the light, and he towered over even the tallest detective or officer by at least five inches. Tonelli was ex-special ops and had made his bones early on in his blue career by cracking The High-Rise Hellraiser case, which involved an attacker gaining entry into uptown high-rise buildings housing the city's power people, sabotaging the elevators, and then assaulting ten women in the stairwells. The *Hellraiser* reference came into play because the perp had so many piercings in his face and ears the detectives likened him to the movie's infamous villain Pinhead who himself had pins sticking out of his entire face and scalp.

Tonelli clapped his hands together once, the sound like the register of a starter pistol. The milling detectives and beat cops dipped down into seats as Tonelli's voice, thin and nasally from a nasty sinus infection and the only thing that did not match his tough exterior, filled the conference office. He stood to the left of a whiteboard with red marker etchings scrawled across it. At first glance, much of it looked like some strange cryptic code to be deciphered as a whole. Closer inspection revealed them to be cell phone numbers. Names associated and tied to the numbers themselves. There was also a pair of photographs taped to the center of the board, as if all other details written there were spawned from the pair.

A man. A woman. Early twenties.

The woman skeletal and pale skinned, with thin red hair swept in a ponytail over her right shoulder. The photograph had been cropped, part of the arm of someone standing beside her in the posed picture jutting into the frame from the right. Rivells knew the arm belonged to the young woman's husband, also missing.

The man's photo was a black and white mugshot from years ago, the most recent picture of him. He looked squirrely except for his unusually full lips and small, opal eyes. He had a hooked nose, like an anteater's snout, and long, greasy dark curls nearly obscuring his thin, sallow cheeks. Rivells knew him for what he was. *The one who pulls the strings.*

Tonelli began, brandishing his hand towards the pair of photographs on the board. "These are our suspects in the Jack Post Kidnapping-slash-Assault-slash-Murder Case! A lot of slashes, people! The case has fleshed out in the last twenty-four hours, and these two perps have really expanded their horizons. They started out with kidnapping the female perp's husband, then hiding in plain sight inside a church local to the Post's residence. Then they literally drove *down the lane* to the Bentley estate where they mortally wounded a nurse living there, assaulted Will Bentley's girlfriend, and then made off with the family dog. Now some of you have been scratching your heads over how this case landed in our lap. We're a Philly squad, after all. I'll tell you this! The Comstock police department, our neighbor to the north, lost two of their officers while they were investigating the church. That means *we* lost two officers. To further elaborate on this connection between departments and precincts, and to trace the roots of this case back to its earliest stages, we have Detective Rivells, temporarily on loan to us from the Sixth Precinct. Detective?"

Rivells outlined the details of her interview with Jodi Dare and her mother regarding a sexual assault at the young girl's work. From there, she connected the dots to her temporary partnership with SVU Detective Jones, the investigation of Jodi Dare's old cell phone and how it led them to the

Post residence. She explained with something of a lingering frustration how she and Darnel had only just missed what was an obvious struggle between Mrs. Post, her husband, and her accomplice.

She pointed to the mugshot of Karl Tarlick. "This man here, as we've come to learn. More about him in a moment." Rivells explained the fender-bender in the parking lot of a convenience store, one involving the male accomplice and a customer. How the customer's prompt reporting of the accident, her description of the man and the car, put Rivells and Jones back on the scent of the suspects. It had also prompted them to reestablish an APB in Comstock and its surrounding counties, as well as a series of road-blocks at all entrances into the area.

Detective Jones interjected, aiding Rivells in her summary. He took up the story where the suspects ambushed Mina Cohen and Katherine Danforth outside Will Bentley's estate. At that point, a beat officer raised his hand. Sensing the question's content, Jones supplied a preemptive response: "Yes, *that* Will Bentley. Pulitzer-Prize winning author." This satisfied the cop, whose hand slipped back down as he nodded, gloating at the cop seated beside him.

Jones went on, "We believe Stella Post, pictured here, and Karl Tarlick, here, then holed themselves up in St. Alphonsus Catholic Church. You may remember the events which transpired there two months prior. It was all over the news. A national story for a day or two. An allegedly abusive pedophile priest was brutally murdered in the church by a group of vengeful parishioners in a late night slaughter. Here is where the dots really start to connect, but not in a logical way.

"Will Bentley and his dog, the animal abducted by our accomplices, were the ones who happened upon the slaughter of the priest the night at the church. Bentley sustained injuries trying to stop the murder. His dog was beaten so severely it slipped into a coma and remained in that state for a month before only recently waking up. Now at this time, the only connection we can make between this crime and the one which took place two months before is the correlation of *vicinity*. Bentley's estate is only a block away from St. Alphonsus, where the murder of the priest and the most recent events have taken place. Had someone else been living there, there would be no such connection. *Vicinity*, people. Nothing more, unless new details prove otherwise. Now, where are we with Karl Tarlick's backstory?"

A male detective with severe acne scars stitched across his cheeks and a black box haircut with silver along the temples raised his hand and squinted down at the notepad in his lap. "Karl Tarlick was released a little over a month ago from Berrysburg Prison to a halfway house in Croydon

Township. He was there on a work-release program because he was such a *good boy* in the clink. The house moderator, a Mr. Tolby, informed me Tarlick was very briefly employed at Mac's Car Wash. He also received a number of phone calls at the halfway house from a woman, who most likely is our female perp. Mr. Tolby also wanted to go on record as stating he did not, in his opinion, believe Tarlick was rehabilitated and quite possibly suffered from the disorder Asperger's Syndrome. It's an inability for a subject to accurately interpret other's emotions or to respond to them appropriately. He got into a lot of arguments with other men in the house and, according to Tolby, even when it came to near blows, Tarlick would laugh like some kind of hyena and walk away like he just got off a good joke. Mr. Tolby said he reported to Tarlick's parole officer once he discovered Tarlick had quit his job. Walked off, rather. This was a violation of his parole, and when he confronted Tarlick it became heated, and Tolby did have to attempt to restrain Tarlick when he became physically 'unhinged'. Apparently, Tarlick overpowered him and was able to escape the house before his parole officer or police could reach it. Mr. Tolby said he hasn't seen Tarlick since. That's what we got on his movements leading up to his arrival at the Post house."

Rivells stepped forward only to be interrupted by the previous speaker in a regretful tone.

"An hour ago, I received an urgent call from Mr. Tolby. Apparently, two more residents have come up missing from the same halfway house Tarlick escaped from. Patrick "Bluto" Blutawskowicz and Henry Brisbane. Mr. Blutaw ... we'll call him Bluto for the sake of brevity, was in Berrysburg with Tarlick, as was Mr. Brisbane. Bluto went in for armed robbery. Brisbane's the lightweight of the bunch. Dealer. According to Mr. Tolby, these two were the only guys there who got along with Tarlick. Tolby found them talking together in whispers a lot. In one another's rooms most evenings. Real pals. Tolby told me a call came in from Bluto's parole officer yesterday. Tolby answered the call. He suspected they weren't who they said they were, but Tolby didn't put too much stock in the suspicion. But hindsight is twenty-twenty, huh? Bluto and Brisbane were gone hours after the call came in."

Captain Tonelli approached the board, pinned two blank pages in place, labeled with the two fugitives names respectively. He pinned them beneath the mugshot of Tarlick, produced a red erasable marker and drew lines connecting Bluto and Brisbane to the curly-haired ringleader above them.

"We'll have mugshots for both these guys any minute. Then we circulate them through the usual mass-media outlets. We're looking for four perps now. Bluto and Brisbane may have only broken their parole, but we suspect they plan to reunite with Tarlick at some point. We gotta pin them down immediately before their damned numbers swell any further."

A uniformed officer raised a hand in the back of the room. "Are we talking *cult-status*?"

"No ... no, I'm not seeing that here," Tonelli said, then stepped away from the board and motioned to Rivells. "We keep their numbers down ... that's the point."

Rivells stepped up once more and laid out a detailed character sketch of Stella Post, whom she referred to as a "kept woman" by her husband, Jack Post. "According to her neighbors, she has exhibited very clear signs of agoraphobia, fear of leaving the house, and acute depression. They've seen her sneak furtive glances out the window throughout the day, and when any neighbor noticed her, she would quickly disappear back behind the curtain. The husband was quite the opposite, a *dream neighbor*. Always willing to help the elderly neighbors with task and chores. He made an appearance, sans his wife, at a block party a year ago. It is possible Stella Post is being psychologically manipulated by Tarlick. He may have even threatened her into submission. Either way, our victim, Mina Cohen, did say during our interview Stella Post did offer something of a weak-willed apology right before she and Tarlick drove off with her dog after their altercation. If there is a way we could separate one from the other, it could be beneficial to use such a rift, no matter how small. I think we could get her on our side, working against Tarlick. As a matter of fact, I would even go so far as to say we could receive a call from her."

"You suspect she wants out?" Captain Tonelli asked.

"If not now, she will want out very shortly. Yes."

"Have we tried to contact her via cell-phone?" Tonelli asked, crossing his arms over his chest.

"Right to automated voice mail. No luck," Rivells replied.

Jones slipped back into the exchange. "Along those lines, where are we with the list of cell phone numbers from Jack Post's Bird Book? Any significant contact made?"

A young, lithe blonde with a pixie cut and tailored black pantsuit spoke up from the rear of the meeting area. She consulted a clipboard in her hands. "Detective Nolan and I ..." she nodded to a handsome young man beside her who appeared all too happy to leave this bit of reporting to his counterpart. "... placed calls to all twelve of the numbers inscribed in the book titled *The Aviary Enthusiast's Handbook* recovered from Jack Post's library. Our results varied.

"Of the twelve cell numbers, five were listed as out-of-service, which can be taken to mean the victim changed their number or asked their carrier to put it out of rotation. One was listed to a new customer, who was understandably perturbed we were calling them in the first place. One was listed to the most recent victim who approached Detective Rivells. Jodi Dare. However, there were three cell phone numbers we called where we were actually able to make some kind of contact with the victim herself, or someone close to them. One woman, a Terry Matarese answered, but she hung up on us once she understood the reason for our reaching out. Another number, listed to a Madeline Tarry, is still registered to her, but it seems her boyfriend has been screening her calls because he was the one who answered when we called. We asked for Ms. Tarry and her as-yet-unidentified boyfriend said, 'Who wants to know? Who the *bleep* is this?'"

At that point, we did explain the nature of our call without revealing the crime in question, in the event the boyfriend had no idea it ever happened. But he knew all too well Ms. Tarry had been assaulted. He said, and I quote 'I'm handling it! You people had your chance, and your follow-up was for shit!' I tried to find out who she reported the assault to, but he wouldn't give up a name. If what he's saying is true, someone will want to dig deeper on that because it's looking like this assault was reported to someone and fumbled somewhere along the chain of command. I don't know. Not trying to tell anyone how to do their job, but now we've got a vigilante boyfriend on our hands because nothing was done. Maybe someone should reach out to Ms. Tarry again and try to talk her boyfriend out of whatever revenge he may have up his sleeve. Just saying."

Jones flinched at the sudden sound of his cell phone ringing inside his suit jacket. He nodded his apology towards the others in attendance, fished his cell out, thumbed the silence button, and quickly checked his iPhone screen. His expression was neutral, unreadable as he ducked out of the area and into the adjoining hall leading to the staging area.

The blonde detective lobbed the ball over to her partner, Detective Nolan, taking him off-guard it would seem. He smiled thinly, stepped into the silence of the moment and picked up the ball to finish their report.

"The remaining two victims answered and conversation began cordially enough. They seemed to want to cooperate. They even sounded somewhat relieved we were giving them a voice after what happened to them. But, something strange happened with both women. Nancy Rose and Yvette Vaughn. Both women would begin to tell us what happened, but they'd get as far as who it might have been and they shut down. It's a strange thing. Both Detective Rose and I think the victims knew their attacker. It would seem almost some of them, at least two of them, felt some sort of need to *protect* his identity? Of course, we're still working on this theory. Gathering more evidence to support or dismantle it."

Captain Tonelli spoke up, wincing, like the theory caused him great abdominal pain. "You think this is some kind of Stockholm-syndrome type situation where they feel an allegiance to their attacker?"

Detective Nolan smoothed down her blonde hair in the back. "Only a theory at this point."

Jones slipped back into the meeting area, sidling up beside Rivells. He held up his cell phone, "I just received a call from the DA who prosecuted Karl Tarlick nine years ago. He was able to provide more details regarding Tarlick's crimes. I want to add Tarlick and Stella Post were romantically involved, and it's possible they saw no further need to keep Jack Post alive. He was the odd-man-out from the very beginning. The third wheel. It's fair to say if they haven't killed him and disposed of him yet, it's coming soon."

From there, Jones provided the sordid, disturbing details centering around the kidnapping and ritual execution of neighborhood cats and dogs from Tarlick's hometown neighborhood. The arrangement of the animal's corpses into elaborate, personifying displays after Tarlick hung them, strangled them with his bare hands, sawed off their limbs while they were still alive, poked out their eyes, or buried them alive under four feet of dirt before returning to the scene of their burial site in the woods behind his house to exhume them. Even the most seasoned officers in attendance could not disguise how appalling Tarlick's exploits as a disturbed teenager were laid out in plain, horrid detail. A darkness seemed to sweep through the meeting area. It wasn't until Jones finished, the lot of them remembered to breathe and look around.

Captain Tonelli cleared his throat. "Folks, I want all of you to harness your contempt and disgust into bringing this to a quick close. We have to collar these four fugitives, and we have to do it yesterday. While it would be … *preferable* … to recover Jack Post alive, should it come down to a situation where an officer or detective's life is in danger and you have to make a split-second decision … you know which way I'll back. You all have your assignments and your follow-up. Snap to it, people! Quick and yesterday!"

60. *ALBERTA IN CHAINS*, PART II

Alberta stirred, the spider webs of a deep slumber clouding her vision, and invisible fingers tugging at her eyelids. It was an odd sensation, one she had never known without aid of anesthesia. Her body at rest for a long enough period of time she actually felt *rested*.

The grogginess melted away, and she became more keenly attuned to the throbbing at the base of her skull, where she had hit it against an object in the trunk. She was chained to something hard and stinking of oil. Rubber.

She recognized snatches of sound remnants inside her head like clothing belonging to another. She heard the Inside Man talking while she lingered in the black. At times feverish, other times, even and docile. Alberta only knew the meaning of certain words.

The man had spoken for a long time.

That wasn't the only thing.

Alberta swore she had heard the sound of The Man Before. Not inside her mind. Apart from it. Speaking with the Inside Man. She *swore* it was him. His voice.

The Man Before.

Will?

The sound of The Man Before had put her at ease just enough she not only slept, but she slept to rest and to dream.

Awakening within the cramped, pungent trunk snapped her back into the horridness of her surroundings and her situation. Suddenly. Alberta knew only hunger and the pangs of an empty stomach. She had emptied her bowels and bladder in the trunk while she slept. She was hungry again. Alberta felt her stomach lurch, her mind cloud over once more. Then she remembered the taste of the two men back at the church. She knew it was a *church* because The Man Before had added this to her vocabulary some time ago as one of the places she liked to walk, and he liked to take her.

Church.

Only now, Alberta made the unconscious association between *Church* and hunger.

And *human flesh*.

Sustenance.

Alberta scrambled around, half stooped as she struggled to avoid her mess beside her. After some time, she managed to find some comfort in the arrangement of her body against the rubber tire.

The sounds she made were inarguably human.

Human agony.

61. INSULT TO INJURY

Stella Post couldn't let it go because she couldn't wrap her mind around what Karl was telling her. "I don't see how this is possible. I mean, I know what I saw back at the church. But … I can't imagine Jack … is somewhere inside that dog's mind like some kind of captive spectator. It's impossible? It's—"

She almost said *amazing* but held back. No, this was nothing short of horrifying in its intent and execution, its shocking implication. It felt for Stella like she had just garnered solid proof there is life after death, *but* it is a life of eternal torture and damnation, a paradox from Hell.

Karl cut across two lanes on I-95, a breakdown lane, a strip of median grass, and just barely angled the Cutlass onto the Atlantic City off-ramp. The smell of sand and surf, intermingled with the overriding scent of sewage, filled the interior of the car. Stella could remember the handful of trips as a child with her alcoholic parents down the shore and how her mother, sloppy as early as nine in the morning, would tell her and her dad to roll down their windows as they drove over the bridge connecting the beach community to the rest of the Garden State.

"Smell the ocean air!" Stella cracked the Cutlass's passenger window, but it wasn't long before Karl told her to close it up again. Something about being allergic to shellfish and the smell of it?

Karl drummed the side of the wheel. "Screw the scientific mind. It's limiting as shit! Step outside your … understanding of fixed fucking … what's the word? … *parameters* for what's possible." He paused, a dawning look coming over him. "*Palo mayombe* scares people because it's outside the Three Major Faiths. Your Christian. Muslim. Jew. But it's the same hodge-podge of mystery and mysticism and magic, no matter how you slice it or celebrate it. *Palo Mayombe* doesn't try to dress itself up in a pretty Sunday school pattern and sensible shoes. It's gritty. It's real. It doesn't fuck around. People … they're monkey's with day planners. They pretend, until something happens to them to ruin their day. Then, you see the devil behind their eyes. *Palo mayombe. The Santeria faith.* It's just as true. Honest. And it appeals to everyone, or it will, because everyone craves revenge at least one time in their life. If you're looking for a word to describe what we're doing, try *liberation.*"

Stella didn't say anything, as she stared blankly out the passenger window. She knew what she wanted to say next, but the words wouldn't come. They were fully formed in her mind. She just simply could not bring herself to say them, because it would mean she has to admit this feeling of fear was tied directly to the ever-developing realization she *never really knew* this man sitting beside her.

I thought he loved me. Stupid, stupid girl!

Stella smoothed down the nape of her neck, whipping her red ponytail away from the irritated, hackled skin. "What happened to the police officers was a horrible mistake. You know it. They were innocent."

"You really gonna make me say it? I don't want to say it because it's a stupid saying but I will—"

"I knew both of those officers," Stella said. "They were good men. Families. And children."

"All right … you gotta break some eggs to make a cake. See, I hate that saying but you drove me to it."

"Jokes," Stella said nervously. "You're making jokes? It's—"

"It's what? A tragedy?"

Stella sucked wind. "It's revolting."

"All right, so *I'm* revolting too. Just a disgusting hunk of meat?"

"I'm saying … *this* … what we're doing … the *act* … the-the-plan! *That* is revolting."

"All right, let's talk it through. Would it surprise you if I said I had more than a few *attacks of conscience* back when I was collecting the animals as a kid? Assembling them? Arranging them so they'd hold their poses for when the exhibit was eventually discovered. I mean, I knew whatever idiot first came across my *showing* out there in the forest was going to have a knee-jerk reaction to what they saw. Even the toughest critics have their first negative response, and then they get some … ah … *perspective* by the time they sit down to write a review. I knew the right *people* would get what I was trying to put across. I had to give myself a lot of these *mini* pep talks because I lost my nerve for the whole thing more times than I can count. I cried. I cut myself. I *almost* walked into the police station and made a confession before I finished putting the whole damned exhibit together. But … all the self-doubt … and … the little voice in the back of my head that started trying to hold me back … that all left me alone when I walked to the library and took out a book on the lives of Van Gogh and Dali. Two fucking *mad men* whose art was just as misunderstood as I knew mine would be." He smiled out through the windshield, his knuckles white against the black vinyl of the Cutlass's steering wheel. "Afterward … the voice in my head … they just … *fucking* died.

"And the voice … I know who it was. It wasn't mine. It was never me, Stell."

333

"Who … who was it?"

"Dear ol' dad," Karl said. "He died. In my head, he was already rotting."

She nodded, but the last of his revelation faded, crowded out by the sound of pumping blood between her ears. From Karl's perspective, Stella looked to be gazing out the window into the harsh gleam of red and white traffic lights.

Stella was actually staring down at the passenger door controls. The window button, Lock-Unlock. She started hashing out some rudimentary math and guesswork in her head. *How many seconds—split seconds—from my tapping the unlock button on the door before he realizes what I did? Then, how many seconds—split seconds, dammit—will it take for him to grab me and hold me in before I can crank open the door and just roll and roll?*

"… for you?"

Stella jerked her face towards him. "Huh?'

"I said … is that good enough for you? Or do you need more?"

"No-no … I'm fine. Just …"

"Enough about the cops. You're starting to make me feel bad!"

Really? A small flame of hope lit at the base of her spine.

Karl laughed thickly. "I will say this about the cops. They don't deserve so much as an ounce of my sympathy. The way they bad-mouthed my work. Dismissed me as just another headcase with … what did they call it? *Delusions of grandeur!* I mean, who farted, right? If you're thinking I'm going to leave cops out of it from here on out if they get in our way, I'm telling you I'll pile their blue bodies to the fucking sky if I have to. And I don't give a shit about their families or their kids."

Two seconds—I hit the Unlock switch—then another two seconds—so I—

"Mm-hmm," she said, and slowly inched her fingers towards the button.

Suddenly, the Cutlass's engine sped up and sounded like it was strangling under the hood. The car lurched forward violently, and Karl laughed as he gunned it through a red light. Horns blared from every direction, and the smell of burnt rubber assaulted Stella's nose as the insane squeal of a thousand tires screamed in the disconcerting surround. Karl's laugh peaked into a high, terrifying cry, and it did not break in his throat until they emerged miraculously unharmed through the intersection.

Karl kept the speed up. Stella saw the needle in the dash pinned at 90 miles-per-hour and felt her bowels loosen.

He knew what I was going to do! Goddam him! He knew, and he's fucking with me!

"Oh Lordy!" he cried through a devilish, ever-widening smile.

"What? *What?* YOU TRYING TO KILL US?'"

"Not at all! Just excited!"

"Why!?"

Karl glanced over at her, a thin but animated light dancing in his black eyes. "We're close. Your GPS says two minutes away."

Then, he started humming the melody to "I Want Candy!" and Stella knew. She almost threw up in the wheel well.

It was 1:30 a.m.

62. LAST CHANCE, NEXT EXIT

Will Bentley knew he could be dead wrong about the assumption, his *educated guess* about where the millennial Bonnie and Clyde were headed first. He thought about what he would do and how he would visit the women on the IDs. In what order. Will decided he would start close and work his way outward to the furthest point or address. From there, he would just *keep on keeping on*, since there could be no way he would be able to return to Comstock. Hell, if Will were *them*, he'd jump on the nearest on-ramp south to Mexico.

The closest coordinate happened to be in the Society Hill section of Philadelphia. The girl's name was Jodi Dare, according to Jack Post's dictated list. *If I'm off track, it will be time lost. That's what's killing me right now, the possibility I could be way off or driving in the opposite direction of where they're headed.* At the same time, he had to deal with the more frequent warm tingling in his cheek, immediately followed by the voice of his Sarge in the prefrontal cortex of his brain.

Soldier, something doesn't feel right about this. You got four names and addresses. This is a crap-shoot right now! There's got to be a way you can narrow this down, eliminate some of them for the time being. Narrow your focus some.

"First things first," Will said, and decided to pull over into the parking lot of a Uni-Mart.

The spaces were empty at such a late hour, the interior of the overly-brightened interior equally vacant save a short, spindly looking man with

335

flyaway white hair, and a look of vacancy to match the store as he pushed a broom up and down the aisles.

"Sarge, it could be useful to have an army. More firepower. More eyes. Don't you agree?"

They aren't just gonna welcome you into their fold, Soldier! You damn well know it! And if you're thinking of pooling information with them, I can tell you it's only gonna flow in one direction—from you to them! They ain't gonna share shit with you beyond the usual scant details that'll keep you believing they're on the case! You're seriously thinking of calling that detective?

"So you would prefer an extraction with this? It's perfectly fine if it comes down to that, but I have to track them effectively. I can't lose track of them, and I can't guess incorrectly." The consequences for following an erroneous trail made his cheeks burn with frustration. This feeling of control slipping away reminded him of how he had felt during the month Alberta was in a coma. He could do nothing to help her. To revive her. He could only put his trust and surrender himself to the vet staff at St. Pio's Clinic.

Granted, they saved Albie.

Only to have her face down this new nightmare! I'll tell you what, I'm going to leave these two fucks wherever I find them.

Will took out his phone and punched up Detective Rivell's phone number.

Keep it vague, soldier—get something out of her you can use, but you play your cards close!

"Rivells."

"Detective Rivells," Will said. "Will Bentley."

"Uh … yeah-yeah … Mr. Bentley. What can I help you with?" She sounded both breathless and mildly perturbed.

"I wanted to touch base with you to see if there are any new developments."

"We're working round-the-clock on this, I can assure you. We've got a number of leads, and the suspects were last spotted an hour ago at a toll stop headed into New Jersey."

"New Jersey?" Will cried, the tumblers falling into place with a satisfying series of clicks. "Really?"

"We're presently working in coordination with their police force and cordoning off major roadways. I hope you're near your girlfriend, and you two can hold each other while we work to get this resolved."

New Jersey. There's only one person on the list living in New Jersey. Atlantic City to be exact. Sonofabitch! I almost drove to fucking Old City

336

Philly for nothing.

"I'm on my way back to the hospital now to be with her."

"Oh, Mr. Bentley? I'm actually glad you called. I wanted to ask you a few more questions, if you have a second."

"Sure, sure."

"It's about your dog."

"What do you need to know?"

"Well, if she's had her rabies shots, for one. And if she's ever shown a history of aggression or violence."

"No … no, never." It was strange. Will had never seen Albie flex her temper, but his answer still tasted like a lie. He loved Albie like a parent loves a child, but there had always resided a small flame of dread burning way down at the bottom of his soul whenever he thought about the things he did not know about his dog's history. It had always been there, this feeling. It wasn't her fault, and he knew it. Still, Will often wondered if the proverbial shoe would ever come to drop with Albie. "Never. Why do you ask?"

"We lost two police officers during the course of the investigation. They were investigating a location where the two perps were suspected of holing up. Both were viciously attacked at the site in question. But their wounds, the way they were killed, is consistent with an animal attack. More specifically, a dog. We won't know definitively until after the autopsy has been performed, but as it stands now we have no choice but to treat your dog as hostile and dangerous."

"That's impossible!" Will cried. "You've got it all wrong. My Albie would *never* hurt another human being unless she felt her life was threatened. I mean, she was a *war dog*. They undergo some training to support the troops in their unit, but she's peaceful. She's a damned teddy bear, for God's sakes!"

"Maybe your animal feared for her life when she came across the officers. They may have had their guns drawn and your dog misinterpreted their intent. Now, you said your animal was a *war dog*? She served over in Iraq with you?"

"Yeah! Decorated!"

"Was she born and bred in the United States and brought over with a team, or is she native to the Middle Eastern region?"

"My unit found her as a stray while we were liberating a town. She never exhibited any sort of penchant for aggression. We had a soldier on staff who trained her how to protect and defend, but not at will. *Never* at will. No, she operated under strict protocol and only responded to a series of specific, classified words to call her into action during combat. *Classified* commands!

337

So unless either of those two fuckwits you're chasing have access to classified material like that, they would have no idea how to activate her."

"Mr. Bentley, your choice in words there is … a bit telling. Alarming even."

"Meaning what?"

"You've used words like *activate* and *control* when talking about your dog. It almost sounds like your animal is some kind of *weaponized creature.*"

"No, you've got it all wrong," Will said, pleading then.

"Well." Rivells sighed. "I'm hoping so. We're all hoping for a peaceful resolution to this situation. I'm hoping to return your dog safely into your custody. I will … I'll do my best. All things considered."

All things considered?

"What are you saying? Are you going to kill my dog?"

"No, of course we're hoping to avoid that."

"*Avoid that?*"

"Mr. Bentley, rest assured we're doing everything we can. Let us do our job and I'll be in touch as things—"

Will Bentley hung up the phone.

Then, he brought up the GPS on his phone, punched in the address for the woman in Atlantic City. The route planned for him, Will drove east towards his fate.

63. CANDY WHITBY

Anaconda Road was five blocks from the Atlantic City boardwalk, with its glittering and hypnotic flurry of beckoning lights and decadent ambience. The side streets of the boardwalk's surrounding neighborhoods crisscrossed dizzyingly all the way up the boardwalk on-ramps. The streets still buzzed at such an obscenely late hour with clusters of tourists, gamblers, winos, and prostitutes, none of whom had any concrete plans with a pillow and blanket until the soft, winter sun rose in a few hours. Anaconda Road itself consisted of a row of blue and white ranches, with driveways of crushed white stone and cramped, but neatly trimmed squares of lawn bordering narrow walk-ups onto humble little patios. Every house flew the flag at dawn and took it down at dusk, a holder affixed to at least one patio support beam.

A wood and crème stucco bungalow stood at the corner of Anaconda and Llanview Roads. The bungalow housed two inhabitants, upstairs and down. The grass was threadbare and grey in comparison to the neighboring properties. The sidewalks leading up to the two private entryways were cracked and crumbling away. Some of its dust frosted the tips of dead grass lining either side.

Inside, Candy Whitby was dreaming of a miracle product called The Deviled Egg Delight. She was in the audience watching some D-list celebrity fawning over all of the wonderful ways this new and upcoming invention could dice deviled eggs and turn them into beautiful, enchanting side-garnishes. The audience was on their feet, chanting and playing up to the director stage side and holding up a sign with the word APPLAUSE. The audience hooted and hollered. Candy remained seated. She was weeping to herself. She was cradling a dead kitten in her lap, stroking its matted fur and mixing her tears into it, working the wetness into the pelt of the animal. It kept startling, seizing in her lap, and then turning stiff again. Over and over. Resurrecting itself only to die. Repeat. Repeat. She wiped her eyes, lay the cat on the empty seat beside her. The seats occupant was on their feet and cheering like The Beatles just reunited, even the dead ones in their funeral shrouds, come back to bang out "I Am the Walrus" one last time.

It would have been a dream she didn't mind having.

This was madness. Disjointed. Disconnected. And like most dreamers unaware they are dreaming, she fell in line and filled her role as best she could. She stood up, suddenly interested in what was unfolding on the stage down below. The D-list celebrity, along with a pretty little blonde who served as the demonstrator of the product, continued their orgasmic response to the miracle of The Deviled Egg Delight.

"It can garnish and slice, neat as you please," the blonde demonstrator said, snapping a quick and sassy smile at the camera, which revealed a toothless mouth and slick, bleeding gums, like her teeth had only just been plucked before she took the stage for this middle-of-the-night infomercial.

"Who would like a close-up demonstration?" The hands of twenty-five people in the audience flailed in the air like fish drowning out of water. Candy's hand shot up. The blonde on stage laughed all the way from her sensible high heels and shouted. "Okay, you-you-YOU! THE FUCKING NUTJOB IN THE BACK ON THE RIGHT AISLE! COME ON UP, YOU CRAZY BITCH! If you can put one foot in front of the other, you bipolar whackaDOO!"

The remaining audience members let their dead-fish hands drop back into their laps. What felt like a thousand eyes swiveled around, staring up at Candy. She was standing at her seat, alone. Candy smiled down at the

339

people on the stage and made her way down. Then, she remembered she had forgotten something. She had left something on the seat beside her.

"Don't worry, weirdo!" the D-list actor called to her. "We had one of our producers bring your kittycat down to the stage. They also managed to revive it. Our producer is a consummate professional, as well as a Messiah on the side. A Christ. He raised your cat from the dead, just long enough to participate in our little demonstration. Come on down, you sick bitch! Hurry up!"

The words did not sting like they would have if she were awake. In the dream, they were mere sounds. She trundled her way down the steps and walked onto the cramped staging area. There was a mock backdrop of a sunny kitchen, complete with a stainless steel refrigerator and a window with bright yellow curtains, and a stupid painted sunrise emerging outside in all its cheesy acrylic splendor. Candy approached the display table where Mr. D-List and the small, insulting blonde were gathered. The table was choked with all manner of deviled egg dishes and fancy garnishes.

Candy barely batted an eyelash when Mr. D-List suddenly swept everything off the display table with a wide, vicious sweep of his arm. Everything came crashing down on the left side of the display table. The blonde smiled, all sunshine and rainbows, and dipped down underneath the display table. When she stood up again, she grasped Candy's cat, alive once more, by the generous tortoise-shell fur of its scruff. It hung limply, its eyes white and milk-glazed. The blonde set the cat down on the display table and beckoned Candy to come closer. "Come here, dickhead! Have a look at what else the Deviled-Egg Delight does!"

On cue, Mr. D-List dipped down to search beneath the display table. He brought out a much larger version of the deviled-egg slicer machine. It was nearly as big as the display table itself. He grasped the handle on the left side of the slicer, lifted it, and the ten parallel razor-sharp knives rose a foot above the bowl of the slicer itself. The blonde stepped into Mr. D-List, pivoting before him as she set the cat down in the bowl of the slicer; with the other hand she groped Mr. D-List's noticeably prominent erection tenting the crotch of his slacks. "I can't help it, Dolores," he said to the blonde. "This kind of thing gives me wood!"

Candy managed to snap out of the fog of her dream-state enough to realize what was about to happen. She shoved her way towards the slicer and the cat, who had laid down inside the bowl like it was a comfortable cat bed. "I don't want you to—"

Dolores the Blonde's face reddened, and she flashed a set of perfectly white teeth, sharpened to points like a picket fence behind her lips.

"You're next—they're coming inside right now, and you're so stupid-dosed you don't even know it—dumb bitch!"

"But I don't want—"

The audience groaned when Mr. D-List slammed the handle of the slicer downward and the blades did their job—

Iwanttowakeupwanttowakeupwantowantto.

Candy Whitby had fallen asleep under the same gold and brown afghan blanket her dead mother knitted for her when she was twelve. She lay with her knees tucked up into her belly. She rarely made it to the twin bed in the other room, crashing hard and fast on the sofa as the Late Show with Jimmy Kimmel gave way to a series of benign, repulsive infomercials that cast white and gray castes all about the wood-paneled walls of her living room.

She snapped awake.

The TV was blaring. Louder than she would have had it, especially since she had anticipated it lulling her to sleep, as it had so many nights before.

The medicine she took for her bipolar condition, a strong and sedating antipsychotic called Geodon, plagued her with these same nightmares; a comingling of the stimuli provided to her subconscious, compliments of the infomercials. The medicine did the rest, providing claws to an otherwise stupid half-hour sales pitch. The medicine also deadened her to the point she barely woke in the middle of the night, and even after having gained eight hours of solid shuteye, Candy still craved her bed for much of the day like some zonked vampire. The only thing which kept her from fucking up at the casino, where she worked as a bartender, was the espresso machine in her kitchen she bought secondhand at Goodwill. She brought thermoses of the strong, pungent Italian drink with her to work and nipped at it during her breaks. Otherwise, she would have dumped drinks in many a lap and botched many a mixed beverage.

She couldn't lose this job. Her boss had even offered her the opportunity to *move up* if she was willing to attend a Card Dealer Certification course. She'd have to foot the bill, but the casino would reimburse her once she produced the certificate of completion. Classes started next Wednesday.

With all of these things spinning around in her head, Candy yawned loudly and thrust the afghan off her. She walked to the blaring television set across the room. She switched it off and found she could breathe again.

Her chest unclenched, and she felt the wave of anxiety building within filter out of her by way of her fingertips.

Candy stood there in the dark. The red-letter digital clock on top of the tv read 2:36 a.m.

hudda-hudda-hudda-hudda-hudda

She hadn't heard it right away after turning off the tv, but now it sounded like it was right inside her ear canal. A panting.

hudda-hudda-hudda-hudda-hudda

Candy spun toward the source of the sound. It seemed to somehow be playing games with her sense of hearing. She swore she heard it here, there. Everywhere. A siege. The room was bathed in gentle low light, a series of edges and planes coming up blue and gray here and there as her eyes adjusted. Nothing she could identify as being out of place. Coffee table. Uncomfortable La-Z-Boy recliner. An Ikea bookshelf behind that, boasting a generous paperback collection ranging from Dean Koontz to Christopher Marlowe.

Nothing strange.

And still the *hudda-hudda-hudda-hudd.*

Then, she heard something else on top of that.

Someone whispering. Quick, staccato sounds of a muted voice.

"Hello?" she asked the darkness.

It suddenly dawned on her if someone were standing nearby in her house, they could probably see her a hell of a lot better than she could see them.

The next thing she said was something her stepfather once told her to say if ever she feared someone had broken into her house. How had he known it would come to serve her someday?

"I have a gun," she said calmly.

The whispering cut off, but the panting sped up and swelled in volume.

Candy's heart pounded. She felt light-headed, drunk from a lack of oxygen as her chest tightened and her lungs struggled. Still, she was in full fight-or-flight mode.

"I'll blow your head off if you don't just … just leave my house … *right now!*"

That's when someone peeled themselves away from the wall to her immediate right. Pale skin. Skeletal. Eyes alight with something which immediately frightened her. It stopped her heart. She flinched away from the shape, which became a woman standing a mere three feet from her.

The woman's voice was shuddery, weepy and lamenting. "Do you know Jack Post?"

Candy's breath hitched, confusion staying her fear for a moment. *Jack. Post. That … that enabler! I'm still trying to forget about him, and here comes a woman in my house–*

"Who are you? What are you doing in my house?"

"Did you *fuck* Jack Post?"

"You see my hand?" Candy said, reaching behind for her jeans waistband. "I'm going for my gun, and I *will* shoot you if you don't get the hell out of my house!"

A man's voice, twangy and sarcastic sounded further away, near the kitchen alcove. "You got shit, lady! Ask her whatever you want, Stell. This is how you get your peace of mind. You go on ahead."

This must be the one whose shadow Candy saw hunkering down in the filtered light of the moon sifting through the curtains.

Candy felt a fluttering behind her ribcage. It was unlike any sort of feeling she had ever known before. Her heart was not beating as heavily anymore. It felt like a caged bird, but not a frenzied one. It knew it would get out. Knew there was a freedom coming, and it was more nervous than frightened. This was a sense of resolve. She had talked about this moment so many times with her therapist.

She anticipated this final moment where she would die a violent death. Candy always expected this, irrational as her therapist had tried to convince her. *It's an irrational fear. Nothing is going to happen to you. You were violated. You were raped, yes, but you still choose to come and keep your appointments with me every week. That is saying something. It is your battle cry, your* never say die *declaration, every time you come here and sit with me and talk to me. You're going to live a long life because you want to live a long life.* She wondered absently what her therapist would say about this present situation. Would she apologize? Offer a refund?

Of course, Candy would have much rather been wrong about her fears. She would have much rather lived a long life, but the fear melted away and calm covered it over like a drenching spring rain. All of these years, ever since her early adolescence, her phobia had been preparing her for this moment and it was not so bad.

The woman took a step towards Candy. "Did you fuck Jack Post?"

Candy swallowed hard and brought her hands around to her sides. "He told me he loved me. It was … nothing … in the end. He … played games with me." She looked at the woman, noted the hazy flyaway hairs stirring along the top of her head as the heating vent above tickled them. "Are you his … girlfriend—"

"Oh-no-no-*no*-I'm his wife. Don't insult me—"

"I'm not. I-I wouldn't."

"Are you HIV positive, Candy?"

"How do you know my name?"

"Because he talked about you all the time. How much you two were in love—"

"Okay-*okay*. I'm sorry—"

The man piped up in the burgeoning low light. "You a stripper, Candy? It's a stripper name … *Candy!* Your *Christian* name?"

hudda-hudda-hudda-hudda

"Is that a … a dog I hear?" Candy asked, certain she had identified the sound.

The man continued, his voice dripping with delight. "Who is going to miss you when you're gone? Who's gonna pay for your burial? Anyone? Who do you have? You got a roster of folks to stand graveside, or is your death gonna be more like a tree falling in the woods with no one around to hear it? Doesn't matter? Never happened?"

"W-who–a-are–you?" Candy stammered, the warmth of calm fizzling and her belly turning cold.

"Folks back in high school used to call me *Moonshadow*, on account I guess they all thought I look like that guy who wrote 70s folk songs, Cat Stevens. He's a Muslim now, I think. It's not even his name anymore. But you can call me Moonshadow. It'll be fun."

I want this to be over. Either I live or I die. Can't bear this drawing it out. "What are you going to do?"

hudda-hudda-hudda-hudda.

Candy felt the blade pierce her side, but she didn't know what was happening to her until it bumped up against the bottom rung of her right rib cage. The woman had come closer, nose to nose with her in an instant. There were tears in the woman's squinty eyes. Her mouth was a painful leer, and she winced right along with Candy as she twisted the knife and widened the wound. The woman sighed, "Nothing. It's … nothing. It'll be over soon."

"Don't lie to the poor slut!" the man cried.

Both women looked down at the blade in Candy's side, appalled by the action in seemingly equal measure. Then the women raised their eyes once more, and this was where their matched motion and response split.

Stella gasped. "I'm sorry."

Candy Whitby screamed, but it died in her throat as the pain of her wound overwhelmed her. Her right side, from the top of her thigh all the way down the pant leg was drenched in thick blood glistening in the shallow light. She felt the world tip over, and she went with it. Revoltingly, she found herself having no choice but to grab for the sleeve of the very woman who had just stabbed her. Candy expected the woman to back away. Instead, the woman accepted her weight and even steadied her with both hands. Candy

344

heard the knife fall to the rug with a muted thunk! She felt the cold enter her body, originating from the opening in her side, and widening ever upward until her whole right side felt numb, like she had been leaning it up against the cold steel door of a meat locker.

The strength left Candy. There had not been much to begin with. The calm had been there before, and it would see her through. *Please, let this be it. Let this be the extent of it. I can ... I can deal with this. It feels like sitting down inside of a cool bath.* The woman steadying her, her murderer, and slowly guided her towards the sofa she had risen from moments before. Candy felt herself lowering onto the sofa with the precarious guidance of the woman and then she was putting all her weight, meager as it was, into the cushions.

The woman lingered near Candy. Her voice was the sound of small stones at the bottom of a mason jar. "You never answered my question."

Candy dropped her head back against the cushions, lolled it over to the side with building exhaustion as the life ran out of her. "What ... what are you ... talking ... about?"

The woman's voice flared as she repeated her question. "Do you have AIDS?"

"N-n-no ... of course not ..."

The bath water is turning cold. I don't mind it ... don't mind at all.

The woman hesitated, lingering longer. "Oh. I ... I'm sorry. I—"

The man spoke up behind her, his voice closer. The dog's panting closer as well.

hudda-hudda-hudda-huddahuddahudda

"Jack?" the man called out.

This confused Candy, but not too much. She was slipping the mortal coil.

"Jack? I know you're in there! Everything that's about to happen? It's your fault. And you got a front row seat, Jack! I hope this slut was worth it! Most of all—"

Candy heard the sound of something snap a few inches away from her head. She smelled something like raw hamburger. *Huddahuddahudda-huddahuddahudda.*

SNAP!

Teeth—it's ... it's teeth snapping shut.

"Most of all, Jack? I hope you loved this one! It'll hurt so much more, you piece of garbage!"

Candy felt the dog's teeth clamp down into the taut flesh of her throat and wrench away.

345

64. THE ONE

When it was over and they put him (and the dog, of course) back in the trunk, Jack Post pulled himself into a fetal position and wept, with his back against the invisible black barrier of the dog's mind. He had tried so hard not to watch, and there was a great deal he successfully bypassed by hiding his eyes. But the sounds were ever present, and even with his hands clapped over his ears as he lay shuddering and sick, Jack could not successfully shut out the screams, the gurgling, and finally, the death throes from the woman he had once thought of leaving Stella for years before. This woman, Candy was her name, had been *the one*.

Jack's *one*.

Now, there would be no reunion or reconciliation. She would be buried, most likely in pieces of gnawed, separated body parts, and the coffin would be closed. He had heard Karl Tarlick (*psycho demon fuck!*) ask Candy if she would have people at her funeral who would bear witness to her life and death. Jack knew the answer to that question. Candy Whitby was estranged from everyone in her family, immediate and extended. She had been estranged from them all when Jack met her at the Sands Cocktail Bar two years ago. He was quite certain Candy still lived a solitary, lonely existence.

The type of sad, insipid life not even her quack of a therapist could save her from.

I couldn't save this bird. I tried. This is not *my f*ault!

You broke her.

Yes, but I was going to fix her—I swear!

But you broke her!

Not my fault! They did this to her! I was going to fix her again.

Jack screamed loud and long, his cry a wail which made the dog whimper and moan at the sound of it echoing throughout the caverns of the animal's fracturing mind.

Jack was remembering snatches of the three-month relationship he and Candy shared. It was all too much, too *damned* much, but he could not stop the images and the pieces of conversation as they returned to haunt him one last time. Their romance had begun as most true ones ought to, without the first night roll in the bed sheets. No, Jack insisted they take their time getting there, and he knew this would only endear him to Candy all the more.

Jack had known for years about his *strange magnetism*, as he had come to call it. The uncanny, unconscious ability to draw only deeply troubled women (*girls* in high school) to him. He barely had to try. They al-

346

ways approached him, sensing something about him they probably couldn't quite place, other than it was a comforting, nurturing thing they could draw strength from. He gave them their strength. Jack loved his *birds*, no matter how battered their wings or blunted their beaks. He worked ceaselessly, just like he had with Candy, and they gave themselves over to him. Physically. Psychically. Mentally. Everything.

Until something clicked inside of them.

The women, his *birds*, would come to realize, as had Candy, Jack was no longer *enough* for them. Not capable of helping them, and if anything, he was further crippling them. Holding their heads under water so they would not swim away. The women then sought out professional help, and the professional always poisoned them against Jack. Suddenly, the vocabulary of his *birds* had stretched to include such new words and concepts as "enabler" and "Munchausen-by-proxy."

So it had been with Candy Whitby.

Jack's *one*.

The other relationships did not last nearly as long as what he had with her. Towards the end especially, they barely lasted longer than a week or a few days. They turned to mere *trysts*, but Jack never ceased to put his heart into each and every one of them. He imagined they simply started to form their false notions about him (enabler) earlier than before. He must have been putting out the wrong vibes. Had he more time, had none of this befallen him, Jack was certain he could have reworked his approach and helped more *birds*. Widened the span of his *flock*.

Now, he was *killing* them. Slaughtering the birds. One by one.

Candy Whitby, the first.

It had pained him far worse having to listen to Candy being ravaged and shredded, far more than when he'd come back to visit her for the *breaking down* two years ago. He never thought of these return visits, the unexpected ones which disarmed each woman, as *rapes*. Jack always thought of them more as the equivalent of hitting the *reset button* for each of his birds.

So he had thought.

Candy Whitby.

Memories.

Jack lay there in a crumpled heap, shrouded in the blackness of the dog's mind, and wept until he exhausted himself into something of a waking sleep. He remembered the regatta he had attended with Candy a month into their relationship. They were snapping complimentary photographs of all the couples at the event, and Jack could remember how he had protested for some time before Candy eventually convinced him to pose for one with her.

He hadn't wanted any sort of documented proof of an affair, but for her, Jack had found he was easy when it came to what she wanted. He even kept the photograph, storing it in his private photo album. Locking *that* away in his closet safe.

Who will fix the broken birds, if not me?

The memory of his time at the regatta gala with Candy had already turned fuzzy with age, and he hadn't thought about it for some time. Now, Jack heard only the screams and the cries and the death of his *one*.

He screamed and wept. Screamed. Wept.

The dog whimpered and moaned. Whimpered. Moaned.

The Cutlass drove on, east towards Maryland.

65. CLARITY

Stella had snuck two Xanax before they started their journey to Candy Whitby's shore bungalow. She knew her limits and the amount she needed to take in order to soften her mind, to knead its dough into something pliable and pudgy. She had been hoping for a complete lack of sharpness. At the Whitby house, she needed more than a little bit of coercion from Karl to exit the vehicle and enter the house. To *take part* in the ritual. Stella had relented, slipped inside the house with not nearly the same amount of silent grace as Karl and the dog.

She hadn't planned on doing what she did to Candy until the knife in her hand plunged into the woman's side and that warm, sticky blood cascaded over her knuckles.

The woman set Stella with a look which seemed to ask *Why?*

She and the woman were praying for the same thing right then. A quick death.

Please let this be the end of it! No more suffering or violence. Let her die, just like this. Quietly, and peacefully. No need for the—

Then, Karl had unleashed the dog upon Candy and the belt of sanity spinning inside Stella's mind snapped. It flung itself around and flailed wide inside her skull and she knew it would only continue on like this. A chain of deaths stretched out over a series of twenty-four hours or so. A road trip with a trail of blood and entrails in its wake. She had run out of the house, her hands clapped firmly over her ears. No screaming. It was still dark out. Late.

Now, curled up in the stolen car's passenger seat, Stella entertained only one thought spiraling endlessly through her mind. Haunting and plaguing her. *Why did you get back in the car with him? Why didn't you run? Why didn't you ... WHY?*

She had no answer, nothing to satisfy her fractured mind. Like most unanswered questions, it continued on and carried like an echo down a dark, stone corridor. Stella had come to understand something more since the events unfolded at the Candy Whitby bungalow.

He's not planning for any kind of revolt against him. He's still deluded into believing the two of you are in love. What if I rose up ... or ... turned the knife inward— he's got the dog under his command; under his thumb.

The inside of the car was a nauseating comingling of sweat and blood, slowly cooking as the heat hissed out of the console on full blast. Stella held her cheek against the cold glass of the passenger window, her eyes cast sideways out at the seemingly endless corridor of skyscraper pines lining the turnpike, ushering them further towards the great state of Maryland. Her eyes gauged the darkness at the base of the treeline, trapped and contained there like a treacherous animal brought to a temporary heel. She once more imagined herself working the door lock open and bursting out of the passenger side. Dropping and rolling, like someone on fire. Spinning down into the grass gulley dropping down and away from the breakdown lane, charging right into the pitch forest beyond. She thought of how long she could survive in the woods, and this, in turn, transported her back to the two to three months she had spent as a child in her local Brownie Troop. She had learned how to make fire from the friction of sticks rubbing together, but there had been little time for anything else she could make use of out in the wilderness. Slowly, begrudgingly, Stella's mind abandoned the possibility of tramping out into the woods and fending for herself rather than riding along.

Riding along.

No!

I don't want to die. I can't remember the last time I was in charge of anything in my life. There were moments I tricked myself into believing I was in the driver seat, finally taking control. This situation—this revenge scenario—I was never in charge. I know that now.

Death is personal. It's sacred. It ought to belong to the one doing the dying, right?

"Yes," she said, softly. Prayerfully. "Yes."

Karl didn't hear her. He had the local rock station turned up loud. Filter's "Hey Man, Nice Shot!" screeched through the speakers of the console like a captive screaming from under the hood as the gears ground them into a bloody sludge.

She had no idea what Karl's *magic words* were, the ones which called the dog to heel and then unleashed hell. Stella had tried to listen in on some of the chants, but none of it made sense. She was sure she could not pronounce them effectively if she tried. So she could not hijack the animal to turn it on Karl. For all intents and purposes, the dog was Karl's weapon, and his alone.

Still, she could bring the roof crashing down on Karl's head in other ways. Stella didn't blame the dog. She felt sorry for it; she had seen something in the animal, a cringing and naked fear in the animal's eyes when she and Karl had first come across it. The dog was not inherently evil, only its master at the moment. Dogs are inherently good, despite their primal wolf roots.

She drew her face away from the cold glass. "Can we stop somewhere for the night?"

The radio was still blaring: "Don't Cry" by Guns N' Roses.

She laid a hand on Karl's arm. "Hey!"

Karl was entranced by the swirling carousel of Axl Rose's vocals. His face swiveled towards her, eyes wide and enchanted. "What? Bad dream?"

"I wasn't sleeping."

"Then what?"

"Can we stop somewhere and bed down for a couple hours?"

"Oh yeah … sure."

She nudged his arm. "I'm serious!" she cried.

Karl spun the volume knob all the way down. "We're barely fifty miles outside of Comstock, little dummy! You *can't* be serious!"

Little dummy?

Stella rolled her shoulders, bit her bottom lip. "I need to sleep or you're going to have to carry me into the next address."

"Nah, you got things to say to all these ladies. You got to be up and at em' and sharp until we wrap this up. Just having the chance to confront these pigs ought to be enough to keep you energized."

"I know my part, Karl."

"You're tired, huh? You taking your Xanax?"

Stella hesitated. "Why?"

"*Why?*" Karl said, smirking. "Why-why-why? What do I care anymore?"

"It wouldn't matter anyhow, Karl. Tired is tired."

"All right, then we'll stop at the next rest stop motel. How would that be?"

She smiled, thinly. Laid her hands, folded in her lap. "It would be fine."

Karl pressed down on the gas. The Oldsmobile engine screamed in protest, and the car lurched from 50 mph to 70 mph in an instant. "You know, Stella? I'm not sure you understand what it is we're *really* doing here yet. Guess I'm gonna have to try harder to drive it all home for you. It's okay. I don't mind. Not at all." He palmed the wheel onto the upcoming rest stop exit only to veer wildly back onto the highway. Stella screamed. The dog in the trunk wailed. And Karl laughed from his gut. "So, we do one more stop then we sleep! Hopefully, *hopefully* our next visit will drive home the seriousness of it all! Ever been to Delaware?"

66. PROFILE

Detectives Jones and Rivells had only just crossed the bridge into the New Jersey Meadowlands when her cell phone buzzed along her hip. She answered it and mimed for Jones to lower the volume.

"Rivells."

"Top of the early morning to you, Glynna," a female voice said, surprisingly chipper and laced with an Irish brogue. Lily O'Connor, the staff psychologist from her precinct. A genuine Irish rose with curly, striking red hair and alabaster skin. She had greeted Rivells with such a stereotypical phrase to play off the fact she was about as Irish-looking and sounding as they come. "Reporting back regarding your serial rapist, Jack Post."

"Yes, my lovely, what do you have on *Broken Bird Syndrome*?" Rivells sat up straight in the passenger seat.

"I've treated it in a handful of my private patients, but I know it by another name. *Broken Woman Syndrome*. It's most prevalent in females, but there's a name for it when men exhibit symptoms. It's called *Broken Soldier Syndrome*. The symptoms differ in terms of exhibition between the sexes. You mentioned you were calling about women. Plural. I pulled out some of my older files and dusted them off. I compiled some new notes to share with you, and this flurry of activity was sponsored in part by an overused espresso machine in my office and a generalized condition of insomnia that's gone untreated for the last six months."

"Thanks for doing this, Lil. My partner and I believe we're dealing with a rapist who operates under the motivations of someone who thinks he *attracts* broken women and is tasked with trying to fix them."

351

"See, that's not your typical scenario in these cases. Normally, men can sniff out the warning signs when they're out on a first date with a *broken woman,* and they'll run for the hills. They don't normally stick it out or *embrace* it. Not to generalize too much, but these women typically suffer from a deep sense of depression and anxiety, and their insecurities are seeded on that. A *broken woman* will frame their lives as if their best days are behind them. She'll often use and cite friends who are more successful than herself to validate her own existence. The spark of vitality, that light in people's eyes which stays lit for most of us, has extinguished itself like a pilot light gone out. These women just never arrive at any reason to relight it. They dwell almost exclusively on past trespasses from former lovers, parents, or anyone they had come to trust completely. These women require a great deal of love and affection. Reassurance. Almost a constant influx of the latter. They're painfully shy. Many become shut-ins as a result of this painful condition."

That's our gal. Our Stella. For God's sakes, it's like Lily O'Connor met Stella Post before and evaluated her. Rivells thought of the blue curtains facing out onto the street where the Post's lived. The twitch at the bottom floor curtains throughout the day as Stella Post snuck a peek outside and then flitted away like a fly away from a bug zapper.

"Our perp even referred to his victims as *broken birds* in one of the books we recovered from his home office," Rivells said. "Their names were inscribed on the pages of a birdwatcher book. He's not just aware of the condition in women, this nutbag believes he attracts these types of women exclusively. He thinks of himself as some kind of healer for the broken *women* who come to him seeking repair. He married a woman with extreme depression and anxiety. We know very little yet about the other women whose names we found in the Bird Book."

"There's a pattern when you do manage to gather profile characteristics on the others. Histories of psychotropic drug prescriptions written for them. Visits to therapists and a number of these false-starts where they never go back. Some do try harder and keep up a regular routine of visits with professionals. These women want to get better, but it's tricky. It's difficult to predict when and how they're going to one day decide they've had enough of the whole *damsel in distress* lives they have been leading, and they want to take the reins. They decide they want to get better and seek out help from a licensed professional. They enter clinics for short stays. They get on the right meds. Now, this is good, but then you've got to ask yourself, if this epiphany takes place while they're *involved* with this 'Healer of Broken Birds,' what happens from then on? How does their relationship change? Because I can tell you, on more than one occasion, I've counseled one of my patients who

352

fit this psychosis to leave their significant other because it became quite clear the boyfriend or husband was keeping them from helping themselves. Hindering therapy visits. Withholding medicine. That sort of thing. They were clearly threatened their little *wifey or girlfriend* wouldn't need them as much as they used to."

"That's who I think we're dealing with," Rivells said. "Jack Post. We think he had a number of extra-marital affairs with a series of women who fit these characteristics, and they sought him out, more often than not. Shit, is this guy putting out some kind of unidentified pheromone these specific women are picking up on? The 'I can fix you' musk?"

Lily O'Connor tittered. "If only it were so convenient to explain this phenomenon."

"The problem is our perp doesn't just go on his merry way once these women reject him in favor of getting better. We suspect he makes a return visit to them in a disguise and assaults them. Takes their driver's license and their cell phone numbers, even though he already has the digits."

"That I've not yet encountered," Lily O'Connor said. "He's clearly breaking the women down again so they will come crawling back to him and therapy will fail them. This is very much like what pimps do to their new women. They break them down and make it so these young girls redevelop in a more wilted, bent, damaged, and completely dependent vessel upon their pimp. He gets them addicted to drugs. He convinces them he is the only one who stands between a cruel world and safety."

Rivells cast a wary glance over at Jones, who caught it at the last minute and kept his gaze on the side of her face. Her jaw was tight and tense.

"Wait a minute," Rivells said. "So … oh shit, so if I'm putting this together right, all the women who were attacked by our perp *knew* him beforehand? Dated him for some period of time?"

"I'd stake my license on it."

"Christ," Rivells sighed.

Detective Jones mouthed *what* at her, but her thoughts were already a couple steps ahead of the *why* and the *how*.

"All right," Rivells said. "Thanks again, Lil! I owe you a dinner at La Scala whenever you're free!"

"It's a date, my dear!"

Rivells stared down at her cell phone screen, agitation suddenly taking hold of her so much she stabbed her index finger repeatedly into the *Hang up* icon. It wasn't working fast enough for her. "Dammit, come on!" Then, once her home screen finally reappeared, she dialed another number and waited. Jones kept shooting her questioning glances, but she didn't want to lose her momentum on this.

The thing of it was, they would most likely have to turn the car around at the next exit.

"Answer your phone, chick!" Rivells's foot tapped the bottom of her footwell impatiently. "Come on—oh great, *voicemail!* All right then … Jodi, this is Detective Rivells calling. We need to talk as soon as possible. If I don't hear back from you in the next ten minutes, I'm going to come to you. I'll hit up your work and your house until we touch base. It's very important we speak right away!"

As soon as Rivells hung up, Jones started. "We can't turn around—"

"Jodi Dare knew her attacker. And I think a part of her knows this but was afraid to alert us to it. This changes everything. We've got to get to her as soon as possible."

"So … I *am* turning this bitch around?"

"You are," Rivells said. "She's one of the *birds*, Jones. And we're not going to wait ten minutes."

"Why don't we have them send a squad car so we can continue on to the Whitby house?"

"That's a given. Radio it in, but I'm still going back. I have to. This started with a conversation I had with her, and I promised her from the very beginning I would keep her safe. That's what this is about. That … and the truth. All of it, no matter how unpleasant."

67. THE LEAVINGS

Will's roughened left cheek flared with a white heat for much of the ride to Atlantic City. Sergeant Karns burned in Will's mind like never before, the disembodied, gravelly voice of his long-dead superior alternating from commands to inspiring words to downright bullying verbal tactics to get Will's blood up. This was the time, the context of place and situation, within which he most craved his Sarge's counsel. Will was going to war and it didn't matter he was going it alone. It didn't bother him how cliché his actions and his mindset felt, the whole *Rambo-one-man-army* tunnel vision focus fueled by total destruction of his adversaries.

One dog, man's best friend, delivered from evil.

Quite literally.

We can't wait until the sun finally rises in three hours, soldier.

Karns's voice scraped like a snow shovel on concrete. *We gotta find a sporting goods store or a gun shop on the way to where we're going. Do a search on your cell for a place—and we're gonna do what needs doing! Don't shy away from this, now! Forget law and order! We need to arm up, soldier! Tranquilizer gun. Long-range rifle of your choice, soldier. You want to become the night—make it your friend. Grab a baseball cap and sunglasses for the daylight hours! Better to have and* not *need than to* need and not have—

"We're twenty minutes out, Sarge," Will countered. "Exit's coming up. I have to try and beat them to Candy Whitby's house. If there's a shred of a chance I can head them off I have to try—"

She's already dead, soldier!

"No, I don't accept that!"

Dead and gone. All you're going to find is their leavings—they had an hour head start on you, soldier!

"I gotta try!"

What is your malfunction, soldier?

Will didn't even try to rebut his Sarge. He drove on in silence, praying against all fate he was right and his Sarge wrong.

For once.

Will stood under the threshold separating Candy Whitby's kitchen nook from the rec room and felt his stomach somersaulting. He bit his lower lip as he surveyed the scene before him, smeared across the ratty beige carpeting of Candy's rented duplex apartment like fruit spread across a slice of bread.

He felt drunk.

Unsteady.

Defeated.

Not an option, soldier! Stand up straight! Find your spine! Line it up!

In what felt like an encapsulating fog which distanced him from his own actions, Will approached the remains of the woman. He braced the back of a nearby ratty recliner and lowered himself down to do what needed doing just the same. An examination of sorts.

Candy Whitby's body looked like a pack of wolves had surrounded her and taken chunks out of her. Her left leg was separated from the rest of her body just below the knee. The tattered shreds of her nightgown, now a red sheet wrapped around her midsection, barely clung to her outer thighs. It looked more like a funeral shroud than sleep apparel. One of her sizeable breasts had been gouged out of her chest, leaving a gaping, gleaming hole in its place. Teeth marks framed her side all the way up and down as if one of the *wolves* had at first sampled her before snapping its

355

jaws deep down into flesh.

Will leaned in, something even more strange drawing his attention. One wound stood out among the many others. It was nothing canine teeth had made, but rather a knife or some other instrument. It looked cleaner in its entry. Roughly two inches in diameter, stabbed into the woman's right side just below the bottom cleft of her ribcage. *One of them cut her before ... before—*

Your dog did this, soldier! There's no denying! But you know this ain't her—not Alberta! Problem is, they're going to shoot to kill when they find her with them! They're going to put her down because this is no search and rescue Albie *mission! That motivation evaporated soon as Albie killed the two officers back at the church!*

The sheer viciousness of the attack left Will breathless. The murder scene told the story, revealed a bit more of the iceberg beneath the arctic waves of what Will knew of his own dog's mentality. Not only had Candy been massacred, she had also been stomped and ground into the rug like the kidnappers, or (God forbid) his dog, had tread on her remains repeatedly, working it into the very fibers of the crusty rug. Candy's throat was ripped away, leaving a chewed white gleam of spinal bone poking out of the ravaged flesh.

Oddly enough, aside from smears of blood across her cheeks, Candy's face was perfectly intact. Not one bite mark or wound of any kind to her face. If the rest of her remains were covered and tucked underneath her chin, it would have been easy to assume she was only sleeping. *A pretty woman. With her eyes standing open like that, she looks kind of like the actress Jessica Lange.* A shudder shook him from the base of his spine to the nape of his neck. He reached out, shut her eyes, and stood up.

You understand now?

"I always understood," he muttered, turning away and walking back into the kitchen. "I have to get to Albie first. They're going to treat her like a *cop killer*."

No mercy, soldier.

"Christ," he sighed. "When I find her, I can … I can hit her with a knock-out syringe and take her away in the crate. An extraction. But … I understand more about this than I wish I had to. They're going to force me to put her down."

The cops are not your friends in this situation! Now you're getting it! You gotta ask yourself, how much do you love Alberta?

"It's not her fault … those bastards did something to her. Baited her in some way."

356

How much do you love your dog, soldier?

"I'll hide her—she doesn't deserve to die."

How? Much?

"Enough to protect her from my fellow man," Will said. "Once I find her, of course." He suddenly understood he would need to break and enter into veterinary clinic *as well as* a sporting goods store. They don't exactly sell tranquilizing medications over the counter at your local CVS. *This means I have to get started right this second, before the sun comes up in a couple hours. And that means ... dammit ... they're going to kill someone else before I can get to them in time. Maybe more than one victim. Unless I act fast and don't run into other problems or obstructions.*

Will took out his cell phone. His iPhone was at 25 percent. He would need to charge it in his truck and was fairly certain he had his portable charging cord stashed inside his glove box. *Gotta get going. Can't leave a trace I was ever here.* He thumbed the GPS tab and searched for local vet clinics in the immediate and surrounding areas of Candy Whitby's neighborhood. He found one roughly five miles southwest of his present location: Sand Bar Veterinary Clinic and Hospital. The clinic did not have hours for the coming day, Wednesday. This would allow him more time to ransack the clinic for the anesthesia he needed, but he wasn't stupid. *I'm not going to drag my feet. I won't be able to anyhow, since I'll most likely be triggering an alarm.* Will saved this location to his Favorites and moved on.

Next, he ran a Google search for a gun shop. Eleven miles north: Tanner's Guns and Ammo. They opened at nine. Another blessing, widening the amount of time he had to make the rounds from place to place before getting back on the scent of Alberta and her captors. *Save.*

Two B and E's, soldier! That's something else! Best get going!

One more thing to do.

He turned halfway towards the tv room, unable to look at the scene of the massacre again. He'd seen things, terrible things. Nothing like what lay beyond the threshold.

It was saying a lot.

Will walked over to the phone on the wall hanging just above the stove. He punched in 911. He laid the phone down on the counter and went out into the evaporating night.

68. MAEVE STAPLES

The sky had softened and the sun's pink veins were beginning to bleed into the navy blue sky hovering above the rooftops of the lightly dozing side street. Jack Post stared blearily out of the dog's eyes as Karl Tarlick rousted the animal, then drew it out of the car's trunk. The dog raised its head, and Jack caught a momentary glimpse of Karl's fierce, angry stare before his hand swatted at the animal's snout. It growled low in its throat. Then, Karl took a knee next to the dog and hissed into its right ear.

Karl's tone was admonishing, fierce. Jack could only assume he was referencing the stinking mess the animal had made in the trunk. The dog had evacuated in the trunk. It had thrown up numerous times. Jack heard it, and he felt it. Every clenching of the animal's muscles and heave of her stomach as it drove anything and everything out of her body from top to bottom.

Jack stood up inside the dog's mind and moved towards the two windows of the dog's eyes. He exploded a torrent of words at Karl Tarlick, unaware the sonofabitch could hear none of it.

"This dog was sick before this! You piece of garbage! You're killing this animal! It's dying! I can smell death all around in here! It's in this dog's pores, for God's sakes! Just. Stop. This!" It was true, the smell of the animal's mortality clung to her like a terrible musk. It permeated the dog's mind as well, like an invisible gas wafting in to poison Jack in his dark, dank cell.

The dog goes ... I go with it. I wink out into the ether, and this will all be over. I know we're probably going to different places when the light goes out, but I'll stick with the dog until the fires come nipping at my heels.

Karl rose and closed the trunk, mindful not to slam it. He lowered the hatch and slipped the hasp into the latch until he heard a satisfying click.

"Good girl," he muttered down to the dog and yanked at the chain around her neck. Jack felt the tug, the animal's head and body falling in line and step. "No hard feelings. Don't matter much to me anyhow. I'm not the one's gotta ride back there for the rest of the trip. You've done it to yourself, girl. And, uh, by the way, we're going solo on this one. It seems our lady passenger doesn't have the stomach for what needs to be done. She's gonna wait in the car on this one. Deal with her later, I suppose. And ... it's looking like we're gonna have to bring the other two into the fold sooner than I planned."

Other two? Who? This just gets worse and worse ...

The chain-link leash rattled alongside the dog's head hypnotically. She looked to her right then left, a slow sweep. It was enough for Jack to gather something of a working knowledge for where they were. The cement walkway lined on either side by neat, narrow beds of dirty, white stones, with gray weeds poking out every few inches or so. A sad little row of dead flowers lay in wilted decay along the perimeter of the building. The only sign of life, a prickly, evergreen box shrub which seemed to thrive despite the freezing temperatures. *I remember these stones. Dirty stones, flecked with mud like flawed pearls. I remember telling Maeve her landlord has taste out the ass going with a stone front yard instead of grass. I remember telling her how* ugly *it looks. Oh ... no ... you can't—*

"No," Jack cried, rushing towards the windows of the dog's eyes. "No, not her! She's a good girl! She's got a lot of problems! This was my fault! This was my fault! Don't take it out on her like this! Don't punish her for the things I did! Punish me! *Punish me!*"

They *were* punishing him. That was the idea.

Maeve Staples.

Jack once believed he loved every single one of his *birds*, only in different ways and for different reasons. Like a parent loves their children, and all the while one of their offspring is indulged over the others without any conscious decision having been made. Before this early morning visit to Maeve Staples's house, Jack had been so certain he loved them all the same, even this one. Then, it dawned on him like a building nausea, he had neglected this one more than the others. The last time he saw Maeve, he was wearing a dog mask. *Oh God, was that really the last time I saw her? The re-setting ceremony?* It was. Maeve had called him after the *resetting* (attack). She had begged for him to come. She had told him she was suicidal, and her therapist was threatening to have her committed if she didn't try a procedure called ECT. She was terrified of the procedure, which involved the passing of electrical currents through the brain for the aim of reversing certain aspects of Maeve's ever-present bipolar condition. She was frightened of the mini seizures it caused. She had Googled everything she could about the procedure, Electroconvulsive Therapy, until she scared herself enough to call Jack with a plea for help.

I failed her. I reset her. She came back to me after rejecting my help. My love. But ... I didn't follow through on my end. I never made it back down to Dover. I called her back and promised I would come. I set dates with her and broke them. I left her. What kind of woman have I left behind? Is she still alive?

When Jack met her three years ago, Maeve was working as an escort for a company called Blue Orchid Enterprises. Jack was in town scouting out a wide-receiver at James Baldwin High School who had been breaking state records for the last two years like they were going out of style. The bellhop at the Hyatt who'd shown him to his room on the fourteenth floor doubled as something of a *hook-up* for drugs and women. Jack had discovered this quite by accident when he dropped a harmless hint to him and suddenly the young, towheaded boy in an ill-fitting beige bellhop uniform scribbled a number onto the back of Jack's receipt and pressed it into his hand with a sly smile and a quick farewell. A half hour later a tall, leggy, woman with long, wavy black hair and baby blue eyes was knocking back highballs while lounging across Jack's rented king-size bed and laughing at his corny jokes. It was all going so swimmingly until Maeve made a move to unzip him, and he begged off and told her he didn't want to sleep with her. He wanted to *lay* with her. To *talk*.

She wanted to leave, right then and there. She snatched up her purse and made a rush for the door, but Jack barred her exit. Not in an aggressive way. The most effective way he knew how, borne of years of practice. Of trial and error. The words, scripted and stiff on anyone else's lips, dripped from Jack's tongue like honey.

"I asked for you by name, Maeve. What would you do if I told you this didn't have to be forever? What would you do if I told you I could get you out of this life? Not for me ... for you. No strings attached. Just a promise of freedom. I would pay your way from here on out, until you figured out what you *really* want to do with your life. School? A dream you have been putting off? Come, just hear me out. I'll pay you double ... just for your time. Come ..." They must have talked the dark out of the sky and the sun up again. The spring sunrise in New Castle, glinting off the metal and steel of the industrialized neighborhood, Jack and Maeve slipped from conversation into each other's arms, and with an unspoken consent and submission to his promises, he slipped inside of her.

Love?

Maeve had cried after they orgasmed together. She crept out of the bed and into the bathroom, sobbing in the white bowl of the hotel bathtub in the dark, until he went to her. *Another bird to save. Another for my collection. Only ... I failed to love this one as well as the others. I ... I suppose I deserve what comes next ...*

The dog raised her snout and her eyes found Karl's hands, fumbling at the lock with what looked like a metal coil. The lock popped and clicked. The door groaned, then sighed open an inch.

Jack wanted to scream. He knew in his heart of hearts it would go unheard. It would only vex the animal all the more. He stood before the windows of the dog's eyes and waited. Held his breath and prayed for some kind of interloper to obstruct Karl's plans. A wild card. Anything? He tried to remember if Maeve owned a gun and thought better of this. *With her mental history, she'd never pass a background check!*

The house was dark but a column of light reached across the rug of the living room just beyond the hallway adjoining the foyer to the interior of the apartment. Karl stooped and spoke into the dog's ear. Once more, a lot of gibberish which made zero sense to Jack. He suspected he would have been able to understand every word if he were listening with a human mind, trained in the linguistics and vocabulary of English. Unless, of course, Karl was speaking an alien language altogether. The words did not seem to belong to any language belonging to earth or its beings. It was severe. It did not roll off the tongue, but rather stabbed at it like tiny pinpricks.

Jack felt it in the soles of his feet as he stood there. Karl's words were speeding up the animal's heart. He heard the animal's calm breaths turn to belabored gasps. *This is some kind of spell? I don't know. But it's changing her. Vexing her.*

Karl stood and led the dog through the hallway, then out the other side to the living room where a foldable card table against the west wall, and a pair of rickety wooden chairs, served as the dining area. A hunter green recliner and another of those wooden chairs sat on either side of a low end table. A retractable light was clipped to its edge, coiled like a snake. Four pill bottles littered the surface of the end table, some on their sides and opened. Empty. The finest accent of the room happened to be the oriental rug flung across the open space between the chair and end table arrangement and the forty-inch television perched atop a tv tray opposite.

The dog took it all in, its tongue dropping out of the side of its mouth like a hunk of raw meat.

hudda-hudda-hudda-hudda-hudda.

Something stirred across the room, behind the tv set. It was a rustling of sorts. Karl yanked the dog's chain, cinching it further around her throat. Karl drew it towards him as he ducked and inched towards the source of the sound. The dog was already searching the dark, and she found it on the floor tucked into a corner of the room before Karl even knew what he was seeing.

Of course. She still has them. Her two hamsters. Will and Grace. A good sign she's doing well. She can care for other living things.

The little steel cage was lined in straw and one of the little brown and white hamsters trounced about within while its buddy lay asleep in a drift of sedge.

The dog groaned low in its throat. It was menacing. Frightening.

"No, girl," Jack said, trying to calm her. "Don't you do it. They're innocent. She's innocent, too. Please, listen to me, girl. Just *heel!* Do you understand *heel?* *Hold! Wait! Heel! Please, girl—"*

"DON'T! STOP! WHY ARE YOU DOING THIS TO ME? LEMME-GO-LEMME-GO-LEMME ..."

Maeve's screams exploded throughout the apartment. Karl jumped and the dog assumed a pounce stance, instantly. Her growl swelled like a rapidly inflating balloon.

"No, wait—just wait, girl!" Jack cried, appealing to the dog. "She's only having a nightmare! She has a lot of nightmares! Night terrors! For as long as I've known her!"

Maeve suffered from this terrible condition and according to her, it had been her dark passenger for much of her life. Dating back to when she was six or seven years old.

"She's no threat. She's having a nightmare."

The dog lunged forward, driving her head down as the chain leash strained against her matted fur. She pulled Karl out of step. The animal jerked violently towards the direction of the screams. The bedroom. A black rectangle in the right corner of the room near the rustling little pen of hamsters on the ground.

It gaped, the door opened wide.

Karl pulled back on the chain, annoyed. "You wait until I say, or this is gonna go a whole other way. You hear?"

Jack's voice broke as he pleaded with the animal to yield. "Please just HEAR ME! HEAR ME! HEEL! JUST *HEEL—"*

Karl stooped down to the frenzied animal, uttered a nonsensical word into her left ear.

Then Karl let loose the chain leash.

Now, it was Jack's turn to scream. "STOP! *STOP! STOP!"*

This time, he did not turn away. He would not allow himself to shield his eyes as he had at Candy's house. The fact he had done it gnawed at him for some time afterward. He would bear witness. After all, these women were his birds, and someone should see them out of this world and into the next. No matter how gruesome their departure. He lowered himself down onto the bottom blackness of the animal's mind. He crossed his legs like someone sitting around a campfire. He rocked himself, slowly. The massacre unfolded before his eyes like a horror film bleeding across twin screens. The chain, loose from Karl's hand, clanked across the hardwood floor of the bedroom as the dog launched herself at the single bed in the center of the room. Maeve woke up seconds before the dog's teeth seized her by the throat. The clipped tweet of a scream interrupted as the dog shredded her voice box.

Then, the terrible sound of drowning out of water, a common sound shared between this attack and Candy Whitby's as the dog sent pint after pint of blood down into Maeve's heaving, panicked lungs. *This woman had tried to kill herself so many times, in so many ways. Yet, the fear and terror in her eyes right now as death comes to finally claim her is so complete and shocking and total!*

The head came away from the torso and rolled off the side of the bed, like a bowling ball. The dog started on the side of her body, just beneath her left arm pit.

Only then, when Jack couldn't look into Maeve's eyes any longer because they were across the room, did he allow himself to look away. To curl up. To cry.

Poor Maeve.

My birds.

You're killing them ...

69. B AND E'S

Will stopped at the nearest ATM and withdrew three-thousand dollars from his checking account. Then, he commenced with his breaking and entering spree, a gnawing feeling of guilt pinching his insides all the while. He knew the best way to hold this guilt at bay would be to call to mind different endearing and memorable moments spent with Alberta. It would act as fuel in the tank, spurring him onward in the face of his searing Catholic remorse.

Armed with his Glock, a silencer, the tire iron from behind the seat of his truck, and a black baseball bag slung over his shoulder, Will pulled into the alley behind the Tanner Guns and Ammo with his lights out. There were no street lamps in the rear of the small, ramshackle building, and he enjoyed the advantage of wrapping himself in shadow as he made surprisingly quick work entering the rear door. He pulled on black leather gloves and pried at the steel door with the sharp end of the tire iron. When this proved useless, he screwed the silencer onto the end of his Glock and fired two shots into the right side of the door. It yawned backward and he kicked it open the rest of the way with the flat, unforgiving soles of his combat boots.

The alarm hit his eardrums like a cuff of the fist to the side of the skull. He gritted his teeth and surged into the breach, a shadowy storage room comprised of iron shelves with bins of merchandise and glints of gunmetal peeking out at him from a few ragged boxes. The shrill sound of the pulsating alarm conducted up and down the column of his spine as he raced into the main storeroom. No time to search boxes or crates for what he needed. Better to take items right off their shelves, or out of the glass display cases running along the east wall of the sales floor. He located the night vision goggles. He swung the tire iron into the display glass. This triggered a second, more intense alarm which sounded like it was exploding right over his head. It sickened him as he grabbed the goggles out through the jagged opening he had created.

A few more seconds.

Next he skirted the display case and slipped behind it where a number of different caliber rifles and snipers hung suspended from a wall-length harness. He knew his weapons on sight, something he never thought would serve him as well as it did right then. He knew what he wanted and took it down off the wall. An M24 Sniper Weapon, the color of graphite and oily to the touch. Further down the wall, he found a dart gun. He would be picking up the ammo for that particular weapon at his next stop. The ammo for the M24 was stored in a locked wooden crate directly beneath where the sniper hung. He bashed the lock with the tire iron and quickly rifled through the boxes until he drew his hands out with two boxes of ten rounds.

While rummaging through the boxes of ammo, Will uncovered a large, black box hidden underneath. Concealed for some reason.

You know these places always hide the good *stuff away. The illegal stash. And it stays hidden until a certain somebody makes the owner's acquaintance and knows* just *what to ask for ...*

"All right," Will said, "I'll bite. But fast."

The alarm swirled around the room and sounded impossibly louder.

Quickly, Will found the edges of the black box and pulled it out of the ammo bin. It was roughly as long as his arm and wide as the type of box a vase might come in. When Will turned it on its side, he saw a simple block lettering logo running across: **R56 COMMUNICATION**. Underneath the logo, it read in bold white lettering: **DETECTOR-S**.

"Shit," he said to himself, "I read about these not too long ago. No wonder they're keeping this hidden away. You remember, Karns?"

That there is a radar the police and military are using that can actually see through walls.

"Controversial, because the ACLU has an issue with invasion of privacy," Will said. "You know what I have to say about that right now?"

That's affirmative, soldier. The people who took our Albie? Fuck their privacy!

"Hope this thing comes with directions." He tucked it down into the bag and zipped it up. It sagged on his shoulder and he hoisted it up higher. He checked his watch. *Four minutes, gone.*

He slapped the three grand down onto the counter, tucked it under an edge of the cash register.

Not too bad. Not so bad.

Will nosed his truck out the opposite mouth of the alley just as the sirens blared around the front of the surplus store. He tapped the ceiling of his cab, crossed himself for the first time in years, and drove on to the vet clinic.

The police scanner in Will's truck cab was buzzing like a living thing by the time he slipped out of the Sand Bar Veterinary Clinic a half hour later. There had been an alarm there, no surprise. But he was pressed for time more so at his second stop in relation to the first. He had stirred the beehive and the cops were on high alert all at once. The operator alerting the different cruisers and units in the vicinity spoke with a quick staccato delivery, the officers in snipped, curt responses. *10-4. En route. Copy that!* The sound of the scanner elevated Will's heart rate while he drove, pinning the speedometer to a steady 80 mph.

The locked medicine storage cabinet, located inside one of the veterinary doctor's offices, had given him more trouble than anything at the Army Surplus. He must have hammered the metal door with the blunt end of the tire iron at least fifteen times before it swung open. Inside, the storage cabinet was deeply recessed into the wall. Will had to dig and rummage for some time before he found the plastic wrapped pair of syringes he was looking for. Two shots of Thiopental, typically used as a general anesthetic in dogs over one-hundred pounds.

Then there was the other item Will retrieved from the clinic.

This was the item which ultimately held him up. Nearly got him caught red-handed standing right there in the rear of the clinic with a washed and conflicted look on his face. He nearly left without the item. Nearly lost his nerve. The thought of taking something like this, let alone traveling with it made him sick.

That wasn't even the worst part.

It was what he was going to use it for that tore Will apart from the inside out.

You're going to need it. Just think of how it could save Albie's life if the plan works! Keep reminding yourself what it will be for ...

As the first peals of a siren rounded the corner three blocks north,

Will pulled open the door to the large stainless-steel freezer and peered in-side, through the cold mist swirling out at him. It smelled pungent, the strong scent of formaldehyde nearly throwing him into a gagging fit. He reached inside. It was awful, feeling his terrible way through each of them until he found one the right size. *Jesus, how can I do this to her? What kind of man am I? I'm no better than the people who have her.*

Soldier, you couldn't be MORE WRONG! MORE OFF-BASE! WAKE UP, SOLDIER! MOVE-MOVE-MOVE!

As soon as Will felt what seemed to be the right size, he grabbed it up like a football player snatching a fumble. He shut the freezer door, and holding the small, plastic wrapped package against his chest, he ran back out to his truck and eased away from the curb. No gunning the engine. No laying rubber off the tires. A slow, easy drifting back into the now spotty traffic of the early morning. The package lay on the passenger seat. It could have been anything, wound round and round in the heavy plastic sheathing. A loaf of marble rye. A sandwich.

How Will's stomach had roiled and was still somersaulting as he hopped back on I-95 towards Baltimore.

70. MOTEL 6

At 6 a.m., Karl and Stella pulled into a rest stop twenty-five miles outside Baltimore, Maryland. They didn't park the stolen Oldsmobile Cutlass in the parking lot of the Motel 6. They couldn't take the chance of the dog in the trunk alerting any passersby should the animal start barking inside the cramped compartment. Stella suggested to Karl he leave her at the front curb and meet her after he parked the car in the stand of trees some thirty yards from the rest stop area. He didn't answer her. He did not pull up out front of the Motel 6. He hopped the far right curb of the rest stop and slowly rolled the car over to a stand of trees. He nosed it behind the trees and killed the engine.

It was evident to Stella he had no intention of letting her out of his sight.

Karl hurried her along, told her to "grab her shit." They bustled around in the back seat on either side of the vehicle, gathering their bags and stuffing any loose items into whatever square inch of space remained in a duffel or suitcase. Anyone watching them from the road would have thought them hitchhikers. Vagabonds. Hippies. The look of Karl would have further cemented the latter of these guesses, his long, curly tresses slippery with oil as they dangled in his face and framed his starved jawline. A thin strand had plastered itself across his brow and dangled at an odd angle. He blew upward, unseating it. He smoothed it away from his face and barked a command at Stella, who was struggling with her bags and sinking beneath them.

They came to the Motel 6 lobby, a siege of sweat and profanities, then feigned smiles and forced chatter between the two of them for the benefit of putting the tired-looking Indian clerk behind the counter at ease.

A small flat-screen flashed behind him on a countertop, the sound on mute. The image was as colorful as it was animated and featured a number of dancing Bollywood actors. Stella's attention, as scattered and disconnected as it was after an evening without sleep, somehow managed to seize on the glitterati of the tv screen. Karl asked for three twenty-dollar bills from her. Stella produced the money from her purse, absently thumbed the bills out, and handed it to him. She couldn't tear her eyes away from the screen. She missed Karl shaking his head dismissively at her as he turned back around, paid for the room, and gave their "road names" to the bleary-eyed clerk.

"Mr. and Mrs. Sherwood Schwartz."

Stella heard the name and could have sworn she had seen it somewhere before.

She would remember it while she was on the phone to the police out back behind the motel building a short while later.

Stella turned on the flat-screen in their room immediately after setting her things down in the corner by the door. She plopped down on the edge of the bed, remote control aimed at the cable box. She surfed and surfed, barely hearing much of what Karl was having on about. Something about "that dog better keep quiet while she's out there or there'll be hell to pay." She nearly answered him, letting loose the first thing that popped into her head: "Like you're any match for the Frankenstein's Monster you created! She'll tear your scrawny ass limb from limb!" She bit back the words and thought, *He really thinks he's in charge of the situation. It's funny as it is tragic.*

"—leave the tv, will you! Honest to Christ, you're like a child!"

"I'm trying to find that show the clerk was watching downstairs."

"You serious?" Karl cackled, coming out of the bathroom and picking at his gums haphazardly with a toothpick he had picked up at the reception desk. He was completely naked, chicken-wing shoulder blades and pale, rail-thin body, like a waifish mannequin. "What was that shit he had on? Some multi-colored Ali Baba shit?"

367

Stella held her tongue, thumb stabbing incessantly at the Channel button.

"Hey!" Karl squawked. "You just passed by a porno! Like, three channels back!"

Shaking her head, Stella kept surfing. She anticipated the slap on the side of her face, her cheek muscles dancing and jittering. It would come. She would take it. It would be the last time he got away with it. Well, one of the last, depending on how soon they responded to her 911 call. "Just let me look for it—"

It wasn't Karl's open palm that suddenly slapped into the side of her face.

She felt the slimy trail along the curve of her nose as the tip of Karl's flaccid, but nevertheless dripping penis pressed up against her profile.

"Kiss it," Karl said. "It feels like we're losing our connection. The mindmeld we had for so long .. its weakening. We gotta build it back up again. So, I need you to kiss it. Take it all. And don't spill a drop."

Stella sat, still as a statue. Her thumb remained poised over the Channel button, her hand shuddering. But it wasn't fear or trepidation which caused the palsy; it was anger. Building and building, blotting out the black sky of her consciousness and tearing a hole in the heavens for the first lone shards of sunshine to break through. She tasted each word as it passed from her lips. "My period. It's heavy right now."

"You think I'm squeamish about blood then you haven't been paying much attention."

"I'm … I'd feel uncomfortable. Can you understand that?" *Does it even matter, you crazy prick?* Then, before she realized she was speaking out loud, Stella said in a tone of unwavering finality, "I'm not going to fuck you, Karl."

"Oh …"

Karl stepped back from her, cupping his genitals like he feared they would fall off.

Don't you dare ask him if that's ok? It's what you want, and that's all the ok you need, Stella.

"I just want to unwind and watch some tv—"

His hand flew to her face. The hand which had been cupping his cock and balls a second ago was now clamped over her mouth. The tips of his fingers dug into her cheeks. She envisioned blood pooling out from under them as his fingernails suddenly stabbed down into the thick, ruddy flesh of her face. She tried to jerk her face away and felt his nails cut deeper. Karl held fast to her. His eyes were closed, mouth wide as he started to pant. His ribs heaved against the taut skin of his abdomen. The thin slivers of muscles leaped and writhed along his arms and chest, thighs and legs. With his left hand, he masturbated with all the concentration of a swami trying to rise off the ground while sitting cross-legged.

"I. Want. Mine." Karl squeezed the lower half of Stella's face so fiercely she feared he would tear her jawbone away from her skull. *What kind of mark will he leave on my face when he climaxes?* Karl held her face in place, oddly unworried about the possibility of her hands coming up to scratch at his eyes or tear ribbons of flesh away from his face as he clutched her so viciously. *He knows—he* thinks—*I won't hurt him or resist! How does he know that? And why aren't I resisting?*

His whole body spasmed, Karl's hand a vice. "This is *power* … you can't *buy!"*

The hot fluid struck her in the ear, pooled in the cartilage.

Karl's hand fell away from her face. "Don't worry about it," he muttered, turning his back on her and walking back into the bathroom. "I don't need to stick it in you to *know* I'm in you." She heard him lick his lips, a slathering sound. "Gimme your cell phone? Is it in your bag?"

She didn't answer him, eyes straight ahead and tongue a lump of useless flesh between her teeth. In her periphery, she saw him ransacking her handbag. At first, he rooted. Then, when he came up empty-handed, Karl upended the bag onto the floor and snatched up the cheap, silver flip phone nestled among used tissues and a tube of lipstick, which had come uncapped and bloodied the pocket mirror and part of a silver bracelet. A handful of tampons and carry-on Listerine—the contents of a dead woman's purse.

After a few seconds, Stella tossed the remote onto the bed and clasped her hands in her lap. She was afraid to touch her face. It could hurt to the touch. Then she would know she had a bruise of some kind. Her jaw felt like it had been unseated, off-track. She sat there in the burgeoning silence, listening to the sound of cloth rubbing and blotting flesh in the bathroom.

There was no fan, and she could hear everything. The sounds of Karl wiping himself clean, clearing his throat here and there.

The bathtub faucet came on.

He'll pin most of it on you and maybe they'll believe what he has to tell them because he's got a gift. They're not going to forget about you. Did you think for one second you'd get a pass for calling them? If that's why you're doing it then you might as well take it into your own hands. You're no stranger to this option. Think of all you've done—tally it up—think of what you did to your cat for God's sakes! Betsy—whatever happened to Baby Betsy?

She would call the authorities. There are other ways to make a call. Once the shower kicked on, she slipped out of the motel room.

Stella drummed her fingers along the lip of the clerk's desk as he swiveled away from her, picked up the telephone console on the adjacent desk, and stretched its cord so he could set it down before her. She stared down at it, hesitated, then slid the telephone back towards him. "Do you have a pay-phone on the premises?"

The teller cocked his head. "What? No phone?"

"No, thank you," she stammered. "It's just I need some privacy. Something outside? Around the corner maybe?"

"Free call if you do it in here. This phone here."

"Oh, I don't mind." *You don't have to worry about it, Stell. All calls to 911 are free.*

He shrugged, moved the phone back to the other side desk, and settled back down into his chair. It groaned under his meager weight. Then, as if he remembered an unanswered question hung heavy in the air between them, the teller whisked his hand behind him. "Payphone out at the road."

Stella thanked him and hurried out. She snuck a furtive glance back towards her motel room. The door was still closed. The morning was coming up unseasonably warm. Her breath still managed to plume out before her as she hurried across the blacktop, towards the glint of steel of the payphone waiting for her right where the teller said it would be. A white boat of an Oldsmobile lumbered past her, trailing a blue cloud of noxious smoke, which hit her in the face and choked her.

Being out in the open air of a burgeoning morning after the events of the previous evening seemed sacrilegious as it was daring. Stupid, even. She felt naked, skinned. Every nerve exposed and every guilty thought sprouting above her head in one of those thought balloons in comic strips. *I am a murderer and an accomplice to murder. I did nothing to stop the second killing, and I stabbed the first victim. I waited in the car during the second murder, but it doesn't excuse me from what I've been involved in. I'm travelling with a man who at one point during our many prison conversations told me he couldn't decide whether he was Jesus Christ or Michelangelo reborn. I laughed it off like a schoolgirl dismissing a crude joke told in mixed company.*

"I'm doing something now," she muttered to herself, shuddering at the distant trickle of a small child's laughter from the front doors of an adjacent Roy Rogers. A little girl held fast to the hands of her mother and father, flanking her on either side like sentries. *Guarding their child against the*

370

likes of myself and my company. Oh God, what have I become?

"But I'm doing something now," she repeated.

The black receiver was like a block of ice when she picked it up from its cradle and put it to her ear. It numbed the side of her head. She punched in the *nine*. The o*ne*. Then it happened. Jack used to call it getting her *stuck in neutral*. Usually, he would be the one to jam her up like this, to cause her mental gears to stick, to grind so she could barely draw a new breath. His cruel taunts. The sexual domination. The *mindmeld*.

Mindfucks! She couldn't punch in the last number. Stella knew she could always hang up before the operator picked up, but she had watched enough cop shows to know they usually responded to hang-ups and treated them like distress calls, just the same. They would show up at the Motel 6, and they would investigate. There would be no way to *unring* the bell.

She heard the sound of the little girl across the parking lot, now more of a delighted chortling as she climbed up into the back seat of her parent's Subaru Forester. Then, the dad leaned across her to strap his child in. Stella watched, enthralled. Something sizeable stuck in her throat. Tears rose in her eyes. *I'm doing something now!*

With a sudden certainty and stiff index finger, Stella punched in the *one* and waited. She turned herself away from the front row of rooms of the Motel 6 facing the highway.

A man's voice, teenager in pitch, filled the earpiece. "Nine-one-one, what is your emergency?"

"Yes ... uhm ... my name is Stella Post. Could you connect me with the Comstock Township Police Department. It's in Pennsylvania." Stella croaked.

"Ma'am, I can take your information and determine who I can send out to your location in the shortest amount of time. What is your emergency?"

"I ... I-I want to turn myself in," she said. "Myself and my travelling companion."

"You want to turn yourself in? Are authorities currently in pursuit?"

"Yes, I'm sure they're looking for us."

"You said your name is Stella *Post?*"

"Yes."

"Could you spell your last name, ma'am?"

"No."

"No?"

"No, I'm not going to do that. You get with your people, and they can give you the information."

Silence on the other end of the line. "All right, Stella?"

371

"Yes, I'm here."

"What is the name of the person you said you're travelling with?"

"Karl Tarlick. He's ..."

"Ma'am, could you—"

"He's out of control. Could you please come? He-he's not done yet. And I'm ... I'm really scared he's going to kill me."

"Ok-ok-*ma'am,* are you near this individual right now?"

Stella tasted her heart in her mouth; she thought she might faint. A fluttering inside her brain. "I'm going to run. I'm going to leave him. But he'll be here when you come. And if he's not, it'll be because I'm calling you right now, and he's forced to change his plans. Regroup. He said if he has to regroup, he said he's going "back to where it all started." That's where he's going if anything goes wrong, and this may be considered something going wrong. Probably means St. Alphonsus Church in Comstock. Pennsylvania—"

"Ma'am, I want you to remove yourself to a safe location. I have you at the rest stop in Bridgton, near Mile Marker 238. Is that correct?"

"I believe so."

"Can you remove yourself to a safe location?"

Sure thing, Mr. Pencil-dick! How about I duck into the Roy Rogers, order myself a couple roast beef sandwiches, and hole up until the cavalry comes? "I have to run. I have to go. He's in room 125. And ... and ... I'm just going to tell you if he tries to stop me or anything, I'm going to move on him. I changed my mind. I don't want to lay down and die for him. I changed my mind, and I want it my way."

"Ma'am, do not engage the suspect! I want you to remove yourself to a safe location! There are many options at this truck stop according to the information I've got here. Choose as public a location as you can and sit tight. I'm sending units to your location now!"

"He's got a dog with him," Stella said.

"A dog, ma'am?"

"Not exactly rabid? Not exactly Lassie either. You're going to want to send an animal control unit along, too."

"This dog is dangerous, ma'am?"

"That's not even the word for it."

"All right, ma'am—"

"I'm going to run now. You may find him alive. You may find him dead. Maybe you'll find me dead. You may be the last decent human being I ever speak to. So ... I don't know ... could you take my last words down? Could you make a note of it? I-I mean, I doubt nine-one-one operators are ever asked to do such a thing, but—"

"You're going to be fine, ma'am."

"Will you write this down?"

"Ma'am?"

"Hell may be hot, but it's got to be better than this. I'm sorry."

Stella laid the phone down on the steel shelf of the phone booth and stepped away from it. The earpiece was squawking and buzzing with the frantic exhortations of the operator, who had tried so hard to be comforting and ended up sounding as wooden and scripted as every other man she had ever known. She walked away from the booth, back towards the motel room and her fate. Whatever it could be.

A crisp, wintry wind played at the bottom of her jeans as she crossed the parking lot, then decided to angle towards a line of birch trees planted along the perimeter of the motel grounds. They were leafless, spindly brown skeletons. Stella walked to the nearest tree, reached a full foot above her head, and curled her hands around the lowest hanging branch. It was about as thick in diameter as a toddler's arm. She lifted herself off the ground, drew her weight up then down on it until she heard the delightful sound of the wood weakening and giving way. She aimed her toes back down at the frozen ground and slowly lowered onto her feet. She wrenched it the rest of the way, twisting at the wooden husk until it came away and she was holding a formidable, albeit primitive, weapon in her hands.

Anything can be a weapon if you hold it the right way. I'm gathering my things and cutting out. I'll walk a mile down the road and then hitch it somewhere. Hopefully, he'll still be showering.

She envisioned herself using it on Karl if he tried to attack her, and suddenly Stella found she felt less vulnerable as she made her way back towards the room. Cutting across the narrow cement patio, and past the five rooms before she reached Room 125. She tapped the branch into her open palm, relishing how solid and blunt it felt against the webbing of her skin.

Thumbing the key fob out of her jeans pocket, Stella let herself back inside the room. The whole unit was steamy, tendrils of it tumbling through the thick air. The mirror beside the tv was fogged over. Oddly enough, the television was still on and tuned to the colorful Bollywood movie Stella had tuned it to earlier. The sound was muted, and it hadn't been before. The shower was done and Karl had already come out, leaving the bathroom door ajar so as to steam up the motel room. *He's out. He's—*

Stella moved to raise the branch over her right shoulder like a star hitter when something stopped it in mid-air. Then, the branch left her hands, neatly as if it were greased and torn away. Almost simultaneously, she felt something cinch around her throat. Karl's face leered over her left shoulder as her air cut off, rapidly.

"We'll be together … in paradise!" he said, just as the string of the blinds affixed to the nearby window cut into her windpipe and dropped her down into a seemingly bottomless pit of black.

Something over my mouth. Tape. I can't talk. I can't scream.

Oh God ... the smell!

Stella lay on her side. Karl had taped her mouth. She pushed up with her knees at the black canopy above, only to find it mere inches above her head. Her hands were bound in twine. Her ankles itched from the binding wound around them as well. Once her nose fully awoke to the smells surrounding her, Stella gagged so violently the muscles in her chest locked up. Acidic bile rose in her throat, only for her to swallow it back down as the tape obstructed its exit. She smelled motor oil. Vomit, tangy with a meaty putrescence. Feces. She knew none of it belonged to her, was not of her.

Stella understood exactly where she was.

She saw the eyes in the darkness, their subtle red caste glowing and hovering inches from her face. Poised for something. Waiting.

Hudda-hudda-hudda-hudda-hudda.

"Stell?"

Karl's voice, softened by the metal of the trunk hood separating the two of them, rained down on her like a cold, February rain.

"Stell? I know she hasn't killed you yet because I haven't given her the order. You're still alive. I didn't choke you that hard. I know you're taped so just make a sound to let me know you hear me, huh?"

"*Plsssssssss!*" The front of her throat lit up with pain like a Christmas tree and her voice gave way to violent coughing made far worse by the fact she could not breathe out of her mouth. She dared not try again to make a sound louder than a whimper.

"This sucks, Stella," Karl said. "The whole thing. It sucks. We could have gone on and on if you didn't make that call. You know? We can't come back from this now. I had to call in a couple unsavories to help finish the job. You didn't leave me any choice."

She felt an inner struggle between her defeated self and a more primal urge to fight her circumstances. Odd as it was, she waited for Karl's next words. She prayed they would not be an incantation, calling the dog into ravenous motion against her. When he spoke again, it was sullen. Crestfallen. It confused her. *Is this sympathy? How can this be?*

"You know, this isn't me turning off my love for you like some kind of light switch. I don't work that way. It isn't how I'm wired. I thought you understood. But then you went and you made your phone call, and you made a real statement with it. You said to me 'Karl, you're just as sick and twisted as everyone always said and thought you were.' You believe it now too, right? So … now I gotta turn my back on you. You don't deserve any kind of enlightenment. Why educate someone about to die? Kind of like polishing a turd, don't you think?" He paused, knocked on the trunk hood twice. "I love you. Still … I love you, Stella. You were the last building standing in my city of rubble and shit and piss, baby. But I gotta say good night—"

"*Mmmmmmmmm-ah-mmmmm-nnnnnn*"

"Nah-nah-nah-NO!" Karl cried, hammering against the trunk door.

"*Krrrrrlllllllll–krl–krl–*"

Hudda-hudda-hudda-hudda-hudda.

Stella felt the dog's hot, stinking breath blooming against the side of her neck now. The damp from the dog's tongue nearly touching her skin, transferring the wet through the small gap like some kind of cosmic transference.

Then, she heard the unfamiliar words she had so dreaded. Karl's words, spoken in a low but steady, rhythmic delivery that caused the dog to clench from snout to tail in an instant. She felt it. A change in the cramped atmosphere of the trunk, like electricity in the air right before a thunderstorm. *I won't resist. I know I'll cry out. I know because it's unavoidable, but I won't give him the satisfaction in knowing I'm going into this terrified.*

The snap of the dog's jaws as they closed and then opened again, terrorizing her.

Fire erupted at the base of her throat, and she was drowning.

Her mind took her out of the moment, protecting her in its final moments of functionality. She was sinking slowly to the bottom of Macasaw River where she and her dog Moxie used to go swimming together in the full blaze of the August summer sun. She reached for his paws as a building weight pressed down on the top of her and invisible hands squeezed her lungs. Her air sacs filled with water, and she tasted the woodsy filth of the water in her mouth. Down her throat. She tasted hot copper. It all burned going down.

Moxie … show me the way … I'm going down … down … down …

71. THE BURIED STORY

Detective Jones had called for a squad car to meet Detective Rivells and him at Jodi Dare's apartment complex. By the time their black Ford Explorer rolled up along the front sidewalk, a pair of officers were stationed across the street in their cruiser. They emerged, one with a Dunkin' Donuts coffee whose name tag read Officer Cumia while the other, whose tag read Officer Hughes, muttered something into the CB pinned to his blue lapel.

Officers Cumia and Hughes followed the detectives into the lobby of the apartment complex. Cumia sipped at his coffee and rubbed at the bridge of his nose. Rivells read the gesture all too well. *Guy's probably pulling a double, and it's his first time doing it.* The four of them stood in front of a row of tenant mailboxes.

"So you got us for eight hours, then we're gonna have to switch out for another pair of blues. They haven't confirmed they can send two other guys yet. Captain needs us elsewhere later on, though. He let you know about this?" Officer Tired Eyes said.

Rivells shook her head. "Neither of you are to leave your posts outside Ms. Dare's apartment door until you're relieving officers show up. Just all there is to it."

Jones nodded, hands squarely on his hips and his brows jutting downward. "Absolutely correct. Not looking to jam you up, but we gotta work together here. We need your help. I gotta head down to AC to see about a precinct setting up two cops at a residence there. I have to do this in two more states after that. I'll be connecting the dots in Delaware and Maryland when all is said and done."

"If there's any kind of lapse you gotta take it up with our captain?" Hughes said, clearly establishing himself as the lead while his partner continued nipping at his coffee like a caffeine miser.

"Your captain's on board," Rivells said.

Cumia said, "We'll do what we gotta do."

Rivells knew perfectly well it was *double-speak*. Could mean one of two things. *All I know is don't trust either of them. I hate to read them that way, but it's what I see.*

She made her decision.

Jones nodded, satisfied. "Then you'll ride back with me, Detective Rivells. Have your quick word with Ms. Dare, and then we'll hit it. These officers are here for at least the next eight hours. Two more unis don't show up to relieve the two of you before you split, we all know what's going to happen to *all four of you.* I don't even have to spell it out because I trust you two know protocol. Your captain, also."

Cumia sniffed, either a cough or a scoff. "You ever met our cap?"

"Enough times to know he doesn't play nice with our department. But I'm running on fumes right now and I'll tell you, officers, I'm almost hoping to have to lock horns with him over at Internal Affairs once we have our perps behind bars. Any dereliction of duty will do."

Cumia nodded stiffly.

"I'll go up and talk to her, but I'm also going stay behind," Rivells said.

Jones shifted his stance, put off by this change of plans. "I need you with me, Detective. She's in good hands here."

"I know-I know," Rivells lied. *These two are going to fuck up somehow. My sensors are going haywire.* "I live in this building. My car's parked right underground. I'll meet up with you once I verify two more unis are in place to relieve these gentlemen. Eight hours."

Jones hesitated. "You need me up there for the interview?"

"No," Rivells said, "it's a conversation. Anybody shows up uninvited, I'm sure we can handle it. The three of us."

"All right," Jones relented, "I'm going to try the Atlantic City precinct again to see about the detail over at the Whitby house." He nodded to them all before turning on his heel and stalking back out onto the street, cell phone at his ear and posture pristine.

Rivells led the two officers up the three flights of stairs. The elevator had been broken for a month, and Rivells had learned to abide the inconvenience by treating it as an opportunity for cardio exercise.

The walk up was silent and somewhat tense. The two officers didn't say anything to her. Nothing along the lines of small talk, but they muttered amongst themselves. Rivells didn't consider herself overly sensitive, the polar opposite as a matter of fact. But the two officers seemed to have bristled the moment she said she would stay behind. Their body language said more, their eyes practically glued to Jones' face even when Rivells spoke. *Would it have killed them to look at me?* Male officers, detectives, administrators froze her out in certain situations during which she was poised as a dominant figure. These two were no different, and it wasn't a paranoid reaction. Rivells learned a long time ago how to differentiate paranoia from a legitimate sixth sense.

The chill from the other officers had the same sort of effect on Rivells as with every other situation she had come across during her career in law enforcement. It emboldened her. She reached the stairwell with barely a winded feeling in her lungs. The officers trailed her by a floor. This pleased her all the more, fanning the little flame of satisfaction jittering within.

"You guys all right?" she called down the stairwell to them.

Cumia grunted an indecipherable response as the two of them rounded the corner. Another muted statement passed between the two officers, eliciting a flutter of laughter before they met Rivells on the third floor landing.

"It's number three-one-three. Right here."

Rivells knocked three times on the apartment door.

Officer Hughes asked, "You sure she's even home? You call ahead?"

"I did," Rivells said. "She's a barista. Works nights, mostly. I live in this building also. We're friends."

"Friends, huh?" Cumia said and tilted his head back to dump the remainder of his coffee down his throat.

No answer.

Rivells knocked twice more. She called through the door. "Jodi? It's Detective Rivells!"

Something heavy thumped against a wall inside the apartment.

Cumia set down his empty Dunkin' Donuts Styrofoam cup and thumbed the hasp off the butt of his service revolver. Hughes did the same.

Rivells drew her weapon, disengaged the safety as well. She leaned closer to the door.

"Jodi? We're coming in!" She stepped back, aware of the glances exchanged between the two officers beside her. They were taken aback she intended to knock the door in herself. *I know just where to land my shoulder against the door—the sweet spot for these types of doors.*

The deadbolt slid back, and the door cranked open mere seconds before Rivells launched herself. The chain was fastened. Jodi Dare peeked through the narrow opening. Even the small, visible sliver of the young girl's face revealed sleep-worn eyes, cheeks puffy from having just risen off the pillow.

"What's wrong?" Jodi asked, squeezing her words through an ever-widening yawn. "What's happening?"

"Jodi, I'm here with Officers Cumia and Hughes," Rivells said. "They're here to protect you. You're in danger. Let me in and I'll explain everything."

"Wha-what are you talking about?"

"Jodi, we don't have time to do this through the door. Just let me in. I'll tell you everything."

Jodi stood there, silent but alert. She nodded, threw the chain, and opened the door wide. Rivells told the officers to man the door. Then it was their turn to stare blankly at her. Cumia nodded his assent, a curt twitch around his eyes betraying his resentment.

Rivells stepped inside Jodi's apartment behind her.

"You have any coffee?" Rivells asked. "I'll settle for instant."

"Sure," Jodi responded, her tone flat and hollow.

The young girl, clad in her rumpled sleep gear of cow print pajama bottoms and a blue Strath Haven High School t-shirt, cut a path into the kitchen. Rivells followed and realized the girl was truly petrified when Jodi suddenly took to turning from countertop to refrigerator to the sink, and then round in a circle like she barely knew where she was or what Rivells had even asked of her.

"Ok," Rivells said, taking Jodi by the shoulders. "Nevermind. That was stupid of me. Why don't we go sit?"

"*No*-no! I-I got it. Instant. Instant. I have it. Just … give me a minute."

"All right," Rivells said, stepping away. "That's fine. It's fine. How about we talk while you make it. Why don't you have some tea? Coffee might not be the best thing for your nerves right now."

Jodi nodded. She stepped to it, the barista within calling her to motion. While she set the teapot to boil and readied two mugs, one with a generous dollop of honey and the other with half-and-half.

Rivells leaned against the opposite wall of the narrow kitchen nook. "Do you know a man named Jack Post, Jodi?"

There it was.

Jodi and Rivells were suddenly looking into one another eyes across the kitchen. Jodi's eyes looked pinched around the edges like pie crust. She didn't blink. "Asshole," she said. "He was a manipulative … he was an *asshole*. We dated for a few weeks. Then I kicked him to the curb."

"All right," Rivells said, crossing her arms. "And that was the end of it?"

"I wish it was," Jodi said, leaning against the counter. "I talked it over with one of my friends at work. She helped me to see there was just something off about Jack. He's hot. It draws you in. But once you get past it, he's all cliché sayings and these condescending little 'You got this, girl!' snippets of advice that just got old real quick. I started to see he was trying to build me up, sure, when I started to show my cracks, but then he'd insert these little backhanded compliments here and there that added up quickly until I couldn't ignore them anymore. He was trying to make me strong, but just strong enough I wouldn't outgrow him. That's what Linda at work helped me figure out because she has an ex-husband like that who killed himself a year after their divorce. Guys like Jack? They realize after a while what makes them tick is bullshit. Always was. Then, they just kind of wink out like a candle flame. Fake people get sick of themselves eventually. That was Jack. A sadist."

"Sadist?"

"I broke it off with him after my talk with Linda at Starbucks. I did it through a text message. I know, probably not the best way to do it. But I had no idea it would make him stalk me like he did for a whole week after. Coming into my work. Not talking to me directly, but ordering drinks and sitting in a far corner. He tried to make it look like he wasn't staring at me across the shop, but he was. Then, he'd just … *leave*. I think it would have been better if he *did* say something. At least then, I would have had the chance to tell him to leave me the hell alone and get some kind of feel for whether or not he *got* what I was saying to him. This way, I started to develop a higher level of anxiety than I've ever had before. I hated him for it."

"Would you mind if I asked you a personal question, Jodi?"

Jodi shrugged, her eyes immediately dipping down to examining Rivells's shoes.

"Do you have a history of mental illness?"

The young girl smiled at nothing in particular. "My senior year, I was diagnosed Bipolar Type Two," she said in a small voice. "Not as bad as Type One, but not exactly a good thing. Not a better thing. I take … um … I take medicine. A couple pills at night and first thing in the morning. They make me really tired. Hence, the way I look right now. I sleep a lot when I'm not studying or working. More than I'd like, but it's a trade-off. Feel like a maniac or just sleep more than most people."

"You ever tell Jack about your condition?"

"He knew before I could tell him," Jodi said, just as the kettle whistle started to work its way to a shrill scream. She spun around and quickly set about pouring the hot drinks. "He even knew it was Type Two, not One. I remember asking him how, and he just cracked a joke about it. Something about his mother had a 'potpourri of mental illnesses,' and he became an expert early on. A *psychic for the brainsick*. That's how he put it. He also tried to convince me the pills were making me worse, and I should stop taking them. He got pretty adamant about it during a few conversations." She turned around, holding both mugs. She offered Rivells her tea and cocked her head. "Detective Rivells, you said I was in danger. What does all this have to do with … *that*?"

"You know, Jodi."

"Jack? But why would he come here? I never got the impression he

380

would hurt me. Just he wanted to scare me. Psych me out or something."

Rivells sipped at the rim of her mug, relishing it. "Your attacker," she said. "I want you to think back. And I wouldn't be asking you to revisit the incident if it wasn't important you understand why I'm here. That you understand how sick Jack Post is. Even though … he's not the one coming for you."

"Then … who?"

"What do you remember about your attacker?" Rivells pressed. "Anything about his body. Parts he showed to you. Did he say anything?"

"I thought you said we don't have *time* for this—"

"I said not through your apartment door," Rivells said. "But I'm here. You've got two officers posted outside. They've got photographs of our suspects. You don't have to worry now. But, you need to think back."

"You're staying with me, right?"

"I am," Rivells said. "You've got me for at most eight hours."

Jodi paused, then began. "He disguised his voice. And he didn't really have to alter it all that much because the dog mask muffled it even more. Then, when he forced the dog mask down over my head, I couldn't really hear him at all. He was really into it, but he was just kind of doing this panting thing. Maybe getting into the whole *dog mask* thing." Jodi paused, thinking. "He did say my name, but I thought about that, too. I thought he could have been anyone I ever served a drink to because I wear a name tag. So, nothing really there." Then, the ghost of a smile played at her lips before disappearing abruptly, as if she were ashamed in having worn it at all. "There was one other thing …"

"Mm?"

"His penis hurt when he forced it in …"

"He was rough? Is that why?"

"No."

"Um," Rivells said, her cheeks hot. "Was he … larger than average."

"No, it—it curved upward."

"Okay."

"No … like … *severely* upward! It hurt."

"All right," Rivells said.

When the light in Jodi's eyes glistened, Rivells knew the last piece of the puzzle had just clicked into place for the young girl.

Jodi looked up at Rivells, naked and abashed knowing in her eyes. "No."

"Jack Post. What was sex with him like? I'm just going to ask."

"It hurt."

"Why?"

"He … he said he had something called Peyronie's Disease. It's a painful bending of the penis. He said he had it since puberty. I lied to him and told him it made it feel better when we were together. But … to be honest … it was another reason I wanted to break it off."

"The sex sucked?"

"It hurt. I mean *fucking really* hurt. No pleasure."

"You understand?"

Jodi's bottom lip started to quiver. Water flooded her eyes. "Jack … he raped me?"

"Yes."

"But … you said he's not the one coming?"

"No." Rivells sighed and lowered her mug to the counter dividing the living room from the kitchen. "But this is all because of the man Jack Post has been. The ugly, sick, and vicious creep he's been probably all his life."

The air seemed to thicken around them. Jodi cast her overflowing eyes down to the tiles of her kitchen. "I knew it. I knew something was off about him. But I never-never thought he could be violent. Just … creepy."

"Well, it's a good thing you were brave enough to come forward with this. Otherwise, it's possible he would still be preying on young women. Fragile young women like yourself."

"He's a fucking … a *fucking wolf*, isn't he?"

"He is," Rivells said, her tongue thickening with anger. "But we're going to find him and shut him down. Him and the rest of his … entourage."

"Who are the others? Who's coming for me, then, if not him?"

Rivells hesitated sharing this with Jodi, then rationalized it could not possibly harm their investigation or jeopardize it in any way. "Jack Post is married. His wife and her boyfriend. They're the ones we are watching out for." *I'm not even going to mention the other two ex-cons. It'll scare the shit out of her even more.*

"He's married?" Jodi cried. Then, all at once, the temper downgraded to sullenness. "Jesus, why should that surprise me after figuring all the rest of this out?" She sipped cautiously at her tea and shrugged. "I don't suppose it would do any good to try and reason with Jack's wife if they were to come here. I don't know … try to explain I had no idea he was married. He never wore a ring." She shook her head. "No, it sounds typical. Lame, even coming from me."

"Jodi, I can promise no harm will come to you. But you should call out of work for tonight if you're scheduled. I do not want you setting foot outside this apartment building until we've got confirmation we have these people in custody. All right? That's how you can help yourself. By being smart."

The young girl nodded. Then, she did something at odds with the situation. It both amused Rivells and unnerved her, for a reason she could not directly identify. *Foreboding?*

"So a lazy day, then? Just us girls. You ever watch *The Notebook*? I figure those cops are right outside. No reason we can't make this ... enjoyable on some level? Besides, Ryan Gosling is well worth watching the movie again. This will be my fifteenth time."

The young girl's smile was infectious, in spite of Rivells's stoicism. She smiled back. "Damn, girl. I'm more of a comic book girl. You have *The Dark Knight? Avengers: Civil War?*" But she knew the answer to both.

Negative. Negative.

72. DOLLAR SHORT

Will Bentley eased his foot down on the brake the minute he turned the corner onto Maeve Staples's street. The front of her apartment complex was clogged with police vehicles and a hearse. The cruisers were a flurry of overlapping red, white, and blue dome lights across the dark wood and siding of the building itself and its the neighboring houses. The sun had started out high and bright at dawn, but by the time Will reached the residence and eased his truck into a parking spot half a block away from the chaos, the morning had taken a turn for the gloomy. Clouds shifted and slid over one another. Rain spit on his windshield. His heart sank.

Men in drab grey and brown rumpled suits milled around on the front sidewalk, stood in what looked like a stone garden, which took up the whole front yard in the place of grass. One of them stared up at the structure like he had never seen an apartment building of such a particular architecture before. Two were engaged in heated conversation, while another appeared to be holding himself free of the fray. Two uniformed officers strode out the front door of the building, followed close behind by another two wheeling a body in a black canvas bag down the center walk. One officer flanked them from the back, a washed out look in his face. He couldn't have been more than twenty-two years old. The officer betrayed his age and amateur status further when he hurried over to a box-cut bush along the front of the building and vomited violently into the prickly leaves.

They rolled the gurney down the sidewalk towards the opened mouth of a waiting hearse's cargo area. They slid the gurney inside and slammed the hatch shut.

That's Maeve Staples. God in heaven, if Albie did this, she didn't understand. They did something to her ... they ... I don't know—they fucked with her. They shook her and shook her until a shred of some terrible memory came loose and turned her inside out.

He didn't want to think about it. But it was impossible for Will to stop the rapid slideshow of images as they flashed across his mind. The body of Candy Whitby. The vicious rending and tearing wounds of her flesh. The lake of blood spilled across the rug of her living room, still gleaming fresh. The bite marks up and down her sides. The nibbles. The more predominant piercings, upper and lower jaws having clamped down and met completely as they tore into the skin. He knew if he were to unzip the contents of the body bag travelling down the road, away to the autopsy table and then the makeup chair for her final *close-up* in a viewing room, he'd find the body in the same state of complete and utter disarray. The wounds would match.

Then would come that awful, if not fleeting, sickness towards his dog Will stuffed back down because he knew it was not Albie's fault. It was not Albie.

This is a Catch-22 if ever there was one. Dammit! His face felt hot as he mulled it over. Sitting there in the brittle warmth of his truck cab, Will found he had no idea where he ought to drive to next. The fact of the matter struck him, turning his blood cold and still in his veins. He realized his chances for finding the killers would improve profoundly as more and more victims were erased from the equation. The chances of his choosing the right address would improve only in direct correlation with the number of victims left breathing and unharmed.

Will dug into the pocket of his jacket and brought out the list of names and addresses Jack Post had dictated to him in that grimy hotel room back in Comstock. *Three women left: Christine Taylor in New Castle, Delaware; Elizabeth Allender in Media, Pennsylvania; And Jodi Dare Philadelphia. The Society Hill section, according to Jack.* His gut told him to follow his previous line of reasoning, connecting the dots in a circuitous route. So far, he had been spot on with this approach, but it could fall apart if the killers went another way. Not to mention, his pursuit could prove ultimately fruitless and arbitrary if he continued to show up after the murders were already a thing of the past. Will knew he needed a break. A string of good luck. *Christine Taylor. I feel like the next logical stop for them would be New*

Castle. Same state as Maeve Staples'. New Castle is not far from here.

He snatched up his cell phone and thumbed open the app for Google Maps. He plugged in Christine Taylor's address and waited for the screen to feed him the information he was after. Estimated time of arrival and distance.

44 miles, 49 minutes.

"Sonofabitch!" Will whipped his head from side to side, angrily. He wrenched the stick out of Park and into first gear. Mindful to not spin his wheels or draw attention to himself, Will pulled out of his parking spot and into the right lane. Only when he cleared the cluster of emergency responder vehicles parked hodgepodge in front of the Staples residence did he give it serious gas. The truck shot forward like a hunk of red metal out of a cannon.

His cell phone started to dance an Irish jig across the bucket of his passenger seat. Pearl Jam's "Alive" screamed out of the phone's small speakers, loud enough to startle Will out of his ever-tightening focus. *Gotta get there—gotta get there—gotta get there.*

He snatched up his cell phone, pressed the Call-Accept icon and jammed it into his ear. "Yeah?" He hadn't bothered to check who was calling. The phone number. Anything. Starting a blind conversation.

"Will? This is Detective Rivells! You got a minute?"

"Yeah, yeah," he said. "Any news? Did you find them?"

His face suddenly burned like someone had just held a fiery brand to his left cheek.

Sergeant Karns blotted out the detective's response.

You don't want the police finding them. That'll mean Alberta's been put down. You know this! Don't sound so hopeful! It ain't what you want, soldier!

"… you haven't been to see her at all since yesterday or called—"

"Who?" Will asked, befuddled.

A pause on the other end. *Was that a sigh?* "Mina," Rivells said. "She called me because she was concerned you might have gone off and tried to take matters into your own hands. You haven't called her or gone in to see her since yesterday. She said that's not like you, and wanting to handle this on your own is *exactly* like you. So now I'm concerned. Where are you?"

"Driving."

"All right," Rivells said. "Where you going, Will?"

"Will you answer me a question, Detective?"

Hesitation. "We can trade question for question, but mine's the first in queue. So where are you going, Will?"

"Are you going to take my dog alive, or are you going to shoot to kill?"

"Of course we wouldn't want any harm to come to your dog," Rivells said. "But if the animal—"

"Alberta."

"What?"

"Her name's Alberta. We call her Albie."

"All right, we would try our very best to preserve the life of Alberta, but if she presents an eminent threat to any of our officers, we would have to take the necessary measures to—"

"That's probably going to happen," Will said angrily. "But I need you to understand if I can get to her first, then I can rein her in the only way I know how, there won't be any need for you to kill her."

"We wouldn't shoot to kill, Will. We would sedate her with a tranquilizer shot."

"Bullshit, all due respect."

"Mr. Bentley—"

"Alberta killed two of your own. Isn't that correct?"

"How do you know?"

"Never mind how I know it. It happened. And you know as well as I do she's going to be treated with extreme prejudice because of it. She's been labeled a cop killer in the eyes of your colleagues, and they won't hesitate to shoot her dead if given the opportunity for plausible deniability. C'mon, Detective! I'm a writer. I'm trained to think five steps ahead of the present tense."

"All well and good, but you need to stand down right now," Rivells said, any last lingering charm gone from her voice. "You need to let us do our job and injecting yourself into the investigation could do more harm than good."

Soldier, just tell her what she wants to hear if it'll get her off the phone and out of your ear!

"I'll turn around then," Will said, following the signs for the nearest I-95 on-ramp. "I guess it won't hurt to tell you those two murdering pigs killed two women already. I've been to both of their addresses. Too late. Each time. But I'm getting warmer. So I ask you, should I keep pulling this U-ie I'm turning into right now or would you rather have another capable person on their tail."

"Just how in the hell do you know where to go? Where did you get the women's names?"

"Research," Will said. "And I gotta tell you, I have always hated doing any kind of research for my books. This time around, it was a pleasure getting the goods and gathering the details. I've got a leg up.

386

I don't understand why it's so unfathomable to you I would get involved. I mean, none of you give a shit about my dog. All due respect, I'm finished with trying to sell you on why I'm in this all the way."

"I knew you wouldn't dare turn around and head back home," Rivells said glumly. "But I'm warning you to stay out of the way of our people so we can do our jobs."

"There are three women left."

"I know," Rivells spat, but Will wasn't so sure she knew any such thing until right then.

"Christine Taylor. Elizabeth Allender. And Jodi Dare—"

"I'm with Jodi Dare as we speak, Will. She's fine, and I plan on keeping her that way."

"You're going to sit on her? What about the others?"

"Don't tell me how to do my job, and I'll stop telling you to back the hell off. Are we agreed?"

"Wait … are you serious?"

"I never said that," Rivells said. "Are we clear?"

"Crystal."

"Good," Rivells said. "Then you don't worry about Jodi. Chalk her off your list. Worry about the other two. We've got cruisers at both their addresses already. Stay clear whenever possible."

"I'll stop by *there* after I check the next Delaware address," Will said. "You'll see me soon."

"Goddammit, I just said—"

"Call it a feeling," Will said. "And I haven't been *wrong* yet. Just … too damned late. But I'm getting warmer."

He hung up and turned his attention back to the road.

73. NEW CASTLE, DELAWARE - PART I

Alberta didn't have the strength, nor the will, to whimper, even though every fiber of her being cried out for it. The part barring her from being able to find her animal voice and express the pain she felt was the sizeable portion of her brain which catered exclusively to the now-crazed man trapped between her ears. She could not see him. No idea what he looked like. But she knew his voice nearly as well as she knew The Man Before's voice.

Far worse, Alberta knew the sounds of the man's screams. They were now something she was forced to live with.

That did not mean the fits and starts of the man's tantrums and pleadings, and screams and cries were not tearing her mind apart. The dog felt herself regressing more and more often to the horrid existence she had known in the Land of Sand. The time before The Man Before found her and rescued her from the Land of Sand.

Between the shouts of the man trapped between her ears, Alberta suffered flashes of remembrance and images from her life in such a nightmarish, distant land.

I'm cured, don't you see? Isn't that what you wanted? I recognize my wrongs! Just stop killing them—PLEASE—I'M CURED!

Girl! HEY, GIRL! CAN YOU HEAR ME?

Alberta recognized the *girl* name. The Man Before used to call her *girl* when they would be out walking and she nosed into something he wanted her to leave alone. She had never come to associate it with anything negative or punitive, simply another name for her. A warm, compassionate one. So when the man between her ears called her by the *other name*, she felt disarmed and soothed by its usage.

GIRL? LISTEN TO ME, PLEASE! It is all up to you, and you alone can make this stop! You can fight back against them, instead of killing innocent people! Fight the man! You've got to fight the man! WILL YOU JUST FUCKING FIGHT HIM—TURN YOUR ANGER AGAINST HIM! HE'S THE MOTHERFUCK WHO DESERVES IT—

The trunk door opened.

Another man stood there peering down at Alberta.

She had never seen him before.

74. NEW CASTLE, DELAWARE-PART II

Karl Tarlick knocked twice on the back door of the Taylor house. He listened to the sound of Doc. Marten's soles along the tiles just beyond the closed door. The back door opened a crack. The fat face of a man wearing a boat captain's hat, complete with gold anchor stitched above the wide brim, peered out at Karl. His beard was black and bushy, threaded with scraggly wisps of gray. He breathed heavy as an asthmatic. His eyes were bloodshot, blinkless. No eyebrows. Karl knew the man hated his eyebrows and had taken to shaving them years ago. Karl also knew the man liked to be called

"Bluto," and that was easier to remember. The sonofabitch looked just like the cartoon character. Living, breathing, committed to it.

Bluto's voice was thin and reedy. It did not jibe with the way he looked. But who was going to tell Bluto he sounded like a girl? Only Karl would dare.

"Well, then … I guess … here we go, eh?" Bluto asked.

"Any problems?" Karl slipped inside. He strode past Bluto down the hallway into the kitchen nook.

"Some."

"Really?" Karl asked.

The sounds of Bluto's boots pounding along the tiles of the hallway were steady and attentive, in step behind Karl as he entered on the much bloodier scene in the cooking area.

At least, more bloody than he had expected.

Leaning forward with his elbows resting on the countertop in the center of the kitchen, a man perhaps too handsome for his surroundings and the circumstances, stared at Karl as he filed inside the room. The handsome man was tall, his body lean from a sporadic eating habit and the heroin which had only just recently been shot into his veins after years of going without while inside Berrysburg Prison walls. He had a long face with sunken cheekbones. *Heroin chic?* A brownish-blonde swathe of hair hung above his head like a wave just about to break. In prison, this man, whose name was Henry Brisbane, had looked healthier. More meat on him. He ate a regular breakfast, lunch, and dinner. Karl could see Henry had already settled back into all his bad habits.

Judging by the blood on Henry's hands and up his forearms, the footprints and handprints slapped against the tiles, and the puddle stretched out just behind where Henry was leaning, Karl was certain the pretty boy had also graduated to murder. He was not a killer when Karl met him at Berrysburg. He was a pusher then.

"Is there a body on the floor behind you, Henry?" Karl asked, monotone and even.

"Not her. Not the one you're thinking of, so don't worry."

"Then who?" Karl lunging past Henry and cast his eyes down upon the body lying in the center of the blood puddle.

"Who's she then?" Karl demanded, planting his hands on his hips and staring down at the mess.

"The caregiver," Bluto answered, coming up alongside Karl. "This Taylor lady's already in bad shape. Wait 'til you see her?"

Karl nodded. "Why'd you see the need to scalp this woman? And which one of you has her … scalp?"

Bluto nodded over at Henry, who came away from the counter raking his hand through his hair.

"Thought it would do some good to add a little something to the crime scene that don't match the others," Henry explained. "As far as I understand it, you didn't take any of the other lady's scalps, did you?"

Karl glared at Henry. He didn't blink. Once he realized Henry Brisbane developed a bit of palsy around his wrists, Karl waved his hand at the woman on the floor. "No one's ever gonna put together the how or the why about any of this. Not unless any of them learn how to speak *dog*. Don't see it happening any time soon. Our killer's a canine."

Bluto bristled beside Karl. "You want her staged?"

Karl dug in his pocket and brought out the keys to his car. He tossed them to Bluto. "Go get the dog. And be quick about it. The sun's up, and there's eyes to worry about now."

"The dog safe?" Bluto asked uneasy, failing to hide it despite his size and reputation.

"Unless I turn her otherwise. Go on." He turned to Henry, who was yawning into his hand. "Put this one's head in the oven. Turn it on. And hammer her scalp to the wall where you walk in."

Henry nodded stiffly and set to work.

Karl stood there, taking the kitchen nook in just as the first rays of sunlight cut through window panes to converge in the center of the little room as if to form some centrifuge there. He thought of Stella. She didn't look happy or sad. More indifferent than anything else. But her eyes clung to Karl, unwavering and blinkless. They asked a question. He laughed to himself, knowing full well how to answer her and trying at the same time to ignore the tearing in his gut. *Her wishy-washy bullshit's the reason I ever even needed this Plan B. These two fucks! She sold me out. She knew what that would mean. I'm not the bad guy.*

Snapping out of his reverie, Karl turned to Henry who was in the midst of hauling the body of the caregiver over to the oven in the corner of the kitchen. Karl caught a glimpse of the woman's face. It was a mask of blood, the older woman's eyes wide and shocked, staring through the glistening crimson.

"Henry, where's Christine Taylor?"

Henry grunted, balancing the caregiver across his knees with one hand while working the door to the oven open with the other. "She's … ah, she's down the basement. Lots of cobwebs. Cold as hell down there. Bound. Gagged. She's scared shitless of her own basement. You should've seen her.

Door's right behind you."

"It ain't the only thing that threw a fright into her, I'm sure," Karl said. He turned and opened the door to the basement.

He walked down the cement steps. The sounds of struggling and panting were present the moment he had opened the door to the basement, but by the third step down it intensified, and Karl could hear Christine Taylor screaming arbitrarily against something over her mouth.

A muted scream sounds more animal than not.

Karl rounded the corner of the wall separating the shallow stairwell from the rest of the basement.

He saw her, hanging from a water pipe mounted to the ceiling by her bound hands, dangling like a slab of beef in a freezer.

"Christine?" Karl asked. "Good to know you."

Christine Taylor was the shortest of the women Karl had come across in this gory odyssey. She wore a pink bathrobe, which had probably at one point been warm and comfortable to wear. It was stained with blotches of red under her armpit. Her crotch area. Her right hip. The bathrobe tie at the waist was knotted. Its cinch was gone and hung loose, and the robe barely covered her naked body underneath. Her panties clung around her ankles. They were soiled. Bloody. Christine's hair was pinned back into a black ponytail. Karl could see a good bit of the scalp through the thinning hair. The woman's face was thin. Starved. She was sick. Her skin was yellow. Sallow and awful to behold.

When Karl took another step towards her, Christine writhed and twisted her body against her restraints. Her ankles were tied with rope. Her mouth was covered by duct tape. The effort of this exhausted her, and she fell limp against her bindings, her head dropped down into her thin throat.

"Nah, I'm not going to hurt you," Karl said, holding up his hands palms out. "It's just I see you got blood around your … your privates. Your panties. I want to make sure neither of my men did anything … unforgivable to you. That's not why they were sent here. Did they hurt you in—in *that* way?"

Christine didn't move. She sniffled and squawked like a chicken.

"Is that a *yes?*" Karl asked, moving closer to her.

Her eyes widened. She lifted her head just as Karl reached for her and took her chin between his thumb and forefinger.

"*Yes* or *no*? Tell me, and I'll take care of it."

Karl loosened his grip so she could shake her head in the affirmative or the negative.

Christine shook her head left to right.

Karl let go of her and took a step backward. He planted his hands on his hips and studied her from head to toe. Then it dawned on him. It had been a gnawing at first, a nipping at the front of his brain like baby bird bites.

"You … look like my sister."

Tears slid from the corners of Christine's eyes. She shook her head, forlornly.

"You look *just* like my Blaise!"

He moved closer again. He sniffed at the air hanging before Christine. He wrinkled his nose. Then, he was tearing up himself and arming his eyes. Wiping away the tears coming fast and strong. "You smell like sick. Are you sick … Blaise? Are you … *sick?*"

You know damn well what this is, Karl!

Karl's sadness quickly boiled over to rage. His hand flew to his mouth. He dropped his eyes, tore his gaze away.

"He infected you. This is his AIDS. Blaise … you tell me … and I'll … I'll make it right."

How you gonna do that, big brother? The damage is already done! It's been done for a long time! Jack killed me back then, and he's killing me all over again now! You see it, don't you?

"I do, Blaise—"

"Mr. Tarlick? Who you talking to?"

hudda-hudda-hudda-hudda.

Karl wheeled around to find Bluto standing at the foot of the stairs. Beside him, the dog stood with her long pink tongue heaving in and out of her mouth as she panted ceaselessly. The chain looped around her neck hung silent, but still menacing to behold. Bluto was staring at Karl, his curious expression hooded slightly by the shadow cast from the brim of his sailor cap. He was easily twice Karl's size, and for some reason this never occurred to him before then. It felt good to know with certainty Bluto was indeed one of Karl's greedy faithful and would never raise a hand to him in anger.

At least, not until their transaction was completed.

No need to worry about it. So long as Bluto and Henry think they got a pot o' gold waiting at the end of this rainbow all will be well, and they'll do as I say.

He had promised them money.

Lots of it.

"We're going to leave this one," Karl said, almost prayerfully. "Take the dog out. Put her back in the trunk and move on to the next address. It's Philly. Take Henry with you, so long as he's done with the caregiver." His mouth worked, as he tried to say something more. Then, he abandoned the effort.

He stepped in front of Christine, opened his denim jacket, drew the hunting knife out Stella had used to stab Candy Whitby only a day before, and quickly carved a smile into the woman's supple throat. "Blaise …" he sighed and turned his back on her. He stalked back towards the wooden staircase, feeling Bluto's eyes as they bore into his downturned face, past the thick brown curls lumped along his cheeks.

"Man, why'd you—"

Karl shoved past him, stowing the bloody knife back inside his coat.

"Shut the fuck up," he muttered, his voice shuddery with tears. "Do what I said."

75. CONVERGENCE

Bluto and Henry took it surprisingly well after they climbed into the Dodge Caravan they'd parked a block away from the Taylor house and the engine wouldn't turn over. Henry drove because Bluto never got his license. Driving a car was his self-professed Achilles heel and damned if he knew why. He only knew it freaked him out, to trust every other motorist around you with your life sight unseen. *One of them could be suicidal and steer their car into yours! Could be high? Drunk! Psycho! Who knows?* Henry touched the wires together for the tenth time, and the two of them sat in the stolen Caravan's front seats, listening to the engine grind down and down until it was nothing more than a series of clicks.

Henry flung the wires back under the steering column and collapsed back against his seat. "I knew this car wouldn't take us far. The moment we laid eyes on it in that Walmart parking lot, I knew we were stealing a piece of utter shit. And here we are. No getaway car. No way to Philly, unless we—"

"You shitting me, Henry?"

"It sound that way to you, motherfucker?"

"We got other options. And if we weren't in such a hurry, I'd let you figure it out. Since we're in the thick of things, I'm just gonna tell you there's the caregiver's car. I seen it parked in the garage when I went out there looking for rope and duct tape. It's gotta be the nurse's car because there ain't no way the sick lady still drives anywhere."

"What the hell are we waiting for?" Henry cranked his door open.

393

A blast of arctic wind slapped him across the face, and he recoiled before stepping out and slamming the door shut again. He slapped the side of the Caravan, a simple goodbye to a piece-of-shit that had gotten them this far in their short, bloody odyssey. He walked around the back of the minivan and found Bluto already stalking back in the direction of the Taylor house.

Henry hurried after Bluto, who was already a few yards out from the rear yard fence of the Taylor house. Casting his eyes this way and that, pleasantly surprised at the absence of eyes in the immediate vicinity, Henry moved with more confidence in his step. The stores of the nearby strip mall were still shuttered for the morning. Many of them would not open for another two hours.

There was still time to salvage things.

He was coming up on the fence to the Taylor yard. He shoved it open, the metal links along the bottom of it catching on the grass and wedging it.

Bluto already slipped back inside the house.

"Thanks for waiting up, you fat fuck—"

Two quick shots from inside the house.

Tap-tap.

"Shit!" Henry cried. He hustled across the yard, skipping the split paving stones leading up to the front steps. The door hung open a crack. *I got a hunting knife. For God's sakes—this'll be a challenge!*

"Onward and upward," Henry breached the door. Just as quickly, he recoiled back behind its threshold.

"*Hen*-ry! *Henry*—"

Another man's voice cut off Bluto's pleading. A voice Henry did not recognize. "You're helping *me* now, Beard!"

The side wood paneling of the front door exploded into splinters right next to Henry's head.

The stranger in the house called to him by name.

"Hey, Henry! Have you seen my dog? Come on in, and we'll have a talk about it!"

Henry broke away from the front door, sprinted across the ratty front lawn to the waist high fence, and hopped it with a complete absence of grace. He didn't turn around, just maintained a mad dash with no immediate destination. *Hide in the Caravan? Yeah, I think so—I think so!* He knew the stranger was standing in the opened front door to the Taylor house, staring him all the way down the road. *He ain't gonna shoot! Not out in public! Get to the Caravan and, sorry to say, but fuck Bluto! Call Tarlick—call Tarlick* ...

76. BLUTO

"Bluto? Really?"

Will Bentley circled the bulbous, oversized man tied to one of the kitchen chairs in the middle of the living room. The chair looked second-hand, maybe even thirdhand, and might have collapsed once Bluto saw fit to fight his restraints. But the two bullets Will had initially fired into the big man's kneecaps swept him off his feet. It also humbled him on contact. Bluto turned docile as a lamb once he found he couldn't stand, walk, or run away. Will was quick to give Big Bluto a knock upside his skull, which drove the big man down into the darkness just long enough for Will to tie him to the chair with the same rope he and his accomplice had used to bind Christine Taylor in the basement.

The big man came to in an immediate frenzy. He shoved against the inch-thick rope wrapped around his chest and ankles, securing him and his dead legs to the chair legs. Bluto's eyes were wild, stitched in blood. They rolled over and back again like his head were a slot machine that just had its crank yanked. He screamed and brayed against the duct tape over his mouth. His own muted, pointless voice drove him all the more insane.

"It's not your name," Will said, stopping in front of the big man. He tapped the business-end of his Glock against the big man's forehead. "And I'd like to know your first name at least. It only makes sense, seeing as how the two of us are going to be working together from here on out." He withdrew the gun, resumed his pacing once more. "I wasn't counting on running into you or ... Henry is it? I have to admit. I was under the assumption there were only two, a man and a woman. And ... of course, my dog. Her name's Alberta. Did you know that? No ... I don't think it's possible, unless you read the papers. Something tells me you're not much of a reader of *anything*. So, I'm going to remove your duct tape. I'm making you a promise we're partners from here on out, but you've got to be honest with me. I want to know everything. Then, and only then, will it put us on an equal footing. Partners. Until you tell me everything and we're on the same page, I'm going to maintain this relationship we have going right here. The man with the gun and the shithead trying not to catch a bullet in the brain. So ... start with your name."

Will stopped in front of the big man once more, and ripped off the duct tape.

"I am gonna eat your fucking heart! Everyone you love—everyone

you ever even said *hello to your whole life! I'm gonna eat their hearts! And I'm gonna split your fucking dog down the middle like a wishbone!*

Will's hand was a blur, a dark trail that came from his side. Then, the big man's right eye socket was throbbing with pain far surpassing the wounds in his kneecaps. Bluto started wailing. His right eye had come unseated. It no longer matched its twin in movement or focus. It roamed separate from the other eye.

"We can't be partners. That's off the table. But you can still save your own life by telling me everything. We can't be friends now, but you could still ... well, *crawl* away from this. And ... I thought about it, and I could give a shit what your name is."

He jammed the barrel of the Glock into the big man's screaming, opened mouth. The big man's teeth clacked against the oily steel.

"I *want* to kill you, big guy," Will said evenly. "You know it, don't you? I'm so ... damned ... close." He curled his finger around the trigger. "Remember to swallow hard."

"Awwwwwhy–awwwwhyyyyy–awhy"

Will removed the gun. "What'd you say?"

"All right–all right, I'll tell you! I'll tell you!"

"Tell me." Will folded his arms, the Glock across his chest. "How do you know the other two people? The man and woman?"

"I don't know nothing about the woman, only she's dead. Karl had to turn her into dog food because she called the cops and tried to rat them both out. He was going to do her eventually, anyway. Karl used her to get to her husband. Really played the *long game,* man. In prison. For years. He had us in queue the whole time, but he didn't think he'd need to call us out to meet him so soon. Didn't think he'd have to kill her so fast. We met him at the halfway house just outside Comstock."

"Why'd you agree to help him with this? What's in it for you?"

"A half a million dollars each. M-me and Henry. Karl told us his poor old mother is living all alone in the family A-frame over in Levittown. Sister's dead. Karl's dad died on the job. He was this construction foreman. Something about a falling girder. Karl said he heard it cut his old man clean in half. The company his old man worked for paid out on his insurance. Wrongful death. A lawsuit on top of that. In the end ... in-in the end, his old man ended up sitting on a pile of dough. She don't believe in banks ... Karl told us ... and the money's still there. Buried in the ground under the .. the woodpile behind the backyard shed. Plastic bag."

"You believe him?"

"You ever been to prison?" Bluto cried, red snot bubbling in one nostril. "How about a fucking halfway house? You'd do anything for *anybody* if there's even a *chance* you can come out clean and free on the other side of extradition in another country. Money'll make that happen. I been in and out of the system all my life, so don't … don't fucking stand there staring down at me like I'm some pile of shit!"

Will's itchy trigger finger slipped back behind the guard.

The big man saw it. He was acutely observant of Will's every move. Shiver. Facial expression as it changed.

Everything.

"So that's where you were headed? You and that pussy, Henry?"

"He is … he is one *dead pussy*," the big man said, casting a hateful glance toward the front door. "You let me out of here alive, I will take care of him."

"You're a cripple. What are you going to do to him? Tiny Tim would pose more of a threat than you right about now, big man!"

"I'll get his ass."

"Fine," Will said. "Where was your next stop?"

The big man looked up at Will, his left eye mismatched. The broken eyeball stared off into space, disconnected. "Philly," the big man spat. "Society Hill section. Then onto the Tarlick house. So we get paid."

"That would be …?"

Will had to stop himself from saying the name out loud, but the tumblers nevertheless fell perfectly into place.

Jodi Dare.

He had to get on the phone. His suspicions, an inner gnawing, had been spot on. He suspected Karl and Alberta would hit the Dare house next, and now he had definitive proof. There was the off chance Detective Rivells would bypass his call or send it through to voicemail, but he had to try. First things first.

"All right?" the big man shrieked. "You got what you need?"

"Yeah … so I'll be on my way."

Soldier, your directives are clear as crystal! This is a take-no-prisoners mission. Leave no one breathing on the battlefield. Fulfill your oath as a soldier of the highest standards and neutralize this sonofabitch!

"He *is* neutralized," Will said. "He'll never walk again."

"Oh, I'll walk again!" the big man said, suddenly renewing the struggle against his restraints. "I'm in your life. From here on out. Once you put two in my legs, you brought me in, and I ain't going nowhere. I got a new life's purpose. To see you in the ground. To make sure you don't get an open casket. You got me?"

"Not for him," Will said, his gaze having transformed into something of a thousand-yard stare which unnerved the big man. "No."

I am your sergeant, and this is a direct order! Now execute this prick!

"No."

"Who you talking to? You some kind of kook?"

Will lowered himself onto his haunches, lining himself up eye-to-eye with the big man. "I'm going to go now."

"Yeah, it's all well and fine, but *this ain't the end between us!*"

"Then I guess I'll be looking over my shoulder for the rest of my life," Will said. "But something tells me we'll never see each other again."

"Fuck you!"

Will sighed and stood. He shook his head, holstered his Glock, and lowered his coat over it. "See, now, it's just like I said. No conscience. Never a conscience. You were just … I don't know … *born bad.* But I've got no bullets for you. Only for one. And I'll be seeing him soon. You? It'd be a waste of ammunition for you, and I've already spent two slugs on your knees."

"You lose."

"Maybe."

"*Fucking loser!*"

Will turned and strode towards the front door. He turned back around under the threshold and shrugged. "Maybe."

He walked out.

Philly.

By the time he climbed into his truck, Will had his phone to his ear, and he was listening intently to the ringing sound of Rivell's cell. *One, two, three, four, five, six …*

77. NO PARTICULAR PLACE TO GO

The minivan was so cold Henry felt the nubs of his nipples standing up against his ripped Minor Threat t-shirt, the chill reaching its hands all the way underneath his coat. Henry worked his cell phone, a burner, out of his tight jeans pocket. They clung so firmly to his thighs and legs he worried the phone would come out of his pocket in pieces of shattered glass and wires. He flipped it open, punched in the only number stored, and waited.

There was the chance Karl might not answer. When he had left them at the Taylor house, his eyes were puffy with tears, and he was more ornery than usual. He said little on his way out the door with the dog on the chain. Henry watched him yank hard on the chain when the dog seemed to be dragging behind him. The motion elicited a guttural growl like thick fabric tearing down the middle. The dog hacked and gasped.

He could be standing right outside the van—answer, Karl—you mother—

"Yeah?" Karl's sodden, stuffy voice filled Henry's ear. The ex-con hadn't felt so relieved to hear the little creep's voice since said little creep had made the initial proposition to Henry and Bluto back at the halfway house. *Murder. Torture. And a pot o' gold at the end of the rainbow. Are you in?*

"Karl, it's Henry, brother. We got a problem."

"Why're you whispering? Can't hear a fucking word!"

Henry raised his voice, just above a church whisper. No louder. "Things are fucked over here at the Taylor house. Somebody showed up while we were getting ready to shove off, and Bluto got shot."

"What the hell you talking about?"

"An ambush. That's what I'm talking about!"

"Was it the cops? Couldn't have been anybody else because nobody knows a damned thing about what we're trying to do with all this."

"I don't think he was a cop. He came alone. He's a good shot. Bluto got it, and I had to leave him or the guy would have taken both of us."

"You left him behind?"

Karl's words dropped Henry's stomach ten floors as he realized the cowardice of his actions. His shame spun into anger. "I did what you would have wanted me to do, Karl. I preserved the mission. This guy got a hold of me and there's no fucking telling what kind of tactics he would have used to find out everything I know. For all I know—"

"Bluto's giving everything up right this second," Karl said. He fell into silence, clearly brooding on his end. "Giving it all up. And ... well, hell ... we're almost done! Jack Post's own personal 'shit show' is nearly over. Then I was gonna let him die."

"Who?" He heard it. He swore he heard it. Right outside the sliding side door of the Caravan. Boots on gravel. Footsteps on the street. *Swore I heard it. I swear. Waited too fucking long!*

"Never mind," Karl said, his words winding down to an odd, grinding growl that reminded Henry more of the rabid dog on the chain. "You wanna tell me what kept you two, that I left you both forty-five minutes ago, and you're just calling me now to deliver the bad news?"

Oh bitch, if I didn't need the money—if I didn't already know *where*

I was running to in Mexico I'd tell this prick what to do and where to go!

Henry swallowed hard. It hurt, the sizeable lump stuck there. "We boosted a car with a shot engine."

"So get another car!"

"Karl, now sounds about as good enough a time as any for you to swear out an oath to me about the money, because this wasn't how it was supposed to go."

"An oath? You fucking *kidding* me?"

"How do you know your mother hasn't already gone and spent all the money she made in the settlement! Swear out a promise when we get to your old house the money'll still be where you said it is. In the ground under the firewood pile!"

Hesitation on the other end. "Mom's dead. She followed my daddy by about six months. Broken heart. Dead ... *daughter passed?* Son behind bars? And now a husband gone away? She died before she could spend any of it."

Don't press this any further, you don't know much about this guy; you probably don't know the half of what this guy's about. But I gotta—this changes shit even more.

Henry's back straightened. He clutched the cell phone with both hands. "Wait a minute! You're telling me your mother doesn't live at that house anymore? The one we're headed to when all this was finished?"

Silence, other than the distant thrum of an engine running in the background as Karl drove on. Then, "Mm-hmm."

"So ... then someone else lives there?"

"Maybe a whole family," Karl said, sounding bored by his own logistics.

"So ... wait ... wait ... we're doing the whole home invasion thing?

"Of course."

"In broad fucking daylight?"

"It'll have to be."

Henry searched for the words. For some reason his thoughts drifted to Charles Manson, the murders on Cielo Drive in Hollywood resulting in a dead actress and a shocked nation. The event which ushered in the end of the Hippie era. "What about the ones who live there? What if there's kids living there?"

"Well," Karl said sleepily, "all I can say about that is I hope their mother taught her children well. Otherwise ... I can't be sure. I can't be responsible for what will happen. But I imagine they'll be out playing."

"Dammit, it's Sunday!"

400

"Church, then."

"Don't fuck with me, Tarlick!"

"You burn me on this and not only will there be no payout in the end, but you'll know the true meaning of being *fucked*. Now ... you're going to head to my house. The address is 2870 Calliope Lane. Levittown. Not New York. This is in Pennsylvania. Talking maybe fifteen miles from the halfway house. But no one will see you coming. Don't you worry! If my ma were still living there, I'd say there's good reason for caution. That isn't the case, so I want you to go there, and I want you to clear the way."

"Clear the way?"

"If they're at home, you'll need to clear them all out," Karl said.

"All right, all right, but what if I just try to sneak out back to the woodpile and snag the money without being noticed?"

"What if there's no woodpile anymore? What if there's an inground pool dug out back there and a nice Jacuzzi where the woodpile *used* to be? Lot of what-if's."

"How long ago your mother die?"

"Two years ago."

"Mother-*fuck!*"

"This is a helluva lot better for what I need done. You're not whispering anymore, and you sound downright pissed off! Just hold on to your venom and make sure you spray it in the right direction. Not at me! I'm not the one. I'm the banker for the rest of your life. You gonna spit in your banker's eye?"

Henry fell silent, sullenness swelling within.

"Clear the path," Karl said. "This is the endgame, Henry. And I'm gonna make you rich when it's all over. All right now?"

"If they put up a fight at the house ... how far you want me to go with this?"

"Hmmm ... depends on how much your own survival and the money stash mean to you. That's how far you go."

The line went dead.

78. SOMETIMES, ALL IT TAKES IS
A LITTLE PUSH ...

Kelly Lin felt her handbag slipping down her shoulder as she stood at the Septa bus stop with about ten other people and gave it a firm yank back up her arm. The heavyset gentleman behind her, wearing a stained short sleeved shirt and cargo shorts despite the freezing temperatures was quite the mouth breather. Kelly could hear his slogging respiration, wet and clogged, like the inside of a washing machine all sudsed up. *He's sick. Sounds like the flu and he* still *comes out of the house dressed like it's mid-July!* Her coworkers over at Citizens Bank on Third Street just off Vine and the Parkway came in sick all the time, turning the entire teller station into an enclosed petri dish of illness. The bulletproof glass partition shut them all in with whatever airborne sickness one of the other employees decided to bring in to share with the rest of them. Now, this mouth breather! She was thankful to be wearing the knitted scarf her mother sent to her from her childhood home in Albany. It was stitched in her favorite three colors (gold, blue, and silver), and it warmed like a friendly hot palm across the back of her neck. It also kept the phlegm off pretty well.

Mouth Breather hacked, loosely covering his mouth with the side of his hand. All this managed to do was fan out the germs to everyone standing near him. The other people waiting for the bus were not nearly as tolerant as Kelly and flat out told Mouth Breather to "cough into your armpit, man!" or "take yourself to the ER and grab a stretcher, *muh-fuh*!"

Mouth Breather laughed it off. "Gotta get to work. Pizzas ain't going to deliver themselves!"

"You deliver pizzas? Sounding like that? I wanna know where you work so I never order from there!" a young black woman to Kelly's left said.

Kelly flinched. She was the sensitive type. Her mother worried about her, how she was faring in the big city. Philadelphia. When Kelly was fourteen, she was diagnosed as *excitable* and *sensitive to excessive external stimuli.* Socially anxious, in layman's terms. Her mother didn't understand how it could be, nor her father. Her mother was a native of China, easily one of the most externally stimulating nations on the planet. So many people. So many cars. Kelly had never gone to China, largely because of her condition.

But she could live in Philadelphia, despite the noise and the sirens and the traffic and the horns and the sick fat men standing in your personal space talking about how they'll never tell the name of the pizza parlor where they work right before hacking up what sounds like a golf ball sized loogie.

Her parents insisted she live in the nicest section of Philadelphia. Society Hill, where the self-professed *intelligentsia* lived and jogged and walked their dogs, or combined the two with earbuds stuck in their ears and a bottle of Fiji water in one hand. They knew she could not possibly pay for such an expensive apartment and insisted on covering her rent, a number upwards of two-grand a month. Her banker's salary afforded her many luxuries, but smaller and more manageable ones. Nothing like a car. It didn't really matter, though. *No one drives a car in the city. And if they do, they have their own garage.* Kelly did not.

So she rode Septa everywhere she went.

Damn strap. Kelly hiked her bag up her shoulder again.

Mouth Breather was arguing with a teenager, maybe a college kid. He sounded smart enough to shut down Mouth Breather with little cognitive effort. No profanity, whatsoever. *Maybe Temple? Drexel?* He was handsome too! Kelly let her eyes linger on the young man, wash over his blonde wavy hair and green eyes. Cute spray of freckles across the bridge of his nose.

"Smells like snow, don't it?"

Someone nudged into her. Kelly turned to find a much different looking man standing beside her than the good looking college preppie boy. This man was about her height, she was not tall by any stretch. Five-four. He looked slight of frame with shoulders bowing inward. Thick curled husks of brown hair hung in his face. His eyes were dark and piercing. Opals. Full lips, like a woman addicted to Botox plumping. His smile was strange, like he had borrowed it from somebody else and tried to pass it off as his own. He cast his eyes skyward, blinked up at the slate grey canopy above.

"Don't it?" he repeated.

His mouth kept moving, but Kelly missed the last half of what he said. The wheezing transmission and squeal of an approaching Septa bus's brakes muted his voice. Kelly was never more relieved to hear the arrival of the gas-guzzling behemoth in all her time in the city. She turned towards it. She felt the crowd of people around her shift to the left. She knew this move. They were trying to angle themselves towards the exact spot where the doors to the bus would open up. Kelly moved with the crowd, shoving without irritating those around her.

"Don't it?" the man repeated, so close he could have licked the side of her neck.

I think I might actually get on first. I think it's going to stop right in front of me.

A hand slid around her waist, under her peacoat and seized her by the hip. Another hand curled around the other side.

403

Those hands shoved her out in front of the bus.

She stumbled. Her left shoe heel split, and she went head over feet.

The last thing Kelly Lin saw was the massively wide tire inches from her head. The rubber treads, nearly worn all the way down to baldness.

79. "THE NOTEBOOK"

By the time Ryan Gosling stripped his shirt off for the second time in "The Notebook," Rivells was fully convinced he just wasn't her type. She had dated both black and white men, and the more she thought about it, Rivells never once had a good time with a blonde-hair blue-eyed guy. Not once. The two she'd gone out for drinks with had wandering eyes, and she always seemed to catch them scanning the bar for the next *best* thing.

Although Jodi had coaxed her out of the kitchen where she had been sitting, with one hand on the butt of her holstered gun and the other curled around a mug of strong Colombian coffee, Rivells's attention was still properly divided between the romantic drivel unfolding across Jodi's flat-screen and the slightest sound issuing from just behind the door to the Dare residence.

The chatter outside the door was sparse. The cops had run out of shit to talk about. Rivells was surprised. She was certain they were both full of endless bullshit and trivial banter, which would have been just as at home in their locker room or favorite cop bar as the hallway of a victim's apartment building. *They're bored! We should invite them in for a dose of this sappy rom-drama drivel!*

"So hot," Jodi sighed, her legs tucked underneath her as she sat perched on the edge of a comfy-looking recliner. She was nursing a pint of Ben & Jerry's Cherry Garcia with a long spoon. "Ryan freakin' Gosling."

"Any brothers in this movie, Jodi?" Rivells asked. "I'm not feeling your man right now. No offense."

"Oh, well, there's got to be!"

Jodi snatched up her cell phone from the nearby end table and her talon-like manicured nails tap-tap-tapped her iPhone screen. "Says here on IMdB—"

It stopped Jodi dead.

The sound of it.

A gut-wrenching sound of vehicle brakes screaming to a stop. Then, the shrieks and cries of men and women from the street rang out in the distance. Rivells and Jodi leapt off the furniture and crowded into the nearest window, Jodi yanking back the vertical blinds. They chittered in her hands like old bones. Rivells and Jodi craned to see. It hadn't happened right outside, but somewhere down the block to the right, towards Fourth and Chestnut. People were running in that direction on both sides of the street.

"Can you see anything?" Jodi asked, her nose pressed to the cold windowpane.

"Not a thing. Just people running."

Dammit!

Suddenly, someone was hammering at the door to Jodi's apartment.

Rivells's hand fell hard against the hasp of her holstered weapon. "Go hide in your bedroom! Lock the door and don't come out unless I tell you to. And if I use these words—Jodi!"

"Yeah?"

"I know you're scared, but I need you to listen to this especially. This is important. If I call to you inside your bedroom, and I use the words 'It's all clear, you can come out,' then do NOT come out. It'll be code it's not safe. Only if I say the words 'You can come out' are you to unlock that door and come to me. Do you understand?"

"HEY, DETECTIVE RIVELLS!"

One of the cops outside the apartment door.

"OPEN THE DOOR! WE GOT A SITUATION!"

Rivells took Jodi by the shoulders, squeezed them gently and gave her a small smile, enough to offer the girl some comfort. "So if I say 'It's all clear, you can come out,' what does it mean, honey?"

"It-it-it means d-*don't* come out! It's not safe!"

"Good," Rivells said. "Now, go on."

Jodi did as she was told, and it wasn't long before Rivells heard the door to the young woman's bedroom door slam shut and the simple thumb button in the doorknob click into a locked position. *It wouldn't keep an eight-year-old out, but it'll slow them down long enough to take a bullet or five!*

Rivells rushed over to the apartment door, threw back the deadbolt, kept the chain lock in place, and opened the door a crack. Officer Cumia's caffeinated breath blew in at her as he pressed his face into the opening. "There's been an accident about a block away southbound. Some kid just buzzed himself into the building. Told us it's bad. Lady needs CPR stat. We gotta go!"

"You gotta *go?*" Rivells cried. She unlinked the chain on the door and stepped out into the hallway to find them already stomping down the stairwell. *Sonofabitch!* "Both of you need to go? At least one of you stay, for God's sakes!"

Officer Cumia held up his hands and waved them around like some kind of placating maestro. "We gotta go have a look to see if we can lend a hand. We're both certified. A woman's head almost went all the way under a Septa bus wheel, Detective! This is protocol! I already got the OK from the precinct. You're here. You're an armed police officer. You can hold the line until we get back. Captain's orders."

If the apartment door opposite Jodi Dare's didn't crank open at that exact moment, and an old woman in pink fluffy slippers and baby-blue housedress didn't step out into the landing with her hand scratching incessantly at a tuft of gray hair atop her head, Rivells would have put up some protest.

"You hear that?" the old woman cried. "Sounded like a building falling down? Officer?"

Cumia flashed two rows of coffee-stained shark teeth and turned his back on Rivells to face the old woman full on. "Me and my partner are heading to the scene right now. Don't worry! Go back in your apartment."

The woman switched her gaze between Rivells' pinched, fierce expression and Cumia's utter mask of servitude. She shrugged and put herself right back behind her apartment door and bolted the door. Rivells heard the chain lock slide into place.

Before Rivells could snag Cumia by the scruff of his pressed blue collar, the officer disappeared down the stairwell and out of sight.

Standing there on the third-floor landing of Jodi's apartment building, Rivells felt a strange sense of foreboding. It struck her as a kneading of the intestines, a clamping and releasing not unlike a menstrual cramp. She wasn't due for that, and knew it for what it was. A sixth sense. An odd additional alert from within that all cops develop over time. Rivells knew something was coming, only because she had been left to guard against it. This was a reckoning.

Call it what you will, time to batten down the hatches!

She slipped back inside Jodi's apartment and locked the door. She walked into the kitchen nook and dragged one of the two simple chairs arranged at a small, circular table down the hallway to the front door. She wedged the top of the chair, a wrought-iron build, under the doorknob. Tested it for any wiggle room and then satisfied, Rivells rushed back into the kitchen. A low serving bar separated the kitchen from the living room, and its wall offered a direct view down the entry hall to the front door. Rivells hoisted herself up onto it.

"Jodi? You good?" she called to the nearby bedroom door.

Nothing, then, "Yeah. You?"

I don't know why I find it funny she'd be worried about me?

"I'm good, honey. Stay in there. Don't make a sound. Maybe get inside your closet if you can fit."

"I can't. Too narrow."

"It's all right. Just don't come out. Until you hear the right words from me."

"All right."

Rivells moved to unholster her weapon when her cell phone buzzed on her hip.

She moved to snatch it up. She read the name.

WILL BENTLEY.

She took the call, her cheeks burning.

"Mr. Bentley?"

"He's on his way there!" Will yelled. "Right now. You gotta get out of there with Jodi!"

"Wait a minute, *wait a minute*, who's coming here? Tarlick?"

"Tarlick is on his way there if he's not in the city already! You have to move Jodi out of there!"

"It's too late! How do you *know* this? What have you been doing?"

Will told her exactly what he had been up to. The murder of Stella, the addition of two more far deadlier accomplices to Tarlick's fold, and finally his apprehension and disabling of one of the accomplices at the Taylor house in New Castle, Delaware. By the time he finished, Rivells was chewing the inside of her cheek as a mixture of consternation and dread swirled around in her head.

"You're going to get yourself killed, Will! You keep going like this instead of letting the police do their job!"

"I have to protect my dog," Will said. "I gotta get to her before your people do. No offense, but I'm not on your side. The only reason I'm calling to warn you is I like you as a person, and I don't want to see any more people die."

Rivells massaged the bridge of her nose. *Time to let this rogue in.* She shut her eyes and breathed deep. "All right. How far out are you from Society Hill? You know the address here?"

"I do."

How the hell does he know all this?

Rivells chewed her cheek some more, holding back from asking the question flaring inside of her.

"How far?"

"A good thirty minutes according to Google Maps."

"And how long ago did Tarlick leave the Taylor house."

"Dammit, I don't know," Will said. "By the time I got there he was gone, and his boys were cleaning up the mess. They were just about to fly when I caught them. And one of them did manage to get away."

"Do you know his name?"

"There was a big guy. Fat. Wears a boat captain's hat. Like … I don't know, Bluto from the Popeye comics? And the other guy. Sounds strange, but he looked like a damned underwear model for Gap! According to Bluto, they met Tarlick at the halfway house where they were all staying. He promised them money from a settlement from when Tarlick's father got crushed by a falling girder on a construction job. Apparently, and this could be total bullshit, Tarlick's mother never trusted banks and the money is buried in bags underneath a woodpile in Tarlick's backyard. The house where he grew up."

"Mother would have spent it."

"Mother's in the ether, according to what Tarlick told Bluto and the model-looking guy. The money's still there. Buried. But a new family probably lives there now."

"Oh … Jesus … don't tell me they're headed there."

"The model-looking guy is," Will said. "Tarlick's on his way to you. You have to go!"

"The Taylor woman … is she—"

"Yes," Will said. "But I will say, she didn't die like the rest of them. She had her throat cut."

"All right," Rivells said. *So he's de-escalating? A sign of internal stress. Panic, even. His plan could be breaking down. He could be running out of gas.*

"I'm coming to you—"

Rivells heard the explosion before the door to the apartment came down, as if the two events were separate from one another. It sounded so loud in her ears she could have sworn it sounded like an upstairs neighbor had come crashing through the ceiling along with their stove or refrigerator. Wood splinters blew inward. One caught Rivells in the forehead, piercing the taut flesh and producing a single droplet of blood. She had dropped her cell phone without realizing, Will Bentley's panicked cries crackled through the earpiece. Her cell smacked the kitchen tiles, its screen spidered instantly.

She already had her gun out.

They may as well have been on a fast-moving belt, propelling the little

408

man and the *demon* towards her. They were upon her so rapidly, it would not have been outside the realm of speculation they were spring-loaded and shot through the door. Cast upon Rivells like a scourge from hell. She knew she fired on them, had squeezed the trigger more than once. But it didn't slow either of them. *Oh God, I missed—I missed!*

Someone behind her screamed. Some shrill sort of battle cry.

"Jodi! No!"

"Bastards*! Get out of my apartment!*"

Rivells dove off the bartop, gracelessly landing on her side and jamming her hip good on the ground. Her head whipped around just in time to catch Jodi standing in front of her. She held something out before her, and it was spraying a thin but potent stream of what looked like water (but most certainly was *not)* into the air before her. The little man's screams were dreadful, partly cries of pain and laughs of twisted pleasure as he swayed to and fro on his knees before Jodi. His hands were clapped over his eyes, plump lips split into a sneering smile. "Bitch-bitch-*bitch!*"

Pepper spray! Pepper spray beats maniac? Holy shit!

She grasped her gun and rolled over into a marksman stance beside the serving bar. One knee up, the other under. She raised her gun and sighted down on Karl Tarlick, the little man with the curly dark hair that looked like it was turning to a scalp full of dreadlocks. Two things happened right then.

The pepper spray hit her eyes and blinded her with her own tears.

Rivells heard what she would later describe as a human voice warbled and impeded by the growling, guttural vocalizations of an animal. A dog. It was a tortured, agonized noise, issuing just behind the serving bar. English words rose up above the broken, dreadful language of the wounded animal like buoys, only to duck down below the waves once more— *CURED! LET ME DIE! PLEASE!* She had never heard anything like it in her life, the hybrid of human and creature pressed into one vocal cord and snout-mouth.

"Rivells!" Jodi cried. "I'm out! Shoot him! Shoot *them!*"

Rivells heard the clink sound of something cast down to the kitchen tiles. *The empty pepper spray canister!*

"SHOOT HIM! GLYNNNAAA!"

Fuckfuckfuckfuck

No time to arm the tears out of her eyes. She blinked and took her shot. It clipped the little man's back just as he lunged forward on his hands and knees, grabbing Jodi around the knees. He yanked her forward, bending her down. Rivells fired again just as Jodi toppled over into the waiting arms of the little man. Karl Tarlick. He laughed and cringed and wept all at once, and the sound was nearly as maddening to hear as the strange, unimaginable noises coming from the blinded animal on the kitchen floor. The shot just missed the crown of Jodi's head, and she shrieked. Karl's arms curled around her and spun Jodi like a top so her back was shoved up into his chest. Then, he worked her into a sleeper hold.

"Don't do it! I've got you pinned, Tarlick!" Rivells yelled.

"Come on, now!" he said. "You're blind as shit!"

Karl reached down beside him and yanked something upward. It made a chinking sound, like shackles clanging together. Then, as if on command, the dog's half-human half-creature lament ceased, and Rivells heard the unmistakable sound of a canine rustling around on the kitchen tiles.

Jodi screamed. "Rivells! Shoot him!"

"I might miss and hit you instead! I can't, *goddammit!*"

"Good forward thinking!" Karl said and rammed Jodi's head into the corner paneling of the serving bar. Rivells heard the sickening sound of her skull fracturing, or at least egg-shelling. The young girl went limp in Karl's grasp. "Now, don't shoot because now I can move her into any damned position. I'll make her a goddam bullet sponge if I have to."

"You won't make it out of here! You missed the police car parked out front. They're all over this block, and they'll take you down the minute you poke your head out. Sniper's on the roof!"

Karl laughed. "Not for a guy like me. And it looks like your guards left their posts. Some kind of accident around the corner. Woman got thrown in front of a bus. Head came apart like a casaba melon."

"A guy like *you* killed two cops!"

"Nope, not *me!* The dog!" Then, standing just inside the threshold, Tarlick called out a string of completely incomprehensible words. Comprised of clicks of the tongue against the roof of the mouth. A snapping of the inside of the cheek. A chattering of the teeth. Abhorrent sounding vowels and consonants sharp enough to slice the air as he pushed them out of his mouth. The very sound of it offended Rivells's ears, and she felt nausea build and rise at the base of her stomach before Tarlick finished.

Who the hell is he talking to?

Inside the kitchen, Rivells heard the sound of a dog finding its feet. The jangling of chains around its thick, impossible neck.

Rivells inched forward, gun trained before her. Sighted down the barrel. She tried to bring Karl and the unconscious Jodi into her line of fire.

Then, the dog rounded the corner of the serving bar.

It locked eyes with Rivells.

Her focus scrambled. She felt fear like she had not known since the first time she watched the original *Texas Chainsaw Massacre* movie at an eighth grade sleepover. The quickening of the pulse. Shortness of breath. Dry mouth. Fleeting flashes of a short life lived. She saw the face of her mother, but her face didn't come between Rivells and her clear, dreadful view of the *demon* locked into a seemingly unbreakable gaze with her.

My God, the eyes! The eyes! Red eyes! Bloody mouth! The stench of it.

"That's *not* Will Bentley's dog," she said, a thought she could not help but to give voice to. "That's … a monster. A *demon."*

Rivells raised her gun to shoot, laid the crosshairs squarely on the dog's forehead.

Tarlick's voice snapped her out of the reverie. It also snapped the dog out of its own deadly focus.

The dog (demon) turned tail and went to Tarlick. They disappeared behind the apartment door.

Rivells's hands were shaking violently.

Jodi's screams rang up the stairwell, but they were muffled and muted by what could have been Tarlick's hand. Rivells heard doors open up and down the stairwell, imagined the other tenants with questioning glances and furrowed brows as they tried to make sense of the whirlwind that just whipped around the railing and disappeared out into the afternoon. Rivells lunged towards the apartment door and ripped it open. She emerged on the landing and took to the stairs, her head still plagued by the residual image of the burning red eyes of the Bentley dog. She rushed past the rubberneckers lingering outside their doors, shuffling around.

"Go back inside your apartment!" she told them. "Lock your doors!" She touched down in the lobby with no memory of how she got there.

A man in a duster and black horn rims, clutching a small stack of mail against his chest, pointed one long and trembling finger towards the back hallway. The emergency exit at the end of a narrow service hallway.

Rivells surged down the hallway. She exploded through the emergency exit door, instantly sounding an alarm she barely heard. She had lived in this apartment building for five years and had never once given notice to this alternate exit. It gave onto a back alleyway, sort of the concealed skeleton of the complex itself with spindly steel fire escapes bolted up its side and brickwork badly in need of a power wash. She turned to her left, her right. A garbage bin and litter strewn around it. Puddles. No sounds of any footfalls bouncing off the sidewalk in either direction. She broke to the left and ran until she emerged on Chestnut Street.

A police car blew past her, its siren blaring. She followed it a half black down to where it screeched to a halt. A deep cluster of people were

411

gathered there, milling about or exchanging quick words with one another. An older woman wearing a fur coat and knee-high leather boots leaned into a man who held her with one hand across her back and spoke into a cell phone with the other. The woman was sobbing, shuddering against him. Rivells ran towards the gathering of cop cars and people. *Please tell me they're in the middle of that mess ... and Jodi is okay!* Then she remembered the little evil man's words back upstairs in the apartment. *Someone fell in front of a Septa bus.*

"No," Rivells breathed. The blunt nose of an ambulance jutted out halfway across the intersection of Chestnut and Eighth. Then, as she came closer, Rivells saw the Septa bus, stopped curbside. The sounds of women crying. Shrieking. Children, the same. Men doing what men did in the midst of such a tragedy, turning all about with shocked and vacant looks on their faces.

"No."

It would have been so easy for them to get away with this going on—because he pushed the woman in front of the bus.

"No."

Nearby, Rivells heard the sound of car tires screaming down the street in the opposite direction.

Away from the scene of the accident.

"I need my phone. Right now!"

Rivells retraced her steps as quickly as she could. The man who had flattened himself against the mailboxes inside the apartment complex was gone when she ran past again. A few tenants were still lingering in the hall-way despite her previous command to put themselves behind locked doors. She ignored them and bounded up the stairs until she made it back into Jodi's apartment.

Inside smelled of dog slobber and wet pennies.

She quickly located her cell phone on the kitchen tiles. The screen was spidered, but the phone was still useable.

"Hello?"

No one on the other end.

Then, the phone buzzed and *screed* in her hands like a thing brought back to life.

She pressed the Call Accept button.

"Hello? *Will?*"

"Are you all right?"

"He was here! H-He took Jodi! And ... your dog!"

"Is she all right? She didn't hurt you, did she?"

412

She didn't hurt me, but your dog is not *all right.*

"Your dog is with Karl Tarlick. They got away from me!"

"Shit!"

"Do you know where they're going? I'll send all units! But you've got to be sure!"

"I don't know," Will said. "Not yet. I'm still trying to get that out of this Bluto prick."

"You don't know yet?"

"I'm working this. I'll get it! Then you'll get my call."

"What? Will?"

End of conversation.

Rivells squeezed her phone so tight between her fists the frame clicked. She stood in the kitchen of the Dare apartment, seething and unable to chart her next move. But it stalled her for barely a moment before she punched in her next call to Detective Jones. He picked up on the tenth ring, his breathing labored and tone agitated. "Yeah, Rivells? You all right?"

"Two things," she said, flatly. "One, I want you to find out Karl Tarlick's boyhood address. It's where they're going—"

"—got a mess over here, Rivells—"

"—and two, promise when we catch up to Will Bentley, you'll put him in cuffs and throw the book at him."

"Wait now, isn't he the dog's owner?"

"That *dog* isn't a *dog* anymore. And he's done nothing but obstruct this entire investigation from beginning to end. I want him prosecuted. Promise me, Jones!"

80. ALL OF US ARE DYING

Karl Tarlick turned up the radio and found it all too easy to align his thoughts and feelings to the song blaring out of the console. It was The Doors' "When The Music's Over." Jim Morrison's vocals boiled over with rage as he spouted what sounded like the perfect impromptu rantings. He hammered the side of the wheel. He stomped his left foot down into the wheel well next to the brake and slid the car onto I-95 North, with a frenzy burning in his brain the likes of which he had not felt since the police came to drag him out of his house when he was a teenager. The inside of the car was sweltering. He had the heat all the way up. Liked it that way. He liked there was no longer a *Stella* to compromise with when it came to the temperature inside the car.

He could hear the girl lying on the floor of the backseat moaning and sniffling against the duct tape over her mouth. Karl snuck a glance behind him and down at the Dare girl.

"I'll rip off the duct tape if you want to sing along, Jodi! Would you like that?"

Jodi lifted her head and screamed against the sticky adhesive. She wriggled helplessly against her twine-tied hands and turned her legs this way and that against the bindings.

Karl shook his head at her. "All right, forget I said anything."

He grasped the wheel with one hand, turned his full attention back to the highway before him, and gauged the space between himself and any other cars on the road. Then, Karl punched around the passenger seat and down into Jodi's face. He felt her nose crunch against the ridge of his knuckles. She gasped and choked.

The Dare girl fell silent.

The song ended, giving way to a car dealer commercial complete with some barking loon and honking horns Karl thought might have been someone tailgating him, until he checked his rearview and saw the car behind him idling along a mile back.

He switched off the radio and quickly regretted it.

The dog. *The fucking dog!* It was howling in the trunk, a mournful and drawn out sound like a wolf perched on the edge of a cliff with a full moon glowing fat and ominous behind it. *The thing's cracking! You can hear it! There ain't much action left in her! She's like a gun that's been fired too many times! A two-by-four cracked across one too many skulls!* Whatever there was left to do, Karl knew it needed to be done within a few hours. He also knew if the dog kept on like that, he'd have to pull over into the breakdown lane and either whisper to it or crack it good like he had to do to the Dare girl.

The dog could go rogue at any time, man! You try to hurt her, and she just might tear you apart! Tread lightly, Karl! Your little Frankenstein's Monster isn't going to play nice with you for much longer!

Someone patted his right leg. He cried out. He turned to find a starved-looking, petite young girl sitting in the passenger seat next to him. She wore a pair of jean cut-offs and a white Tori Amos Tour shirt billowing out around her upper body like a cloud with sleeves. Her long, pale legs crossed as they extended down into the wheel well. She wore black, low-top Chuck Taylor Converse. She was a ginger, a trail of vivid freckles stamped across the bridge of her thin, pinched nose. Her left eye burned bright with

414

amber and flecks of gold, her most beautiful and disarming feature. When she turned to look at him full on, Karl nearly lost his grip on the wheel. The right eye was a milky, depthless orb. A hole was eaten clear through her right cheek and spiders skittered in and out of the opening. She smiled at him, nodded, and cast her eyes back to the road.

"Blaise," Karl breathed.

Blaise Tarlick folded her arms across what was a surprisingly ample bosom for such a small girl. Karl always suspected *those things* would one day get her into a heap of trouble. Pregnant. The wolves would gather at the door just to get at *those things*.

Sometimes Karl had wondered stupid, simple thoughts alone in his prison cell when there was nothing left to do but ponder in the darkness. *If she was flat as a board, maybe a motherfucker like Jack Post never would've looked her way twice! God set her up for a bad end, didn't He? He sure as hell did!*

"Don't blame it on my tits, you idiot!" Blaise said, smirking out at the cloudy sky and the grey highway. "All that tells me … all that kind of thinking ever showed me was *you* were the one who wanted to touch them. More than anybody else. I'm surprised you never snuck a feel."

Karl moved to backhand her with his right hand and struck the cushioning of the upholstery where Blaise's head was. "You *don't* talk like that! A filthy thing to say!"

"What? You always wanted to fuck your own sister, and when Jack Post beat you to it, it drove you clear out of your mind?"

"Ah, so you're with *them*? The people who think I'm nuts? You want to know what people back in high school used to call you? I wasn't getting into fights every other day for my health, little girl! It was always about defending you when they all wanted to call you filthy words! After you *gave it away* to Jack-fucking-Post … that's when it all started. The names they called you! He bragged all about it to everyone."

"I didn't know it then," she said, airily. "I'm well aware of it now."

"That's right. He showed you a face, and he had another one for everybody else. An ugly face. And you were the first one he done this to, but it started with you, and it never woulda' ended unless I showed him all this."

"And what is *all this*?"

Karl glanced at her, his mouth working. His tongue suddenly tasted like it had swelled to three times its size. "All *this*? It's for you, Blaise."

"Oh," Blaise said, smoothing down the front of her t-shirt and sucking her bottom lip. "Okay."

"Wha–don't you like it?"

415

"I don't get all this ... *showmanship*. This *ceremony*. Why didn't you just cut Jack's throat and have done with him?"

"Too easy!" Karl yelled, slapping the side of the wheel. "C'mon now. You can't be serious, Blaise!"

Blaise wheeled on him, just in time for Karl to catch a quick glimpse of something with a hundred legs inch its way out from under her dead eyelid and skitter around her cheek to burrow into her mottled ear. "You're an idiot, Karl! Don't you see how messed up this is, I mean, beyond the obvious? You're punishing Jack's victims!"

"I'm *punishing* him!"

"Toh-may-toh, toh-mah-toh!"

"Dammit, Blaise!"

"And I even showed myself to you back at the poor sick woman's house! You saw my face in hers, and you *still* killed her! I thought it would have stopped you, to see me in her ... but no!"

"You did that?"

"I tried," she said, turning away from him once more. "I failed."

Karl drove on and let the radio fill what otherwise would have been silence. They sat through half of Foo Fighter's "Times Like These" before he stammered his way into something else to say. His eyes were bulging.

"They were all whores. To sleep with a married man ... and—and one of them gave him AIDS! Then Jack ... he went and brought it home to his wife!"

"Hmm ... I seem to remember you shagging a married woman on her living room floor while her husband was away. As a matter of fact, this was only a couple days ago, Karl."

"Not the same thing."

"How's it different?"

"Because it was all according to plan. You know it!"

"I don't know any such thing. Why don't you enlighten me, big brother?"

Disgust tugged downward at the corners of Karl's mouth as he stared glumly out the windshield at the white Mack truck favoring its brake a bit too heavily for the fast lane. "All of it. The whole funny business I carried on with Stella? From the first letter I sent to her from prison to the last minutes of her life when I finally locked her in the trunk with the dog? All according to plan. I needed to get to her husband to punish him, and the only way to do that was to go through her. Because I promised myself—promised you—I would get Jack Post back for what he did to you. For making you kill yourself."

416

"Oh, brother, *brother,* you *really* played the *long* game, didn't you?"

Karl nodded, gripping the wheel fiercely. "Damn right. Four years of writing letters, talking through plexiglass every Sunday afternoon. Having to listen to her sad sack-o'-shit stories about how Jack would *mindfuck* her all the time. She wouldn't leave him. Of course not. Because that would only make sense, and you women don't deal in good common sense. Don't get me wrong, I'm no *woman hater.* I just got no patience for ordinary stupidity. But I got out, and she brought me right in. None of this happened by accident. There were no coincidences, Blaise. So you can imagine my disappointment when I still haven't heard so much as a *thank you* come out of you since you decided to hitch a ride with me."

Blaise glanced over at Karl, her eyes sodden, her mouth tight-knit. "Thank you, Karl. Now pull off onto the next exit, and let this girl go. You made your point."

"Oh yeah? How so?"

"Because, brother-Karl, Jack Post has been lying dead in a seedy motel room for the last hour. He's not even *in* the animal anymore. He is *no more.* So it's over. You don't have an audience for this any longer. Roll the credits. End the show."

"Bullshit!" Karl jerked the wheel to the right, forcing his way into the next lane.

"He is, though," Blaise said evenly, like she was talking to a preschooler.

"Well, even if he *is,* it don't mean he's not still trapped inside the dog's mind! So the show must go on!"

"I'm telling you, Karl. He's gone. I don't know where he is at this point, but he's gone from this particular plane of existence. You said you were doing this for me. Then listen to me. End it. I'm asking you to do this."

"Yeah, well … ask all you want. But you're gonna want to take the ride with me to where we're all going."

"I know where you're going. And I'm begging you to *not* continue. I'm *begging* you to call Henry—"

"Not my friend. Business partner."

"And your business is *what?"*

"Smartass," he said, and pressed the gas pedal to the floor.

"I'm asking you to call Henry off. Tell him you'll pay him what you promised. Just don't bother the people who live there."

"Blaise, you're my sister. I love you very much. But if you're going to ride along, I'm going to need you to shut your mouth. I'm not interested. You'll thank me when this is all over. Trust me."

417

81. INVASION

Cynthia and Ryan Riley knew all about the family who had lived in the Levittown red and white A-frame before them. The details were thrust on them during a dinner date at Applebee's when they agreed to go out for drinks and pub eats with their next-door neighbors, The Chimas. The Chimas, twice the age of Cynthia and Ryan (both of them mid-thirties), were retired teachers who seemed always on the verge of a blowout argument. Ryan had told Cynthia he was never going to retire from his cushy engineering gig if it meant being home alone together every day would amount to that sort of animosity.

When the Chimas were not busy clipping off one another's statements, they were all-in together when it came to sharing neighborhood gossip with the Rileys. They talked about Gus Stapleton, a sixties widower, who brought home prostitutes every Tuesday night and drank enough Guinness he should own stock in the ale company.

The youngest Pinner girl had gotten pregnant at fifteen by the boy next door, an eighteen-year-old dropout named Casey Foster, and one way or another that *baby* never saw the light of day. *Abortion or miscarriage.*

An hour into the eighth round of lagers at Applebee's that night eight months ago, Gilbert Chima had simply come out with it.

The Tarlick family. Their *curse*, as Gilbert Chima put it.

"Maniac son who kidnapped neighborhood pets and slaughtered them in the woods behind our houses. Our cat Darcy was an inside cat at the time. Otherwise he would have gotten her too. Daughter kills herself a year after they put the boy away. Then, a construction accident kills the father. The mother supposedly won big in a settlement with the firm overseeing the construction job. Dies before anyone saw so much as a new car in her driveway or new landscape dug into the front yard. That was the Tarlicks."

The Rileys had two more beers with their neighbors before splitting the bill and calling it a night. At Applebee's, the Rileys had done their best to mask their astonishment and disgust involving this new information. The real estate agent hadn't mentioned any of it, more concerned with her commission than full disclosure. That night, eight months ago, Cynthia and Ryan each snuck into their children's room and hugged them while they sleep. They hugged RJ (Ryan Junior), who had just turned twelve the week before. They crossed the bedroom to hug Ava, the three year old with her blonde, unruly curls fanning across her pillow like bird feathers. She had only just discovered the sustenance her own thumb provided her when she stuck it in her mouth. Cynthia had been trying to break the little girl of the habit before it really set in because she heard it could cause a speech impediment later on in life.

After that, they brushed and washed up before creeping into bed next to one another.

Cynthia confessed the new information filled her with dread. She thought it might give her bad dreams, and she was right. She didn't sleep soundly for a week, a twentysomething man leaning over her with his face a mere inches away from hers. Of course, she had no idea what the young man of the house looked like, the one her mind conjured up was frightful enough to stir her blood. Then after a week, Cynthia Riley simply decided she would not allow *anyone* to rob her and her family of enjoying and loving their new home. The dreams stopped. She believed she had willed them to stop. A power of the mind.

Ryan had listened to his wife cry out and rustle in the dark beside him all week. The news about the Tarlicks had a different effect on him. For him, it prompted a call to action on his part. It was a summoning to safeguard his home and family against any sort of threat that could crop up. The Chimas told him the sister, mother, and father were all dead. That left one Tarlick walking the earth. Granted, he was in prison. Ryan scoured the internet for any information relating to the Tarlick boy's release date. There was nothing. The information was quite obviously sealed. And it was the *not* knowing that prompted Ryan Riley to make the first major decision apart from his wife since they got married.

Not knowing is not an option!

Ryan bought a full-service pistol recommended for best home defense by the retailer. A SIG 226. He bought a gun safe, took a course on gun safety and handling, and hit the gun range enough times after work until he was satisfied with his ability to aim and fire effectively. Then the SIG went away into the gun safe. The gun safe has remained in the back of Ryan Riley's walk-in closet for the last six months.

Untouched.

The Riley's settled into their lives and their new home. Any dark cloud which had held reign above the A-frame in Levittown must have lifted. It's what they chose to believe. What else could they do? Vigilance is healthy, but when overdone it is paralyzing. Exhausting. They let their guard down and lived their lives.

On Sunday, December 23, at approximately 11:30 a.m., the Rileys were just about to depart for Mass down at St. Cyril's Catholic Church. It was game day for the Philadelphia Eagles and despite Cynthia's protests, Ryan and RJ

419

planned on wearing their jerseys to church. Father Abe had emboldened the Eagles fans in his parish by encouraging them to support the home team, even if it was in God's house.

"God, no doubt, is a Carson Wentz fan, so have at it, congregants!" Father Abe said. The parishioners loved Father Abe, and not just because he loosened the dress code on game days.

RJ was holding the family up because he couldn't find his jersey.

"Mom! Is it in the wash? It wasn't even dirty!" RJ was halfway under his bed, rifling through the cluster of discarded clothing kicked under there at some point.

"Oh really, little man?" Cynthia countered, ducking into his bedroom and fastening an especially tricky clasp earring to her right lobe. "You were living in it for a week straight after they beat the Cowboys. It was starting to smell like you were wearing it for underpants!"

RJ skittered out from under the bed and sat up, his cheeks red. He armed his eyes. Not tears–allergies. A lot of dust bunnies under there. "What am I gonna do now?"

"You'll just have to put on one of your nice button-downs." Before he could protest, Cynthia moved towards the stairwell. In her wake, she heard him grumbling but mindful not to let slip any of the bad words she knew he used liberally when he played "Call of Duty" with his friends. "We're already late. I don't want us to have to stand in the back like a family of hobos!"

More grumbling. RJ slammed his door shut to pull on one of his loathsome Abercrombie shirts and a pullover sweater itching the nape of his neck like nobody's business.

Ryan was just about to call up the stairs to his family when the stunning vision of his wife in red chiffon, her hair wound up into a bun that looked tasty enough to eat, made her way down to him. He took her hand and led her the rest of the way to the bottom where they stood together in the foyer.

He offered her an Eskimo kiss and then stepped back. "You know, I didn't mean what I said last night," Ryan told her. "If you're brother needs a place to stay for a little while to get himself together, I'm fine with it."

"You weren't last night," Cynthia said. "You called him a beach bum."

"I was just curious as to how he went from getting a sizeable loan to start up a parasailing business to sleeping on the beach under a busted canoe? Where did all the money go? How do you fail at starting a parasailing business in Malibu?"

"I don't know, Ryan. Why don't we ask God to enlighten us about why Corey is such a screw up. Maybe he'll have some answers. I have none. Now, we're going to be late, and all you're doing is reviving a tense exchange from the night before."

"I don't look down on your brother."

"I believe you," Cynthia said, her tone lifting at the end into a lie.

"Can we not stretch this out into a week-long standoff? I said it was okay if he comes."

"Yes, well, I'll go you one better, honey."

"What does that mean?" Ryan said, stiffening.

"He's on his way here already. Should be pulling up in a cab later on today."

Ryan scratched the line of his jaw, a line he noticed was softening of late. "All right ... don't you think we might've done better finishing up the conversation first before you told him to get on a plane? I mean, shit ... wait a minute, that's an eight-hour flight. You—you had to have told him to come before you even talked to me about it! Dammit, Cynthia! What are you trying to do?"

"Me? I'm trying to make it to noon Mass. You want to do that with me? Help get the kids down here before I lose my temper!"

Ryan swallowed a very sizeable lump, shrugged on his charcoal overcoat, and walked halfway up the stairs with his lips pulled into a bloodless line he would not show his wife.

"We'll talk later then," he muttered down to her. He projected his voice up to the second floor, the timber of his tone darkening to the no-nonsense. "Kids, we're leaving now. If you're not on the wagon train when we pull out, it's a month inside. No games. No internet. No phone, RJ!"

The little girl, Ava, emerged from around the corner at the top of the stairs. She held fast to her Powerpuff Girl doll and plucked absently at the doll's hair as she felt blindly for the banister and made her way down to her parents. Her mouth was screwed up into a knot of concentration, and she looked to Mom and Dad like one of those monkeys that picks nits out of another's fur while they perch on a branch together.

"There's a dead spider in Bay-bay's hair, Daddy!" she announced, suddenly lifting her eyes to gaze down the rest of the step at her father. "Can you get it out? It's gross!"

"Let me have a look," Cynthia said and worked it out of their daughter's arms. "I doubt it's a spider, honey." Cynthia, now herself plucking at the fake, slippery hair of the Powderpuff doll, spoke in a curt voice to her husband. "Could you hurry your son along? And maybe we don't wear our jerseys to church anymore? It seems to cause more problems than it's worth at this point."

"Sure," Ryan said, ascending the stairs.

"Come on, honey," Cynthia said, clicking her black high heels down the center hallway into the kitchen. Ava followed in her mother's wake, breaking into an impromptu skip before coming to a stop just behind her mother as Cynthia stood at the kitchen sink. Ava watched her mother turn on the tap and move to hold the doll's hair under the flow of water.

Ava tugged angrily on her mother's coat. "You're gonna ruin it. Her hair, mama!"

But Cynthia wasn't listening to her daughter at all. She laid the doll down on the countertop. She was staring at something outside the small window over the kitchen sink. The pane which looked out onto the backyard. She forgot to breathe. Cynthia felt for Ava's little shoulder beside her and squeezed it. "Honey, would you go get your father?"

"What's wrong, Mommy?"

"Right now. Fast. Go get daddy. Tell him mommy wants him right away."

"Emergency?" Ava asked, sounding out the word by breaking it down into syllables. She barely knew what the word meant, only it usually carried with it a serious tone in her parent's voices.

"That's right," Cynthia said. She let go of Ava, and her hand went to her throat. She massaged the taut flesh there, smoothing it over and over. She could not swallow until she did this. "That's right."

She kept looking out the window into the yard, her gaze fixed upon one spot. Her pupils pinpricks as the wintry sun, strong and stark, stung her eyes. She gripped the lip of the countertop and felt the slow, agonizing ticking away of time as she stood there. In her mind, she wondered how many seconds, or fractions of a second, it would take for her to lay her hands on one of the steak knives in the drawer behind her. Literally a turnaround and a lunge towards the drawer. Then something she had honestly never once thought about in all her thirty-four years sent waves of shock and nausea outward from her hammering heart into the rigid limbs of her arms and legs. *How easily would a steak knife stab into a man's back? Looks like there's a lot of muscle and tendon back there! It would take a couple slashes—*

"What's up?"

"Look outside, Ryan," she said, her husband sidling up beside her.

"Who the *hell's* that? What's he doing in our backyard?"

"I don't know," Cynthia said. "He hasn't moved an inch from the way you're seeing him right now."

"It—it almost looks like he's trying to find something in the grass behind the shed."

"He hasn't turned around. He's not wearing a uniform. You know, like a cable guy or a meter reader. I have no idea what this is."

Ryan took a deep breath. "All right. I want you and the kids to go up into RJ's bedroom and lock yourselves in. Just to be safe."

"Ryan—"

"It's all right; it's fine. Probably just a simple misunderstanding. Just do as I said. Take the kids and don't open the door for anyone, not even me. I have a key to the door hidden so you won't need to let me in if the coast is clear, which I'm sure it will be. Don't worry. It's probably a homeless man or something. Maybe the guy's got Alzheimer's, and I just have to walk him back home. Okay, babe?"

Cynthia turned, latched onto her husband's Eagles jersey, along the short-sleeved hems. "He doesn't look old enough to have Alzheimer's, Ryan!"

"Go," Ryan said and hugged his wife. "Go. I'll be fine."

She tried to say his name again. Something tugged at the pit of her stomach. Ryan was adapting to this strange situation as if he had practically grown up with curious-looking men wandering into the backyard of his childhood home. Cynthia could have sworn she even detected something of excitement flickering behind her husband's big blue eyes.

Anticipation?

The Rileys walked up the stairs, their hands clasped tightly together, until it came time to separate. Cynthia crept towards RJ's room where she found little Ava now sucked into the search for her big brother's missing Eagles jersey. She smiled at both of her children and slipped inside, shutting and locking the door behind her.

Ryan hung a right. He charged into the master bedroom, tore the closet doors open wide. He drove his hands through his hanging work shirts and felt for the little hidden hasp hidden behind them, set into the wall. He flicked the hasp with his thumb and felt the little door open outward as far as the hanging clothes would allow. Ryan parted the hanging dress shirts wide enough he could open the door all the way. He brought out the gun safe and walked it over to the bed. The combination was the last four digits of his childhood phone number.

8-7-4-2.

The box lock clicked. Ryan opened it up and took out the SIG handgun, easing it out of its snug foam compartment. Next, he withdrew the box of bullets from the compartment in the wall. He checked the safety and loaded the weapon to capacity. He jacked a round into the chamber, sighted down its crosshair. He gathered his bearings and stalked out of the bedroom. Ryan stopped outside RJ's door, knocked lightly. "I'll be right back, guys. RJ, calm the ladies down. Everything's fine."

"Dad?" It was RJ.

But Ryan was already on his way back down the stairs.

There was no need for Ryan to keep it quiet when he exited the house into the backyard.

The stranger in his yard was standing now. He had turned around and was looking right at Ryan with something of irritation. It was an expression which unnerved Ryan if for no other reason than the sonofabitch had the audacity to eyeball *him,* like Ryan was where *he* didn't belong. The stranger did not look like any run-of-the-mill crazy. He was surprisingly handsome, his hair a brown wave, luxuriant just above the man's low, tanned brow. His eyebrows even looked like they had been plucked and maintained rather recently. His stare was not clouded by any sort of drug fog. In fact, they were alert and expressive. He wore a black Carhartt jacket, khaki chinos, and motorcycle boots. The black leather polish was off the boots, Ryan noticed. They were discolored, in fact, by something lighter enough in shade to show a contrast. Crimson. A tint of it, maybe.

The stranger had his hands thrust deep down into his pockets. His head was cocked to the side, as if he were appraising Ryan while the homeowner made his slow, steady approach across the frozen ground of the yard.

I'm going to have the first word. And the last. This is my house. My family's scared.

"You're trespassing on private property," Ryan said. He brought out the gun from behind his right thigh, laid it against the side of his leg. *Just letting him know it's here.* "You lost?"

"Where's the woodpile, my man?" the stranger asked. His voice was burnout, dope smoker. Condescending. *Damn if this prick doesn't remind me of Cynthia's piece-of-shit brother, Corey. Same cocksure attitude, and nothing to show for it!*

Ryan ignored the knocking of his heart against his ribcage. He tapped the barrel of the SIG against his leg, cocked an eyebrow. "Woodpile? You're in *my* backyard, man! That's all you should be concerned about."

"What're you gonna shoot me?"

Yeah, he sounds like Corey. Motherfucker.

"You want to get shot?"

"Oh ... oh, man ... big bad suburban *Dad* thinks he's got the shit

424

inside him to kill somebody. I'm gonna ask *you* again. Where the fuck is your woodpile? You ain't got a woodpile? It's the dead of winter, dude! Is this how big bad suburban *Dad* provides for his family?" The stranger's gaze raked their way up the back of the house. Ryan didn't like the way the stranger's eyes suddenly narrowed, fixed on something. "Gang's all home, huh?"

Ryan knew without having to look, to follow the stranger's line of sight, Cynthia and his children were peering out RJ's window down into the yard. Watching the stand-off. It stung Ryan just knowing the stranger had laid eyes on Ryan's prizes, his reasons for living. When the stranger licked his lips, leaving a slick along them that made Ryan's stomach lurch, he decided it was time to firm his statements up some. Clear and concise *threats*, not to be misunderstood by even the lamest of the lame.

He brought the gun up and aimed it at the stranger's chest. "I'm telling you one last time. Leave my yard. Get off this street. As a matter of fact, you'd be smart to cross county lines. Maybe even state lines. Or I'm going to put two in your chest."

"You know what a *cuck* is, my man?" The stranger smirked at Ryan, hands on his hips.

"Listen, I'm giving you one last—"

"I think *you're* a *cuck* ... don't you want to know what it is?"

Ryan curled his finger around the trigger, the steel cold and slick.

"I'll tell you," the stranger said. "A *cuck* is a guy who likes to watch better looking, hung guys fuck his wife or girlfriend while he watches."

Shoot him-shoot him-shoot him!

He had only ever fired his Sig at a paper target at the range. Granted, he learned early on he was a surprisingly good shot, the heart section of the paper target usually obliterated by the time he rolled it back to inspect it. He could punch two grapefruit-size holes into the man's chest. But he couldn't. At first, he thought it could be a malfunction, the trigger sticking against his finger.

If this guy doesn't show me some kind of weapon, this whole damned thing'll turn around me afterward. He's got to show me something!

His brain, his conscience, his rational mind was the only thing sticking in that moment. It stopped him. He had this annoying habit of thinking not just three to four steps ahead of actions, but ten to twelve steps. He always thought this would help him to act as a responsible gun owner, as opposed to the other *gun nuts* who shoot first and ask questions later.

Now, Ryan was sober to the fact this posed a real danger to him and his family.

Show me something! A gun! Hell, a knife! I NEED YOU TO SHOW ME!

This insight.

This damnable rational mind!

Shoot him-shoot him-shoot! (that's the voice I want to listen to, goddammit)

The stranger was suddenly two feet closer to Ryan than he had been.

"I'm gonna fuck your wife in front of you if you don't tell me what happened to the fucking woodpile that's *supposed* to be behind the shed over there!"

FUCK IT!

The first shot rattled Ryan's hand like nothing he had ever experienced at the firing range. It felt different, the recoil. More intensified. Maybe the outside air? Maybe the fact he had just fired at a human being for the first time? *Who gives a shit, really!* The left side of the stranger's bulky Carhartt coat blew open, like a mouth opened wide. White cotton exploded out of the gape. The white was pure. No red.

No blood.

I nicked him.

The stranger lunged at Ryan, blotting out the soft overcast light of the Sunday afternoon. He swung an arm wide just as Ryan squeezed the trigger again. The gun fired wide as it left Ryan's hands, blasting a portion of the second floor rain gutter clear away. A snakelike cluster of condensed dead leaves dumped out of the opening and plopped down onto the patio like a dead body. The Sig Sauer landed next to the swing set ladder leading up to the top of a small slide. Ryan drove his knee up into what he could only hope was the man's groin. His kneecap struck the stranger much lower. Ryan tried to roll over underneath the man, aiming to somehow gain all fours. A move stored in muscle memory from his time on the middle school wrestling squad. The stranger worked his other arm much like the first, as a blunt club by which to bash Ryan in the side of the head. Ryan dumped down onto his stomach, his vision going in and out of focus.

He felt the weight descend on him even before he smelled the grass and the dirt pushing up his nose as the stranger drove his face down into the earth. Faintly, and it could have been a hallucination much like the spots and stars spinning and spiraling before his eyes, Ryan swore he could hear his wife calling down from the second floor window. Screaming his name. *Leave him alone! Please don't hurt my husband!* Real or imagined, the next thing he felt was not so much imaginary as it was shocking in its intention the moment he felt it enter just below his left shoulder blade.

This gave way immediately to a bigger, blacker pain which fanned outward from the point of initial contact. Then, a deadening of the area, muscles unresponsive. Wet and sloshing. Ryan moved to try and flip himself over again. Something punctured or popped inside his chest, instantly immobilizing him.

A knife in my back.

Deep. Hilt-deep.

I'm going to die.

"Your wife'll know," the stranger said, straddling Ryan as he inched the blade deeper and deeper into the groove it had created. "Your children, maybe. You don't know shit. That's why you're dying right now. And … I *am* gonna *fuck your wife.* So, take that with you on your way down, my man …"

Ryan dug his fingernails into the ground, burrowing.

Burrowing.

"Don't … please … just … stop …"

Then, his fingers stopped, poised inside the rivets of dug-up dirt. He thought he was begging for his life long after his brain shut down, like a record player needle whinnying to a slow, terrible stop.

82. PASSION OF THE RILEYS

Henry left Cynthia Riley tied to the bedposts of the bed she had shared with her husband for eleven years and twenty days. Actually, nineteen and a half days, to be exact. Before everything changed. For Ryan, left in a crumpled heap on the frozen grass in the backyard. For Cynthia, the stranger's semen drying on her inner thigh as she lay bound and gagged. For her children, both stowed away in the downstairs coat closet with a run of rope tied around the handles until the young boy and girl could do nothing more than rattle the wooden foldaway doors inside their tracks. The Rileys were a fractured family, but not broken.

Cynthia would not allow for the fracture to break.

She would not let this man hurt her children. He had done his worst to her. *Death would have been better than rape!* She knew that now. Cynthia had never been violated before, but she knew it was all about power and nothing to do with lust. Nothing like what her husband had experienced in his final moments before the stranger overpowered him.

The stranger hovered just outside the master bedroom. He was on the phone. Having some difficulty, from what she could hear. A disagreement. She knew his name because he had forced her to beg for it, to call it out like someone in the throes of ecstasy. Henry, *big bad Henry*, was coming unglued. Getting scared. He would get sloppy.

This is our house, and I'm going to kill you! Some way! Somehow, I'm going to fuck *you right back, and harder than you could ever do it to me!*

For now, Cynthia listened and bit back the pain.

Henry crossed in front of the master bedroom door, sneaking a twitchy look inside at the half-naked woman on the bed tied to the bedpost, before trudging past. To and fro. Pacing.

"—the guy was a great shot," Henry hissed into the phone. "I only got a quick look at him, but he was wearing all black. Looked like SWAT ... but if he was ... then ... that's what I'm trying to say ... he wouldn't have stormed the house back there by himself. He woulda' come with a whole fleet and a shitload of *goodnight-nurse* artillery, you know what I mean?"

Silence.

Cynthia tried the twine around her wrist, wriggling against it. It only dug deeper divots into her skin.

"—*shitting me*? We got Rambo's *dog?* You sure know how to pick em', don't you?"

Silence.

"But it might not be the guy from the newspaper. Could just be a ... fuck ... *fuck ... I don't know who the else he could be!* What the hell have you got us into? You got Bluto dead! I cut up a father of two, and I ain't never killed anybody before. What are you doing to *me?* I got a family here in *your house that ain't your house anymore* ... yeah ... that's *right* ... and you still haven't told me what to do with them?"

You knew what you wanted to do to me before you even checked in with your boss, now isn't that right? Cynthia could only assume Henry added rape to the agenda on his own. The Bitch-Boy could somehow do some thinking on his own, it turned out.

"No—NO THEY DON'T KNOW WHAT THE FUCK I'M TALKING ABOUT—I TOLD YOU!"

Henry charged back into the bedroom. He stalked towards the bed, seized her by the chin and squeezed. "Bitch, what happened to the woodpile behind your shed? I'm only going to ask you one more time, and then I'm going to start dissecting your pretty ass!"

Tell him what he wants to know. Buy yourself more time. Give him something to do. Some digging.

428

"When–when we first moved in … there-there *was* a woodpile there, *okay?* A—and there was a big nest of wolf spiders inside the pile. They kept coming into the house and scaring the children! Ryan had the pile removed by some landscapers about a year back. No more … wolf spiders."

Henry put the phone back up to his ear. "You hear that? And there isn't any bare earth where the pile would've been. Nothing to mark the spot. Now you know the backside of the shed is easily about fifteen feet wide, so *now what*? Where was the pile when you lived here? You … *you … you fucking serious?* You're going to have to *show me?* SHOW ME? What are you, fucking Blackbeard or something? Just … just *tell me … nevermind …* I'm going to start digging back there after I get them all down the basement. No … I'm not going to do *that … you want them dead, you kill them.* You got me, Tarlick? Just get here, will you? I got a bad feeling, like there's something I don't know, like the dog's owner's already fucking here … paranoid? … we'll see!"

Henry kicked the side of the bed. Cynthia bared her teeth at him like a feral animal.

He leaned in so close she could smell the menthol cigarettes and black coffee on his breath. "Tell me I'm the biggest you ever had. Tell me it hurt going in."

Cynthia turned her eyes to the bedroom windows. *I'm not going to cry. Fuck him!*

Henry's hand shot out and took hold of her chin once more. He wrenched her face towards his and locked eyes. "I'm going to put you and the kids down in the basement. Now I rode you hard, it's time to hang you up wet. And the kids better behave. You better tell them the score. Then you're gonna tell me where your hubby's shovels are. Garage? Shed?"

83. TIME BOUGHT

Will Bentley parked his truck just inside the tree line of an especially dense cluster of woods after verifying the house he was after lay just beyond the wooded border. A hundred yards out, give or take. The woods closed off one cul-de-sac from another to the left of the dark, dense forestry. A quiet neighborhood, wallowing in the sweet lethargy of a Sunday afternoon. The wintry winds were still whipping about and snapping their jaws. On the drive over, Will had actually felt it pulling his truck out of its proper driving lane.

The forest was a gift. The natural cover of trees banking the left hand perimeter of the house in question; the trunks grown so close together they provided significant camouflage despite their barren branches. He could set himself up just inside, gather some coordinates through the use of the police radar he had brought along. He had given the directions a quick and cursory glance and found the radar was fairly simple to use. It also worked up to fifty yards away from the wall and the detectable human subjects behind it. Also, the radar could detect human breath as it stirs the air in front of someone's mouth. As morbid a thought as it was, the radar would allow for Will to detect only the *living* inside the house. The dead would not emit a signature, if there were any casualties to be had.

The sudden shockwave of electric pulses in the left side of his cheek caught him off-guard for the first time in a long time.

Glad you took the radar like I advised, soldier? See, I'm gone, but I ain't so far gone!

"I'll give you that," Will conceded, rubbing his temples. The first flares of a headache were blooming on both sides of his skull. "But you need to back off so I can strategize."

Together, soldier! We work this together! If you ever needed your sergeant, it's now—

"I need to think," Will said. "Need to think. Why don't you … I don't know … slip back into the part of my mind that likes tits and ass. Hang out and pore over whatever's still lingering, and I'll call you out when I need you."

You can't distract your sergeant with pussy, soldier!

"Back! BACK!"

The sergeant's rebuttal split apart into something incomprehensible, and thankfully less distracting.

Will checked his watch—11:40.

He took his cell phone and thumbed open his GPS device. He brought up the most recent address he had punched in, and Jodi Dare's came up second to the address of the house just beyond the tree line. Will started the GPS routing from his present location to the Dare house in Philadelphia's Society Hill section. Fifty miles. Fifty minutes.

Fifty minutes.

Can I get it done in that amount of time?

Will Bentley decided he would have to.

He swiped the app closed and brought up a number from his recent call list.

Waited through seven rings and then started talking right over Detective Rivells.

"I'm going to tell you exactly where to find Karl Tarlick and the Dare girl." *But not my dog ... no, you'll be too late for her!*

"You're already fucking there, aren't you?"

Will hesitated. "I am."

"Mm-hmm, and what happened to the fucking *phone call* you promised to place to me once you *got it out of him*?"

"I couldn't get a signal."

"Couldn't get a ... sonofabitch—"

"It's the truth, Detective. I swear on my sergeant!"

Do what you got to do, soldier!

"And you're looking for what, Will? A medal for finally cooperating with investigators? You're going down when this is all over, and we're going to be the ones to bring it to a close. Not you! Do we understand each other? You are to *stand down,* or we will treat you as hostile right along with the rest of them!"

"If you think I'm going to do that, you haven't been listening to anything I've been saying."

"Let me make this clear as crystal for you, Will! You have *no power* in this situation. You are a private citizen who is about to get in way over his head. Then you'll be begging for police assistance. And quite possibly, emergency assistance, as well! I'm telling you to give me the address to your location, and then I want you back in Comstock, or I'm going to make sure they throw the book at you. You should be bedside with Mina right now. Not playing one-man army!"

"Listen to me," Will said. "I'm going to walk out of here with my dog. I'm making a promise to you right here and now I will neutralize the *bad actors* so by the time you get here, all you need to do is establish a perimeter and Mirandize whoever's still breathing. What I can't promise is there will be any bad guys left to read their rights to. If they present a problem, I'm going to steamroll right over them. I won't even think twice about it, Detective. But I want your word if I make good on my end with what I've just promised, you won't pursue me any further. And you won't euthanize my dog."

"Will, your dog is a cop killer. Your *dog* poses a threat to the public at large. Domestic pets have been put down for far less than what your dog's been involved with. The local precinct there will have an address any second. They're already doing a search."

"Albie's under some kind of influence. I know it sounds crazy. I do. But this is not my dog. And I guess I'm just going to have to step it up a notch."

"And I'd be willing to bet Animal Control has heard that same

431

characterization of dangerous pets time and again. But they have their directives, and I've got mine." Silence on both sides of the line.

Will's headache was starting to spread its wings across both hemispheres of his brain. Then, Detective Rivells broke the spell of silence.

"Will, I came face-to-face with your ... your *dog*. I hate to tell you this, you're your dog is not how you probably remember it. Something's come over it. In fact, when I was staring it dead in the eyes, and, by the way, Will, her eyes were completely red all the way across, I found it very difficult to believe it was ever a dog at all. It looked like some kind of ... some kind of demon—"

"*She*, dammit! Not *It, she!*"

"I'm not so sure, Will."

Remember your *directive, soldier. You're here to protect you and yours. No one else. We decided this beforehand and you put your name to it. So tell this lady where to go.*

Exactly what I'm not going to do—not at this point.

"Well, then I guess I'm going to have to further adapt things to your change of approach. You were going to safeguard my dog. Now it sounds like you wouldn't mind being the one to put a bullet in her head yourself if given the chance."

"You're way off!"

"Am I!"

"Show me some good faith! It's all I need from you!"

Rivells paused. "Will ... what is it about you and this ... this *dog?*"

"You wouldn't understand."

"Oh, I betcha' I would. I grew up in a house full of dogs, cats, and birds. My mother was quite the animal lover. She taught me how to care for all God's creatures."

"There's no time for stories or vignettes or little anecdotes which could convince you why my dog's life is worth saving," Will said, now clutching the side of his head where the throbbing of his migraine was now a force to be reckoned with. "All I can tell you is this dog is suffering from the same kind of PTSD a soldier comes home with after about four or five tours in the desert. And, that's only the part of her history I'm sure of. Her life over there is a mystery to me. I can't identify where the wound is, so damned if I can heal it. But I can tell you anything she's been doing, and I saw some of her *handiwork* ... sickened me ... but ... it would be like losing my child. It would be like someone shooting my child dead."

"All right ... all right, Will," Detective Rivells said. "I may have something."

"What do you mean?"

"Give me the address, and I'll tell you what I'm thinking."

"I–I–"

"We've got to learn how to trust each other if we're going to save anymore lives."

"Wait–wait a minute—I think I've got eyes on Karl Tarlick."

"Are you serious?"

Will ducked down in his seat, clutched the cell phone with white knuckles. He watched the slow, staggering approach of the battered brown Oldsmobile Cutlass as it rolled down the street towards Will, then cut a sharp turn into the double driveway of the house beyond the trees.

"Yes! He's here."

"Holy shit, you've got him."

"Not yet … but the address is 7238 Turling Road, Levittown, PA."

"All right, thank you, Will. We'll be there directly. Keep your eyes on him and answer me this, I read the article in the paper about your dog's coma. She just came out of it. I imagine she's been on certain medications since then which could have played a role in changing her personality. Would I be correct she's been on some form of medication? Daily medication?"

"Y-yeah," Will said. "A brain nutrient med. I forget the name of it."

He was watching the Cutlass's driver's side like a hungry hunter. It seemed like a full twenty-four hours more before the brown door cranked open. The man who emerged from the driver's side was not even close to matching what Will had expected to see when he finally laid eyes on him. This was a crawling rat fresh from a flooded sewer.

Long hair that almost completely concealed his eyes when he snuck a furtive glance all about before digging in his denim sheepskin jacket pocket for what revealed themselves by their gleam to be keys. His shoulders were as sunken as a broken clothesline and projected what Will had always been told by his mother growing up was a sense of deep insecurity. Something told Will this little man was more headstrong than his bowed shoulders would portray. He crossed to the back of the car, and the swagger of his gait was enough to prove Will's suspicions about this. This man was small, but a bulwark to be reckoned with. Short guys always overcompensate for their height. Will had even seen evidence of it in the Corps, but it was nothing he could ever relate to. He stood at a solid and secure five-ten.

Detective Rivells' voice snapped him back into the conversation. "You see him? Definite positive ID?"

"I'm looking right at him," Will said, his voice a whisper. "Got out of a Cutlass."

433

"Yes! That's him!"

"If you say so. I—"

"You were expecting someone … more?"

"It just occurred to me. If he *were* actually something more, he wouldn't have needed my dog to do all the killing. He would have been able to do it himself. Little creepy fuck!"

"So you understand what I'm saying about Alberta?"

"Yes," Will said. "You're going to float the theory the medicine had an adverse reaction."

"A gravely unfortunate reaction that was not her fault."

"Thank you."

His eyes fattened in their sockets at the sight of what he could only assume was his Albie at the end of a heavy steel chain with Creepy Fuck leading her like The Dog Whisperer. "Oh my God—"

"You see Alberta?"

"Oh. God."

"Okay-*okay*-Will, I know this is hard, and you don't want to listen to anything I'm saying to you right now, but *you have to hold yourself back!*"

Will's left hand moved to the door handle, fingers curled around it. *How does she know what I'm thinking? What I want to do right now? Because she's been through this probably more times than you could ever imagine!*

"Will, there could be bystanders outside, and if you and this maniac get into it, an innocent could get hurt! I know you've probably got a small arsenal with you, and God knows what *he* has besides your dog, or even to keep your dog in line. Please, *just listen to me, and I know this isn't going to make any sense, but I know how this goes down.* Let him go into the house."

"Let him go inside? Let him put four walls around him? Are you kidding me?"

"You've got to trust me on this! It would be better to storm the home, *not you,* but I know that's not going to stop you. But you're going to want him in a tight spot because he's going to feel less in control. As a matter of fact, he's going to feel the power slip away by degrees until he's desperate. Desperate people do stupid things. They make mistakes. And that's when— and if you tell anyone I said this I will deny it—you will do what you were trained to do in the Marines. Understood?"

He understood enough to not crank the driver's side door open as he watched Creepy Fuck lead his dog up onto the front porch. The porch spanned the length of the inside of the living room. A number of empty flowerpots were arranged here and there. A couple's swing stood in the center and swung to and fro, the wind having its way with the empty lounger. Creepy Fuck looped his end of the chain leash around of the foundational poles near the front door. He wound it round and round and drew the end through the other bindings, locking Alberta to the pole.

When the Creepy Fuck bent down and whispered something into the dog's ear, Will bit down hard and tasted blood pool on his tongue. *What are you saying to* my dog, *you sonofabitch!*

Alberta lowered her flank. Her tongue dropped out the side of her snout. Her eyes did not follow Creepy Fuck when he returned to the car in the driveway. Alberta's eyes seemed to lack any sense of concentration or focus, and her gaze drifted lazily about like a blind animal's eyes.

"Will? I'm in my car, and I'm driving to you, along with local Levittown police, SWAT, and two FBI. The murder of two police officers hit their radar pretty much right away. We'll all be there soon."

"All right—"

Jesus, look at the girl.

"I have eyes on the Dare girl now."

"Is she alive?"

"He's got her up and walking, with his arm around her waist. She's got her mouth taped. Hands bound in front of her. And ..."

This feels WRONG!

"... and I'm watching him enter the house now with Alberta and the girl. No one let him in. Looks like the door was left open for him."

"So somebody beat him there."

"Yeah, the Henry guy I heard about from the other one, Bluto."

"Bluto?"

"You heard right."

"Well, if Henry wasn't at the door to let Tarlick in with the dog and the girl, he's either busy or one of the people in the house overpowered him."

"And this street is dead. No one saw any of this freakshow."

"It's a Sunday. Early afternoon. Everyone's at Church or a flea market or a movie. Something. Laziest day of the week."

"No rest for the wicked, of course."

"Will?" Rivells said, her voice strained.

"Yeah?"

"Be gone by the time we get there. Work fast."

"What have you done with the *real* Detective Rivells, lady?"

Connection broken.

84. COREY SNELL—PRODIGAL BROTHER

Corey Snell's Uber driver didn't want to talk. For that, Corey was thankful. He was five days off the meth and two days off the bourbon, and it had been those two key ingredients which once spurred on his larger-than-life personality and slacker-chic charisma. True or not, Corey had not the will nor the way to even string sentences together. Not into anything remotely interesting or original. Corey had always prided himself on striving to be an original, and yet there he was on the way back to Levittown with his tail between his legs. Back to his hometown to move in with his sister, their two children he had never met, and Ryan Riley, *Pennsylvania's Answer to Ryan Reynolds!*

There Corey was a character in a never-released John Hughes movie, fumbling in his hash-weave wallet for the Visa credit card he was pretty sure was not maxed out. The Uber driver slid his black Ford Focus sedan along the curb outside the handsome-looking blue A-frame house. The middle-aged driver cranked the stick shift into Park and cleared his throat. He pressed a series of buttons on the digital readout mounted into the dashboard. He asked Corey to have a look at the readout, to verify the amount owed.

Corey was busy flipping through the small deck of business cards, folded receipts, a couple grocery value-shopper cards, before coming across his Visa. He slid it out and leaned forward to both hand it up to the driver and to have a look at the amount due. The ride from Philadelphia International cost him $73.25. *That card fucks me over right now, and I'm breaking for the woods over there next to sis's house.* This was not a casual, benign little thought! Not when it came to Corey Snell. He had done far worse in tighter spots than this.

The driver slid the Visa through the magnetic strip attached to his cell phone and waited.

Corey waited with a tightening in his narrow chest. He clutched his satchel up against his ribcage. He surveyed the tree line in the distance. *Is that a truck parked inside the woods there? What the fucking-fuck? Maybe key's left in the truck? Maybe the engine running? Stranger things have happened and providence isn't always such a bitch to me, so you never know!* Corey tried to see if there were any exhaust fumes pouring out of the truck's tailpipe. *My suitcase is in the trunk. Might have to part with it if it comes down to it, but Cindy'll help me get some new threads. Toiletries—*

"Mr. Snell?"

Corey snapped back. "Yeah? Sorry … somewhere else."

"You want a paper receipt, or you want it emailed?"

Thank God!

"Oh, I'll take the paper one."

The driver handed it back over his shoulder to Corey, not even craning his neck in Corey's direction. "You got your bag in the back. Come around, and I'll get it."

"Roger that, brother," Corey said, relishing the way *brother* made the driver's eyes crinkle up like foil wrap at the edges. He smiled to himself, cranked open the back door, and stepped out behind the driver who was circling around the back of the Focus towards the trunk. It was already opened wide.

Corey's eyes swept across the front of the property. There was a rusted out brown boat-of-a-vehicle parked next to the Riley family's black Honda CRV. A beauty and the beast situation if ever there was one. The big, ugly car tickled his ribs, stirred a handful of butterflies inside his stomach. *It's a hoop-dee car! I never could have predicted The Riley's know anyone poor enough to be puttering around in such a piece of shit, let alone having them over for Sunday brunch!* Then again, they were agreeable to letting Corey, Cynthia's Prodigal Brother, crash on their couch until he could find his feet again, financially and spiritually.

"Mr. Snell?" the driver barked from the rear of the vehicle. "I got a schedule to keep!"

"Oh, right-right!" Corey hurried to the rear of the car and accepted his suitcase from the driver, who had surprisingly already pulled it out of the trunk. "Thanks, man! Appreciate it!"

The driver nodded stiffly, slammed the trunk shut, and left Corey Snell standing there while he climbed back into the Focus. He idled there, clearly waiting for Corey to get his ass up onto the sidewalk. Corey's eyes had crept back to the brown Cutlass in the driveway.

It was a strange fixation, something he hadn't experienced sober anyway!

The driver honked the horn. Corey waved at the driver and moved up onto the sidewalk, satchel sagging on his left shoulder and his suitcase tugging down the right as he clutched the fifty-pound weight of personal items. He set them both down to make some adjustments. He pulled his maroon knitted cap down lower, lining up with his dark eyebrows. He pulled his fingerless gray texting gloves back, exposing more of the tips so he could maneuver and grasp his suitcase handle better. Finally, he buttoned his green army jacket, fastening the top button snugly against the soft bulge of a black scarf knotted at his throat.

All right, you suburbanoids, here I come ...

Corey gathered up his items and started to walk. He thought of trudging right up the center of the gray but full front lawn of the Riley house, then decided he wanted to have a closer look at the car in the driveway. *Don't ask me why? But ... man, I'm feeling a serious disruption in The Force just looking at the fucking thing!* A mere three feet from the trunk of the brown boat, Corey felt a strong urge to turn himself around and hit the sidewalk again. To put as much distance between himself and his sister's house as he could.

He stood there, staring at the rear of the car. The bile rose in his throat.

There were handprints slapped all over the outside of the trunk. They were everywhere. Two even curled around the bumper.

Muddy prints?

Gotta be mud ... I mean ... right?

"Corey, stop being such a puss, will you?" he told himself, and shook his head against the rapidly ascending wall of dreadful thoughts rising inside his mind. "This isn't the Spahn Ranch for god sakes!"

He straightened up and strode past the car, still shaking his head. He stepped up onto the front porch. Reached to ring the doorbell—

Something cold and hard pressed into the back of his head, imprinting in the wool of his cap.

A voice came from behind him, hushed and affectless. "Don't turn around. Just back up as fast as you can. I'll guide you."

"What the—"

"You have no idea how close you just came. Move it. Come on."

Corey did as he was told, flinching as the stranger behind him took him by his right shoulder and guided him back down off the porch. Back across the driveway. Then, into the grass along the right side of the Riley house.

Towards the woods.

"What did I just come *close to?*" Corey managed. "At least tell me that much."

"Back into the tree line and then you can turn around. I'm serious."

Corey felt his feet crunch down into dead leaves and tangled underbrush. He felt the stranger's hand fall away from his shoulder. He turned around and saw a man standing there in front of him, dressed all in black. Roughly Corey's height with a thicker, far more muscular build that filled out the black fatigues he was wearing. Black hair stood up in zig-zag spikes along his head, and he looked more punk rock than commando. A graying beard rode all the way up past the divots of his sunken cheekbones. Green eyes lit with razor-sharp focus. The thing the stranger had pressed into the back of Corey's head dangled down by the man's hip. A hefty, lethal looking handgun.

"What's your name," the stranger asked

"Corey."

"I'm Will."

"Will, does this … does this have something to do with the shitty ass heap of metal parked in the driveway of my sister's house?"

Will's lips twitched at this. "Everything to do with it."

Then he brought Corey Snell into the fold. Just like that.

85. A HOUSE ONLY EVER REALLY HAS ONE OWNER

"Henry, why don't you tell me what it is you're looking for, huh?"

Henry found Karl Tarlick's false, affected twang to be just about the most annoying thing he could think of right then. If he hadn't wanted out of the halfway house and clear away from its moderator who propositioned him for some off-the-record *suck-offs* in his car, Henry might have done his full time and then found his way into maybe tapping some of his old acquaintances for an apprenticeship into the steamfitters union. It all went to shit the first time he turned down Mr. Uppington's advances, and nearly threatened him with an unmerciful beating. *Shit, man, I mean is everyone in the penal system a perv? It's looking more and more like a safe haven for these bastards and their power! Reminds me of the priesthood …*

"Where'd you stash the … people?" Karl pressed, standing just inside the entrance to the family garage. "Time to catch me up, Henry."

"I'm looking for a fucking shovel and a pickaxe if they got one," Henry said, a sting in his voice. "The wife wouldn't tell me shit."

"How come?"

"Sore at me, I guess." The smell of engine oil and cement reminded Henry of his time working on cycles in a Philly repair shop in Fishtown. The guys who worked there were down-to-earth, didn't put on fake-ass accents, and devoted zero minutes to any kind of bullshit. They also didn't ask a whole lot of questions. They trusted he knew what went where on a bike, what it needed. Parts and labor costs. *Karl Tarlick is asking more questions, and I can't remember the last time he* answered *any of mine, so I think I'll let him stew there. Him and that fucking creepy ass dog.*

The dog was at Karl Tarlick's side. Henry didn't even have to turn around to know so.

hudda-hudda-hudda-hudda.

"You know, that dog smells like a thousand asses?" Henry threw a cursory glance over his shoulder, still digging around inside a big plastic container that sprouted lawn tools like a leaf rake, tiller, and bulged with a stack of blue plastic tarps. Somewhere in there, tucked away, Henry knew he'd find a shovel at the very least. Then, once he laid hands on it, he would demand Karl accompany him into the backyard and show exactly where the fucking money was buried. If Karl held back, Henry knew he'd have no hesitation swiping the business end of the shovel across Karl's skull. Then, the dog's skull, of course.

"That's no way to talk about our guest of honor, Henry." Karl tugged on the chain in his hands. The dog's tongue slapped against the top of her snout and then dropped back down. "Anybody see you come in? You know of?"

hudda-hudda-hudda-hudda.

"Not that I know of," Henry snapped. He felt his hands graze something that felt like it could have been a gardening tool, one of those hand shovels. "The man of the house found me out in the yard. I tried to stay out of sight while I had a look behind the shed, but somehow they caught a glimpse of me inside. Next thing you know, the big bad *man of the house* comes out pointing a gun at me across the yard. These houses are set pretty far apart, so no worries." Henry sniggered. "I knew the minute I laid eyes on him with that piece of steel in his hands, he was scared shitless about having to actually fire the damned thing at me."

"You coulda' been wrong. You rush him, I guess? That coulda' gone wrong, and then we would have had a whole other thing going on here. Something involving a cop telling me to 'watch my head' as he guides me down into the back seat of his police car. You should know I don't like not getting closure. It's an imbalance. It turns me out. It makes me sick inside, and then people pay for it. You would've had to pay out the ass, Henry."

"That so? You think it's really all that productive waxing over what *could have been* instead of what is?"

"Where's the guy's body?"

"Down basement," Henry said. "I strung him up by the wrists along the water pipe. Right between his wife and the two kids."

"They dead too?"

"Nope," Henry said, laying hands on a small hand-held sickle tool he immediately wrenched out from inside the big plastic container. He turned around, wielding the item like he meant to bury its four rusted spikes in the

440

nearest brain. "Just the dad. I hung him between them to send a message. To keep them in line. You know, the way a king impales his enemies' heads on the front gate spikes leading into his kingdom. *This'll be you if you put up any kind of fight.* You know?"

"Well, you're right," Karl said. "See, they thought all this time they were *actually* home. That this was their place. All this time they were only visiting. Squatters. If there's one thing I know, a home only ever really has *one,* and I mean *only* one, owner its whole existence. The people who lay their heads down inside it once its built. Everyone who comes after … squatters. Like I said." He paused, shook his head, and added, "You mentioned they changed things behind the shed in the backyard?"

"They did, man. It's why I'm going to need you to show me where exactly your mother buried her money. I'm going to dig it up while you do your thing with the girl … and wrap things up with the family. After all … squatters are lawbreakers. They ought to be punished right?" *That's it! Tell the little creep exactly what he wants to hear! Corroborate! Then get him to show you where the money is and ... well, you and Bluto had your plans for Karl Tarlick once he handed over your share of the money. Minus Bluto, you're just going to have to tie the knot up yourself. But, it won't be much of a challenge for you ... especially if you have to listen to him yap for much longer.*

"I'm going to make good on that," Karl said. "Don't worry. So long as no one saw you come in, so far as you can tell, we don't have to hurry it along."

"You're forgetting about something. Some*one*, Karl."

"Who? What's that?"

Henry cocked his head, his brow knitting downward into a divot of confusion. *You serious?* "You serious? What about the fucking commando dude who surprised us at the house back in New Castle? You don't think he got something out of Bluto? Pulled some kind of advanced interrogation shit maybe? I'm telling you, this guy looked like Special Ops with the shit he was wearing. He was not fucking around. And you say *that's* his *dog?* Fuck me, dude! *Who?* Really? You're going to have to do better than that!"

"I think it's about time I pull the weed, Henry."

"What? What are you talking about?"

"The one you got up your ass. The one that's got you talking to me like I'm one of your jailhouse bitches back in Berrysburg Detentional." Karl jiggled the chain, and the dog's back went rigid. "I'll do it, if it's got to be done. But I thought we might remain friends when all this was said and done. My best girl let me down. Sold me out. I don't know how I'd handle it if my best man were to turn around and give me the same kind of shit. So I'm asking, we gonna part friends, or is the house going to become some kind of Thunderdome for the two of us where *two men enter and one man leaves*?"

"Karl—"

"You ever see that movie? Mel Gibson? Classic!"

Henry looked down at the dog. The animal stood still as a statue. "What are you trying to say here, man? You *know* you need me in this until the end just as much as I need you. We split apart instead of pooling our resources, we're done. I'm just looking for my share, and you can't blame me for being a little … a bit put off by the fact the yard's been fucking redone."

Karl smirked, crossed the garage to where a wooden panel was nailed into the wall. A trike and a Huffy dangled from a pair of plastic hangers mounted into the wood. He reached out, gripped the oversized plastic front wheel of the Huffy, spun it. Stepped back, stared at the sparkling spokes until it stopped dead. Then, he regarded the entire display before him. "You see the wood board nailed up there? The one these bikes are hanging from? My daddy put it up when we lived here! And … they kept it the way it was. They *kept* it. They coulda' ripped it down and just lined up the bikes along the rear wall or something."

Henry tapped the trowel against his hip. "Why's that?"

"Because someone here whispered in their ear or … or maybe they come into one of their dreams. Whispered some things ought to stay the same way they were before. If it ain't broke, don't fix it just because you want to say you done it, right? Damn … I think that's what happened. Probably Blaise. She got in the daddy or the momma's ear when they weren't expecting it and just sort of … I don't know … blew a little bit of influence into their ear. And damned if it didn't have *some* influence." Karl's eyes took on an empty, airy gaze, fixed upon nothing in particular. "I wonder if they know anything about the false chimney downstairs. What's … shit, what's behind it? I wonder … if they *fucked* with it or left it alone."

A woman's scream came from inside the house. Henry jerked in spite of himself. *Karl jumped too. Motherfucker was just as spooked!* But Henry hadn't seen any such thing. Not even so much as a rattle of the chain showing the dog or the man had jumped in any way.

"That's your girl down basement, Henry," Karl said, as if relegating responsibility. "Mine has her mouth gagged and taped. Maybe we should see to her and the kids."

"In a minute."

"Then, go tell your bitch to shut up, Henry."

"All right," Henry said, stalking across the cracked cement of the garage and ascending back up into the foyer. He threw open the door across the hall, leaned in, shouted, "SHUT UP, BITCH!*"* This was met with the tinkling murmur of a child's crying. "That's better!" He slammed the basement door shut.

When Henry turned around, Karl and the dog were practically upon him.

Mere inches away.

huddahuddahuddahuddahudda ... hudda ...

Karl laid a hand on Henry's shoulder. "I got a skinny, disease-spreading whore on the living room floor I need your help with carrying down into the cellar. And as far as the folks downstairs being *my people*? I don't want any parts of them unless they get in my way. They're all yours. I don't have any hand or part in killing them. That's all ... eh, extra-curricular. Bad enough I was forced off course having to let the dog kill two cops. This dog should only have a taste for whore-flesh. Nothing else."

Whore-flesh. Aren't they all *whores when the lights go out?*

"Sure," Henry said. "Then I gotta think about this. They can identify us 's the problem." He paused. Smiled broadly like the sun had just come up behind his brain. "I'm definitely going to take a second helping of the mother's pie no matter what I decide." Henry, already sensing the blood as it began its mad rush downward into his lap, turned and flung the door to the basement open again.

Karl did not follow him down.

"You ... you took ... *a helping*? Henry?" Karl clutched the chain so tight it carved links into the palm of his hand. He tasted the words, whispering them. As the blood was rushing into Henry's erection, Karl's blood flooded his cheeks and burned them. "A *helping?"* Karl felt his voice rise to more of a trill, trembling in the back of his throat. "Henry?" Louder. "*HENRY!"*

When Henry tramped back up the basement's cement stairs, he nearly bounded right into Karl, who was still standing his ground in the hallway and filling the space with the dog beside him. "Jesus Christ man! Scared the shit out of me—"

"I've got the girl in the living room on my own. Don't worry about her. I'll ... I'll bring her down myself. You just tend to the family downstairs. And ... *remind* them this is *not* their home. It's mine. It was always mine. You understand?"

"I'll drill it into their heads ... somehow."

"Use a *real* drill if any of them have a hard time *getting* it, Henry. I'll be right down with the whore."

They stood there studying one another until Henry leered with a mouthful of what looked like too many teeth and bounded back down into the basement. His entrance was marked by the shriek of both the mother and the little girl. The boy must have spent the short time left alone down there to grow somewhat used to the fact he was now the man of the house and protector of the homestead. Karl made his way up the steps and thought he heard the boy say "I'm gonna fucking kill you, dickbag!"

Karl strode into the living room on what felt like stilted legs. He had felt the heady wash of nostalgia upon entering the house, but right then it was a full-on assault to his senses as his eyes crept from one corner of the room to the next. Faded memories of a child-size, red-varnished rocking chair his parents called the "Baddie Chair." Whenever he or Blaise misbe-haved, which mostly involved speaking out of turn at the dinner table, they were confined to the "Baddie Chair" for an hour, and no one else in the house was permitted to speak to them or even acknowledge their presence. Karl remembered his time in the chair as some of the most excruciating blocks of time he'd ever experienced (yes, even worse than his term served in Ber-rysburg). It felt like he had been erased from existence. Smudged out by the Great Hand of an unmerciful God. The chair, of course, was gone. Had most likely been broken down at some point and given to the fire or trash truck. He was thankful. Still, this memory caused a lag in his attention.

Then he heard the girl struggling on the narrow carpeted area be-tween glass coffee table and the foot of the maroon sofa. Jodi Dare was rolling back and forth, butting up against the table and the sofa like a rat in a cage with her hands and feet bound up tight in twine. She screamed a mut-ed, incomprehensible noise against her gagged and duct-taped mouth. Her blonde hair had gone fuzzy as it rubbed itself frizzy against the carpeting.

Karl moved in, straddled her across her tightly wound midsection. He snatched at her chin and snagged it between his fingers. He held it still, but the girl's blue eyes still bulged at the sound of the screaming and crying filtering up from the basement in terrible fits and starts.

"Ssh-ssh-*sssssshhhhhh*—I gotta talk to you," Karl said, in an eerily doting tone. "We gotta talk to each other. I'm gonna take off your gag, but you gotta promise me … *promise* ... *me* ... you won't go apeshit like the ones downstairs. You keep yourself calm and cool and we can have our-selves a quick back and forth. It'll be worth your while."

But Jodi Dare only knew how to strain and pull against the hold of Karl's hands on her chin. He felt the resistance through the tips of his fingers. Her eyes were so big in the sockets Karl thought they would pop out of her face like olive pits.

Karl bent down, pressing his face into hers. His voice was a teakettle hiss right before the whistle. "I'm trying to tell you I changed my mind. I'm changing teams. *Your* with *me! You understand?* You can be on *my team* now! Do you want that? Do you?"

Then, as if a switch was thrown, Jodi was trying to nod. Karl loosened his grip on her chin, allowing her the room to make the affirmative movement.

"All right, then. I'm gonna take off the gag. Remember? Quiet."

Jodi's body went rigid.

Karl peeled back the duct tape from her mouth. He plucked out the dirty oil rag he found in the trunk, under the spare tire. Jodi Dare's head sprang up off the carpet as she coughed and spit. Trying to lose the taste of 10W-30 motor oil permeating all the way to the back of her throat.

"Ssh-ssh-*sssssshhhhh-shhh*—we gotta get on this now, so listen up. You haven't met Henry yet, but I can predict the two of you aren't gonna get along. Hell, *I* can barely stomach to look at the *rapist sonofabitch*. I'll tell you what, I wish I could put him in the Baddie Chair so we could all just forget about him. Forget he exists. It'd kill him. Guy like Henry ... he *needs to be known*. He's one of the *people who needs people*. He's not like you and me. I can see about you. You like to be alone. You like your thoughts and your feelings because you know they're good company. That's why I want you on my team. So ... we're gonna play a little trick on Henry. You help me out with it, you play nice ... and I'll let you go."

"I don't believe you."

Karl's seized her by the chin, fingers like pincers. "What do you got to lose? You do this ... I won't feed you to my dog. You tell me? You want to be shitted out later by a mutt, or you wanna walk out the front door?"

Lines of fear sprang across Jodi's brow.

Karl sat up, still straddling her and holding fast to the chain leash containing the dog. The animal had been standing beside the sofa, stoic and panting. Karl folded his arms like a truculent child.

"I'll wait."

86. THE BUNDLE

Will Bentley was worried the towheaded beach dude who said his name was Corey would need a second rundown of what was happening in his sister's house just beyond the trees. He had given Corey what he considered to be enough time to process what Will had just explained to him, had even stood by for an additional minute or two while Corey paced back and forth through the leaves, tossing them up behind him as his heels fell and then lifted violently. He'd heard the beginning of what might have been tears building in the young man's eyes as he asked the beginnings of questions only to abandon them.

Will licked his chapped bottom lip where the skin had cracked and said in a low, but firm voice, "We don't have time for another explanation. I know this is a lot for you to process, but you have to man up, and you have to do it fast. I need your help if I'm going to get into the house without somebody dying who has no business dying today. You get me?"

Corey stopped pacing, patted down his army jacket breast pocket and slid a crumpled pack of Winstons out, along with a lighter featuring a Jimi Hendrix "Are You Experienced" miniature mural wrapped around its cylinder. He got a cigarette going with two trembling fingers. "We got no idea what the hell is happening in there. Could be anything! That's my sister inside … RJ … little Ava … fuck."

"Now you're here, I've got a better chance of pulling this off without any innocent people getting hurt. I was going to pull the whole load myself. The odds are in our favor now. You'll be my eyes, right here. I'm going to give you a crash course in how to use the police radar device I have. It uses sonar to see through walls. You'll have x-ray eyes. Like some kind of surfer Superman."

Will lowered the black baseball bag off his shoulder. He moved it into Corey's view, unzipped it, and brought out the army green handheld police radar device. Will read Corey's gaze as a question unspoken, and answered it for him.

"They'll let you see anyone, any of their movements, and what their locations are inside the house. Up to fifty yards. It can see through wood, steel, even down into the ground up to three feet in density."

Corey pinched off his cigarette, then accepted the handheld device and turned it over and over in his hands.

"Shit, you're right. Like Superman. Looking through walls."

"So I'm going to know how many are in there and where before I enter. I won't necessarily know whose who, but you can give me coordinates. They'll appear as blips on the screen there. Like a sonar reading." Will dug deeper into the bag, brought out twin CBs that mount to one's collar. He handed one to Corey. "Snap one of these onto your jacket lapel. We can communicate this way. You'll give me all the coordinates you can detect.

Good deal?"

"Y-Yeah. What if I … fuck up? Get you ambushed?"

"There'll be a diversion. To help clear the way and distract the men inside. Don't worry about what it'll be. Just pray it'll work. Now give me a minute."

Will rummaged in the baseball bag on the ground and brought out his gear piece by piece. Before anything, he loaded three out of four of his weapons, racked a bullet into each chamber, and then set their safeties on. The situation didn't call for the Blasé Sniper Rifle and he decided to forego it. He strapped the Beretta into his shoulder holster. He secured the .357 Magnum to his ankle. He led with his Glock out before him. He left the grenades behind as well. No call for them either as far as he could tell.

Lastly, Will slipped the bundle from the veterinary hospital out of the bag and tucked it inside his flak jacket. He zipped it up all the way.

The bundle was cold against his chest. He thought he felt it lurch, exhale against him, and it nearly split his mind in half.

When Will turned his attention to Corey once more, he discovered the young man had shed some of the palsy in his hands. "You a little better?"

"I dunno. Man, just … show me how to use this stuff. I don't want to fuck this up. It would be nice to be of some use. Not to mention … what would you have done if I didn't come along?"

The left side of Will's cheek lit up with an intense static sensation.

Don't mention me, or I swear you will regret it, soldier! You came damn close to outing me at that stupid meet-and-greet, but you're not gonna make the mistake here! Not with this beach bum junkie hippie asshole! Not here! No way! Sergeant Karns voice was blistering in its anger. Karns wanted out so badly, to own a body and to move that body. To swing his arms in a tantrum. It was obvious. *We would have been just fine* without *this Flower Child, and if you think for one second this boy ain't gonna get your head blown off or cut off then you're more whackadoo than I ever could've imagined! Send him away now, and we'll do it ourselves! This is your sergeant, and I am giving you a direct order!*

"Somehow I would have managed," Will said. "I planned on taking a quick reading with the radar there *before* going inside and hoping their coordinates wouldn't change that much by the time I breached. But judging by the number of people inside, it would have been too many variables for something not to shift. To maybe turn things against me when it's too late to turn back and regroup."

Will explained the functions of the police radar device in a calm, professorial manner. When Corey seemed comfortable enough with how it worked, Will told him to scan the woods all around them. "Hold it out in front of you," Will said, "and watch the screen. If there's any wildlife within the reach of the radar, they'll show up as a blip. Those circles fanning out from the edges of the screen over and over like that? The animal's mass will interrupt their signals. What you'll see are these interruptions. They're the animals. The people. Anything and anyone breathing. Clear?"

Corey held the radar out before him. He turned in slow revolutions, eyes fixed upon the screen. "There's something over there." He waved his hand towards the deeper section of trees. "Something on the ground ... there. *Right there!*" Corey jabbed an index finger towards a thick piling of leaves and underbrush. "Inside there. Hiding."

"I'm not surprised. This is more ruckus than they're probably used to. You can sit or you can stretch out on your stomach, just as long as your CB isn't getting crushed against your lapel."

"I'll sit. Don't feel like eating dirt, man." Corey lowered himself down into the leaves and the brambles.

"Now, I want you to aim it at the house. Move it around a little bit until you pick up some shapes inside."

Corey slowly panned the device from left to right. Back and forth. Over and over.

Will leaned in, checking the screen. "What's the matter?"

"I-I ... it's not picking anything up. You sure they're inside?"

Will bit his bottom lip, regained his composure. "I'm sure," he said, flatly. "All right. That can only mean the radar's reach isn't what it's supposed to be."

"What happened to *fifty feet*?" Corey wheeled on Will, his brow drawn downward.

"Listen to me, Corey. We've already taken up far too much time with this then I'm comfortable with. Change of plans now. You're going to have to stand right next to the house and hold the radar up against the siding. It's the only way we're going to get a dependable read."

"You want me *that close*? Are you shitting me?"

"I'll come with you," Will told him. "And I'll be armed. Soon as we verify the radar is working and it can detect the people inside I'm going to head in, and you're going to follow the shapes on the screen. They move out of your reach, you move with them. You should be able to keep a read on them at all times. And you're going to keep me in the loop as far as how many are in my proximity. I'll make a quick, sporadic movement when I get in there so you'll be able to differentiate which shape is me. Are we good?"

Corey's face was washed out. After a short time, he nodded his head rather stiffly and licked his dry lips back to a shine.

Will clamped a hand on Corey's shoulder. "All right, let's cross the yard. Stay behind me until we reach the side of the house."

They broke from the forest. Will bounded across the gray grass in a hunch, and Corey adopted the same stance like a child imitating their older sibling. In twenty or so paces, they gathered along the side of the house in a low huddle. Without having to be told, Corey pressed the flat side of the radar against the rib-like bumps of the siding.

Together, they watched the screen in anticipation.

The shapes materialized on the screen like magic.

Corey's breathing slowed somewhat. "Looks like … five … down the basement right here at our feet. Yeah … five. One of them looks like they're walking on air and lowering themselves down to the ground … oh, wait … they're walking downstairs into the basement."

"All right," Will said. "Move it up until it's at eye level. That'll show us the first floor."

"How are we going to get a read on the second floor?"

"We can't. It's going to be one big blind spot. Nothing we can do about it."

"Shit. I got eyes on someone else, man. Standing right near … shit … I don't even understand what I'm seeing here. None of this shit makes *any sense!*"

"What? Come on!"

Pause. "It looks like two masses are—I dunno—bouncing off each other over and over. Someone is … sitting *on top* of someone else. Either that, or a couple people inside are … you know. Either way, they're both moving. Looks fucking weird. Like they're struggling on the ground. Wrestling."

"I doubt they're wrestling, kid," Will said. "The one on top is dominating the one on bottom. Keep looking. You see anyone else on the first floor?"

"No one else."

"All right, seven inside. Including Albie. I won't know which one is her until I get in there. We got four down the basement. Three on the first floor." He took a deep breath, squeezed the grip of his Glock. "Don't leave your post. Stay on the side of the house unless I radio you otherwise. I'm heading in by way of the back door."

Corey swabbed at his runny nose and nodded. "I'll wait to hear from you. I'll stay here. Promise, man."

But Will was already on the move.

449

87. RUSE

Karl could sense how surprised the girl was when he cut most of the twine away from her wrists. Not all of it. That was part of the plan. Before he did it, he warned her the dog was under his command, and he taught the animal certain prompts to have it at her throat in an instant, ripping away her windpipe faster than a child tearing wrapping paper away from a Christmas present. Jodi took one look at the dog, with its red-clotted fur and empty, crimson eyes as it bit at its flank with a strange ferocity, and nodded her assent. She held her hands in the same position they had been tied into moments before.

Jodi's eyes flashed with water. "You'll *really* let me go? You promise—"

She flinched when Karl scooped her up and draped her over his shoulder. Jodi let her body go limp. Karl reminded her to keep her wrists together to hold the now-compromised twine around them in place. He moved towards the entrance to the basement stairwell. The dog was captivated and thoroughly distracted by the rending of its own flesh. Karl could see as he moved past her she had actually opened up a considerable wound in her back. Blood slowly oozed from the circular bitemark.

"I'm going to slip a knife into the back of your pants like I said. You cover it with your shirt. You won't know it until you feel the cold steel against your spine. Then, you'll know for sure. I'll put it there right before you need to use it. You'll know when because I'll turn my head to the left, like I seen something out of the corner of my eye. Watch for it then grab for the knife, and do what I said. I'd do it myself, but Henry already doesn't trust me. He'd see me coming a mile away."

Karl heard the screeching sound of the little girl Henry had hog-tied to a water pipe down basement. The sounds she was making while Henry attempted God-knows-what called the pale, freckled face of Karl's sister Blaise to mind. Her features bled into his brainpan, forming into a sight which weakened his knees momentarily. He couldn't abide another second of the sound. The distress call.

Enough's enough.

"Henry! Turns out I *do* need a little help with this one up here! Fuckin' live one! Like trying to hold smoke! I'm at the top of the stairs!"

"Knew you couldn't do it alone!" Henry called up the stairwell. "What're you, a buck twenty-five soaking wet, Karl?"

Karl sucked the inside of his right cheek. He lowered the girl off his shoulders, held her before him by the shoulders so he could look her dead in the eyes for some confirmation, and pressed her down onto her knees. Karl took her by the wrists, held her. Jodi started to struggle against him, writhing against his leg and pretending to bite at his hands. *Making a good go of it*, Karl had to admit.

Just the kind of show that pressed Henry into quick motion when he saw the girl on the ground pitching a fit. He wrestled her out of Karl's loose grip. He forced her onto her back, the girl's body stretched out at a downward angle along the stairwell. The wooden lips of the steps jutted upward into her spine, and she cried out. Henry tightened his grip on her. He spit a thick wad of yellow phlegm into her mouth when she opened it to scream. Jodi turned her head aside, spitting and gagging.

Karl laughed at the gesture. "I'm gonna take her around the knees. Let me get around her and lift her up."

"Do what you got to do."

Karl slipped alongside her, taking the steps carefully as he did so. He slid his arms around her knees, bore her up, and slid the knife down into the back hem of her pants.

She felt it. The girl snuck a quick, furtive glance up at Karl, then continued to struggle.

They made a stiff, unsteady go of carrying the girl down the stairwell that wound around a wall before it descended fully into the cold, cement basement. Karl supplied the *stiff* and *unsteady* aspect of the haul, pulling against Henry's pull and grunting the whole way. They touched down on the cement floor of the basement. Karl could hear the other captives down there with them, but averted his eyes and tried desperately to shut out their cries and screams. They were not a part of his plans.

Granted, he would have to deal with them in the end, but that was for later.

"Thanks, Henry," Karl muttered.

Henry lowered his end and turned away to tend to the screaming little girl behind him, who was praying the *Hail Mary* at her mother's instruction.

The girl ripped her wrists free. The twine snapped and fell away.

She looked at Karl, who had turned his head to the left.

The Dare girl seized the knife tucked into the back of her pants, rolled over onto her knees, and stood up behind Henry.

She reached around and carved a lopsided smile across Henry's throat.

The Rileys erupted into a cacophony of heartrending screams. Henry's carotid blood fanned across the little girl's face. Mother and daughter burst into maniacal tears. Henry grabbed for his throat with both hands and affected what amounted to a half turn before his legs gave out, and he folded over onto the cold cement floor. His fingers clawed at the gushing line carved into his throat. His mouth worked, producing a sickly drowning-out-of-water *"Gwaaaaahhhhhhh-gaaaaawaaaahhh"*

Karl stepped up and leaned over Henry, hands planted on his narrow, bony hips. His eyes trained on Henry as he bled out, Karl addressed Cynthia Riley. "He wasn't supposed to violate you, ma'am. Wasn't part of the plan. Once he told me what he did to you, I decided he had to die. I can't tolerate a rapist. Otherwise, nothing I've done up until now would make any goddamn sense. I'm trying to *punish* a rapist. I never wanted one on my team. I apologize for him. I hope you can forgive me."

When Jodi found her sense of balance and her faculties returned, she turned on Karl. "I want to go now. You promised. I'm going …"

88. TRIGGERED

"How am I looking, Corey?" Will offered an obligatory wave as he stepped up onto the wooden deck adjoining the back of the house. He doubted the motion would show up with any clearness on the small radar screen, but it was worth a shot. "Do I have a clear path? I'm coming up on the back door."

A brief pause, then a soft crackling of static before Corey's voice bled through the CB. "There's only one left on the first floor. Someone came upstairs, and then it looked like three of them moved back downstairs again. And, Will? I got a feeling about the one shape still on the first floor. Call it a hunch. Something about the way their moving around. It could be your dog. Don't hold me to that, though. If anything changes, I'll give you a holler. Over."

Will thumbed down the CB volume at his throat, then approached the back door head-on in a squat. He was hoping for the absence of a deadbolt, something more flimsy like one of those cheap bronze jobs from Home Depot with an ornate handle and a locking mechanism which couldn't confound a two year old. Eyeballing the slat between the door and the jamb, Will found his hopes dashed. Nothing he could do to snap through a lock like that. If he had to (and this was a last resort as well as a bad idea) Will would crash through the door with the sole of his steel-tip boots. Just like he'd done to countless bolted doors inside the seemingly endless miles of hovels and abandoned buildings along the Gaza Strip.

He squat-walked along the rear of the house. He had to skirt a bulky green sandbox in the shape of a turtle before he found himself standing before a pair of regular-sized windows facing out onto the rear yard. They were curtained with a crème-colored window dressing. He was free to stand, if only halfway. *Okay, kids live here. Corey told me that much. It's my hope maybe one of them opened the window and the screen. Then they shut it and forgot to latch it. But ... if Dad's smart, he's the kind of guy who checks all the windows and the doors are locked and latched before even thinking about going to bed for the night. Its what my stepdad always did at our house. Hell, it was a like an OCD thing for him. All depends—*

He slipped his fingertips into the narrow divot between the screen and its frame. He inched the long tips of his fingernails, thankfully neglected for a few weeks, and felt them lodge beneath the screen's bottom edge. Now or never. Will lifted with his fingernails. The screen gave with surprising ease and when he garnered enough of an opening, Will slipped his fingers all the way under and slid the screen open all the way. It offered an obnoxious, but instantaneous squeak that made Will bite his bottom lip. Then, it jammed.

No sound of footfalls within, angry and aggressive. No belligerent screams of murder.

The window. Divine Providence. Come on, God! I tried to save one of your guys and it almost cost me and my dog our lives! I tried, though. Help me out here ... come on—help me—

The CB squawked to life, splintering Will's iron will. "You all right? You been standing there awhile."

Dammit!

Swallowing his instinct to bark back at Corey, he gathered himself and told Corey he was fine. He breathed out slow and easy, then worked his fingers back into the narrow slit between the bottom of the windowpane and the jamb itself. *Gimme movement–gimme-gimme–come-on—*

A splintery snap!

The sweet, whoosh of the window along its tracks as it glided upward. Opening.

He widened the opening just enough to squeeze himself through. This would be a bit tricky. He was transporting the bundle underneath his flak jacket, and he could not compress the bundle against the pane or ... *well, it wouldn't be good.* He set down his Glock on the windowsill for a second. Will left his feet and managed to slide inside. The bulge beneath his flak jacket nearly scraped the pane, but he held the bundle clear for the most part.

Will braced himself along the way and landed headfirst in a welcome plush of pillows scattered across a comfortable hunter-green sofa arranged right under the window. He sprang up, retrieved the Glock off the sill.

I'm in.

That's when he saw her.

"Albie."

The sight of her stole his breath.

Her condition.

The reunion did not go nearly as Will wanted it to. Alberta's ears did not perk up. She took no notice of him when he planted his feet not even five feet away from her. Her coat was not its usual lovely brindle color. A black slimy substance had rubbed itself into her fur from head to toe. He could smell it for what it was. Motor oil. She was biting at her body, her effort accentuated by the groans and low, guttural growls rolling out of her throat while she worked. Bit. Gnawed. He saw a wound about the size of a half-dollar had been opened along her hindquarters, the fur there ripped away and a gash of gleaming blood oozing. She nosed around it for a moment, lapped at the blood like it was a wellspring of water, before the self-assault.

"Oh God … Albie."

Empty, red and slit eyes.

"Please girl … stop."

Ears flattened against her head.

I have to go to her. Can't—she's not Albie—I have to rouse her.

"Ok," he said to himself. "Ok."

The sounds of a struggle, then the all-too-familiar gagging of a human being choking on their own blood filtered up from the basement and stalked the first floor like a menacing evil.

His CB squawked. Will's hand flew to it, cupping the speaker grate with his palm to deaden the sound.

"Will, something's happening down the basement! I can't be sure … the way they're all moving … jerking … looks like they're all freaking the fuck out!"

But Will could hear it. The screams. Women and a young girl. A young boy, prepubescent tenor of his voice.

And a gravelly, lazy-sounding voice.

Will would have had no way of knowing, but he was certain it was Karl Tarlick.

"Dude, I'd do what you're gonna do and get out with your dog. One of them is gonna be up there soon. I know it. Over."

"Copy," Will said, with an edge.

454

Now.

He unzipped his flak jacket all the way down, drew out the football-sized package against his breast. He laid it down before him.

Alberta stiffened. Her massive head stopped in mid-motion. Swiveled around. Life flashed within her dead eyes, a spark. She started panting. *Hudda-hudda-hudda-hudda.*

"That's right, girl. I found her, Albie. She needs you."

Will unwound the plastic shroud from around it. The smell was putrid. It's smell. He covered his nose.

"Albie, I found her for you. She needs you."

Albie started towards Will and the thing on the carpet before him.

89. *FALLUJAH/ LIVING IN YOUR BRAIN-PART II*

Excerpt taken from *I Can Hear the Shiite Weeping*, by Jack R. Bentley, 2008, Pgs.35-40:

The dog followed our platoon, the Clean-Sweep Crew, all the way down Highway 10 in Fallujah proper. The gunfire that came in fits and starts as we soon turned to shooting at shadows and phantoms did not scare the animal off. In fact, the dog seemed even to know its place among our ranks, holding to the tail end of the formation. This was an animal with instinct unlike any I had ever seen, almost like it carried within its bones and flesh a formerly living, breathing soldier cut down earlier on in the war and then reincarnated in her starved-looking body.

"The thing's carrying one of them dead pups in its jaws," Private Mueller said a few men back. "One of em' that got flung down to the street back there. Musta' been one of hers! You seeing this?"

We weren't supposed to turn to our rear unless the mission or an emergency called for such a change in protocol. A downed soldier, which would call for five of our men to encircle them while our medic worked on him under cover of our human stronghold. As I could have predicted, Sergeant Moons, our platoon leader, told Private Mueller to "Shut the fuck up!" in the kindest terms any military leader could muster while sweeping a terrorist hotbed in the middle of a warzone. Of course, we had snipers stationed on the rooftops every couple of buildings. They were our eyes in the sky, and our death from above. Unseen and as final as an eighth nail in a coffin lid.

But Private Mueller had rung a bell, and there was no way to un*ring* it for any of us. He painted a picture in our heads we had to see to believe. One by one, the lot of us snuck a quick glance over our shoulders at the German Shepherd capping our rear formation. I knew they probably longed to laugh out of a desperate fear, or to cry for the same reason, but it would have been met with the most severe of reprimands from Sergeant Moon. So, they stole their glances, turned and continued along as if they had seen nothing especially interesting about the dog behind them carrying a stillborn puppy carcass.

When I turned around, the dog was yelping and frantic, which caused all of our infantry to sneak another look behind them. Her cries were panicked shrieks. Quick, sharp jabs at the brain of the line of soldiers. She must have lost the puppy she was carrying between her teeth, lost her grip on it, and it had fallen into the earthy dust. Consequently, the anxiety set in, stirring the animal crazy.

I said it before I knew I even opened my mouth to speak. "Sergeant? Permission to aid the animal?"

"What, soldier? Aid the *what?*"

"Permission to aid the distressed animal?"

"You have *got* to be shitting me, Private Bentley! Is that what you're doing right now? Because we still have about a quarter mile of road to clear before nightfall! Forget about the fucking dog—it's half-dead as it is!"

"Sir! Permission to speak?" another infantryman (I think it was Garcia) spoke up towards the rear of the line.

"Make it quick or not at all, Private Garcia!"

"The dog is alerting the enemy of our exact location the longer we let it carry on like this, sir! Can we form a barrier around it and give it back its pup? It will quiet it down, then we can proceed undetected—*"

My boot knocked against something. Soft. It gave a little against the strike of my hard leather.

"Sir, I have located the pup right here, next to my boot!" I scooped it up. The carcass was no bigger than a football. It was layered in a dusty coating, gone sticky in spots as the blood and gore mixed to a sticky substance with the desert sand. "Sergeant, I have the carcass in-hand!"

Another one of us, a farm boy named Private Pillweed, who allegedly shit his pants his first night at basic training, offered to shoot the dog. "That'll put an end to his crying … *sir!*"

Sergeant Mueller's boots continued to stomp the dirt, leading our formation. I was put off by his silence, unnerved by it. I feared he had taken to actually considering Farmboy Asshole's suggestion, chewing on it. Then,

456

his voice rained down, "Private Pill-head, that may be how you and your *pappy* handle animals back on the farm in Ally-bama, but here we are the civilization this territory is crying out for. And civilized people *do not shoot dogs without good reason, especially dogs in mourning!*"

Pillweed's unfortunate nickname of *Pill-head* was his own fault. He was an open book to the other men in the platoon, more so than it was necessary to be. He confessed to a couple of us on a long, lonely night in the trenches how his *pappy* forced him into the Marines because the old man was at his wit's end with his only son, who developed a wicked methamphetamine addiction. Apparently, his *pappy* thought the Corps would not only turn him into a soldier but would also serve as a clinic to clean him up. For free!

Hence, the shitting in Pillweed's pants his first night on the island. He was still coming off the last of his withdrawal.

"Private Bentley move to the rear of the formation, and give the dog its newborn! Pillweed! Garcia! Mendelssohn! Bradley! You circle around him while he does it and return to your position once it's complete! Do it now!" It happened mechanically, and I soon found myself surrounded by a human shield of fellow soldiers closing all gaps around me.

In the middle of the circle, I moved alongside the German Shepherd. She had stopped crying, her eyes transfixed upon the dead puppy in my hands. I held it out to her. "I found her," I said, measuring the dog's anxiety and longing as they raged within her. "I found her. She's right here. She needs you—"

She snapped her snout forward and accepted the dead puppy, ensnaring the shriveled, sticky nape of its neck between her sharp front canines.

Something passed between us. I am not a spiritual man, even though many men I served with later turned their hearts and minds towards religion so fervently when I met up with them later, more than a few becoming ordained or born-again, submitting to Allah. The transformation never touched my mind or my heart. The writing bug had already crawled into my ear instead, and it hasn't left since. Neither has my connection to that dog from the desert whom I now call my *best friend* with the greatest of ease and the warmest of intentions. I knew I had made her my responsibility from that moment on. I remember how much I seethed with hate for Pill-weed, and how it embarrassed me in my private moments how I longed to beat him for what he had suggested to the sergeant as easily as if he were suggesting crème in someone's coffee.

She's here. I have her here. She needs you ...

457

90. NEED

Will wasn't sure Alberta entirely *flipped her switch* until she came within a foot of him, whimpering as she dipped her snout downward to nose at the carcass on the rug. She nudged it around and around, as if willing it to find its own legs and unleash a whimper of its own. Will's chest tightened with a mixture of heartbreak and rage. This close to the animal, Will would have been able to sense any malice or danger coming from her. His body would have felt it, sensed it deep down like a primal musk. A deadly, invisible mist.

He raised a hand to touch Alberta. His hand lingered just above her head. She looked sickly. She smelled horrible. It didn't matter. The terrible things she had been made to do did not infect Will's feelings for her. He loved her as strongly as he had before she was taken, perhaps more.

When he lowered his hand to the dog's head, a rumble burred seemingly from her core, and Will drew his hand back. "All right, honey," he said. "It's all right. I understand. I'm here. You just tend to your baby."

He remembered just then the rest of the people in the house were down basement, and yet he had heard nothing for a couple minutes. *Don't tell me he killed them all, please!* Just as Alberta seized the carcass by its nape, like she had done in the desert so many years ago, Will switched the safety off his Glock with one hand and grabbed for the CB with the other. "Corey, you there?"

Will cupped the CB's grating, softening the gurgle of static before Corey's attentive voice vibrated against his palm. "Here, Will."

"I need you to come take the dog out the back door. Meet me where I am right now. I'll turn her over to you."

"Wait a second, man," Corey hissed. "Isn't she dangerous?"

"Not anymore," Will said. The sickness, whatever it was, appeared to be draining out of her like a poison. "She'll be good. Just make sure she holds onto her baby."

"Baby?"

"You'll see. Hurry, brother. Don't knock when you get to the back door. I'll crack the door. You get her out. Both of you lock yourself inside my truck and stay there!"

"But then I can't be your eyes."

"They're all still down the basement, right?"

Pause. "Yeah ... but—"

"What?"

"Well, it almost looks like ... can't be ... unless there's ..."

"Tell me! What?!" Will held the dog in his periphery as he cast a glance towards the dark, gaping opening which was the door leading down to the basement.

"Two of them ... looks like one of them is leading her deeper down into the ground. They're, like, a half-floor lower than the rest of them. I think there might be another room there? No idea."

A deeper room? Another room, lower than the basement?

"Doesn't make any sense. Your sister ever mention any kind of ... I don't know, a fallout shelter?"

"Nope, only they were still getting used to living in the house. They only moved in like a year ago. You know how it is when you first move into a new home or rent a new place. Feels weird."

"Ok, come grab Albie, and get her away from here! Over and out!"

So from here on, I'm going to have to head down into the basement, blind and open to attack from some alcove. Will listened for any sound from the basement, keenly sharpening his sense of hearing for so much as a footfall upon the cement stairwell. It would be hard to detect, if someone was softening their step. But the deeper room? If the woman of the house couldn't point him in the direction of where Tarlick and Jodi had hidden, if she was blindfolded and hadn't seen their escape, Will would be hard-pressed to locate the *lower alcove.*

Maybe a false chimney giving onto a hidden room? Survivalists favor this kind of addition to their house's layout, stocking secret rooms with food, cots, even a couple board games in preparation for the end times. Tarlick's father could have been one of those types, mistaking paranoia for good preemptive sense. *It would add up if the guy was crazy like his son ... genetics, right?*

The basement's silence was unnerving. Will felt his stomach try to turn sideways, but the Marine in him disallowed it from happening. Instead, his abdomen hardened to a stone of resolve.

The CB sighed at Will's shoulder. "Here. Send her out."

Ok ... here goes nothing.

Will moved his hand towards Alberta. She was down on her side, taken to licking the grime and gunk off the carcass. He touched her head and held his breath.

No groan. No growl.

A lamentable moan.

Then Will felt the dog move her big head into his hand, wanting more.

"Ok, girl, it's your dad," he spoke into her ear. "Up. Dad wants you to stand up. All right?"

They stared at one another, and there was a moment when time stood still.

It could have gone either way.

The dog sniffed, licked at Will's sleeve, and rose onto all fours with the puppy carcass clenched between her teeth. Will nudged her towards the back door leading out into the back yard. Corey Snell's shadow shifted around just outside the door, trying to steal a look into the house. Will, still low to the ground, turned the doorknob and eased the door open.

"Ok, take her."

Alberta's body tensed tight as a sailor's knot. Corey stood there just beyond the threshold, arms outstretched. Maybe he spooked her in some way. She backpedaled furiously. Her ears perked up. Her head swiveled around. Her body followed suit. Alberta greased herself through Will's hands. She slipped Will's grasp, his hands sliding down her long, lean body and trying to snatch at her tail before it escaped his hands, and Alberta bolted away from him.

"No! *NO! DON'T GO DOWN THERE, ALBIE! NO!*"

The big German Shepherd disappeared down the basement stairwell, called by something far more powerful than motherhood or a dead puppy.

She had dropped the carcass halfway across the living room.

Time sped up for Will. He shot to his feet and unfastened his flak jacket so he could get at the Beretta APX pistol nestled in his shoulder holster. He pressed it into Corey's palsied hands. "Stand by, Corey. I'm going down there!"

"But you got no idea what's down there waiting for you!"

"It doesn't matter. I'm finishing this, and I'm getting my dog, and then I'll leave you to care for your family. I know you can do it. You ever fire a gun?"

"Actually … yeah."

"Good. The safety's on—see this right here—but you can disengage it by doing this." He showed Corey with a flick of his finger. "If I call you, I'm going to need you to come. It'll mean I'm overwhelmed, and I need backup. You got me?"

Corey looked down at the gun in his hands like a newly sprouted appendage.

"Corey!" Will seized the limp noodle of the beach dude by his narrow shoulders, squeezed. "Look at me! Remember, your family's down there too! All right?"

"Okay, I got you. I got you."

Will chased his dog down into the basement, boots clacking furiously against the cement steps like a torrent of firecrackers going off.

91. LINES CROSSED

"Sergeant Malone!" Rivells shouted into her cell phone, white-knuckling it as she peeled down I-95 in search of Exit 39 to Levittown, "Rivells. How far out from the Riley house are you and your men?"

Malone's gruff, cigarette-husky voice filled the earpiece. "I got five officers, and I got SWAT en route ahead of us. We never had a home invasion in our township. Not ever, and I wanna put this down as quickly and cleanly as possible."

"I'm twenty minutes out. Now, what about Animal Control?"

"Uh … they're on their way, too!"

Rivells sensed the hesitation in Malone's voice. "Can I get an ETA on their arrival?"

"Sure you can. They'll be around when they get there, and that's all I got for you, Detective!"

"You never called them, did you?"

"Course I did. I know protocol when it comes to a dangerous animal. I think you're forgetting yourself, Detective—"

"I haven't forgotten a damned thing, but it sounds to me you've decided to forgo protocol, and I'd be willing to stake my career on the fact you told your men to shoot to kill the dog if given the opportunity!"

"Now you listen here, you uppity bitch! All I know is this piece of shit mutt killed two of ours! Nearly decapitated one of them. Not telling you anything you don't already know! Now you want me to get on my cell, and tell Animal Control to step on the gas so they can be the first ones on the scene to *sedate* a cop-killing animal?"

"The animal had no idea what it was doing, Sergeant. It's not rabid. This is an extreme negative reaction to its PTSD medicine regimen. She's a war dog. Served in Iraq alongside our Marines and special forces. You're telling me you'll be able to sleep better tonight putting down the equivalent of a war hero?"

"A veteran, huh?" Sergeant Malone barked, a bit of his Philly lethargic accent breaking through. "You're talking to a Vietnam Veteran. A decorated veteran. You putting me in the same league as a fucking dog, you better walk it back before your superiors hear about your insubordinate talk!"

"You can't blame her for this—the animal has no history of violent behavior—"

"*Listen and comprehend*! I *called* Animal Control, and they're on their way. If they don't make it there before my men and SWAT, even before you for that matter, then I can promise you the animal will be dealt with as I see fit. Not you! As it stands now, she poses a very clear and present threat to the community of Levittown the longer she's able to draw breath. My job is to keep the citizens of this county safe, sound, and free from dog attacks. So I will see you there, De-tec-tive, and you and I can continue our little *convo* on the scene if you like. Just know, I won't abide one more comparison drawn between myself and my fellow vets with the likes of that murdering, maniac animal!"

Connection broken.

Fuck-fuck-fuck.

Rivells pushed the gas to the floor and shot out in front of a slow-moving Miata.

92. DOWN BELOW

The basement weakened Will's nerve and his legs all at once.

Where is God? How does God mix a monster like Tarlick in with the rest of us? I don't see any greater good, or higher plan on display here! Nothing! NOTHING!

The little girl huddled in a far corner of the basement, her face between her knees as she rocked back and forth. Her little body shuddered as she wept softly to herself. Will went to her, averting his eyes from the three people hanging by their arms from a low-hanging water pipe in the ceiling.

Sooner or later, he would have to look.

Later.

Just a minute ...

"TARLICK! YOU MOTHER—"

Remember the little girl.

"TAR-LICK!"

For the moment, what mattered was comforting the little girl, holding her close as she would let him, and most importantly getting her to her

Uncle Corey. Up and out as soon as possible.

He pulled the CB up and away from his lapel. "Corey, I have your little niece down here. I need you to come down here and take her out. Take … Jesus … *take* her to my truck."

"You want me to … come down there? Is it safe?"

"It's … this is as safe as it's going to get. Now get down here, and get this kid. She's in tatters. I'll cover you while you make the extraction."

"Wait, did he … did he kill them?"

"Yes. O-over." He flung the CB away from his mouth. Tears pricked at the corners of his eyes.

Will approached the little girl. He hunkered down before her, touched her knee. The little girl flinched, lifted her face away from between her knees, and peeked with her little blue eyes between splayed tiny fingers at Will. Her nose was red, clogged. Her lips had shriveled up into a terrified sneer. "The man … kilt them …"

"I know-I know—but you're safe now. I'm here to get you out of here. You can trust me. Can I … can I pick you up?"

"The man says my name isn't Ava," she whimpered.

"Is that your name? Ava?"

"The man kilt them … and he made me say my name wasn't Ava."

"All right. What did he make you say your name was?"

"Blaise. But he made me tell a lie. I'm gonna get in trouble."

It's probably the only reason he spared you.

"No … your name is Ava, sweetheart," Will said. "Can I pick you up? I'm going to take you to your Uncle Corey. He's here. He wanted to surprise you. You're going to stay with him while I sort all this out. Would that be okay with you?"

Ava burst into a fresh bout of tears as she held out her hands, fingers curling and uncurling in the air in such a way it broke Will's heart. There was no time for commiseration. He would cry with her afterwards, and he would hold her if she wanted him to. For now, Will scooped her up, surprised at how light she felt in his arms. She clutched at him for dear life, burrowed her face into his flak jacket as she sniffed, and moaned against his shoulder. He gripped her with one hand and led with the butt of his Glock as he moved across the basement floor. He felt his body sag with the profound sadness tearing the little girl up from the inside out.

At the top of the stairs, Corey called to them.

Will walked the little girl up to her uncle, inching along with his back against the wall. He aimed the Glock down the stairwell as he handed the little girl off. She stiffened at first and then allowed herself to be transferred from one pair of loving arms to another. "Ava, it's okay. I swear to you it's going to be okay." Will's words rang hollow, even though he meant every syllable.

The little girl craned around as Will turned to tramp back down the cement stairwell. "When my mommy and daddy and brother wake up from their naps ... will you tell them where I am?"

God in Heaven ... where the hell are You in all this?

Stiffly, Will nodded and charged back down into the basement.

For better or worse, he could now have a better look at Karl Tarlick's handiwork. He made a quick examination of the three Riley family members, hanging all in a row like sides of beef in a freezer. The father's chest was crisscrossed with at least ten bludgeoning wounds. The front of his Eagles jersey had been transformed from green to a deep, dark red. The player number shone like a ghost in the scarlet overlay. His head hung down like he had been called into prayer, but Will noticed much to his sickening dismay, the man's tongue hanging out the side of his mouth, like a dead deer on the side of the road. The mother possessed an old-time, platinum actress quality of Hollywood's Golden Age, from the soft bob and curl worked into her short ashen tresses to the sunken but lovely cheekbones. Her throat smiled a ghastly red grin, and the front of her white turtleneck sweater looked like someone had squeezed a sponge fat with blood over her and let it rain down. The tears Will had been holding back suddenly wet his cheeks. *For what? FOR WHAT?*

He found he could not even look at the boy for longer than a second. His emotions bent him over to the point he had to hold his rubber band knees and ride out his own weeping until it slowly dissolved and then warmed over into a deep, burning of rage and bloodlust of his own. The boy had suffered the age-old *death by a thousand cuts*, it would seem. Slashes from his brow to his ankles. Seeping from every inch of his body.

"Help ... *help* ..." A mere rasp.

The boy's eyes were slitted, but open and quivering. His mouth, the corners of it cut wider like the Joker, worked like a stroke-victim. Barely detectable, but producing sounds of late distress. Will moved in towards him. This young boy had somehow hung on to life. He lifted the boy up so as to take the weight off of his hanging, bound hands. With his other hand, Will worked at the knotting of deep twine wound round the boy's hands and suspending him from the water pipe. "Hold on, just hold on—listen to my voice. You're going to make it—just hold on—listen to the sound of my voice-listen—"

"Help ... help ... my mom ... hehhhhhhhhhh ..."

464

"No-no-no! Don't you go—wait!"

But Will felt the life, a spark of vitality, as it fled the boy's body in his arms.

The twine finally gave, and Will bore the dead boy down slowly, gingerly to the cement floor. He arranged the boy on his back, folded his arms over his heart.

Will stood there, his muscles and tendons leaping and writhing under the skin like enraged snakes as adrenaline animated each and every one of them into motion.

The basement burned red in Will's vision.

His cheeks burned with blood, engorged.

He turned around and around, his hungry gaze searching the slate-grey brick walls for some kind of opening. The basement's parameters spanned the entire first floor in length and width.

Sonofabitch.

A small wooden door set into the brick face along the far east wall. Shrouded in shadow. No larger than the entrance to a crawl space.

It hid there ten yards away like a living thing, daring for Will to see. To understand. A sliver of light cast by a weak light bulb bled across the right side of the door, revealing the contrast of wood against faded red brick.

See and understand.

He thought of Alberta.

Oh Christ! Jesus Christ …

He felt his heart quicken, hammering at his rib cage like a bird throwing itself at its confinement. To fly off.

Once more, Will wondered where God was.

Will crossed the basement in what felt like two wide-arching leaps. He fell upon the door, curled his hands around its small knob, and yanked.

93. FALLOUT

Jodi Dare lay in the dimness of light cast by a 40 watt bulb encased in what looked like a shell of chicken wire. She couldn't stand. Jodi could not have even pulled herself up onto all fours if she tried. Her midsection felt like a crane had just driven a wrecking ball into it. The pain held no mystery. She had felt for herself, driven her hand down inside her cow print pajama bottoms, and when she drew it out again, the strong smell of copper attacked her nostrils immediately. The man had dragged her through the little doorway, forced her through to the other side. It happened then. The roughness of it. He handled her like one would handle a sack of potatoes. No regard.

I lost it. I lost the baby.

She felt the blood between her thighs, a sticky adhesive now. Jodi felt it draining out of her, life's blood. She shivered along the cold cement floor, her body fast going cold. Rigid. Immobile. Had she the strength to turn her head away from them, Jodi would have. She turned her eyes aside. They closed, only to spring open again. To find them only a few feet away from her. Engaged in something strange. Deeply unsettling.

It looked to her as if they were … coupling? The little man and the big dog. She watched, growing ever more detached. *I'm not here. My body is gone. Mind is nothing.* The little man applied what meager weight he boasted on top of the strangely submissive dog lying on her back beneath him. A long, low croon reached her where she lay. She listened to the wretched sound. No choice.

Jodi could not determine which one of them was making the sound. Man or animal.

It was what frightened her the most, perhaps. Something unholy unfolding before her. If Jodi could have wished herself dead as opposed to having to bear witness to what was happening in the middle of the grimy, neglected floor of the fallout shelter she would have.

Her hand crept to her inner thigh, the dampness thicker along her fingertips. *Yeah, this could be it for me, and … it's okay.*

The little wooden door by her head started rattling furiously in its hinges.

Jodi felt for her chest at the sudden, terrifying clamor, but her heart was not there. It was between her teeth.

94. ONE SWIFT AND CERTAIN SWING

"Jodi! If you can hear me, get clear of the door! NOW!"

Will waited a beat and fired three quick rounds into the doorknob.

Inside, the Dare girl shrieked and wept with the same amount of strength the dead boy had used to utter his last words to Will.

"Jodi!"

He wrenched the door open, took to his knees, and stooped to inch his way inside while leading with his Glock.

It was darker inside the shelter wing. Stray light from the basement proper bled across its floor in a short column of paleness. Will strained to see clearly. He caught a glimpse of fur. Then, a palsied hand as it clawed and clambered along the floor of the shelter like a seizuring white spider. The two figures writhed together along the filthy floor, locked into some bizarre vertical dance.

"Make him stop." Jodi cried, her voice a forced wheeze. "Please … make it stop …"

The Dare girl lay against the right wall. She was on her side, clutching at her midsection, which was mottled with bloody handprints she had made herself. She reached to Will. It reminded him of the way the little girl had reached for him, and this startled him out of his paralysis.

The room smelled of feces, wet dog, and depraved human. He could taste the blood hanging in the air, a dirty coin on the tip of his tongue. The room could not have been more than ten by ten, and the smells swirling around within seemed spring-loaded to burst across his face like a backhand to the face. He swabbed at his nose, breathed through his mouth, and swung the gun towards the others.

A beast with two backs!

Will surged forward and pressed the the Glock against the back of Tarlick's greasy, curly head.

It happened with breathtaking shutter speed.

Karl Tarlick craned his neck around, the gun muzzle raking through his hair and bending his ear back until it pressed against his cheek. His eyes blazed red. There was no white in them, and it looked like someone forced two red pool balls into the sockets, forcing them into openings half their size. Tarlick's mouth yawned open with a hiss and Will caught a glimpse of long side teeth before he felt the bite of another set of canines as they sank into his ankle. Alberta's muzzle unclamped from his leg, and the animal wriggled out from under Karl Tarlick. The dog raised herself onto all four legs and rocketed towards the shelter opening before Will knew what was happening.

"What—what'd you do?"

Alberta trailed a suffering cry behind her as she exited the basement. Thoroughly human.

"What'd you—"

Karl let loose with a guttural, unhinged burst of barks and growls that blew Will's hair back.

Flash of side-teeth. Tarlick looked like a werewolf trying to smile.

Red eyes, burning to the core of Will's sanity.

Will pulled the trigger. Tarlick's head snapped back, and a snotty blob of white and crimson splashed across the wall behind him.

The barking ceased.

Alberta cried and wailed, like a poltergeist haunting the upstairs floor, until Will heard the crash of a windowpane.

Then nothing but the soft trickle of Jodi's whimpering behind him.

95. FLASH OF BRINDLE FUR

Corey Snell turned the heat up in the cab of Will's truck. He hadn't ever really spent that much time around children, let alone his niece or nephew. The little girl was shivering in the passenger seat. She had crammed her little body up against the door like she meant to make a break for it. "Here, honey, it'll be warm in here soon. What else can I do for you?"

Little Ava Riley didn't answer. She shoved her hands deep into her armpits. She was coatless, dressed only in a little pink Eagles jersey, jeans, and white Keds. Absently, Corey remembered reading the Philadelphia Eagles were favored to clinch the NFC Championship. He imagined the whole family dressed in their Eagles garb. Then it came to him. How to drum up some sort of easy, light conversation. Anything to draw her thoughts away from the nightmare images no doubt looping through her feeble, little mind.

"So ... who's your favorite Eagles player, Ava?"

He swore he saw her offer a slight shrug before turning her little face against the cold glass.

Try again. C'mon, man, you gotta keep at it!

"Do you have one?" he pressed gently, and in a lilted tone he was not used to using. When he lived in the area, the quarterback was Randall Cunningham. And he could even recall the big running back Reggie White. He also knew White had died a few years back. He wished right then he had kept up with it, possessed some kind of working knowledge. The circles he ran in across the county in Malibu County weren't the sporting news types. They knew their music. They knew the best blend of cannabis. Little else. "I heard a lot about the quarterback. He's got an arm on him, man oh man. What's *his* name, Ava? I can't remember."

"Carson Wentz," she answered in a small, quavering voice.

"That's it! Right on the tip of my tongue. You! You're good, kiddo!" He sighed.

"He's my favorite," she added, shifting around some in her seat. She came away from the door. "Mommy ... she says he's got a *big heart*."

"Yeah? That's what I heard about him too. There's a big game today, right?"

Ava snuck a quick, wet glance at her uncle and shook her head.

You have to talk about it, carefully, but you have to.

"Honey," he said. "I'm your mommy's brother. That makes me your uncle. Your family. I know ... I know you're scared right now. I know you're feeling all alone right now. I promise you you're not. Not even close. I'm here, and I'm not going anywhere. I'll keep right by your side, and we *will* get through this. Together. I don't even know if you're hearing everything I'm saying right now, and it's okay too. But you're going to see ... you're going to find ... I'm there at every turn if you want me there. Only if you want me there. I mean, if you want to go with one of the police officers or something when they get here ... like, a lady or something ... I won't be mad at you. I'll understand. You tell me to get lost, and you're wish is my command, kiddo. But ... if you—"

He wasn't ready for the little girl to leap into his arms, but he knew how to give a hug and mean it without having to think about it. It's what made him Uncle Corey. Useless Uncle Corey who couldn't even sell a bar of Sex Wax in a surfing community. Important to another human being. He felt his heart shiver inside. He felt it leap, never having known such a feeling before. *So small. This little kid ... so small. With a broken heart and a haunted mind.* She burst into fresh tears, curling her tiny arms around Uncle Corey's neck. "Don't go away. Please ... stay with me. I'm scared."

"I won't, I *promise*. I'm here."

"Will you help me wake mommy up? She won't listen to me. Maybe she can't hear me."

She pulled back, and her little blue eyes, red, seemed to search him for something. Honesty, maybe. *Can kids do that?* "I-I'll try. I will."

"And Daddy?"

Corey swabbed at his eyes, now overflowing themselves. His head hurt. "Yeah, I'll try my best—"

"And AJ?"

"Yes-yes–I will *try*."

"I want the bad man to leave. Will you make him go away? *Please?*"

I'm not that man. Dammit, I wish I was.

"I have a feeling he's already gone," Corey said. She was a running watercolor image on his lap. "You remember that man—the nice one—who brought you to me? He made the other man leave! It's why he came. And I think he made the bad man hit the road."

"*HE'S NOT COMING OUT HERE! HE'S GONNA GET ME! I'M SCARED—*"

"Oh-no-no-*no* I won't let anything happen to you! He's gotta go through your Uncle Corey to get to you, and I'll beat his … I'll beat his butt if he tries anything! But I *really* think the good man in the house made him go away. I really believe that! Do you believe it? You ever … you ever read *Peter Pan* with mommy? It says in there if you *really* believe something … *really, truly* … you can make it happen! So believe it with me! Will you do that?"

"Ok … ok. I … believe … the bad man is gone."

"That's good," Corey said, sniffling and laughing. He swore he saw the ghost of a smile cross the little girl's lips before vanishing. "It must be true, then. Now—"

"A doggie! LOOK, UNCLE COREY!" The little girl twitched her arms and legs, trying to stand up in his lap. Her hand shot out, index pointing out the driver's side window. "RUNNING IN THE WOODS! LOOK-LOOK-*LOOK!*"

Corey jerked his face towards the window. He caught the flash of brindle fur, weaving around the maze of trees. Then, he saw legs running at a steady pace as the animal took full form, bounding through the underbrush and kicking it up in its frenzied wake. The dog from the house.

Will had wanted him to catch the dog.

Ava banged on the window. "DOGGIE! COME HERE! I WANN' PET YOU, DOGGIE! SO PRETTY!"

"Ava-wait!"

"DOGGIE—C'MERE!"

The CB clipped to Corey's Army jacket lapel burped to life.

"Corey … you there?"

Corey yanked the CB up to his face. "Will, did you get him?"

"Ten-four, but forget that for now! You have eyes on my dog?"

Ava crowed, hopping up and down. "TELL HIM! DOGGIE-DOG-GIE!"

"You heard her, Will," Corey said. "She's running through the woods."

"Okay … I want you to listen to me very carefully, Corey."

"Is she … all good now?"

"NO-NO-NO-DO NOT LET HER ANYWHERE NEAR THE LIT-TLE GIRL UNTIL AFTER YOU DO THIS!"

I knew it!

470

"Ok, tell me."
Will told him.

96. TIMID

Will had no idea how the moment down basement was affected when the pain came, carving its way into the left side of his face like razors inserted into his cheek one-by-one, overtop of one another like tectonic plates. He had no idea whether or not he blacked out in the moment and would not come to realize he had lost time until later when the voice of Sergeant Karns, ten times louder in its resolution between his ears than ever before and far more callous in its delivery, exploded in his head like a sudden, crippling migraine. Will felt Sarge's voice flick at his eardrums like taunting fingers. He felt it rattle his brain. The Sarge would be heard. And he would be obeyed.

Will would not have had it any other way.

Will stumbled running out of the basement. He stalled, intense trepidation wobbling his legs and bending his knees. He grabbed for the handrail, but his fingers merely grazed it and grabbed at the air. His hand slid down the cold brick wall, and he tried to call his breath into a more normalized rhythm. It wouldn't come. He started to hyperventilate, his lungs seeming to shrink with every in and out.

He had no idea whether or not he blacked out in the moment. The pain might have done it when it came on, carving its way into the left side of his face like razors inserted into his cheek one-by-one, overtop of each other like tectonic plates. The voice of Sergeant Karns, ten times louder than ever before and far more callous, exploded in his head like a brain embolism.

All right, you've got my attention—I thought you were gone—so tell me before I suffocate.

Sorry I had to do it this way, but it's better than a kick to the balls, so consider yourself lucky I'm only a voice in your head. Here's what ... I want you to think back to the summer of 2005. July 4th of that year, to be exact. I'm not talking about the morning sex you had with Mina followed by the farmer's omelettes you made afterward to ring in the morning. Ain't going to help your dog. No, I want you to fast-forward to later on. Nightfall. Maybe eight o'clock in the evening. You got it into your head you were gonna treat Mina and Alberta to some kind of amateur fireworks show in the backyard. You bought all different kinds of T n' T over at the stand they have at Rice's

471

Flea Market. Fountain works. Crackers. Snakes (boy, did they suck!), and smoke bombs. Cherry bombs, to be exact. You called them out onto the back porch. You were so excited! They were excited because you were excited. You remember how Albie was circling 'round you when you lit the first round of fireworks. She was feeding off your happiness!

But then, after the first line of crackers went off, what did Albie do? She ran back across the yard—she went back up on the porch.

More like Albie hid behind Mina, and she tried to tell you maybe this wasn't such a good idea. But you had it in your head everybody's gonna enjoy this fireworks show no matter what. Sometimes, soldier, you're stubborn to a major fuckin' fault. Anyway, no use in guilting you now. There's a reason I'm refreshing your memory about this. You tried calling Albie back. You and Mina had a little back and forth. You clipped off the disagreement by saying, "I'm going to combine a couple of these, and you're going to love it. I'm going to set them off for maximum effect just like the guy at the store recommended. C'mon! It's the 4th! This is what it's all about, ladies!" You were irritated by both of them. Your little family and in that moment you wanted to curse them for being so ungrateful for what you planned for their entertainment! Again, not trying to guilt you, soldier—

Then get on with it—It was one time, and I kept my cool.

Fair enough, soldier! You set off ten novelties. Red, white and blue. That's how they lit up the sky. I gotta say, it made my heart skip a beat for a minute there. But then, on top of that, you lit red, white, and blue smoke bombs—ten in a row. More than you needed to get the effect you needed, but this was your first time putting on a fireworks show so you get a pass. By this time though, Mina was shouting to you from the porch. She sounded mad. Maybe you knew what she was yelling, maybe not. Either way, you lit the smoke bombs, then you strode back up towards the porch through the smoke. And, soldier, there was so much smoke, on any other night Comstock Ladder 15 would've suspected a four alarm fire over at the Bentley residence. As you came up closer to the porch, you could hear Mina even though you couldn't see her. ... she's scared to death, Will! Why didn't you listen to me! You should see her."

How was I supposed to know, Sarge?

Not saying you were supposed to put it all together right then and there, but you remember smoking all those insurgents out of their hiding places back in the desert. You remember who went in first to those little hidey-holes after you guys threw the flash bangs and smoke bombs in? You didn't put it together until you saw Alberta lying there on the patio stones in a ball, her front paws over her ears. Whimpering. Crying. Mina bent over

472

her, trying to comfort her. You're putting it together now, too. You under-
stand, soldier? Do you see?

       Sarge, wasn't it enough I fucked with her head with the puppy car-
cass?

       Then you tell me what's more cruel: playing off your dog's PTSD
so you can contain her or letting her take a bullet or twenty from a horde of
angry, vengeful police officers? They're here now too! And you got SWAT
swarming this house! But, by all means, you go ahead and think about it!
I'll wait.

       Will reached for his CB.

97. "WARZONE"

Will told Corey where to find them. Behind the seat in the cab, on the driver's side. Wound tightly inside a Panera Bread bag that was tucked into the
black duffel Will used to transport his guns. Will said one was a flash bang,
the other two smoke grenades.

       It took Corey way too long to convince little Ava to stay in the truck
when there was a seemingly lovable *doggie* racing back and forth inside the
forest, practically teasing her to run to it and pet its head. The little girl pout-
ed. The tears came, and her nose bubbled over with snot. Corey leaned into
the cab, hands in his pockets to secure the three items he had secured inside
his coat, and he reached for her hands. She surrendered one hand across the
seat to him and wiped her snotty nose with the other. For this, Corey was
grateful.

       "I'm gonna go see if I can get the doggie to come back here and
leave with us. I'll even ask her if she wouldn't mind you petting her. How's
that sound?"

       "*YAY! YAAAAAAY!*" It was like a thrown switch. It always amazed
Corey how resilient children are. She had just witnessed what was most
likely the brutal murder of her whole family, but a dog sighting somehow
succeeded in softening the blow. "*Make sure she comes with us! Please-*
please—PLEASE!"

       He promised her. "I'm going to shut the door now. If you come out
of the cab you'll scare her off, and she'll run away. Then she won't be able
to come with us. Okay, honey?"

       Ava Riley crossed her heart, clapped her hands, and smiled from ear to ear as Corey Snell slammed the door to the truck. Quickly, he sidled around to the back of the truck. He held his hands overtop of the three small cylinders stowed inside the inner pocket of his army jacket. He lifted the latch and lowered the truck's tailgate. He fished the paper bag of grenades out of his jacket, carefully eased them out of the bag to arrange them side-by-side on the gate. The smoke grenades were wire-pull devices encased in a black cylinder as long as Corey's hand. The frag grenade, labeled FRAG up its bronze side looked far more lethal, *like a grenade.*

"Your job is to disorient Alberta," Will told him. "That will trigger panic, and I know how she handles this certain type of trigger. She doesn't lash out. She puts her tail between her legs and curls up into a ball. She turns submissive. By that time, I'll be out there to help you gather her up."

Shit, if only this worked for all crazy, wild dogs out there in the world! There'd be a lot less of them put down. Corey had no idea why this particular sort of stimulation would tame the dog temporarily, but Will sounded sure enough Corey had no reason not to trust it.

Corey gathered up the grenades into his coat once more and climbed up into the truck bed.

A large steel dog crate was shoved up against the rear window of the cab. It was collapsed and banded down so as not to shift all over the truck bed during the drive. He took a knee and unfastened the three bands securing the crate. He tossed them aside, then focused on the crate itself. It was oblong. Looked awkward to carry. *Should I open it first and then carry it into the woods?*

He turned it on its side with a grunt, carted it to the edge of the truck gate and hopped down to lower it onto the ground.

The temperature felt like it must have dropped a full ten degrees since he had first holed himself up in the truck with his niece. His bones felt the cold, beneath his three layers of clothing. He could almost feel them grinding uncomfortably at the joints as he carted the dog crate into the forest. He whipped his head from right to left, occasionally dropping his gaze to the terrain before him to avoid tripping over a branch or stumbling into a rabbit hole concealed by leaves or brambles.

Then, he heard the dog at his heels and could not turn around fast enough before teeth sank into the taut bulb of his right calf muscle.

He dropped the dog crate. It made a splashing sound when it dumped down into leaves and flung them up into the air.

Corey sat down hard and clawed at the spot where he was bitten. The dog had taken a chunk out of him and then sprinted off in the opposite direction, as if it were playing with him. He heard the sound of a man's laughter, actually more of a chortling or a guffaw. *There's a man out here, too? And he's laughing? I thought Will cleared the bad guys out!* The rugged denim of his jeans was torn away where he had been bitten. A dark red smear peeked out from inside the pant leg. He thought of rabies. "Fuck," he grunted, crawling up the side of a nearby tree stump until he found he could stand so long as he applied the better part of his weight onto his good leg.

His heart pounding and mouth dry, Corey cast his eyes all about the forest around him. He ventured in deep enough he could no longer see the truck where his niece was locked away. He felt like a man drifting out at sea, his eyes finding nothing of land in any direction. A slow, building panic he could not afford.

The dog was as fast as it had been covert.

And I can still hear a man laughing in the distance! Who the hell is that?

The CB burped to life at his collar. "How we doing out there, Corey? You got the crate set up yet?"

Corey clawed at the CB as if angry at it. "N-no. Working on it. Your dog got my leg pretty good. She got all her shots?"

"Of course."

"All right. I-I'm doing it now."

"I'll be right out there," Will said. "I'm coming out with the girl they kidnapped. She's a tough gal, but she's scared. I only now just got her to come along with me."

Corey heard none of it. There was only a phantom buzzing in his ears.

And the man's laughter.

Coming closer.

Closer.

"Not again, motherfuck!" he cried and moved to the dog crate lying in the brush. He lifted it up and with a series of jerks and grunts, Corey Snell at first struggled with unfolding the crate and then the latches which would force the crate to hold its sturdy rectangular shape.

...HUDDA-HUDDA-HUDDA-HIPPIE-FAGGOT-GONNA KILL-HUDDA-HUDDA-HUDDA-*HUDDA.*

The last latch wouldn't slide into place. It was bent what looked like a fraction of a centimeter, but just enough not to engage the thin upper bar in a flush fashion. He wriggled madly at it, forcing it. Bending it further out of shape. It would never line up now. The rest of the crate stood. Held.

HUDDA-HUDDA-BURNOUT-FUCK-HUDDA-HUDDA-HUDDA.

Corey's head jerked to the left, and he found himself staring into the blackest eyes this side of hell. They bore down on him. He smelled rotten

475

meat and shit and motor oil until all three seemed to wrap themselves around him like one big filthy, flowing overcoat of grisliness. His right hand shot upward, and he somehow seized the animal by the front of its wide throat. The dog's snout surged downward, teeth snapping so viciously an inch from his nose he thought the animal had actually broken its side teeth against one another. Corey squeezed the dog's throat, felt the inner workings of muscle and cartilage beneath the fur and flesh as they engaged at once to aid the dog in breaking his hold and taking out Corey's throat.

He knew he'd have a greater chance of holding the dog off if he used both hands on its throat. But he needed the grenades inside his coat. The dog stood with its back legs on his lower abdomen while Corey staved off the animal's incessant lunges down at his face. Corey laid hands on one of the grenades in his coat just as the dog's side teeth snapped right next to his left ear. The animal was bending Corey's arm at the elbow, applying more force than Corey's resistance could match.

It was tricky.

Corey worked his thumb into the ring at the top of the grenade and tried to extend it upward sharply enough to pull it out. The ring held.

HUDDAHUDDAHUDDA-KILLYOU-KILLYOU-KILLY-OU-HUDDA-HUDDA-HUDDA-HUDDA-HUDDA

He shoved his thumb upward and out again.

The ring held.

The dog's rank breath swarmed up his nose now, no more than an inch away from his face.

Black eyes. Dead eyes. But so fucking alive!

Snap of the side teeth.

Corey felt the sting of something along the side of his throat. *It got me. Next bite–next bite–I'm dead–can't be a next bite.*

He flicked the grenade's ring once more. It pinged out of its slot and flew across the forest.

Then, Corey felt himself choking on sulfur. He could not see more than a foot in front of him, and it looked like a cloud had swept down from the sky and somehow scooped him up into its billowy white fluff. The weight of the dog's back legs against his groin was gone. The billowy white pulled back the dog's snout from snapping at his face like a large mousetrap. But, he could still hear the animal nearby.

That and the sudden shrill of police sirens in the distance. A veritable army of them, if Corey trusted his ears.

Don't stop. Just because the dog pulled back. You have to overwhelm her like Will said.

Without hesitation, Corey pulled himself up onto his knees. Sulfurous smoke enshrouded him. Concealed him. He heard the dog, whimpering. He wrenched open his coat and took out the remaining smoke bomb and the flash bang grenade. It didn't matter which one he chose to use next.

He decided on the frag and set it off just as red and blue lights washed across the side of him and the shout of police officers and car doors slamming invaded the afternoon.

98. TUNNELS OF MEMORY

Alberta bolted, making no effort to avoid the clustered trees and ramming her head into the stumps at full force. It emboldened the Man hiding inside her skull, screaming at her. Commanding her. She had understood the trigger words, the ones in that strange language The Man would whisper in her ear right before her world went dark, and she could only taste and crave the syrupy sweetness of human blood. Now The Man somehow entered her skull, he reverted to more recognizable trigger words. *Kill. Sic.* These were words she learned a long time ago, back in the land of the sandstorms.

The Man berated her.

Kill.

Sic.

They sounded more like words of admonishment than commands, and she felt her tail tuck between her legs as he shouted at her, broiling her brain. She rammed her head over and over. Blood ran into her eyes. Spots danced before her vision like low-hanging black stars. She tasted another essence on her tongue. She smelled it. All around her. It swarmed her like a dark heavy blanket. Over her head. To cover her eyes.

Death.

Alberta knew she was dying. She only wanted to somehow expel The Man from her skull. This seemed the only way to make it so. The Man yelled at her, commanding her to stop this madness. She found she could ignore him if she tried hard enough.

The blackout came.

Her vision failed. All at once, someone else was driving. Rendering her a passenger once more. This is how it worked. Every time. Then, she heard the scream of a man outside her mind. She felt herself leap and land on something that reeked of human stink and sweat. She heard her jaws snapping. Her neck craning to somehow extend beyond its reach. But there was no taste of blood. The queer craving for the thick, rich liquid to hit the back of her throat.

She lunged and lunged.

She saw nothing of what she was doing, her eyes blinded.

Alberta remembered the men who had abused her in the land of the soft ground. Their eyes had glowed in the pitch black like dying embers on a neglected fire pit. She heard the rapid back and forth of their dialogue as they argued. The two men often argued. Sometimes, they hit each other. Drew blood. Then they would turn their anger on her, and Alberta remembered as well. All too clearly.

The man on the ground was—
The men from the land of the soft ground—
They had melded—
No differentiation.
Kill.
Sic!

Alberta felt her body peel away from the man on the ground. She was choking on smoke. It was everywhere. It was inside her, billowing about inside her lungs. She coughed and choked. Smoke plumed out of her snout. She dropped onto her side. Rolled onto her back. Her mind was an echo chamber of voices now. The Man, yes. He was ever-present. But somehow his screams had diminished to more of a whisper. A hiss, rather than the rantings of a lunatic.

She heard the voice of The Woman from Before. The kind woman. Her mind's eye opened to reveal a veritable collage of people and settings and actions bleeding into one another like a kaleidoscope of memories. She heard the woman's voice, saw a snatch of her black hair with the one white stripe tucked behind her ear. "It's all right, honey. No more fireworks. Finished! I promise! *Will? No more! You're scaring her!*" The Woman's black hair bled into the darkness as Alberta descended into a narrow opening barely wide enough to accommodate her as she charged down the cement steps into a low-lit hovel where a barrage of human voices collided with one another. She heard herself barking, vicious and threatening. She felt her nose sniffing out the people inside, and she lunged at one of them. A voice behind her, male and gruff: "*Sic! Sic! Albie, girl! Sic! Sniff em' all out, girl!*" The Man from Before. She felt the burn of sand in her eyes, the grains in her mouth, up her nose. She charged at one of the people inside, flanking her left side and heard the loud staccato of explosions at the same moment a searing pain announced itself in her left flank. "*Albie! Out, girl! Out! Now!*

478

Out, girl! Jesus, she's hit—she's hit!" She felt hands on her as the back half of her body sagged, and her legs buckled. The smoke. All around her. Up her nose. In her mouth.

A deafening bang.

Great burst of light.

Alberta's body went limp as a wet rag. She curled up.

Then there were hands hauling her up out of the leaves and twigs. She only heard the onrush of other men as they charged past her. She heard the voice of The Man From Before in her ear. "I got you! I got you, girl! It's all right! It's all right—"

Then the smell of wet earth. Mud. Detritus. She burrowed her nose into it.

No idea who, what, or where.

Only she is dying.

And it is not so terrible.

99. CAGE

The Dare girl was weak and had lost a lot of blood. Will holstered his Glock and carefully bore her up off the sticky cement. She shrieked in his ear. Her arms curled around his neck and clung to him like the two of them were suspended over a dark, depthless pit. He comforted her as best he could, and his words smacked of the same things he would say to Alberta whenever she was frightened. "It's all right. I got you. You're going to be okay." She sighed into the side of his neck when he told her he was taking her out of there. She wept against him when they heard the sounds of sirens converging in the distance.

I have to get out there! Christ, I can only hope Detective Rivells is with them! She'll stop them!

"I will be as careful as I possibly can," he told her, as they took to the stairwell leading up and out of the basement, "but we have to get out here as soon as possible. I promise I will try not to jostle you, but we have to move."

"Please," Jodi whimpered into his ear, "just get me … out of here …"

He tightened his grip on her, somehow managed to free a hand to depress the button on the side of his CB. "Corey, come in! Come in, brother!"

Jodi hissed. "Ow … *ow-ow-ow-ow-ow!*"

"Sorry," he mouthed to her. *Corey, what are you doing? Answer!*

479

Dammit! They rounded the wall and climbed the remaining steps. He pressed the CB button. "Corey? Come in! What's going on? Over!"

Nothing.

Jodi dug her nails into the back of Will's neck. "Who's … Corey?"

"Ah … he could be the hero of the day if only I could—*Corey–Corey–come in*!"

"Will, the cops are here! SWAT! A whole fleet of them! I-I did what you said, and it worked but she won't go into the cage—don't wanna force her, but—"

"PUT YOUR HANDS UP! NOW! DO IT NOW!"

Shit, it's happening! Will simply knew with a cold, strangely clairvoyant certainty Detective Rivells was not outside. She had not beaten the local police force there.

The CB gurgled at Will's throat. "I gotta go, or they're gonna shoot me—"

"Corey! COREY!"

Will hustled towards the front door at the opposite end of the corridor. "I'm sorry, we gotta go—we gotta, Jodi! Hold on tight as you can!"

100. TO HELL

The residential road in front of the Riley house looked like a festively lit obstacle course by the time Rivells arrived. There had to have been seven cruisers, including a state trooper vehicle and SWAT van, parked every which way. They backloaded the entrance to the once sleepy little route so Rivells had to maneuver her black SUV around the vehicles with a constant palming of the wheel and padding of the brake until she somehow squeezed herself into a narrow opening between two Levittown cruisers. She shot out of her vehicle, one hand on her holstered weapon. She needed past this police barricade and fast. A flash of the badge and ID on a chain around her neck would allow her swift movement deeper into the fray without obstruction. It was the last thing she needed. Pushback from any of them, no matter their rank.

This was a tense situation. Home invasions always were, largely because of the high number of variables involved and the reckless nature of the perp who chooses to enter a private residence in the middle of the day without regard for consequence or retribution.

She rushed past a cluster of unis at the curb, their shoulders squared and jaws set as they switched their glances from one another then deep into the forest just off the road. Rivells joined up with the state trooper towing the line at the forest border along with another green-looking uni. "Detective Rivells." She flashed her lanyard. "What do we know?"

The state trooper's face was a stitch of broken blood vessels up his cheeks and across the bridge of his nose, but his eyes flashed battleship grey alertness as he leveled his steeled gaze upon Rivells. The uni scratched his sharp jawline, turned halfway aside of Rivells to stare into the maze of thin, clustered trees. The state trooper nodded towards the woods. From a distance, Rivells had thought the woods rather transparent. Up close, it appeared to deepen into an ever-darkening labyrinth.

"What we got is the strangest standoff I seen in a long time," the state trooper said to Rivells, licking his severely chapped bottom lip. He jabbed a thumb over at the house to the right of the forest, the site of the home invasion. "SWAT just stormed the house, but they didn't cross paths with your guy. Mr. Bentley. He's either on his way out with his hands up, or he's made his getaway. Looks like they just missed each other."

"The girl? Jodi Dare?"

"SWAT hasn't seen the Dare girl, or any girl who fits her description inside the house, but …" The state trooper stalled. Rivells could have sworn she saw the barrel-chested trooper's bottom lip push out like a petulant child. His eye glistened then cleared in an instant. He leveled his gaze, hardened once more, upon Rivells. "They found three bodies in the basement. All of em', hung up … from a pipe. Father stabbed. Mother with her throat cut. But … the boy … no more than ten years old … for some reason, he got it the worst. Numerous stabs and lacerations all over his body. Overkill."

"Oh God," Rivells said, her stomach plummeting.

The uni standing by the trooper wheeled on them both, his hand clutching the CB clipped to his black, pressed lapel. "Trooper, one of our guys has eyes on the little girl. She's locked inside a truck parked in the woods. Red truck. They're trying to gain entry. She won't let them in."

"That's the missing Riley girl," the trooper said. "Thank Christ."

Rivells tried to gain a deeper focus into the woods. She caught a blur of motion, dark clothing. Then, as her ears adjusted, she heard the shouts. The clipped, affirmative commands which are the trademark of an officer in the midst of a standoff. It was one-sided, the shouting. Rivells heard no resistant shouting from a perp, which told her it would be contained shortly. But she heard no mention of—

"Trooper?" Rivells said.

"State Trooper Gerundsen."

"What's happening in the woods? Have your men come across a German Shepherd, full grown, roughly ten years old?"

Trooper Gerundsen's facial muscles strained along the soft line of his jaw. "Detective, I got four officers in the woods right now. They all got their guns trained on that *dog*. They've got another unsub in handcuffs. He gave up pretty easily. But the dog? They're keeping their distance. Apparently, the animal's in some kind of manic, hyper-charged state."

"Can they contain the animal with rubber bullets? Has Animal Control arrived yet?"

"They'll be along … but they've been instructed this will be a recovery for them. There isn't going to be any rescue or containment of the animal," Trooper Gerundsen said.

"Trooper Gerundsen—"

"It's already been decided," he said, clipping her off and raising an oversized callused palm. "This animal is responsible for the deaths of two fellow officers, and … last count … four women. In their homes. Unsuspecting. Massacred. So, if you're looking to plead for the animal's life, you'd best get your priorities in better order. Your duty—*our duty*—is to uphold the law and to protect the general public. We're not beholden to put the welfare of some rabid animal ahead of any human life? You wanna report me to PETA, I'll lend you my cell phone. But I can bet they'd back me up on this, too! I'm sorry, but just … don't … Detective."

"This dog is a war hero, Trooper Gerundsen. She's not rabid. The animal's suffering from the effects of an extremely potent, character-altering drug to counteract the residual effects of the coma she was in for two months."

"Detective—"

"No, you've got to listen," Rivells pressed, somewhat surprised at her own persistence. *This is your mother shining through. Your mother loved animals. All animals. She preferred them to the company of people any day of the week.* "Can we sedate her then verify what could be wrong with her. She may very well have been unaware of her actions, or impaired in some way. Mr. Bentley came all this way for this *dog,* and he has most likely saved more than a few lives by staying on the scent of Tarlick and his accomplices. We owe him this! Please, don't shoot to kill—sedate, and then we'll regroup!"

Stoic as a programmed android, Trooper Gerundsen held to his mantra, squaring his shoulders. His gaze darkened, like a black cloud passing over a weak autumn sun. "It's already been decided—"

"Ah, *to hell with what's been decided!*" Rivells broke past the trooper, gun drawn, and charged into the woods. "Shoot me *too* then!"

101. A CLEAR VIEW

Will exited the backyard with the Dare girl slung over his shoulder. He saw the SWAT team members already heading him off on the side of the house, their assault rifles aimed at his chest and forehead. He didn't hear what they were shouting at him, but imagined it to *Stand down!* or *Lower the girl to the ground!* Any number of exclamations would have filled their opened mouths, cold breaths bursting out of their mouths, and it would have worked. Will would have been more than happy to comply. But the woods were neither dark nor deep enough to conceal what was an all-too-clear view into it from his vantage point.

What he saw changed his plans for surrender in an instant.

He increased his grip on the Dare girl. He would not put up his hands, sink to his knees, and hand himself over to the authorities. They would shoot him if he held out for very long. But no matter what, he would hold onto the girl in his arms. It's not like Will had decided to commit *suicide by cop*.

Not at all.

"I can see into the woods, boys," he said in a loud, plaintive voice like he was addressing his old platoon. "You better get your officers to lower their weapons and walk out, or this is not going to end well. If they hurt my dog, I'm going to make this even messier for all of you. I know just how to do it."

I've come so far, so very far ...

One SWAT team member, shifting his weight aggressively from right to left foot, shook his head. "You got a shot?" Will understood he was talking to his partner a couple paces to his left. "You take it."

"You take the shot," Will cried, pointing to the center of his flak jacket. "And I promise you the C-4 belt I got on under this will level half the block, boys."

Will heard the side gate clang and instantly pivoted toward its sounds, all the while holding fast to Jodi Dare who hung like a slab of meat over his right shoulder. Three more SWAT, rifles on Will, as they filed out of the back yard and flanked him on his left side. One of them spoke into a thin black twig poking out from under his black skull cap. "We've got Bentley pinned. Left side of the residence."

"I'm telling you boys for the last time!" Will shouted. "You get the fuck back and call your men out of the woods, or I'm going to kill all of us and a few people just getting back from Church on top of that! You want to test me? Let's see how high you boys can fly!"

The SWAT switching from his left to right foot twitched around the mouth. Gritted his teeth. "Matson? You see a bulge from your vantage?"

"Can't be sure," Matson, the SWAT to the speaker's left admitted, the snub nose of his AK15 never wavering.

"Ma'am?" the SWAT speaker called. "Are you alert? Are you with us, ma'am?"

"It's all right, Jodi. The man's talking to you," Will said.

"Ma'am?" the SWAT speaker repeated, finally planting his left foot.

"Yes ... I-I'm ... bleeding."

"Ma'am, did this man hurt you?"

"No ... n-no ... he saved me. He carried me ... out of there. Please ... I'm losing blood because I miscarried!"

The SWAT speaker motioned to something above their heads, raising his hand and closing it into a tight fist before dropping it back down to the stock of his weapon. Will knew he was motioning to a sniper out of sight. They had worked it in an identical way over in Fallujah and beyond. *Eyes in the sky at all times*! "You would let this young lady bleed out before surrendering? Sounds to all of us like you're not the villain here, but you're becoming one right before our eyes! I read your book, Bentley! You're looking at a member of your warrior tribe, soldier! I don't want to be forced to take out one of my brothers in arms. Don't make me do it! Don't *you* make me do it!"

"That so?"

"It *is* so?"

"Then you know all about my dog, Alberta? You know she was right in there with us, clearing out hovels! Sniffing out bombs! She was a war dog! You read my book, you know this isn't how you handle a war dog! A hero! You owe her more than a bullet behind the ear ... *soldier!*"

"I'll see what I can do. But you gotta show some seriously *good* faith here, or I *will* put you down. Lay the girl down. Hands up. Then ... and only *then* can we talk about who gets spared!"

Then Will heard her, the voice he had only ever heard through his cell phone. "WILL BENTLEY! THIS IS DETECTIVE GLYNNA RIVELLS HERE! THE ANIMAL IS SAFE! SHE WILL REMAIN SO AS LONG AS YOU COMPLY WITH AUTHORITIES. RELEASE MS. DARE, AND GET DOWN ON YOUR KNEES WITH YOUR HANDS HIGH! I REPEAT; I

HAVE EYES ON YOUR DOG, AND SHE IS SAFE!"

She made it! Thank God, she made it here! This makes it so much easier.

You're gonna trust this woman you barely know from fucking Eve, soldier? Don't you dare lay down for any of them! No-NO! THEY'RE GONNA TURN YOU INTO A BULLET CUSHION, SOLDIER! DO! NOT! SURRENDER!

Will was certain the left side of his face had to be glowing red as a stop light, but none of the SWAT men seemed to notice. It felt like Sergeant Karnes had finally decided to birth himself out of the side of Will's skull, slipping him like a chick cracking out of an egg.

Yet, it was not enough to stop him from stooping slowly over and lowering Jodi to the ground.

Then, everything happened very fast.

102. DENOUEMENT

"We *are* the only Animal Control here right now," the officer shouted as he edged closer and closer towards the dog on the ground. He had his service weapon drawn, aimed at the animal, who had not come up off its back. The dog writhed among the brambles and twigs and crumbly dropped leaves as sounds of utter torment ripped their way out of its half-opened muzzle. The officer could see the animal's eyes were wide and projected to the thin canopy of naked treetops above their heads, as if it were tracking the ascent of some angel come down to show it the way to heaven. Its body appeared to move independent of its head, slithering and twitching. "This dog's rabid! No doubt in my mind! We're *not* taking any chances! You need to back off from this, Detective!"

"I am *not* telling you to drop your weapon! I'm telling you to exercise restraint! You are *not* Animal Control, and they're en route as we speak!" Rivells said, hand hovering over her holstered weapon, tramped through the leaves. She inched along, tramping as lightly as possible. But the ground clicked and snapped beneath her every footfall. "I'm asking for restraint!" She lowered her voice. "Just relax. You can see this animal's sick. It may already be dying."

"This mutt *bitch* killed two of our own, Detective! Is your memory that impaired, or just your judgment?"

Rivells saw the red band of angry flesh just above the lead officer's dark blue starched collar. "I know what happened, officer. I was there. But this animal has just come out of a two-month coma after attempting to save the life of a priest who was being ripped to shreds inside his own church. By his own parishioners."

"So you're trying to sell me on sparing this bitch's life on the fact it *also* tried to protect a pedophile in black robes? You're not making a very good case, detective!"

"All right-all right, this animal was also trained and served in Iraq as a war dog. She saved the lives of countless servicemen. Marines. Something obviously went wrong here. She was manipulated by her captors. Possibly tortured beyond reason. We don't know. But I, for one, would like to learn mor,e and I think we can if we find it within ourselves to *spare* this dog. I think we'll find she was a victim in all this as well!"

Rivells came up alongside the lead officer. They locked eyes for a split second before he continued to sight down his handgun towards the animal. Rivells could see the dog's ears were caked in blood. A good bit of it had leaked out onto the forest floor. The top of its head also looked tinged in red. It's skull also appeared misshapen, badly sunken in between the ears. "What happened to her head?"

"Damned thing was ramming its head into the trees when we got here? I'm talking full-force running right into them." He cast a quick glance towards Rivells. "The dog stands, and I'm duty-bound to put it down."

"Look at her," Rivells said. "She's not getting up."

"I dunno."

"What's your name, officer?"

"Grady. Officer Grady."

"Officer Grady, I want you to look past the trees on the side of the lawn. Two o'clock. You'll find there's a standoff happening, and it's got everything to do with the fact you look like you're about to shoot that dog. Go on, take a look. I'll keep an eye on the dog." Rivells waited for the officer to do so, then she went on. "I'm going to call to the man holding the girl over his shoulder. I'm going to tell him, assure him, his dog is safe from harm. And that's going to mean you will need to lower your firearm at least in the time it takes for him to surrender the girl he's holding and put up his hands."

"What the hell is SWAT waiting for? They probably got a red dot on his forehead right now, but no one's taking a shot! What is this shit?"

"I take full responsibility for anything the animal does from here on out. I'm staking my career on a gut instinct about a damned dog, so could you maybe work with me here. I'm trying to help defuse a situation with a lot of dangerous moving parts."

Officer Grady's green, pinched eyes flinched once more towards her, lingered a little longer, and he lowered his service weapon. He did not holster it. "You better be right about this."

No shit, Officer Blarney Stone!

"And I don't need a bullhorn. We don't need any more police stomping into these woods towards this man's animal just to hand me one." With that Rivells called to Will Bentley in a loud, stern voice: "WILL BENTLEY! THIS IS DETECTIVE GLYNNA RIVELLS HERE! THE ANIMAL IS SAFE! SHE WILL REMAIN SO AS LONG AS YOU COMPLY WITH AUTHORITIES. RELEASE MS. DARE, AND GET DOWN ON YOUR KNEES WITH YOUR HANDS HIGH! I REPEAT; I HAVE EYES ON YOUR DOG, AND SHE IS SAFE!"

Rivells' chest tightened as she watched Will's hesitation, her muscles only oozing into calm once more when she saw him lower the girl off his shoulders and lower himself onto his knees before the SWAT team encircling him.

In mere seconds the men closed ranks around him, and Will Bentley disappeared.

"All right," she said, with a belabored sigh. *They won't hurt him. Nothing a veteran can't handle, anyway.* "Now, I need you to radio your sergeant and get an ETA for Animal Control. We're going to sit on the animal until they arrive—"

The big German Shepherd stood in the time it would take to close a hand into a fist.

Officer Grady's gun toting hand rocketed up from his side, as if spring-loaded.

Rivells launched herself at him, her hands seizing his wrists and shoving the officer's hands, the gun, wide and flailing away from the animal. The gun discharged up into the canopy of trees. "Wait!" she cried. "She's not coming for us! She's gone off towards eleven o'clock!"

The sudden excited flurry of voices and calls to action stirred at the tree line parallel to the road where the rest of the officers and their bosses were gathered with bated breath.

"JUST WAIT!" Even as she wrestled with Officer Grady, Rivells knew she could be ending what was a short but decorated career as a Philadelphia Special Victims Unit detective. She felt its passing with every flex of her muscles as she tried not so much to disarm the uni but to stay his trigger finger somehow. She mourned her job in an instant. *All on a promise to keep the guy's dog safe! A lousy, two-bit promise.*

Then again, she knew there was no such thing as a *two-bit promise.* Not in her universe.

The animal took a running charge at an especially wide stump, butting the top of her skull against its bark and knocking a good bit of it away to reveal smooth, crème flesh underneath. Rivells heard the audible crack of the dog's skull, and it was sickening to hear.

It was far worse to watch the dog drop onto its side.

The dog's chest did not rise and fall again.

The dog's tongue dropped out the side of her snout.

And two men were standing there nearby who hadn't been there a moment before. Their shapes were softened, fuzzy, and translucent. The one with the longer curly hair, was backed up against the tree the dog had just butted up against. He looked as disoriented as he was curious. The other man peeked his head out from behind the same tree. He was a good bit taller than the other man, and a great deal more handsome.

Rivells and Officer Grady stopped their struggling, both of them slack jawed in the presence of the two thin spirits standing before them.

"Oh … God …" Rivells breathed.

Karl Tarlick.

And Jack Post.

Officer Grady found his feet, told the two men to put their hands up.

The ethereal form of Karl Tarlick held out his hands before him, stared down at them. He did not raise his arms. He wiped his hands off on his jeans. He didn't say anything.

Rivells stared. Time seemed to tick down, like its hour and minute hands were trying to click through tar. A part of her knew they were intangible, both men. By degrees, she understood the danger was no longer something any of them could measure or gauge.

Jack Post broke from the cover of the tree he was hiding behind and ran off, his shoes merely skimming the ground. Tarlick stood there for a few moments, his gaze far removed. He moved his arms out from his sides, tilted his head back, and looked like someone on the verge of levitation. Then, Karl Tarlick shook his head at them, stiltedly and dismissively before stalking off in the direction of his counterpart.

Grady and the other officers took pursuit, charging after them with their guns at the ready.

Rivells knew better.

She strode towards the animal lying in the leaves a few feet away.

I tried. I really tried. But he's not going to believe me.

She hunkered down beside Alberta. She reached out, laid a hand on the dog's side.

"Holy … " She couldn't complete the thought.

The dog's chest inflated, slow and laborious, beneath her hand.

Still alive! Only … barely …

Rivells breath quickened in and out of her lungs. She smoothed down the animal's fur. It was sticky to the touch and every swipe of her hand drew the fur up into spikes and hackles. She drew her hand away once enough of the anonymous substance had rubbed off into the palm of her hand.

Behind her, one of them spoke up in an almost gloating, misogynistic voice. "Is the thing dead?"

Rivells bit her bottom lip and didn't answer. Her eyes were suddenly drawn to a thin tendril of smoke rising up from what at first looked like the ground, crowded with twigs, broken branches, and shit-brown leaves. Maybe a couple of brambles somehow rubbed together in just the right way, creating a certain friction which produced the line of rising smoke. The notion fizzled as she edged closer towards Alberta's head. The tendril of smoke was rising from her left ear. It confused Rivells at first. Then, all at once, there was no question. Only bafflement. *What the hell … is … that?*

It looked at first glance like a small charcoal briquette sticking out of Alberta's left ear. The smoke was rising off of it, producing the odd illusion of Alberta's ear emitting a toxic fume. Rivells moved her hand within an inch of the smoking *briquette* jutting out of the dog's ear. She felt the subtle heat it was giving off and thought of leaving it in place. But it looked to be hurting the animal. *Maybe if I take it out, it'll help her. Or it could open up a blood geyser, for God's sakes!* Before the rest of them crowded around her, and it could be any moment, Rivells decided.

She expected it to burn her hand, even gritted her teeth as she extracted the thing from the dog's left ear. It was warm, like a cookie right out of the oven. The dog snuffled, her eyes closed. The piece was no larger than a golf ball. It looked like a chunk of granite.

Granite formed by layers compacted over time.

Or that had once been soft.

Fleshy.

Pinkish-grey.

When Detective Rivells turned it over in her hand, she knew she was right. A small section of the piece was uncharred. Raw.

A small, pale oval that looked like fat worms stuck to one another to form a cushiony cluster.

She felt someone leaning over her. Something bumped her back.

489

Their leg or something.

"What the hell's that?"

Detective Jones.

She angled around to find him standing over her, lines of worry stitched across his brow like etchings from a switchblade.

I don't know. Frontal. Cerebral Cortex. Knocked loose somehow by the dog's collision with the stump. And ... when it was jarred loose ... they *... appeared. Tarlick and Post.*

"I don't know how much longer this dog has," Rivells said, rising and showing the thing in her hands to Jones. "But we've got to try."

"But this dog ... she's dangerous."

"It wasn't her, Jones," Rivells insisted. "It never was." She pointed at the small broiled section of brain matter in Jones's hands as he turned it over and over. "It was this." She cast her eyes out across the woods to her back. It could have been her imagination, but in the moment the terrain looked darker and denser than it had moments before. *It was this.*

And them.

103. YOU KEEP ME HANGING ON

It baffled both of them. How large the woods were. They seemed to run on forever in every direction. Neither one could talk to the other. They discovered this by accident. The thoughts were there for both of them, but neither could give voice to what they were thinking. Consequently, their feelings of frustration and disorientation developed into something of a fugue state for them. The shorter, curly-haired one turned his ankle in a hidden foxhole, concealed beneath a high pile of rubbish. There was no pain, but it annoyed the little man just the same. He thought of cursing the hole. Stringing new and fantastical sentences of glorious profanity together, brilliant enough to light up the woods and frighten every bird from every branch. But he opened his mouth, and a monotone hum escaped his lips. He tried harder, and the hum became the static of an empty AM radio frequency until he abandoned the effort and kept charging and stomping about. The other man kept his distance.

But that would not last long.

Sooner or later, they would converge.

What would come of it, no mortal could know.

104. CLIPPINGS

Excerpt from *USA Today*, pg.5, dated February 10, 2017

(Bucks County, PA.) The New Hope War Dog Cemetery was opened to the public this past Saturday afternoon during what was a cold, overcast morning. The wintry weather did not keep the hundreds of tourists, veterans, locals, and public officials away, though. Also in attendance was State Congressman Kevin Fitzpatrick, State Senator Gene Digiralomo, and Pulitzer Prize winning author Will Bentley who funded the establishment of the cemetery with his own money.

Speeches were delivered at the foot of the "Cappy" Doberman statue, a replica of the monument that stands at the entrance to the National War Dog Cemetery at Naval Base Guam. "Cappy" was a Doberman Pinscher war dog credited with saving the lives of 250 Marines when he warned them of a massive Japanese force near their camp near the close of World War II. Mr. Bentley and his wife, Mina, commissioned local sculptor Donna Vrango to replicate the statue of the famous war dog. Ms. Vrango was also in attendance, which included the unveiling of the "Cappy" statue at the beginning of the ceremony.

For Will Bentley, 41, the event was bittersweet as this was a day he had fought long and hard for. "The events leading up to my dog Alberta's death have been widely publicized so there's no need to rehash any of it. I do want to be clear when I tell you Alberta was a victim of circumstance in the most literal sense of the word. She was abducted and abused beyond reason by her captors. A veterinarian later determined she had developed a brain tumor which wreaked further havoc on her impulse control and distorted her perception of reality. These details have been conveniently left out of the national coverage of her story, and I'm here to set the record straight, not just to lay her to rest where she rightly belongs."

In December of 2016, Alberta was abducted and participated in a two-day rampage which resulted in the slayings of five young women in the states of Maryland, Delaware, New Jersey, and brought to a violent end in Levittown, Pennsylvania when the dog's captors perpetrated a home invasion and the subsequent executions of three of its four residents. Mr. Bentley followed the clues to his dog and her captors. He tracked them to the house in Levittown and killed the suspected ringleader of the killing spree, parolee Karl Lee Tarlick, 25. Tarlick's killing was ultimately ruled as self-defense.

But it is for Alberta's acts of valor during the Iraq War Bentley wants his twelve-year old German Shepherd to be both remembered and honored. "I'm not going to name names here, but I will say there was a great deal of pushback and red tape I had to contend with just to get *permission* to bury Alberta here. There were people who contested she receive a *hero's burial* after what happened. There was even a petition that went around in ten different townships across the tri-state, barring her remains from being buried here. This cemetery would've been established no matter what happened. I mean, I believe the state of Pennsylvania ought to have such a memorial park. The Revolutionary War saw its first sparks in the Philly taverns not twenty miles from here. I almost caved when I got a phone call from one of the officer's wives who was killed. How do you argue with a grieving police widow? You can't! You *don't!* But then I got a call one night from Lieutenant Colonel Avery Karns. I knew his father. I served under the man for three tours and greatly admired him. His son was a teen at the time, and when he told me who he was I had to take a few deep breaths. It was a very emotional phone call for both of us. I'm not going to get into the more private exchanges, but Colonel Karns assured me he would be taking the matter all the way to the top if he had to. He's well acquainted with Military General Agee. Once he told me he would have *his* ear about the whole thing, I knew Alberta would be laid to rest with full honors. This is a dog who saved the lives of fifty or more men during the course of three years. On routine scouting expeditions. Night watch duties. This dog had a hellish life, but in good times, and around her family, she was a comfort to myself and my wife despite all the terrible memories. Anyone who tries to tell you a pet cannot possibly equal that of a child, never knew the love or the loyalty of a dog like my Alberta."

Alberta's ashes were laid to rest with full military honors. She is the first Marine service dog to be interred in the memorial park, and her name the only one inscribed on the "Cappy" statue's adjoining bronze plaque. Her remains were accompanied into burial grounds by a full military procession. "TAPS" was played by a trio of bagpipes while Will and Mina Bentley, along with so many others wishing to pay their respects, hugged one another and wiped away tears. The New Hope War Dog Cemetery is open daily from dawn to dusk, Monday through Saturday.

Excerpt from *The Philadelphia Inquirer,* pg. 10, July 5th, 2017

Residents in Levittown, Bucks County, are reeling with fear after five separate sightings in Teague Woods of two men engaged in what has been described by witnesses as a "bloody and incomprehensible" altercation. The first to stumble across the two as-yet unidentified men was thirty-two-year-old Harris Weintraub and his four year-old son, Jerry, who were cutting through the woods to fish for minnows in a small creek adjoining the wooded area. "I know this is going to sound like some episode of *Black Mirror,* but when we first saw the two guys, one guy had the other *literally* impaled on a tree branch. And he was … pushing him further and further back onto it. The other guy was screaming and screaming. He shouldn't have been able to do that. I remember I picked up my son, who was just shaking and crying, and we ran back the way we came. He even left his pole behind. I went back to get it a little time later, and I was with a couple officers. The two guys were gone. I tried to find the branch, figuring it was probably stained red. But I couldn't find it."

Police are scratching their heads over this mystery, even though four other eyewitnesses, who wished to remain anonymous, placed calls to 911 over the course of the three-day holiday weekend. Two teenagers whose houses border Teague Woods went to retrieve a baseball and came across the same two men, according to the descriptions they gave to police. "One of them had this long, greasy hair, and I couldn't see his face, but the other dude was on top of him and just hammering him over and over in the head. It didn't stop. They didn't notice me or my friend, and we were, like, almost right up on them. But the weird part was when we turned to run away; I looked over my shoulder, and both the dudes were up and standing there next to each other, and they were watching us run away. They didn't run after us. And they both looked really messed up, like a couple of UFC fighters if they were allowed to bring knives into the octagon."

Residents have also described sounds of screaming and other sounds of distress coming from Teague Woods, some lasting for hours upon hours and at random times of day. Police are currently patrolling Teague Woods, as well as the residential roads which border it. Some residents are concerned there could be a connection to the events that have now come to be called the Riley Family Massacre. Investigators at this point have no reason to believe the two events are connected in any way. Authorities are still searching for both men, described as in their mid-twenties, one short with long and dark hair, while the other is taller and rail thin with short, chestnut hair. If you have any information regarding this story or the two men described herein, please call 911 or email our staff editors at phillyinquirer.crimecenter.com.

DRINK WITH ME TO DAYS GONE BY ...

"So how often," Will asked his guests over four beer glasses overflowing with dark Guinness, "have you gotten together with people from your past cases to break bread and get buzzed?"

Darnell Jones snuck a playful glance at Glynna Rivells, who sat on the chaise lounge beside his. "Well, that would be *never*. For either of us. It's funny you mention that because she and I were talking about this very topic on the drive over to your house. But we were both free for the 4th of July, so ... why the hell not. Right?" He found her hand, the one not clutching the tall beer glass as she slurped at the top foam, and squeezed it.

Will and Mina Bentley had known early on they wanted to spend the holiday with Glynna and Darnell. Once the smoke cleared away and the case closed in terms of Will's involvement (and thanks almost completely to the constant lobbying on his behalf by Glynna Rivells), both couples found themselves trading phone calls or playing phone tag more and more often regarding things which did not even remotely relate to the matters which had transpired over the course of late 2016. Mina started meeting Glynna for daiquiris every Friday night in the city. Darnell and Will, both Villanova University graduates, bonded quickly over the school's men's basketball team once the chances of a national win came more within reach. They attended a handful of games at the school. They drank and shared another fondness for Black and Tan brew. They watched every game they didn't see up close either on Will's 48-inch screen or Darnell's awe-inspiring 60 inch. By the time the Ballantine Blazers choked against Florida State in the Final Four showdown come March, Darnell and Will were already close and well-acquainted friends. Will had given up on making new friends of the male variety at his age.

He thought he'd live out the rest of his days with his wife as his only friend, aside from his agent who even then had a vested financial stake in knowing him and handling his affairs.

Darnell Jones surprised the hell out of Will Bentley when he slipped rather seamlessly into the role of *best friend* for the writer.

So Will's questions seemed almost preposterous given the history of friendship the two couples had already established in such a short time.

Mina traced the rim of her beer glass, thoughtfully. "We reached out to Corey Snell and little Ava. We invited them over, too. Will was going to buy some high-tech fireworks and dazzle the little lady with a display back here in the yard. But …"

Will sighed. "She's not doing well in foster care."

Glynna shook her head, gazed blankly out at the distant line of trees at the far rear of Will's property. "Still not talking."

"According to Corey, she hasn't spoken since that day." Will felt pressure at the corners of his eyelids. "Once Corey told her Alberta died … she just … shut off. That's how he put it. He said she was really excited when she first saw her running around in the woods. Then she was crushed."

Darnell lowered his beer glass down to rest it precariously on his knee. "I hate to say it, but she's going to be in the damned system until *somebody else* besides her uncle materializes to prove competency and the means to adopt her."

Glynna scoffed. "Her uncle's working now. Steady income. He has an apartment in Oxford Valley. He's gotten himself situated in the area just so he can prove to the courts he can take care of the little girl. It's pure bull-shit they wouldn't at least allow him the opportunity to."

"Babe," Darnell said, "he still dresses like a burnout, even if he's walking the straight and narrow. The guy's gotta dress the part, not just walk the walk."

"Then maybe Mina and I will show up on his doorstep one of these days and hit King of Prussia Mall for a whole new wardrobe. Our treat. You game, Meen?"

Mina raised her glass, nodded with a glazed look in her eyes. This was her second beer, and she was a self-professed lightweight. All one hundred twenty-five pounds of her. "I'll bring the Gold Card. You bring the AmEx, girl!"

"See?" she beamed, shining on Darnell who smiled down at his white Chuck Taylors.

They sat there for a spell in silence on the brick patio. Will and Mina sat at the patio table, the umbrella in its center still raised despite the hour. It's steel stalk started shuddering and knocking against its stabilizing ring set into the glass of the table as a chill swept across the patio. Glynna zipped up her jogging top and pulled up the collar to cut the cold. She shivered and nuzzled sideways into Darnell's shoulder, which met her halfway as he moved towards her at the same time. Will's seat faced the side lawn, enclosed by a wooded area not unlike the tract of forest bordering the Riley house. The tract where his dog had died, winding down like an old time-piece. He stared intently into the obscure ink black between the trees.

Looking for them, when he knew with more certainty than the others sitting there, the two ghosts had not and would never find him. They would never come to frolic and fight and bludgeon and ravage one another over and over in Will's woods. They were confined to the woods bordering the Riley house. For all time. Will knew this.

He had been told this.

An undisclosed source.

Will swept his palm across his left cheek. The smoothness of its contour still surprised him, even though he had had the surgery months ago.

The remaining microscopic bone fragments of Sergeant Karns had been removed for a whopping total of $10,000. His insurance company deemed it cosmetic procedure and therefore an unnecessary surgery. They refused coverage, but it did nothing to Will's intent in seeing it through. He shelled out the entire amount without batting an eye. Surprisingly, Karns's voice did not leave him all at once. It was not gone from his mind when he woke from the anesthesia as he had expected it would. No, Karns sulked. He griped. Then, he made peace with Will, leaving him with only one condition that was non-negotiable. Sergeant Karns wanted to dictate a note to his son, now the esteemed colonel, and have Will deliver it. Will took the dictation, much of it framed from the point of view of a man who was still living and merely penning a last letter to his son "in case of," so when it came time for his son to read it, the letter would not come across like it was from beyond the grave. Will mailed it out, spoke with the colonel briefly the day it reached his house in Roanoke, hashed out old fond memories of Sergeant Karns, and they politely hung up with one another forever.

After the phone call ended, Will both felt and mourned the total and complete absence of Karns in his head.

Never a word from Karns since that day.

Silence, and a smooth jawline.

Was it worth it? Yes, I believe it was.

He heard Mina's voice, a distant chirp across the table. "—he won't even tell me what he's working on now, so I know it's something serious.

Right, Will?"

"Huh? What?"

"Oh, honey, where'd you go?" Mina asked.

"Into the woods … again."

"How did I know?"

Glynna and Darnell laughed. Darnell leaned forward, tapping the tip of his fingernail against the side of his glass. "So, is that code for something? This whole *into the woods* saying?"

Mina said, "It's what we call it when Will slips into one of his creative daydreams. Or … in this case … what would it be? Nightdreams?"

Glynna nodded. "So long as they're pleasant. You don't need to be torturing yourself with any bad memories. They'll fade, if you let them."

"Oh," Will said, straightening in his seat like someone who has quite literally startled out of a nap, "I know that. They hang on. The things that happened. The things I had to do."

Glynna laughed. "The push and pull you and I went through the whole way. I know why you kept me a little way away, but damned if I'll ever understand how you managed to always stay one step ahead of us. I mean, were you working with some informant we don't know about."

Partly, but then I had him surgically plucked from my cheek, piece by little piece …

"No, it was a lot of trial and more error, to be honest. Otherwise, I would have been able to save the other four women, instead of just the Dare girl. I always seemed to get there after the damage was done. And *that* is what haunts me more than anything. The aftermath I would walk into when the scent of those bastards still hung in the air like they had just been there seconds before. The things that … the bodies …"

Mina cut in. "Okay, we said we'd steer clear of this stuff."

Glynna stood, ruffled and embarrassed. "I'm sorry. I didn't mean to lead you back into it."

Will waved it off, even though a part of him had tramped back *into the woods* again. *You won't find them. She told you they can't come here. They're not strong enough. They're imprisoned. What is your obsession?*

Mina stood and walked over to Glynna, linking arms with her. "Why don't we see about some more drinks and finger food. I've got lots more to bring out. We'll let the two men lick their wounds over Villanova for a little bit."

Glynna nodded, and the two women slipped back into the house by way of a sliding glass door.

After a moment, Darnell decided to cross the patio and grab a chair

497

across from Will. The legs of the patio chair scraped along the red brick and drew Will's attention away from the tree line long enough for him to realize his friend was sitting there staring at him. He smiled thinly and straightened again in his chair. "Sorry," he offered, "this is kind of the process. Sliding in and out of the moment. When I start working out a book in my head. Blessing and a curse. I don't know how the hell Mina puts up with it."

"You look …" Darnell stopped himself, as if trying to find the right word.

But I know he knows exactly what the right word is. Mina has said the exact same thing about me from time to time.

"You can say it," Will said.

"My man, you look … haunted."

"I am."

Darnell nodded, pulled the rest of his dark beer down his throat and belched into his palm. "So I was asking Mina about what you're writing these days. You were somewhere else and thinking about the very same thing. What are you working on these days?"

Don't tell him—you promised me you wouldn't breathe a word until we were finished.

I won't—I'll keep it nice and vague.

"I started a couple weeks back, and it's coming very fast. Tight and fast. The writing, it's like a wellspring I can't cap off when I'm not sitting in front of my computer screen. It spills over into my life, takes me away. Anyway, I came across a story not too long ago. Just the surface details. On some online news source. I do a lot of surfing to try and see what'll resonate. This story did. I read it, and it was like the words were suddenly rising up my body, shaking the bones and tickling the skin, like I had turned into this living and breathing *tuning fork*. Best way I can describe it."

"Damn," Darnell laughed. "You writer folk really know how to explain things in an off-the-wall kind of way. And *right-on* at the same time! Shit!"

But Will didn't smile this time. He had forgotten to, even though it should have been what came next in the social exchange. Instead, he shoved his glass of beer back away from him, and went on. "It was interesting to me because a part of the story deals with the phenomenon of *Broken Bird Syndrome*. You and Glynna explained it to me a little ways back, and it really resonated with me, this calculated and devastating targeting of damaged women by men who want to *fix them* and end up breaking them beyond any repair in the end. This girl I'm writing about, she became one of those *broken* people, and her story doesn't end happily. There's no phoenix at the end of this story rising out of a pile of ash. I felt compelled to tell her story."

"We talking one of the victims in all this?" Darnell asked.

"No," Will lied without hesitation. "I came across her story quite by accident." This was the truth, as it turned out.

Darnell nodded. "Well, if you need me to help open any law enforcement doors for your research you let me know. I have a pretty good reach. Wide and far."

"Research," Will said, chewing on the word. "That's already in motion. Thank you. though."

Glynna and Darnell stayed until a little after 1 a.m. Mina confirmed her Girl's Night Out for next Friday with Glynna. They were going to do some drinking at a new watering hole which just opened up by Penn's Landing. Something about the ritual stirred Will's stomach with a heavy wooden spoon until he called for calm and got it. He made plans with Darnell to check out the new Christopher Nolan movie at The Barn Cineplex next Thursday, the night of its release. Then a sports bar where they could try their hands at eating enough wings to win themselves a free dinner. Plans made. iPhone calendars updated. Hands shaken. Hugs. Kisses where applicable.

They separated. Mina shut the door and turned around to lean against its white slab in the low foyer light. She stifled a yawn behind her hand. "I'm hitting it. Hard."

Will saw the look on her face, expectancy which she knew better than to voice. She wanted him to come to bed with her, right then and there. Maybe there would be sex. There usually was, and it was just fine with Will. But she knew this was the time he earmarked to work on his new project. Will was thankful she understood and put up with the strange hours he had been keeping ever since the idea first struck him. One thing he made sure of was Mina was doted on, more so than perhaps was needed. They made love five days a week and would have done so that night if not for the lateness of the hour.

"I know," Mina said, moving in for a hug.

Will pulled her close, smelling the Pantene dreaminess still lingering in the crown of her black hair. The press of her breasts against his chest caused a stirring in his loins, but he ignored it. She was only then starting to put some of her natural weight back on. After everything that happened, Mina had been like the incredible shrinking woman. They were in psychotherapy. Separately. It was slow to yield results, at least for him. But he would stick to it.

"Love you, Meen."

"Mm … love you too." Mina offered him a closing squeeze before separating from him and slipping soundlessly up the stairs to bed.

From there, Will went to the kitchen and set about preparing his mug of Earl Grey tea. He lingered, waiting for the kettle to scream, and when it did he quickly made his drink. He stirred in a dollop of honey and a splash of milk. Then he stirred it as he weaved his way through the meandering hallways of the downstairs into his darkened study. The green-visored desk lamp, which still reminded him of the sort which would seem more at home on a card table with players throwing down or staying as cigar smoke swirled about their sweat soaked heads. He set down the tea beside his laptop and flipped it open.

He punched in his password. A screensaver which would have no doubt raised Mina's eyebrow flashed across the screen.

It was a yearbook photo of a young girl. The full color of the photograph worked wonders for the girl's appearance, which if it had been printed in black and white, would have washed out what was already a pale and freckled face. Will had gained access to the yearbook photo during a visit to Halloran High School, legitimizing his visit by explaining to the principal who he was and what he was going to be writing about. Of course, there was always a *quid pro quo* when it came to hashing out such arrangements. When Will left, he had made a promise to visit the school and speak to the student body about his *Shiite Weeping*, which was actually being taught in one of the school's AP courses. He had shaken hands. That was it. He had snapped a picture of the girl's photo with his iPhone, then scanned it into his computer when he got home.

The girl's smile looked desperate, like she had practiced it in the mirror the night before it was taken over and over before deciding it would simply have to appear as a put-on. Her eyes, small and green like those of a salamander, squinted even smaller before the camera. Her nose was thin, aquiline. Her hair was red, straight and severely parted down the center of her small skull. Her bowed shoulders betrayed her insecurity more so than anything else about her appearance. They jutted forward, like two blunt objects ready to strike out at anyone who could hurt her.

I always hated that picture—do you have to keep it up there, Will?

"It's got to be total immersion if I'm going to tell your story," Will said, lowering himself down into his writing chair. "Sorry, my dear. You were the one who decided to … board me like a cruise ship down in the basement of your house."

I don't like the title, either.

"Well," Will said, "consider it a working title, then."

500

Yeah, but … The Broken Bird? Makes me sound like a pathetic, flapping, squawking weakling.

"Why don't we get started for the night."

Will swiveled his chair around so he was facing the leather divan behind him. It looked like something a psychotherapist would have patients stretch out on. Will had bought it recently at a secondhand antique store in New Hope. One Mina recommended.

A young girl with red hair fanned out across the top of the divan lay on the leather upholstery, her hands folded over one another as if in death. She stared up at the ceiling, eyes wide and searching for something unfathomable. The girl from the yearbook photo.

"Where did we stop?" she asked, complacently.

Will told her.

"All right," she said. "And you're leaving my name out?"

"As promised," Will said. "Unless you change your mind."

"Blaise Tarlick," she bemoaned. "What an ugly name. *Blaise!* I don't know. Let's see how this turns out."

"You know how it turns out."

"Smartass … okay. I want to tell you about my dad. And the bomb shelter. Down basement."

"The room where you decided to end your life. Are you sure?"

"I want it out of the way."

"Then that's where we'll pick up."

Will swiveled back around.

Blaise started to talk.

He typed, trying to keep up and doing a pretty good job at it.

November 12, 2016-
March 5, 2018
Bensalem, Pennsylvania

ACKNOWLEDGEMENTS

Writers don't know everything, and people need people.

This is why I want to thank Samantha Dugan for reading the earliest draft of this novel and providing her invaluable advice and keen feedback.

This civilian also wants to thank Lance Fling, police retired, for always and often answering questions about police procedure and protocol.

Thank you to Larissa and Tara Bennett for the tireless hours they devoted towards turning this *story* into something worthy of being called a *novel*.

Much gratitude to Donelle Pardee Whiting for catching the inconsistencies and remaining an *editor's* editor of the highest caliber.

Lisa Vasquez, thank you for being a wonderful mentor, friend, and for turning it all around for me.

Mucho love to the SSP family.

Last but not least, I want to thank *you*, The Chance-Taker, for laying your hard-earned money down to read *Broken Birds*. It means more than you could possibly imagine!

P.M.

BIOGRAPHY

Peter Molnar is an author, singer-songwriter, musician, educator, and editor. His short stories have appeared in *City Slab: Urban Tales of the Grotesque, Necrotic Shorts, Hydrophobia: A Charity Anthology to Benefit Hurricane Harvey Victims*, and the upcoming *Tenebrous Tales Anthology*. His blog, "As the Shadow Stirs", is a mashup of music, movies, horror, and superheroes and can be found on his home webpage. *Broken Birds* is his debut novel. He lives and works in Southeastern Pennsylvania with his wife, daughter, and two cats. Currently, he is at work on his next book and a slew of new short entries. Visit Peter at the following sites:

www.petermolnarauthor.com
www.facebook.petermolnarauthor.com
www.PMolnarAuthor/twitter
www.instagram.com/pmolnar423